WOLF SOLENT

by John Cowper Powys

"The book is a poem as well as a novel. I am in the presence of genius. . . . Above all, the book is unique. Fresh, unhackneyed in everything, in language, similes, method, content, and philosophy; poet and philosopher, pagan and saint have come together to make it."—Will Durant

"*Wolf Solent* [is] the only book in the language to rival Tolstoy." —George Steiner.

"In the beauty and freshness of its imagery and the sustained interest of its narrative its power is without question. Its prose often rises to the cadence of poetry. And beyond beauty, it sinks shafts through the unique personalities and provincial setting with which it deals, to a core of truth which is the stuff of human experience. . . ."—*The New York Herald Tribune*

"He has made his novel one of the most beautiful and powerful written in our language in this century."—*Bookman*

Also by John Cowper Powys
in Colophon Books

WEYMOUTH SANDS

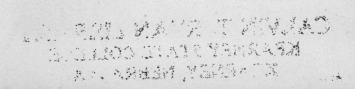

WOLF SOLENT

JOHN COWPER POWYS

HARPER COLOPHON BOOKS
Harper & Row, Publishers
New York, Cambridge, Philadelphia, San Francisco,
London, Mexico City, São Paulo, Singapore, Sydney

A hardcover edition of this book was published by Simon & Schuster, Inc. in the United States in 1929 and Macdonald & Co. (Publishers) Ltd. in Great Britain in 1961. It is here reprinted by arrangement with The Estate of John Cowper Powys.

First HARPER COLOPHON edition published 1984.

Library of Congress Cataloging in Publication Data
Powys, John Cowper, 1872–1963.
  Wolf Solent.
  (Harper colophon books ; CN 1163)
  I. Title.
PR6031.0867W5 1984   823'.912   84-47672
ISBN 0-06-091163-8 (pbk.)

84 85 86 87 88 10 9 8 7 6 5 4 3 2 1

INTRODUCTION

THE task of the writer of an introduction is, as I see it, to bring the prospective reader and the writer together, hoping that they will like one another, and become friends. He knows the writer, who is already a friend of his, even if they have never met, or are separated by several centuries; he does not know the prospective reader, but he hopes that this possible reader is a congenial spirit who will like his friend the author. So what should he say?

Surely he should be an enthusiast for the book in question, and invite the prospective reader to share an experience he himself has treasured for some time.

This presents no difficulty to me in introducing *Wolf Solent*, or indeed any of the novels of John Cowper Powys, for I have admired him, and felt warm gratitude toward him, for something like fifty years. I have returned to his work, always with increased pleasure, for all of my life as a reader. He is not one of the most widely known writers of this century, but many people think he is one of the greatest, and, although he is not one of the most easily accessible of novelists, he is unforgettable. What he leaves in the mind of the reader becomes, in time, part of the fabric of that mind.

Who was he? He was not one of those writers whose name appears in countless books of literary reminiscence as a member of a special circle, the hero of paper love-affairs and the originator of quips and judgments that have become part of the century's literary gossip. He was born at Shirley, in Derbyshire, England, in 1872, and he ended his long life in the small town of Blaenau Ffestiniog, in North Wales, in 1963; twenty-five of the intervening years, more or less, he spent in the U.S.A. Much that is important is contained in those facts. Born an Englishman, descended from a notable Welsh family that had lived in England for centuries, he insisted that in spirit and literary sensibility he was Welsh. Well acquainted with the United States, he held that country in deep affection, and embraced its spirit, having come to know a wide range of its people. His life was long, reaching into his ninety-first year, and his literary development was slow, though as a member of an upper-class, educated family which in his generation produced two other distinguished writers (his brothers Llewelyn and Theodore) out of a total of eleven children, literature was bone of his bone from childhood. Indeed, his literary affinity extended even to his ancestry, for on his mother's side he was descended from John Donne (1571–1631) and William Cowper (1731–1800). Like all people of the English-speaking group, his ancestry was mixed, but out of the mixture he chose the Welsh strain, and insisted, with increasing vehemence as his life progressed, that he was Welsh, and that what Welshness meant to him was dominant in his work.

What was it, this Welshness? He wrote:

> ... Bad Welshmen are about as bad as human nature can be, while good Welshmen have a magnanimity and generosity that is almost disconcerting. Nor is it exactly *saintly* generosity, in the conventional Christian sense. It is a kind of magical generosity, capable of going to an excess which causes the well-meaning Saxon to call up memories of his childhood's wildest fairy-tales.

There are words here which will come into your mind again and again as you read Powys: magnanimity, generosity, disconcerting, excess and above all, magical. His is not the easy magic of science fiction; it is the revelation of what all nature, and human nature in particular, reveals to such a Shakespearean sensibility as his. For there is something Shakespearean about him; what he said of a friend, in his own splendid *Autobiography,* applies fully to Powys—"He combined skepticism of everything with credulity about everything, and I am convinced this is the true Shakespearean way wherewith to take life." People who must always be grouping and ranking authors have sometimes placed Powys with Hardy and D. H. Lawrence, but as we read him we find that it is this Shakespearean breadth, this mingling of acceptance and irony, that makes him like nobody but himself.

The book in your hand, *Wolf Solent,* was written in 1929 when he was already fifty-seven, but it was the first of his books in which he spoke in his authentic voice. He wrote for thirty years more, with growing power. For twenty-five years he had rushed about the North American continent, making what his manager called "mean jumps" from town to town, lecturing on every aspect of Western literature and Western culture, for he allowed his audiences to choose his subjects. As a lecturer he was what it is now fashionable to call charismatic; the tall, gaunt, eagle-like man, clad in his Cambridge gown, never spoke from notes; he *thought* in front of his audience, shouting, wooing, accusing and wowing 'em in a rhapsodic flow that might go on for an hour and a half, reaching to the highest shelves of his extraordinary literary range for allusions and examples from Homer, Dante, Rabelais, Dickens, Balzac and all the great of Western culture that would illumine his theme. He demanded response, and his favourite audiences were Jews, blacks and New Americans who were not afraid to weep, to shout approval, to shout disagreement, to yield themselves to him and his Welsh magic. Powys was never the darling of the great American universities; they found him "unscholarly" and did not care that Powys did what scholars rarely do; he brought a sense of the greatness and splendour of literature as an enrichment of life to people who wanted precisely that. It was in the smaller universities, in the women's clubs, in the synagogues and labour halls that his delighted audiences were found, where people wanted to feel, as well as think.

It is in this rhapsodic, enchanter's voice that you must read this book, hearing every word and savouring every cadence and nuance with the inner ear. Powys is not for the speed-reader, the rapist of the printed page, the person who does not much like reading a book but wishes to say that he has read it. Only thus will you find what Powys has to give, which he called "a full, over-brimming, personal consciousness of life." Only thus can you share in Powys's great theme, which he declared to be the purpose and essence and inmost being of *Wolf Solent,* and that is the necessity of opposites, the element of compensation in the pattern of life. Life and Death, Good and Evil, Matter and Spirit, Body and Soul, Reality and Appearance are contraries that cannot exist in solitude. In this book Lenty Pool is not Evil if the Reserved Sacrament is not in the church; the delight of the lovers in each other is deepened quite as much by the stench from the pigstyes as by the sweetness of the summer grass. The sensuality of the book, its evocation of sights, sounds, textures and smells, is part of its fabric and must be sensed by the reader. Powys, as much as any novelist, reminds us that it is not how much we read, but how we read it, that assures us of the pleasure of literature.

Have I forgotten to give you the "Message" of the book—something which, if you are a student, you can use in your essay? I am sorry. Of course it is The Compensatory Function of Contrarieties, and if you want to pursue it at length, you may do so in the twenty volumes of the Collected Works of Dr. C. G. Jung of Zürich, where it is admirably explored. Or, on the other hand, you can simply read and re-read *Wolf Solent* attentively, hearkening to the inner rhapsodic, Welsh voice, and then go on to read the other great novels of this great man.

ROBERTSON DAVIES

Massey College,
University of Toronto

May 1, 1984

CONTENTS

Affectionately Dedicated
To
Father Hamilton Cowper Johnson

THE FACE ON THE WATERLOO STEPS

From Waterloo Station to the small country town of Ramsgard in Dorset is a journey of not more than three or four hours, but having by good luck found a compartment to himself, Wolf Solent was able to indulge in such an orgy of concentrated thought, that these three or four hours lengthened themselves out into something beyond all human measurement.

A bluebottle fly buzzed up and down above his head, every now and then settling on one of the coloured advertisements of seaside resorts—Weymouth, Swanage, Lulworth, and Poole—cleaning its front legs upon the masts of painted ships or upon the sands of impossibly cerulean waters.

Through the open window near which he sat, facing the engine, the sweet airs of an unusually relaxed March morning visited his nostrils, carrying fragrances of young green shoots, of wet muddy ditches, of hazel-copses full of damp moss, and of primroses on warm grassy hedge-banks.

Solent was not an ill-favoured man; but on the other hand he was not a prepossessing one. His short, stubbly hair was of a bleached tow-colour. His forehead as well as his rather shapeless chin had a tendency to slope backward, a peculiarity which had the effect of throwing the weight of his character upon the curve of his hooked nose and upon the rough, thick eyebrows that over-arched his deeply-sunken grey eyes.

He was tall and lean; and as he stretched out his legs and clasped his hands in front of him and bowed his head over his bony wrists, it would have been difficult to tell whether the goblinish grimaces that occasionally wrinkled his physiognomy were fits of sardonic chuckling or spasms of reckless desperation.

His mood, whatever its elements may have been, was obviously connected with a crumpled letter which he more than once drew forth from his side-pocket, rapidly glanced over, and replaced, only to relapse into the same pose as before.

The letter which thus affected him was written in a meticulously small hand, and ran as follows:

My Dear Sir,

Will you be so kind as to arrive at Ramsgard on Thursday in time to meet my friend, Mr. Darnley Otter, about five o'clock, in the tea-room of the Lovelace Hotel? He will be driving over to King's Barton that afternoon and will convey you to his mother's house, where for the present you will have your room. If it is convenient I would regard it as a favour if you will come up and dine with me on the night of your arrival. I dine at eight o'clock; and we shall be able to talk things over.

I must again express my pleasure at your so prompt acceptance of my poor offer.

Yours faithfully,

JOHN URQUHART

He re-invoked the extraordinary incident which had led to his 'prompt acceptance' of Mr. Urquhart's 'poor offer.'

He was now thirty-five, and for ten years he had laboriously taught History at a small institution in the city of London, living peacefully under the despotic affection of his mother, with whom, when he was only a child of ten, he had left Dorsetshire, and along with Dorsetshire all the agitating memories of his dead father.

As it happened, his new post, as literary assistant to the Squire of King's Barton, brought him to the very scene of these disturbing memories; for it was from a respectable position as History Master in Ramsgard School that his father had descended, by a series of mysterious headlong plunges, until he lay dead in the cemetery of that town, a byword of scandalous depravity.

It was only the fact that the Squire of King's Barton was a relative of Lord Carfax, a cousin of Wolf's mother, that had made it possible for him to find a retreat, suitable to his not very comprehensive abilities, after the astounding *dénouement* of his London life.

He could visualize now, as if it had occurred that very day instead of two months ago, the outraged anger upon his mother's face when he communicated to her what had happened. He had danced his 'malice-dance' – that is how he himself expressed it – in the middle of an innocent discourse on the reign of Queen Anne. He was telling his pupils quite quietly about Dean Swift; and all of a sudden some mental screen or lid or dam in his own mind completely collapsed and he found himself pouring forth a torrent of wild, indecent invectives upon every aspect of modern civilization.

He had, in fact, so at least he told his mother, danced his

2

'malice-dance' on that quiet platform to so abandoned a tune, that no 'authorities,' in so far as they retained their natural instincts at all, could possibly condone it.

And now, with that event behind him, he was escaping from the weight of maternal disapproval into the very region where the grand disaster of his mother's life had occurred.

They had had some very turbulent scenes after the receipt of Mr. Urquhart's first answer to his appeal. But as she had no income, and only very limited savings, the sheer weight of economic necessity drove her into submission.

'You shall come down to me there when I've got a cottage,' he had flung out; and her agitated, handsome face, beneath its disordered mass of wavy, grey hair, had hardened itself under the impact of those words, as if he had taken up her most precious tea-set and dashed it into fragments at her feet.

One of the suppressed emotions that had burst forth on that January afternoon had had to do with the appalling misery of so many of his fellow Londoners. He recalled the figure of a man he had seen on the steps outside Waterloo Station. The inert despair upon the face that this figure had turned towards him came between him now and a hillside covered with budding beeches. The face was repeated many times among those great curving masses of emerald-clear foliage. It was an English face; and it was also a Chinese face, a Russian face, an Indian face. It had the variableness of that Protean wine of the priestess Bacbuc. It was just the face of a man, of a mortal man, against whom Providence had grown as malignant as a mad dog. And the woe upon the face was of such a character that Wolf knew at once that no conceivable social readjustments or ameliorative revolutions could ever atone for it – could ever make up for the simple irremediable fact that it *had* been as it had been!

By the time the hill of beeches had disappeared, he caught sight of a powerful motor-lorry clanging its way along a narrow road, leaving a cloud of dust behind it, and the sight of this thing gave his thought a new direction. There arose before him, complicated and inhuman, like a moving tower of instruments and appliances, the monstrous Apparition of Modern Invention.

He felt as though, with aeroplanes spying down upon every retreat like ubiquitous vultures, with the lanes invaded by iron-clad motors like colossal beetles, with no sea, no lake, no river free from throbbing, thudding engines, the one thing most precious of all in the world was being steadily assassinated.

3

In the dusty, sunlit space of that small tobacco-stained carriage he seemed to see, floating and helpless, an image of the whole round earth! And he saw it bleeding and victimized, like a smooth-bellied, vivisected frog. He saw it scooped and gouged and scraped and harrowed. He saw it hawked at out of the humming air. He saw it netted in a quivering entanglement of vibrations, heaving and shuddering under the weight of iron and stone.

Where, he asked himself, as for the twentieth time he took out and put back Mr. Urquhart's letter – where, in such a vivisected frog's-belly of a world, would there be a place left for a person to think any single thought that was leisurely and easy? And, as he asked himself this, and mentally formed a visual image of what he considered 'thought,' such 'thought' took the form of slowly stirring, vegetable leaves, big as elephants' feet, hanging from succulent and cold stalks on the edges of woodland swamps.

And then, stretching out his legs still further and leaning back against the dusty cushions, he set himself to measure the resources of his spirit against these accursed mechanisms. He did this quite gravely, with no comic uneasiness at the arrogance of such a proceeding. Why should he not pit his individual magnetic strength against the tyrannous machinery invented by other men?

In fact, the thrill of malicious exultation that passed through his nerves as he thought of these things had a curious resemblance to the strange ecstasy he used to derive from certain godlike mythological legends. He would never have confessed to any living person the intoxicating enlargement of personality that used to come to him from imagining himself a sort of demiurgic force, drawing its power from the heart of Nature herself.

And it was just that sort of enlargement he experienced now, when he felt the mysterious depths of his soul stirred and excited by his defiance of these modern inventions. It was not as though he fell back on any traditional archaic obstinacy. What he fell back upon was a crafty, elusive cunning of his own, a cunning both slippery and serpentine, a cunning that could flow like air, sink like rain-water, rise like green sap, root itself like invisible spores of moss, float like filmy pond-scum, yield and retreat, retreat and yield, yet remain unconquered and inviolable!

As he stared through the open window and watched each span of telegraph-wires sink slowly down till the next telegraph-post pulled them upward with a jerk, he indulged himself in a sensation which always gave him a peculiar pleasure, the sensation of imagining himself to be a prehistoric giant who, with an effortless ease, ran along by the side of the train, leaping over hedges, ditches lanes, and ponds, and easily rivalled, in natural-born silent speed, the noisy mechanism of all those pistons and cog-wheels!

He felt himself watching this other self, this leaping giant, with the positive satisfaction of a hooded snake, thrusting out a flickering forked tongue from coils that shimmered in the sun. And yet as the train rushed forward, it seemed to him as if his real self were neither giant nor snake; but rather that black-budded ash tree, still in the rearward of its leafy companions, whose hushed grey branches threw so contorted a shadow upon the railway bank.

Soon the train that carried him ran rapidly past the queer-looking tower of Basingstoke Church, and his thoughts took yet another turn. There was a tethered cow eating grass in the churchyard; and as for the space of a quarter of a minute he watched this cow, it gathered to itself such an inviolable placidity that its feet seemed planted in a green pool of quietness that was older than life itself.

But the Basingstoke Church tower substituted itself for the image of the cow; and it seemed to Solent as though all the religions in the world were nothing but so many creaking and splashing barges, whereon the souls of men ferried themselves over those lakes of primal silence, disturbing the swaying water-plants that grew there and driving away the shy water-fowl!

He told himself that every church-tower in the land overlooked a graveyard, and that in every graveyard was a vast empty grave waiting for the 'Jealous Father of Men' who lived in the church. He knew there was just such a church-tower at King's Barton, and another one at Ramsgard, and yet another at Blacksod, the town on the further side of Mr. Urquhart's village.

He sat very upright now, as the train approached Andover; and the idea came into his head, as he fixed his gaze on his fellow traveller, the bluebottle fly, who was cleaning his front legs on a picture of Swanage pier, that from tower to tower of these West Country churches there might be sent, one gusty November night, a long-drawn melancholy cry, a cry heard only by dogs and horses and geese and cattle and village-idiots, the real death-cry of a god – dead at last of extreme old age!

'Christ is different from God,' he said to himself. 'Only when God is really dead will Christ be known for what He is. Christ will take the place of God then.'

As a sort of deliberate retort to these wild fancies, the tall spire of Salisbury Cathedral rose suddenly before him. Here the train

5

stopped; and though even here – possibly because his absorption in his thoughts gave him a morose and uncongenial appearance – no one entered his third-class carriage, the stream of his cogitations began to grow less turbid, less violent, less destructive. The austerity of Salisbury Plain yielded now to the glamour of Blackmore Vale. Dairy-farms took the place of sheep-farms; lush pastures of bare chalk-downs; enclosed orchards of open cornfields; and park-like moss-grown oaks of wind-swept naked thorn-bushes.

The green, heavily-grassed meadows through which the train moved now, the slow, brown, alder-shaded streams, the tall hedgerows, the pollarded elms – all these things made Solent realize how completely he had passed from the sphere of his mother's energetic ambitions into the more relaxed world, rich and soft and vaporous as the airs that hung over those mossy ditches, that had been the native land of the man in the Ramsgard cemetery.

His mother's grievances, posthumous and belated, but full of an undying vigour, had never really made him hate his father; and somehow the outburst that had ended his scholastic career had released certain latent instincts in him which now turned, with a fling of rebellious satisfaction, to the wavering image of his sinister begetter.

Children, he knew, were often completely different from both their progenitors, but Wolf had a shrewd suspicion that there was very little in him that did not revert, on one side or the other, to his two parents. He was now thirty-five, a grim, harassed-looking, clean-shaven man, with sunken eye-sockets; but he felt his heart beating with keen excitement, as, after an absence of a quarter of a century, he returned to his native pastures.

What would he find in that house of 'Darnley Otter's mother?' Who was this Darnley Otter? What had he to do with Mr. Urquhart? And what would Mr. Urquhart reveal that evening as to the form his own services were to take?

As the train drew up at Semley, he read the words, 'For Shaftesbury,' upon the notice-board; and very soon the high grassy battlements of the great heathen fortress loomed against the sky-line.

Staring at those turf-covered bastions, and drawing into his lungs lovely breathings from damp moss and cold primroses – breathings that seemed to float up and down that valley on airy journeys of their own – he found himself gathering his mental resources together so as to face with a concentrated spirit whatever awaited him in these pleasant places. . . . 'Christ is not a man;

6

He never *was* a man,' he thought. 'And He will be more than a god when God is dead. . . . Three church-towers . . . three. Ramsgard . . . King's Barton . . . Blacksod . . . it's quaint to think that I've absolutely no idea what I shall be feeling when I touch with my hand the masonry of those three towers . . . or what people I shall know! I hope I shall find some girl who'll let me make love to her . . . tall and slim and white! I'd like her to be *very* white . . . with a tiny little mole, like Imogen's, upon her left breast. . . . I'd like to make love to her out-of-doors . . . among elder-bushes . . . among elder-bushes and herb Robert. . . .'

He pulled in his legs and clasped his hands over his knees, leaning forward, frowning and intent. 'I don't care whether I make money. I don't care whether I get fame. I don't care whether I leave any work behind me when I die. All I want is certain sensations!' And with all the power of his wits he set himself to try and analyse what these sensations were that he wanted beyond everything.

The first thing he did was to attempt to analyse a mental device he was in the habit of resorting to – a device that supplied him with the secret substratum of his whole life. This was a certain trick he had of doing what he called 'sinking into his soul' This trick had been a furtive custom with him from very early days. In his childhood his mother had often rallied him about it in her light-hearted way, and had applied to these trances, or these fits of absent-mindedness, an amusing but rather indecent nursery name. His father, on the other hand, had encouraged him in these moods, taking them very gravely, and treating him, when under their spell, as if he were a sort of infant magician.

It was, however, when staying in his grandmother's house at Weymouth that the word had come to him which he now always used in his own mind to describe these obsessions. It was the word 'mythology'; and he used it entirely in a private sense of his own. He could remember very well where he first came upon the word. It was in a curious room, called 'the ante-room,' which was connected by folding-doors with his grandmother's drawing-room, and which was filled with the sort of ornamental débris that middle-class people were in the habit of acquiring in the early years of Queen Victoria. The window of his grandmother's room opened upon the sea; and Wolf, carrying the word 'mythology' into this bow-window, allowed it to become his own secret name for his own secret habit.

7

This 'sinking into his soul' – this sensation which he called 'mythology' – consisted of a certain summoning-up, to the surface of his mind, of a subconscious magnetic power which from those very early Weymouth days, as he watched the glitter of sun and moon upon the waters from that bow-window, had seemed prepared to answer such a summons.

This secret practice was always accompanied by an arrogant mental idea – the idea, namely, that he was taking part in some occult cosmic struggle – some struggle between what he liked to think of as 'good' and what he liked to think of as 'evil' in those remote depths.

How it came about that the mere indulgence in a sensation that was as thrilling as a secret vice should have the power of rousing so bold an arrogance, Wolf himself was never able to explain; for his 'mythology,' as he called it, had no outlet in any sort of action. It was limited entirely to a secret sensation in his own mind, such as he would have been hard put to it to explain in intelligible words to any living person.

But such as it was, his profoundest personal pride – what might be called his dominant *life-illusion* – depended entirely upon it.

Not only had he no ambition for action; he had no ambition for any sort of literary or intellectual achievement. He hid, deep down in his being, a contempt that was actually *malicious* in its pride for all the human phenomena of worldly success. It was as if he had been some changeling from a different planet, a planet where the issues of life – the great dualistic struggles between life and death – never emerged from the charmed circle of the individual's private consciousness.

Wolf himself, if pressed to describe it, would have used some simple earthly metaphor. He would have said that his magnetic impulses resembled the expanding of great vegetable leaves over a still pool – leaves nourished by hushed noons, by liquid, transparent nights, by all the movements of the elements – but making some inexplicable difference, merely by their spontaneous expansion, to the great hidden struggle always going on in Nature between the good and the evil forces.

Outward things, such as that terrible face on the Waterloo steps, or that tethered cow he had seen at Basingstoke, were to him like faintly-limned images in a mirror, the true reality of which lay all the while in his mind – in these hushed, expanding leaves – in this secret vegetation – the roots of whose being hid themselves beneath the dark waters of his consciousness.

8

What he experienced now was a vague wonder as to whether the events that awaited him – these new scenes – these unknown people – would be able to do what no outward events had yet done – break up this mirror of half-reality and drop great stones of real reality – drop them and lodge them – hard, brutal, material stones – down there among those dark waters and that mental foliage.

'Perhaps I've never known reality as other human beings know it,' he thought. 'My life has been industrious, monotonous, patient. I've carried my load like a camel. And I've been able to do this because it hasn't been my real life at all! My "mythology" has been my real life.'

The bluebottle fly moved slowly and cautiously across Weymouth Bay, apparently seeking some invisible atom of sustenance, seeking it now off Redcliff, now off Ringstead, now off White Nore.

A sudden nervousness came upon him and he shivered a little. 'What if this new reality, when it does come, smashes up my whole secret life? But perhaps it won't be like a rock or stone . . . perhaps it won't be like a tank or lorry or an aeroplane. . . .'

He clasped his bony fingers tightly together. 'Some girl who'll let me make love to her . . . "white as a peeled willow-wand" . . . make love to her in the middle of a hazel wood . . . green moss . . . primroses . . . moschatel . . . whiteness. . . .' He unclasped his fingers, and then clasped them again, this time with the left hand above the right hand.

It was nearly twelve o'clock when the train drew up at Longborne Port, a village which he knew was the last stop before he reached Ramsgard.

He rose from his seat and took down his things from the rack, causing, as he did so, so much agitation to his only travelling-companion, the bluebottle fly, that it escaped with an indignant humming through the window into the unfamiliar air-fields of Dorsetshire.

A young, lanky, bareheaded porter, with a countenance of whimsical inanity, bawled out at the top of his voice, as he rattled his milk-cans: 'Longborne Port! Longborne Port!'

Nobody issued from the train. Nothing was put out of the train except empty milk-cans. The young man's voice, harsh as a corncrake's, seemed unable to disturb the impenetrable security which hung, like yellow pollen upon a drooping catkin, over those ancient orchards and muddy lanes.

9

And there suddenly broke in upon the traveller, as he resumed his seat, with his coat and stick and bag spread out before him, the thought of how those particular syllables – 'Longborne Port!' – mingling with the clatter of milk-cans, would reproduce to some long-dead human skull, roused to sudden consciousness after centuries of non-existence, the very essence of the familiar life upon earth!

What dark November twilights, what drowsy August noons, what squirtings of white milk into shining pails, would those homely syllables summon forth!

He lay back, breathing rather quickly, as the train moved out of that small station. For the last time he took from his pocket Mr. Urquhart's letter. 'Darnley Otter!' he said to himself. 'It's odd to think how little that name means now, and how much it may mean to-morrow!' Why was it that, when the future was very likely all there already, stretched out like the great Wessex Fosse-way in front of him, he didn't get some sort of second-sight about it by merely reading those words in Mr. Urquhart's neat hand? What kind of man was Darnley Otter? Was he a plain, middle-aged man like himself, or was he a beautiful youth? The idea of beautiful youths made his mind once more revert to 'peeled willow-wands,' but he easily suppressed this thought in the excitement of the moment.

Ay! There were the ruins of the great Elizabethan's castle. And *there* was the wide grassy expanse where the town held its annual agricultural show, and where the Ramsgard schoolboys were wont in old days to run their steeplechase!

How it all came back! Twenty-five years it was since he left it, frightened and bewildered by his parents' separation; and how little it had changed!

He let his gaze wander over the high tops of the park beech trees till it lost itself in the blue sky.

Millions of miles of blue sky; and beyond that, millions of miles of sky that could scarcely be called blue or any other colour – pure unalloyed emptiness, stretching outwards from where he sat – with his stick and coat opposite him – to no conceivable boundary or end! Didn't that almost prove that the whole affair was a matter of thought?

Suppose he were now, at this moment, some Ramsgard boy returning to school? Suppose he were Solent Major instead of Wolf Solent? And suppose some genial house-master, meeting him on the platform, were to say to him: 'Well, Solent, and what have *you* made of your twenty-five years' holiday?' What would he answer to that?

As the train began to lessen its pace by the muddy banks of the River Lunt, he hurriedly, and as if from fear of that imaginary master, formulated his reply.

'I've learnt, sir, to get my happiness out of sensation. I've learnt, sir, when to think and when not to think. I've learnt . . .'

But at this point his excitement at catching sight of the familiar shape of the Lovelace Hotel, across the public gardens, was so overwhelming that the imaginary catechism came to an end in mid-air.

'I shall send my things over in the bus,' he thought, standing up and grasping his bag. 'And then I shall go and see if Selena Gault is still alive!'

'CHRIST! I'VE HAD A HAPPY LIFE!'

His excitement grew rather than diminished as he got out of the train.

He gave up his ticket to an elderly station-master, whose air, at once fussily inquisitive and mildly deferential, suggested the manner of a cathedral verger. He watched his luggage being deposited on the Lovelace bus; and there came over him a vague recollection of some incident of those early years, wherein his mother, standing by that same shabby vehicle, or one exactly resembling it, with a look of contemptuous derision on her formidable face, said something hard and ironical to him which lashed his self-love like a whip.

Opposite the station were the railed-in public gardens. These also brought to his mind certain isolated trivial occurrences of his childish days; and it struck him, even in his excitement, just then as being strange that what he remembered were things that had hurt his feelings rather than things that had thrilled him.

In place of following the bus round the west of the gardens, where the road led to the hotel, and then on past the police-station to the abbey, he turned to the east and made his way across a small river-bridge. Here, again, the look of a certain old wall against the water, and certain patches of arrow-head leaves within the water, stirred his memory with a sudden unexpected agitation.

It was over this very bridge that twenty-five years ago he had leaned with his father, while William Solent showed him the difference between loach and gudgeon, and in a funny, rambling, querulous voice deplored the number of castaway tins that lay in the muddy stream.

But Wolf did not lean over the bridge this time. He heard the abbey clock striking one, and he hurried on up Saint Aldhelm's Street. Newly-budded plane trees cast curious little shadows, like deformed butterflies, upon the yellowish paving-stones; and over the top of an uneven wall at his side protruded occasional branch-ends of pear-blossom.

He came at last to a green door in the wall.

'Is it possible,' he wondered uneasily, 'that Selena Gault lives here still?'

He allowed a baker's cart to rattle negligently past him while he made two separate hesitating movements of his hand towards the handle of the green door.

It was queer that he should have had an instinct to look sharply both up and down the street before he brought himself to turn that handle. It was almost as though he felt himself to be a hunted criminal, taking refuge with Selena Gault! But the street was quite deserted now, and with a quick movement he boldly opened the gate and entered the garden.

A narrow stone path led up to the door of the house, which resembled a doll's house, brilliantly painted with blues and greens. Blue and white hyacinths grew in masses on either side of the path; and their scent, caught and suspended in that enclosed space, had a fainting, ecstatic voluptuousness which was at variance with the prim neatness around them. A diminutive servant, very old but very alert, with the nervous outward-staring eyes of a yellow-hammer, opened the door to him, and without demur ushered him into the drawing-room.

He gave his name and waited. Almost immediately the little servant came back and begged him to take a chair and make himself comfortable. Miss Gault would see him in a few minutes. Those few minutes lengthened themselves into a quarter of an hour, and he had time to meditate on all the possibilities of this strange encounter. Miss Gault was the daughter of the late headmaster of Ramsgard; and Wolf had heard his mother for twenty-five years utter airy sarcasms at her expense. It appeared she had had some tender relation with his father; had even attended William Solent's death-bed in the workhouse, and seen him buried in the cemetery.

Wolf sat on Miss Gault's sofa and set himself to wonder what this rival of his mother's would look like when she entered the room. The servant had not quite closed the door; and when fifteen minutes had elapsed it opened silently, and Wolf, rising quickly to greet his hostess, found himself confronted by three cats, who walked gravely and gingerly, one after another, into the centre of the apartment. He made some awkward gesture of welcome to these animals, who resembled one another in shape, size, breed, and temperament – in everything except colour, being respectively white, black, and grey; but instead of responding to his advances they each leapt into a separate chair, coiled themselves up, and surveyed, with half-closed languid eyes, the door through which they had entered. He felt as if he were in the house of the Marquis of Carabas and that the three cats were three Lord Chamberlains.

He sank back upon the sofa and stared morosely at each cat in turn. He decided that he liked the black one best and the grey one least. He decided that the white one was its mistress's favourite.

He was occupied in this harmless manner when Selena Gault herself came in. He rose and advanced towards her with outstretched hand. But it was impossible for him to eliminate from his expression the shock that her appearance gave him; and it did not lessen his surprise when she received his gesture with a formal bow and a stiff rejection of his hand.

She was a tall, bony woman, with a face so strikingly ugly that it was impossible to avoid an immediate consciousness of its ugliness; and it was borne in upon him, as their conversation proceeded, that if only he *had* been able to contemplate her countenance with unconcern, she would have enjoyed one of the happiest moments of her life.

She made a sign for him to resume his seat; but as she herself stood erect in front of the fire, which in spite of the warmth of the day still burned on the hearth, he preferred to remain on his feet. Like a flash he thought to himself, 'Can my father have actually embraced this extraordinary person?' And then he thought to himself, 'The poor woman! Why, she can't be able to meet a single stranger anywhere without giving them a shock like this.' But he had already begun speaking quietly and naturally to her, even while he was thinking these things.

'I knew you would know who I was,' he said gently. 'I've just been invited down here. I'm going to do some work—I can't tell you quite what it is – out at King's Barton. I'm going to drive over there this afternoon; but I thought I would come and see you first.'

While she listened to him, he noticed that she kept pulling her white woollen shawl tighter and tighter round her black silk dress. The effect of this was to give her the appearance of someone caught unawares in some sort of fancy costume – some costume that rendered her ashamed and even ridiculous.

'And so I just came straight in,' he went on, beginning to feel a very odd sensation, a sensation as if he were addressing someone who was listening all the time in a kind of panic to a third person's voice – 'straight in through your little green door and between those hyacinths.'

She still made no observation, and he noticed that one marked quality of her ugliness was the dusky sallowness of her cheeks combined with the ghastly pallor of her upper lip, which projected from her face very much as certain funguses project from the brown bark of a dead tree.

'I've decided that your favourite cat is the white one,' he brought out after an uncomfortable pause.

She did relax at this, and, moving to the chair occupied by the grey cat, took up the animal in her arms and sat down, holding it on her lap.

'You're wrong, wrong, wrong!' she whispered hoarsely. 'Isn't he wrong, Matthew?'

The cat took not the least notice of this remark, or of the fingers that caressed him; but it did impinge upon the consciousness of Miss Gault's visitor that this singular woman's hands were of a surprising beauty.

'What are the names of the others?' Solent enquired.

'The black one is Mark,' replied the lady.

'And the white one Luke?' he hazarded.

She nodded; and then, quite suddenly, with an effort as though a gust of wind had swept aside a mass of dead leaves, uncovering the fresh verdure below, her whole face relaxed into a smile of disarming sweetness.

'I've never had a John,' she said. 'And I never will.'

Wolf Solent was quick enough to take advantage of this change of mood. He moved across to her, bent down over her chair, and scratched Matthew's head. 'I thought I'd like to go over and see where the grave is.' His words were low-pitched, but without any emotional stress. His intonation could hardly have been different if he had said, 'I think I'll go to the abbey presently.'

Selena Gault gave a deep sigh, but it seemed to Solent like a sigh of relief rather than sadness.

'Quite right, quite proper,' he heard her murmur, with her head held low and her hands occupied in smoothing out the shawl beneath the body of the somnolent cat.

'The best thing you could do,' she added.

Since she said nothing more and persisted in keeping her head lowered – a position which accentuated the enormity of her upper lip and the dark sallowness of her face – Wolf began to feel as if he were an impertinent intruder stroking the pet animal of some proud, secretive being whose peculiarity it was to prefer beasts to men.

He straightened himself and squared his shoulders with a sigh. Then he moved across to the sofa and laid his hand on his hat and stick which he was rather surprised to notice he had brought with him into the room.

'I suppose,' he said, as he turned round with these objects in his hand, 'there'll be someone out there at the cemetery, some gardener or caretaker, who'll know where the grave is? I shouldn't like to get out there and not be able to find it. But I don't want to let this day pass without trying to find it.'

Selena Gault tossed the grey cat from her lap and rose to her feet.

'I'll come with you,' she said.

She uttered the words quite quietly, but he noticed that she avoided looking him in the face.

She stood for a time staring out of the window, motionless and abstracted.

'If it would be a bother to you – ' he began.

But she suddenly turned her distorted countenance full upon him.

'Sit down, boy,' she rapped out. 'Do you think I'd let you go there alone, if there were fifty gardeners?'

She stared at him for a second after this with a look that seemed to turn his bodily presence into the frame of a doorway, through which she gazed into the remote past.

'Sit down, sit down,' she said more gently. 'I'll be ready soon.'

The door had not closed behind her for many minutes when the elderly servant entered, carrying a silver tray, upon which was a plate of Huntley and Palmer's oaten biscuits and a decanter of sherry. Wolf had poured himself out as many as three glasses of this excellent wine, and had swallowed nearly all the biscuits, before Miss Gault returned. She found him stroking Mark, the black cat.

Her appearance in hat and cloak was just as peculiar as before, but more distinguished; and Wolf soon found out, when presently they passed the front of the abbey, where several townspeople greeted her, that the power of her personality was fully appreciated in Ramsgard.

Their way to the cemetery took them straight past the work-house. This building was on the further side of the road; but Solent was unable to retrain an impulse to turn his head towards it. The edifice was rather less gloomy than such erections usually

16

are, owing to the fact that some indulgent authority had permitted its façade to be overgrown with Virginia creeper.

He found himself reducing his pace so that he might familiarize himself with every aspect of that heavy, sombre building behind iron gates. As he lingered he became suddenly aware that his companion had slipped her gloved hand upon his arm. This natural gesture, instead of pleasing him or rousing his sympathy, made him feel curiously irritable. He quickened his pace; and her hand fell away so quickly that he might easily have supposed that light pressure to have been a pure accident.

They walked side by side now, with such swinging steps that it was not long before they were beyond the houses and out into what was almost open country. It annoyed him that she remained so silent. Did she suppose he had come to see his father's grave in a vein of sentimental commiseration?

'What's *that!*' he exclaimed, pointing to a ramshackle group of sheds that seemed fenced off from the road with some unnatural and sinister precaution.

Selena Gault's reply made his touchiness seem captious and misplaced.

'Can't you see what that is, boy? It's the slaughter-house! You've only to take the shadiest, quietest road to find 'em in any town!'

They were soon skirting the edge of the neat oak palings that ran along the leafy purlieus of Ramsgard Cemetery.

'I let them bury him at the paupers' end,' she remarked gravely. 'It's nearer. It's quieter. It's hardly ever disturbed. This is the way I generally go in.' With a sly, quick glance up and down the road, a glance that gave an emphasis to the whites of her eyes such as made her companion think of a crafty dray-horse edging into a field of clover, Miss Gault stooped down and propelled herself under a rough obstruction that blocked a gap in the oak palings.

Solent followed her, confused, a little surly, but no longer hostile.

She did not wait for him, but made her way with long, rapid strides to the extreme corner of the enclosure. Her swinging arms, her gaunt figure, her erratic gait, set the man's mind thinking once more of various non-human animals.

He came up to her just as she reached her goal. 'William Solent,' he read, on the upright slab of sandstone; and then, under the date of birth and death, the words, '*Mors est mihi vita.*'

Wolf had no difficulty in recognizing the particular hyacinths that stood in an earthenware pot. 'She must have come here for twenty-five years!' he thought, with a gasp of astonishment; and he gave her a hurried, furtive, prying look from under his bushy eyebrows.

She certainly did nothing on this occasion to cause him any discomfort. She just muttered in quite a conventional tone, 'I never like to see plantains in the grass'; and bending down she proceeded to pull up certain small weeds, making a little pile of them behind the headstone.

Swaying thus above the mound, and scrabbling with outstretched arms among the grass-blades, her figure in the misty afternoon sunshine took on, as Wolf stood there, a kind of portentous unreality. There was something outlandish in the whole scene, something monstrous and bizarre that destroyed all ordinary pathos. Twenty-five years? If she had come here regularly for all that time, how could there be any plaintains, or any clover, or any moss either, left upon his father's grave? He was so conscious of the personality of this woman, so amazed at a tenacity of feeling that seemed to pass all limits of what was due, that his own sensibility became hard and rigid.

But though his emotions were cold, his imagination worked freely. The few feet of Dorsetshire clay, the half-inch of brittle, West-country elm-wood, that separated him from the upturned skull of his begetter, were like so much transparent glass. He looked down into William Solent's empty eye-sockets, and the empty eye-sockets looked back at him. Steadily, patiently, indifferently they looked back; and between the head without a nose looking up and the head with so prominent a nose looking down, there passed a sardonic wordless dialogue. 'So be it,' the son said to himself. 'I won't forget. Whether there are plantains or whether there aren't plantains, the universe shan't fool me.' 'Fool me; fool me,' echoed the fleshless skull from below.

'There!' sighed Selena Gault, rising to her natural perpendicular position. 'There! There won't be any more of *them* for a fortnight. Shall we go back now, boy?'

When they were once more in the road Miss Gault became a little more talkative.

'You're not like him, of course – not in any way. He really was uncommonly handsome. Not that *that* had any weight with *me*. But it had with some. It had with Mr. Urquhart!' She paused and glanced almost mischievously at her companion. 'I'm sure I don't know,' she remarked, with a funny little laugh, 'what Mr. Urquhart will make of *you*!'

'The idea seems to be,' said Wolf gravely, while his estimate of his new friend's perspicacity became more respectful, 'that I should help him with some historical researches. It appears he is writing a "History of Dorset." '

'History of fiddlestick!' snapped the lady. And then, in a more amiable tone, 'But he's no idiot. He *has* read a little. You'll enjoy going through his library.'

Wolf felt himself experiencing a rather cowardly hope that his companion would pass the slaughter-house this time without comment. The hope was not fulfilled.

'I suppose *you* eat them?' she asked in a hoarse whisper; and Wolf, turning towards her a startled face, was struck by an expression of actual *animal fear* upon her extraordinary physiognomy. But she did not linger; and it was not long before they were once more opposite the workhouse.

'Do you know what he said when he was dying?' she began suddenly. 'He didn't say it particularly to me. I just happened to be there. He said it to every one in general. He said, "Christ! I've enjoyed my life!" He used the word "Christ!" just in that way, as an exclamation. There was a young clergyman there, straight down from Cambridge, an athlete of some sort; and when your father cried out "Christ!" like that – and he was dead the next second – I heard him mutter, "Good for you, sir!" as if it had been a fine hit at a cricket-match.'

Wolf would have been entirely responsive now if Miss Gault had touched his arm or even taken his arm, but she walked forward without making any sign.

'I expect your mother has abused me pretty thoroughly to you since you were a child,' she said presently. 'Ann and I were never fond of each other. We were enemies even before your father came. She cut me out, of course, at every turn; but that didn't bring her round! She couldn't forgive me for being the head-master's daughter. You've no idea of the savage jealousies that go on in a place like this. But wherever *we* were we should have hated each other. Ann is flippant where I'm serious, and I'm flippant where Ann is serious.'

Wolf tried in vain to imagine on what occasions Miss Gault would display flippancy, but he knew well enough what that word meant in regard to his mother. He was seized at that moment with an irresistible temptation to reveal to this woman the picture of her character with which he had been regaled for the last twenty-five years. It was a picture so extraordinarily different from the reality, that it made him wonder if all women, whether flippant or otherwise, were personal to the point of insanity in their judgments of one another. What his mother had told him was not even a caricature of Selena Gault. It referred to another person altogether.

'My mother has a lot of friends in town,' he began, rather lamely. Miss Gault cut him short.

'Of course she has! She's a brave, high-spirited, ambitious woman. Of course she has!' And then, in a low, meditative voice that seemed to float wistfully over the years, 'She was very much in love with your father.'

This last remark, coming at the moment when the abbey clock above their heads struck four, produced considerable bewilderment in Wolf's mind. The idea of his estranged parents having been 'in love' with each other made him feel curiously in the cold, and strangely alien to both of them. In some obscure way he felt as if Selena Gault were practising an indecent treachery, but a treachery so subtle that he couldn't lay his finger upon it!

'Let's go in here for a minute!' he said. 'And then I must keep my appointment with Mr. Otter.'

They entered the great nave of the abbey church and sat down. The high, cool, vaulted roof, with its famous fan-tracery, seemed to offer itself to his mind as if it were some 'branch-charmed' vista of verdurous silence, along which his spirit might drift and float at large, a leaf among leaves!

There was a faint greenish mist in that high roof, the effect of some cavernous contrast with the mellow warmth of the horizontal sun pouring through the coloured windows below; and into that world of undulating carving and greenish dimness Wolf now permitted his mind to wander, till he began to feel once again that mysterious sensation which he called his 'mythology.'

He felt free of his mother, and yet tender and indulgent towards her. He felt bound up in some strange affiliation with that skeleton in the cemetery. He felt in whimsical and easy harmony with the queer lady seated by his side. The only thing that troubled him at all just then was a faint doubt as to what effect this return to the land of his birth would have upon his furtive, private, hidden existence. Would he be crafty enough to keep that secretive life-illusion out of the reach of danger? Would his inner world of hushed Cimmerian ecstasies remain uninvaded by these Otters and Urquharts?

20

He felt as though he were tightening his muscles for a plunge into very treacherous waters. All manner of unknown voices seemed calling to him out of this warm spring air; mocking voices, beguiling voices, insidious voices – voices that threatened unguessed-at disturbances to that underground life of his which was like a cherished vice. It was not as though he heard the tones of these voices so that he could have recognized them again. It was as though a wavering crowd of featureless human figures on the further side of some thick, opaque lattice-work were conferring together in conspiring awareness of his immediate appearance among them!

The atmosphere was cooler when they came out of the church. Its taste was the taste of an air that has been blown over leagues and leagues of green stalks full of chilly sap. It made Solent think of water-buttercups in windy ponds, and the splash of moor-hens over dark gurgling weirs.

He parted from his companion by a grotesque little statue under the lime trees representing the debonair ancestor of the Lovelaces, whose name, though intimately associated with Ramsgard, had slipped into something legendary and remote. Selena Gault gave him her hand with a stately inclination of her unlovely head.

'You'll come in and see me and my cats before long and tell me your impressions of all those people?'

'I certainly will, Miss Gault,' he answered. 'You've been very good to me.'

'Tut, tut, boy! Good is not the word! When I come to think of it, standing like that with your hat off, you *have* a kind of look – '

'That's under *your* influence, Miss Gault,' he hurriedly said, and they took their separate ways.

There was far less embarrassment for Wolf in his encounter with Mr. Darnley Otter than he had expected. They were the only men in that massive old-world sitting-room, decorated with hunting-scenes and large solemn prints of Conservative statesmen, and they found it easy and natural to sit down opposite each other at a round table and to enjoy an excellent tea. Wolf was hungry. The bread-and-butter was fresh and plentiful. The solidity of the teapot was matched by the thinness of the cups; and the waiter, who seemed to know Mr. Otter well, treated them with a dignified obsequiousness which had about it the mellow beauty of centuries of feudal service.

He was a clean-shaven man, this waiter, with an aristocratic stoop and a face that resembled that of Lord Shaftesbury, the great philanthropist; and Wolf felt an obscure longing to sit opposite him in his own snug parlour – wherever that was – and draw out of him the hidden sources of that superb respectfulness – to be the object of which, even for a brief hour's tea-drinking, was to be reconciled not only to oneself, but also in some curious way to the whole human race!

'We haven't seen Mr. Urquhart down here lately,' the waiter was saying to Wolf's new acquaintance. 'His health keeps up, I hope, sir?'

'Perfectly,' responded Mr. Otter. 'Perfectly, Stalbridge. I hope you yourself are all right, Stalbridge?'

Wolf had never seen a physical human movement more expressive, more adjusted, more appropriate, than the gesture with which the elderly servant balanced the back of his hand against the edge of their table and leaned forward to reply to this personal question. He noticed this gesture all the more vividly because of a curiously-shaped white scar that crossed the back of the man's hand. But he now became aware of something else about this waiter – something that surprised and rather disturbed him. The fellow's countenance did not only remind him of Lord Shaftesbury. It reminded him of that face by the Waterloo steps!

'I've nothing to complain of, sir, thank you, sir, since I settled that little legal trouble of mine. It's the mind, sir, that keeps us up; and except for the malice and mischief that comes to all, I've no grievance against the Almighty.'

The air of courteous magnanimity with which the old waiter exonerated Providence made Wolf feel ashamed of every peevishness he had ever indulged. But why did he make him think of that Waterloo-steps face?

When Mr. Stalbridge had left them to look after some other guests, both the men, as they finished their tea and lit their cigarettes, began to feel more comfortable and reassured in their attitude to each other.

Darnley Otter was in every respect more of a classified 'gentleman' than Solent. He had a trim, pointed, Van Dyck beard of a light-chestnut colour. His finger-nails were exquisitely clean. His necktie, of a dark-blue shade, had evidently been very carefully chosen. His grey tweed suit, neither too faded nor too new, fitted his slender figure to a nicety. His features were sharply cut and very delicately moulded, his hands thin and firm and nervous.

22

When he smiled, his rather grave countenance wrinkled itself into a thousand amiable wrinkles; but he very rarely smiled, and for some reason it was impossible for Solent to imagine him laughing. One facial trick he had which Wolf found a little disconcerting – since his own method was to stare so very steadily from under his bushy eyebrows – a trick of hanging his head and letting his eyelids droop over his eyes as he talked. This habit was so constant with him that it wasn't until the dialogue with the waiter occurred that Wolf realized what his eyes were like. They were of a tint that Wolf had never seen before in any human face. They were like the blue markings upon the sides of freshly-caught mackerel.

But what struck Wolf most deeply was not the colour of Mr. Otter's eyes. It was their look. He had never in the whole course of his life seen anything so harassed, so anxious, as the expression in those eyes, when their owner was unable any longer to avoid giving a direct glance. Nor was it just simply that the man was of a worrying turn of mind. The curious thing about the anxiety in Mr. Otter's eyes was that it was unnatural. There was a sort of puzzled surprise in it, a sort of indignant moral bewilderment, quite different from any constitutional nervousness. His expression seemed to protest against something that had been inflicted on him, something unexpected, something that struck his natural acceptance of life as both monstrous and inexplicable.

It was when he spoke to the waiter that his unhappy expression was caught most off-guard, and Wolf explained this to himself on the theory that the waiter's abysmal tact unconsciously relieved his interlocutor from the strain of habitual reticence.

Their meal once over, it did not take them long to get mounted, with all Wolf Solent's luggage, in Mr. Urquhart's dog-cart. That afternoon's drive from Ramsgard to King's Barton was a memorable event in Wolf's life. He had come already to feel a definite attraction toward this scrupulously-dressed, punctilious gentleman with the troubled mackerel-dark eyes; and as they sat side by side in that dog-cart, jogging leisurely along behind an ancient dapple-grey horse, he made up his mind that if it was to be in Darnley Otter's company that his free hours were to pass, they would pass very harmoniously indeed.

The evening itself, through which they drove, following a road parallel to and a little to the right of that one which had ended with the cemetery, was beautiful with an exceptional kind of beauty. It was one of those spring evenings which are neither golden from the direct rays of the sinking sun, nor opalescent from their indirect diffused reflection. A chilly wind had arisen, covering the western sky, into which they were driving, with a thick bank of clouds. The result of this complete extinction of the sunset was that the world became a world in which every green thing upon its surface received a fivefold addition to its greenness. It was as if an enormous green tidal wave, composed of a substance more translucent than water, had flowed over the whole earth; or rather as if some diaphanous essence of all the greenness created by long days of rain had evaporated during this one noon, only to fall down, with the approach of twilight, in a cold, dark, emerald-coloured dew. The road they thus followed, heading for that rain-heavy western horizon, was a road that ran along the southern slope of an arable upland – an upland that lay midway between the pastoral Dorset valley, which was terminated by the hills and woods of High Stoy, and the yet wider Somersetshire valley that spread away into the marshes of Sedgemoor.

Solent learned from a few courteous but very abrupt explanations interjected by his companion that the only other occupants of the house to which they were proceeding were Darnley's elder brother, Jason, and his mother, Mrs. Otter. He also gathered that Darnley himself, except on Saturdays and Sundays, worked as a classical under-master in a small grammar-school in Blacksod. By one means and another – Wolf was quick at such surmises – he obtained an impression that this work in Blacksod was anything but congenial to his reserved companion. He also began to divine, though certainly with no help from his well-bred friend, that these scholastic activities of his were almost the sole financial support of the family at Pond Cottage.

'I do wish I could persuade you,' Solent began, when they were still some two and a half miles from their destination, 'to give me some sort of notion of what Mr. Urquhart really expects from me. I've never made any historical researches in my life. I've only compiled wretched summaries from books that every one can get. What will he want me to do? Go searching round in parish-registers and so on?'

The driver's gaze, directed obstinately to the grey tail of their slow-moving horse, remained unresponsive to the querulousness of this appeal.

'I have a notion, Solent,' he remarked, 'that you'll get light on a great many things as soon as you've seen Mr. Urquhart.'

Wolf pulled down the corners of his mouth and lifted his thick eyebrows.

'The devil!' he thought. 'That's just about what my friend Miss Gault hinted.'

He raised his voice and gave it a more serious tone.

'Tell me, Otter, is Mr. Urquhart what you might call eccentric – queer, in fact?'

Darnley did turn his bearded profile at this. 'That depends,' he said, 'what you mean by "queer." I've always found him very civil. My brother can't bear the sight of him.'

Wolf made his favourite grimace again at this.

'I hope your brother will approve of *me*,' he said. 'I confess I begin to be a bit frightened.'

'Jason is a poet,' remarked Mr. Otter gravely, and his tone had enough of a rebuke in it to rouse a flicker of malice in his companion.

'I hope Mr. Urquhart isn't a poet, too,' he said.

Mr. Otter took no notice of this retort except to fall into a deeper silence than ever; and Wolf's attention reverted to what he could see of the famous Vale of Blackmore. Every time the hedge grew low, as they jogged along, every time a gate or a gap interrupted its green undulating rampart, he caught a glimpse of that great valley, gathering the twilight about it as a dying god might gather to his heart the cold, wet ashes of his last holocaust.

More and more did the feeling grow upon him that he was entering into a new world where he must leave behind the customs, the grooves, the habits of fifteen long years of his life. 'There's one thing,' he thought to himself, while a sudden chilliness struck his face as their road drew nearer the course of the river, 'that I'll never give up . . . not even for the sake of the slenderest "peeled willow-wand" in Dorset.' As this thought crossed his mind he actually tightened his two bony hands tenaciously over his legs just above his knees, as if he were fortifying himself against some unknown threat to his treasured vice. And then, in a kind of self-protective reassembling of his memories, as if by the erection of a great barrier of mental earthworks he could ward off any attack upon his secret, he set himself to recall certain notable landmarks among his experiences of the world up to the hour of this exciting plunge into the unknown.

He recalled various agitating and shameful scenes between his high-spirited mother and his drifting, unscrupulous father. He summoned up, as opposed to these, his own delicious memories of long, irresponsible holidays, lovely uninterrupted weeks of idleness, by the sea at Weymouth, when he read so many thrilling books in the sunlit bow-window at Brunswick Terrace. How clearly he could see now the Jubilee clock on the Esplanade, the pompous statue of George the Third, the White Nore, the White Horse, the wave-washed outline of Portland breakwater! How he could recall his childish preference for the great shimmering expanse of wet sand, out beyond the bathing-machines, over the hot, dry sand under the sea-wall, where the donkeys stood and Punch and Judy was played!

'I am within twenty miles of Weymouth here,' he thought. '*That's* where my real life began . . . *that's* the place I love . . . in spite of its lack of hedges and trees!'

Then he recalled his tedious, uninspired youth in London, the hateful day-school, the hateful overcrowded college, the interminable routine of his ten years of teaching. 'A double life! A double life!' he muttered under his breath, staring at the grey rump of Mr. Urquhart's nag, as it swayed before him, and moving his own body a little forward, as he tightened his grip still more fiercely upon his own bony thighs.

Was he going to be plunged now into another world of commonplace tedium, full of the same flat, conventional ambitions, the same sickening clevernesses? It couldn't be so! It couldn't . . . it couldn't . . . with this enchanted springtime stirring in all these leaves and grasses. . . .

What a country this was!

To his right, as they drove along, the ground sloped upwards – cornfield after cornfield of young green shoots – to the great main ridge between Dorset and Somerset, along which – only a mile or so away, his companion told him – lay the main highway, famous in West-country history, between Ramsgard and Blacksod, and also between – so Mr. Otter assured him – Salisbury and Exeter!

To his left the Vale of Blackmore beckoned to him out of its meadows – meadows that were full of faint grassy odours which carried a vague taste of river-mud in their savour because of the nearness of the banks of the Lunt. From Shaftesbury, on the north, to the isolated eminence of Melbury Bub, to the south, that valley stretched away, whispering, so it seemed, some inexplicable prophetic greeting to its returned native-born.

As he listened to the noise of the horse's hooves steadily clicking, clicking, clicking, with every now and then a bluish spark rising in the dusk of the road, as iron struck against flint; as he watched the horizon in front of him grow each moment more fluid, more wavering; as he saw detached fragments of the earth's surface – hill-curves, copses, far-away fields and hedges – blend with fragments of cloud and fragments of cloudless space, it came over him with a mounting confidence that this wonderful country must surely deepen, intensify, enrich his furtive inner life, rather than threaten or destroy it.

Thus, clutching his legs as if to assure himself of his own identity, thus leaning eagerly forward by his companion's side, his eyebrows contracted into a fixed frown and his nostrils twitching, Wolf felt the familiar mystic sensation surging up even now from its hidden retreat. Up, up it rose, like some great moonlight-coloured fish from fathomless watery depths, like some wide-winged marsh-bird from dark untraversed pools! The airs of this new world that met its rising were full of the coolness of mosses, full of the faint unsheathing of fern-fronds. Whatever this mysterious emotion was, it leaped forward now towards the new element as if conscious that it carried with it a power as formidable, as incalculable, as anything that it could encounter there.

3

A DORSET CHRONICLE

'So this is to be your room,' said Mrs. Otter. 'I knew you'd want to see it at once; as you have to dress, of course, for dining at the House? It's not large, but I think it's rather comfortable. My son Jason said only just now that he felt quite envious of it. His own room is just opposite, looking on the back garden, as yours does on the front. I think we might show him Jason's room, don't you, Darnley? It's so very characteristic! At least we try to keep it so, don't we, Darnley? Darnley and I do it ourselves, when he's out.' Her voice, as the two men stood in the doorway staring at Solent's pieces of shabby luggage, which they had just carried in, sank into a confidential whisper. 'He's out now,' she added. They both moved aside as she proceeded to make her way across the small passage. 'There!' she exclaimed, opening a door; and Wol peered into complete and rather stuffy darkness. 'There! Perhaps you have a match, Darnley?'

Darnley obediently struck a match and proceeded to set alight two ornate candles that stood on a chest of drawers. The whole look of the chamber thus revealed was detestable to the visitor.

Above the bed hung an enormous Arundel print of a richly-gilded picture by Benozzo Gozzoli; and above the fireplace, where a few red coals still smouldered, was a morbidly sanctimonious Holy Family by Filippino Lippi.

'I'd better open the window a little, mother, hadn't I?' said Darnley, moving across the room.

'No – no, dear!' cried the lady hurriedly. 'He feels the draught so terribly when he's indoors. It's only cigarette smoke – and a little incense,' she added, turning to Wolf. 'He finds incense refreshing. We order it from the Stores. Darnley and I don't care for it. So a little lasts a long time.'

'He must have gone to Blacksod again,' remarked the son grimly, glancing at his watch and looking very significantly at his mother.

'If he has, I'm sure I hope they'll be nicer to him than they were last time,' murmured the lady.

'At the Three Peewits?' retorted her son drily. 'Too nice, I daresay! I wish he'd stick to Farmer's Rest.'

'We are referring to the inns in this neighbourhood where my son meets his friends,' remarked the mother; and Wolf, contemplating the thin, peaked face, the smooth, high forehead, the neatly-brushed, pale hair, the nun-like dress of the little woman, felt ashamed of the first rush of inconsiderate contempt that her manner of speech had provoked in him.

'There's something funny about all this,' he thought to himself. 'I'll be interested to see this confounded incense-burner.'

Left to himself to unpack his things, he looked round with anxious concern at the room that was to be his base of operations, his secret fox's hole, for so prolonged a time. There was a Leighton over the mantelpiece, and a huge Alma Tadema between the two windows; and he divined at once that the spare bedroom was used as a depository by this household for mid-Victorian works of art.

He leaned out of one of the windows. A sharp scent of jonquils was wafted up from some flower-bed below; but the night was so dark he could see nothing except a row of what looked like poplar trees and a clump of thick bushes.

He quickly unpacked his clothes and put them away in easily-opening, agreeably-papered drawers. There was a vase of rust-tinted polyanthuses on the dressing-table; and he thought to himself, 'The poet's mother knows how to manage things!'

He decided at first to confine himself to a dinner-jacket, but realizing that he had only one pair of black trousers, and that these went best with the tail-coat, he changed his mind and put on full evening-dress.

As he finally tied his white tie into a bow at the small mahogany-framed looking-glass, he could not help thinking of the many unknown events that would occupy his thoughts as he stood just there in future days – events that were only now so many airy images, floating, drifting, upon the sea of the unborn.

'How will Mr. Urquhart receive me?' his thoughts ran on. 'This brother of Otter's doesn't like him; but that's nothing. . . . I'll deal with these awful pictures later!' And he carefully extinguished his candles and stepped out on the landing.

The little dining-room of Pond Cottage faced the drawing-room at the foot of the stairs; and when he stood in the hall, hesitating over which room to enter, he was surp ised to fin himself beckoned to, eagerly and surreptitiously, by a bent old woman in a blue apron, laying the dinner. He crossed the threshold in answer to this appeal.

'I know'd yer,' the crone whispered. 'I know'd 'twas none o' they, soon as I did hear yer feet. Looksy here. Mister! Master Darnley'll want to go up to Squire's with 'ee. Don't 'ee let 'un go! That's what I've got to say to 'ee. Don't 'ee let 'un go! 'Tis no walk up to House. 'Tis straight along Pond Lane and down Lenty, and there 'a be! Just 'ee go off now, quiet-like, afore they be comed downstairs. I'll certify to Missus that I telled 'ee the way to House. Don't 'ee stand staring at a person toad-struck and pondering! Off with 'ee now! Be an angel of a sweet young gent! There! Don't 'ee wait a minute. They'll be down, afore 'ee can holler yer own name. Out wi' 'ee, and God bless 'ee. Straight to the end of Pond, and then down Lenty!'

It was the nature of Wolf Solent, when other things were equal, to be easy, flexible, obliging. So without asking any questions he silently and expeditiously obeyed the old servant. He snatched up his hat and his overcoat, and vanished into the darkness of the night.

'I suppose this is Pond Lane,' he said to himself, as he made his way in the direction pointed out by the old woman. 'But if it isn't, I can't help it. They're all on the jump about that chap's coming home. She wanted to keep Otter in the house to deal with the beggar.'

Fortune favoured him more than he might have expected. Just where Pond Lane turned into Lenty, he met a group of children, and under their direction he had no difficulty in finding the drive-entrance to King's Barton Manor.

It was not a long drive and it did not lead to a big house. Built in the reign of James the First, Barton Manor had always remained a small and unimportant dwelling. Its chief glory was its large and rambling garden – a garden that needed more hands to keep it in order than the present owner was able to afford.

And, standing on the top of the weather-stained, lichen-spotted stone steps, after he had rung the bell, Wolf Solent had time, before anyone answered his ring, to imbibe something of the beauty of this new surrounding. The sky had cleared a little, and from a few open spaces, crowded with small, faint stars, a pallid luminosity revealed the outlines of several wide, velvety lawns, intersected by box-hedges, themselves divided by stone-flagged paths. Wolf could see at one end of these lawns a long, high yew-hedge, looking in that uncertain light so mysterious and ill-omened that it was easy to imagine that on the further side of it all manner of phantasmal figures moved, ready to vanish at cock-crow!

For one moment he had a queer sensation that that wretched human face he had seen on the Waterloo steps hung there – there also, between the branches of a tall obscure tree that grew at the end of that yew-hedge. But even as he looked, the face faded; and instead of it, so wrought-upon were his nerves at that moment, there appeared to him the worried, anxious, mackerel-coloured eyes of Darnley Otter.

He was disturbed in these fancies by the opening of the carved Jacobean door. The man-servant who admitted him was, to his surprise, dressed in rough working-clothes. He was an extremely powerful man, and had a swarthy, gipsy-like complexion and coal-black hair.

'Excuse me, sir,' he said with a melancholy smile, as he took the visitor's coat and laid it on a great oak chest that stood in the hall. 'Excuse me, Mr. Solent, but I've been working till a few minutes ago in the stable. He never likes me to apologize to gentlemen who come; but that's the way I am; and I hope you'll excuse me, sir.'

Even at the very moment he was muttering an appropriate reply to this somewhat unusual greeting, and allowing his thoughts, below the surface of his words, to reflect how oddly the servants in King's Barton behaved, Wolf became aware of the approach of an imposing personage coming down the long hallway towards them. This figure, limping very much and leaning upon a stick, was in evening-dress; and as he approached he muttered, over and over again, in a low, soft, satiny voice: 'What's this I hear, eh? What's this I hear, eh? What's this I hear, eh?'

The tall coachman, or gardener, or whatever he was, did not wait for his master's arrival. With one quick glance at Solent and a final 'Excuse me, sir!' he vanished through a side-door, leaving Wolf to face his host without any official announcement.

'Mr. Solent? Very good. Mr. Wolf Solent? Very, very good. You received my letter and you came at once? Excellent. Very, very good.'

Uttering these words in the same low voice that made Wolf think of the unrolling of some great, rich bundle of Chinese silk, he offered his left hand to his visitor and kept his right still leaning upon the handle of the stick that supported him.

The impression Wolf got from Mr. Urquhart's face was extremely complicated. Heavy eyelids, and pendulous, baggy foldings below the eyes, made one aspect of it. Greenish-blackness in the eyes themselves, and something profoundly suspicious in their intense questioning gaze, made another. An air of agitated restlessness, amounting to something that might have been described as a hunted look, made yet a third. The features of the face, taken in their general outlines, were massive and refined. It was in the expression that flitted across them that Wolf detected something that puzzled and perturbed him. One thing was certain. Both Mr. Urquhart's head and Mr. Urquhart's stomach were unnaturally large – far too large for his feeble legs. His hair, which was almost as black as that of his man-servant, caused Wolf to wonder whether or not he wore a wig.

Dropping his visitor's hand, he suddenly stood stock-still, in the attitude of one who listens. Wolf had no idea whether he was arrested by sounds in the garden outside or sounds in the kitchen inside. He himself heard nothing but the ticking of the hall-clock.

Presently the squire spoke again. 'They didn't come with you, then? They didn't bring you to the door, then?' He spoke with what Wolf fancied was a tone of nervous relief.

'I found my way very easily,' was all the visitor could reply.

'What's that? You came alone? They let you come alone?' The man gave him a quick, suspicious glance, and limped a step or two towards the front door. Wolf received an impression that he wasn't believed, and that Mr. Urquhart thought that, if the door were opened and he called loud enough, someone would respond at once out of the darkness.

'Didn't Darnley come *any* of the way with you?' This was said with such a querulous, suspicious accent that Wolf looked him straight in the face.

'They didn't even know I had left the house,' he remarked sternly.

Mr. Urquhart glanced at the door through which the servant had vanished.

'I told him to lay three places,' he remarked. 'I made sure they wouldn't let you come alone.'

Wolf, at this, lifted one of his thick eyebrows; and a flicker of a smile crossed his mouth.

'Would you like me to run over and fetch him?' he said.

'What's that, eh? Fetch him? Did you say fetch him? Of course not! Come, come. Let's go in. Monk will have everything ready by now. Come along. This is the way.'

He led his visitor down the hall and into a small oak-panelled room. The table *was* laid for three; and no sooner were they seated, than Roger Monk, re-garbed as if by magic in a plain dark suit, and accompanied by a young maid in cap and apron, brought in two steaming soup-plates. The dinner that followed was an exceptionally good one, and so also was the wine. Both host and guest drank quite freely; so that by the time the servants left them to their own devices, there had emerged not only a fairly complete understanding as to the character of the work which Wolf was to undertake in that remarkable establishment, but also a certain *rapport* between their personalities.

Staring contentedly at a large monumental landscape by Gainsborough, where what might have been called the spiritual idea of a country road lost itself between avenues of park-like trees and vistas of mysterious terrace-walks, Wolf began to experience, as he sipped his port wine and listened to his host's mellow discourse, a more delicious sense of actual physical well-being than he had known for many a long year.

He soon discovered that he was to labour at his particular share of their grandiose enterprise in a window-seat of the big library of the house, while Mr. Urquhart pursued independent researches in a room he called 'the study.' This was excellent news to the new secretary. Very vividly he conjured up an image of that window-seat, ensconced behind mullion-panes of armorial glass, and opening upon an umbrageous vista resembling that picture by Gainsborough!

'Our History will be an entirely new genre,' Mr. Urquhart was saying. 'What I want to do is to isolate the particular portion of the earth's surface called "Dorset"; as if it were possible to decipher there a palimpsest of successive strata, one inscribed below another, of human impression. Such impressions are for ever being made and for ever being obliterated in the ebb and flow of events; and the chronicle of them should be continuous, not episodic.' He paused in his discourse to light a cigarette, which, when it was lit, he waved to and fro, forming curves and squares and patterns. His hand holding the cigarette was white and plump, like the hand of a priest; and, as he wrote on the air, a trail of filmy smoke followed the movements of his arm.

'Of course, a genuine continuity,' he went on, 'would occupy several lifetimes in the telling of it. What's to be done then, eh? D'ye see the problem? Eh? What's to be done?'

Solent indicated as well as he could by discreet facial signs that he did see the problem, but left its solution to the profound intelligence in front of him.

Mr. Urquhart proceeded. 'We must select, my friend. We must select. All history lies in selection. We can't put in everything. We must put in only what's got pith and sap and salt. Things like adulteries, murders, and fornications.'

'Are we to have any method of selection?' Wolf enquired.

Mr. Urquhart chuckled. 'Do you know what I've thought?' he said. 'I've thought that I'd like to get the sort of perspective on human occurrences that the bedposts in brothels must come to possess – and the counters of bar-rooms – and the butlers' pantries in old houses – and the muddy ditches in long-frequented lovers' lanes.'

'It's in fact a sort of Rabelaisian chronicle you wish to write?' threw in Wolf.

Mr. Urquhart smiled and leant back in his chair. He drained his wine-cup to the dregs, and with half-shut, malignant eyes, full of a strange inward unction, he squinnied at his interlocutor. The lines of his face, as he sat there contemplating his imaginary History, took to themselves the emphatic dignity of a picture by Holbein. The parchment-like skin stretched itself tightly and firmly round the bony structure of the cheeks, as though it had been vellum over a mysterious folio. A veil of almost sacerdotal cunning hovered, like a drooping gonfalon, over the man's heavy eyelids and the loose wrinkles that gathered beneath his eyes. What still puzzled Wolf more than anything else was the youthful glossiness of his host's hair, which contrasted very oddly not only with the extreme pallor of his flesh, but also with the deeply-indented contours of his Holbein-like countenance. Mr. Urquhart's coiffure seemed, in fact, an obtrusive and unnatural ornament designed to set off quite a different type of face from the one it actually surmounted.

'Is it or isn't it a wig?' Wolf caught himself wondering again. But each furtive glance he took at the raven-black cranium opposite him made such a supposition less and less credible; for by the flicker of the candles he seemed to detect the presence of actual individual hairs, coarsely and strongly growing, on either side of the 'parting' in the centre of that massive skull. While he was considering this phenomenon, he became conscious that Mr. Urquhart had left the matter of Dorset Chronicles and was speaking of religion.

34

'I was brought up an Anglican and I shall die an Anglican,' he was saying. 'That doesn't in the least mean that I believe in the Christian religion.'

There was a pause at this point, while the squire refilled his own glass and that of his visitor.

'I like the altar,' the man continued. 'The altar, Mr. Solent, is the one absolutely satisfactory object of worship left in our degenerate days.' There came into Mr. Urquhart's face, as he uttered these words, an expression that struck Wolf as nothing less than Satanic.

'It – does – not – matter – to you then, sir,' threw out Wolf cautiously, 'what the altar represents?'

Mr. Urquhart smiled. 'Eh?' he muttered. 'Represents – did you say?' And then in a vague, dreamy, detached manner he repeated the word 'represents' several times, as if he were mentally examining it, as a connoisseur might examine some small object; but his voice, as he did this, grew fainter and fainter, and presently died away altogether.

The new secretary bowed discreetly over his plate of almonds and raisins. He suspected that if it had not been for the excellence of the wine, the great swaying pontifical head in front of him would have been more reserved in its unusual credo.

'Is the church in King's Barton ritualistic enough for your taste, sir?' he enquired.

And then straight out of the air there came into his mind the image of Mr. John Urquhart, stark naked, with a protuberant belly like Punch or Napoleon, kneeling in the dead of night, while a storm of rain lashed the windows, before the altar of a small dark, unfrequented edifice.

'Eh? What's that?' grumbled his entertainer. 'The church here? Oh, Tilly-Valley's all right. Tilly-Valley's as docile as a ewe-lamb.' He leaned forward with a sardonic leer, lowering his head between the candles as if he possessed a pair of sacred horns. 'Tilly-Valley's afraid of me; just simply afraid.' His voice sank into a whisper. 'I make him say Mass every morning. D'ye hear? I make him say Mass whether there's anyone there or not.'

The tone in which Mr. Urquhart uttered these words roused a definite hostility in Wolf's nerves. There came over him a feeling as if he had been permitted, on an airless night, to catch a glimpse of monstrous human lineaments behind the heavy rumble of a particular clap of thunder. There was something abominably menacing in this great wrinkled white face, with its glossy, carefully parted hair, its pendulous eyelids, its baggy eyefolds, butting at him between the candle-flames.

It presented itself to his mind as a clear issue, that he had now really come across a person who, in that mysterious mythopœic world in which his own imagination insisted on moving, was a serious antagonist – an antagonist who embodied a depth of actual evil such as was a completely new experience in his life. This idea, as it slowly dawned upon his wine-befogged brain, was at once an agitating threat and an exciting challenge. He deliberately stiffened the muscles of his body to meet this menace. He straightened his shoulders and glanced carelessly round the room. He composed his countenance into an expression of cautious reserve. He stretched out his legs. He threw one of his arms over the back of his chair. He clenched together the fingers of his other hand, as it lay on his knee beneath the table. He knew well enough that what Mr. Urquhart saw in these manifestations was an access of casual *bonhomie* in his new secretary, a *bonhomie* amounting to something almost like youthful bravado. He knew that what he did not see was a furtive gathering together of the forces of an alien soul, a soul composed of metaphysical chemicals directly antipodal to those out of which his own was compounded.

What Wolf felt in his own mind just then summed itself up in vague half-articulated words uttered in that margin of his consciousness where the rational fades away into the irrational. 'This Dorsetshire adventure is going to be serious,' he said to himself. And then he became suddenly aware that though quite ignorant of all that was occurring in the mind and nerves of his visitor, the squire of King's Barton had grown alive to the fact that his remarks were not meeting with the same magnetic response that they had met with at first. After a minute or two of silence, Mr. Urquhart rose and limped towards the door of the dining-room. He opened the door for Wolf and they both went out into the hall.

'I think,' he said, as they stood at the foot of the stately Jacobean staircase, 'I think I will not show you the library to-night. You have had a tiring day, and if I take you upstairs there's no knowing when we shall separate! By Jove' – and he glanced at the hall-clock – 'it's past ten already! Better say good night before we start talking again, eh? You've got a walk before you, too. Better say good night before we get too interested in each other, eh?

What? Where'd that idiot put your things? Oh, good! Very good. Well, come again by ten o'clock to-morrow morning and we'll settle everything. I am very relieved to find how much we've got in common. My History will not be betrayed by *your* assistance as it was by my last helper.'

Wolf walked to the place where his coat had been laid down by the man-servant, and after he had put it on, and picked up his hat and stick, he turned to his host, who kept uttering meaningless monosyllables in a silky, propitiatory whisper, as if he were ushering out a madman or a policeman, and asked him point-blank who this ill-advised predecessor of his was, turning as he did so the handle of the front door. The question seemed to disturb Mr. Urquhart's mental equanimity as much as the chilly March wind that blew in with a gust when the door was opened disturbed his physical balance.

'Eh? What? What's that? Didn't Darnley tell you? The boy ruined my History at the start. I had to tear up every scrap. He dropped it and went – all in a minute. Eh? What? Didn't Darnley tell you? He left it in chaos. He played hop-scotch with it!'

Struggling with the heavy door and the gusty wind, Solent muttered a propitiatory reply.

'Very annoying – I hope, indeed, I shall do better, sir! You had to get rid of him, then?'

The wind whistled past him as he spoke, so that his host's final word was scarcely audible. In fact, the last thing he saw of Mr. Urquhart was a feeble attempt the man seemed to be making to cover his rotund stomach with the flaps of his dress-suit.

When at last the great door had really closed between them and he was striding down the stone steps, he found his mind full of the impression which that inarticulate final word had made upon him; and before he reached the end of the drive and passed through the iron gates into Lenty Lane, he had come to the startling conclusion that his predecessor in the study of Dorset Chronicles had died, as they say in that county, 'in the het of his job.'

'Good Lord!' he thought, as he turned into Pond Lane. 'If all he feels for his assistants when they die at their post is anger like that, he must be a queer chap to deal with. Or did he mean something quite different? Dead? Dead? But that wasn't the word he used. What *was* the word he used?' And he continued worrying over the wind-blown sarcasm he had caught in the doorway, without coming to any solution of the riddle. 'If it wasn't that he meant the fellow was dead, what *did* he mean?'

His mind was so full of this problem that he arrived at the gate into the small garden of Pond Cottage before he was aware of it. There was a feint reddish light in the window of what he knew was his own bedroom. 'She's given me a fire!' he thought to himself; and he looked forward with keen anticipation to his first night in Dorset after twenty-five years.

Opening the door quietly, he lit a match as soon as he was inside, and turned the key in the lock. He then took the precaution of taking off his shoes; and lightly and stealthily he slipped upstairs and entered his room.

He had no sooner done so than a figure rose up from a chair by the fire and stumbled towards him. It was a middle-aged man, in a long, white, old-fashioned night-shirt, with a woollen shawl wrapped about his shoulders. There was no light but the firelight in the room; and the man's countenance was a mere blur above the folded shawl.

'Was writing poetry . . . let my fire out . . . came before expected . . . humbly apologize . . . hope you'll sleep well. . . .' Without further explanation the man pushed past him and went out, leaving these broken sentences humming in the air like the murmur of some thick, muffled, mechanical instrument. Once more Wolf found himself alone with the Landseer and the Alma Tadema pictures.

'This is too much!' he muttered furiously. 'If I can't have my room to myself I'll go somewhere else,' he thought. 'Does this incense-burner suppose that everyone in the world must humour his whimsies?' He opened both windows wide and lit the candles on his dressing-table.

Apparently Jason Otter had retired quietly to his bedroom, for the house was now as silent as the darkness outside it. He began slowly undressing. For a while his irritation was prolonged by the way the wind kept making the candles flare; but gradually, in the freshness of the cool garden-smells, his accustomed equanimity returned. After all, there would be plenty of time to adjust all these things! He must propitiate these people to the limit at present, and feel his way. It would be silly to show touchiness and cantankerousness at the very start.

By the time he had blown out the flickering candles and was safe in bed, his habitual mood had quite reasserted itself. He went over in his mind his conversation with Mr. Urquhart, and wondered how far his imagination had led him on to exaggerate the sinister element in the man. He wished intensely that he had caught the drift of that final word about his predecessor. Was he dead? Or was it only that he had been ignominiously dismissed?

As he grew sleepy, all manner of trivial occurrences and objects of this adventurous day began rising up before him, emphasizing themselves, out of all proportion to the rest, in a strange half-feverish panorama. The long, enchanted road revealed in that Gainsborough picture hovered before him and beckoned him to follow it. The abrupt apologies of Roger Monk melted into the furtive exhortations of the old woman in the blue apron. Framed in the darkness that closed in upon him, the coarse black hairs, that had refused to be reduced to a wig, metamorphosed themselves into similar hairs, growing, as he knew they *could* grow, upon a long-dead human skull! The jogging, grey haunches of the mare that had brought him from Ramsgard confused themselves with the grey paws of the cat upon Selena Gault's knees.

Very vividly, more vividly than anything else, he saw the waiter at the Lovelace, as he leaned heavily upon their tea-table. He remembered now both the queer whitish scar on the back of that hand and the resemblance to the Waterloo-steps face.

And then, all suddenly, it seemed that he could think of nothing else but the completely unknown personality – apparently that of the clergyman of the place – referred to so contemptuously by Mr. Urquhart as 'Tilly-Valley.' While the syllables 'Tilly-Valley' repeated themselves in his brain, the person concealed behind that odd appellation ceased to be a man. He became some queer-shaped floating object that could not be put into words, and yet was of the utmost importance. What was of importance was that an obstinate bend in that floating object should be straightened out. Something was preventing it from being straightened out, something that emanated from a black wig and a woollen shawl, and was extremely thick and heavy, and had a taste like port wine!

But there was another thing, far down, far off, covered up, as if by masses of dead leaves, a thing that was stirring, gathering, rising, a thing that, in a minute more, would give him illimitable reassurance and strength. When this thing rose to the surface, the bent twig would be straightened out – and all would be well! This 'all being well' implied that that calm, placid cow which was eating plantain-leaves under Basingstoke church tower, should stop eating and lie down. The cow lying down would be a beautiful green mound covered with plantains – plantains that grew larger and larger, till they became enormous succulent leaves as big as elephants' ears; but the cow couldn't quite lie down. Something thick and heavy and sticky, like port wine, impeded its movements. . . .

Everything in the world was material now. Thoughts were material. Feelings were material. It was a world of material objects, of which his mind was one. His mind was a little bluish-coloured thing, soft, fluffy, like blue cotton-wool; and what was rising out of the dead leaves was blue too, but the sticky impeding thing was brown, and the bent twig was brown. . . .

It was as if in that slow sinking into sleep his soul had to pass all the long, previous, evolutionary stages of planetary life, and be conscious with the consciousness of vegetable things and mineral things. This is what made every material substance of such supernal importance to him – of an importance which perhaps material substances really *did* possess, if all were known.

GERDA

The first sensation to which Wolf awoke in a morning of rainy wind and drifting clouds, was a sensation of discomfort. As his mind began concentrating on this discomfort, he realized it proceeded from those two heavily-framed pictures which gave to his chamber a sort of reading-room or club-room aspect. Harmless enough in themselves had they awaited him in the parlour of an hotel, they seemed no less than an outrage upon his senses when associated with this simple and quiet bedroom. He resolved to issue an ultimatum at once. He hadn't come to Dorsetshire to be oppressed by the ponderous labours of Royal Academicians. And he would also make it clear that his bedroom was to be his sanctuary. No night-shirted intruder should run in and out at his pleasure!

He leapt from the bed and proceeded to turn to the wall both of the mid-Victorian masterpieces. That done, he lay down again and gave himself up to the rainy air, full of the smell of young leaves and wet garden-mould. Lying stretched out upon his back, he set himself with a deliberate effort to gather up his recent impressions and relate them as well as he could to the mood of yesterday's drive. With clear awareness of most of the things that had happened to him since he left his mother at the door of their little flat in Hammersmith, he was oddly conscious that all his deepest instincts were still passive, expectant, waiting. He was like a man who recovers from the shock of a shipwreck, and who, drying himself in the security of some alien beach, hesitates, in a grateful placid lethargy, to begin his hunt for berries or fruits or fresh water.

Detail by detail he reviewed the events of the previous day; and as the images of all these people – of Miss Gault, of Darnley, of Mr. Urquhart – passed in procession before him, he was surprised at the light in which he saw them, so different from the way in which they had appeared only some eight or nine hours ago. The importance of material objects – their mystical importance – had been his last impression before sleeping; but now everything appeared in a cold, unmystical light. It was always thus when he awoke from sleep; but the fact that he recognized the transitoriness of the mood did not diminish its power. He was never more cynically clairvoyant than on these occasions. He surveyed at such times his dearest friends through a sort of unsympathetic magnifying-glass in which there was not one of their frailties that did not stand out in exaggerated relief. The port-hole, so to speak, of the malign consciousness through which he saw them was at the same time telescopic and microscopic. It was surrounded, too, by a thick, circular obscurity. He was abnormally sensitive at such times, but with a curtailed and reduced sensibility. Each particular thing as it presented itself dominated the whole field of vision. Nor was this sensitiveness itself an altogether normal receptivity. It was primarily physiological. It had few nervous chords; and no spiritual or psychic ones. Everything that approached it approached it on the bodily plane, as something – even if it were a mental image – to be actually grasped with the five senses.

And so, as he lay there, knowing that a long while must pass before he would have any chance of breakfast, or even of a cup of tea, he made a stronger effort than usual to get his thoughts into focus. The wet airs blowing in through the open windows helped him in this attempt. It was as if he stole away from that little round port-hole and shuffled off to some upper deck, where he could feel the wide horizons. His mind kept reverting to what he had felt during the drive with Darnley, and he tried to analyse what sort of philosophy it was that remained with him during all the normal hours when his 'mythology' – his secret spiritual vice – lay quiescent. He fumbled about in his mind for some clue to his normal attitude to life – some clue-word that he could use to describe it, if any of his new friends began questioning him; and the word he hit upon at last was the word *fetish-worship*. That was it! His normal attitude to life was just that – or nearer that than anything else!

It was a worship of all the separate, mysterious, living souls he approached: 'souls' of grass, trees, stones, animals, birds, fish; 'souls' of planetary bodies and of the bodies of men and women; the 'souls,' even, of all manner of inanimate little things; the 'souls' of all those strange, chemical groupings that give a living identity to houses, towns, places, countrysides. . . .

'Am I inhuman in some appallingly incurable manner?' he thought. 'Is the affection I have for human beings less important to me than the shadows of leaves and the flowing of waters?'

42

He gazed intently at the window-sills of his open windows, above which the tassels of the blinds swayed to and fro in the damp gusts of wind. He thought of the grotesque and obsessed figure of Selena Gault, as she pulled up plantains from his father's grave. No! Whatever this fetish-worship might be, it certainly was different from 'love.' Love was a possessive, feverish, exacting emotion. It demanded a response. It called for mutual activity. It entailed responsibility. The thrilling delight with which he was wont to contemplate his mother's face under certain conditions, the deep satisfaction he derived from the sight of Miss Gault and her cats, the pleasure with which he had surveyed the blue eyes and pointed beard of Darnley Otter – these things had nothing in them that was either possessive or responsible. And yet, he lost all thought of himself in watching these things, just as he used to do in watching the mossy roots of the chestnuts and sycamores in the avenues at Hampton Court! It seemed then that what he felt for both things and people, as he saw them under certain lights, was a kind of exultant blending of vision and sympathy. Their beauty held him in a magical enchantment; and between his soul and the 'soul,' as it were, of whatever it was he happened to be regarding, there seemed to be established a tremulous and subtle reciprocity.

He was pleased at having thought of the word 'fetish-worship' in this connection. And it was in the pleasure of this thought that he now leapt out of bed and, putting on his overcoat, began hurriedly to shave himself, using as he did so the cold water in his jug.

He had not got very far with this, however, when there was a sound in the passage outside that reminded him of the rattle of the milk-cans on the Longborne Port platform. This was followed by a gentle knock at his door. Opening it cautiously, he was surprised to see Mrs. Otter herself standing there, while beside her was a wide tin bath and a can of hot water.

'I was waiting till I heard you move,' she said. 'Darnley has had his breakfast and gone. He goes to Blacksod early. Jason does not get up till late. Dimity and I will be ready for you when you come down.'

Wolf hovered at the door, his face lathered, his safety-razor in his hand. He suddenly felt no better than a lout in the presence of this faded old lady.

She smiled at him pleasantly. 'I hope you'll be happy with us,' she said. 'You'll get used to us soon. Poor Mr. Redfern got quite used to us before he died.'

43

'Mr. Redfern?'

'The gentleman who helped the Squire with his book. But you must have your bath now. Do you think you can be ready in about half an hour?'

Wolf bowed his lathered face and she went off. While he was dragging the bath into his room, she turned at the head of the stairs.

'Would you like a cup of tea at once, Mr. Solent, or will you wait till you come down?'

'I'll wait, thank you! Thank you *very* much!' he shouted; and jerking both bath and can into his fortress, he shut the door and prepared to wash and dress.

The whole process of his ablution and his dressing was now a mechanical accompaniment to absent-minded fantastic thoughts on the subject of the dead Mr. Redfern.

'This was the fellow's room, no doubt,' he said to himself. 'I suppose he died here. A nice death, with those monstrous pictures lying like lead on his consciousness!'

It was on Mr. Redfern's behalf now that Wolf scowled at the backs of these pictures, as he sponged himself in the tin bath. Mr. Redfern dominated that half-hour, to the exclusion of all other thoughts. Wolf saw him lying stone-dead on the pillows he himself had just quitted. He saw him as a pale, emaciated youth, with beautifully moulded features. He wondered if he had been buried by the person Mr. Urquhart called 'Tilly-Valley.' He decided he would look for his grave in the King's Barton churchyard. His dead face took during that half-hour the most curious forms. It became the soap. It became the sponge. It became the spilt water upon the floor. It became the slop-pail. It became the untidy heap of Wolf's dress-clothes. Wolf was not relieved from it, in fact, till he found himself drinking delicious cups of tea and eating incredibly fresh eggs under the care of his hostess in their pleasant dining-room. The pictures here were of the kind that no philosopher could quarrel with. Old-fashioned prints, old-fashioned pastels, old-fashioned engravings, gave the room a spirit that seemed to emerge from centuries of placidity and stretch out consolatory hands to every kind of wayfarer.

'This is *my* room,' said Mrs. Otter, looking very pleased when Wolf explained to her what he felt about it. 'These things came from my own home in Cornwall. The best things in the house belonged to my husband. They're in the drawing-room; very valuable things. But I like this room myself, and I'm glad you do. Mr. Redfern used to love to read and write at this table. I believe if he'd done all his work here he'd never have got that terrible illness. That library of Mr. Urquhart's was too learned for him, poor, dear, young man! And he *was* so good-looking! My son Jason used to call him by the names of all the heathen gods, one after another! Jason was extremely upset when he died so suddenly.'

The visitor to King's Barton found his attention wandering several times after this. Mrs. Otter began to drift into rambling stories about her native Cornwall, and it was only Wolf's power of automatically putting a convincing animation into his heavy countenance that prevented her from realizing how far away his thoughts had flown.

Hostess and guest were interrupted in their rather one-sided *tête-à-tête* by the sound of footsteps descending the stairs. Mrs. Otter jumped up at once.

'It's Jason!' she cried. 'We must have disturbed him. I was talking too much. I'll go and tell Dimity she need not clear away. I expect Jason will like to have a smoke with you.'

She disappeared through the door into the kitchen at the very moment when her elder son entered the room. Wolf was astonished at the difference between the figure he had seen the night before and the figure he rose to shake hands with now. Dressed in neat, dark-blue serge, Jason Otter had the quiet, self-composed air of a much-travelled man of the world. His clean-shaven face, framed by prematurely grey hair, was massively and yet abnormally expressive. Forehead and chin were imposing and commanding; but this effect was diminished and almost negated by the peculiar kind of restless misery displayed in the lines of the mouth. The man's eyes were large and grey; and instead of glancing aside in the way Darnley's did, they seemed to cry out for help without cessation or intermission.

He and Wolf sat opposite each other at Mr. Redfern's favourite table, and, lighting their cigarettes, looked each other up and down in silence. Jason Otter was decidedly nervous. Wolf saw his hand shaking as he lit a match.

There was, indeed, something almost indecent about the sensitiveness of this man's lined and indented face. It made Wolf feel as though at all costs the possessor of such a countenance must be protected from nervous shocks. Was it in taking care of him that Darnley's blue eyes had acquired their curious expression? Jason's own eyes were not tragic. They were something worse. They were exposed; they were stripped bare; they seemed

45

to peer forth helplessly from the human skull behind them, as though some protective filaments that ought to have been there were *not* there!

'I saw you'd turned our pictures to the wall,' he began, fixing his pleading eyes upon Wolf's face as if asking for permission to humble himself to the ground. 'I'll have them taken away. I'll have them put in the privy or in the passage.'

'Oh, it's all right, Mr. Otter,' returned Wolf. 'It's only that I never can sleep in a room with large pictures. It's a peculiarity of mine.'

No sooner had Jason heard this expression, 'a peculiarity of mine,' than his whole visage changed. A childish mischievousness illuminated his pallid physiognomy, and he chuckled audibly, nodding his head.

'A peculiarity? That's excellent. That's what Bluebeard used to say. "It's a peculiarity of mine." I think that's one of the prettiest excuses I've ever heard.'

This explosion was so surprising to Wolf that all he could do was to open his mouth and stare at the man. But the humour passed as quickly as it had come. The face unwrinkled itself. The eyes became supplicatory. The mouth tightened in solemn misery.

'I don't want anyone to be bothered about the moving of those pictures, Mr. Otter,' said Wolf, for he seemed to see with terrible distinctness the devoted lady of the house struggling alone with those heavy frames. 'You must allow me to do it myself. In fact,' he went on, in what he tried to make a casual, airy tone, 'I'm going to beg Mrs. Otter to let me treat that room as if it were an unfurnished flat of my own.'

The head opposite him was so grey that he felt as if he were addressing this hint to Mrs. Otter's husband rather than to her son.

Very gently, moving delicately, like Agag before Samuel, Jason rose to his feet. 'I think we'd better get those pictures changed now,' he whispered earnestly, in a grave, conspiring voice.

Wolf tried to retain his airy, casual manner in the face of this gravity.

'I'll do it like a shot,' he said, rising and moving towards the door. 'Just tell me where to put them!'

The two men went up together, and under Jason's directions the Landseer and the Alma Tadema were deposited in a vacant room at the back of the pantry.

46

'Come upstairs for a minute,' said Mr. Otter, when this trans-action was completed; and stepping softly and quietly, as if there were a dead person somewhere in the house, he led the way into his own room.

Wolf felt the same uneasy sensations in this chamber as he had experienced the evening before. Sinking into a luxurious armchair, and accepting a cigarette, he found himself bold enough to make a faint protest against his host's Arundel prints, whose ceremonious piety he found so distasteful.

'I couldn't work in this room,' he murmured – and felt as he spoke that his tone was cantankerous and impolite.

But Jason Otter showed not the least annoyance or even surprise at his guest's rudeness.

'I expect not! I expect not!' he cried cheerfully. 'There are few people who *could*. I myself could work in a church or in a museum. I welcome anything that acts as a shield. It's like having a band of retainers, a sort of papal guard, to keep the populace at bay.'

As he spoke, he looked proudly and complacently round the room, as if conscious of the protection of the antique French chair in which he had ensconced himself. There was a Boule table at his side, and he proceeded to dust it with a large silk handkerchief.

'I suppose you've never read any books on Hindoo mythology?' he said suddenly.

The word 'mythology' gave Wolf an uncomfortable shock. He felt as a Catholic might feel if he heard a Methodist refer to the Virgin Mary.

He shook his head.

'I've only read one myself,' went on the poet, with a chuckle; 'so you needn't feel a fool. It was by that man who went to Tibet. But in it he mentions Mukalog, the god of rain.'

'The god of rain?' responded Wolf, beginning to feel reassured.

'That's what the man says,' continued the other. 'Of course, we know what these travellers are; but he had a lot of letters after his name, so I suppose he passed some examination.' Jason put his hand in front of his mouth as he said this; and his face was wrinkled with amusement. 'He knows Latin, anyway. He brings it in on the first page,' he added.

'It sounds like a real idol ... Mukalog, the god of rain ...' murmured Wolf.

Jason's countenance suddenly grew solemn and confidential. 'I've got it here,' he whispered. 'I bought it for thirty shillings from Mr. Malakite, the bookseller. *He* bought it at a sale from some

47

fool who thought it was nothing. . . . It's brought me all my luck.
. . .' He lowered his voice still further, so that Wolf could scarcely
hear him. 'These priests look for God in the clouds, but I never
do that. . . . I look for Him . . .'

'I beg your pardon?' questioned Wolf, leaning attentively forward. 'You say you look for Him . . .?'

There was a pause, and the expression of the man changed from
extreme gravity to hobgoblinish humour.

'*In the mud!*' he shouted.

Then, once more grave, he rose to his feet and fetched from its
pedestal a hideous East Indian idol, about six inches high, and
placed it in the middle of the Boule table, just opposite Wolf.

'It's his stomach that makes him so shocking,' said Jason
Otter; 'but the ways of God aren't as dainty as those of the
Bishop of Salisbury. In this world Truth flies downward, not
upward!'

Hardly aware of what he was doing, so occupied was his mind
with the whole problem of his host's personality, Wolf rose, and,
leaning over the table, picked up Mukalog, the god of rain.
Holding it absent-mindedly in his fingers for a while, he finally
made a foolish schoolboy-like attempt to balance it upside-down
on the flat skull of its monstrous head.

This proceeding brought a flash of real anger into Jason's
eyes. He snatched the thing away with a nervous clutch, and,
hurrying to the back of the room, replaced it on its jade pedestal,
which Wolf noticed now, with no great surprise, was standing
near a carved brazier containing some still-smouldering ashes –
doubtless the ashes of that very incense which had to be 'ordered
from the Stores'!

While his host returned in silence to his French chair, and in
profound dejection took out his cigarette-case, Wolf, still staring
in a sort of hypnotized trance at the 'god of rain,' set himself to
wonder why it was that the kind of evil which emanated from this
idol should be so much more distasteful than the kind of evil that
emanated from Mr. Urquhart.

He came to the conclusion that although it is impossible for any
living human being to obliterate all elements of good from itself,
it *is* possible for an artist, or for a writer, or even for the anonymous
creative energy of the race itself, to create an image of evil that
should be *entirely evil*.

But why should this Hindoo idol seem so much more sinister
than any Chinese or Japanese monster? Was it because in India

the cult of spirituality, both for good and evil, had been carried to a greater length than anywhere else in the world?

'You'd better not listen to any tales about me that old Urquhart tells you,' said the poet suddenly, fixing his sorrowful eyes upon the visitor.

The name of his employer made Wolf rise hurriedly from his armchair.

'Certainly not,' he said brusquely, moving to the door. As he placed his hand on the door-handle, he felt as though the evil spirit of Mukalog were serpentining towards him over the poet's shoulders and over the smooth Boule table.

'I'm not one to listen to tales from anyone, Mr. Otter,' he said as he went out.

He crossed the landing and entered his own room. Now that he was alone, he fell into a very grave meditation, as he slowly laced up his boots. 'No wonder,' he said to himself, 'that poor chap Redfern committed suicide! What with this man's demon and Mr. Urquhart's devilish History, this place doesn't seem a paradisal retreat. Well! Well! We shall see what we shall see.'

He carried his coat and hat quietly downstairs and managed to get out of the house unobserved by either Mrs. Otter or the old servant.

The current of his mood was running more normally and gently by the time he found himself being escorted by his eccentric employer to the great isolated library which was now to be the scene of his labours. His dream of the writing-table by a mullioned window 'blushing with the blood of kings and queens' turned out to be a literal presentiment. The view he got from his seat at that window surpassed the Gainsborough itself. The manor-garden melted away into herbaceous terraces and shadowy orchards. These in their turn faded into a green pasture-land, on the further side of which, faint in the distance, he could make out the high ridge of ploughed fields along the top of which ran the main road from Blacksod to Ramsgard.

Mr. Urquhart, however, seemed in a fussy, preoccupied, fidgety mood that morning. He kept bringing books from the shelves and placing them on his secretary's table; and then, after he had opened them and read a passage or two, muttering 'That's good, isn't it? That's the kind of thing we want, isn't it?' he would return them to the shelves and bring back others. Wolf was not very much helped by these manoeuvres. In fact, he was teased and nonplussed. He was anxious to find out exactly how much

49

of a free hand he was going to be allowed, and he was also anxious to find out what definite ideas the Squire of King's Barton already had. This erratic tumbling about of old folios, this hunting for nothing but whimsical and scandalous passages, seemed waste of time on that first morning.

'Have you any plan, any synopsis, made out, sir, such as I could enlarge upon?'

These words greeted Mr. Urquhart when, with a satyrish leer on his face and a thick folio pressed against his stomach, he came limping up to the table for the fourth or fifth time.

'Eh? What's that? "Plan" did you say? "Synopsis" did you say? By Jove! my young friend, I mustn't make such a tosspot of 'ee again the night before we set to work. Didn't I make it clear to you that our book was going to develop along organic lines, not along logical lines? Didn't I make it clear that what we had to aim at was something quite new, an altogether new genre; and that it was to represent the pell-mell of life? It's a sort of Diary of the Dead we're aiming at, Solent. Your plans and your skeletons would spoil it utterly. What I want you to do is to saturate yourself with Dorset Chronicles, especially the more scandalous of them – the old houses, Solent, the old houses! – and then, when you've got the drift of it in your blood, what we'll aim at shall be a sort of West-country *Comédie humaine*. Do you get my meaning? What you've got to do now, Solent, is to help me collect material and to take notes. I'll show you my notes to-morrow. They'll make my meaning clearer. The *last* thing we must think of is arrangement. My book must grow like a living thing, till it frightens us by its reality.'

Wolf listened patiently and dutifully to this discourse. What he thought in his mind was: 'This whole business is evidently just an old man's hobby. I must give up any idea of taking it seriously. I must play with it, just as he's playing with it.'

With this intention in his mind, as soon as he was alone in his window, he spread open before him that monument of scurrilous scandal, *The History of the Abbotsbury Family*, and gave himself up to leisurely note-making. He transcribed in as lively a way as he could the most outrageous of the misdeeds of this remarkable race, as they are narrated by the sly Doctor Tarrant. He exaggerated, where it was possible, the Doctor's unctuous commentaries, and he added a few of his own. He began before long to think that the Squire was not so devoid of all sagacity in this unusual method as he had at first supposed.

Half the morning had already passed in this way when Mr. Urquhart came limping in in a state of impetuous excitement.

'I must send you off at once to Blacksod,' he began. 'Eh? What? You don't mind walking a few miles, eh? Roger says he can't spare the trap. You can lunch in the town at my expense. I've got a bill at the Three Peewits, and you can come back at your leisure. You don't object, eh? It's nothing for a young man like you, and there's very good ale at the Peewits.'

Wolf folded up his notes and replaced Doctor Tarrant's *History*. He expressed himself as more than delighted to walk to Blacksod, and he enquired what it was that Mr. Urquhart wanted done.

'Well, there are two things that have come up, both of them rather important. I've just heard from my bookseller down there. You'll easily find him. His name's Malakite. He's in Cerne Street. He says he's got hold of the Evershot Letters. That's the book for us, Solent! Privately printed and full of allusions to the Brambledown Case! He says there's a man in London after it already. That may be a lie. You'll have to find out. Sometimes Malakite's let me have the use of a book and then sold it afterwards. You'll have to find out, Solent. Eh? What? You'll have to be a diplomatist, a Talleyrand, and that sort of thing, eh?'

Wolf composed his countenance as intelligently as he could and enquired what the other thing was.

Mr. Urquhart lifted his eyebrows, as if the question had been impertinent.

'The other thing?' he murmured dreamily.

But the next moment, as Wolf leaned back against the arm of his chair and looked straight into the man's eyes, there was a startling change in that supercilious face. A flicker, a shadow, a nothing, passed from one to the other; one of those exposures of secret thoughts that seem to bring together levels of consciousness beyond rational thought. It was all over in a moment; and with a quick alteration of his position, and a shuffling of his stick, the lame man recovered his composure.

'Ah yes,' he murmured, with a smiling inclination of his head that resembled the bow of a great gentleman confessing a lapse of memory. 'Ah yes, you are perfectly right, Solent. There *was* another little thing that you might as well attend to while you're about it. It's not of any pressing importance; but, as I say, if you have time, and feel energetic, it might be a good thing to jolt the memory of Mr. Torp. Eh? What's that? Torp, the stone-cutter. Torp of Chequers Street. You'll easily find the fellow.

He's a Jack-of-all-trades – does undertaking and grave-digging as well as stone-cutting.'

Mr. Urquhart became silent, but the expression upon his face was like that of some courtly prince-prelate of old times, who desired his subordinate to obey instructions that he was unwilling to put into vulgar speech.

'Mr. Torp?' repeated Wolf, patiently and interrogatively.

'Just a little matter of a headstone,' went on the other. 'Tilly-Valley's quarrelled with our sexton here. So I've had to use Torp as both sexton and undertaker. He has been disgracefully dilatory.' Mr. Urquhart shuffled to the bookcase, leaning heavily on his stick. He changed the position of one or two of the books; and as he did so, with his back to his secretary, he finished his sentence: 'He's been as dilatory about Redfern's headstone as he was about digging his grave.'

Once more there was a silence in the library of King's Barton Manor. But when the Squire turned round, he seemed in the best of spirits. 'It's not your job, of course, this kind of thing. But I'm an old man, and I don't think you're touchy about trifles. Jog the memory of the good Torp, then, will you? What? Jolt the torpid Torp. That's the word, eh? Tell the beggar in good clear English that I'll go to Dorchester for that stone if he doesn't set it up within the week. You can do that for me, Solent? But it's not important. If it's a bother, let it go! But have a good luncheon at the Three Peewits anyway! Make 'em give 'ee their own ale. It's good. It's excellent. That individual down at Pond Cottage gets drunk on it every night, Monk tells me.'

Turning again to the bookcase, Mr. Urquhart made as though the conversation had terminated; and Wolf, after a moment or two of that awkward hesitation which a subordinate feel when he is uncertain as to what particular gesture of parting is required, went straight out of the room, without a word, and ran downstairs.

He had found his hat and stick, and was on the point of letting himself out of the house, when the little side-door leading to the kitchen hurriedly opened, and Roger Monk made himself visible. He did this with the precipitation of a man reckless with anxiety, and he plunged at once into rapid speech.

'You'll excuse me, Mr. Solent, for troubling you, but the truth of the matter is, sir, that this house will be upset by breakfast-time to-morrow, unless you – unless you – would be so kind, sir, as to help Mrs. Martin and myself.'

'What on earth is coming now?' thought Wolf. 'These King's Barton servants seem pretty hard put to it.'

''Tisn't as though I didn't know that it's above my province to speak,' went on the agitated man. 'But speak I must; and if you're the kind of young gentleman I think you are, you'll listen to my words.'

Wolf contemplated the swarthy giant, who, dressed in his gardener's clothes, with bare throat and bare arms, had the torso of a classical athlete. Beads of perspiration stood out on his forehead, and his great sunburnt hands made weak fumbling gestures in the air.

'Certainly, Roger. By all means, Roger. I shall be delighted to help you and Mrs. Martin in any way I can. What is it I can do for you?'

The tall servant's face relaxed instantaneously, and he smiled sweetly. His smile was like the smile of some melancholy slave in a Greek play. His voice sank into a confidential whisper.

'It's sausages, sir, asking you to excuse me, it's sausages. Mr. Urquhart *has* to have 'em these days for breakfast, and there ain't none of 'em in the house; and I am too set out, what with horses to clean and artichokes to plant and pigs in the yard to feed, to go to town myself.'

Wolf smiled in as grave and well-bred a manner as he could. 'I'll be very glad to bring you home some sausages, Monk,' he said amiably.

'At Weevil's,' cried the other, full of relief and joy. 'At Weevil's in High Street. And be sure you get fresh ones, Mr. Solent. Tell Bob Weevil they're for me. He knows me and I know him. Don't mention Squire. Say they're for Mr. Monk. He'll know! Two pounds of sausages; and you can tell Weevil to put 'em down. Thank 'ee more than I can say, sir, for doing this. It eases a man's mind. I was downright distraught in thinking of it. Squire's like that. What he puts his heart on he puts his heart on, and none can turn him. I've been with other gentlemen – mostly in stable-work, you understand – but I've never worked for one like Squire. Doesn't do to contravene Squire when his heart is fixed, and so I thank 'ee kindly, Mr. Solent.' And the man vanished with the same precipitation with which he appeared.

Wolf set out down the drive in extremely good spirits. Nothing suited him better than to have the day to himself. It seemed to extend before him, this day, and gather volume and freedom, as if it were many days rolled into one. It didn't worry him that it was Friday. The nature of the day, its cloudiness, its gustiness, its greyness, suited his mood completely. It seemed to carry his mind far, far back – back beyond any definite recollections. The look of the oak palings; the look of the mud; the look of the branches, with their scarcely budded embryo leaves swaying in the wind – all these things hit his imagination with a sudden accumulated force. He rubbed his hands; he prodded the ground with his stick; he strode forward with great strides.

This melancholy day, with its gustily-blown elm branches, seemed to extend itself before him along a road that was something more than an ordinary road. Fragmentary images, made up out of fantastic names – the name of Torp, the name of Malakite – hovered in front of him, mingled with the foam of dark-brown ale and the peculiar, bare, smooth look of uncooked sausages. And over and above such images floated the ambiguous presence of his father, William Solent. He felt as if everything that might chance to happen on this grey phantom-like day would happen under the direct influence of this dead man. He loved his father at that moment, not with any idealistic emotion, but with an earthy, sensual, heathen piety which allowed for much equivocal indulgence.

At the foot of the drive he turned into Lenty Lane, passing at the corner a trim little cottage, whose garden of rich black earth was full of daffodils. He stopped for a moment to stare at the window of this neat lodge – thinking in his mind, 'That must be where Roger Monk lives' – and without being seriously disturbed, he was a little startled when, by reason of some impish trick of light and shade, it seemed to him that he saw an image of himself standing just inside one of the lower windows.

But he walked on in undiminished good spirits, and in about a quarter of an hour found himself in the centre of the village of King's Barton.

All the cottages he saw here had protective cornices, carved above windows and doors, chiselled and moulded with as much elaboration as if they were ornamenting some noble mansion or abbey. Many of these cottage-doors stood ajar, as Wolf passed by, and it was easy for him to observe their quaintly-furnished interiors: the china dogs upon the mantelpieces, the grandfather's clocks, the highly-coloured lithographs of war and religion, the shining pots and pans, the well-scrubbed deal tables, the deeply-indented wooden steps leading to the rooms above. Almost all of them had large flagstones, of the same mellow, yellowish tint, laid between the doorstep and the path; and in many cases this stone was as deeply hollowed out, under the passing feet of the generations, as was the actual doorstep which rose above it.

Beyond these cottages his road led him past the low wall of the parish church. Here he stopped for a while to view the graves and to enjoy the look of that solid and yet proud edifice whose massive masonry and tall square tower gathered up into themselves so many of the characteristics of that countryside.

Wolf wondered vaguely in what part of the churchyard his predecessor's body lay – that hiding-place without a headstone! He also wondered whether by some stroke of good luck he should get a glimpse of that submissive clergyman, satirically styled 'Tilly-Valley,' pottering about the place.

But the church remained lonely and unfrequented at that mid-morning hour. Nothing moved there but a heavy rack of dark-grey, wind-blown clouds, sailing swiftly above the four foliated pinnacles that rose from the corners of the tower. Close to the church he perceived what was evidently the parsonage; but there was no sign of life there either.

The cottages grew more scattered now. Some of them were really small dairy-farms, through the gates of whose muddy yards he could see pigs and poultry, and sometimes a young bull or an excited flock of geese.

At last he had passed the last house of the village and was drifting leisurely along a lonely country road. The hedges were already in full leaf; but many of the trees, especially the oaks and ashes, were yet quite bare. The ditches on both sides of the road contained gleaming patches of celandines.

As Wolf walked along, an extraordinary happiness took possession of him. He seemed to derive satisfaction from the mere mechanical achievement of putting one foot in front of the other. It seemed a delicious privilege to him merely to feel his boots sinking in the wet mud – merely to feel the gusts of cold air blowing upon his face.

He asked himself lazily why it was that he found nature, especially this simple pastoral nature that made no attempt to be grandiose or even picturesque, so much more thrilling than any human society he had ever met. He felt as if he enjoyed at that hour some primitive life-feeling that was identical with what these pollarded elms felt, against whose ribbed trunks the gusts of wind were blowing, or with what these shiny celandine-leaves felt, whose world was limited to tree-roots and fern-fronds and damp, dark mud!

The town of Blacksod stands in the midst of a richly-green valley, at the point where the Dorsetshire Blackmore Vale, following the loamy banks of the River Lunt, carries its umbrageous fertility into the great Somersetshire plain. Blacksod is not only the centre of a large agricultural district, it is the energetic and bustling emporium of many small but enterprising factories. Cheeses are made here and also shoes. Sausages are made here and also leather gloves. Ironmongers, saddlers, shops dealing in every sort of farm-implement and farm-produce, abound in the streets of Blacksod side by side with haberdashers, grocers, fishmongers; and up and down its narrow pavements farmers and labourers jostle with factory-hands and burgesses.

After walking for about two miles, Wolf became conscious that this lively agglomeration of West-country trade was about to reveal itself. The hedges became lower, the ditches shallower, the blackbirds and thrushes less voluble. Neat little villas began to appear at the roadside, with trim but rather exposed gardens, where daffodils nodded with a splendid negligence, as if ready in their royal largesse to do what they could for the patient clerks and humble shop-assistants who had weeded the earth about their proud stems.

Soon there began to be manifested certain signs of borough traffic. Motor-cars showed themselves, and even motor-lorries. Bakers' carts and butchers' carts came swiftly past him. He overtook maids and mothers returning from shopping, with perambulators where the infant riders were almost lost beneath the heaps of parcels piled up around them. He observed a couple of tramps taking off their boots under the hedge, their long, brown, peevish fingers untwisting dirty linen, their furtive, suspicious eyes watching the passers-by with the look of sick jackals.

And then he found himself in an actual street. It was a new street, composed of spick-and-span jerry-built houses, each exactly like the other. But it gave Wolf a mysterious satisfaction. The neatness, the abnormal cleanliness of the brickwork and of the wretched sham-Gothic ornamentation did not displease him. The little gardens, behind low, brightly-painted, wooden palings, were delicious to him, with their crocuses and jonquils and budding polyanthuses.

He surveyed these little houses and gardens – doubtless the homes of artisans and factory-hands – with a feeling of almost maudlin delight. He imagined himself as living in one of these places, and he realized exactly with what deep sensual pleasure he would enjoy the rain and the intermittent sunshine. There would be nothing artistic or over-cluttered there, to prevent every delicate vibration of air and sky from reaching the skin of his very soul. He loved the muslin curtains over the parlour-windows, and the ferns and flowerpots on the window-sills. He loved the quaint names of these little toy houses – names like Rosecot, Woodbine, Bankside, Primrose Villa. He tried to fancy what it would be like to sit in the bow-window of any one of these, drinking tea and eating bread-and-honey, while the spring afternoon slowly darkened towards twilight.

He roused himself presently from these imaginations to observe that some of the real business of the town was becoming manifest. The little houses began to be interspersed with wood-sheds and timber-yards, by grocers' shops and coal-yards. He became alert now – that faint sort of 'second-sight,' which almost all contemplative people possess, warning him that Mr. Torp's establishment was not far off. He knew he was in Chequers Street. It only remained for him to keep his eyes open. He walked very slowly now, peering at the yards and shops on both sides of the road; and as he walked, a curious trance-like sensation came over him, the nature of which was very complicated, though no doubt it had something to do with the emptiness of his stomach. But it took the form of making him feel as if he were retracing some sequence of events through which long ago he had already passed.

Ah! There it was! 'Torp, Stone-cutter.' He gazed with interest at the various monuments for the dead, which lay about on the ground or stood erect and challenging against the wall. It produced a queer impression, this crowd of anonymous tombstones, the owners and possessors whereof were even now cheerfully walking about the earth.

'I must get this Torp to show me what he's done for poor Redfern,' he thought, as he passed on to the door of the house.

He knocked at the door and was so instantaneously admitted that it was with a certain degree of confusion that he found himself in the very heart of the stone-cutter's household.

They had evidently just finished their midday meal. Mrs. Torp, a lean, cadaverous woman, was clearing the table. The stone-cutter himself, a plump, lethargic man, with a whimsical eye, was smoking his pipe by the fire. A handsome boy of about eleven, who had evidently just opened the door to let himself out, fell back now and stared at the stranger with a bold impertinence.

'What can I do for 'ee, sir?' said Mr. Torp, not making any attempt to rise, but smiling amiably at the intruder.

'Get on! Get off! Don't worry the gentleman, Lob!' murmured the woman to the spellbound boy.

And then it was that Wolf became aware of another member of the family.

No sooner was he conscious of her presence than he felt himself becoming as speechless with astonishment as the boy was at his own appearance. She sat on a stool opposite her father, leaning her shoulders against the edge of a high-backed settle. She was a young girl of about eighteen, and her beauty was so startling that it seemed to destroy in a moment all ordinary human relations. Her wide-open grey eyes were fringed with long, dark eyelashes. Her voluptuous throat resembled an arum lily before it has unsheathed its petals. She wore a simple close-fitting dress, more suited to the summer than to a chilly day in spring; but the peculiarity of this dress lay in the way it emphasized the extraordinary suppleness of her shoulders and the delicate Artemis-like beauty of her young breasts.

'I've come from King's Barton,' began Wolf, moving towards the stone-cutter. 'I believe I have the honour to have taken the place of the gentleman for whom you have just designed one of your monuments.'

'Sit 'ee down, mister. Sit 'ee down, sir!' cried the man cheerfully. 'Give the gentleman a chair, missus!' He spoke in a tone that implied that his own obesity must be accepted as a pleasant excuse for his retaining a sitting posture.

But Mrs. Torp had already left the room with a tray; and Wolf, as he seated himself with his face to the girl, could hear the woman muttering viciously to herself and clattering angrily with the plates behind the kitchen-door – a door she seemed to have left open on purpose, so that she might combine the pleasure of listening to the conversation with the pleasure of disturbing it.

'Missus be cantiferous wi' I 'cos them 'taties be so terrible rotted,' remarked the man, in a loud, hoarse whisper, leaning forward towards his guest and confidentially tapping his knee with his pipe. 'And them onions what she been and cooked all morning, she've a-boiled all taste out o' they. Them onions might as well be hog-roots for all the Christian juice what be left in 'un.'

Wolf, who had found it difficult to keep his eyes away from the girl by the settle, now suddenly became aware that she was fully conscious of his agitation and was regarding him with grave amusement.

'I suppose *you* don't do any of the cooking?' he said, rather faintly, meeting her gaze.

She changed her position into one that emphasized her beauty with a kind of innocent wantonness, smiled straight into his eyes, but remained silent.

'She?' put in her father. 'Save us and help us! Gerda do the cooking? Why, mister, that girl ain't got the gumption to comb her own hair. That's the Lord's own truth, mister, what I'm telling 'ee. She ain't got the durned consideration to comb her own hair; and it be mighty silky, too, when it be combed out. But her mother have to do it. There ain't nothing in this blessed house what that poor woman hasn't to do; and her own daughter sitting round, strong as a Maypole. Now you be off to school, Lob Torp! Don't yer trouble the gentleman.'

This last remark was due to the fact that the handsome boy had edged himself quite close to Wolf and was gazing at him with a mixture of admiration and insolence.

'What be that on your chain?' he enquired. 'Be that a real girt seal, like what King John throwed into the Wash?'

Wolf put his arm round the child's waist; but as he did so, he looked steadily at Gerda. At that moment Mrs. Torp re-entered the room.

'Well, John?' she said. 'Aren't yer going into the yard? That stone for Mr. Manley's mother's been waiting since Sunday. He comes to see 'un five times a day. He'll be a crazed-man like, if 'tisn't up afore to-morrow.'

Wolf rose to his feet.

'What shall I tell Mr. Urquhart about the headstone for Mr. Redfern?'

He uttered these words in a more decided and less propitiatory tone than he had yet used, and all the family stared at him with placid surprise.

'Oh, that!' cried Mr. Torp. 'So you came about that, did yer? I had thought maybe you knowed some wealthy folk out in country what had a waiting corpse. Do 'ee come from these parts, mister, or be 'ee from Lunnon, as this 'ere Redfern were? . . . Lunnon, eh? Well, 'tis strange that two young men same as you be should come to Blacksod; and both be Lunnoners! But that's what I tells our Gerda here. Maids what won't help their mothers in house, maids what do nought but walk out wi' lads, had best be in Lunnon their own selves! That there Metropolis must be summat wonderful to look at, I reckon. I expect they makes their own moniments in them parts?'

Wolf nodded, with a shrug of his shoulders, to imply that there was little need at present for Mr. Torp to think of extending his activities.

'Could you show me what you've done for Redfern?' he asked abruptly.

'Well, there ain't no harm in that, is there, missus?' said the stone-cutter, looking appealingly at his wife.

'Best show him,' said the lady briefly. 'Best show him. But let 'un understand that Mr. Manley's mother is what comes first.'

The obese stone-cutter rose with an effort and led the way into the yard. Wolf stepped aside to permit the girl to follow her father; and as she passed him, she gave him a glance that resembled the sudden trembling of a white-lilac branch, heavy with rain and sweetness. Her languorous personality dominated the whole occasion for him; and as he watched her swaying body moving between those oblong stones in that cold enclosure, the thought rose within him that if his subterranean vice couldn't find a place for loveliness like this, there must be something really inhuman in its exactions.

With an incredible rapidity he began laying plots to see this girl again. Did Mr. Urquhart know of her existence? Had Darnley Otter ever seen her? . . . He was roused from his amorous thoughts by an abrupt gesture of Mr. Torp.

'There 'a be!' said the carver. ''Tis Ham Hill stone, as Squire Urquhart said for'n to be. I does better jobs in marble; and marble's what most of 'em likes. But that's the order; and the young gent what it's chipped for can't help 'isself.'

Wolf regarded the upright yellow slab, upon the top of which was a vigorous 'Here Lies,' and at the foot of which was an even more vigorous 'John Torp, Monument-maker.'

'You haven't got very far, Mr. Torp,' he remarked drily.

'Won't take me more'n a couple o' afternoons to finish it up,' replied the other. 'And you can tell Mr. Urquhart that as soon as Mr. Manley be satisfied – Mr. Manley of Willum's Mill, tell 'un! – I'll get to work on his young friend and make a clean job of he.'

There did not seem any excuse just then for prolonging this interview. Wolf's mind hurried backwards and forwards like a rat trying to find a hole into a pantry. He thought, 'Would they let her show me the way to the Three Peewits?' and then immediately afterwards he thought, 'They'll send the boy, and I'll never get rid of him!'

In the end he went off with an abruptness that was almost rude. He patted Lob on the head, nodded at the stone-cutter, plunged into the eyes of Gerda as a diver plunges into water, and strode away down Chequers Street.

It was not long before he was seated at a spotless white cloth in the commercial dining-room of the famous West-country inn. In front of him rose a massive mahogany sideboard, which served as a sort of sacred pedestal for the ancient silver plate of three generations of sagacious landlords. In the centre of this silver were two symbolic objects – an immense uncut ham, adorned with a white paper frill, and a large half-eaten apple-tart.

Wolf was so late for luncheon that he and a solitary waiter had the whole dusky, sober room entirely to themselves. They were, however, looked down upon by the ferocious eye of a stuffed pike, and by the supercilious eye of Queen Victoria, who, wearing the blue ribbon of the Garter, conveyed, but only by the flicker of an eyelid, her ineffable disdain for all members of the human race who were not subjects of the House of Hanover.

And as he lingered over his meal, drinking that dark, foamy liquor that seemed the dedicated antidote to a grey March day, he permitted his fancy to run riot with the loveliness of Gerda Torp. How remarkable that she had never once opened her lips! And yet in her silence she had compelled both that room and that yard to serve as mere frames to her personality. He tilted back in his chair, and pressed the palms of his hands against the edge of the table, revolving every detail of that queer scene, and becoming so absorbed that it was only after a perceptible interval that he began to taste the cigarettes which he went on unconsciously smoking.

The girl was not the particular physical type that appealed to him most, or that had, whenever he had come across it, the most provocative effect upon his senses; but the effect upon him of a beauty so overpowering, so absolute in its flawlessness, was great enough to sweep out of sight all previous predilections. And now, as he conjured up the vision of what she was like, it seemed that nothing more desirable could possibly happen to him than to enjoy such beauty.

He made up his mind that by hook or by crook he would possess her. He knew perfectly well that he could not, properly speaking, be said to have fallen in love with her. He was like a man who suddenly finds out that he has suffered all his life from thirst, and simultaneously with this discovery stumbles upon a cool cellar of the rarest wine. To have caught sight of her at all was to be dominated by an insatiable craving for her – a craving that made him feel as if he had some sixth sense, some sense that *must* be satisfied by the possession of her, and that nothing but the possession of her *could* satisfy.

Drugged and dazed with the Three Peewits' ale and with these amorous contemplations, Wolf sat on beneath that picture of Queen Victoria in a species of erotic trance. His rugged face, with its high cheek-bones and hawk-like nose, nodded over his plate with half-shut lecherous eyes. Every now and then he ran his fingers through his short, stiff, fair hair, till it stood up erect upon his head.

'Well, well,' he said to himself at last, 'this won't do!' And rising abruptly from his chair, he gave the waiter, who in his preoccupation had been to him a mere white blur above a black coat, an extravagant tip – half a crown, in fact – and, taking up his hat and stick, told them to put down his meal to Mr. Urquhart's account, and stepped out into the street.

The cold, gusty wind, when he got outside, cleared his brain at once. He made up his mind that he would leave the bookseller to the last; and, stopping one of the passers-by, he enquired the way to Weevil's grocery.

Never did he forget that first lingering stroll though the centre of Blacksod! The country people seemed to be doing their shopping as if it were some special *fête*. Parsons, squires, farmers, villagers – all were receiving obsequious and yet quizzical welcome from the sly shopkeepers and their irresponsible assistants. The image of Gerda Torp moved with him as he drifted slowly through this animated scene. Her sweetness flowed through his senses and flowed out around him, heightening his interest in everything he looked at, making everything seem rich and mellow, as if it were seen through a diffused golden light, like that of the pictures of Claude Lorraine.

And all the while over the slate roofs the great grey clouds rushed upon their arbitrary way. His spirit, drunk with the sweetness of Gerda and the fumes of the Three Peewits' ale, rose in exultation to follow those clouds.

Whirling along with them in this exultant freedom of his spirit, while his human figure with its oak walking-stick tapped the edge of the pavement, he felt a queer need, now, to carry this maddeningly sweet burden of his to that mound in the Ramsgard cemetery.

'*He* would chuckle over this,' thought Wolf, as he recalled that profane death-bed cry. '*He* would push me on to snatch most scandalously at this girl, let the result be as it may!'

His mind dropped now like a leaden plummet into all manner of erotic thoughts. Would her silence go on . . . with its indrawing magnetic secrecy . . . even if he were making love to her? Would that glaucous greyness in her eyes darken, or grow more luminous, as he caressed her? Gerda certainly couldn't be called a 'peeled willow-wand,' for her limbs were rounded and voluptuous, just as her face had something of that lethargic sulkiness that is seen sometimes in ancient Greek sculpture.

It was just at this point that, looking round for a suitable person to enquire of again concerning the sausage-shop, he felt himself jerked by the elbow; and there, in front of him, smiling up into his face, was the handsome, mischievous countenance of Lob Torp.

'I see'd 'ee, mister!' burst out the boy breathlessly. 'I see'd 'ee long afore 'ee could see I! Say now, mister, have 'ee any cigarette-pictures on 'ee?'

Wolf surveyed the excited child thoughtfully. Surely the gods were on his side this day!

'If I haven't, I soon *will* have,' he brought out with a nervous smile, searching hurriedly in his pockets.

It appeared that he did have a couple of half-used packages, containing the desired little bits of stiff, shiny paper.

'There, there's two, at any rate!' he said, handing them over.

Lob Torp scrutinized the two cards with a disappointed eye. 'They ain't Three Castles,' he said sadly. 'Them others bain't as pretty as they Three Castles be.' He meditated for a moment, with his hands in his pockets. 'Say, mister,' he began eagerly, with radiant eyes. 'Tell 'ee what I'll do for 'ee. I'll sell 'ee the photo of Sis, what I be taking down to Bob Weevil's. He were a-going to gie I summat for'n, but like enough it'll be worth more to a gent like yourself. Come now, mister, gie I a sixpence and I'll gie 'ee the picture and say nought to Bob.'

The ingratiating smile with which Lob uttered these words would have been worthy of an Algerian street-arab. Wolf made a humorous grimace at him, under the mask of which he hid annoyance, uneasiness, curiosity.

The boy continued: ''Tis a wonderful pretty picture, mister. I tooked it me own self. She be ridin' astride one of them wold tombstones in Dad's yard, just the same as 'twere a girt 'oss,'

'I don't mind looking at it,' said Wolf, after a pause, pulling the boy into the door of a shop. But Lob Torp was evidently an adept in the ways of infatuated gentlemen.

'Threepence for a look, mister, and sixpence for to keep,' he said resolutely.

It was on the tip of Wolf's tongue to cry, 'Hand it over, boy. I'll keep it!' But an instinct of suspicious dignity restrained him, and he assumed a non-committal, negligent air. But under this air the ancient, sly cunning of the predatory demon began to fumble at the springs of his intention. 'I'll get Bob Weevil to show it to me,' the Machiavellian monitor whispered. 'I shall have it in my hands then without being indebted to this rascally little blackmailer!'

He turned to the boy and took him by the arm. 'Come on, youngster!' he said. 'Never mind about the picture. Much better give it to your friend! I'm going to Weevil's shop now myself, and you can show me the way. I'll give you your sixpence for *that*!' He pulled the child forward with him and made him walk by his side, his arm thrown lightly and casually round Lobbie's neck. But all this sagacious hypocrisy no more deceived the cynical intelligence of Gerda's brother than did the unction of that arm about his shoulder!

The child slipped out of his grasp like a little eel. 'Don't 'ee hold on to I, mister. I ain't going to rin nowhere. I ain't a-gived school the go-by for to play marbles. I be goin' fishing with Bob Weevil, present. He lets I hold his net for'n.'

'Oh, is there any fishing about here?' enquired Wolf blandly, accepting his defeat. The boy skipped a pace or two like a young rabbit.

"Tain't what *you'd* call fishing, mister. Nought but minnies and stickles, 'cept when us do go to Willum's Mill. Woops-I! But them girt chub be hard to hook. And Mister Manley he likes to keep *them* for the gentry. 'Tis when us be down to Willum's of an evening, when farmer be feeding 'issrlf, that Bob and me do a bit of real fishing.'

Wolf surveyed the good-looking urchin with benevolent irony. 'Have you ever landed any of those big chub?' he asked. And then he suddenly became conscious that the nervous, hunted eye of a very shabby clergyman was observing them both, with startled interest, from the edge of the pavement.

'We're near where us wants to go now, sir,' was the boy's irrelevant response, uttered in a surprisingly loud voice.

When they had advanced a little further, the child turned round to his companion and whispered furtively. 'Yon Passon were the Reverend T. E. Valley, mister, from King's Barton. 'Ee do talk to I sometimes about helping he with them holy services up to church; but Dad he says all them things be gammon. He's what you might call blasphemious, my Dad is; and I be blasphemious, too, I reckon; though Bob says that High Church be a religion what lets a person play cricket on Sundays. But I takes no stock o' that, being as cricket and such-like ain't nought to I.'

'Tilly-Valley! Tilly-Valley!' muttered Wolf under his breath, recalling the contemptuous allusion of Mr. Urquhart.

'Here we be, mister!' cried Lobbie Torp, pausing before a capacious old-fashioned shop, over which was written in dignified lettering, 'Robert Weevil and Son.'

They entered together, and the boy was at once greeted by a young man behind the counter, a young man with black hair and a pasty complexion.

'Hullo, Lob! Come to see if there's fishing to-night?'

Wolf advanced in as easy and natural a manner as he could assume. 'I must propitiate my rival,' he said grimly to himself. 'My name is Solent, Mr. Weevil,' he said aloud, 'and I come on behalf of Mr. Urquhart of King's Barton.'

'Yes, sir, quite so, sir; and what can I do for you, sir?' said the young man politely, bowing with a professional smirk over the polished counter.

'The gentleman's been to see Dad,' put in Lobbie, in his high treble. 'And he saw Sis, too, and Sis seed him, too; and I rinned after him and showed him the way!'

'And what can I do for you, sir, or for Mr. Urquhart, sir?' repeated the young grocer.

'To tell you the truth, Mr. Weevil, it was Monk, the man up there, who asked me to come to you. It appears he's run out of sausages – your especial sausages – and he begged me to take back a pound or two for him.'

'I'll do them up at once for you,' said the grocer benignantly. 'I've just had a new lot in.'

It was not very surprising to Wolf to notice that his young guide hurriedly followed Mr. Weevil into the recesses of the shop. From where he stood he could see the two of them quite clearly through an open door, the dark head and the fair head close together, poring over some object that certainly was not sausages!

65

A shameless and scandalous curiosity seized him to share in that colloquy. The various paraphernalia of the shop, the piled-up tins of Reading biscuits, the great copper canisters of Indian teas, the noble erections of Blacksod cheeses – all melted – all grew vague and indistinct.

'Mounted astride of a girt tombstone,' he repeated to himself; and the thought of the cool whiteness of that girl's skin and its contact with that chiselled marble reduced everything else in the world to a kind of irrelevance, to something that fell into the category of the tedious and the negligible.

There came at last an outburst of merriment from the back of the shop that actually caused him to make a few hurried steps in that direction; but he stopped short, interdicted by his sense of personal dignity. 'I really can't join in libidinous jesting with the Blacksod populace *just* at present!' he thought to himself. 'But there's plenty of time. I've no doubt *William* Solent would have had no such hesitation!' And the thought came over him how ridiculous these dignified withdrawings of his would appear to that grinning skull in the cemetery.

But the youth and the boy came back again now gravely enough to the front of the shop.

'There you are, sir!' said Bob Weevil, handing him a lusty package, and puffing out his cheeks as he did so. 'I think Mr. Urquhart will find those to his taste.' He paused and gave Wolf's companion a glance of complicated significance. 'Don't tell Gerdie what I said about that picture, Lob, will you?' he added.

There was a tone in this remark that caused Wolf's face to stiffen and his eyebrows to rise. 'And now perhaps you can tell me,' he said, 'where I can find Malakite's, the bookshop?'

The two friends exchanged a puzzled and baffled glance, not unmixed with disapproval. Books were evidently something for which they both entertained a hostile suspicion. But the young grocer gave him detailed instructions, to which Lob Torp listened with satiric condescension. 'See you both again soon!' murmured Wolf, with dignified amiability, as he left the shop.

He walked very slowly this time along the Blacksod pavements, and he found himself buttoning his overcoat tightly and turning up his collar; for the wind had veered from north-west to due north, and the air that blew against his face now had whistled across the sheep-tracks of Salisbury Plain.

Ah! *There* was the second-hand bookshop, with the single, curious word, 'Malakite,' written above it. He paused for a second to gaze in at the window, and was both surprised and delighted by the number and rarity of the works exposed there for sale. The house itself was a solidly-constructed, sturdily-built mid-Victorian erection, with a grey slate roof; and there was a little open passage at one side of it leading, he could see, into a small walled-in garden at the back.

He pushed open the door and entered the shop. At first he found it difficult to see clearly; for it was already nearly four o'clock, the sky heavily overcast, the place ill-lighted, the gas-jets unlit. But after a moment of suspense, he made out a tall, gaunt, bearded old man, with sunken cheeks, hollow eye-sockets, closely-cropped grizzled hair, seated in a corner of the shop upon a rough, faded horse-hair chair, with a little round table in front of him, carefully gumming together the loose leaves of a large folio which he held upon his knee. The old man's head was bent low over his work, and he made no sign of having heard anyone enter.

'Mr. Malakite?' said Wolf quietly, advancing towards him between rows of books. His approach was so easy and natural in that dim light that his astonishment may be imagined when the old man let the folio fall to the ground, and stumbled to his feet with such agitated violence that the round table collapsed also, tossing the glue-pot upon the floor. In that twilit place it was almost spectral to see the eyes in that old furrowed face staring forth like black holes burnt in a wooden panel.

'I startled you, sir,' muttered Wolf gently, drawing back a little. 'It's a dark, cold afternoon. I'm afraid I disturbed you. I am very sorry.'

For one second the old bookseller seemed to totter and sway, as if to follow his folio to the ground; but he mastered himself, and, leaning against the arm of his horse-hair chair, spoke in a dry, collected voice. His words were as unexpected to his visitor as his agitation had been.

'Who *are* you, young man?' he said sternly. 'Who were your parents?'

Not Dante himself, when in the Inferno he heard a similar question from that proud tomb, could have been more startled than Wolf was at this extraordinary enquiry.

'My name is Wolf Solent, Mr. Malakite,' he answered humbly. 'My father's name was William Solent. He was a master at Ramsgard School. My mother lives in London. I am acting now as secretary for Mr. Urquhart.'

The old man, hearing these words, gave vent to a curious rattling sigh, deep down in his throat, like the sound of the wind through a patch of dead thistle-heads. He made a feeble gesture with one of his long, bony hands, half apologetic, half sorrowful, and sank back again upon his chair.

'You must forgive me, sir,' he said, after a pause. 'You must forgive me, Mr. Solent. The truth is, your voice, coming suddenly upon me like that, reminded me of things that ought to be – reminded me of – of too many things.' The old man's voice rose at the words 'too many,' but his next remark was quiet and natural. 'I knew your father quite well, sir. We were intimate friends. His death was a great blow to me. Your father, Mr. Solent, was a very remarkable man.'

Wolf, on hearing these words, moved up to the bookseller's side, and with an easy and spontaneous gesture laid his hand upon the hand of the old man as it rested upon the arm of his chair.

'You are the second friend of my father's that I have met lately,' said he. 'The other was Miss Selena Gault.'

The old man hardly seemed to listen to these words. He kept staring at him, out of his sunken eye-sockets, with deprecatory intensity.

Wolf, beginning to feel a little uncomfortable, bent down and occupied himself by picking up the fallen table, the glue-pot, and the folio. As he did this he began to grow aware of a sensation resembling that which he had felt in Mr. Urquhart's library – the sensation of the presence of forms of human obliquity completely new in his experience.

He had no sooner got the folio safe back upon the table than the shop-door swung open behind him and closed with a resounding noise. He glanced round; and there, to his surprise, stood Darnley Otter. This quiet gentleman brought in with him such an air of ease and orderliness that Wolf felt a wave of very agreeable reassurance pass through his nerves. He was, in fact, thoroughly relieved to see that yellow beard and gracious reticence. The man's reserved manner and courtly smile gave him a comfortable sense of a return to those normal and natural conventions from which he felt as if he had departed very far since he left the tea-room of the Lovelace Hotel yesterday.

The two young men exchanged greetings, while the owner of the bookshop observed them with a sort of patient bewilderment. He then rose slowly to his feet.

68

'It's time for tea,' he said, in a carefully measured voice. 'I generally lock the place up now and go upstairs. I don't know –' He hesitated, looking from one to the other. 'I don't know whether it would be asking too much – if I asked you both to come upstairs with me?'

Wolf and Mr. Otter simultaneously expressed their extreme desire to drink a cup of tea with him.

'I'll go and warn my daughter, then,' he said eagerly. 'You know, Mr. Otter, I feel as if this young gentleman and myself were already old friends. By the way, this folio, sir' – and he turned to Solent – 'is the book I wrote to Mr. Urquhart about. I think I shall have to trust it with you. It's a treasure. But Mr. Urquhart is a good customer of mine. I don't think he'll want to purchase it, though. Its price is higher than he usually cares to give. Will you excuse me, then, gentlemen?'

So saying, he opened a door at the rear of the shop and vanished from view. The two men looked at each other with that particular look which normal people exchange when an extraordinary person has suddenly left them.

'A remarkable old chap,' observed Wolf quietly.

Darnley shrugged his shoulders and looked round the shop.

'You don't think so?' pursued Solent.

'Oh, he's all right,' admitted the other.

'You don't like him, then?'

The only reply to this was an almost Gallic gesture, implying avoidance of an unpleasant subject.

'Why, what's wrong?' said Solent, pressing him.

'Oh, well,' responded the Latin-teacher, driven to make himself more explicit. 'There's a rather sinister legend attached to Mr. Malakite in regard to his wife.'

'His wife?' echoed Wolf.

'He is said to have killed her with shame.'

'Shame? Do people die of shame?'

'They have been known to do so,' said the schoolmaster, drily, 'at least in classical times. You've probably heard of Œdipus, Solent?'

'But Œdipus *didn't* die. That was the whole point. The gods carried him away,'

'Well, perhaps the gods will carry Mr. Malakite away.'

'What do you mean?' enquired Wolf, with great interest, lowering his voice.

'Oh, I daresay we make too much of these things. But there was a quarrel between this man and his wife, connected with his fondness for their daughter, this young Christie's elder sister . . . and . . . well . . . there was a child born, too.'

'And the wife died?'

'The wife died. The girl was packed off to Australia. It seems she couldn't bear the sight of her child, and it was taken away from her. I can't tell you whether the case got as far as the law-courts, or whether it was hushed up. Your friend Miss Gault knows all about it.'

Wolf was silent, meditating upon all this.

'Not a very pleasant background for the other daughter!' he brought out at last.

'Oh, she's a funny little thing,' said Darnley, smiling. 'She lives so completely in books that I don't think she takes anything that happens in the real world very seriously. She always seems to me, when I meet her, as if she'd just come out of a deep trance and wanted to return to it. She and I get on splendidly. Well, you'll see her in a minute, and can judge for yourself.'

Wolf was silent again. He was thinking of the friendship between this old man and his father. He pondered in his mind whether or not to reveal to Darnley the unexpected agitation which his appearance had excited. For some reason he felt reluctant to do this. He felt vaguely that his new closeness to his cynical progenitor committed him to a certain caution. He was on the edge of all manner of dark entanglements. Well! He would use what discernment he had; but at any rate he would keep the whole problem to himself.

'I went to Torp's yard,' he remarked, anxious to change the subject. 'The fellow doesn't seem to have got very far with Redfern's headstone.'

Darnley Otter lifted his heavy eyelids and fixed upon him a sudden, piercing look from his mackerel-blue eyes.

'Did Urquhart talk to you about Redfern?' he asked.

'Only to grumble at him for doing something about the book that didn't suit his ideas. Did *you* know him? Did he die suddenly?'

Mr. Otter, instead of replying, turned his back, put his hands in his pockets, and began pacing up and down the floor of the shop, which seemed to get darker and darker around them.

He stopped suddenly and pulled at his trim beard.

'I cursed my wretched school-work to you yesterday,' he said. 'But when I think of the misery that human beings cause one another in this world, I am thankful that I can teach Latin, and let it all go. But I daresay I exaggerate; I daresay I exaggerate.'

At that moment the door at the back of the shop opened, and the old bookseller, standing in the entrance, called out to them in a calm, well-bred voice.

'Will you come, gentlemen? Will you come?'

They followed him in silence into a little unlit passage. Preceding them with a slow, careful shuffle, he led them up a flight of steps to a landing above, where there were several closed doors and one open door. At this open door he stood aside and beckoned them to enter.

The room, when they found themselves within it, was lighted by a pleasant, green-shaded lamp. There was a warm fire burning in the grate, in front of which was a dainty tea-table with an old-fashioned urn, a silver teapot, some cups and saucers of Dresden china, and a large plate of thin bread-and-butter.

From beside this table a fragile-looking girl, who might have been anything between twenty and twenty-five, rose to welcome them. Darnley Otter greeted this young person in the manner of a benevolent uncle, and while Wolf and she were shaking hands, retained her left hand affectionately in his own.

Solent had received, since he left King's Barton, so many disturbing impressions that he was glad enough to yield himself up now, in this peaceful room, to what was really a vague, formless anodyne of almost Quakerish serenity. What he felt was undoubtedly due to the personality of Christie Malakite; but as he sank down in an armchair by her side, the impression he received of her appearance was confined to an awareness of smoothly-parted hair, of a quaint, pointed chin, and of a figure so slight and sexless that it resembled those meagre, androgynous forms that can be seen sometimes in early Italian pictures.

For several minutes Wolf permitted the conversation to pass lightly and easily between Darnley and Christie, while he occupied himself in enjoying his tea. He did not, however, hesitate to cast every now and then surreptitious glances at the extraordinary countenance of the old man, who, at a little distance from the table, was reposing in a kind of abstracted coma, his bony hands clasped around one of his thin knees, and his eyes half closed.

Then, all in a moment, Wolf found himself describing his visit to the stone-cutter's yard, and without the least embarrassment enlarging upon the hypnotic charm that had been cast upon him by the loveliness of Gerda.

It appeared, for some mysterious reason, that he could talk more freely to these two people than he had ever talked in his life.

71

He had come, little as he had yet seen of him, to have a genuine regard for Darnley Otter, a regard that he had reason to feel was quite as strongly reciprocated. And in addition to this there seemed to be something about the pale, indefinite profile of the girl by his side, the patient slenderness of her neck, the cool detachment of her whole attitude, that unloosed the flow of his speech and threw around him an unforced consciousness of being at one with himself and at one with the general stream of life.

Darnley rallied him with a dry shamelessness about his confessed infatuation for the stone-cutter's daughter; and Christie, turning every now and then an almost elfish smile toward his voluble talk, actually offered, as she filled his cup for the third or fourth time, to help him in his adventure by inviting the young woman herself, whom she said she knew perfectly well, to have tea with him any afternoon he liked to name!

'She *is* beautiful,' the girl repeated. 'I love to watch her. But I warn you, Mr. Solent, you'll have many rivals.'

'She's worse than a flirt,' remarked Darnley, gravely. 'She's got something in her that I have always fancied Helen of Troy must have had – a sort of terrible passivity. I know for a fact that she's had three lovers already. One of them was a young Oxonian who, they tell me, was a terrific rake. Another, so they say, was your predecessor, young Redfern. But none of them – forgive me, Christie dear! – seems to have, as they say down here, "got her into trouble." None of them seems to have made the least impression upon her! I doubt if she possesses what you call a heart. Certainly not a heart that you, Solent' – he smiled one of his gentlest ironic smiles – 'are likely to break. So go ahead, my friend! We shall watch the course of your *furtivos amores*, as Catullus would say, with the most cold-blooded interest. Shan't we, Christie?'

The young girl turned upon Wolf her steady, unprovocative, indulgent gaze. 'Perhaps,' she said quietly, after a moment in which Wolf felt as though his mind had encountered her mind like two bodiless shadows in a flowing river – 'perhaps in this case it will be different. Would you marry her if it were different?' These words were added in a tone that had the sort of faint aqueous mischief in it, such as a water-nymph might have indulged in, contemplating the rather heavy earth-loves of a pair of mortals.

'Oh, confound it, *that*'s going a little too fast, even for me!' Wolf protested. And, in the silence that followed, it seemed to him as if these two people, this Darnley and this Christie, had managed between them, in some sort of subtle conspiracy, to take off the delicious edge of his furtive obsession.

'Damn them!' he muttered to himself. 'I was a fool to talk about it. But there it is! None of their chatter can make the sweetness of Gerda less entrancing.' But even as he formulated this revolt with a half-humorous irritation, he was aware that his mood *had* in some imperceptible way changed. Under cover of the friendly badinage that was going on between Darnley and Christie, he once or twice encountered the silent observation of the old bookseller, who had now lighted his pipe and was watching them all with a cloudy intentness; and it occurred to him that it was quite as much due to the shock of what he had heard about the old man that this change had come, as to anything that these two had said.

'But to the devil with them all!' he muttered to himself, as he and Darnley rose to go. 'I've never seen anything as desirable as that girl's body, and I'm not going to be teased into giving it up.'

Before he left the house the old bookseller wrapped the folio in paper and cardboard and placed it in his hands, making, as he did so, an automatic reference to his professional concern about its well-being. But the expression in Mr. Malakite's hollow eyes, as this transaction took place, seemed to Wolf to have some quite different significance – some significance in no way connected with the History of the Evershot Family.

All the way back to King's Barton, as the two men walked side by side in friendly fragmentary speech, Wolf kept making spasmodic attempts to adjust the folio and the sausages so as to leave his right hand free for his oak stick. He rejected all offers of assistance from his companion with a kind of obstinate pride, declaring that he 'liked' carrying parcels; but the physical difficulty of these adjustments had the effect of diminishing his response both to the influence of the night and to the conversation of his friend.

It was quite dark now; and the north wind, whistling through the blackthorn-hedges, sighing through the tops of the trees, whimpering in the telegraph-wires, had begun to acquire that peculiar burden of impersonal sadness which seems to combine the natural sorrows of the human generations with some strange planetary grief whose character is unrevealed.

The influence of this dirge-like wind did by degrees, in spite of the numbness of his obstinate clutch upon his packages, come to affect Wolf's mind. He seemed to rush backward on the wings of this wind, to the two human heads – to the fleshless head of William Solent buried in the earth and to the despairing head of that son of perdition crouching at Waterloo Station.

He mentally compared, as he shouted his replies to his companion's remarks against the blustering gusts, the sardonic aplomb of the skull under the clay with that ghastly despair of the living, and he flung over the thorn-hedge a savage comment upon the ways of God.

The trim beard of Darnley Otter might wag on . . . like a brave bowsprit 'stemming nightly to the pole' . . . but the keel of every human vessel had a leak . . . it was only a question of chance . . . just pure chance . . . how far that leak would go . . . any wagging beard . . . any brave chin might have to cry, at any moment, 'Hold, enough!' . . .

And suddenly, in the covering darkness, Wolf took off his hat and stretched back his head, straining his neck as far as it would go, so that without relaxing the movement of walking, his up-turned face might become horizontal. In this position he made a hideous grimace into infinity – a grimace directed at the Governing Power of the Universe. What he desired to express in this grimace was an announcement that his own secret happiness had not 'squared' him. . . .

His mind rushed upwards like a rocket among those distant stars. He imagined himself standing on some incredible promontory on the faintest star he could see. Even from that vantage he wanted to repeat his defiance – not 'squared' yet, O crafty universe! – not 'squared' yet!

5

THE BLACKBIRD'S SONG

The destinies certainly did appear anxious to 'square' him; for when that evening, after dinner with the Otters, he repaired to the Manor House with his packages, Mr. Urquhart turned out to be so delighted with the book that he commissioned him to return to the bookseller the very next morning and make the old man a liberal offer.

Wolf awoke, therefore, on this day of Saturn, in that vague, delicious mood wherein the sense of happiness-to-come seems, like a great melted pearl, to cover every immediate object and person with a liquid glamour.

He took his bath with unalloyed satisfaction between the four bare walls, whereon certain dimly-outlined squares in the extended whiteness indicated the exile of all art except that of the air, the sun, and the wind.

He saw nothing of either of the brothers. Jason had not yet appeared; and though there had been some vague reference to his accompanying Darnley in his early start, it was now clear that the younger Otter wished his morning walk to be free of human intercourse.

This was all agreeable enough to Wolf, who, like most conspirators, had a furtive desire to be left to his own devices; and he resolved, without putting his resolution into any formal shape, that as soon as his business with Malakite was settled, he would make his way to the stone-cutter's yard.

From his conversation at breakfast with Mrs. Otter, he learnt that it was possible to reach the portion of the town where the bookseller lived without following the whole length of Chequers Street. This suited him well, as he wished to time his appearance at the Torp *ménage* so as to be certain of finding the girl at home.

He had discovered, laid carefully at the edge of his plate, a letter from his mother, and another letter, with a Ramsgard postmark, that he suspected to be from Selena Gault. Both these epistles he hurriedly thrust into his coat-pocket, afraid of any ill-omened side-tracking of his plans for that auspicious day.

It lacked about an hour of noon, when, armed with permission to bid as high as five pounds for the Evershot chronicle, Wolf entered for the second time the establishment of Mr. John Malakite.

The old man received him without the remotest trace of the emotion of the preceding day. He agreed so quickly to accept Mr. Urquhart's offer that Wolf felt a little ashamed of his own skill as a business intermediary. But he was glad to escape the tedium of haggling, and was preparing to bid the bookseller farewell when the man asked in a blank and neutral voice, as if the proposal were a mechanical form of politeness, 'Will you come upstairs with me, Mr. Solent, and have a glass of something?'

Knowing that there was no immediate hurry, if he were to time his visit to the Torps so as to catch them at their midday meal, Wolf assented to this suggestion, and, as on the former occasion, followed the man up the dark stairway with unquestioning docility.

He found Christie in a long blue apron, dusting the little sitting-room. Wolf was touched by the grave awkwardness with which she pulled this garment over her head and flung it down before offering him her hand. The dress she now appeared in was of a sombre brown, and so tightly fitting that it not only enhanced her slenderness, but also gave her an almost hieratic look. With her smoothly-parted hair and abstracted brown eyes, she resembled some withdrawn priestess of Artemis, interrupted in some sacred rite.

No sooner was the guest seated than Mr. Malakite muttered some inarticulate apology and went down to his shop.

The girl stood for a while in silence, looking down upon her visitor, who returned her scrutiny without embarrassment. A delicious sense of age-long intimacy and ease flowed over him.

'Well, Mr. Solent,' she murmured, 'I suppose you're not going to leave Blacksod without seeing Gerda?'

'I thought of waiting till their dinner-time,' he said, 'when I would be certain of finding her. Redfern's headstone can be dragged in again as an excuse.'

Christie nodded gravely. 'I wrote to her yesterday,' she said, 'after you went. If I'd known you were coming in to-day, I might have asked her to tea. But I daresay she'll come, anyway. She often does pay me visits.'

While the girl uttered these words, Wolf became aware for the first time of the extraordinary key in which her voice was pitched. It was a key so faint and so unresonant as to suggest some actual deficiency in her vocal cords. As soon as he became conscious of this peculiarity, he found his attention wandering from the meaning of her speech and focusing itself upon her curious intonation.

But she moved to the fireplace now and bent her back over it, striking a little lump of coal with an extremely large silver poker.

'That girl must be sick of admiration,' observed Wolf, 'wouldn't you think so? Her mother must have an anxious time.'

'I expect her mother knows how well she can take care of herself,' retorted Christie, glancing sideways at him while she rested on the handle of the poker. A couple of thin, loose tresses of silky brown hair hung down across her brow, her nose, her mouth, her chin, giving the impression that she was peering out at him through the drooping tendrils of some sort of wild vegetation.

Her remark, as may well be imagined, was not received with any great ardour by her guest.

'What an expression!' he cried petulantly. 'Take care of herself! Why the devil *shouldn't* she take care of herself?' And it occurred to him to wonder how it was that this sophisticated young lady had ever made friends with the stone-cutter's daughter. Christie's manners were so well-bred that it was difficult to associate her with a family like the Torps.

The girl smiled as she replaced the silver poker by the side of the hearth. 'Gerda knows well enough that *I* don't worry about her,' she said. 'Pardon me a minute,' she added, slipping past him into an alcove that adjoined the room.

Wolf took advantage of her absence to move across to a bookshelf which already had attracted his attention. What first arrested his interest now was an edition of Sir Thomas Browne's *Hydriotaphia or Urn-Burial*. He took this book down from the shelf, and was dreamily turning its pages when the girl returned with a glass of claret in her hand. Hurriedly replacing the book in its place, and raising the wine to his lips, he could not resist commenting upon some other, more abstruse, volumes that her bookshelf contained.

'I see you read Leibnitz, Miss Malakite,' he said. 'Don't you find those "monads" of his hard to understand? You've got Hegel there, too, I notice. I've always been rather attracted to *him* – though just why I'd be puzzled to tell you.'

He settled himself again in his wicker chair, wine-glass in hand.

'You're fond of philosophy?' he added, scowling amiably at her. His thick eyebrows contracted as he did this, and his eyes grew narrow and small.

She seated herself near him upon the sofa and smoothed out her brown skirt thoughtfully with her fingers. She was evidently

77

anxious to answer this important question with a becoming scrupulousness.

With this new gravity upon the features of its mistress, it seemed to Wolf as if the little sitting-room itself awoke from somnolence and asserted its individuality. He observed the unadulterated mid-century style of its cut-glass chandeliers, of its antimacassars, of its rosewood chairs, of its Geneva clock, and of the heavy gold frames of its water-colour pictures. The room, as the morning light fell upon these things across the grey slate roofs and the yellow pansies in the window-box, certainly did posses as charming character of its own, a character to which the thick, dusky carpet and the great mahogany curtain-rod across the window gave the final touches.

'I don't understand half of what I read,' Christie began, speaking with extreme precision. 'All I know is that every one of those old books has its own atmosphere for me.'

'Atmosphere?' questioned Wolf.

'I suppose it's funny to talk in such a way,' she went on, 'but all these queer non-human abstractions, like Spinoza's "substance" and Leibnitz's "monads" and Hegel's "idea," don't stay hard and logical to me. They seem to melt.'

She stopped and looked at Wolf with a faint smile, as if deprecating her extravagant pedantry.

'What do you mean – melt?' he murmured.

'I mean as I say,' she answered, with a shade of querulousness, as if the physical utterance of words were difficult to her and she expected her interlocutor to get her meaning independently of them. 'I mean they turn into what I call "atmosphere." '

'The tone of thought,' he threw in, 'that suits you best, I suppose?'

She looked at him as if she had been blowing soap-bubbles, and he had thrown his stick at one of them.

'I'm afraid I'm hopeless at expressing myself,' she said. 'I don't think I regard philosophy in the light of "truth" at all.'

'How do you regard it then?'

Christie Malakite sighed. 'There are so many of them!' she murmured irrelevantly.

'So many?'

'So many truths. But don't tease yourself trying to follow my awkward ways of putting things, Mr. Solent.'

'I'm following you with the greatest interest,' said Wolf.

'What I mean to say *is*,' she went on, with a little gasp, flinging out the words almost fiercely, 'I regard each philosophy, not as the "truth," but just as a particular country, in which I can go about – countries with their own peculiar light, their Gothic buildings, their pointed roofs, their avenues of trees – But I'm afraid I'm tiring you with all this!'

'Go on, for heaven's sake!' he pleaded. 'It's just what I want to hear.'

'I mean that it's like the way you feel about things,' she explained, 'when you hear the rain outside, while you're reading a book. You know what I mean? Oh, I can't put it into words! When you get a sudden feeling of life going on outside . . . far away from where you sit . . . over wide tracts of country . . . as if you were driving in a carriage and all the things you passed were . . . life itself . . . parapets of bridges, with dead leaves blowing over them . . . trees at crossroads . . . park-railings . . . lamp-lights on ponds. . . . I don't mean, of course,' she went on, 'that philosophy is the same as life . . . but – Oh! Can't you *see* what I mean?' She broke off with an angry gesture of impatience.

Wolf bit his lip to suppress a smile. At that moment he could have hugged the nervous little figure before him.

'I know perfectly well what you mean,' he said eagerly. 'Philosophy to you, and to me, too, isn't science at all! It's life winnowed and heightened. It's the essence of life caught on the wing. It's life *framed* . . . framed in room-windows . . . in carriage-windows . . . in mirrors . . . in our "brown studies," when we look up from absorbing books . . . in waking dreams – I do know perfectly well what you mean!'

Christie drew up her feet beneath her on the sofa and turned her head, so that all he could see of her face was its delicate profile, a profile which, in that particular position, reminded him of a portrait of the philosopher Descartes!

He changed the conversation back to himself. 'It's queer,' he remarked, 'that I can confide in you so completely about Gerda.'

'Why? she threw out.

'Don't you see that what I'm admitting is an unscrupulous desire to make love to your young friend?'

'Oh!' She uttered this exclamation in a faint, meditative sigh, like a wistful little wind sinking down among feathery reeds. 'You mean that you might make her unhappy?'

He gave a deprecatory shake of the head.

'But you leave out so many things in all this,' she went on. 'You leave out the character of Gerda; and you leave out your own character, which, for all I know' – she spoke in a tone whose irony was barely perceptible – 'may be so interesting that the advantage of contact with it might even counterbalance – your lack of scruple!'

Wolf withdrew his hands, which were clasped so close to Christie's elbows as almost to touch them. He interlocked his fingers now, round the back of his head, tilting his chair a little. 'Forgive me, Miss Malakite,' he said ruefully. 'I do blunder into unpardonable lapses sometimes. I oughtn't to have said *that* to you . . . so bluntly. It's because I seem to have . . . a sort of . . . curiosity. At least, I *think* it's curiosity!'

'It's all right. Don't you mind!' She spoke these words with a tenderness that was as gentle as a caress – a caress which might have been given to a disgraced animal that required reassuring; and as she spoke she leaned forward and made a little movement of her hand towards him. It was the faintest of gestures. Her fingers immediately afterwards lay clasped on her lap. But he did not miss the movement, and it pleased him well. Another thing he did not miss was that under any stress of emotion a certain wavering shapelessness in her countenance disappeared. Mouth, nose, cheeks, chin, all these features, chaotic and inchoate when left to themselves, at such moments attained a harmony of expression which approached, if it did not actually reach, the verge of the beautiful.

Wolf brought down his tilted chair upon the floor with a jerk. 'I'm forgiven then?' he said, and paused for a second, searching gravely in her brown eyes for a clue to her secret thoughts. 'It must be all those books you read,' he went on, 'that makes you take my scandalous confessions so calmly.' He stopped once more. 'I suppose,' he flung out, 'the most amazing perversities wouldn't shock you in the least!' As soon as he had uttered these words he remembered what Darnley had told him, and he caught his breath in dismay. But Christie Malakite gave no sign of being distressed. She even smiled faintly.

'I don't know,' she said, 'that it's my readings that have made me what I am. In a sense I *am* conventional. You're wrong there. But in another sense I am . . . what you might call . . . *outside the pale.*'

'Do you mean . . . inhuman?'

She turned this over gravely.

'I certainly don't like it when things get too human,' she said. 'That's probably why I can't *bear* the Bible. I like to be able to escape into parts of Nature that are lovely and cool, untouched and free.'

Wolf nodded sympathetically; but he got up now to take his leave, and allowed these words of hers to float away unanswered.

He allowed them, as he moved to the door, to sink down among the old-fashioned furniture about her, as if they were a chilly, moonlight dew mingling with warm, dusty sun-motes. His final impression was that the ancient objects in her room were pondering mutely and disapprovingly upon this fragile, heathen challenge to the anthropomorphism of the Scriptures!

Once out in the street – and strangely enough before his mind reverted to Gerda at all – Wolf found himself recalling something he had hardly noticed at the time, but which now assumed a curious importance. Between the pages of the volume of the *Urn-Burial* which he had taken down from Christie's shelf, there had lain a grey feather. 'Her marker, I suppose!' he said to himself, as he made his way back to the High Street.

But soon enough, now, in the hard metallic sunshine and the sharp wind, his obsession for the stone-cutter's daughter rose up again and dominated his consciousness. With rapid strides he made his way through the chief thoroughfares of the town, witnessing on every side all manner of bustling, lively preparations for the Saturday afternoon's marketing.

When he was within a few hundred yards of the Torp yard he glanced at his watch and realized that he was still a good deal too early. It would be, he felt, a great blunder to present himself at that house and find no Gerda! Looking around for a resting-place, he espied a small patch of grass behind some rickety palings, in the centre of which was a stone water-trough. He clambered through the palings and sat down on the ground, with his back to this object. It was then, as he lit a cigarette, that he remembered that he had not yet read his letters.

He opened them one by one. They were both short. Miss Gault's ran as follows:

My dear Boy,

If I were not so eccentric a person and *striking*, I may say, in more senses than one, I should take for granted that you had forgotten all about me – but since I know that both my manners and my cats *must* have made *some* impression upon you, I am not at all afraid of this! I am writing to ask you whether you will care to come over to tea with me on Sunday afternoon? I will not reveal in advance whether there will be only myself and my cats. . . .

Yrs. affectionately,
SELENA GAULT

81

Mrs. Solent's letter was even more laconic.

My dearest Wolf,

Carter has begun to fuss about the rent. What does he think
we are? And why did you run up that bill at Walpole's? That's
the one kind of luxury which ought always to be paid for in cash.
I have refused to pay till the summer. Better let it be understood that you're away on a holiday! I think I shall join you at
King's Barton quite soon; in fact, as soon as you can assure me
that you've discovered a clean, small cottage, with a neat, small
garden. I think it will do me good to do a little gardening.
How lovely, my dear, it will be to see you again!

Your loving mother,

ANN HAGGARD SOLENT

Wolf pushed out his under-lip and drew down the corners of
his mouth as he replaced these two documents in his pocket.
Then he got up upon his feet and shivered. He looked at his
watch again. 'I'll go in,' he said to himself, 'when it's five minutes
to one.'

He pulled his greatcoat tighter around him, and, removing his
cloth cap, sat down upon it very gravely, as if it had been a
wishing-carpet.

The passers-by upon the pavement hardly turned to notice the
bareheaded man with an oak stick across his knees. They were
Blacksod burgesses and had their own affairs to attend to. A tuft
of vividly green grass grew between some uneven bricks in front
of him; and he regarded its sturdy, transparent blades with concentrated interest.

'Grass and clay!' he thought to himself. 'From clay to grass and
then from grass to clay!' And once more that peculiar kind of
shivering ran through him, which a coincidence of physical cold
with amorous excitement is apt to produce, especially when some
fatal step of unknown consequence is trembling in suspension.

And with extraordinary clearness he realized that particular
moment in the passing of time, as he sat there, a hunched-up
gaunt figure, wrapped in a faded brown overcoat, waiting with a
beating heart his entrance to the yard of Mr. Torp.

His mind, after his fashion, conjured up in geographical simultaneousness all the scenes around him. He saw the long, low
ridge of upland, on the east slope of which lay the village of King's

82

Barton, and along the top of which ran the high road linking together the scholastic retreats of Ramsgard with the shops and tanneries of Blacksod. He saw the rich, pastoral Dorsetshire valley on his right. He saw the willows and the reeds of the Somerset salt-marshes away there on his left. And it came into his mind how strange it was that while he at this moment was shivering with amorous expectation at the idea of entering that yard of half-made tombstones, far off in the Blackmore Vale many old ploughmen, weather-stained as the gates they were even now leisurely setting open, were moving their horses from one furrowed field to another after their midday's rest and meal. And probably almost all of them had relations who would come to Mr. Torp's yard on their behalf one day.

'I'll go to Miss Gault on Sunday,' he said to himself, 'and I'll look around for a place for mother.'

Swinging his mind from these resolutions with an abrupt turn, emphasized by a dagger-like thrust into the earth with the end of his stick, he now struggled to his feet, and without glancing again at his watch clambered over the palings and strode down the road.

The appearance of Torp's yard seemed to have changed in the night. It looked smaller, less imposing. The headstones themselves looked second-rate; but Wolf, as he made for the door, wondered which of them it was that had served the girl for a hobby-horse, and this doubt once more lent them dignity.

He knocked boldly at the door; but he had time, while the vibrations of the sound were dying down, to notice that there was a crack in one of the door-panels, and in the middle of this crack a tiny globule of dirty paint.

The door was opened by Mrs. Torp. There they all were, just beginning their meal! Gerda was evidently disposing of no small helping of Yorkshire pudding. But she swallowed her mouthful at one gallant gulp and regarded her admirer with a smile of pleasure.

The first words uttered by Wolf, when Mrs. Torp had shut the door behind him, were directed at the head of the family, whose mouth and eyes were simultaneously so wide open as to suggest sheer panic.

'I haven't come about business to-day. I only happened to be passing and I thought I'd look in. Mr. Urquhart was very pleased to hear how well you're getting on with that monument. I saw him last night.'

Mr. Torp turned his countenance toward his wife, a proceeding which seemed to announce to everyone round the table that he was too cautious even to commit himself to a word until reassured as to what was expected of him.

'Just passing, and thought to look in,' repeated Mrs. Torp, avoiding her husband's appeal.

'We seed three girt woppers down to Willum's Mill. We dursn't pull 'em out, cos Mr. Manley his own self were casting. He were fishing proper, he were. But Bob says maybe Mr. Manley won't be at the job, come Monday. So then us'll try again.'

These hurried words from young Lob eased the atmosphere a little.

Mrs. Torp looked at the sirloin in front of her husband and at the Yorkshire pudding in front of herself.

'Thought to look in,' she repeated, resuming her seat.

Wolf began to feel something of a fool. He also began to feel extremely hungry. He laid his hand on the shoulder of the boy, and was on the point of saying something about perch and chub to cover his embarrassment, when he detected a quick interchange of glances between mother and daughter, followed by the appearance of a faint flush on the girl's cheeks.

'Since you *were* passing, you'd be best to sit 'ee down and take a bit of summat,' said the woman reluctantly. 'Father, cut the young gentleman a slice. Get a plate from the dresser, Lob.' Thus speaking, she thrust a chair beneath the table, with more violence than was necessary, and having added a very moderate portion of Yorkshire pudding to the immense slice of beef carved by the monument-maker, she caught up her own empty plate and retired into the scullery.

When once his guest was seated at the table, between the silent Gerda and himself, the obese stone-cutter relaxed into most free pleasantry.

'Injoy theeself like the wheel at the cistern, be my text, Mr. Redfern, I beg pardon, Mr. Solent. The Lord gives beef, but us must go to the Devil for sauce, as my grand-dad used to murmur. I warrant this meat were well fed and well killed, as you might say. 'Taint always so wi' they Darset farmers.'

Wolf listened in silence to these and other similar remarks while he ate his meal. He was so close to Gerda that he could catch the faint susurration of her deep, even breathing.

'I'm glad she doesn't speak,' he thought to himself, in that sensualized level of consciousness which is just below the threshold of mental words; 'for unless I could talk to her alone – '

'And so thik beast went to the hammer.' The thread of Mr. Torp's carnivorous discourse had begun to pass Wolf by, when the foregoing sentence fell like a veritable pole-axe upon his ear. Like a flash he recalled Selena Gault's words outside the slaughter-house. 'Damn it!' he said to himself. 'The woman's right.'

'Be there any apple-tart, mammie?' cried Lob, in a shrill voice.

The door of the scullery was opened about three inches, in which space the beckoning forefinger of Joan Torp summoned her son to her side.

Very slowly the beautiful profile on Wolf's right turned towards her father.

"Tisn't no use your coaxing of I, missie,' responded the stone-cutter. 'What yer mummie says, yer mummie says. I reckon she's just got enough o' that there pasty to comfort Lob. Us and Mr. Redfern must swetten our bellies by talking sweet; and what's more, my pet, if I don't get out in thik yard afore I gets to sleep, there'll be no pleasing Squire *or* Mr. Manley!'

Saying this, the man rose from his chair, glanced at Wolf with a leer like the famous uncle of Cressid, and shuffled out of the house, closing the door behind him.

Wolf and Gerda were left alone, seated side by side in uncomfortable silence. He moved his chair back a little and glanced toward the scullery door. The voice of the woman and her son reached him in an obscure murmur. His eye caught the devastated piece of meat at the end of the table, and it brought to his mind the terrifying story of how the flesh of the Oxen of the Sun uttered articulate murmurs as the companions of Odysseus roasted it at their impious camp-fire.

'I *must* say something,' he thought. 'This silence is beginning to grow comic.'

He began to search his pockets for cigarettes. It seemed absurd to ask leave of this young girl, and yet it was likely enough that her shrewish mother detested tobacco.

'You don't mind if I smoke?' he said.

Gerda smilingly shook her head.

'I suppose you've often been told that you're as lovely as the girl who was the cause of the Trojan War?'

'What a way of breaking the ice!' he thought to himself, and felt a pang of mental humiliation. 'If the wench is going to dull my wits to this extent, I'll miss my chance and be just where I was yesterday.' Under cover of what Darnley had called the girl's terrible passivity, which was indeed just then like the quiescence of a great unpicked white phlox in a sun-warmed garden, he lit his cigarette and ransacked his brain for a line of action.

Desperately he hit upon the most obvious one. 'Have you got anything to put on within reach?' he whispered rapidly. 'I want to see something more of you. Let's step out while we've got the chance and go for a stroll somewhere!'

The girl remained for a moment in motionless indecision, listening intently to the murmuring voices in the scullery. Then, with a grave nod, she rose to her feet and stepped lightly to a curtained recess, behind which she vanished. Returning in less than a minute she presented herself in hat and cloak.

Wolf, trembling with a nervous excitement that made his stomach feel sick, seized his own coat and stick and moved boldly to the door.

'Come on!' he whispered. 'Come on!'

They slipped out together and the girl closed the door behind them with cautious celerity.

The stone-cutter's chisel could be heard in his open shed; but his back must have been turned to them, and they did not cast a glance in his direction. Into the street they passed, Wolf taking care not to let the latch of the gate click. Instinctively he led his captive to the right, away from the town. They walked rapidly side by side, and Wolf noted with surprise the absence of finery in the things worn by his silent companion. The hat was of cream-coloured felt, surrounded by a blue band; the cloak of some soft plain stuff, also cream-coloured. Wolf kept walking a good deal faster than circumstances seemed to demand, but he repeatedly fancied he heard the light steps of the intrusive Lob running in pursuit of them.

Before long they reached a place where a broad road branched to the left at the foot of a considerable hill. Wolf had not remembered passing this turn on the preceding day; but his attention must have been occupied with the row of little villas on the other side.

Following his instinct again, he turned up this road and slackened his pace. Still his companion remained perfectly silent; but she appeared quite untroubled by the rapidity of their movement, and she swung along by his side lightly and easily, every now and then brushing the budding hedge on her right with her bare hand.

For about half a mile they advanced up the long, steady hill, meeting no one and seeing nothing but snatches of sloping meadow-land as they passed various five-barred gates.

86

Then there came a turn to the left, and all of a sudden, over a well-worn wooden stile, the top bar of which was shiny as a piece of old furniture, they found themselves overlooking the whole town of Blacksod, and, away beyond that, the pollard-bordered course of the sluggish Lunt, as it crossed the invisible border-line between Dorset and Somerset.

'What do you call this hill, missie?' he murmured, as he re-covered his breath. It seemed impertinent to use her Christian name quite so quickly; but no stretch of politeness could have induced him just then to utter the syllable Torp.

'Babylon Hill,' she replied quite naturally and easily; for she was less out of breath than he.

'Babylon? What an extraordinary name!' he cried. 'Why Babylon?'

But at that she shrugged her young shoulders and contemplated the blue distances of Somersetshire. To her mind the extraordinary thing evidently was that anyone could be surprised that Babylon Hill was called Babylon Hill!

From the stile over which they were leaning a little field-path ran along the sloping greensward and lost itself in a small hazel copse that overshadowed one end of a rounded table-land of turf-covered earthworks.

'Come on,' he cried. 'Skip over, child; and let's see where *that* leads!'

She swung herself across without any assistance, and Wolf noticed that in the open country the movements of her body were entirely free from languor or voluptuousness. They became the swift, unconscious movements of a very healthy young animal.

'Has *this* got any name?' he remarked, as they clambered up the turfy slope of the grassy rampart.

'Poll's Camp,' she answered. And then, after a pause:

> 'When Poll his rain-cap has got on
> They'll get their drink at Dunderton!'

She repeated this in the peculiar sing-song drawl of a children's game.

There was something in her intonation that struck Wolf as queerly touching. It didn't harmonize with her ladylike attire. It suggested the simple finery of a thousand West-country fairs.

'Poll-Poll-Poll,' he repeated. And there came over him a deep wonder about the origin of this laborious piece of human toil. Were they Celts or Romans who actually, with their blunt, primitive spades, had changed the face of this hill? Was this silent, beautiful girl beside him the descendant of some Ionian soldier who had come in the train of the legionaries?

Dallying with these thoughts – which probably would never have come into his head at all, if a certain childishness in the girl hadn't, in a very subtle manner, lessened the bite of his lust – Wolf was slower than she in reaching the top of the ridge. When he did reach the top, and looked down into the rounded hollow below, he was astonished to see no sign of his companion.

'Good Lord!' he thought, 'has she gone round to the right or to the left?'

He ran down into the bottom of the little artificial valley and stood hesitating.

How like a child, to play him a trick of this kind!

His thoughts shaped themselves quickly now. His hope of finding her depended on how far he could sound her basic instincts. If she were of a hare-like nature she would double on her tracks, which in this case would mean turning to the left or right; if she were of the feline tribe she would pursue her course, which in this case would mean climbing the opposing earthwork. Wolf turned to the right and followed the narrow green hollow as it wound round the hill.

Ah, there she was!

Gerda lay supine, her arms outstretched, her cream-coloured hat clutched tight in one of her hands, her knees bare.

She waited till Wolf was so close that he could see that her eyes were shut. Then, catching the vibration of his tread upon the turf, she leapt to her feet and was off again, running like Atalanta, and soon vanishing from sight. Wolf pursued her; but he thought to himself, 'I won't run *quite* as fast as I could! She'll better enjoy being caught if she has had a good race.'

As a matter of fact, so swift-footed was the damsel that by following this method of leisurely pursuit he soon lost her altogether. The hollow trench ran straight into the heart of a thick coppice which from this point outwards had overgrown the whole of the camp. Here, in the heavy undergrowth, composed of brambles, elder-bushes, dead bracken, stunted sycamores, and newly-budded hazels, all ordinary paths disappeared completely. All he could have done was to have followed obstinately the bottom of the trench; and that was so overgrown that it was un-believable she should have forced a way there. But if he didn't follow the trench, where the devil should he go? Where, under the sky, had *she* gone? 'The earth hath bubbles as the water hath,' he quoted to himself, amused, irritated, and completely nonplussed. Teased into doing what he knew was the last thing calculated to bring her back, he began calling her name; at first gently and hesitatingly; at last loudly and indignantly. The girl, no doubt panting like a hunted fawn somewhere quite close to him, must have been especially delighted by this issue to the affair; for one of the peculiarities of Poll's Camp was the presence of an echo; and now, over and over again, this echo taunted him. 'Ger-da – Ger-da!' it flung across the valley.

He would have been more philosophical at this juncture if he hadn't, at that brief moment of overtaking her, caught sight of those incredibly white knees. But the impatience in his senses was at least mitigated by his appreciation of the immemorial quality of his pursuit! He looked round helplessly and whimsically at the thick undergrowth and sturdy hazel-twigs; and he played with the fancy that, like another Daphne or Syrinx, his maid might have undergone some miraculous vegetable transformation.

'Ger-da! Ger-da!' The echo returned to him again; whereupon, once more, the image of those bare knees destroyed the spirit of philosophical patience.

But he sat down then, with his back against a young sycamore, and lit a cigarette, wrapping his overcoat carefully round him and resolving to make the best of a bad job.

'If she *has* run away from me,' he thought, 'and just gone back to Chequers Street, there's no doubt she'll come out with me again. She certainly seemed at ease with me.' Thus spoke one voice within him. Another voice said: 'She thinks you're the father of all fools. You'll never have the gall to ask her to go out with you again.' And then, as he extinguished his third cigarette against a piece of chalk, moving aside the tiny green buds of an infinitesimal spray of milkwort, he became aware that a black-bird, in the dark twilight of hazel-stems, was uttering notes of an extraordinary purity and poignance.

He listened, fascinated. That particular intonation of the black-bird's note, more full of the spirits of air and of water than any sound upon earth, had always possessed a mysterious attraction for him. It seemed to hold, in the sphere of sound, what amber-paved pools surrounded by hart's-tongue ferns contain in the sphere of substance. It seemed to embrace in it all the sadness that it is possible to experience without crossing the subtle line into the region where sadness becomes misery.

He listened, spellbound, forgetting hamadryads, Daphne's pearl-white knees and everything.

The delicious notes hovered through the wood – hovered over the scented turf where he lay – and went wavering down the hollow valley. It was like the voice of the very spirit of Poll's Camp, unseduced by Roman or by Saxon, pouring forth to a sky whose peculiar tint of indescribable greyness exactly suited the essence of its identity, the happiness of that sorrow which knows nothing of misery. Wolf sat entranced, just giving himself up to listen; forgetting all else. He was utterly unmusical; and it may have been for that very reason that the quality of certain sounds in the world melted the very core of his soul. Certain sounds could do it; not very many. But the blackbird's note was one of them. And then it was that without rising from the ground he straightened his back against the sycamore-tree and got furiously red under his rugged cheeks. Even his tow-coloured hair, protruding from the front of his cap, seemed conscious of his humiliation. Waves of electricity shivered through it; while beads of perspiration ran down his forehead into his scowling eyebrows.

For he realized, in one rush of shame, that Gerda was the blackbird!

He realized this before she made a sound other than that long-sustained tremulous whistle. He realized it instantaneously by a kind of sudden absolute knowledge, like a slap in the face.

And then, immediately afterwards, she came forward, quite calmly and coolly, pushing aside the hazels and the elder-bushes.

He found her a different being, when she stood there in front of him, smiling down upon him and removing bits of moss and twigs from her hair. She had lost something from the outermost sheath of her habitual reserve; and like a plant that has unloosed its perianth she displayed some inner petal of her personality that had, until that moment, been quite concealed from him.

'*Gerda!*' he exclaimed reproachfully, too disordered to assume any sagacious reticence; 'how on earth did you learn to whistle like that?'

She continued placidly to clear the wood-rubble out of her fair hair; and the only reply she vouchsafed to his question was to toss down her cream-coloured hat at his feet.

Very deliberately, when her hair was in order, she proceeded to lift up the hem of her skirt and pick out the burs from that. Then she quickly turned away from him. 'Brush my back, will you?' she said.

He had to get up upon his feet at this; but he obeyed her with all patience, carefully removing from the cream-coloured jacket every vestige of her escapade.

'There!' he said, when he had finished; and taking her by the shoulders, he swung her around.

In the very act of doing this he had determined to kiss her; but something about the extraordinary loveliness of her face, when she did confront him, deterred him.

This was a surprise to himself at the moment; but later, analysing it, he came to the conclusion that although beauty, up to a certain point, is provocative of lust, beyond a certain point it is destructive of lust; and it is this, whether the possessor of such beauty be in a chaste mood or not.

If only – so he thought to himself later – Gerda's face had been a little less flawless in its beauty, the beauty of her body would have remained as maddening to his senses as it was at the beginning. But the more he had seen of her the more beautiful her face had grown; until it had now reached that magical level of loveliness which absorbs with a kind of absoluteness the whole æsthetic sense, paralysing the erotic sensibility.

Instead of kissing her he sat down again with his back to the sycamore; while Gerda, lying on her stomach at his feet, her chin propped upon the palms of her hands, began to talk to him in unconscious, easy, almost boyish freedom.

'I wouldn't have run away,' she said, 'so you needn't scold. I *would* have if it had been anyone else. I always *do* run away. I hide first and then slip off. Father's quite tired of seeing me come back into the yard after I've started for a walk with someone. That's because I always like people at the beginning, when they're frightened of me and don't try to touch me. But when they stop being frightened, and get familiar, I just hate them. Can you understand what I mean, or can't you?'

Wolf surveyed the beautiful face in front of him and recalled what Darnley had said about the three lovers.

'But, Gerda – ' he began.

'Well?' she said, smiling. 'Say it out! I know it's something bad.'

'You must have had *some* love-affairs, being the sort of girl you are. You can't make me believe you've always run away.'

She nodded her head vigorously.

'I have,' she said. 'I have, always. Though the boys I know never will believe it. Directly they touch me I run away. I want them to want me. It's a lovely feeling to be wanted like that. It's like floating on a wave. But when they try any of their games, messing a person about and rumpling a person's clothes, I can't bear it. I *won't* bear it, either!'

Wolf lifted his thick eyebrows and let them fall again, wrinkling them so that a great puckered fold established itself above his hooked nose. His ruddy face, under its rough crop of coarse, bleached hair, resembled a red sandstone cliff on the top of which a whitish-yellow patch of withered grass bowed before the wind.

The girl clambered to her feet, and, smoothing out her skirt beneath her, sat down on the ground by his side, hugging her knees.

'I found out I could whistle like that,' she began again, this time in a slow, meditative voice, 'when I used to play with Bob in the Lunt ditches, down Longmead. I fooled him endless times doing different birds. Listen to this. Do you know what this is?' And with her mouth pursed up into the form of a crimson sea-anemone, she imitated the cry of the female plover when any strange foot, of man or beast, approaches her nest on the ground.

'Wonderful!' cried Wolf, enraptured by that long-drawn familiar scream borne away upon the wind. 'How *did* you learn to do it?'

'I fooled Bob with that; but I fooled Dick – he was an Oxford gentleman – with a silly owl's-hooting which old Bob would have known at once.'

'Did you let the Oxford gentleman make love to you, Gerda?'

As soon as he had uttered the words, he felt a sense of shame that was like a pricking sore lodged under the cell-lobes in the front of his brain.

'There – don't answer!' he whispered hurriedly. 'That was a gross remark of mine.'

But the half-profile which she had turned upon him showed no traces of anger.

'I told you, didn't I?' was all she said. 'I ran away. I hid. I hid in the hedge under Ramsbottom. Dick was furious. He went past me several times. I heard him damning me like a sergeant – Ramsbottom's miles away. We'd taken our lunch. He had to go home without me and he told mother. Mother hit me with the broom when I got back. Dick was an "honourable"; so mother wanted me to marry him.'

Wolf was reduced to silence. He watched the flutterings of a greenfinch over some young elder-bush saplings. Then he turned towards her and spoke with solemn emphasis.

'I wish you'd make that blackbird-noise for me now, Gerda.'

He detected from her expression that this was a crisis between them. Her smile was suspended and hung like a faltering wraith over every feature of her face. She seemed to hesitate; and her hesitation brought a depth into her eyes that darkened their colour so that they became a deep violet.

'I've never *once* whistled for anybody,' she said slowly.

Wolf sent a wordless cry of appeal down into the abysses of his consciousness. They were ready to help him, those powers in the hidden levels of his being. They responded to his cry and he knew that they responded. In the repetition of his request there was a magnetic tone of power that reassured himself.

'Come on, Gerda!' he said. 'That's all the more reason. Come on! Whistle that song!'

Turning her face away from him, so that he could see nothing of her mouth, she began at once.

He could hardly believe his ears. It was like a miracle. It was as if she had swiftly summoned one of those yellow-beaked birds out of its leafy retreat. It seemed easier that a bird should be decoyed out of a wood than that a human throat should utter actual, unmistakable bird-notes.

'Go on! Go on!' cried Wolf, in an ecstasy of pleasure, the moment there was any cessation of this stream of cool, liquid, tremulous melody.

Over the turf-ramparts of Poll's Camp it swelled and sank, that wistful, immortal strain. Away down the grassy slopes it floated forth upon the March wind. No conceivable sky but one of that particular greyness could have formed the right kind of roof for the utterance of this sound. Wolf cared nothing that the whistler kept her face turned aside as she whistled. He gave himself up so completely to the voice that the girl Gerda became no more than a voice herself. At length it did really cease, and silence seemed to fall down upon that place like large grey feathers from some inaccessible height.

Both the man and the girl remained absolutely motionless for a while.

Then Gerda leapt to her feet.

'Let's go down to Longmead and watch the water-rats swim the Lunt!' she cried. 'We can get down there from here easily. There's a lovely little field-path I know. And we shan't meet anyone, for Bob and Lobbie are going to Willum's Mill.'

Wolf rose stiffly. He had sat so long in petrified delight that he was a little cramped. His mind felt drugged and cramped too, and felicitously stupid.

'Wherever you like, Gerda dear,' he said, looking at her with hypnotized admiration.

She took him by the hand, and together they climbed the embankment.

The wind was gentler now, and a very curious diffusion of thin, watery, greenish light seemed to have melted into the grey stretches of sky above their heads. The immense Somersetshire plain, with patches of olive-green marsh-land and patches of moss-green meadow-land, lost itself in a pale, sad horizon, where, like a king's sepulchre, rose the hill-ruin of Glastonbury. The path by which Gerda guided him down to the valley was indeed an ideal one for two companions who desired no interruption. Starting from a pheasants' 'drive' in the lower half of the hazel copse, it wound its way down the incline along a series of grassy terraces dotted by patches of young bracken fronds that had only very recently sprouted up among the great dead brown leaves.

Arrived at the foot of the hill, they struck a narrow cattle-drove where the deep winter ditches were still full of water and where huge half-fallen willow-trunks lay across old lichen-covered palings.

Advancing up this lane hand in hand with his companion, Wolf felt his soul invaded by that peculiar kind of melancholy which emanates, at the end of a spring day, from all the elements of earth and water. It is a sadness unlike all others, and has perhaps some mysterious connection with the swift, sudden recognition, by myriads and myriads of growing things. of the strange fatality that pursues all earthly life, whether clothed in flesh or clothed in vegetable fibre. It is a sadness accentuated by grey skies, grey water, and grey horizons; but it does not seem to attain its most significant meaning until the pressure of the spring adds to these elemental wraiths the intense wistfulness of young new life.

It seemed to Wolf, as they plodded along side by side through that muddy lane, that the light-green buds of those aged willow-trunks were framed in a more appropriate setting under that cold forlorn sky than any sunshine could give to them. Later seasons would warm them and cherish them. November rains would turn them yellow and bring them down into the mud.

But no other sky would hang above them with the cold floating weight of sadness as this one did – a weight like a mass of grey seaweed beneath a silent sea. No other sky would be cold enough and motionless enough actually to *listen* to the rising of the green sap within them, that infinitesimal flowing, flowing, flowing, that for non-human ears must have made strange, low gurglings and susurrations all day long.

At last they came to the bank of the River Lunt.

'Hush!' whispered Gerda. 'Don't make a noise! It's so lovely when you can make a water-rat flop in and see it swim across.'

It was along the edge of a small tributary full of marsh-marigolds that they approached the river-bank. Gerda was so impatient to hear a water-rat splash that she scarcely glanced at these great yellow orbs rising from thick, moist, mud-stained stalks and burnished leaves; but to Wolf, as he passed them by, there came rushing headlong out of that ditch, like an invisible company of tossing-maned air-horses, a whole herd of ancient memories! Indescribable! Indescribable! They had to do with wild rain-drenched escapes beneath banks of sombre clouds, of escapes along old backwaters and by forsaken sea-estuaries, of escapes along wet, deserted moor-paths and by sighing pond-reeds; along melancholy quarry-pools and by quagmires of livid moss. Indescribable! Indescribable! But memories of this kind were – and he had long known it! – the very essence of his life. They were more important to him than any outward event. They were more sacred to him than any living person. They were his friends, his gods, his secret religion. Like a mad botanist, like a crazed butterfly-collector, he hunted these filmy growths, these wild wanderers, and stored them up in his mind. For what purpose did he store them up? For *no* purpose! And yet these things were connected in some mysterious way with that mythopœic fatality which drove him on and on and on.

'There's one! There's one! There's one! Oh, throw something to make it go faster. Throw something! Quick! Quick! Quick! No – I don't mean to *hit* it. I don't mean to *hurt* it. To make it swim faster! There! I *can't* throw straight. Oh, do look at its head breathing and puffing! Oh, what ripples it makes!'

Conjured in this way to join in this sport, Wolf did pick up an enormous piece of wet mud and hurled it in the trail of the swimming rat.

The muddy ripples from this missile came rushing up behind that pointed little head, came splashing against those pointed little ears. Gerda clasped her hands. 'Swim! Swim! Swim!' she called out; and then in her excitement she pouted her mouth into a reed-mouth and uttered a long, strange, low, liquid cry that was like no sound Wolf had ever heard in his life.

'It's gone! It's done it!' she sighed at last, when the rat, emerging from the water without so much as one shake of its sleek sides, slid off along its mud-channel to its bed in the reed-roots. 'It's gone! And you *did* make it swim! I liked to see it. Let's go rat-swimming often. It's wonderful!'

She began walking along the river-bank in the direction leading away from Blacksod, gazing intently and rapturously at the sluggish brown stream.

Wolf followed her, but he surreptitiously glanced at his watch, and discovered, as he suspected, that it was already late in the afternoon.

'You can't tell when twilight begins,' he thought to himself, 'when the sky is *all* twilight.'

'Hush!' The sound reached him rather by implication than by ear. But the girl had crouched down under an overhanging alder and was staring at the water, her long cream-coloured arms supporting half the weight of her body.

He sat down himself and waited patiently. It satisfied his nature with an ineffable satisfaction to watch that steady flow of the brown water, gurling round the willow-roots and the muddy concavities of the bank. He felt glad that the Lunt, where he was now watching it, had left the town behind and was now to meet with nothing else really contaminating until it mingled with the Bristol Channel. He had already begun to feel a peculiar personal friendliness toward this patient muddy stream; and it gave him pleasure to think that its troubles were really over, when itself might so easily be fearing another Blacksod somewhere between these green meadows and the salt sea to which it ran! Looking quite as intently at these brown waters as Gerda herself was doing, it occurred to him how different a thing the personality of a river is from the personality of a sea. The water of the sea, though broken up into tides and waves, really remains the same identical mass of waters; whereas the water of a river is at every succeeding moment a completely different body. No particles of it are ever the same, unless they get waylaid in some side-stream or ditch or weir.

Wolf tried to visualize the whole course of the Lunt, so as to win for it some sort of coherent personality. By thinking *of all its waters together*, from start to finish, this unity could be achieved; for between the actual water before him now, into which he could thrust his hand, and the water of that tiny streamlet among the mid-Dorset hills from which it sprang, there was no spatial gap.

The one flowed continuously into the other. They were as completely united as the head and tail of a snake! The more he stared at the Lunt the more he liked the Lunt. He liked its infinite variety; the extraordinary number of its curves and hollows and shelving ledges and pools and currents; the extraordinary variety of organic patterns in the roots and twigs and branches and land-plants and water-plants which diversified its course.

While he was thinking all this he had turned his attention away from Gerda; but now, glancing up the river, he was struck by a gleam of living whiteness amid the greenery. The huntress of water-rats had slipped off her shoes and stockings and was dabbling her bare feet in the chilly brown water. Her face was bent down. She was not being provocative this time. He felt sure of that. Or, if so, the provocation was directed to something older and less rational than the senses of man. She was giving way to some immemorial girlish desire to expose warm, naked limbs to the cold embraces of the elements.

He rose to his feet, and, moving slowly up to her side, sat down by her. He was struck by the fact that she made no movement to pull her skirts down over her knees. But once again he was made aware, he could not quite tell how, that there was no provocation in this. She had indeed, as Darnley had said, something of the 'terrible passivity' of the famous daughter of Leda. Certainly Wolf had never seen, in picture, in marble, or in life, anything as flawless as the loveliness thus revealed to him. It was amazing to him that she did not shiver with the cold. The whole scene, as the hour of twilight grew near, had that kind of unblurred, enamelled distinctness such as one sees in the work of certain old English painters. The leaf-buds of the alder under which she sat were of that shade of green that seems to have something almost unnatural in its metallic opacity; and the line of southern sky against which the opposite bank was outlined was of that livid steel-grey which seems to hold within it a suppressed whiteness, like the whiteness of a sword that lies in shadow.

'You're sure you're not cold?' Wolf asked.

'Of course I'm cold, silly! I'm doing this *to* feel cold!'

'What a sensualist you are!'

'Better say nothing if you can't say anything nicer than that.'

'Gerda.'

'Well?'

'Have you enjoyed yourself to-day?'

'What do you mean?'

97

'Have you been happy to-day?'

She did not answer.

All about those white ankles and those white knees the greenness of the earth gathered – the greyness of the sky descended. It was as if such vague non-human powers, made up of green shadows and grey shadows, drew the girl back and away – back and away from all his human words, back and away from all his personal desires.

Commonplace and irrelevant seemed both his sentiment and his cunning in the face of these two great silent Presences – that of the earth and that of the sky – which were closing in upon her and upon himself.

But it was getting too cold. He must make her put on her things and come home.

'That's enough now,' he said. 'On with your stockings, like a good girl. I don't know when your people expect you back; but anyhow I mustn't keep Mrs. Otter waiting.'

He took her by the wrist and pulled her up the bank. Then he began vigorously rubbing her ice-cold ankles with his hands.

'You do take care of me nicely,' she said, when finally he pulled her frock over her knees and smoothed out the wrinkles from her cream-coloured coat. 'Bob never used to stop for a minute. He was always doing up his tackle or washing his fish or something. And if I *did* ask him to stop, he thought I wanted him to mess me about – you know? – when it was only, like now, that I just *couldn't* get my boots on! They get so stiff and funny when you take them off. I never understand why.'

But Wolf's mind was in no mood to deal with the abstract problem of damp leather. He was wondering in his heart whether Gerda's mania for water-rats had anything to do with the close resemblance between Mr. Weevil and these harmless rodents.

'What we've got to think about now,' he said, 'is the shortest way to Blacksod.'

'Oh, don't worry! We can be at my house in three-quarters of an hour, and then you can take the short cut to Barton.'

Wolf was very much struck by the competent geographical skill with which she now proceeded to guide him, over hedge and over ditch, until they reached a navigable lane.

'We'll be home in half an hour now,' she said, and the two walked rapidly side by side between the cold, fresh shoots of the hawthorn hedges and the dark sheen of the celandine leaves.

'I think I'd be all right now, married to *you*,' said Gerda, suddenly.

98

She made the remark in as unemotional and matter-of-fact a tone as if she had said, 'I think I'd be all right now if I used low-heeled boots.'

In that chilly twilight, with the white mist rising around them, everything seemed so phantasmal, that this surprising observation gave him no kind of shock. But he did remember how startled he had felt when Christie Malakite introduced the same idea.

'I wonder how I should feel married to *you!*' murmured Wolf in response, deliberately putting a nuance of irresponsible lightness into his tone.

'I think we'd get on splendidly,' she retorted, with an emphasis that was more boyish than girlish. They walked for a while in silence after this, and Wolf became vividly aware how completely a definite responsible project of such a kind tended to break the delicious spell of care-free intimacy. It broke it for him, anyway. But it must have been just the reverse with her. The beauty of the situation with her evidently had to find its justification in some continuity of events beyond the mere pleasure of the passing moment.

But it was impossible to prevent his thoughts hovering round this bold idea, now it *had* been flung into the air. Christie Malakite had been the first to toss the fatal little puffball upon the wind. *She* had done it with the utmost gravity, the gravity of some remote being altogether outside the stream of events. He remembered the peculiar steady look of her brown eyes as she uttered the words. But that this airy nothing of speculation should have received a new impetus from Gerda herself was another matter. He began to wonder what kind of relations existed between these two young girls.

Splashing up the water from a puddle on his right with the end of his stick, he hazarded a direct question on this point.

'I had tea yesterday with Christie Malakite,' he said, 'and she told me she was a friend of yours. I liked her so very much.'

'Oh, I shan't ever be jealous of Christie!' was his companion's reply to this. 'I don't care if you have tea with Christie every day of your life. *She's for no man,* as the game says.'

'What game, Gerda?'

'Oh, don't you know? That old game! Kids play it together. *We* called it "Boys and Girls"; but likely enough where you come from they call it something else! But it's the same old game, I reckon.'

'Why do you say Christie Malakite's "for no man," Gerda?'

99

'Don't ask so many questions, Mr. Wolf Solent. *That's* your fault – asking questions! *That's* what'll make me cross when we're married, more than anything else.'

'But it's such a queer expression – "She's for no man." Does it mean she's got lovers who aren't human? Does it mean she's got demon lovers?'

He spoke in a mocking, exaggerated manner, and his tone was irritating to his companion.

'Men think too much of themselves,' she replied laconically. 'I like Christie very much, and she likes me very much.'

This silenced Wolf, and they walked together in less harmony than at any previous moment in that afternoon.

They hit the town by a narrow alley between the town hall and Chequers Street. Wolf looked at his watch and compared it with the town hall clock. It was a quarter past six. There was still plenty of time for him to reach Pond Cottage before eight, when the Otters dined.

They drifted slowly down Chequers Street, Gerda making all manner of quaint, humorous remarks about the people and things they passed; and yet, through it all, Wolf was perfectly aware that she had not forgiven him the hard, frivolous tone he had adopted about her friend. That she was able to chatter and delay as she was now doing had something magnanimously pathetic and even boyish about it. Most girls, as he well knew, would have punished him for the little discordance between them by hurrying home in silence and shutting him out without the comfort of any further appointments. To act in any other way would have seemed to such minds to be lacking in proper pride. But Gerda appeared to have no pride at all in this sense. Or was it that her pride was really something that actually did resemble that high, passive nonchalance which permitted the old classical women to speak of themselves quite calmly, as if they were external to themselves; as if they saw their life as an irresponsible fate upon which they could, as it were, lie back without incurring any human blame?

They said good-bye at the gate of Torp's yard; and when Wolf enquired how soon he could see her again, 'Oh, any day you like, except to-morrow and Monday,' she replied. 'I've enjoyed myself very much,' she added, as she held out her hand. 'I'm glad you made me go.'

Wolf was on the point of asking her what her engagements were on Sunday and Monday, but he thought better of it in time, and taking off his cap and waving his stick he turned and strode away.

It was very nearly dark when the last little villa on the King's Barton road was left behind.

He walked slowly forward under a starless sky, revolving his adventure. He recognized clearly enough that his first infatuation had changed its quality not a little. Gerda was now not only a maddeningly desirable girl, she was a girl with a definite personality of her own. That bird-like whistling! Never had he known such a thing was possible! It accounted as nothing else could do for her queer, unembarrassed silences. In fact, it was the expression of her silences – and not only of hers! It was, as he recalled its full effect upon him, the expression of just those mysterious silences in Nature which all his life he had, so to speak, waited upon and worshipped. That strange whistling was the voice of those green pastures and those blackthorn-hedges, not as they were when human beings were conscious of them, but as they were in that indescribable hour just before dawn, when they awoke in the darkness to hear the faint, faint stirrings – upon the air – of the departing of the non-human powers of the night!

He was so absorbed in his thoughts that it was with quite a startled leap of the heart that he became conscious of hurried, uneven steps behind him. What kind of steps were they? They didn't sound like the steps of a grown-up person – either man or woman – they were so light in the dark road. And yet somehow they didn't resemble the footsteps of a child. Wolf became aware of an odd feeling of uneasiness. With all his habitual mysticism he was a man little subject to what are called *psychic* impressions. Yet on this occasion he could not help a somewhat discomfortable beating of his heart. The last thing he desired was to be overtaken by something unearthly on that pleasant Dorset road! Had the extraordinary phenomenon of the girl's whistling unsettled his nerves more than he realized?

His first simple and cowardly instinct was to quicken his own steps. In fact, it was with a quite definite effort that he prevented himself from setting off at a run! What was it? Who was it? He listened intently as he walked, and this listening in itself induced him to diminish his speed rather than to increase it.

At last the mysterious maker of this uncertain wavering series of footsteps arrived close at his heels.

Wolf swung round, grasping his stick tightly. Nothing on earth could have prevented a certain strained unnaturalness in his voice as he challenged this pursuer.

'Hullo!' he cried.

There was no answer, and the figure came steadily along till it was parallel with him.

Then he did, in a rush of relief, recognize this night-walker's identity.

Even in the darkness he recognized that shabby, derelict personality he had seen in the street with Lob Torp the day before. It was the Vicar of King's Barton!

He was surprised afterwards at this sudden recognition; though it was not the only occasion in his life when he had used a kind of sixth sense.

But whatever may have been its cause, Wolf's clairvoyance on this occasion was not shared by his overtaker.

'It . . . is . . . very . . . dark . . . to-night,' said the clergyman, in a voice so husky and hoarse that it resembled the voice attributed to the discomposed visage of the King of Chaos by the poet Milton.

Wolf's own voice was quite natural now.

'So dark that I took *you* for some kind of ghost,' he said grimly.

'Hee! Hee! Hee!' The Vicar laughed with the laugh of a man who makes a mechanical, appreciative noise. This hollow sound would doubtless have passed harmlessly enough in the daylight. In the darkness it was ghastly.

'You came up very quickly,' remarked Wolf. 'You must be a good walker, Mr. Valley.'

'Who . . . are . . . you . . . if . . . you . . . don't . . . mind . . . my . . . asking?'

'Not at all, Mr. Valley. I am the new secretary at the Squire's.'

The man stopped dead-still in the road; and, in natural politeness, Wolf stopped too.

'You are . . . the . . . other . . . one . . . Then . . . I . . . must . . . see you later . . . I buried him. . . . I said prayers for him every day. . . . He . . . was . . . very kind to me. I must see you . . . later. . . .' Having uttered these words, the Vicar seemed to gather up out of the dark some new kind of strength, for he moved forward by Wolf's side with a firmer step.

For nearly half a mile they walked side by side in silence.

Then the quavering voice out of the obscurity began again.

'Valley . . . is my name. . . . You've got it quite right. T. E. Valley. . . . I . . . drink more than's good for me. . . . I'm a little drunk to-night . . . but you'll excuse me. In the dark it isn't noticeable. But you're quite right. T. E. Valley is quite right. I was in the Eleven at Ramsgard. . . . I play still. . . . I play with the boys. . . .'

Once more there was no sound but that of the two men's feet in the road and the thud – thud – thud of Wolf's stick.

Then the voice recommenced. 'The poor people here are very kind to me . . . very kind to T. E. Valley. But for the rest. . . .'

He again stopped dead-still in the road, and Wolf stopped with him.

'For the rest . . . except . . . Darnley . . . they are all . . . You won't tell them, will you? They are all devils! Devils! Devils!' His voice rose in a kind of helpless fury. Then, after a moment's pause: 'But they can't hurt T. E. Valley. None of 'em can . . . drunk or sober . . . and that's because I'm God's Priest in this place. . . . God's Priest, sir! However you like to take it!'

This final outburst seemed to restore the shadowy little man to his senses, for until Wolf brought him to the gate of the Vicarage and bade him farewell there, his words became steadily more coherent – his intonation more normal and more sober.

The door of Pond Cottage was opened for Wolf by Dimity Stone.

'I've kept dinner back till it's as good as ruined,' grumbled the old woman.

'Where are – ' Wolf began.

'In there . . . waiting!' she answered, as she moved off.

He opened the drawing-room door.

'I am so very sorry, Mrs. Otter,' he said humbly.

They all rose from their seats; but it was Jason who spoke first. '*Everything*'s only waiting,' he chuckled grimly. 'That sofa is a better place for waiting than a head master's study!'

'My son doesn't mean that you've kept us a minute,' said Mrs. Otter. 'Dimity's only just ready. But we'll sit down at the table while you wash your hands, so that you can feel quite happy.'

'Don't be long, Solent!' cried Darnley, as Wolf turned to go upstairs. 'Mother won't let us touch a morsel till you come.'

As he entered his bedroom he heard Mrs. Otter's voice. 'Dimity! Dimity! We're quite ready!' And then, just as he was closing the door he caught something about 'these secretaries' from Jason.

6

BAR SINISTER

Breakfast in Pond Cottage on that Sunday morning proved to be the pleasantest meal that Wolf had yet enjoyed under the Otter roof.

Mrs. Otter, dressed in stiff puce-coloured silk, and happy to have both her sons at the table, spoke at some length to their guest about the morning service in the church to which she and Darnley were presently to go. She explained to him how much she liked the quiet, reverent manner in which Mr. Valley conducted the worship of the parish.

'He makes me sad at other times,' she said. 'He's an unhappy little man, and everyone knows how he drinks. He ought to have a wife to look after him, or at least a housekeeper. He's got no one in the house. How he gets enough to eat I can't imagine.'

'Mother thinks no household can get on for a day without a woman in it,' said Darnley.

Jason Otter's pallid face reddened a little. 'Of course, we know he wants to be the only man that any of the village-boys admire. It's human nature – that's what it is. These country clergymen are all the same.'

'There are the bells!' cried Mrs. Otter, thankful for the opportunity of staving off discord between the brothers. They all four listened in silence, while the faint notes from the Henry the Seventh tower penetrated the walls of Pond Cottage.

'That means it's ten o'clock,' said Darnley. 'They ring again at half-past, don't they, mother?'

Wolf felt an extraordinary sense of peacefulness in the air that morning. The sound of the bells accentuated it; and he wondered vaguely to himself whether he wouldn't offer to go to church with the mother and the son.

'By the way,' he remarked, 'may I ask you people a question, while I think of it?'

They all three awoke from their individual meditations and gave him their undivided attention. Mrs. Otter did this with serene complacency, evidently assuming that the nature of his remark would prove harmless and agreeable. Jason did it with nervous concern, touched with a flicker of what looked like personal fear. Darnley did it with an expression of weary politeness, as much as to say, 'Oh, God! Oh, God! Am I not going to have even Sunday free from other people's problems?'

'It's a simple enough thing,' Wolf said quickly, realizing that he had made more stir than he intended. 'I only wanted to know why this house of yours is called Pond Cottage, when there's no trace of a pond.'

There was an instantaneous sign of startled agitation all the way round the table.

'The pond is there all right,' said Darnley, quietly. 'It's over that hedge, just outside our gate, the other side of the lane. It's rather an uncomfortable topic with us, Solent; because at least three times James Redfern thought of drowning himself in it. He may have thought of it more times than that. Jason found him there three times. We don't like the pond for that reason. That's all!'

Jason Otter got up from his chair. 'I'll go and put on my boots,' he remarked to Wolf, 'and we'll go and visit the pond. You ought to see it. And there are other things I can show you, too, while mother and Darnley are in church. You've got your boots on, I think? Well! I won't keep you very long.'

He left the room as he spoke, and Mrs. Otter looked appealingly at her younger son.

'Don't worry, mother dear,' said Darnley gravely, laying his hand upon her knees.

He turned to Wolf. 'You must help us in keeping my brother in good spirits, Solent,' he said. 'But I know I can trust you.'

When Wolf and Jason did finally cross the lane together and enter the opposite field – which they achieved by climbing up a steep bank and pushing their way through a gap in the hedge – the sense of peacefulness in the whole air of the place had intensified to a degree that was so enchanting to Wolf that nothing seemed able to disturb his contentment.

The field he found himself in was a very large one, and only a broken, wavering line of willows and poplars at the further end of it gave any indication of the presence of water. The atmosphere was deliciously hushed and misty; no wind was stirring; and the placid morning sun fell upon the grass and the trees with a sort of largeness of indifference, as if it were too happy, in some secretive way of its own, to care whether its warmth gave pleasure or the reverse to the lives that thrived under its influence. It seemed to possess the secret of complete detachment, this sunshine; but it seemed also to possess the secret of projecting the clue to such detachment into the heart of every living existence that its vaporous warmth approached.

Wolf was suddenly aware of a rising to the surface of his mind of that trance-like 'mythology' of his. All the little outward things that met his gaze seemed to form so many material moulds into which this magnetic current set itself to run.

He surveyed a patch of sun-dried cattle-dung upon which the abstracted Jason had inadvertently planted his foot, and across which was slowly moving with exquisite precaution a brilliantly green beetle. He surveyed a group of small crimson-topped daisies, over which a sturdy, flowerless thistle threw a faint and patient shadow. He surveyed the disordered flight of a flock of starlings, heading away from the pond towards the village. But of all these things what arrested him most was the least obvious, the least noticeable. It was, in fact, no more than a certain ridge of rough unevenness in the ground at his feet; a nameless unevenness, which assumed, as the misty sunlight wavered over it, the predominant place in this accidental pattern of impressions.

Jason said nothing at all as they walked together slowly across the field. The man had ostentatiously avoided any approach to Sunday clothes that morning; and, without hat or stick, in a very shabby overcoat, he presented rather a lamentable figure as he led the way forward towards Lenty Pond.

They reached the willows and poplars at last; and Wolf stared in astonishment at what he saw. He found himself standing on the brink of an expanse of water that was nearly as large as a small lake. The opposite side of it was entirely covered with a bed of thick reeds, among which he could see the little red-and-black shapes of several moor-hens moving; but from where he stood, under these willows, right away to the pond's centre, the water was deep and dark, and even on that placid Sunday a little menacing.

'He could have done it easily if he'd wanted to, couldn't he?' said Jason, gazing at the water. 'The truth is he *didn't* want to! Darnley's a sentimental fool. Redfern *didn't* want to drown himself. Not a bit of it. What did he come here for, then? He came to rouse pity, to make people's minds go crazy with pity.'

'The man must have been thinking of saying just this to me all the way across the field,' thought Wolf. But Jason jerked out now a much more disturbing sentence.

'The boy did upset *one* person's mind. He made one person's mind feel like a weed in this water! And you'd be surprised to hear who that person was.'

But Wolf just then felt it very hard to give him his complete attention. For although the mystical ecstasy he had just experienced had faded, everything about the day had become momentous in his hidden secretive life; and he felt detached, remote, disembodied, for all his Sunday clothes. He could hear the cawing of a couple of rooks high up in the sky; and even when they ceased cawing, the creaking of their wings seemed like the indolence of the very day itself. 'A weed in the water,' he echoed mechanically; while his mind, voyaging over those hushed West-country pastures, followed the creaking wings.

'Who was it, Mr. Otter, who was so upset by Redfern?'

The appeal in Jason's miserable eyes grew still more disturbing. The man's soul seemed to come waveringly forward, like a grey vapour, out of its eye-sockets, till it formed itself into a shadowy double of the person who stood by Wolf's side.

'Can't you guess?' murmured Jason Otter. 'It was I . . . I . . . I . . . You're surprised. Well, anyone *would* be. You wouldn't have thought of that, though you *are* Mr. Urquhart's secretary and *have* come from a college! But you needn't look like that; for it's true! Darnley sentimentalizes about his death, which was unfortunate, of course, but perfectly natural – he died of pneumonia, as any of us might! – but what drove me to distraction was this playing upon a person's pity. He always did it – from the very first day. Darnley yielded to it at once, though he never liked the boy. I resisted it. I am of iron in these things. I know too much. But by degrees, can't you understand, though I didn't yield to it, it began to bother my mind. Pity's the most cruel trap ever invented. You can see that, I suppose? Take it that there were only one unhappy person left, why, it might spoil all the delight in the world! That is why I'd like to kill pity – why I'd like to make people see what madness it is.'

Wolf drew away from him a step or two, till he stood at the very edge of the pond, and then he remarked abruptly, 'Your mother told me that Redfern was one of the most good-looking young men she has ever seen.'

Having flung out these words, he began flicking the dark, brimming water with the end of his stick, watching the ripples which he caused spreading far out towards the centre. Exactly why he made that remark just then he would have found it hard to explain. The wraith-like phantom-soul that had emerged from Jason's eye-sockets drew back instantaneously, like a puppet pulled by a string; and over the two apertures into which it withdrew there formed a glacial film of guarded suspicion.

'*I* have seen better-looking ones,' said Jason Otter drily. 'He used to help that fool Valley in his High Church services. I don't know whether the Virgin Mary ever appeared to him; but I know he used to take her flowers, because he used to steal them out of our garden! My mother let him steal because it was – Hullo! What's up now? Who's this?'

Wolf swung round and observed to his surprise the tall figure of Roger Monk advancing towards them across the field.

'It's something for you. It's something about you,' said Jason, hurriedly. 'I think I'll walk round the pond.'

'Why do that?' protested Wolf. 'There'll be no secret about it, even if it *is* for me.'

'He'll like to find you alone best. These servants of these landowners always do,' replied the other. 'Besides, Mr. Urquhart hates me. He knows I know what he is. He's not a common kind of fool. He likes having good meals and good wine, but he's ready to risk all that for I don't know what!'

'I tell you I have no secrets with Urquhart,' rejoined Wolf. 'There's absolutely no need for you to leave us.'

'This gardener looked at me very suspiciously yesterday,' whispered Jason. 'I saw him through the hedge, in his garden. He was planting something, but he kept looking at the hedge. He must have known I was there. He must have been wondering whether he dared shoot at me with a shotgun. So good-bye! I'm going to walk round the pond very slowly.'

Wolf moved toward Mr. Monk, leaving his companion to shuffle off as he pleased. The gigantic servant looked like a respectable prize-fighter in his Sunday clothes. When the two men met he took from his pocket a telegram and handed it to Wolf, touching his hat politely as he did so.

'This came early,' he said. 'But there was no one else to send; and I had to tend to things before I could bring it myself. If there's any answer, 'twill have to go by way of Blacksod, for our office shuts at noon.'

Wolf opened the telegram. It was from his mother, and ran as follows:

'ARRIVE RAMSGARD SEVEN O'CLOCK SUNDAY NIGHT TRADESMEN HAVE NO SENSE COULD SLEEP AT LOVELACE.'

'There's no answer, Monk,' he said gravely; and then, after prodding the ground thoughtfully with his stick, and looking at the figure of Jason Otter, which was now stationary behind a poplar tree, 'This is from my mother,' he added. 'She is coming down from town to-night.'

'Very nice for you, sir, I'm sure,' murmured the man. "Tain't every gentleman has *got* a mother.'

'But the difficulty is, Monk,' Wolf went on, 'that my mother wants to stay down here. You don't happen to know of any cottage or any rooms in a cottage that we could get for a time, do you?'

Roger Monk looked at him thoughtfully. 'Not that I knows of, sir,' he began, his gipsy-like eyes wandering from Wolf's face to the landscape in front of him, a portion of which landscape included the figure of Mr. Otter, hiding behind the poplar tree.

'That is to say, sir, unless by any chance . . . but that ain't likely, sir. . . .'

'What do you mean, Monk?' enquired the other, eagerly.

"Twere only that I myself live lonesome-like in me own place . . . and seeing you're helping Squire with his writings . . . and Lenty Cottage be neat set up, I were just thinking – '

Wolf swung his stick. 'The very thing!' he cried excitedly. In a flash his imagination became abnormally active. He visualized this gardener's house in all its details. He saw himself, as well as his mother, snugly ensconced there for years and years . . . perhaps for the rest of their lives!

'But we should be a nuisance to you, Monk, even if the Squire *were* amenable, shouldn't we?'

The man shook his head.

'Well, I'll come straight home with you now, Monk, if I may,' said Wolf impatiently. 'Were you going home now?'

'I was.'

'Well, I'll just run and tell Mr. Otter; and then I'll come with you.'

He left the man standing where they had been talking, and hurried round the edge of the pond. There was something peculiarly appealing to him in the idea of this cottage. How pleasant it would be, he thought, when he and his mother were living together there some five years hence, if he happened to say to her, as he came in to tea from his Sunday walk, with a bunch of primroses in his hand, 'I came past Lenty Pond to-day, mother, where I first heard about the chance of our settling here!'

He found Jason sitting on the roots of the poplar, leaning his back against the tree-trunk and holding the tails of his overcoat stretched tightly over his knees, so that he should be entirely concealed from view.

'That man hasn't gone,' was his greeting to Wolf. 'He's standing there still.'

'I know he is, Otter. He's brought a telegram for me. My mother's coming down to-night. Monk says he doesn't see any reason why she and I shouldn't take rooms in his cottage.'

Jason looked up at him from where he sat upon the poplar-root, and the whimsical manner in which he hugged his coat-tails was accentuated by a smile of hobgoblinish merriment.

'You mean to live in it?' he remarked. 'You and your mother? I don't believe old Urquhart would consider such a thing for a moment! These squires like to show off their servants' quarters. They like to take their guests round and say: "That's where my head-gardener lives. He works at *his* garden when he's finished with mine! Those are 'Boule de neige' roses!" But when it comes to honest people lodging in places like that – goodness! Urquhart wouldn't consider it. But you can try. But my advice to you is to be very careful in this matter. You never know what troubles you'll have when you deal with people like this Monk. But you can try. There! you'd better go off with him. He's peeping and spying at this moment. He's thinking I'm holding you back because of the money you pay us.'

Wolf shook his head and made a movement to be gone, but the other bent forward a little and whispered up at him: 'I'll walk slowly round the pond; *then* if he looks back he won't think you ought to wait for me.'

With this complicated and obscure sentence floating on the surface of his mind, Wolf left his companion to his own devices and rejoined Roger Monk.

Not more than twenty minutes' walk brought them to the gardener's cottage. To Wolf's great satisfaction the place proved to be quite out of sight of the manor-house on the Ramsgard side of the orchards and the kitchen gardens. It stood, indeed, in Lenty Lane, a little east of the drive gates, and turned out to be a solid little cottage, pleasantly coated with white paint, and approached from the lane by a neat gravel path, on either side of which was a row of carefully whitewashed small round stones. Wolf for some reason didn't like the look of those white stones. Once more he regarded Lenty Cottage. The idea of its excessive neatness and tidiness, combined with the idea of its being so long empty except for this one man, troubled his nerves in some odd way. What *did* it suggest to him? Ah, he had it! It suggested the peculiar lonely trimness . . . so extraordinarily forbidding . . . of a gaoler's house outside a prison-gate, or a keeper's house outside a lunatic asylum.

'Well, let's see the inside,' he said, turning to his companion. 'Mr. Urquhart might as well have put me up here at first.'

The other gave him one of his equivocal glances. "Twere the matter of meals, I expect, sir,' he said cautiously. 'But if the lady comes, things will be different, no doubt.'

'Then you'd be pleased to have us here?'

This time the gardener's look was direct and eager.

'I'd be glad enough to have a gent like yourself sleeping under this here roof,' he cried.

They entered the house together and the matter was soon arranged between them. When things were settled, Wolf observed the man rubbing one of his hands up and down the back of a chair. 'I'd give a hundred pounds to get a place in them Shires again!' he burst out suddenly.

Wolf looked at him in astonishment. 'You don't like it here, Monk?' he murmured.

'Like it?' The man's voice sank to a whisper. "Tis easier to enter a gentleman's service than to leave it, sir, when that gentleman be the sort of Nebuchadnezzar my master be!'

'You aren't a Dorset man, then?' enquired Wolf.

'I were born here,' replied the other, 'but I left home when I were a kiddie, and worked in they Shires.'

This remark made clear to Wolf a great deal about Roger Monk. The upper layers of the man's mind were sophisticated by travel. The deeper ones retained their indigenous imprint.

'Well, I must go back to Pond Cottage now,' Wolf said calmly. 'Mrs. Otter and Mr. Darnley ought to be back from church by this time, and I must talk to them. We'll arrange about terms, Monk, after I've seen Mr. Urquhart. Do you suppose I should find him at home now if I looked in on my way to the cottage?'

A frown of concentrated concern clouded the countenance of the man in front of him.

'It certainly would be best,' he remarked, 'if it could be done. What he'll say to it, I don't know, I'm sure.'

With these words ringing in his ears, Wolf, some fifteen minutes later, found himself admitted to Mr. Urquhart's presence. He discovered his employer in his study, reading with fascinated interest the book which his new secretary had brought him.

'These Evershots will be the making of our History,' he chuckled, in high glee. 'You did well with old Malakite. Five pounds for this? I tell you, it's worth twenty! You're a capital ambassador, Mr. Solent! . . . Eh? What's that? Your mother coming here? . . . Monk's front rooms?'

He straightened out his legs and smoothed back his glossy hair from each side of that carefully-brushed parting. With his great white face drooping a little on one side, with the flabby folds under his eyelids pulsing as if they possessed an independent life of their own, he made an unpleasant impression on Wolf's mind.

Mr. Urquhart's study was a small, dingy room, the walls of which were entirely covered by eighteenth-century prints. The Squire sat in a low, leather chair, with the Evershot Chronicle on his knees; and as Wolf settled himself opposite him in a similar chair, he began to feel that, after all, he was probably exaggerating the peculiarities of King's Barton Manor.

'It's my nervous imagination, I expect,' he said to himself. 'Urquhart's no doubt like hundreds of other eccentric men of leisure. And as for the gardener's chatter – I suppose servants are always glad to grumble to a stranger.'

'Didn't my predecessor live in Monk's house?' he found himself saying.

The Squire lifted his hand from the book he held and half raised it to his well-shaven chin. 'Redfern? A little while, perhaps. I really forget. Not long, anyway. That drunken individual at Pond Cottage persuaded him to go to them. It was with them he died. They told you *that*, I suppose?'

Mr. Urquhart's voice was so placid and casual as he made these remarks that Wolf was seized with a sort of shame for letting his imagination run riot so among all these new acquaintances. 'It's the difference from London! That's what explains it,' he thought to himself.

Mr. Urquhart now stopped scratching his chin with his delicate finger-tips, and, bowing his head a little, fumbled once more with the pages of the book upon his knee. Wolf sank back into his deep armchair and stared at the man's tweed trousers and shiny patent-leather shoes.

He drew a long breath that was something between a sigh of weariness and a sigh of relief. His recent interviews with Jason and Monk had given him the feeling of being on the edge of a psychic maelstrom of morbid conflicts. The comfort of this remote room and the ease of this leather chair made him at once weary of agitations and glad that he still could feel like a spectator rather than a combatant.

After all, why should he worry himself? As the philosophical Duke of Albany murmured in *King Lear*: 'The event! Well . . . The event!'

'How will your mother appreciate sharing her kitchen with my man?' said Urquhart suddenly.

The remark irritated Wolf. What did this easy gentleman know about the shifts of poverty? He was himself so bent upon the arrangement that these little matters seemed quite unimportant.

'Oh, she won't mind that!' he responded carelessly.

'What put all this into Roger's great, stupid, silly head?' the Squire went on, in his silkiest voice. 'Is he tired of my company? Does he want to leave my service and enter your mother's? What's up with the man? It isn't the money. I know *that* much. Roger cares less for money than any man I've ever dealt with. What can he be up to now?'

Wolf remained silent, letting him run on. But in his mind he set himself once more to wonder how far he really *had* exaggerated the sinister element in his employer's character.

But Mr. Urquhart leaned forward now and regarded him intently. 'You won't play me a trick, will you, like the other one? But you're not tricky, Mr. Solent, I can see that! On my soul, I think you're an honest young man. Your face shows it. It has its faults *as* a face; but it isn't tricky. . . . Well . . . well . . . well! . . . When does your mother arrive? I shall be interested to have the honour of meeting her again. My cousin Carfax was at one time – you know, I suppose? – excessively in love with her. . . . Not to-night, eh? Well, perhaps that's as well. Mrs. Martin shall go over there and make everything straight.'

Wolf rose to his feet at this point, anxious to take his leave before the man had time to read him any passages from the Evershot Diary. Once outside the house, he took stock of the situation. He had settled matters with the occupier and with the owner of his new abode. The final arrangement he had to make was with Mrs. Otter. Therefore, off he hurried to Pond Cottage, where he found his hostess just returned from church.

But here he met with nothing but sympathy – whether, in her secret heart, she was glad to get rid of him, Wolf could not say. She may have all the while regretted the loss to her eldest son of that chamber whose walls Wolf had so arbitrarily denuded. Well! They could put those pictures back on those walls now! And he mentally resolved to pay as few visits as possible to the bedroom of Mr. Jason Otter. He had no wish to behold the countenance of that 'god of rain' again!

He left Pond Cottage soon after lunch, explaining that he would return that night, but would have supper in Ramsgard with his mother. The afternoon proved to be as misty and warm as the earlier hours of the day; and as he retraced the track of Thursday's drive with Darnley, he did not permit the various agitations into which he had been plunged to destroy his delight in that relaxed and caressing weather. He found that travelling on foot in full daylight revealed to him many tokens of the spring that he had missed on his evening drive.

Once or twice he descended into the ditches on either side of the road, where the limp whitish-pink stalks of half-hidden primroses drooped above their crinkled leaves, and, with hands and knees embedded in the warm-scented earth, pressed his face against those fragile apparitions.

The sweet, faint odour of these pale flowers made him think of Gerda Torp, and he began worrying his mind a good deal as to the effect of his mother's arrival upon the progress of his adventure.

Long before he reached the outskirts of Ramsgard he was reminded of his approach to the famous West-country school by the various groups of straw-hatted boys – tall, reserved, disdainful – who seemed exploring, like young Norman invaders, these humble pasture-lands of the West Saxons.

One or two of the boys, as they passed him by, made hesitating half-gestures of respectful recognition. One of them actually lifted his straw hat. Wolf became a little embarrassed by these encounters. He wondered what kind of a master these polite neophytes – for it must have been the newcomers at the place who blundered in this way – mistook him for! Did he look like a teacher of French? Or did they take him for one of that high, remote, aristocratic company – not masters at all, but Governors of the ancient School?

When he got closer to the town, he had no difficulty in espying both cemetery and workhouse across an expanse of market-gardens and small enclosed fields. The look of these objects, combined, as they were, with outlying sheds and untidy isolated hovels, gave him a sensation that he was always thrilled to receive

– the peculiar sensation that is evoked by any transitional ground lying between town and country.

He had never approached any town, however insignificant across such a margin, without experiencing a queer and quite special sense of romance. Was it that there was aroused in him some subtle memory of all the intangible sensations that his ancestors had felt, each one of them in his day, as, with so much of the unknown before them, they approached or left, in their West-country wandering, any of these historic places? Did, in fact, some floating 'emanation' of human regrets and human hopes hover inevitably about such marginal tracts – redolent of so many welcomes and so many farewells?

When he arrived at last in the centre of the town and came to the gate of the Abbey, it was a few minutes to four o'clock. There was a languid afternoon service ebbing to its end in the eastern portion of the dusky nave; and, without entering the building, but lingering in the Norman entrance, Wolf contemplated once more that famous fan-tracery roof.

Those lovely organic lines and curves, up there in the greenish dimness, challenged something in his soul that was hardly ever stirred by any work of art; something that was repelled and rendered actually hostile by the kind of thing he had seen in that bedroom of Jason Otter.

This high fan-tracery roof, into whose creation so much calm, quiet mysticism must have been thrown, seemed to appeal with an almost personal sympathy to Wolf's deepest mind. Uplifted there, in the immense stillness of that enclosed space, above the dust and stir of all passing transactions, it seemed to fling forth, like some great ancient fountain in a walled garden, eternal arches of enchanted water that sustained, comforted, and healed. The amplitude of the beauty around him had indeed just then a curious and interesting psychic effect. In place of giving him the sensation that his soul had melted into these high-arched shadows, it gave him the feeling that the core of his being was a little, hard, opaque, round crystal!

Soothed, beyond all expectation, by this experience, and forti-fied with a resolute strength by thinking of his soul after this fashion, Wolf had nearly reached Selena Gault's door, when he remembered that he ought to make sure of a room for his mother at the Lovelace Hotel before he did anything else.

Hurrying round by the station, therefore, where he verified the time of the London train, he entered the office-hall of the famous hostelry. No backwater of rural leisure could have been more pulseless and placid than that mellow interior, with its stuffed fox-heads and mid-Victorian magohany chairs. But it was with a shock of dismay that he learned from the dignified lady in charge of the hotel-books that owing to the approach of the annual Spring Fair every room in the place was already occupied. Wolf cursed the Fair and those horse-loving magnates. But there was nothing for him but to return to Miss Gault's; for the smaller Ramsgard Inn was at the further end of the town, and it was now five o'clock.

He crossed the public gardens. He struck St. Aldhelm's Street just above the bridge and moved westward under the long wall. He pushed open the green door and entered the garden of hyacinths. The mechanical act of opening that little gate, for no other reason than that it was a gate from a street into a private enclosure, brought suddenly into his mind his similar entrance into the Torp yard; and the vein of amorousness in him, like a velvet-padded panther in a blind night, slipped wickedly past all the magic of yesterday's walk and caused his heart to beat at the imaginary image – for he had never actually seen that provocative picture – of the young girl astride the tombstone!

No sooner had the mute servant admitted him into Selena's drawing-room and closed the door behind him, than he realized that his hostess was not alone. Not only were all the cats there, but playing wildly with the cats, like a young Bassarid with young tigers, was a curly-headed, passionate little girl, of olive complexion, who, even before Miss Gault had finished uttering the syllables of her name, seized him by both hands and held up an excited, magnetic mouth to be kissed. Off she went again, however, to her play with the cats, which seemed to arouse her to the limit of her nervous endurance, for her cheeks were feverishly vivid and her dark eyes gleamed like two great gems in the handle of a dagger – a dagger that someone keeps furtively moving backwards and forwards between a red flame and a window open to the night.

As she pulled the cats to and fro and tumbled over them and among them, on sofa and hearth-rug, she kept up an incessant, excitable chatter; a chatter that struck Wolf's mind as resembling, in some odd manner, a substance rather than a *sound*, for it seemed to supply a part of the warm, dusky atmosphere in which she played, and indeed seemed to require no vocal response from the other persons in the room. It was like the swirl of a swollen brook in a picture of Nicolas Poussin, in the foreground of which a young brown goat-herd plays for ever with his goats.

'Olwen Smith!' broke in Miss Gault, when she and Wolf had seated themselves, after their first exchange of greetings, and he had hurriedly given her a description of Mr. Urquhart and Mr. Urquhart's library. 'Olwen Smith!'

The little girl got up from the floor in a moment, and came and stood by her friend's knee.

'You musn't be noisy when a gentleman's here; and, besides, you've got on your Sunday frock. Tell Mr. Solent your name and where you live. Mr. Solent doesn't like noisy little girls, or little girls that talk all the time and interrupt people.'

'I live at Number Eighty-five North Street, Ramsgard,' repeated the child hurriedly. 'I was eleven last Thursday. Grandfather keeps the School hat-shop. Mother went away when I was born. Miss Gault is my greatest friend. Aunt Mattie is my mother now. I like the white cat best!'

The child uttered these sentences as if they had been a lesson which she had learned by heart. She stood obediently by Selena Gault's side; but her dark eyes fixed themselves upon Wolf with an expression that he never afterwards forgot, so wild, so mocking, so rebellious, and yet so appealing did it seem.

'Olwen loves my cats; but not nearly so much as my cats love *her*,' said Selena Gault tenderly.

The little girl cuddled up to the black-gowned figure and laid her head against the old maid's sleeve. Her wild spirit seemed to have ebbed away from every portion of her body except her eyes. These refused to remove themselves from those of the visitor; and as his own mood changed this way and that, these dusky mirrors changed with it, reflecting thoughts that no child's conscious brain could possibly have understood.

'But you know you love your Aunt Mattie as if she *were* your mother,' said Selena Gault. 'She's been so good to you that you'd be a very ungrateful little girl if you didn't love her.'

'I heard grandfather tell Aunt Mattie the other night that she was no more *his* child than I was *her* child,' responded Olwen Smith, mechanically stroking Miss Gault's hand like an affectionate little automaton, while her feverish mocking eyes seemed to say to Wolf, 'There, watch the effect of *that!*'

'Mattie's mother died about twenty-five years ago, child,' expostulated Miss Gault. 'Her name was Lorna. She and your grandfather used to have dreadful quarrels before she died.

That's why Mr. Smith, when he gets angry, says things like that. Of course Mattie is his daughter; and it's very wrong of him to say such things.'

'Aunt Mattie's *funny*,' murmured the little girl.

'Hush, child!'

'But she is, *rather!* Just a tiny little bit funny, isn't she, Miss Gault?'

Selena smiled at Wolf – that peculiar hypnotized smile with which older people, who have given their souls into children's keeping, transform their pets' worst faults into qualities that are irresistibly engaging.

'Aunt Mattie's got a nose like yours,' said Olwen Smith.

'Like mine?' murmured Selena Gault, reproachfully. 'You mustn't be rude, Olwen dear. That's one thing I *can't* have in my house.'

The brown head was buried closer in the black silk gown, but the child's voice sounded clear enough.

'Not like yours, Miss Gault – like *his!* Exactly like his!'

Selena Gault had occasion at that moment to turn clean away from both her visitors; for the mute servant entered the room carrying the tea-tray. The arrangement of this tray was evidently a matter of meticulous ritual in this house, and Wolf surveyed it with silent satisfaction, especially as the turbulent little girl ran off to play with the cats and left Miss Gault free not only to fill his cup, but also to attend unreservedly to his remarks.

The tea-tray was placed upon a round table at Miss Gault's side. A black kitchen kettle – Miss Gault declared that no other kind boiled *good* water – was placed upon the hearth. The servant herself did not retire, as most servants are wont to do at such a juncture, but remained to assist at the ceremony of 'pouring out,' a ceremony which was so deftly accomplished that Wolf soon found all his difficulties and annoyances melting away in the fragrance of the most perfect cup of tea he had ever tasted.

The general effect of Miss Gault's drawing-room, in the pleasant mingling of twilight and firelight, began to take on for his imagination the particular atmosphere that he was wont, in his own mind, to think of as 'the Penn House atmosphere.' This implied that there was something about this room which made him recall that old bow-window in Brunswick Terrace, Weymouth, where in his childhood he used to indulge in these queer, secretive pleasures. There was not a single piece of furniture in this room of Miss Gault's which did not project some essence of the past, tender and mellow as the smell of potpourri.

He broke the silence now by a reference to his conversation with Darnley in the Blacksod bookshop. 'Otter said – ' he began.

'Hush!' cried Selena Gault; and then in a completely different tone, addressing the silent child, who was listening intently: 'Olwen dear, you can go on playing! You can make as much noise as you like now! We've finished our conversation.'

'I don't want to play any more, Miss Gault! I hate all your cats except this one! I want to hear Mr. Solent tell you what Otter said!'

'I'll have to send you home, Olwen, if you don't behave better. It's rude to interfere with grown-up people's conversation.'

'I wasn't interfering; I was listening. I'd never have known about Aunt Mattie not being grandfather's real daughter if I hadn't listened. . . .'

'Be quiet, child!' cried Selena Gault. But the passionate little girl's shrill voice rose to a defiant shriek, as she jumped up from the sofa, flung the cat upon the floor, shook back her tangled curls, and screamed aloud: 'And I'd never have known about Aunt Mattie not being my real mother if I hadn't listened . . .!'

If Miss Gault had not managed the child with perfect tact before, she rose to the occasion now.

'It's all right, Olwen dear,' she said in the calmest and most matter-of-fact voice. 'I daresay it's because grown-up people talk such a lot of nonsense that they get so cross when children listen. There! Look! You've frightened your own favourite!'

It was when matters were at this point of psychic equilibrium that Wolf decided that no more moments must elapse before he informed his hostess of his mother's arrival. The nervous electricity with which the air of the room was already vibrating, encouraged rather than deterred him.

'Miss Gault!' he began suddenly, when the tall black figure had subsided into some kind of peace in her green chair, 'I've just had some rather serious news which I'd better tell you at once.'

Like a weary caryatid, sick of the burden of life, but unyielding in her resolution to bear it without reproach and without complaint, Selena Gault leaned forward towards him.

'You needn't tell me, boy; I can guess it. Ann Haggard's coming down here.'

He nodded in assent to her words, but a look of irritation crossed his face.

'My mother and I have the same name,' he protested.

'When's she coming? Oh, what a mistake you'll make if you let her come! What a mistake you'll make!'

'I've not had much choice,' remarked Wolf drily. 'She's due now in a few minutes.'

'*What?*' gasped the lady, her deformed lip twitching like some curious aquarium specimen that has been prodded by a visitor's stick. 'She's due at seven o'clock.'

'In Ramsgard again – after twenty-seven years! What a thing! What a thing to happen!' gasped Selena Gault.

'I don't know where the deuce I'm going to put her! That's where I want your advice. The Lovelace is all filled up with people come in for the Spring Show.'

Miss Gault's face was like an ancient amphitheatre full of dusky gladiators. She took firm hold of the arms of her chair to steady herself.

But at that moment a diversion offered itself which distracted the attention of both of them. Olwen Smith, who had been listening with fascinated intensity to what they were saying, now burst in upon them.

'O Mr. Solent!' she cried. '*Do* let your mother have our front room for the night. Aunt Mattie takes lodgers, though grandfather does sell the School hats! I *know* Aunt Mattie would love to have your mother. Wouldn't she, Miss Gault? Do tell him she must come to us. Do tell him, Miss Gault! He'll let her come if you'll only say so!' And with that the child sidled up against their hostess's knees with such beguiling cajolery that Wolf was surprised at the coldness with which the woman received her appeal.

She made a very faint movement with her two hands, just as if the child had not been at her side at all – a movement as if she were pressing down a load of invisible earth over the roots of an invisible plant.

'Hush, child!' she said irritably. 'You mustn't interrupt us like that. I've told you so often you mustn't. I'm sure your Aunt Mattie wouldn't wish to have a guest for only one night. No one likes an arrangement of that sort.'

But the child, who had been watching her face with intense scrutiny till this moment, now flung herself down upon the floor and burst into furious crying. 'I – want – her – to – come – to us!' she wailed. 'I want her to come! It's always like this when anything nice happens. You're unkind, Miss Gault! You're very unkind!'

And then quite suddenly her tears stopped, her sobs ceased; and, very solemnly, sitting upon the floor, hugging her knees, looking up at the figure above her with a tragic, lamentable face, 'You are *prejudiced* against me!' she said.

The word 'prejudiced' sounded so unexpected and so queer out of her mouth that it charmed away the old maid's agitation. 'It's all right, my dear,' she murmured, stooping down and lifting her up, and covering her hot forehead with kisses. 'It's all right, Olwen, Mr. Solent shall bring his mother to your house.'

She fell into a deep reverie, staring into vacancy. Past the child's curly head, which she held pressed against her, she stared, past the puzzled and rather sulky profile of Wolf, past the thick green curtains bordered with red-and-gold braid, out into the gathering night, out into many nights lost and gone.

Wolf now rather impatiently looked at his watch and compared it with the clock on the mantelpiece.

'It's half-past six,' he said brusquely, interrupting Miss Gault's thoughts.

The lady nodded gravely, and rising to her feet with the child's hand still in hers, 'I'll tell Emma to take Olwen home,' she said, 'and then she can tell Mattie Smith to expect you. Say good-bye to Mr. Solent, little one.'

Olwen held out her hand with one of the most complicated looks he had ever seen on a child's face. It was repentant, and yet it was triumphant. It was mocking and mischievous, and yet it was, in a queer way, appealing and wistful.

'Well, I'll see you again,' said Wolf, stooping down and kissing the child's feverishly hot little fingers, 'unless they send you off to bed before we get to the house.'

Olwen was obviously immensely relieved that he had refrained from hugging her or kissing her face.

Very sedate and dignified was the curtsey she now gave him, turning round to manœuvre it as Miss Gault opened the door, and he was left with that honourable glow of satisfaction with which clumsy people are sometimes rewarded who have been self-controlled enough to respect the nervous individuality of a child.

When Miss Gault returned and had closed the door, she stood for a space regarding her visitor with the sort of grave, concentrated look, not unmixed with misgiving, that a commander in an involved campaign might give to a trusty but over-impetuous subordinate whose limitations of mind prohibit complete confidence.

'It will be awkward for her to go straight to these Smiths, you know. But she'd have to meet them, I suppose, sooner or later; and it *may* be all right. It's like taking the bull by the horns, anyway; which is what Ann always did.'

Wolf was silent. He was watching the hands of the clock.

'Why did you let her come down here?' the old maid broke out. 'Are you her shadow? Are you tied to her apron-strings? Can't you see what it means to me, and to others who remember *him*, to have to see her, to have to speak to her? Haven't you felt yourself that this is *his* country, his corner of the world, his possession? Haven't you felt that? And yet you let his enemy, his vindictive enemy, invade his very burying-ground!' ...

Wolf's only retort to this impassioned speech was to snatch at the lady's hand and give it a hurried kiss. 'You mustn't take it too seriously,' were his parting words.

When he reached the station, he was met by the news that the train was to be about an hour late.

'This will worry our little Olwen!' he thought in dismay. 'They'll send her to bed for a certainty. They'll think we're not coming at all. They'll think we've changed our minds. And where shall we get supper when we *are* there? Damn these teasing problems! I wish mother had waited till to-morrow.'

The station was not a very pleasant place to spend an hour in; so Wolf mounted the hill which rose behind the parallel tracks of the railroad and the river. Here there was a sort of terrace-road, perched high above the town and itself overshadowed by the grassy eminence known as 'The Slopes,' beyond the summit of which lay the wide-stretching deer-park of the lord of the manor.

Feeling sure that, if the train came sooner than it was expected, he would hear it in time, as soon as he reached the terrace-road below 'The Slopes' he began pacing to and fro along its level security, gazing down on the lights of the town as they twinkled intermittently through the darkened valley beneath him. The sky was overcast; so that these scattered points of light resembled the phantasmal reproduction of a sidereal firmament that had already ceased to exist. Mists that in the darkness were only waftures of chillier air rose up from the muddy banks of the Lunt and brought to his nostrils on this spring night odours that suggested the autumn. As he paced that terrace, inhaling these damp airs, his mind seemed to detach itself from the realistic actualities he was experiencing. It seemed to float off and away on a dark stream of something that was neither air nor water. What he desired at that moment, as he had never desired it before, was a support in which he could lose himself completely – lose himself without obligation or effort! He, the mortal creation of Chance, craved for some immortal creation of Chance, such as he could worship, wilfully, capriciously, blindly. But he stretched out his arms into that darkness in vain. His voice might have been the voice of a belated rook on its way to Babylon Hill, or the scraping of one alder-branch against another above the waters of the Lunt, or the faint infinitesimal slide of tiny grains of gravel, as some minute earthworm in the midst of the empty little path at the top of 'The Slopes' came forth to inhale the spring night! A bubble of airy vibration, his appeal was lost as absolutely as any single drop of water that rolled at that moment down the green back of a frog emerging from the cold surface of Lenty Pond.

He kept visualizing the mud-scented darkness in which he seemed to be floating as a vast banked-up aqueduct composed of granite slabs covered with slippery black moss. Out of the spiritual tide that carried him along, there whirled up, in spurts of phosphorescent illumination, various distorted physical aspects of the people he had met these last few days. But these aspects were all ill-assorted, incongruous, maladjusted. . . . All these morbid evocations culminated finally in the thought of his mother; for what dispersed them and shook them indeed into nothingness now, with an abrupt materialistic shock, was the clear, sharp sound of the clattering gates of the level crossing.

Wolf slid with a jerk into the normal world as he heard this sound, like a man falling plumb down from a skylight upon a creaking floor.

He grasped his stick firmly by its handle, digging it into the ground at every step, and hurried with long strides down the little descent.

Nothing in the world seemed important to him now but to see his mother's face and hear her high-pitched familiar voice. . . .

Standing on the platform, before the train drew in, he found that his heart was beating with excitement.

'I'm simply at an *impasse*,' he thought to himself, 'about what I feel for mother. I don't really want her down here . . . interfering with Gerda . . . interfering with everything. . . . It's odd . . . it's funny . . . it's just like the spouting up of a great white whale . . . spouting up, when no one's thinking of whales . . . when everyone's thinking of the course of the ship!'

When the train actually came in, and he held her at arm's length with both his hands, clutching her wrists almost fiercely, looking her up and down almost irritably, he recognized in a flash that existence without her, however adventurous it might be, would always be half-real ... just as those famous Ramsgard 'Slopes' up there had seemed half-real a few minutes ago!

It was she alone who could give the bitter-sweet tang to reality, to his phantasmal life, and make the ground under his feet firm.

Her coming, now, as of old, had done, at this moment, just this very thing!

As he looked upon her now—that gallant, ruddy, handsome face, those proud lips, those strong, white teeth, that wavy mass of splendid, grey hair—he felt that, though he might love other persons for other reasons, it was she alone who made the world he lived in solid and resistant to the touch. He felt that without her the whole thing might split and tear—as if it had been made of thin paper!

'Oh, it was awful, my dabchick!' the lady cried, kissing him on both cheeks in an exaggerated foreign manner. 'They were all down on us. I never knew what wretches tradesmen could be! They'll be nicely fooled when they find the house shut up. But they deserved it. They behaved abominably. . . .' She caught herself up with a gasp, and turned, full of despotic abruptness, towards the patient Ramsgard porter. 'Those are all mine! Three big ones and three little ones! You can come back for the other people's when you've taken mine out! Is that bus there? It always used to be.'

Wolf took from her a basket she carried, which appeared full of the oddest assortment of objects; and they both followed the loaded little truck, pushed by the docile porter to the front of the station.

'There it is,' cried Mrs. Solent, 'the old Ramsgard bus! Put them in . . . carefully now! Carefully now!'

The porter retired, recompensed by a shilling, which Wolf hurriedly produced from his pocket while his mother was opening her purse. When he had helped her into the interior of the stuffy little vehicle, he gave his order to the man on the box.

'Number Eighty-Five North Street!'

'Where are you taking me?' Mrs. Solent asked, as the bus rumbled off.

'To a room in the town for one night, mother. The Lovelace was full. But I've got a lovely cottage for us at King's Barton, near Mr. Urquhart's drive-gate.'

'Where is this room? I remember every house in North Street.'

'It's at Mr. Smith's, the hatter's.'

Mrs. Solent's dark-brown eyes glowed like the eyes of some excited wood-animal.

'*That* man! Not *that* house, of all houses. You don't mean – ' She broke off and stared at him intently, while an indescribable smile began to touch the corners of her mouth.

Then she leaned forward and rubbed her gloved hands together, while her cheeks glowed with mischief.

'Has the good man by any chance got a daughter called Mattie?'

'*Aunt* Mattie?' murmured Wolf, feeling as if he were struggling to catch two ropes, which, at the same time, dangled before him. 'That *is* what the child called her.'

'The child?' It was his mother's turn to look puzzled now.

'Little Olwen Smith.'

Mrs. Solent's smile died away.

'It can't be the same,' she said. 'Unless Lorna's child's got married.'

'It's the same, all right, mother. It's your man, all right. He was the hatter, wasn't he?'

She nodded.

'Well! It's the same, mother.'

Her inscrutable smile began to return and she leaned back with a sigh.

'To go straight to Albert's house – But it'll be fun. It'll be sport! I'm not going to take it seriously. . . . Aunt Mattie? . . . little Olwen? . . . goodness! But they must have come down in the world, if he lets out rooms to visitors . . . . or did he invite me? Am I destined to be Albert Smith's guest the first night I set foot in this place?'

'Did you and father know him well?' enquired Wolf, as the bus swung round the corner by the ancient conduit.

'Your father knew Lorna well – Albert's minx of a wife. Lorna was even sillier about him than that idiot Selena.'

'What happened, mother?'

'Never mind now, Wolf! I'm in a mood to be amused by *every-thing*. Don't look so sulky! I tell you I'm going to amuse myself here. You don't seem to realize that I lived in this town for ten years.'

'Listen, mother,' said Wolf hurriedly, 'I know what you mean when you talk of "amusing" yourself. Now look here, mother, I won't have you getting into any rows down here! I've got my job here! and you've *got* to be nice to everybody. Do you understand?'

In his excitement he laid his heavy hand upon her knee. 'You've got to be nice to everybody – to everybody!'

The flickering oil-lamp which lit the inside of the bus shone down upon those shining wood-animal eyes. They glowed with excitement. They positively gleamed as the jolting of the vehicle jogged both mother and son up and down on their seats.

'Your father taught me to be unconventional,' she said. 'And I'm not going to be all sugar-and-spice in my old haunts.'

The rambling old conveyance was drawing up now outside number Eighty-Five.

'Mother, you *must* be good, and let bygones be bygones.'

She turned upon him then, while the bus-man ran up the steps of the house to ring the bell.

'Your father never gave up his amusement for me, and I'm not going to give up my amusement for you! I'm going to be just myself with all our old acquaintances. I'm going to begin with Albert! There! Don't be silly! Get out and help me out. We *can't* go anywhere else now. . . . Who's that at the door? Is *that* Lorna's child? . . .'

Just half an hour later Wolf and his mother were seated at a massive mahogany table in the hatter's dining-room, sharing the Smiths' Sunday supper. Olwen was *not* in bed. With feverish cheeks and enormous dark eyes she stood at the elbow of her grandfather, listening to every word of the talk and scanning every detail of Mrs. Solent's appearance.

'I would never have believed it possible,' the grey-haired lady was saying with radiant glances at them all, 'that you should have changed so much, Albert, and that Lorna should have come to life in Mattie. You're not so pretty as your mother, my dear. Of course, we must allow that! But goodness! You've got her figure and her look. How does it feel to be so like someone else? It must be queer – almost as if you inherited their feelings, their troubles, everything! But I *am* glad to see you, Mattie. It gives me – even me – a rather queer feeling. No, you're not as pretty as your mother; but Albert musn't be hurt if I say I think you're much nicer! You needn't scowl at me, Wolf. Mattie doesn't mind, do you? And Albert knows me too well to be surprised at *anything* I say.'

'Times change, Mrs. Solent – times change!' murmured the master of the house, in a low voice. 'I was all shaky when little Olwen said you were coming. It seemed like the dead coming to life. But I feel all right now, as I set eyes upon you.' And he helped

126

himself to a lingering sip of the glass of mild whisky-and-water that stood in front of him.

He was a sad, lean, commonplace little man, with a deprecatory bend of the head and a mingling of rustic cunning and weary obsequiousness in his watery, spectacled eyes. He looked as if he had been spending the day in long Low Church services. The smell of hassocks and stuffy vestries hung about his clothes, and the furtive unction of an official who had collected many threepenny bits in an embroidered bag weighed upon his stooping shoulders.

While Mrs. Solent ate her cold mutton and hot caper-sauce with hungry relish, and rallied the nervous churchwarden, Wolf took the opportunity of studying in quiet self-effacement the expressive countenance of Mr. Smith's daughter. Mattie turned out to be a girl with a fine figure, but an unappealing face. She looked about twenty-five. She was not pretty in any sense at all, in spite of what Mrs. Solent had said. Her thick, prominent nose was out of all proportion to the rest of her face. Her chin, her forehead, her eyes, were all rendered insignificant by the size of this dominant and uncomely feature.

But though Aunt Mattie's eyes were small and of a colour that varied between grey and green, they possessed a certain formidable power. A person gazing into them for the second or third time found himself looking hastily away, as if he had been caught trespassing in a very rigidly preserved estate.

Wolf was surprised how completely at ease the girl showed herself. He had expected her to be extremely disconcerted by this intrusion. But not at all. She replied calmly and with quite the appropriate nuance of humour to his mother's rather exaggerated badinage; and with himself she seemed perfectly natural and unaffected. All this was astonishing to him; though why it should have been so, he would have been ashamed to explain. Perhaps he had expected the Smith family to display social tendencies at variance with those of the upper middle class to which he himself belonged. If so, he was certainly guilty of unjustifiable snobbishness. For though the hatter of Ramsgard School did not behave like a nobleman, he behaved with quite as much dignity and ease as most of the professional gentlemen with whom Wolf was acquainted! This unpremeditated supper-party in that dingy high-ceilinged dining-room, with its great cut-glass chandelier hanging over their heads, and its gold-framed picture of some ancestral Mr. Smith gazing down upon them, was neither awkward nor embarrassed. Mrs. Solent's evident recklessness found no rocks or reefs in the behaviour of the others upon which its mischief could lash itself into foam!

Before the evening was over and it was time for him to start for his night walk back to King's Barton, Wolf had begged more than once for a definite promise from Mattie Smith that she would bring Olwen over to see them when they were established in their new abode at Lenty Cottage. The girl was complaisant and gracious over this invitation, to which the child responded breathlessly; but Wolf knew enough of the ways of women to know that there were subtle withdrawings and qualifications, under that heavy, benevolent mask, into which it would have been unwise to probe.

'Which day does the Spring Fair begin, father?' Mattie said suddenly to the old gentleman.

'The Fair, my dear?' responded the hatter. 'To-morrow, I believe; and it lasts till the end of the week; but someone told me after church – no! it was *before* church – that Thursday is the Horse Show.'

'Oh, that completes it all!' cried Mrs. Solent. 'That's the one last touch. *Don't* I remember the Fair! I'd like to go to-morrow, the moment the gates are open! I'd like to go every day.'

'We'll go on Thursday, mother,' said Wolf. 'Everyone will be there then and you'll be able to see how many of 'em remember you.'

'The Horse Show *is* the great day,' said Mattie Smith acquiescingly.

'I haven't changed very much, then, Albert?' murmured Mrs. Solent in response to a furtive appraising glance from the discreet churchwarden.

Mr. Smith looked a little embarrassed at having been caught observing her.

'No, you haven't changed! You haven't changed!' sighed the weary little man; and the tone in which he uttered these plaintive words seemed drawn from a vast warehouse of accumulated school-hats – shelves upon shelves of hats – the burden of which seemed weighing him down in a Dead Sea of diurnal desolation.

'*Your* mother is your *real* mother, isn't she?' interrupted Olwen in a shrill voice, gazing at Wolf from the protection of Mattie's knees.

Providence came to his rescue with an answer that was really quite an inspiration.

'Mothers *are* as mothers *do*,' he responded.

But he caught, all the same, a reddening of Mattie's cheeks and a hurried turning away of the churchwarden's eyes. Mr. Albert

Smith kept pouring out whisky for himself and for Wolf; but though Mrs. Solent drank only a little coffee, she was the one who held the evening together by her high spirits. Wolf watched Mattie whispering to the child about going to bed; but as he knew well enough that Olwen wouldn't go to bed till the party broke up, he began to look from one to another, waiting till a lapse in the conversation should give him a chance to bid them good-night and start on his walk home.

But Mrs. Solent's excitement was unsubduable; and there seemed something about this unusual supper-party that made him reluctant to bring it to an end. The dark old furniture, the dark old wall-paper, the dark old great-grandfather in his heavy frame, projected some kind of hypnotism upon the sliding moments, that made it as hard for him to move as if he were under a spell.

No sound came from the street outside. No sound came from the rest of the house. Like a group of enchanted people they continued to sit there, facing one another across the table, listening to Mrs. Solent's rich, voluble voice.

Wolf had long begun, in his insatiable manner, to drink up every peculiarity of the room in which they sat – of the furniture upon which the heavily-globed gas-jets of the candelabra shed so mellow a glow. As he grew tired of smoking cigarettes, he became aware of a faint scent of apples. Where this scent originated he could not detect. It seemed to proceed equally from every portion of the apartment. And as he gave himself up to it, it brought to his mind a kind of distilled essence of all the fruit and the flowers that had ever been spread out upon that massive brown table; spread out upon former editions of *The Western Gazette;* editions old enough to contain news of the death of Queen Adelaide or of Queen Charlotte!

'I *must* go now,' he thought. 'I *must* go now.' And he began to suspect that what really held him back from making a start upon his walk was not any attraction in the Smith *ménage*, but simply the great invisible struggle that had already begun between that dead man in the cemetery and this woman who was so extraordinarily alive!

She had come prepared to avenge herself in her own magnificent way – not basely, but still with formidable success. She had not come to Ramsgard to efface herself. And now, being here, being encamped, as Miss Gault said, on the very edge of his burying-ground, she could not refrain, just out of pure, suppressed high spirits, from stirring up the mud of the ambiguous past. Well! the event must work itself out. In *no sense* was he responsible. . . .

He did manage at last to rise and to kiss his mother good-night. He would have kissed Olwen, too, but she impatiently drew away. His final appeal to Mattie to come over and see them, 'any day but Thursday, when we'll all be at the Horse Show,' was received with more warmth and cordiality than this girl had yet displayed.

What *were* the thoughts, day after day, year after year, that beat about in the secretive brain behind that heavily-featured face? What was this queer attraction which he felt for her, so different from the interest excited in him by her father and by the little girl?

Wolf couldn't help pondering on these things as he made his way out of the silent town, accompanied by hardly any mortal sound except the creak of his own heavy boots and the thud of his own heavy stick.

It was not until he was clear of the last houses of Ramsgard, clear of both workhouse and cemetery, that the Smith house, the Smith daughter, the Smith grand-daughter, faded from his brain.

Then, as the grass-scented mists grew cooler against his face, rolling up towards the arable lands from the hushed Blackmore meadows, the old serpent of lecherous desire lifted once more its head in that spacious night. Once more his mind reverted to Gerda Torp – not to Gerda as she was when she sent her bird-call so far over Poll's Camp, but to Gerda as she was to his wicked imagination when he listened to the lewd whisperings of Lobbie Torp and Bob Weevil, to the Gerda he had never seen and perhaps would never see – the Gerda who used a tombstone for a hobby-horse in that littered monument-yard in Chequers Street!

7

YELLOW BRACKEN

Wolf took good care not to reveal to his mother his own secret reservations as to the desirability of Lenty Cottage. But that first impression of something uncannily neat and trim about it still obstinately persisted in his own mind after the stir of their arrival was over.

There was no word spoken about their keeping a servant; but Mrs. Martin, the Squire's housekeeper, promised that their maid, Bessie, should come in two or three times a week to clean up. But how far his mother – who, as Wolf knew, disliked cooking – would be able to deal with their meals, remained to be seen.

On the morning of Wednesday, after their first two nights in their new abode, it struck Wolf that it would be amusing, before entering on his labours with Mr. Urquhart, to pay a visit to King's Barton Vicarage.

He found the clergyman working in his garden, and followed him into his forlorn house, the whitewashed exterior of which was stained with faint yellows, greens and browns by the varied moods of the weather. He followed him up an uncarpeted staircase and across an uncarpeted landing.

The rooms downstairs, the doors of which stood wide open, were evidently used as religious classrooms; for the only furniture they contained was a miserable collection of wooden forms and battered cane-bottomed chairs. Of the rooms at the top of the staircase, the doors of which stood open too, one appeared to be the vicar's bedroom – the bed was unmade, and the floor was littered with tattered magazines – and another the priest's sitting-room or study.

The whole house looked as though its owner had long since relinquished every kind of effort to get that personal happiness out of life which is the inheritance of the meanest. Its shabby desolation seemed to project, in opposition to every human instinct, a forlorn emptiness that was worse than squalor. Its effect upon Wolf's senses was ghastly. No one could conceive a return to such a house as a return 'home!' What it meant was simply that this wretched little priest *had no home*. The basic human necessity for some degree of cheerfulness in one's lair was outraged and violated.

The room into which Wolf was now led had at least the redemption of a small fire of red coals. But except for this, it was not a place where a stranger would wish to prolong his stay. It was littered from end to end with cheap novels. Chairs, tables, and even the floor, were piled up with these vulgarly-bound volumes. The vaporous March light filtering in through dingy muslin curtains threw a watery pallor upon these abortions of human mediocrity.

'You seem to be fond of reading,' remarked Wolf to his host, as he sat down on the only chair that was not in use.

'Mostly stories,' responded T. E. Valley, turning his head round with a whimsical grimace, as he fumbled at the lock of a small cupboard hanging against the wall. 'Mostly stories,' he repeated. Having cleared a chair and the fragment of a table, he sat down opposite his guest with a bottle of brandy between them and two glasses.

'*You* are not unhappy, then,' remarked Wolf, trying to overcome his discomfort. 'Books and brandy . . . and a fire for chilly days. . . . You might be much worse off than you are, Vicar . . . much worse off.'

T. E. Valley smiled wanly. 'Much worse off,' he repeated, re-filling his glass. 'But you know those stories are hardly literature, Solent – hardly theology, Solent. It *is* curious,' he went on, meditatively, resting his chin upon his clenched hands and supporting his elbows on the table. 'It *is* curious that with Urquhart and Jason Otter always working against me, and with most of the parish despising me, I am not more often in despair. Especially as I have so poor a conceit of myself, I know myself through and through, Solent; and I am the weakest, feeblest character alive! And yet, as you say, I really am not, *not at bottom, I mean,* an unhappy person. It is curious, I can't understand it.'

He was silent for a space; while Wolf found himself giving way to a strange, almost sensual spasm of nervous sympathy. There was something about the man's abject humility that excited him in a way he could not have explained.

'It doesn't matter what T. E. Valley does,' he began again, his voice rising to a shrill squeal, like the voice of a prophet among mice. 'It doesn't matter whether I drink or whether I stay sober! The blessed Sacrament remains the same, whatever happens to T. E. Valley!'

Wolf looked at him and exulted in the man's exultation. 'He's got hold of it,' he thought, 'whatever he likes to call it. He's got hold of it. This awful house might be a prison, an asylum, a slave-galley. The fellow's a saint! He's got hold of it!'

But it was his practical reason rather than his nervous sympathy that dictated his next words. 'You don't worry yourself about conduct, then, or about duty?'

The little man's disordered El Greco eyes grew bright within their hollow sockets. 'Not a bit!' he cried. 'Not a bit!'

'And morality?' enquired Wolf.

There was a pause at this; and the light in those animated eyes went out suddenly, just as if Wolf had put an extinguisher over them.

'You mean the matter of unholy love,' murmured T. E. Valley.

'If you call it so,' said Wolf.

'That *is* another question,' the man admitted, and he gave vent to a sigh of infinite sadness. 'Why it should be so, it's hard to tell; but every kind of love, even the most insane and depraved – even incest, for instance – is connected with religion and touches religion. When I get drunk it's a matter of chemistry. When I get angry it's a matter of nerves. But when I love *in the wrong way* –'

The priest of King's Barton rose to his feet. With a shaky hand he deliberately poured back into the decanter his unfinished drink. Then, with awkward shuffling steps, steps that made Wolf aware for the first time that instead of boots he wore large, ragged, leather slippers, he came round the table to his guest's side.

'I'm nothing,' he mumbled almost incoherently. 'I'm nothing. But don't you know,' he said, seizing Wolf's hand in his dirty, feverish fingers, 'don't you know that love sinks down into the roots of the whole world? Don't you know that there are . . . levels . . . in life . . . that . . . that . . . defy nature?'

Wolf's brain became suddenly clearer than it had been all day since he first got out of bed that morning. It seemed to him that between this confessed 'morality' of Tilly-Valley and what he had already divined as the unconfessed 'immorality' of Mr. Urquhart, there was a ghastly reciprocity. He suddenly felt a reaction in favour of the most simple earth-born heathenism. He deliberately finished his glass of brandy, and stood up.

'I don't think any of us knows very much about love,' he mumbled. And then he went on rather lamely: 'I think there are a great many different kinds of love, just as there are a great many different kinds of malice.' He stopped again, his mind struggling with the difficulty of expression. 'I don't think,' he blurted out, 'that most of the kinds of love we run across sink down to the bottom of the universe!'

Having said this, he uttered a short, uncomfortable schoolboy chuckle. 'Well, well,' he added gently, 'I'm not so certain about any of this as to be rude to anyone over it! Well, good-bye, Valley,' and he held out his hand. 'By the bye, my mother will expect a call from you soon. You *will* come, won't you? Drop in at tea-time. I'm generally in then; only don't let it be to-morrow, because we're going to the Show. Shall we see you there?' And he shook the priest's hand with affectionate cordiality, searching his mind with his eyes. . . .

It was just lunch-time when he returned to Lenty Cottage. His mother had been weeding in the garden all the morning; and she brought into the small front room, where they had their light meal, a breath of earth-mould that was very acceptable after his recent conversation.

'You look very well pleased with yourself, Wolf,' she said, as they sat down opposite each other. 'What have you been doing to make you feel so complacent?'

'Acting as oil and wine, mother,' he answered, 'between the Squire and the Vicar.'

She threw back her head and laughed wickedly.

'You're a nice one to settle quarrels! But I suppose you settled this one by shouting them both down, and that's what's given your dear face – as grandmamma used to say – that "beyond yourself" look! There's a letter for you under that book; but you shan't have it till I've finished this good meal and drunk my coffee.'

Wolf looked at the book in question, which was a large edition of Young's *Night Thoughts*, bound like a school prize.

'It's a child's hand,' said his mother, watching his face with gleaming brown eyes. 'Is it from that little Smith girl, do you think? Or have those people you stayed with, those funny Otter people, got any children?'

Wolf shook his head. Could it be from Olwen Smith? It appeared unlikely; but the child did seem to have taken a fancy to him. It was possible. But then, in one of those sudden clairvoyances that emanate so strangely from unopened letters, he felt certain that it wasn't from a child at all. It was from Gerda!

'You're mad to read it, Wolf, I can see that. But I won't have my good lunch spoilt. I think it would be nice if we had our coffee at once, don't you? *Do* go and bring it in! It's on the kitchen stove.'

He obeyed with alacrity, as he always did in these caprices of his mother's, and they sipped their coffee in suspended excitement, their eyes shining across the table like the eyes of two animals.

'Oh, it'll be so amusing, going to the Horse Show,' she cried. 'I wonder how many of them I shall recognize? Albert used to be ever so embarrassed when I made a fuss over him in public. And I did, you know, I often did; just to show I didn't care a fig about Lorna's silliness!'

Obscurely irritated by the flippancy of this allusion to his father's misconduct, and definitely impatient at the enforced delay about the letter, Wolf suddenly burst out: 'I've been to tea with Selena Gault, mother. She wrote and invited me.' He did not say that he had been the first to take the initiative in this affair. He felt it to be revenge enough without that. But Mrs. Solent was a match for him.

'Oh, I'm so glad, Wolf, that you went to cheer up that old monster. That *was* sweet of you! Think of it! My son sitting down to tea with all the Ramsgard old ladies! I'm sure she invited every one of the masters' wives and mothers to meet you. "The son of my old friend, William Solent." I can hear her say it! Well – do tell me, Wolf! For this is really getting interesting. What *did* you think of the great Gault? Of course, you know how it is with me. I never *can* endure deformity! I feel sorry and so forth, but I just can't see it about. It was over the Gault that your father and I had our final quarrel. No, you *must* listen to me! He was as insensitive about things like that as in everything else. He had absolutely no fastidiousness. The Gault had never before met any man who could even look at her. I mean – you know! – look at her as men *do* look at us. And it just went to her poor, dear head. She fell madly in love – if you can call it love, in a monster like that – and the extraordinary thing about it was that it didn't horrify your father. I don't want to be catty; but really – you know! – with a deformity like that – You'd have thought he'd have run to the end of the world. But not at all! What are you doing, Wolf? Take your hands from your head!'

But Wolf, with his long, bony middle fingers pressed against his ears, contented himself with making a shameless grimace at the woman who had given him birth.

Quick as lightning Mrs. Solent ran to the side-table, and, snatching up the letter that was beneath the book, made as though she would throw it in the fire.

This manœuvre was entirely successful. Her son rushed upon her; and the half-playful, half-serious struggle that ensued between them ended in his wresting the letter out of her clenched fingers.

He then pushed her down by main force into an armchair and hurriedly handed her a cigarette and a lighted match.

'Now *please* be good, mother darling!' he pleaded. 'I'll tell you everything when I've read it.'

He sat down in the opposite chair and tore open the letter. His mother puffed great rings of smoke into the air between them and surveyed him with glittering eyes – with eyes that had in their brown depths an almost maudlin passion of affection.

Miss Selena Gault was forgotten.

The letter was written in pencil, and in a handwriting as straggling and unformed as that of a little girl of ten. 'Olwen would have composed a much more grown-up production,' he thought, as he read the following words:

My Dear Mr. Solent,
   I am going out water-rat hunting with a basket for marigolds and to see if there are any moor-hens down there. I'm going to start directly after dinner with Lob and go down-stream just like we did before. Miss Malakite wants us to have tea with her about five. So do come there if you can't come to the Lunt.
   This is from your little friend, Gerda.

'It *is* from a child,' he said as casually as he could, stepping up to his mother's side and waving the letter in front of her. He felt a tremendous reluctance to let her read it; and yet, being the woman she was, he dared not put it straight into his pocket. Nothing of this was hidden from Mrs. Solent; but she had had her little victory in the matter of Miss Gault, and she was in a mood to. be indulgent now.

'All right, Wolf, put it into your pocket. I don't want to see it. I expect you'll find much nicer barmaids in Blacksod than you ever did in Hammersmith. I won't interfere with your light-o'-loves. I never *have*, have I?'

'No, you never have, mother darling,' he responded, with a rush of affection born of immense relief. And slipping Gerda's note into his coat-pocket, he leaned forward and took her handsome, ruddy face between the palms of his hands.

'But I'm off now, my treasure; and don't expect me back till late to-night!' He hesitated for a moment, and then added: 'You'd better not stay awake; though I know you *will*; but I shall be coming home with the Otters, and I'll let myself in quietly.'

He kissed her quickly and placed both his hands for a moment upon the rough mass of her grey hair. She smiled back at him gaily enough, but he wondered if that little sound he seemed conscious of in the cavity of her strong throat was an evidence of some other emotion. If it was, she swallowed it as completely and effectively as if it had been a little silver minnow swallowed by a watchful pike.

'I shall just go to bed, then, and read in bed,' she cried jestingly, when he let her go. 'I'm in the middle of a thrilling story about a young man who has every vice there is! I'm sure he's got *some* vices that even Selena Gault's never heard of. I'll go on with that; and if I want a little variety I'll read the book Cousin Carfax gave me about Chinese Rugs; and if *that* doesn't satisfy me I'll read Casanova's Memoirs. No! I won't! I'll read Canon Pusey's Sermons or something of that sort . . . something that just rambles on and isn't modern or clever! So run off, and don't worry about me. By the way, I had my first caller this morning, when you were over at the Manor.'

'Who was that, mother?' enquired Wolf, flicking his stick against his boot and thinking of the tombstone in Mr. Torp's yard.

'Mrs. Otter!' she cried gaily. 'And I believe we'll get on splendidly. She told me how fond you and her son Jason were of each other.'

'Jason?' muttered Wolf. 'Well, take care of yourself, darling! Don't work too hard in the garden. Remember to-morrow!' And he opened the door hastily and let himself out. 'Jason?' he muttered once more, as he strode down Lenty Lane.

His walk to Blacksod that early afternoon was one long orgy of amorous evocations. He skirted the town in such an absorbed trance that he found himself in the river-meadow before he realized that he'd left the streets behind. Nothing could have been more congruous with his mood that afternoon than this slow following of the waters of the Lunt! Past poplars and willows, past muddy ditches and wooden dams, past deserted cow-sheds and old decrepit barges half-drowned in water, past tall hedges of white-flowering blackthorn, past low thick hedges of scarcely-budded hawthorn, past stupid large-bodied cattle with shiny red hides and enormous horns, past tender, melancholy cattle with liquid eyes and silky brown-and-white flanks, he made his way through those pleasant pastures.

So beautiful was the relaxed spring atmosphere, that by degrees the excitement of his sensuality ebbed a little; and the magic of Nature became of equal importance with the thrill of amorous pursuit.

Though the sky was overcast, it was overcast with such a heavenly 'congregation of vapours' that Wolf would not have had it otherwise. There were filmy clouds floating there that seemed to be drifting like the scattered feathers of enormous albatrosses in a pearl-white sea; and behind these feathery travellers was the milky ocean on which they floated. But even that was not all; for the very ocean seemed broken here and there into hollow spaces, ethereal gulfs in the fleecy whiteness; and through these gulfs was visible a pale yellowish mist, as if the universal air were reflecting millions of primrose buds! Nor was even this vaporous luminosity the final revelation of those veiled heavens. Like the entrance to some great highway of the ether, whose air-spun pavement was not the colour of dust, but the colour of turquoise, there, at one single point above the horizon, the vast blue sky showed through. Transcending both the filmy whiteness and the vaporous yellow-ness, hovering there above the marshes of Sedgemoor, this celestial Toll-Pike of the Infinite seemed to Wolf, as he walked towards it, like some entrance into an unknown dimension, into which it was not impossible to pass! Though in reality it was the background of all the clouds that surrounded it, it seemed in some mysterious way nearer than they were. It seemed like a harbour into which the very waters of the Lunt might flow. That incredible patch of blue seemed something into which he could plunge his hands and draw them forth again, filled like overflowing cups with the very ichor of happiness. Ah! That was the word. It was *pure happiness*, that blue patch! It was the very thing he had tried so clumsily to explain to that poor Tilly-Valley, that both he and Mr. Urquhart so woefully lacked! And this was the thing, he thought, as he walked slowly on through the green, damp grass, after which his whole life was one obstinate quest. Ay! Where did it grow, this happiness? Where did it bubble up free and unspoiled? Not, at any rate, in such 'love' – half sex, half reaction from sex – that these two disordered people were pursuing!

Not in asceticism, nor in vice! Where then? He began to stride forward with all his mind and all his soul fixed on that blue patch over Sedgemoor. Not in any human struggle of that kind! Rather in some large, free, unrestricted recognition of something actually in Nature, something that came and went, something that the mind could evoke, something that required nothing save earth and sky for its fulfilment!

Between himself and that blue patch there stretched now the great trunk of a bending willow, covered, as if by a liquid green mist, with its countless newly-budded twigs. The trunk seemed attracted down to the waters of the Lunt; and the waters of the Lunt seemed to rise a little, as they flowed on, in reciprocal attraction. And through the green buds of this bending trunk the patch of blue looked closer than ever. It was not any opening highway, not any ethereal road, as he had imagined at first. It was actually a pool of unfathomable blue water; a pool in space! As he looked at it now, those green willow-buds became living moss around its blue edge; and a great yellowish fragment of sky that leaned towards it became a tawny-skinned centaur, who, bending down his human head from his animal body, quenched his thirst in its purity. A yellow man-beast drinking draughts of blue water!

Wolf stopped dead-still and gazed at what he saw, as ever more nearly and more nearly what he saw became what he imagined. This was what he wanted! This was what he sought! The brown earth was that tawny-skinned centaur; and the reason why the world was all so green about him was because all living souls – the souls of grass-blades and tree-roots and river-reeds – shared, after their kind, in the drinking up of that blue immensity by the great mouth of clay!

He moved on now again and slowly passed the bent tree. His thoughts relaxed and grew limp after his moment of ecstasy; but such as they were, like languid-winged herons, they flapped heavily over the dykes and ditches of his life.

He felt obstinately glad that through all those detestable London years – the weight of which, like chains that are thrown away, he had never realized till they were over – he had just ploughed through his work at that college, his head bent, his shoulders hunched, his spirit concentrated, stoical, unyielding! What had it been in him that had kept him, for twelve heavy years, stubbornly at work on all that unbelievable drudgery? What had it been in him that had saved him from love-affairs, from marriage – that had made it horrible for him to satisfy his sexual instincts with casual light-o'-loves from tap-rooms and music-halls? What had it been? He looked at a great alder-root that curved snake-like over the brown mud beneath the bank; and in the tenacious flexibility of that smooth phallic serpent of vegetation he seemed to detect an image of his own secretive life, craftily forcing its way forward, through a thousand obstacles, towards the liberation which it craved.

And what was this liberation?

Happiness! But not *any* kind of happiness; not just the happiness of making love to Gerda Torp.

He looked closely at the manner in which the alder-root dipped so adroitly and yet so naturally into the river. Yes! It was a kind of ecstasy he aimed at; the kind that loses itself, that merges itself; the kind that demands nothing in return!

How could this ecstasy be called love? It was more than love. It was the coming to the surface of something unutterable.

And then, like an automatic wheel that revolved in his brain, a wheel from one of whose spokes hung a bodiless human head, his thoughts brought him back to that Living Despair on the Waterloo steps. And he recalled what Jason Otter had said about pity: how if you had pity and there was one miserable consciousness left in the universe, you had no right to be happy. Oh, that was a wicked thought! You had, on the contrary, a desperately punctilious reason to be happy.

That face upon the Waterloo steps *gave* you your happiness. It was the only gift it could give. Between your happiness and that face there was an umbilical cord. All suffering was a martyr's suffering, all happiness was a martyr's happiness, when once you got a glimpse of that cord! It was the existence in the world of those two gross, vulgar parodies of life, *ennui* and *pleasure*, that confused the issues, that blighted the distinctions.

For about half a mile he walked steadily forward, letting the violence of this last thought be smoothed away by the feel of the damp soil under his feet, and the cool touch, imperceptible in detail, through his leather boots – of all the anonymous weeds and grasses that were beginning to feel the release of spring.

Ah, there they were!

He came upon them quite suddenly, as he clambered over a wooden paling between the end of a thick-set hedge and the river-bank, the wooden boards of which, worm-eaten and grey with lichen, jutted out over the water.

They were seated side by side on a fallen elm-tree, arranging the contents of a great wicker basket that lay on the ground between them.

'Hullo!' cried Lob, jumping to his feet.

Wolf took the boy in his arms and began a sort of genial horse-play with him, tumbling him over in the grass and holding him down by force as he kicked and struggled. But Lob soon wearied of this, and, lying quietly under the man's hands, turned his mud-flicked, grass-stained face towards his sister.

'You see I be right, Sis! So hand over thik ninepence. He *be* come, same as I said 'a would. So hand over what I've won!'

Wolf became aware that a fit of sudden shyness had fallen upon both himself and Gerda. He continued to kneel above the prostrate Lob, pinioning the child's arms and putting off the moment when he must rise and face her. Gerda, too, seemed to prolong with unnecessary punctiliousness her fumbling with the ragged recesses of her faded little purse, as she emptied pennies and bits of silver into her lap

'Ninepence! It was ninepence!' the boy kept shouting, as he sought in vain to lift up his eager grass-stained face high enough to see what the girl was doing. 'It was sixpence if he went to Malakite's! It was ninepence if he came here!'

Wolf, bending over his prisoner, found himself watching the progress of a minute ladybird who with infinite precaution was climbing the bent stalk of a small grass-blade close to the boy's head. But he was so conscious of Gerda's presence that a slow, sweet, shivering sensation ran through his nerves, as if in the midst of a great heat his body had been plunged into the cool air of a cavern.

'There, Lob!' said Gerda suddenly, holding out sixpence and three pennies.

Wolf let the child go and stood up.

Their eyes met through the boy's violent scramble and snatch-ing clutch. They met through his cry of 'Finding's keepings, losing's seekings! Bet me enough to make a shilling! I be a prime grand better, *I* be!'

And, as their eyes met, the shyness that they had felt before changed into a thrilling solemnity. For one quick moment they held each other's gaze; and it was as if they had been overtaken simultaneously by an awestruck recognition of some great un-known Immortal, who had suddenly appeared between them, with a hand upon each.

Then the girl turned to her brother.

'I bet you, Lob,' she said, 'you won't find a blackbird's nest round here with eggs in it!'

'How much?' the boy responded, standing in front of her with his hands behind his head, in the pose of a young, indolent conqueror.

'How much? – how much?' mocked Wolf with heavy humour, seating himself on the tree-trunk by Gerda's side. 'What a young miser you are!' As he took his place by her side, the floating barge upon which it seemed to him they were embarked rocked with a motion that gave him a sense of sweet dizziness.

Lob looked at his sister gravely, weighing the matter in his mind.

'You won't hunt rats with *him* when I'm not there?' he bargained.

She shook her head.

'"Tis early for them nesties; but I do know for three o'n already; up along Babylon Hill. They be all hipsy-hor hedges, looks-like, in *this* here field; and blackbirds be fonder o' holly-trees and bramble-bushes. But they bain't so sly, the bloody old yellow-beaks, as them thrushes be. I think I'll do it, Sis.'

'I think I may take her bond,' muttered Wolf under his breath.

'I haven't heard one of them since we came,' said Gerda cunningly. 'They like the hills better than down here on the flat. I wouldn't have betted so much if I wasn't sure I'd win.'

'*I* ain't betted nothink,' said Lob quickly, 'so you can't win anyways. It's either us both loses, or it's me what wins.'

Gerda nodded assent to this unchivalrous issue.

'Well, I may as well have a look round,' decided the boy; 'only mind – no tricks! If you rat-hunt with *him* when I ain't there, 'twill be threepence whatsoever.'

She indicated assent to this also.

Lob began to swagger slowly away.

'I knows why you wants me to shog off,' he called back; and he added an outrageous expression in shrewd Dorset dialect which had the effect of bringing an angry flush to Gerda's cheeks.

'Be off, you rogue,' cried Wolf, 'or you'll get more than you've bargained for!'

But there came flying through the air, from the child's impudent hand, a well-aimed puffball, which burst as it touched Gerda's knee, covering her dress with a thin, powdery brown dust.

Neither she nor Wolf moved a muscle in response to this attack; and Lobbie wandered slowly off till he was lost to sight. Then the girl got up and began shaking her skirt. The cream-coloured cloak hung loose and open, and Wolf saw that she was dressed in an old, tight-fitting, olive-green frock.

When she had finished brushing the puffball-powder from her clothes, she took off her hat and laid it carefully, absent-mindedly, upon the tree-trunk by his side.

He instantaneously threw his arms round her and held her tightly against him, while in the silence between them he felt his heart beating like an invisible underground water-pump.

But she unloosed his hands with deft, cool fingers. 'Not now,' she said. 'Let's talk now.'

In some mysterious way he was grateful to her for this. The last thing he wanted was to spoil the strange, lovely solemnity that had fallen upon them like the falling of slow, thin, noiseless rain.

He rose and took her hand, and they began moving away from the log.

'Wait! I'll leave a signal for that little rascal,' he said, putting his stick and his cloth cap by the side of the cream-coloured hat. But he did not give up her hand; and together they walked carelessly and aimlessly across that wide field, taking a course at right angles to the course taken by her brother. Wolf had hitherto, in his attitude to the girls he had approached, been dominated by an impersonal lust; but what he now felt stealing over him like a sweet, insidious essence, was the actual, inmost identity of this young human animal. And the strange thing was that this conscious presence, this deep-breathing Gerda, moving silently beside him under her cloak, under her olive-green frock, under everything she wore, was not just a girl, not just a white, flexible body, with lovely breasts, slender hips, and a gallant, swinging stride, but a living, conscious soul, different in its entire being from his own identity.

What he felt at that moment was that, hovering in some way around this tangible form, was another form, impalpable and delicate, thrilling him with a kind of mystical awe. It changed everything around him, this new mysterious being at his side, whose physical loveliness was only its outward sheath! It added something to every tiniest detail of that enchanted walk which they took together now over one green field after another. The little earth-thrown mole-hills were different. The reddish leaves of the newly-sprung sorrel were different. The droppings of the cattle, the clumps of dark-green meadow-rushes, all were different! And something in the cold, low-hung clouds themselves seemed to conspire, like a great stretched-out grey wing, to separate Gerda and himself from the peering intrusion of the outer world.

And if the greyness above and the greenness beneath enhanced his consciousness of the virginal beauty of the girl, her own nature at that hour seemed to gather into itself all that most resembled it in that spring twilight.

Gate after gate, leading from one darkening field into another, they opened and passed through, walking unconsciously westward, towards the vast yellowish bank of clouds that had swallowed up that sky-road into space. It was so far only the beginning of twilight, but the undried rains that hung still in motionless water-drops upon millions of grass-blades seemed to welcome the coming on of night – seemed to render the whole surface of the earth less opaque.

Over this cold surface they moved hand in hand, between the unfallen mist of rain in the sky and the diffused mist of rain in the grass, until the man began to feel that they two were left alone alive, of all the people of the earth – that they two, careless of past and future, protected from the very ghosts of the dead by these tutelary vapours, were moving forward, themselves like ghosts, to some vague imponderable sanctuary where none could disturb or trouble them!

They had advanced for more than a mile in this enchanted mood, and were leaning against a wooden gate which they had just shut behind them, when Wolf pointed to an open shed, about a stone's throw away, the floor of which he could make out, from where they stood, to be strewn with a carpet of yellow bracken.

'Shall we try *that* as a shelter?' he asked. The words were simple enough. But Gerda detected in them the old, equivocal challenge of the male pursuer; and as he pulled at her wrist, trying to lead her towards the shed, she stiffened her body, snatching her hand away, and drew back against the protective bars of the gate. Very quickly then, so as to smooth away any hurt to his pride, she began to speak; and since silence rather than words had hitherto been the link between them, the mere utterance of any speech from her at all was a shock strong enough to quell his impetuousness.

'Did you like me directly you saw me, that day in our house?'

He looked at her attentively as, with her fair head bare and her arms spread out along the top bar of the gate, she asked this naïve question.

It suddenly came over him that she had not really the remotest conception as to how rare her beauty was. She regarded herself, of course, as a 'pretty' girl, but she had no notion that she moved through Blacksod like one of those women of antiquity about whose loveliness the noblest legends of the world were made! A certain vein of predatory roguery in him led him to play up to this simplicity.

'I liked you best when you were whistling to me,' he said. But in his senses he thought: 'I should be a madman not to snatch at her!' And in his soul he thought: 'I shall marry her. As sure as to-morrow follows to-day, I shall marry her!'

'I liked *you* best when you were hunting for me at Poll's Camp,' said Gerda. 'But I can't understand – '

'What can't you understand, Gerda?'

'I can't understand why I don't want you to touch me just now. But oh! if you only knew what things they say in the town about girls and men!'

She looked him straight in the face with an ambiguous tilt of her soft, rounded chin. Something had come between them – something that troubled him seriously, though not with the sense of any unscalable barrier.

'What things do they say in the town?' he asked.

At this she clapped her hands to her cheeks, and a look of troubled bewilderment crossed her fixed gaze.

He began to wonder if the girl, for all her coquetries, was not abnormally innocent. Perhaps the extreme lewdness of lads like Bob Weevil had, in some of those furtive conclaves between young people that are always so complete a mystery to older persons, given her some kind of startled shock.

Slowly her hands fell to her sides, and the troubled look faded; but she still faced him with a faint, tremulous frown, while the delicate curves about her eyes took on that expression of monumental beseeching, such as one sees sometimes in antique marbles.

His craving to take her in his arms was checked by a wave of overpowering tenderness.

As she stood there, with her back to the gate, her personality struck home to him with such a sharp, sudden pang of reality, that it made certain tiny little blossoms of the blackthorn hedge become strangely important, as if they had been an apparition of wonderful white swans.

'Well, never mind what they say in the town! You and I are by ourselves now. It's only you and I that count to-day. And I won't tease you, Gerda, you darling – no, not with one least thing you don't like!'

He was silent, and they remained motionless, staring at each other like two stone pillars bearing the solemn weight of the unknown future. Then he possessed himself of one of her hands, and it was a new shock to him to feel how ice-cold her fingers had grown.

'Don't act as if we're strangers, Gerda!' he pleaded. 'I do understand you – much more than you think I do. And I'll take care of you for ever! Isn't as if time mattered one bit. I feel as if I'd known you all my life. I feel as if everything here' – and he glanced round at those strangely important white blossoms – 'were an old story already. It's funny, Gerda, isn't it, how natural and yet how weird it is, that we should have met at all? Only a week ago I was in London, with no remotest idea that you were in the world – or this gate, or this blackthorn hedge, or that shed over there!'

Her cold fingers did respond a little to his pressure now, and her eyes fell and searched the ground at her feet. Without a sigh, without a breath, she pondered, floating upon some inner sea of feeling, of which no one, not even herself, would ever know the depths.

'You *are* glad we've met, Gerda, dear?' he asked.

She raised her eyes. They had the tension of a sudden, difficult resolution in them.

'Do men ever leave girls alone after they've married them?'

The words were so unexpected that he could only press her cold fingers and glance away from those troubled eyes. What his own gaze encountered was a single tarnished celandine, whose bent stalk lay almost flat on a wisp of rain-sodden grass.

'When we're married,' he responded gravely, after a pause, during which he felt as if with his own hands he were launching a rigged ship into a misty sea, 'I'll leave you alone just as much as you want!'

'A girl I know said once that my whistling was only whistling for a lover. *You* don't think that, do you?'

'Good God! I should think not! Your whistling's a wonderful thing. It's your genius. It's your way of expressing what we all want to express.'

'What do we all want to express?'

He chuckled right out at this, and, forgetting all vows and

146

pledges, flung his arms round her shoulders and hugged her tightly to his heart. 'Oh, Gerda, Gerda!' he cried breathlessly, as he let her go, 'you'll be soon making me so damnably fond of you that I'll be completely at your mercy!'

'But what do we all want to express?' she repeated.

He felt such a rush of happiness at the change in her voice that he could only answer at random.

'God! my dear, *I* don't know! Recognition, I suppose. No! not exactly that! Gratitude, perhaps. But that's not quite it. You've asked a hard question, sweetheart, and I'm damned if I can give you the answer.' He drew her towards him as she spoke, and this time she seemed to yield herself as she had never done before. But the warmth of her body, as he pressed it to him, dissolved his tender consideration so quickly that once more she drew back.

Hurriedly anxious to rush in between her thoughts and herself, he began saying the first thing that came into his head.

'I think what we all want to express is . . . something . . . addressed . . . to . . . to the gods . . . some kind of . . . acknowledgment – '

He stopped abruptly; for she had once more fixed upon him that wild, bewildered look.

'You're not angry with me, Gerda, darling?' he blurted out.

She did not take any notice of these words of his, but the look he dreaded began to fade away under the genuine concern of his tone.

She now pulled her cream-coloured cloak tightly across her olive-green frock; and instead of relinquishing the garment when she'd done this, she kept her arms crossed against her breast holding the gathered folds of the woollen stuff. Then her lips moved, and looking away from him, sideways, over the wide field, she said very quietly:

'If you feel it's no good, and you couldn't think of marrying a girl like me, you'd better let me go home now.'

He never forgot the solemn fatality she put into those words; and he answered in the only way he could. He took her head gently between his hands and kissed her upon the forehead. This action, in its grave tenderness and its freedom from any fever of the blood, did seem to reassure her.

But the attraction of her sweetness soon excited his senses again, and he began caressing her in spite of himself. She did not resist him any more; but the reaction from the former tenseness of her nerves broke down her self-control, and he soon became aware of the salt taste of tears upon his lips. She did not cry aloud. She cried silently; but the sobs that shook her showed, in the very power they had over her, the richness and vitality of her youthful blood.

The fact that he had launched his boat and hoisted his sail – the fact that he had already resolved to marry her, come what might – was something that in itself dispelled his scruples.

'It's cold here,' he murmured, when at last she had lifted up her tear-stained face and they had exchanged some long kisses; 'it's cold here, Gerda, darling. Let's just *see* what that shed over there's like! We needn't stay a minute there if it's not a nice sort of place.'

A species of deep, lethargic numbness to everything except the immediate suggestions of his voice and touch seemed to have taken possession of her.

His arm round her, her cream-coloured cloak hanging loose, her cheeks pale, she let herself be led across the intervening tract of grass to the open door of the little shed.

Before they reached it, however, she turned her face round and glanced shyly at him. 'You know I'm quite stupid and ignorant,' she said. 'I know nothing about anything.'

Wolf did not pause to enquire whether this hurried confession referred to what might be named 'the ritual of love' or just simply to her lack of book-learning. His senses were by this time in such a whirl of excitement that the girl's clear-toned voice sounded like the vague humming of a sea-shell in his ears.

'Gerda?' he murmured huskily, with a faint, a very faint interrogation in his tone.

Emotions, feelings, desires, some exalted, some brutal, whirled up from the bottom of his nature, like storm-driven eels roused and stirred from the ooze of a muddy river!

Together they stood at the entrance to that little shed and surveyed the interior in a silence that was like the hovering of some great falcon of fate, suspended between past and future. The place was an empty cow-barn, its roof thatched with river-reeds and its floor thickly strewn with a clean, dry bed of last autumn's yellow bracken.

The queer thing was that as he drew her across that threshold his conscious soul seemed to slip out of his body and to watch them both from the high upper air as if it were itself that falcon of fate. But when, with their feet upon that bracken floor, they faced each other, there suddenly floated into Wolf's mind, like the fluttering of a whirling leaf upon disturbed water, an old Dorset ditty that he had read somewhere, with a refrain about Shaftesbury town.

'I know nothing about anything,' repeated the girl in a low voice; but as he held her tightly against his beating heart, it was not her words but the words of that old song which hummed through his brain:

> 'There'll be yellow bracken beneath your head;
> There'll be yellow bracken about your feet,
> For the lass Long Thomas lays in's bed
> Will have no blanket, will have no sheet.
>
> My mother has sheets of linen white,
> My father has blankets of purple dye.
> But to my true-love have I come to-night
> And in yellow bracken I'll surely lie:
>
> In the yellow bracken he laid her down,
> While the wind blew shrill and the river ran;
> And never again she saw Shaftesbury town,
> Whom Long Thomas had taken for his leman!'

The smell of the bracken rose up from that bed and took the words of this old song and turned them into the wild beating of the very pulse of love.

To the end of his days he associated that moment with these dried-up aromatic leaves and with that remembered rhyme. The sweetness of his paramour, her courage, her confiding trust, her 'fatal passivity,' were blended with the fragrance of those withered ferns and with that old ballad.

Meanwhile the chilly March airs floated in and out of the bare shed where they were lying; and the shades of twilight grew deeper and deeper. Those twilight shades, as they settled down about their heads, became like veritable sentinels of love – wraith-like, reverential, patient. They seemed to be holding back the day, so that it should not peer into their faces. They seemed to be holding back the darkness, so that it should not separate them, the one from the other!

And as they lay – happy and oblivious at last – just as if they were really lying on the deck of some full-sailed ship which a great dark-green wave was uplifting, Wolf found himself unaccountably recalling certain casual little things that he had seen that day – seen without knowing that he had seen them! He recalled the underside of the bark of a torn-off willow-branch that he had caught sight of in his walk by the Lunt. He recalled the peculiar whitish-yellowness hidden in the curves of an opening fern-frond which he had passed somewhere on the road from King's Barton. He recalled the sturdy beauty, full of a rich, harsh, acrid power, of a single chestnut-bud, which he had unconsciously noted in the outskirts of Blacksod. He recalled certain tiny snail-shells clinging to the stalk of some new-grown dock-leaf, whose appearance had struck his mind somewhere in those meadows. . . .

When, after the slow ebbing of what really was a very brief passage of time, but what seemed to Wolf something more than time and different from time, they stood together again outside the hut, there came over him a vague feeling, as if he had actually invaded and possessed something of the virginal aloofness of the now darkened fields.

With his hand over Gerda's shoulder he drank up a great mystery from those cool, wide spaces. His fingers clutched the soft collar of the girl's cloak. He was conscious of her breathing – so steady, so gently, and yet so *living* - like the breath of a warm, soft animal in the velvet darkness. He was conscious of her personality as something quivering and quick, and yet as something solitary, unapproachable.

Suddenly she broke the silence.

'Do you want me to whistle for you?' she asked, in a low, docile voice.

The words reached his ears from an enormous distance. They came travelling to him over rivers, over mountains, over forests; and as they took shape in his consciousness, something quite different from what he had felt for her swelled up in his throat. He took her head between his hands and kissed her as he had never in his life kissed any woman.

'Lob will hear it,' he said with a rough, happy laugh. 'But let him hear it! What does it matter now?'

But she moved a few paces away and he watched her whitish shadowily-blurred face as if it had been the face of an immortal.

And he knew, without *seeing* that it was so, that her expression as she whistled was like the expression of a child asleep, or of a child happily, peacefully dead.

And, though it was into the night that she now poured those

liquid notes, the tone of their drawn-out music was a tone full of the peculiar feeling of one hour alone of all the hours of night and day. It was the tone of the hour just before dawn, the tone of that life which is not sound, but only withheld breath, the breath of cold buds not yet green, of earth-bound bulbs not yet loosed from their sheaths, the tone of the flight of swallows across chilly seas as yet far off from the warm, pebbled beaches towards which they are steering their way.

Gerda's whistling died away now into a silence that seemed to come surging back with a palpable increase of visible darkness in its train.

But the girl remained standing just where she was, quite motionless, about ten paces away from him.

He also remained motionless, where he was, without sign or word.

And just as two straight poplar trees that in some continuous storm had been bent down so that their branches have mingled, when the storm is over rise up erect and are once more completely separate and completely themselves, so this man and this girl, whose relation to each other could never be quite the same again, remained distinct, removed, aloof, each standing like a silent bivouac-watcher, guarding the smouldering camp-fire of their own hidden thoughts.

Thus, and not otherwise, had stood, in the green dews of some umbrageous Thessalian valley at the very dawn of time, Orion and Merope, joined and yet so mysteriously divided by this sweet fatality! So in the same green dews had stood Deucalion and Pyrrha, while the earth waited for its new offspring. They also, those primeval lovers, had pondered thus, content and happy, bewildered and sad, while over their heads the darkness descended upon Mount Pelion, or the white moonlight flooded with silver the precipices of Ossa!

As he thought of these things, he made up his mind that he would refrain from any sentimental attempt to bridge the impassable gulf between what Gerda was feeling then and what he was feeling. . . . No casual words of easy tenderness should spoil the classical simplicity of their rare encounter! For classical it had been, in its arbitrariness, in its abruptness, in its heroic defiance of so many obstacles; as he had always prayed that any great love-affair of his might be.

Their words to each other, when at length they did break the spell, and wander back hand in hand to where they had separated from Lob, were simple and natural – reduced, in fact, to the plain level of prosaic, practical anxieties.

'It's the devil!' grumbled Wolf; 'but there it is, sweetheart, and we've got to face it. It's not only *my* mother, but *your* mother we shall have to deal with. I know only too well that I've never been to Oxford. I know I have no "honourable" in front of my name, and I know that what Mr. Urquhart gives me will be barely enough for three people to live upon. There it is, my sweet, and we've got to face it.'

'I don't think your mother will want to live with us,' said the girl quietly.

Wolf winced at this. Somehow or other he had grown so used to thinking of his mother and himself as one person that it gave him a very queer feeling – as if Gerda had inserted a tiny needle of ice into his heart – to think of the two of them under separate roofs.

A moment later, however, and the feeling passed, crushed under the logic of his reason. It was, of course, inevitable – so he said to himself – that Gerda, young girl though she was, should want a hearth of her own.

'No,' he answered, emphatically enough. 'We must live by overselves.'

'Father won't give us anything,' said Gerda.

'That's all right,' he chuckled, laughing surlily but not maliciously. 'I've no desire to be supported out of tomb-making! No, no, sweetheart; what we've got to find is some tiny shanty of our own, almost as small as our cow-shed, where neither your mother nor my mother can interfere with us.'

'Do you think Mrs. Solent will be *very* angry?' she enquired.

This time her words produced a more serious shock. He felt as if one of his arms or legs had been amputated, and was stuck up as a ninepin for Gerda to throw things at, not knowing what she did.

'I'll deal with her, anyway,' he replied.

'We'll have to have our banns read out in church,' said Gerda.

'We shall!' he conceded, bringing out the syllables like pistol-shots; 'but all that part of it will be awful.'

Gerda snatched her fingers from him and clapped her hands together. 'Don't let's be married!' she cried gaily. 'It'll be far more fun not to be; and if I have a child it'll be a bastard, like the kings in history!'

But Wolf had already formed a very definite image in his mind of the enchanted hovel where he would live with this unparalleled being, free from all care.

'We can't manage it without being married, Gerda, and as for bastards – '

'Hush!' she cried. 'We're talking nonsense. Gipoo Cooper told me I should never have a child.'

Wolf was silenced by this; and then, after a pause, 'I don't believe Urquhart would make any fuss,' he said meditatively. 'It wouldn't interfere with my work.'

'What you don't realize,' she protested in a low voice, 'is how completely different my family is from yours. Why, father never says a word like he'd been educated or been to school.'

But Wolf refused to let this pass.

'Perhaps *you* don't realize, missy,' he flung out, in a clear, emphatic voice, 'that my father died in Ramsgard Workhouse!'

Her commentary upon this information was to snatch his hand and raise it to her lips.

''Tisn't where a gentleman dies,' she responded, 'that makes the difference. 'Tis where he's born.'

'Oh, damn all this!' he cried abruptly. 'I don't care if your father talks his head off with Dorset talk; and all Blacksod knows that my father threw himself to the dogs. I'm going to live for the rest of my life in Dorsetshire, and I'm going to live alone with my sweet Gerda!'

He hugged her to his heart as he spoke.

'I'm very thankful that you like my whistling,' she said, rather breathlessly, when he let her go. 'I don't know what I should have done if you hadn't.'

'Like it!' he cried. 'Oh, Gerda, my Gerda, I can't tell you what it's like. I've never heard anything to touch it and never shall; and that's the long and short of it!'

Thus discoursing, the lovers arrived at the prostrate elm-trunk where they had left their belongings. It looked so familiar and yet so different now, as they stumbled upon it in the darkness, that Wolf received the kind of shock that people get when, after some world-changing adventure, they encounter the reproachful sameness of some well-known aspect of hearth and home. And there was Lob! The boy was crouched in a posture like that of a reproachful goblin. He was engaged in cutting with his pocket-knife – in spite of the darkness – deep, jagged incisions in the handle of Wolf's stick! Much time was to pass before those un-evennesses in the handle of that oak cudgel ceased to compel its owner to recall with bitter-sweet vividness the events of that incredible March Wednesday!

'I know'd you'd go rat-hunting,' was his sulky greeting. Evidently to Lob's mind no other occupation than this could account for their protracted absence from his side. 'I know'd you'd do it. Girls is never to be trusted, girls isn't. 'Tis in their constitution to betray.'

'Good Lord, Lob!' cried Wolf. 'Where did you get that sentence? Have you been composing that speech ever since we left?'

'Look here, Sis,' declared the boy, standing in front of her with the air of a robber-chief. 'You've got to fork out! You've got to give threepence to I, or never no more will I take your word!'

But the girl's tone was now the self-composed, elder sister's tone:

'I hope you only took one egg, Lob; like I always tell you to.'

'I won,' he repeated obstinately. 'I won; so you pays.'

'Show me the egg,' said Gerda. 'Where is it? I hope it *wasn't* the only one. Have you blown it without making that silly big hole you always make? Show it to me, Lob!'

'I can't show it to 'ee, for I ain't got it,' grumbled the boy. 'I got a nest all right, and I got a egg all right. There were four on 'em – all wonderful specks – in thik nest; and I minded what you always says to I, and I only took one.'

'Where is it, then? Show is to us, Lob!'

Lob moved nearer to Wolf. 'You won't let she cheat I of thik threepence,' he pleaded querulously.

'Where is that egg, Lob?' repeated the young girl. 'He's up to something, you mark my words!' she added.

'They girls be never to be trusted, be they?' grumbled the boy, sidling up still closer to Wolf.

'You know perfectly well you can always trust me, Lob!' protested Gerda indignantly. 'It's you who we can't trust now, isn't it, Mr. Solent?'

The man looked from one to the other. It amused him to listen to such contending voices from these two blurred spots of whiteness in the dark; while he himself, full of an unutterably sweet indolence, acted as their languid umpire. He was delighted, too, as well as amazed, by the intense gravity with which Gerda took this trifling disagreement. How quaint girls were! If he had caught Lob stealing his very watch in the darkness, and transferring it to his own pocket, he felt, just then, that he would hardly have noticed the incident!

154

'Haven't I won over she, Mr. Solent?' whined the child. 'I found thik nestie fields and fields away from where us be now. 'Twere in monstrous girt hedge, thik nestie, and I scratched myself cruel getting my hand in.'

'Why haven't you got the egg, then?' insisted the girl, in a hard, accusing voice.

"Cos I broke the bloody thing!' wailed the boy desperately. 'I were crossing one of they darned fields and I treadit in a girt rabbit-gin and came near to breaking me neck, let alone thik bloody egg.'

'Lob, I'm right-down ashamed of you!' cried Gerda, in a voice quivering with moral indignation.

'What be up to now, then?' responded the boy. 'What be all this hullabaloo about, when a person tells straight out what a person gone and done? If it be so turble hard to 'ee to lose three-pence, why did 'ee go rat-hunting with *him* here and leave anyone all lonesome-like? For all *you* care, a chap might have been tossed, this here dark night, by some o' they girt bullicks!'

His voice grew plaintive, but Gerda was unmoved.

'You never found any nest at all, Lob, and you know you didn't.'

Lobbie's voice sounded now as if he very soon might burst into tears.

'I shan't have no shilling! I shan't have no shilling without I gets the threepence you betted wi' I!'

Wolf began fumbling in his pocket, but the girl stopped him with a quick movement.

'Lob,' she said sternly, 'you've never lied to me before, in all the rat-hunts, and nuttings, and blackberryings, and mush-roomings, we've ever had together. What's come over you, Lob? Oh, I *am* ashamed of you!' 'Tisn't as if I were mother or dad. 'Tisn't as if we hadn't always done everything together. You're not nice company, any more, Lob, for people to go about with! I shall always have to say to anyone in the future, "Take care, now, you can never depend upon what Lob Torp says!"'

Wolf, seating himself in the darkness upon the fallen tree-trunk, listened in amazement to this dialogue. The moods of women, except for those of his mother, were a phenomenon the ebbings and flowings of which had hardly presented themselves to his deeper consciousness. He obtained now, in listening to Gerda's righteous anger, an inkling of the supernatural power which these beings have of bringing to bear upon the male conscience exactly that one accusation, of all others, which will pierce it to its heart's core!

He had no conception of how Gerda had found out that the boy was lying, and he felt at that moment a faint and perhaps scandalous wave of sympathy pass through him for Lobbie Torp. Lob himself felt this at once with a child's clairvoyance.

'She's cross about the threepence,' he whispered, leaning against the man's knee, 'but you'll pay it, won't you, Mr. Solent?'

Wolf had grown weary by this time of the whole discussion. He took advantage of the darkness to transfer from his own pocket to that of this fellow wrongdoer at least twice as much as he was demanding.

'Come on,' he said, when the clandestine transaction was accomplished, 'let's get back to the Blacksod road before we're completely benighted!'

He rose and moved on between them, Lob in penitent and rather shamefaced silence carrying the great wicker basket, at the bottom of which reposed a few fading marigolds and some handfuls of watercress.

The excitement of climbing over the railings at the very edge of the river-bank, and the pride she took in being able to show her power of guiding her lover through the darkened fields, quickly restored Gerda's good humour.

'We'll drop Lob at the beginning of Chequers Street,' Wolf said, when they at last felt the hard road from Nevilton to Blacksod under their feet. 'Do you think' he went on, 'that Miss Malakite will expect us still, so long after tea-time?'

'I was going to stay to supper with her,' said Gerda; 'so I don't think it'll matter. She'll give us tea, though, late as we are! She won't have noticed the time at all, very likely. She never does, when her father's away and she's reading.'

With the sister and brother leaning against him naturally and familiarly, each on one of his arms, Wolf, with his oak stick held firmly in the hand adjoining the now somewhat dragging and tired bird's-nester, strode along towards the lights of the town, in a deep, diffused warmth of unalloyed happiness. The days of his life seemed to stretch out before him in a lovely spring-scented perspective.

The few misgivings that remained to him about his marriage fell away in that hedge-scented darkness – a darkness that seemed to separate the earth from the sky with the formless presence of some tremendous but friendly deity, under whose protection he bore those two along. And as he felt Gerda press his arm softly and lightly against her young body, the sensation came over him that he had only to walk on and on . . . on and on . . . just like this . . . in order to bring that secret 'mythology' of his into relation with the whole world.

'Whom Long Thomas had taken for his leman,' he repeated in his heart; and it seemed to him as if the lights of the town, which now began to welcome them, were the lights of a certain imaginary city which from his early childhood had appeared and disappeared on the margin of his mind. It was wont to appear in strange places, this city of his fancy . . . at the bottom of teacups . . . or the window-panes of privies . . . in the soapy water of baths . . . in the dirty marks on wall-papers . . . in the bleak coals of dead summer-grates . . . between the rusty railings of deserted burying-grounds . . . above the miserable patterns of faded carpets . . . among the nameless litter of pavement-gutters. . . . But whenever he had seen it, it was always associated with the first lighting up of lamps, and with the existence, but not necessarily the presence, of someone . . . some girl . . . some boy . . . some unknown . . . whose place in his life would resemble that first lighting of lamps . . . that sense of arriving out of the cold darkness of empty fields and lost ways into the rich, warm, glowing security of that mysterious town. . . .

'Whom Long Thomas has taken for his leman,' he repeated once more. And he thought to himself, 'It's all in that word . . . in that word; and in coming along a dark road to where lamps are lit!'

8

THE THREE PEEWITS

THEY got rid of Lobbie at the corner of Chequers Street, and moved on, side by side, past the lighted shop-windows. It was a further revelation to him of the ways of girls, to notice that Gerda repeatedly stopped him, with a childish clutch at his coat-sleeve, before some trifle in those lighted windows that attracted her attention. Her eyes were dreamy with a soft languorous happiness; while her little cries of pleasure at what she saw made ripples in the surface of her mental trance like the rising of a darting shoal of minnows to the top of deep water.

As for his own mood, the lights of the town, its traffic and its crowds, threw him upon a rich, dark, incredible intimacy with her, whose sweetness reduced everything to a vague reassuring stage-play. Everything became a play whose living puppets seemed so touchingly lovable that he could have wept to behold them, and to know that she was beholding them with him!

When they reached the door of the Malakite bookshop, however, he became conscious of so deep an unwillingness to face the look of Christie's steady brown eyes that he impetuously begged off.

'I can't do it to-night,' he said; 'so don't 'ee press me, my precious!'

Their farewell was grave and tender; but he left her without looking back.

It was then that hunger came upon him; and making his way to the Three Peewits, he ordered a substantial supper, beneath the not altogether sympathetic gaze of Queen Victoria.

He remained for nearly two hours lingering over this meal, while at the back of his mind the ditty about Shaftesbury town and Yellow Bracken mingled with the fragrance of the old hostelry's old wine. When at last he rose from the table, it occurred to him that Darnley Otter had mentioned on the previous day that both the brothers might be here this night. Led by a mysterious desire, just then – not quite understood by himself – for masculine society, he entered the little inner parlour of the Three Peewits. Here he found himself in a thick cloud of tobacco-smoke and a still thicker murmur of men's voices. The change from his erotic musings into so social and crude an atmosphere was more bewildering to his mind than he had expected. He gazed round him, befogged and blinking.

But Darnley Otter rose at once to greet him, leading him to an aperture in the wall, where drinks were served. Standing there by Darnley's side, he made polite, hurried bows to the different members of the company, as his friend mentioned their names, and while his glass was filled and refilled with brandy, he found his eyes turning inevitably to the place where Jason sat – sat as if he had been doing nothing else since he came into that room but wait for Wolf's arrival. The man was watching him intently now, and without a trace of that whimsical humour with which he had departed from him to walk round the edge of Lenty Pond.

Wolf began at once summoning up from the recesses of his own nature all the psychic power he could bring to bear to cope with this new situation. As he chatted at that little counter with Darnley, in the midst of a rambling, incoherent flow of talk from all parts of the room, he deliberately drank glass after glass of brandy, amused at the nervousness with which Darnley observed this proceeding, and growing more and more determined to fathom the mystery of that self-lacerated being on the other side of the room.

It seemed to him now that Jason's head, as he saw it across that smoke-filled space, resembled that of some lost spirit in Dante's *Inferno*, swirling up out of the pit and crying, 'Help! Help! Help!' It was curious to himself how ready he felt then to respond to that cry. 'I must have drunk up this new strength from possessing Gerda,' he thought to himself.

Darnley's trim beard continued to wag with gentlemanly urbanity, as he laughed and jested with various people in different parts of the room, but Wolf could see that he was growing more and more nervous about his brother. Nor was this nervousness without justification. Jason had turned his face to his neighbour, who was a grim farmer from Nevilton, and was uttering words that evidently seemed to startle the man, if not to shock him; for his face grew grimmer than ever, and he kept shifting his chair a little further away.

Things were at this pass when the door opened with a violent swing, and there came in together Mr. Torp, Mr. T. E. Valley, and a tall handsome browbeating individual, who was presently introduced to Wolf as Mr. Manley of Willum's Mill.

The Vicar of King's Barton seemed to have been drinking already, for he staggered straight up to the counter, pulling the plump stone-cutter unceremoniously after him by the lapel of his coat. The heavy-jowled Mr. Manley moved across the room and seated himself by the side of the farmer from Nevilton, whom he addressed loudly and familiarly as Josh Beard. Wolf noticed that Mr. Beard, in a very sour and malicious manner, began at once repeating to this newcomer whatever it had been that Jason Otter had just said to him; while Mr. Manley of Willum's Mill proceeded with equal promptness to cast looks of jocose and jeering brutality at the unfortunate poet.

'My friend Mr. Torp was in the bar-room, so I brought him in,' said T. E. Valley, shaking hands with Wolf as if he had not seen him for years.

"'Tis no impertinence, I hope, for I to come in,' said the stone-cutter, humbly; and it struck Wolf's mind as a kind of mad dream – not a nightmare, but just one of those dreams where men and houses and animals and trees are all involved and interchanged – that this grotesque figure of a man should be the father of Gerda!

'Mr. Torp and I are old friends,' said Wolf, with cordial emphasis, 'and I can't tell you how glad I am to see you again, Vicar! Will you let me order you something? The brandy here seems to me uncommonly good.'

In answer to Wolf's appeal, the barmaid, whose personality, as she appeared and disappeared at that square orifice, grew more and more dreamlike, brought three large glasses of the drink he demanded, two of which he promptly handed to Valley and Torp, while the third he appropriated for himself.

"'Tis wondrous,' remarked Mr. Torp, receiving his glass with unsteady hand; "'tis wondrous for a man what works with chisel and hammer all day, to sit and see what folks be like who never do a stroke. I bain't one o' they myself who do blame the gentry. What I do say be this, and I don't care who hears it. I do say that a man be a man while he lives; and a gent be a gent while he lives. Durn me if that ain't the truth.'

'But when we're dead, Mr. Torp,' called out the voice of Jason from the further end of the room, 'what are we when we're dead?'

'Evenin', Mr. Otter, evenin' to 'ee sir! Dead, say 'ee? I be the man to answer that conundrum. Us be as our tombstone be! Them as has "Torp" writ on 'um in clean, good marble, be with the Lord. They others be with wold Horny.'

Several mellow guffaws greeted this speech, for Gerda's parent was evidently a privileged jester among them; but to the dismay of his brother, who was now talking in a quiet whisper to Wolf, the hollow voice of Jason floated once more across the room.

'Ask that drunk priest over there why he took young Redfern from a good job and turned him into a pious zany.'

There was a vibration in his tone that at once quieted the general clatter of tongues, and everyone looked at Mr. Valley.

'I don't . . . quite . . . understand your . . . question . . . Mr. Otter,' stammered the little man.

The bull-like voice of Mr. Manley of Willum's Mill broke in then.

'His reverence may be hard of hearing. Shall *I* do the asking of him?' And the great bully-boy hesitated not to roar out in thundering tones: 'Mister Otter here be asking of 'ee, and this whole company be waiting to know from 'ee, what god-darned trick you played on young Redfern afore he died.'

'I must beg you, Mr. Manley,' said Darnley Otter, whose face, as Wolf watched it, had become stiff as a mask, 'I must beg you not to make a scene to-night.'

'I am still quite . . . quite . . . at a loss . . . a loss to understand,' began the agitated clergyman, moving forward a step or two towards his aggressor.

But Mr. Torp interrupted him. 'Ask thee bloody questions of thee wone bloody millpond and don't lift up thee's roaring voice among thee's betters!'

There was a considerable hum of applause among the company at this, for Mr. Manley of Willum's Mill was universally disliked.

But the farmer took no heed of this manifestation of public opinion.

'Do 'ee hear what Jack Torp be saying?' he jeered, stretching out his long legs and emptying his glass of gin-and-bitters. 'He's sick as Satan wi' I; and I'll tell 'ee the cause for't.'

There was a general stir in the room and a craning forward of necks. The seasoned cronies of the Three Peewits had long ago discovered that the most delectable of all social delights was a quarrel that just stopped short of physical violence.

'The cause for't be,' went on the master of Willum's Mill, 'that I ordered me mother's stone proper-like from Weymouth. 'stead of ferreting round his dog-gone yard, where there bain't nought but litter and rubbish and paupers' monuments.'

Having thrown out this challenge, the farmer drew in his legs, placed his great hands upon his knees, and leaned forward. There was a dead silence in that ale-embrowned atmosphere, as if the 'private bar' itself, the very walls of which must have been yellow with old leisurely disputes, were aware of something exceptional in that spurt of human venom.

Mr. Torp gave a quick sideways glance to see how the 'gentry' were behaving. But Wolf was discreetly occupied in ordering more drinks – he had already had to tell the barmaid to 'put down' what he ordered, for his pockets were empty – and Darnley was merely pulling at his beard and keeping his eye on the Vicar.

'Thee's mother's stone!' snorted the monument-maker, with resonant contempt. "Twere ready and beauteous, gents all, 'twere ready and beauteous, thik stone! All what passed down street did stop for to see 'un, and did say to theyselves. "Thik fine stone be too good for a farmer's old woman! Thik fine stone be a titled lady's stone!" '

The farmer's gin-dazed wits could only reply to this by a repeated, "Twere a pauper's throw-away; 'twere a workhouse six-foot and nothing!'

Mr. Torp's voice rose higher still. 'This Manley here were afeared to leave his mother in ground for a day without a stone on her. He were afeared the poor woman would come out on's grave to tell tales on him, the old goat-sucker! So while thik fine stone were lying in yard getting weathered-like, as is good for they foreign marbles, this girt vool of a nag's head what must 'a do but drive hay-wagon to Chesil, and bring whoam a silly block o' Portland, same as they fish-folk do cover their bones wi', what have never seed a bit o' marble!'

Under the impact of this eloquent indictment, which excited immense hilarity throughout all the company, Mr. Manley rose unsteadily to his feet and moved towards his enemy. But Mr. Torp, ensconced between Darnley Otter and T. E. Valley, awaited his approach unmoved.

To the surprise of all, the big bully skirted this little group, and, joining Wolf at the liquor-stained counter, bellowed harmlessly for more gin.

It was at this point in the proceedings that more serious trouble began, for Jason Otter, pointing with a shaky forefinger at the Reverend Valley, screamed out in a paroxysm of fury:

'It's you who talk about me to Urquhart and Monk. . . . I've found it out now. . . . It's you who do it!'

The Peewit cronies must have felt that this unexpected clash between two of their 'gentry' rose from more subtle depths than those to which they were accustomed, for they were stricken into a silence, at this juncture, which was by no means a comfortable one.

'Mr. Otter here,' broke in the owner of Willum's Mill, 'Mr. Otter here have been telling pretty little tales of the high doings what go on up at King's Barton. Mr. Otter says Squire Urquhart have sold his soul to that black son-of-a-gun who works in's garden, and that 'tis bookseller Malakite here in Blacksod whose books do larn 'em their deviltries!'

'I think . . . there . . . is . . . some great . . . mistake . . . in your . . . in your mind, Mr. Manley.'

The words were uttered by T. E. Valley in such shaky tones that Wolf was relieved when he saw Darnley take the parson reassuringly by the arm.

'Mistake?' roared the farmer. 'I bain't one for to say what I ain't got chapter nor text for saying! My friend, Josh Beard here, of Nevilton, County of Somerset, be as good a breeder of short-horns as any in Dorset; and 'a do say 'a have heerd such things to-night such as no man's lips should utter; and heerd them, too, from one as we all do know.' And he turned round and leered at Jason Otter with the leer of a tipsy hangman.

'Hold thee's tongue in thee's bullick's-head!' cried the indignant monument-maker. 'A gent's a gent, I tell 'ee; and when a quiet gent, like what's with us to-night, be moderate wambly in's head, owing to liquor, 'tisn't for a girt bull-frog like thee to lift up voice.'

'Bull-frog be – ' grumbled the big farmer, hiding his inability to contend in repartee with Mr. Torp under an increased grossness of speech. 'What do a son-of-a-bitch like thee know of the ways of the gentry?'

'Malakite?' muttered the breeder of shorthorns. 'Bain't Malakite the old beggar what got into trouble with the police some ten years since?'

'So 'twere,' agreed the grateful tenant of Willum's Mill, 'so 'twere, brother Beard. 'A did, as thee dost say, get into the devil's own trouble. 'Twere along of his gals; so some folks said. 'A was one of they hoary wold sinners what Bible do tell of.'

"Twere even so, neighbour; 'twere even so,' echoed Mr. Beard. 'And I *have* heerd that old Bert Smith up at Ramsgard could tell a fine story about thik little job.'

Wolf's mind was too flustered with brandy just then to receive more than a vague shock of confused ambiguity from this startling hint; but the next remark of the man from Nevilton cleared his brains with the violence of a bucket of ice-cold water.

'Bert Smith may sell his grand school-hats all he will; but they do tell out our way – though I know nought of that, seeing I were living at Stamford Orcus in them days – that thik same poor wisp o' bedstraw dursn't call his own gal by his own name, whether 'a be in shop or in church.'

'That's God's own truth you've a-heerd, Josh Beard,' echoed the triumphant Mr. Manley. "Tisn't safe for that poor man to call his own daughter daughter, in the light o' what folks, as knows, do report. If I didn't respect any *real* gentleman' – and to Wolf's consternation the gin-bemused stare of the farmer was turned upon himself – 'and if I weren't churchwarden and hadn't voted Conservative for nigh thirty years, I would show this here stone-chipper the kind of gallimaufry these educated gents will cook for theyselves, afore they're done!'

Wolf's wits, moving now, in spite of the fumes of smoke and alcohol, with restored clarity, achieved a momentous orientation of many obscure matters. He recalled certain complicated hints and hesitations of Selena Gault. He recalled the reckless and embittered gaiety of his mother. With a shaky hand he finished his last glass and laid it down on the counter. Then he looked across the room at the two farmers.

'I don't know whose feelings you are so careful of, Mr. Manley,' he said. 'But since I happen to be myself one of these unfortunate "educated" people, and since Mr. Solent, my father, came to grief in this neighbourhood, I should be very glad indeed to hear anything else you may be anxious to tell us.'

His voice, heard now by the whole company for the first time, had a disquieting tone; and everyone was silent. But Jason Otter rose to his feet, and, in the midst of that silence and under the startled attention of all eyes in the room, walked with short quick steps across the floor till he came close up to Farmer Manley, who was leaning his back against the little counter and who had his hands in his pockets; and there he stopped, facing him. No one but Wolf could see the expression on his countenance; and there were all kinds of different versions afterwards as to what actually happened. But what Wolf himself knew was that the excited man was no longer under the restraint of his natural timidity.

His own intelligence was so clairvoyantly aroused at that moment that he could recall later every flicker of the conflicting impulses that shot through him. The one that dominated the rest was a categorical certainty that some immediate drastic action was necessary. What he did was to take Jason by the shoulders and fling him backwards into an old beer-stained chair that stood unoccupied against the neighbouring wall. In the violence of this action an earthenware jug of water – and Wolf had time to notice the mellow varnish of its surface – fell with a crash upon the floor. There was a hush now throughout the room, and most of the company leaned excitedly forward. Jason himself, huddled limply in a great wooden chair, turned his devastated white face and lamentable eyes full upon his aggressor.

'I . . . I . . . I didn't mean . . .' he gasped.

'It's all right, Solent,' whispered Darnley, accepting a chair by Jason's side, which its owner willingly vacated. 'You couldn't have done anything else.'

'I don't know about that, Otter,' Wolf whispered back. 'I expect we're all a little fuddled. Sit down, won't you, and when he's rested we'll clear out, eh? I've had enough of this.'

All the patrons of the private bar were gathered now in little groups about the room; and before long, with sly, inquisitive glances and many secretive nudges and nods, the bulk of the company drifted out, leaving the room nearly empty.

'I can't . . . understand . . . I didn't see. . . . Was he going to *bite* you?'

The words were from T. E. Valley; and Wolf was so astonished at the expression he used that he answered with a good deal of irritation:

'Do *you* bite people, Mr. Valley?'

The priest's feelings were evidently outraged by this. 'What do you mean?' he protested querulously.

'I mean,' began Wolf. 'Oh, I don't know! But to a stranger down here there does seem a good deal that's funny about you all! You must forgive me, Mr. Valley; but, on my soul, you brought it on yourself. *Bite?* It's rather an odd idea, isn't it? You did say *bite*, didn't you?'

They were interrupted by Mr. Manley of Willum's Mill, who, with Mr. Joshua Beard in tow, was steering for the door.

'Did you hurt the gentleman, sir?' said Mr. Manley to Wolf, in the grave cautious voice of a drunkard anxious to prove his sobriety.

'You drove the gentleman into fold, seems so!' echoed Mr. Beard.

In thus approaching Wolf it was inevitable that the two worthies should jostle the portly frame of Mr. Torp, who, leaning against the back of a chair, with an empty pewter beer-mug trailing by its handle from one of his plump fingers, had fallen into an interlude of peaceful coma.

'Who the bloody hell be 'ee barging into?' murmured Mr. Torp, aroused thus suddenly to normal consciousness.

'Paupers' moniments!' jeered the farmer. 'Nought but paupers' moniments in's yard; and 'a can still talk grand and mighty!'

The stone-cutter struggled to gather his wandering wits together. In his confusion the only friendly shape he could visualize was the form of Mr. Valley, and he promptly made all the use he could of that.

'The Reverend here,' he said, 'can bear witness to I, in the face of all thee's bloody millponds and hay-wagons. The Reverend here do know what they words, "Torp, Moniment-Maker, Black-sod," do signify. The Reverend here did see, for his own self, thik girt stone what I did put up over first young man.' He now removed his bewildered little pig's-eyes from Mr. Valley and fixed them upon Wolf. 'And here be second young man who can bear witness to I; and, darn it, thee'd best do as I do say, Mr. Red-fern Number Two, for thee's been clipping and cuddling our Gerda, 'sknow, and I be only to tell missus on 'ee, and fat be in fire.'

Had not the whole scene become to him by this time incredibly phantasmal, such an unexpected introduction of Gerda's name, on this night of all nights, might have struck a villainous blow at his life-illusion. As it was, however, he could only wonder at the perspicacity of drunken fathers, and pull himself together for an adequate retort.

'My name is Solent, my good sir, as you ought to know,' he said. And then he turned to the two farmers, who were nudging each other and leering at him like a couple of schoolboy bullies. 'Mr. Torp and I are the best of friends,' he remarked sternly.

'Friend of Torp,' chuckled Mr, Manley.

'Torp's friend,' echoed Mr. Beard.

'Thee'd best keep thee's daughter in house, Jack!' continued Mr. Manley. 'Lest t'other one rumple her, same as first one did,' concluded Mr. Beard.

Wolf, beyond his conscious intention, clenched the fingers of his right hand savagely; but his wits were clear now, and he mastered the impulse. 'Whatever happens, I mustn't make an ass of myself to-night,' he thought.

'You'd better go out into the air, gentlemen,' he said quietly, 'and cool your heads, or you'll get into trouble. Come, Mr. Torp. You and I must have a last glass together; and you, too, Vicar.' And he led them away towards the little counter.

The farmers moved slowly toward the door. 'Redfern Number Two, 'a called un,' Wolf heard Mr. Beard saying. 'Now what be the meaning o' *that*, me boy?' He couldn't hear the big farmer's answer; but whatever it was, it ended in a sort of bawdy rhyme, of which all he could catch was the chanted refrain, 'Jimmie Redfern, *he* were there!' And with that the door swung behind them.

He had just time to obtain three more drinks from the barmaid before she pulled down the little wooden slide and indicated in no equivocal manner that eleven o'clock had struck.

Simultaneously with this a serving-boy entered and began to turn down the lights. 'We ought to be starting for home,' said Darnley Otter, from where he sat by his brother, whose great melancholy eyes were fixed upon vacancy. 'And it's none too soon, either!'

'I'll be getting home-along me own self, now this here lad be meddling with they lights,' remarked Mr. Torp, emptying his glass. 'Good night to 'ee all,' he added, taking down his coat and hat from a peg; 'and if I've exceeded in speech to any gent here' – and he glanced anxiously at Wolf and Mr. Valley – 'it be contrary to me nature and contrary to me profession.'

'I . . . suppose . . . you won't mind . . . ' murmured the voice of T. E. Valley, who had remained at the counter, sipping the drink, to which Wolf had treated him, as if it were the first he had tasted that night, 'if I come with you? I don't want to get on anybody's nerves' – and he looked at Jason Otter, who without being asleep seemed to have drifted off into another world – 'but I don't like that walk alone at night.'

'Of course you must come with us, Valley,' said Darnley. 'Though what you can find so frightening in that quiet lane I can't imagine.' Saying this he pulled his brother up upon his feet and helped him into his overcoat.

Half an hour later they were all four making their way past the last houses of Blacksod. Darnley and Jason were walking in front; Wolf and T. E. Valley about six paces to the rear. They were all silent, as if the contrast between the noisy scene they had just left and the hushed quietness of the way were a rebuke to their souls.

In one of the smaller houses, where for some reason neither

curtain nor blind had been drawn, Wolf could see two candles burning on a small table at which someone was still reading.

He touched Mr. Valley's arm, and both the men stood for a time looking at that unconscious reader. It was an elderly woman who read there by those two candles, her chin propped upon one arm, and the other arm lying extended across the table. The woman's face had nothing remarkable about it. The book she read was obviously, from its shape and appearance, a cheap story; but as Wolf stared in upon her, sitting there in that common-place room at midnight, an indescribable sense of the drama of human life passed through him. For leagues and leagues in every direction the great pastoral fields lay quiet in their muffled dew-drenched aloofness. But there, by those two pointed flames, one isolated consciousness kept up the old familiar interest, in love, in birth, in death, all the turbulent chances of mortal events. That simple, pallid, spectacled head became for him at that moment a little island of warm human awareness in the midst of the vast non-human night.

He thought to himself how, in some future time, when these formidable scientific inventions would have changed the face of the earth, some wayward philosopher like himself would still perhaps watch through a window a human head *reading by candle-light*, and find such a sight touching beyond words. Mentally he resolved once more, while to Mr. Valley's surprise he still lingered, staring in at that candle-lit window, that while he lived he would never allow the beauty of things of this sort to be overpowered for him by anything that science could do.

He submitted at last to his companion's uneasiness and walked on. But in his heart he thought: 'That old woman in there might be reading a story about my own life! She might be reading about Shaftesbury town and yellow bracken and Gerda's whistling! She might be reading about Christie and the Malakite bookshop. She might be reading about Mattie – ' His thoughts veered suddenly. 'Mattie? Mattie Smith?' And a wavering suspicion that had been gathering weight for some while in his mind suddenly took to itself an irrefutable shape. 'Lorna and my father. . . . The little girl said we were alike. . . . That's what it is!'

He did not formulate the word 'sister' in any portion of his consciousness where ideas express themselves in words, but across some shadowy mental landscape within him floated and drifted that heavy-faced girl with a new and richly-charged identity! All the vague fragments of association that had gathered here and there in his life around the word 'sister,' hastened now to attach themselves to the personality of Mattie Smith and to give it their peculiar glamour.

'How unreal my life seems to be growing,' he thought. 'London seemed fantastic to me when I lived there, like a tissue of filmy threads; but . . . good Lord! . . . compared with this! – It would be curious if that old woman reading that book were really reading my history and has now perhaps come to my death. Well, as long as old women like that read books by candlelight there'll be *some* romance left!'

His mind withdrew into itself with a jerk at this point, trying to push away a certain image of things that rose discomfortably upon him – the image of a countryside covered from sea to sea by illuminated stations for airships, overspread from sea to sea by thousands of humming aeroplanes!

What would ever become of Tilly-Valley's religion in *that* world, with head-lights flashing along cemented highways, and all existence dominated by electricity? What would become of old women reading by candlelight? What would become of his own life-illusion, his secret 'mythology,' in such a world?

Stubbornly he pushed this vision away. 'I'll live in my own world to the end,' he said to himself. 'Nothing shall make me yield.'

And while a gasping susurration at his side indicated that he was, in his excitement, walking too fast for Mr. Valley, he discovered that that grey feather of Christie's, which served her as a marker in the *Urn Burial*, had risen up again in his mind.

And as he walked along, adapting his steps to his companion's shambling progress, he indulged in the fancy that his soul was like a vast cloudy serpent of writhing vapour that had the power of overreaching every kind of human invention. 'All inventions,' he thought, 'come from man's brains. And man's soul can escape from them, and even while using them, treat them with contempt – treat them *as if they were not*! It can slip through them like a snake, float over them like a mist, burrow under them like a mole!'

He swung his stick excitedly in the darkness, while he gave his arm to Mr. Valley to help him along. He felt as though he were entering upon some desperate, invisible struggle to safeguard everything that was sacred to him, against modern inventions. 'It's queer,' he thought to himself, 'what the sight of that grey feather in the book, and that old woman with the candle, have done to my mind. I've made love to the limit; I've brawled in a tavern to the limit; and here I am, with a tipsy priest on my arm, thinking of nothing but defending I don't know what against motor-cars and aeroplanes!'

He continued vaguely to puzzle himself, as they lurched forward in the darkness, as to what it was in his nature that made his seduction of Gerda, his encounter with Jason, his discovery of Mattie, thus fall away from his consciousness in comparison with that feather and that candle; and he came finally to the conclusion, before they reached King's Barton, that there must be something queer and inhuman in him. 'But there it is,' he finally concluded. 'If I'm like that . . . I *am* like that! We must see what comes of it!'

9

THE HORSE-FAIR

THE first person of their acquaintance they encountered when Wolf and Mrs. Solent mingled with the lively crowd that filled Ramsgard's famous Castle Field that afternoon, was none other than Mr. Albert Smith. Wolf was amazed at the cordiality of his mother's greeting; and so quite evidently was the worthy hatter himself.

Mrs. Solent was fashionably dressed; but what struck her son more than her clothes at that moment was the incredible power of her haughty profile, as she flung out her light badinage, like so many shining javelins, at the nervous tradesman.

The thought rushed across his brain, as he watched her: 'She's never had her chance in life! She was made for large transactions and stirring events!' Letting his gaze wander over the groups about them, Wolf caught sight of Mr. Urquhart's figure in the distance; and he decided that, since sooner or later he would have to greet the man, the best thing he could do was to get it over as soon as possible, so as to be prepared to face his Blacksod friends free of responsibility.

Leaving his companions to themselves, therefore, with a nod at his mother, he plunged into the heart of that motley scene. The day obviously was the culmination of the Wessex Fair. The large expanse of meadow-land lying between the castle ruins and the railway was encircled by booths, stalls, roundabouts, fortune-tellers' tents, toy circuses – all the entertainments, in fact, which the annual horde of migratory peddlers of amusement offered, according to age-old tradition, to their rustic clients.

But the centre portion of this spacious fair-ground was carefully roped off; and it was here that the riding and driving competitions took place that gave so special an interest to this particular afternoon.

One segment of this roped-off circle had been converted into a sort of privileged paddock, corresponding to a racecourse grand-stand, where the aristocracy of the neighbourhood, whose carriages were drawn up under the railway bank, could watch the pro-ceedings in undisturbed security.

The opportunity Wolf had seized of approaching Mr. Urquhart was given him by the fact that the Squire of King's Barton was standing alone, close to the rope, at some little distance from the privileged spot where most of his compeers were gathered.

He was watching with absorbed interest a stately parade of prize stallions, who, adorned with ribbons and other marks of distinction, ambled ponderously by, one after another, as if they were parading in some gigantic super-equine festival that ought to have had super-human spectators! The creatures looked so powerful and so contemptuous beside the stablemen who led them that Wolf, as he approached this procession, saw for a moment the whole human race in an inferior and ignominious light – saw them as some breed of diabolically-clever monkeys, who, by a debased trick of cunning, had been able to reduce to servitude, though not to servility, animals far nobler and more godlike than themselves.

'It makes you feel like a Yahoo, sir,' said Wolf, as he shook hands with Mr. Urquhart. 'I mean it makes *me* feel like a Yahoo. Good Lord! Look at that beast! Don't you get the sensation that those hooves are really making the earth tremble?'

But Mr. Urquhart, though he had grasped his secretary's hand warmly and had seemed pleased to see him, took no more notice of this remark than if it had been some negligible banality uttered by a complete stranger. Wolf, standing by his side, said no more till the procession had passed. His attention began to wander from the great stallions to a mental consideration that made him straighten his own shoulders.

He had suddenly become aware of the felicitous appropriateness of Mr. Urquhart's clothes; and although his own overcoat was a good one and his cloth hat new, he felt somehow badly dressed in the man's company, a feeling that caused him considerable annoyance.

'Damn this accursed snobbishness!' he said to himself, as he contemplated the vast grey flanks of the winner of the third prize. 'Why can't I detach myself absolutely from these things and see them as a visitor from Saturn or Uranus would see them?'

Mr. Urquhart turned to him when the last stallion had passed by. 'Do 'ee know who my man brought with him over here?' he said, smiling.

Wolf could only lift his thick eyebrows interrogatively. He continued to feel uncomfortable under his employer's quizzical gaze. 'He looks me up and down,' he thought to himself, 'as if I were a horse that had disappointed him by not winning even a third prize.'

'You mean Monk?' he said. 'I can't guess whom he brought with him. I thought he was driving *you*.'

'He put her on the box by his side,' went on the Squire. 'It was that old servant of our good Otters. I was compelled to look at the flowers in her bonnet and the tassels on her cape all the way here.'

'You don't mean Dimity Stone?' murmured Wolf; and he contemplated in a rapid inward vision that sly, misogynistic eye fixed sardonically on the old woman's wizened back, and the chivalrous grand air with which the coachman must have conversed with her, as he held the reins.

'I couldn't let her walk,' went on the Squire. 'And the Otters had left her behind. I suppose they hadn't room. They came in a wretched conveyance. I suppose they got it from the hotel.' He swung about and surveyed the crowd with indulgent arrogance. 'I can just see the good Darnley from here,' he said. 'There! – can't you? I wonder where that terrible person who's always drunk has hidden himself! I saw *him*, too, a moment ago. And, by gad, there's Tilly-Valley! Let's go and stir him up. He won't expect me to speak to him. You watch his face, my boy, when I nudge his elbow. Eh? What? Come on.' And greatly to Wolf's annoyance he found himself compelled to support his limping employer on his arm, while the two of them pushed their way towards the clergyman.

'Tally ho! Run to earth!' was the Squire's greeting, as, with Wolf at his elbow, he came up unobserved to where the little priest was standing. 'Afternoon, Valley! Should have thought this sort of thing wasn't in your line; eh? what? Too many horsey rascals about? Too many rowdy young men, eh?'

If Wolf was astonished at Mr. Urquhart's familiar tone, he was still more astonished at the expression on the face of the nervous clergyman.

Stammeringly Mr. Valley found his tongue.

'Fine horses . . . more of them than usual . . . did you see that grey one? . . . the Otters are here . . . they drove over . . . I walked . . . so did others . . . many others . . . it would be nice if there were seats here . . . don't you think so? . . . seats?'

Wolf could hardly bear to listen to these broken utterances of the poor Vicar. There was something about his pinched face, his shapeless nose, his thin neck, his frightened eyes, that produced a profoundly pitiful feeling. This sensation was accentuated by the way a certain vein in the man's throat stood out. Not only did it stand out, it pulsed and vibrated. All the panic that Mr. Urquhart's presence provoked seemed concentrated in that pulsing vein.

'Seats, did you say?' chuckled the Squire. '*You* don't need a seat at your age.' And leaning heavily on his companion's arm, he tapped the priest with the end of his stick with an air of playful familiarity.

It came over Wolf then, with a rush of sheer rage, that he must get his employer away from this man at all costs. Never had he liked Mr. Urquhart less. There was something in his wrinkled white face, at that moment, which suggested an outrush of incredible evil – of evil emerging, like some abominable vapour, from a level of consciousness not often revealed.

Wolf was tolerant enough of the various forms of normal and abnormal sensuality; but what at that instant he got a glimpse of, beneath this man's gentlemanly mask, was something different from viciousness. It was as if some abysmal ooze from the slime of *that which underlies all evil* had been projected to the surface.

'Come along, sir. We must get back to the rope,' Wolf found himself saying in a stern, dry voice. 'They're starting the driving-match and I can't let you miss *that!*'

Mr. Urquhart's hilarity seemed to sink fathom deep at the sound of his secretary's voice. He permitted himself to be pulled away. But Wolf noticed a perceptible increase in his lameness as he drew him along; and glancing sideways at his face, he was startled by the look of almost imbecile vacuity that had replaced what had been there before.

The crowd had thickened perceptibly now; and Wolf realized that he was seeing the most characteristic gathering for that portion of the countryside that he was ever likely to see. Here were smart self-satisfied tradesmen from Ramsgard with their wives and their girls. Here were weather-stained carters from Blackmore; cider-makers and cattle-dealers from Sedgemoor; stalwart melancholy-looking shepherds from the high Quantocks; a sprinkling of well-to-do farmers from the far-off valley of the Frome; sly, whimsical dairymen from the rich pastures of the Stour; and, moving among them all, slow-voiced and slow-footed, but with an infinite zest for enjoyment, the local rustic labourers that tilled the heavy fields watered by the Lunt.

The two men pushed their way back to the taut, vibrating rope, beyond which the driving contest was now proceeding; and as they rested there, Wolf's mind felt liberated from all its agitations, and he drank in the scene before him with unruffled delight. The peculiar smells that came to his nostrils – leather, and straw, and horse-dung, and tobacco-smoke, and cider-sour human breath, and paint, and tar, and half-devoured apples – were all caught up and overpowered by one grand dominant odour, the unique smell of the trodden grass of a fair-field. Let the sun shine as it would from the cold blue heaven! Let the chariots of white clouds race as they pleased under that airy tent! It was from the solid ground under human feet, under equine hooves, that this Dorsetshire world gave forth its autochthonous essence, its bitter-sweet, rank, harsh, terrestrial sweat, comforting beyond conscious knowledge to the heart of man and beast.

Nothing could have been more symbolic of the inmost nature of that countryside than the humorous gravity with which these lean yeomen and plump farmers drove their brightly-painted gigs and high dog-carts round that hoof-trodden paddock! The obvious reciprocity between the men who drove and the animals driven, the magnetic currents of sympathy between the persons looking on and the persons showing off, the way the whole scene was characterized by something casual, non-official, nonchalant – all this produced an effect that only England, and perhaps only that portion of England, could have brought into being. Behind Wolf and his companion surged a pushing, jostling, heterogeneous crowd, giving vent to a low, monotonous murmur; and behind them again could be heard the raucous cries and clangings and whistlings from the noisy whirligigs.

Wolf could make out, here and there among the people round him, the well-known straw hats – manufactured by Mr. Albert Smith – of the boys of Ramsgard School. 'They must be having a "half" to-day,' he thought; and his mind ran upon the various queer, unathletic, unpopular boys among the rest, who must be feeling, just then, so indescribably thankful for this blessed interlude in their hateful life! The thought of the unknown, undiscovered bullies that probably existed in Ramsgard School at that very moment made him feel sick at the pit of his stomach. 'I put my curse on them,' he thought. 'If I have a vestige of occult power, I put my curse upon them!'

A short, stocky man, with powerful wrists, driving a lively but not particularly handsome horse, passed them at that moment inside the paddock. Wolf was wondering why the voices round him were discreetly lowered as this person trotted by, when he noted that the man exchanged a familiar nod with Mr. Urquhart.

'Not a bad turnout for a Lovelace,' muttered this latter, when the equipage had passed; 'but they never can quite do it!'

Once again Wolf felt a prick of shame at the curious interest which this occurrence excited in him. What was Lord Lovelace to him? He glanced furtively at the Squire of King's Barton. The man's baggy eye-wrinkles had, just then, a look that was almost saurian. From one corner of his twitching mouth a trickle of saliva descended, towards which a small fly persistently darted. . . .

Wolf turned away his eyes. The magic of the scene had completely vanished. The smell of the trodden earth was stale in his nostrils. A loathing of the whole spectacle of life took possession of him. And under his breath he repeated that strange classical lament, a tag in his memory from his schooldays, a mere catchword now; but it gave him a certain relief to pronounce the queer-sounding syllables.

'Ailinon! Ailinon!' he muttered to himself, as he leaned his stomach against that vibrant rope. 'Ailinon! Ailinon!' And the very utterance of this tragic cry from the old Greek dramas soothed his mind as if it had been a talisman. But the disgust he felt at the pressure of things at that moment extended itself to this whole fair-ground, extended itself even to the prospect of seeing Gerda again. 'How can I face her in the midst of all this?' he thought; and he recalled the outline of his mother's profile, so contemptuously lifted towards Albert Smith. 'What will she think of the Torp family?' he said to himself, in miserable discomfort.

Struggling against this wretched mood, he straightened his back and clutched the rope with both his hands. Savagely he tried to summon up out of the depths of his spirit some current of defiant magnetism. But the presence of Mr. Urquhart, taciturn and pensive though the Squire had become, seemed to cut off all help from these furtive resources.

So he sought to steady himself by pure reason.

'After all,' he argued, 'those gulfs of watery blue up there are such an unthinkable background to all this, that they . . . that they . . . a trickle of saliva more or less . . . a woman's profile more or less. . . .' And then, as he watched those painted gigs come swinging once more round the enclosure, and heard the exclamations of malicious delight, as a chestnut-coloured mare showed a vicious tendency to back her driver against the rope, a sense of terrified loneliness came upon him. What could Gerda, or his mother, or anyone else – man or woman – really feel toward him so that this loneliness should be eased? Emptiness leered at him, emptiness yawned at him, out of that watery blue; and what pointed spikes of misunderstanding he had to throw himself upon before this bustling day was over!

He ran his fingers along the swaying rope, sticky from the innumerable human hands that had clutched it. His mind seemed to hover above the form of Gerda and above the form of his mother, as if it had been a floating mist gathered about two sundered headlands. That familiar grey head, with those mocking brown eyes, and this other, this new strange head, with its sea-grey gaze and its wild, pursed-up, whistling mouth – what would happen when he brought them together?

It would mean he would have to leave his mother. That's what it would mean. Where was Gerda now, in this confused medley? She must be somewhere about; and perhaps Christie, too!

'You won't care if I go off to look for my mother, sir?' he found himself saying. And the words quite startled him, as if he had spoken in his sleep; for he had made up his mind that he would never speak of his private affairs to this egoistic gentleman.

'Eh? What's that? Tired of the old man, ha? Want to gad after the petticoats? Well! Take me to the enclosure, out of this crowd, and I'll let you go. I suppose it's hopeless to find Monk in this hurly? He was to have come back for me. But Lord! he's got his own little affairs, as well as another. There! That's better. You needn't go at a snail's pace for me. There! That's all right. I'll find Lovelace in the enclosure, I daresay. He'll wait to see the cart-horses.'

Wolf steered the Squire as well as he could through the jostling mob of people, and left him at the entrance to the privileged circle.

'You and I know more about some of these good folks than they know themselves,' remarked Mr. Urquhart, grimly. 'Our History'll make 'em sit up a bit; eh? what? Well, off with 'ee, me boy; and if you want to find your mother, I'd look for her in the refreshment-tent, if I were you. Never know'd but one woman who could see a horse-show out to the end – and she was a tart of Lord Tintinhull's. "Sack" they used to call her; and "sacked" she was, at the finish, poor bitch! Well, good luck to 'ee. We'll do some solid work to-morrow, please God!'

Wolf mumbled some inadequate reply to this and strode away. What struck him just then was the contrast between the silky *tone* of his employer's voice and the toll-pike jocularity of his language.

'Neither tone nor words are the real man,' he thought. 'What seething malice, what fermenting misanthropy, that mask of his does cover!'

Crossing the fair-field to the northward, leaving the paddock to his left and the whirligigs to his right, Wolf speedily found his way to the entrance of the great refreshment-tent.

The place was packed with people, some taking their stimulant at little deal-board tables, others eating and drinking as they stood, others again crowding about the massive serving-counter at the end of the tent, where great silvery receptacles kept hot by oil-flames, were disgorging into earthenware cups a quality of tea that seemed to meet the taste alike of the Lovelaces and of the Torps, so varied were the human types now eagerly swallowing it!

Wolf speedily became aware that Mr. Urquhart's jibe about few petticoats being able to endure a horse-show to the end was not without justification. About three-quarters of the persons filling this huge canvas space were women.

The first familiar form he encountered as he pushed his way in was that of Selena Gault. This lady was seated alone at a small table placed against the canvas wall, where she was drinking her tea and eating her bread-and-butter in sublime indifference to the crowd that surged about her. Wolf hurried to her, snatched an unoccupied chair, and sat down at her side.

He felt, for some reason, a sense of profound physical exhaustion; and underneath the pleasant badinage with which he returned his friend's greetings he found himself positively clinging to this lonely woman.

The lady's costume, to which she had given a vague sporting touch suitable to the occasion, enhanced her grotesque hideousness. But from her deformed visage her eyes gleamed such irresistible affection that his ebbing courage began steadily to revive.

Their complete isolation in the midst of the crowd – for the people jostling past their table gave them little heed – soon led Wolf to plunge shamelessly into what was nearest his heart. Selena Gault's ghastly upper lip quivered perceptibly as he told her of his affair with Gerda and his resolve to get married without delay.

'Why, she's here!' she cried. 'The child's here! She came in with her father a quarter of an hour ago. She certainly is one of the loveliest girls I've ever set eyes upon. I hadn't seen her since she's grown up. I was amazed at her beauty. Well! You *have* made hay while the sun shone. No! it's no use! You can't possibly see her from where you are. Now turn round and look at me; and let's talk about all this, quietly and sensibly. It's as serious as it could be; and I don't know what's to be done about it.'

'There's nothing to be done, I'm afraid, Miss Gault,' said Wolf gravely, forcing himself to accept the situation; 'nothing except to make some money by hook or by crook! Do you think if I put the case to Urquhart he'd give me a little more? We're getting on first-rate with the History.'

Never were human eyelids lifted more whimsically than were those of Wolf's interlocutor at this mild suggestion.

'Oh, my dear boy!' she chuckled. 'You don't know how funny you are. To ask *that* man for money to get married on.'

'No good, eh?' he murmured. 'No, I suppose not. But you don't think he'll show me the door, do you?'

Miss Gault shook her head. 'If he does, we'll put all our wits together and get you something in Ramsgard. There *are* jobs – ' she added, thoughtfully puckering her brows.

But Wolf, having twice twisted his head back into its normal position from a hopeless attempt to see further than a few yards in front of him, felt an irresistible impulse to reveal to this woman certain rather sinister deductions that he found he had been involuntarily making from recent glimpses and hints. Composed originally of the veriest wisps and wefts of fluctuating suspicion, they seemed now to have solidified themselves in unabashed tangibility. What they now amounted to was that Mattie was not Mr. Smith's daughter at all, but William Solent's; and that Olwen, the girl's little protégée, was actually the incestuous child of old Malakite, the bookseller, and of some vanished sister of Christie's. It was the startling nature of these conclusions that tempted him to fire them off point-blank at the lady by his side, whose morbid receptivity made her a dedicated target for such a shock.

'Is it true that I have a sister in this town?' he enquired boldly, looking straight into Miss Gault's eyes.

The appalling upper lip vibrated like the end of a tapir's proboscis, and the grey eyes blinked as if he had shot off a pistol.

'What?' she cried, letting her hands fall heavily upon her knees, like the hands of a flabbergasted sorceress, palms downward and fingers outspread. '*What's* that you're saying, boy?'

'I am saying that I've come to a shrewd certainty,' said Wolf firmly, 'that Mattie Smith and I have the same father.'

Miss Gault astonished him by putting her elbows on to the table and covering her face with her extended fingers; through which her eyes now regarded him. She was not weeping – he could see that. Was she laughing at him? There was something so queer in this gesture, that he felt an uneasy discomfort. It was as if she had suddenly turned into a different person, as different from the Miss Gault he knew as the new Mattie they were talking about was different from the one he had met in that Victorian dining-room.

He wished she would remove those fingers and stop staring at him so discomfortably. When at last she did so, it was to reveal a countenance whose expression he was at a loss to read. Her face certainly wasn't blubbered with crying; but it was flushed and disturbed. The impression he really got from it was of something . . . almost indecent!

He glanced furtively round, and, hurriedly extending his arm, touched one of her wrists.

'You must have known I'd find out sooner or later,' he said. 'It doesn't matter, my knowing does it? *He* couldn't mind. He'd be glad, I should think.' And he gave an awkward little chuckle as he released her hand and began fumbling for a cigarette.

He had only just succeeded in finding the small packet for which he was searching when he caught Miss Gault's eyes lit up in excited recognition.

He swung round. Ah! there they were – making their way straight towards them – the portly figure of Mr. Torp, with Gerda leaning lightly on his arm!

He did not hesitate a moment, but leaping up from his chair with an incoherent apology to his companion, he advanced to meet them, his heart beating fast, but his brain in full command of the situation.

Gerda flushed crimson when she saw him, disengaged her arm from her father's, and, coming to meet him with charming impetuosity, held out her hand.

She was dressed in plain navy-blue serge, and wore a dark, soft hat low down over her fair hair. This unassuming attire heightened her beauty; and the embarrassed yet illuminated look with which she greeted her lover, brought back to his mind so vividly the events of yesterday that for a moment he was struck with a kind of dizziness that reduced everyone in that crowded tent to a floating and eddying mist.

He caught at her hand without a word and held it tightly for a moment, hurting her a little.

He soon dropped it, however, and said very hurriedly and quietly: 'Gerda . . . forgive me . . . but I want to introduce you to my friend, Miss Gault.'

Gerda's eyes must have already encountered those of that lady, for he saw her face stiffen to a conventional and rather strained smile. But at this moment Mr. Torp intervened, coming up very close to Wolf and touching the latter's hand with his plump finger before he could lift it to greet him.

'So you and darter have fixed it up, have 'ee?' he whispered, in a confidential, almost funereal tone. 'Don't 'ee be fretted about I nor the missus, mister. Us be glad in advance, I tell 'ee; and so it be.' He caught hold of Wolf's sleeve and put his face close to his face, while Wolf, with a sidelong glance, became aware that Miss Gault had approached them and had been met half-way by Gerda.

"Tis they wimming's whimsies what us have got to mind, hasn't?' whispered Mr. Torp. 'What they do reckon'll happen to we, 'tis what *will* happen to we, looks so! Don't 'ee take on, mister, about us being poor folks like. Darter's different from we and allus has been, since her were a babe. She's had grand courtiers ere now, though I shouldn't say it. But Gerdie be a good girl, though turble lazy about house. Her mother once did think it 'ud be young Bob Weevil what 'ud get her; but I knewed a thing or two beyond that, I did! I knewed she were one for the gentry, as you might say. 'Twere barn in her, I reckon! I be a climbing man, me wone self. It's like enough she gets it from I!' And before he withdrew his rubicund face to a discreet distance, the stone-cutter gave him a shrewd wink.

It was then that Miss Gault took the opportunity of bringing Gerda up to them. She had evidently said something very gracious to the girl, for Gerda's quaint society-manner had left her, and she looked pleased, though a little bewildered.

'We've made friends already,' said Miss Gault to Wolf, 'and I've told her I knew her well by sight. How do you do, Mr. Torp! I was telling Mr. Solent that I knew your daughter already, though I've never spoken to her; but she's not a young lady one can forget!'

What Mr. Torp's reply to this was Wolf did not hear. Aware that the situation had arranged itself, he found as he kept looking at Gerda's face, as she listened to Miss Gault and her father, that he was beginning to grow nervously hostile to all these explanations. Why couldn't he and Gerda go straight off now, out of this hurly-burly, out anywhere . . . so as to be at peace and alone?

'Well, good-bye,' Gerda was saying. 'Perhaps we'll see you

again later; but father and I haven't half gone the round yet, have we, father?'

'Gone the round! I should think us hadn't!' said Mr. Torp. 'Bain't what used to be, this here fair! I do mind when 'twere so thick wi' gipoos and suchlike, that a person could scarce move. But Gerdie and I will see summat, don't 'ee fear! They whirligigs . . . why there ain't a blessed season since her was a mommet that we ain't rid in they things, is there, my chuck?'

'No, there isn't, father. Good-bye, Miss Gault!' she added, with a straight, confiding, grateful glance at her friend's friend. 'I'll be at home all to-morrow afternoon, Wolf,' she murmured, as she smoothed out her gloves and buttoned her jacket.

Mr. Torp caught the word. 'So she *shall* be!' he cried emphatically. 'I be a turble stern man, for ordering they to do what they've set their hearts on doing! Well, good-bye to 'ee, sir! Good-bye to 'ee, marm! If all and sundry here were to fling at they coceenuts, there'd be few left, I reckon!'

Watching that quaintly assorted couple moving away out of the tent, Wolf felt a glow of almost conceited satisfaction in the discovery that whatever vein of snobbishness it was in him that had made so much of Mr. Urquhart's clothes and Lord Lovelace's appearance, it fell away completely where Gerda was concerned. 'I'm glad the old man is as he is!' he thought, as his eyes followed them into the open air.

'Let's sit down again, shall we?' he said to Miss Gault.

His spirits were a little dashed, however, when he regarded the lady opposite him, as they resumed their seats, for her face seemed to have grown stiff and somewhat remote.

'This is very serious,' she said gravely. And then, with an almost plaintive tone, 'Why is it that men are so ridiculous?'

'But I thought you liked her, Miss Gault! You were so especially sweet to her.'

She sighed and gave him a glance that seemed to say irritably, 'And to cap everything you are an incredible fool!'

'You *did* like her, didn't you?'

'So childish that they think of nothing . . . *nothing* . . . when their desire is aroused.,

'Why is it so serious, Miss Gault?' he said. And then he added rather maliciously, 'My mother would see in a second how refined she is!'

Miss Gault lifted her eyebrows. 'I'm not only thinking of your mother,' she said. 'There's no reason, that I know of, why I should fuss about *her*. I'm thinking of you and the girl herself, and – and of *all* your friends. Listen, boy' – and she bent on him one of the most tender and reproachful looks he had ever seen – 'all this is pure madness – selfish, greedy madness! You *can't* make a girl like that happy – no! not for half a year! Good heavens, child, you're as blind as a – You're as selfish as one of my cats! It's the girl I'm thinking of, I tell you. You'll make her miserable, you and your mother! She's sweet to look at; but Wolf, Wolf! she and you will talk completely different languages! You can't do these things – not in *our* country, anyhow. I've seen it again and again – these things bring misery – just misery. And how are you going to support her, I'd like to know?'

'She has indeed a different language,' cried Wolf, irrelevantly; and his mind reverted to the blackbird of Poll's Camp. And then, as he saw her face droop wearily and her fingers tap the table: 'Why did you take it all so nicely just now. Why did you talk of getting me work in Ramsgard?'

She made no reply to this. But after a moment she burst out: 'Your father would laugh at you . . . he would! . . . He'd just laugh at you!'

'Well, we'd better not talk of it any more,' said Wolf sulkily.

He cast about in the depths of his consciousness, however, with the vindictiveness of defeat, for some line of attack that would disturb and agitate her.

'Miss Gault,' he began, while with her gaze fixed upon vacancy she stared through him and past him into the interior of the great tent, 'do you mind if I ask you a direct question? I know that Mattie Smith is my father's child; but what I want to ask you now is – whose child is Olwen?'

A faint brownish flush ran like a stream of muddy water beneath the surface of the skin of her face. She bent her head over the table; and like a great ruffled bird, in a cage, that has been shaken from the top, she began picking up and lifting to her mouth every crumb of bread in sight. Then, with a shaky hand, she poured some spilt drops of cold tea from her saucer into her cup.

'What I want to know,' repeated Wolf, 'is why my sister Mattie has this child Olwen to look after. Is she a foundling? Is she adopted? Where did she spring from?'

But the daughter of the late head master of Ramsgard School remained obstinately silent. She folded her hands mechanically over the heavy teacup and sat straight in her chair, staring into her lap like an image of Atropos.

'Don't you want to tell me, Miss Gault? Is it something you *can't* tell me?'

Still the lady remained silent, her fingers tightly clenched over the cup.

'I knew there was something queer from the start,' he went on. 'What's the matter with you all? Who *is* this child?'

Then very slowly Miss Gault rose to her feet.

'Come out into the air,' she said brusquely. 'I can't talk to you here.'

They made their way together out of the tent; but they had hardly gone a stone's throw into the cold March sunshine when they encountered, without a possibility of retreat or evasion, Mrs. Solent and Mr. Smith advancing resolutely and blamelessly towards the place they were quitting.

The hatter of Ramsgard School looked pinched and withered in the hard, glaring light. Wolf received a sudden, inexplicable inkling that the man was wretchedly miserable. The look he got from him as they approached seemed grey with weariness. Mrs. Solent was, however, talking gaily. Her brown eyes were shining with mischief. Her cheeks were flushed. And now, at the very moment of salutation, he could see that proud face toss its chin, and that sturdy, well-dressed figure gather itself together for battle. Once more it came over him with a queer kind of remorse, as if he were responsible for it: 'She's had no life at all; and she's made for great, stirring events!'

But it was many days before he forgot the manner in which those two ancient rivals faced each other. It had, this encounter between them, the queer effect upon him of making him recall, as he had once or twice already in Dorsetshire, that passage in *Hamlet* where the ghost cries out from beneath the earth. A piece of horse-dung at his feet, as he instinctively looked away while the two came together, grew large and white and round.

'He can't have a shred of flesh left on him down there,' he thought to himself, with a kind of sullen anger against both the women. But what puzzled him now was that Miss Gault did not rise to the occasion as he had supposed she would have done. To his own personal taste she looked more formidable in her black satin gown than his mother did in her finery; but it was clear to him, as he watched them shaking hands, that his mother's spirit was poised and adjusted to the nicest point of the encounter, whereas Miss Gault's inmost being just then seemed disorganized, disjointed, helpless, unwieldy.

That they shook hands at all, he could see, was owing to his mother. Miss Gault's hands hung down at her sides, like the hands of a large, stuffed doll that has been set up with difficulty in an erect position. And they remained like this until Mrs. Solent's arm had been extended for quite a perceptible passage of time. When Selena *did* raise her wrist and take her enemy's fingers, it was to retain them all the while the two were speaking. But Mrs. Solent told Wolf afterwards that there was no warmth or life in that cold pressure. . . .

'Well, Selena, so it's really you! And I couldn't have believed there'd be so little change. You are at your old tricks again, I see, running off with my son!'

'I hope you are well, Ann,' said Miss Gault. 'You look as handsome as ever.'

'I'd look handsomer still, if my son wasn't so unambitious and lazy,' replied the other, giving Wolf a glance of glowing possessiveness.

'Men can be too ambitious, Ann,' said Miss Gault slowly, speaking as if she were in some kind of trance.

'We passed a *really* pretty girl a minute or two ago,' cried Mrs. Solent suddenly; 'and Albert here says he knows who she is. You ought to go over to the roundabouts, Wolf, and try and find her! She was with a labouring-man of some sort, a stocky, plump little man; but she was pretty as a picture!'

'Do you mean that Dorset labourers *sell* their daughters, mother? Or do you mean that all beauty can be had for the asking? All right; I'll hunt for her through all the tents!'

He felt himself speaking in such a strained, queer voice that he was not surprised to observe Miss Gault glancing nervously at Mrs. Solent to see if she had detected it. But Mrs. Solent was too excited just then to notice so slight a thing as a change of tone. As he spoke with his mother in this way about Gerda, something seemed to rise up in his throat that was like a serpent of fury. He rebelled against the look of his mother's face, the proud outline of her scornful profile. 'I am glad . . . I am glad . . .' he said to himself, 'that Gerda *isn't* a lady, and that her father *is* a stone-cutter!'

And it came over him that it was an imbecility that any human soul should have the power over another soul that his mother had over him. As he looked at her now, he was aware of an angry revolt at the massive resistance which her personality offered.

It did not make it easier for him at this moment that he recognized clearly enough that the very strength in his mother, which had been such security to him in his childhood, was the thing now with which he had to struggle to gain his liberty – that protective, maternal strength, the most formidable of all psychic forces!

She was like a witch – his mother – on the wrong side in the fairy-story of life. She was on the side of fate against chance, and of destiny against random fortune. 'I don't care how she feels when I tell her about Gerda,' he said to himself; and in a flash, looking all the while at his mother's dress, he thought of the yielded loveliness of Gerda's body, and he decided that he would shake off this resistance without the least remorse. 'Shake it off! Pass over it; disregard it!' he said to himself.

'I shall come and see you, Selena, whether you like it or not,' his mother was now saying. 'After twenty-five years people as old as we are ought to be sensible, oughtn't we, Mr. Smith?' she added.

But Mr. Smith had managed to remove himself a pace or two from their company, under cover of a sudden interest in a torn and flapping *Western Gazette*, which he proceeded to push into a trampled mole-hill with the end of his stick.

Mrs. Solent glanced at her son shrewdly and scrutinizingly. 'You look as if you were enjoying yourself, I *must* say! What's come over you? Are you wishing yourself back in London? Well, come on, Albert Smith! I'm longing for a cup of tea. These people have had theirs.'

She was already carrying off her companion, after a nod to Miss Gault, which was received without a sign of response, when Wolf stopped her. 'Where shall we meet, mother, when you're ready to go?'

'Oh, anywhere, child! We can't lose ourselves here.'

'Say over there, then? By the roundabouts, in about an hour?'

'All right; very good! Mr. Smith shall escort me there when we've had our tea. It's strange, Albert, isn't it, that in this place of my whole married life, you're the only friend I've got left?'

Wolf was aware of an expression in her brown eyes, a droop of her straight shoulders, that made him realize that there were strange emotions stirring under the surface of that airy manner.

'The roundabouts, then!' he repeated.

'All right – in an hour or so!' she flung back. 'And why don't you and Selena have a turn at the swings?' she added, as she went off.

Her disappearance seemed to make no difference to Seelna Gault. In absolute immobility the poor lady remained standing there, staring at the grass. It was as if she'd put her foot upon an adder that struck her with sudden paralysis, so that at a touch she would topple over and fall.

Wolf came close to her. 'Don't worry about my mother, Miss Gault, darling,' he whispered earnestly. 'She's not as flippant as she sounds . . . really she's not! She's like that with everyone. She's like that with me.'

Miss Gault looked at him as if his words meant nothing. Her vacant stare seemed to be fixed on something at a remote distance.

'I know; I quite understand,' she murmured; and her hands, coming, as it were, slowly to life, began to pick at the little cloth buttons of the braided jacket she wore over her satin gown. The stiffness of these old-fashioned garments seemed to hold her up. Without their support it looked as if she would have fallen down just where she was – close to the newspaper buried through the nervousness of Mr. Smith!

She seemed to Wolf, as he stood helplessly before her, like a classic image of outrage in grotesque modern clothes. 'She's like an elderly Io,' he thought, 'driven mad by the gadfly of the goddess.'

'Dear Miss Gault! Don't you worry about it any more! I swear to you she isn't as malicious as she seems. You must remember that all this isn't as easy for her as she makes out. She's hard; but she can be really magnanimous . . . you'll see! She doesn't realize people's feelings, that's what it is. She was the same about Gerda. Fancy her noticing her like that!' In his desire to soothe his companion he seized one of the black-gloved hands. As he did so he looked round nervously; for he began to be aware that various persons among the groups who passed them stopped to stare at her perturbed figure.

But his touch brought a flood of colour to the woman's swarthy cheeks. She clasped his hand tightly with both her own, holding it for a moment before she let it fall.

'I can't help it, boy,' she said in a low tone. 'Seeing her brings it all back.' She paused for a moment. 'No one else ever treated me as a woman,' she added, her mouth twitching.

Wolf wrinkled his bushy eyebrows.

'You must let me be as fond of you as he was,' he muttered. 'You must look after me as you looked after him.'

She nodded and smiled a little at that, rearranged the great black hat upon her head, and, after a moment's hesitation, placed her hand on his arm. 'Come,' she said, 'let's go to the roundabouts.'

They moved slowly together across the field. It occurred to him now that he could distract her mind and at the same time satisfy his own curiosity by renewing their interrupted conversation.

'I don't want to tease you with questions,' he began presently. 'But you promised you'd tell me – you know? – about Mattie and Olwen.'

'It's not easy, boy,' said Miss Gault with a sigh.

'I know it isn't. That's why I want *you* to tell me and not anyone else.'

She walked by his side in silence for a while, evidently collecting her thoughts. 'It's the sort of thing one finds so difficult to tell,' she said, looking guardedly round them.

'Well! Let me tell *you!*' he retorted, 'and you correct me, if I'm wrong.'

Miss Gault nodded gravely.

'Mattie's my father's child,' he muttered in a low, clear voice, 'and Olwen is – '

Miss Gault had managed to turn her face so far away from him that he couldn't see her expression.

'Who told you all this, boy? Who told you?' she interrupted, in such a peevish tone that two solemn-faced members of the Sixth Form of the School, with blue ribbons round their straw-hats and sticks in their hands, glanced furtively at her as they passed.

'Olwen's father was old Malakite,' Wolf went on; 'and Olwen's mother was Christie Malakite's sister.'

Miss Gault still kept her face removed from his steady gaze.

'Aren't I right?' he repeated. 'But you needn't tell me. I *know* I am right.' He paused, and they continued to cross the field.

'What's become of the mother?' he continued. 'Is she still alive?'

Miss Gault did turn at this.

'Australia,' she whispered.

'Alive or dead?'

She almost shouted her reply to this, as if with a spasm of savage relief.

'Dead!' she cried.

Wolf held his peace for a moment or two, while his brain worked at top speed.

'What Christie must have gone through!' he murmured audibly, but in a tone as if talking to himself rather than to her. 'What she must have gone through!'

Miss Gault's comment upon this was drowned by the brazen noise issuing from the engine of one of the roundabouts which they were now approaching.

'What did you say?' he shouted in her ear.

'I said that Christie Malakite has no heart!' cried Miss Gault; and her voice was almost as harsh as the raucous whistle that saluted them.

He stopped at this, and they both stood motionless, looking at each other covertly, while a magnetic current of inexplicable antagonism flickered between them.

'It wasn't *her* he loved!' Miss Gault shouted suddenly – so suddenly that Wolf moved backwards, as if she had lifted her hand to hit him.

'Who didn't love whom?' he vociferated in response; while two small boys of the Ramsgard Preparatory School nudged each other and peered at them inquisitively.

'What are you staring for? *Urchins!*' cried Miss Gault.

'All the same they're nice boys,' she muttered. 'Look! I've hurt their feelings now; and they really *are* very polite. Here, children, come here!'

The two little boys, their heads covered with enormous and very new examples of the art of Mr. Albert Smith, pretended not to hear her appeal. They remained in fixed contemplation of a counter of glaring cakes and sweets.

'Come here, you two!' repeated the lady.

They did, at that, sheepishly turn round and begin moving towards her, with an air as if it were a complete accident that their feet carried them in that particular direction rather than in any other.

'I won't hurt you,' she said, as softly as she could in the midst of the terrific noise that whirled round them. 'What are your names, my dears?'

'Stepney Major,' murmured one of the little boys.

'Trelawney Minor,' gasped the other.

'Well, Stepney Major and Trelawney Minor, here's half a crown for you. Only, when you next meet queer-looking people at the Fair, don't stare at them as if they were part of the Show.'

When the two little boys had decamped, radiantly reverential, Miss Gault turned to Wolf.

'Didn't they take off their hats prettily? They *do* bring 'em up well. Little gentlemen they are!'

She seemed glad of the interruption. But Wolf began speaking again.

'What's that, boy?' she rejoined. 'Terrible, this noise, isn't it?'

'Miss Gault!'

'You needn't shout, Wolf. I can hear you. There . . . like that . . . that's better!' And she shifted her position. 'Who didn't love whom? We were talking of the Malakites.'

'My dear boy' – and, as she spoke, a smile of the most complicated humour came into her strange countenance, transforming it into something almost beautiful – 'my dear boy, I wasn't talking of the Malakites! I was talking of your father and Lorna Smith.'

'Mattie's mother, eh? But why did you say – oh, damn that noise! – that Christie had no heart?'

Miss Gault stared at him.

'Haven't you seen her? Didn't you see what she was? Reading the books of that old wretch, keeping house for that old wretch? How can she look the man in the face, I should like to know? They tell me Olwen can't bear the sight of her; and I don't wonder.'

'But Miss Gault, my dear Miss Gault, what has Christie done? I should think she was the one most to be pitied.'

Wolf bent his shaggy eyebrows almost fiercely upon his companion; and after a moment's encounter with his gaze Miss Gault glanced away and contemplated the sweet-stall.

'What has Christie Malakite done to *you?*' asked Wolf sternly.

'Oh, if you must have it, boy, you *shall* have it! Listen. I went over there when all that trouble happened. I had some sort of official position; and things like this, unspeakable things like this, were what I had to deal with. The Society sent me, in fact.'

Wolf lifted his eyebrows very high at this. He began to detect an aspect of Miss Selena Gault's character that hitherto had been concealed from him.

'What society?' he asked.

'The Society for the Care of Delinquent Girls. And I found Miss Christie, let me tell you, both obstinate and impertinent. She actually defended that abominable old wretch! She wanted to keep Olwen in their house. Fortunately the child can't bear the sight of her . . . or of that old monster either. Its instinct, I expect.'

'It doesn't happen to be anything you or Mattie may have let fall?' shouted Wolf in her ear.

'Why, you're defending them now!' Miss Gault retorted, her face dark with anger. 'If you knew all, boy, you wouldn't dare!'

Wolf felt extreme discomfort and distaste.

'What else *is* there for me to know, Miss Gault?' he demanded aloud and in a quieter voice, for there had come a pause in the whistling of the engine.

'That old man was one of the most evil influences in your father's life.'

'Does Mattie know that?' he enquired.

'Oh, Mattie!' she cried contemptuously. 'Mattie knows just as much as we've considered it wise to tell her.'

'Who are we?' said Wolf drily.

'Mr. Smith and myself. Don't you see, boy, we had to make ourselves responsible *to the police* for Olwen's bringing up? It's been an unholy business, the whole affair! It gives me a kind of nausea to talk about it.'

Wolf found that his protective instincts were thoroughly aroused by this .time; and Miss Gault's figure assumed an unattractive shape.

'It's this accursed sex-suppression,' he said to himself; and he suddenly thought with immense relief of his mother, and of her scandalously light touch in the presence of every conceivable human obliquity. 'I must be cautious,' he said to himself. 'I mustn't show my hand. But who would have thought she was like this!' He looked Miss Gault straight in the face.

'Does Mr. Urquhart know the history of my sister and the history of Olwen?' he asked abruptly, leaning so heavily on his stick that it sank deep into the turf.

A flicker of relief crossed the woman's agitated features.

'Mr. Urquhart? Oh, you may be sure he has *his* version, just as all the neighbourhood has! It's been the great scandal of the country.'

The use of this particular word made Wolf explode.

'Greater than the doings of Mattie's father?' he rapped out.

He regretted his maliciousness as soon as the words were uttered. That scene in the cemetery came back to his mind.

'I didn't mean that, dear Miss Gault!' he cried, pulling his stick violently out of the sod. But she had turned her face away from him, and for a little while they stood silently there, side by side, while the crowd jostled them and the engine renewed its whistling. At last she did turn round, and her face was sad and gentle.

'We won't quarrel, will we, Wolf?' she murmured, bending close
to his ear so that he shouldn't lose her words. It was the first time
she had dropped that rather annoying 'boy'; and the use of his
name did much to restore his good temper.

'It's all right,' he whispered back. 'Let's go on now, eh?'

The merry-go-round in front of which they had passed was
isolated from the rest. They proceeded to push their way through
the crowds towards the next one, which was some three hundred
yards further on.

Suddenly they saw before them the anxious little figure of Mrs.
Otter, leaning on Darnley's arm; while Jason, his melancholy
gaze surveying the scene as if he were a Gaulish captive in a
Roman triumph, was standing apart, like one who had no earthly
link with his relations – or with anyone else.

Wolf felt singularly disinclined to cope with these people at
that moment. He had received of late so many contradictory impressions, that his brain felt like an overcrowded stage. But he
gathered his wits together as well as he could, and for a while
they all five stood talking rather wearily, exchanging common-
places as if they had been at a garden-party rather than a fair.

By degrees Wolf managed to edge away from the two ladies,
who were listening to Darnley's criticism of the horse-show, and
began to exchange more piquant remarks with the dilapidated poet.

'Did you see our clergyman?' said Jason.

'Mr. Valley?'

The man nodded.

'Certainly I did. I talked to him when I first got here.'

'Making a fool of himself as usual – '

'Come, Mr. Otter – '

'Well, I daresay it's no affair of ours. It's best to mind one's
own business. That's what God's so good at . . . minding His own
business! Seen Urquhart anywhere?'

'I was with him just now. Monk drove him over.'

Jason Otter's face expressed panic.

'Is *that* man here?' he whispered.

Wolf had already remarked how oddly Jason's fits of mortal
terror assorted with the monumental dignity of his grim and
massive countenance.

'Why not? I understand he gave a lift to your old Mrs. Stone.
You ought to be grateful to him.'

'Urquhart pays him to spy on me, and one day he'll beat me
like a black dog!'

'Incredible, Mr. Otter!' It became more and more difficult for Wolf to take seriously the man's morbid timorousness. It was impossible to make sport of him; but he could not prevent a faint vein of raillery from entering into his reply. 'He looks a powerfully built fellow.'

'I tell you this, Solent, I tell you this' – and Jason clutched Wolf's arm and glanced round to make sure that the others were out of hearing – 'one day I shall be picked up unconscious in a ditch, beaten half-dead by that man!'

But Wolf's mind had wandered.

'By the way, Mr. Otter, if you ever want to sell that Hindoo idol of yours, I'll buy it from you!'

The poet stared at him blankly.

'I'll give five times whatever it cost you!'

'It cost me a pound,' said Jason grimly.

'Very well; I'll buy it for five pounds. Is that agreed?'

Jason pondered a little.

'Why do you want that thing? To bury it?'

'Perhaps that's it! How discerning you are!' And Wolf smiled genially at him.

'Very well, I'll sell it to you.' He paused for a moment. 'And if you could let me have that five pounds to-morrow, I should be very much obliged.'

'Good Lord!' thought Wolf to himself. 'I've done it now! Probably they keep the poor wretch without a penny, to stop him from drinking.'

'I'm not sure that I can manage it to-morrow,' he said affably, 'but you shall have it, Mr. Otter; and I'm sure I'm very grateful to you.'

'Shall you bury it? whispered Jason again, in a voice as sly and furtive as a wicked schoolboy.

'I don't want *you* to have it any longer, anyhow,' said Wolf, laughing.

Jason put his hand to his mouth and chuckled.

'By the way,' Wolf went on, 'I've never yet read a line of your poetry, Mr. Otter.'

The words were no sooner out of his mouth than he stared at the man in bewildered amazement. It was as if a mask had fallen from his face, revealing a totally different human countenance.

'Will you really read something? Will you really?'

The tone in which he said this was so childlike in its eagerness that Wolf felt a sudden unexpected tenderness for the queer man, quite different from his previous amused indulgence. 'How they must have outraged his life-illusion among them all!' he thought.

'But your mother adores your poetry; and your brother likes it too, doesn't he?'

Jason gave him one deep, slow, penetrating look that was like the opening of a sluice-gate.

'My mother ... my brother ...' And the man shrugged his shoulders as if Wolf had referred to the activities of water-flies in relation to human affairs.

'They don't understand it, you mean? They don't get its significance, for all their devotion? Well, I think I realize what you suffer from. But I don't suppose I shall understand it either.'

'I've written lately ... very lately ... last night, in fact – a poem to him.'

'To whom?'

'To him ... to Mukalog.'

Wolf wrinkled his eyebrows and stared intently at him for a moment. 'You'll be altogether happier when you've sold that thing to me, Mr. Otter,' he said.

'You'd like to bury him in your garden,' Jason muttered. And then quite unexpectedly he smiled so disarmingly that Wolf once again experienced that wave of affection.

'I expect lots of people wish I were dead,' he added, with a queer chuckle.

'I don't wish you were dead,' said Wolf, looking into his eyes. 'But I wish you *would* let me throw away that demon!'

A gleam of nervous irritation flashed from Jason's eyes, and his upper lip trembled.

'He's myself!' he murmured. 'He's what I am!' Then after a pause he jerked his thumb towards his brother. 'Darnley's a funny one,' he whispered, nudging Wolf's arm. 'Listen to him talking to the ladies! He ought to have been a Member of Parliament. He loves to behave like a grand gentleman.'

'He *is* a grand gentleman!' said Wolf drily.

'And as for that great bully of yours, Squire Urquhart,' Jason went on, raising his voice, '*he'll* die without any demon to help him. *He's on that road now!*'

These last words were uttered with such concentrated vindictiveness that Wolf opened his eyes wide.

'Did you see how he looked,' went on Jason, 'when those stallions passed him? He had to hang on to the rope to keep himself from falling. . . . I can tell you what crossed his mind then!'

'What?' enquired Wolf.

'To throw himself under their hooves! To be trodden into the ground by fifty stallions!'

'Are ye talking of stallions, gentlemen?' said a well-known voice; and Roger Monk, accompanied by the waiter of the Lovelace Hotel, stood before them, touching his hat politely.

Darnley and Miss Gault moved forward now, and Mrs. Otter began asking Monk about Dimity Stone and thanking him for picking up the old woman.

'Come on,' whispered Jason in Wolf's ear. 'Let's clear out of this! You see what *he* is . . . a great lubberly catchpole, not fit for anything except horse-racing! He's got rid of Dimity and joined up with that waiter with the idea of annoying someone. He wouldn't dare to insult anyone alone; but with that sly dog of a waiter – you know what waiters are – ' He paused and glanced back furtively at his mother and at the two serving-men. 'I'd like,' he added, 'to see Valley well fooled by those rascals. He'd have to go home alone then; and a good thing, too!'

'You've got your knife into us all, Mr. Otter,' said Wolf slowly. 'And I think it's a mistake. It's a waste of energy to hate people at the rate you do.'

But Jason's attention was still so absorbed in watching Monk and the waiter that he listened to him only with half an ear; and, indeed, shortly afterwards he shuffled off with barely a word of farewell.

Shrugging his shoulders under this rebuff, Wolf strode away in pursuit of Darnley and Miss Gault.

When he reached these two, he held out his hand and raised his hat.

'I think I'll leave you now in Mr. Otter's care,' he said to Miss Gault. 'It's about time I began to look for my mother.'

Selena appeared a little disconcerted at his abrupt departure, but Darnley gave him his usual gentle and indulgent smile.

'You always seem to bring me luck, Solent,' he said. 'But *au revoir!* We may meet on the road, for I expect *my* mother will be tired of this soon.'

Wolf shogged off by himself, and as soon as the crowd concealed him from the sight of his friends, he began waving his stick in the air. This was an old trick of his, and he invariably gave way to it when, after any prolonged period of human intercourse, he found himself alone and in the open.

He made his way rapidly to the extreme western corner of the great fair-field, where there were certain small swings patronized rather by children than by grown-up people.

As he threaded his way through all those excitable West-country folk he did his best to reduce to some sort of order the various jolts and jars he had received. So many confused impressions besieged his consciousness that he wished devoutly he were going to return to King's Barton on foot instead of driving.

His thoughts became complicated just at this moment by the teasing necessity of finding some place among those tents where he could make water. Drifting about with this in view, he found himself recalling all manner of former occasions when he had been driven to this kind of search. It took him so long to find what he wanted that when he *had* found it and had re-emerged into the sunshine, he experienced an extraordinary heightening of his spirits.

The acrid, ammoniacal smell of that casual retreat brought back to his mind the public lavatory on the esplanade at Weymouth, into which, from the sun-warmed sands, he used to descend by a flight of spittle stained steps. This memory, combined with an access of pervading physical comfort, drew his mind like a magnet toward his secretive mystical vice. Once more, as he gave himself up to this psychic abandonment, he felt as if he were engaged in some mysterious world-conflict, where the good and the evil ranged themselves on opposite sides.

He rubbed his hands together in the old reckless way as he walked along; and it seemed to him as if all these new impressions of his took their place in this mysterious struggle. That ravaged face of the Waterloo steps mingled its hurt with what Jason, Valley, Christie were all suffering; while the sinister magnetism that emanated from Mr. Urquhart fused its influence with that of Jason's idol, and the cruelty of Miss Gault to Christie, and of his mother to Miss Gault!

When this orgy of mystic emotion passed away, as it presently did, leaving him as limp and relaxed as if he had been walking for hours instead of minutes, he became aware that there were two irritating perplexities still fretting his mind, like stranded jelly-fish left high and dry on a bank of pebbles.

He found himself steering his consciousness with extreme care, as he walked along, so as to avoid contact with these two problems. But, as generally happens, he had not gone far before he was plunged into both of them, mingled confusedly together.

All about him was the smell of trodden grass, of horse-dung, of tar, of paint, of cider, of roasted chestnuts, of boys' new clothes, of rustic sweat, of girls' cheap perfumes, of fried sausages, of brassy machinery, of stale tobacco; and these accumulated odours seemed to resolve themselves into one single odour that became a wavering curtain, behind which these two dangerous thoughts were moving – moving and stirring the curtain into bulging folds – as concealed figures might do on a theatre-stage between the acts of a play.

The first of these thoughts was about his ill-assorted parents. He felt as if there were going on in his spirit an unappeasable rivalry between these two. He felt as if it were that grinning skull in the cemetery, with his 'Christ! I've had a happy life!' that had made him snatch at Gerda so recklessly, with the express purpose of separating him from his mother! It was just what that man would have done had he been alive. How he would have rejoiced in an irresponsible chance-driven offspring!

And then, before he had finished untying this knot of his parents' hostility, he was plunged into the second dangerous thought. This was more troubling to his peace than the other. It was about that grey feather which he had found in that book of Christie's! Why did it rouse such peculiar interest in him, to think of Christie and of Christie's fondness for the works of Sir Thomas Browne? What was Christie to him with her books and her queer tastes? What stability could there be in his love for Gerda when this troubling curiosity stirred within him at the idea of Gerda's friend?

As he thought of all this, his eyes caught sight of the golden face of a little dandelion in the midst of the trodden grass. He touched the edge of its petals rather wearily with the end of his stick, thinking to himself, 'If I leave it there it'll probably be trodden by these people into the mud in a few minutes; and if I pick it up it'll be dead before I get home!'

He decided to give the dandelion a chance to survive. 'After all, it *may* survive,' he thought; 'and if it doesn't – Ailinon! Ailinon! What does it matter?'

Moving on again at random, burdened with perplexities, he suddenly found himself in the midst of a circle of children who were gazing in envious rapture at a gaily-decorated swing that was whirling up and down in full, crowded activity. It was a boat-swing, and the boats were painted azure and scarlet and olive-green. . . .

And there, among the children in the swing, was Olwen, and there, by the side of it, watching Olwen swinging, was Mattie Smith herself! To come bolt-up upon her like this, in the midst of so many agitating thoughts, was a shock. He experienced that sort of mental desperation that one feels when one forces oneself awake from a dream that grows unendurable. And in his knowledge that she was his sister he saw her now as a totally different Mattie. But – what a sad face she had! She was so nervous about Olwen that he could regard her for several long seconds unobserved. What heavy ill-complexioned cheeks! What a disproportioned nose! What a clouded, apathetic brow, and what patient eyes! 'She's had a pretty hard life,' he thought. 'I wonder if she knows or doesn't know?'

Olwen was the first to catch sight of him; and her excited waving made Mattie hurriedly glance round.

She recognized him at once, too, and a flood of colour came into her pale cheeks. Wolf felt a curious embarrassment as they shook hands; and it was almost a relief to him to be forced to take his eyes off her in order to respond to Olwen, who was now waving to him frantically from her flying seat.

The child could not of course stop the machinery of the swing; and when she saw that he had answered her signal, she contented herself with just sweeping him into that rapturous topsy-turvy world – of people, grass, horses, trees, ruins, and hills – which rose and fell around her as she rushed through the air!

The cries of the children, the clang of the machinery, the voices of the showmen, covered Wolf and Mattie with a protective screen of undisturbed privacy. In the light of subsequent events they both looked back upon this moment with peculiar and romantic tenderness.

Directly she gave him her hand – even while he still held it – he had begun to talk to her of their relationship.

'I've known it since I was fifteen,' she said; 'and I'm twenty-five this month. That was what made it so awkward when you and your mother came to our house. *She* knows it, of course; and she let me see that she knew it. But I saw she had kept it from you. Has she told you about it since? What I *cannot* make out is whether father knows. He knows about Olwen, of course. In fact, he and Miss Gault were the ones who took Olwen away from Mr. Malakite.'

She paused, and gave Wolf a quick, furtive look; but what she saw in his face appeared to reassure her, for she smiled faintly.

'It's all so hard to talk about,' she said in a low voice. 'I'd never have thought I could talk to *you* about it. But it seems easy now I'm actually doing it! I was young then, you see . . . only fifteen; and father and Miss Gault thought I knew nothing. But I'd heard the servants talking; and I read about it in the *Western Gazette*. Why do you think it was I wasn't more shocked . . . Wolf?'

The hesitancy with which she brought out his name enchanted him. He snatched at her hand and made a movement as if he would kiss her; but she glanced hurriedly at the swing and drew back.

'I'm pretty hard to shock, too, Mattie dear,' he said. 'I expect we inherit *that!*' he added lightly.

'It was when they brought me to see Olwen at the "Home," ' the girl continued, 'that I made father have her at our house, for Nanny . . . she was my nurse then . . . and me to take care of! I knew she was at the "Home," . . . oh, Wolf, she was such a sweet little thing! . . . for I heard them talking about her. And I made father take me to see her, and we were friends in a second.'

'So it was you that persuaded Mr. Smith to take her into his house?' said Wolf. 'And you were only a child yourself.'

Mattie gave a quaint little chuckle. 'I was a pretty obstinate child, I'm afraid,' she said. 'Besides, Olwen and I both cried terribly and hugged each other. I was mad about children,' she added gravely; 'just mad about them, when I was young.'

'Was your father hard to persuade?' enquired Wolf.

The girl gave him one of her lowering sulkily-humorous glances. 'I made a fuss, you see,' she said solemnly. 'I cried and cried, till he agreed. It was Miss Gault who opposed it most. Oh, Wolf, it's terrible how Miss Gault has made the child hate Christie. Christie has seen her several times. I managed *that* for her! But Miss Gault must have said something. I don't know what. But the last time Olwen would hardly speak to her.'

Wolf frowned. 'Of course, it's possible, I suppose, that it's some kind of instinct in the little girl – ' he began ponderingly.

'No! No!' cried Mattie. 'It's Miss Gault. I know it's Miss Gault!'

'Christie told me she might be here this afternoon,' said Wolf, looking about him from group to group of the noisy young people around them.

'Did she?' said Mattie, with a nervous start. 'Did she really, Wolf?' And she, too, threw an anxious glance round the field. 'I wouldn't like her feelings to be hurt,' she added. 'They *would* be, I know, if she tried to speak to Olwen.'

Wolf's mind reverted violently to the solitary grey feather in the *Urn Burial*. At that moment he felt as though not anyone . . . not Gerda herself . . . could stop him from following that fragile figure if he caught sight of it in this crowd!

But Mattie was now waving her hand to Olwen, whose airy boat had begun to slacken its speed.

They moved together towards the swing; and Wolf rushed forward to help the child to the ground. As he lifted her out, he felt his forehead brushed by the floating ends of her loosened hair.

She put her thin arms round him and hugged him tight as soon as he set her down.

'Oh, I love swinging so! I love swinging so!' she gasped.

'Would you like to have another one?' he said gravely, looking down at that glowing little face.

Her eyes shone with infinite gratitude. 'Aunt Mattie's spent every penny grandfather gave her,' she whispered. 'Would you really give me one more? There! You pay it to that man over there; the one with the funny eyes!'

Wolf handed over the coin and lifted the child back into the painted boat. He waited at her side till the machinery started again and then returned to Mattie.

'Didn't you have the least guess about you and me?' the girl said; and it gave him a thrill of pleasure to see what animation had come into her stolid countenance.

'Not exactly a guess,' he answered. 'But I did have some kind of an odd feeling; as though I understood you and followed your thoughts, even when you were silent. Heavens! Mattie, dear; and you were silent almost all the time!'

'Your mother wasn't very nice to me.'

'Well, one can hardly blame her for that, can one? People do feel rather odd in these situations.'

'But I was nice to *you*, wasn't I?' the girl went on. 'And yet I couldn't bear to think that father wasn't my real father,' she added faintly.

Mattie's face had such a touching expression at that moment – an expression at once so thrilled and so puzzled – that with a quick and sudden movement he flung his arm round her neck and gave her a brusque kiss, full on the mouth.

'Mr. Solent! Wolf!' she protested feebly. 'You mustn't! What will *she* think?'

'Oh, *she'll* think you've found a young man,' he replied, laughing; 'and so you *have*, my dear,' he added affectionately.

But though he laughed at her embarrassment, and though she laughed faintly with him, it was clear enough to his mind, as he glanced at the face of the child in the swing, that their kiss had not been received very happily up there.

Two burning eyes flashed down at him like two quivering poniards, and two fierce little hands clutched the sides of the olive-green boat as if they had been the sides of a war-chariot.

'That child of yours is jealous,' he whispered hurriedly in his companion's ear. 'But don't you worry,' he added. 'It won't last, when she knows me better.'

He moved up to the swing and remained watching the little girl as she whirled past him like a small angry-eyed comet.

By degrees his steady matter-of-fact attention disarmed that jealous heart; and when the swing stopped, and he had gravely kissed her and handed her back to Mattie, all was once more well.

'We must go now and find grandfather,' said Mattie to Olwen. 'I'll come with you,' said Wolf. 'I left my mother with Mr. Smith; so we'll kill two birds with one stone!'

They moved off together, but suddenly, crossing a gap among the people, Wolf caught sight of Bob Weevil and Lobbie Torp.

'You go on, you two – do you mind? We'll meet later. There's someone I *must* run after.'

Both of his companions looked a little hurt at this brusque departure; but with a repeated 'We'll meet later! Good-bye!' he swung off in clumsy haste, pushing his way so impetuously through the crowd that he aroused both anger and derision.

For a time he was afraid that he had lost his quarry completely, so dense had the medley become around the booths; but at last, with a sigh of relief, he came upon them. They were both watching with unashamed delight a young short-skirted gipsy who was dancing wildly to a tambourine. As she danced she beat her knees and threw bold, provocative glances at her audience.

Wolf approached the two boys unobserved and was conscious of a passing spasm of shameless sympathy when he caught the expression of entranced lechery in the concentrated eyes of the young grocer. Lobbie Torp's interest was evidently distracted by the audacious leaps and bounds of the gipsy-wench and by her jangling music; but Mr. Weevil could contemplate nothing but her legs. These moving objects seemed to be on the point of causing him to howl aloud some obscene 'Evoe!' For his mouth was wide open and great beads of perspiration stood out upon his forehead.

The girl stopped, breathless at last, but without a moment's delay began to collect money, holding out her musical instrument with long, bare arms, and indulging in liberal and challenging smiles.

It tickled Wolf's fancy at this juncture to note the beaten-dog expression in Mr. Weevil's countenance as he pulled Lobbie away with him and tried to shuffle off unobserved. In their hurried and rather ignominious retreat they ran straight into Wolf's arms.

'Lordie! Hullo!' stammered Lob.

'It's Mr. Redfern – I mean, Mr. Solent, ain't it?' said Bob Weevil.

Wolf gravely shook hands with them both.

'It's not easy to keep one's money in one's pocket on a day like this,' he remarked casually.

Mr. Weevil gave him a furtive water-rat glance, and Wolf would not have been surprised had the young man taken incontinently to his heels.

'Bob knows all about they gipoos when they do zither like moskitties,' observed Lob slyly.

'Shut up, you kid!' retorted the other, 'or I'll tell Mr. Solent how I caught you kissing a tree.'

'I never kissed no tree,' muttered Lob sulkily.

'*What?*' cried his friend indignantly.

'If I did, 'twere along o' they loveyers us seed in Willum's Lane ditch. 'Twere enough to make a person kiss his wone self, what us did see; and 'twere ye what showed 'em to I.'

'I hope you have both enjoyed yourselves this afternoon,' began Wolf again. 'Christie can't have come,' he thought to himself; and he wondered if he should ask Mr. Weevil point-blank about her.

But Mr. Weevil was bent upon his silly, obstinate bullying of Lobbie. He kept trying to inveigle Wolf in this unamiable game.

'Lob thinks we're all as simple as his mummy in Chequers Street!' continued the youth, with an unpleasant leer.

'Don't 'ee listen to him!' cried Lob. 'Everyone knows what *his* mummy were, afore old man Weevil paid Lawyer Pipe to write "Whereas" in his girt book!'

'Listen, you two – ' expostulated Wolf. 'I want to ask you both a question.'

'He'll answer 'ee, same as my dad answered Mr. Manley when 'a cussed about his mother's gravestone. "Bless us!" said my dad, "and do 'ee take I for King Pharaoh?"' '

'What was it you wanted to ask us, sir?' enquired the older youth, pompously interrupting Lobbie.

'Oh, quite a simple thing, Mr. Weevil. I was only wondering if Miss Malakite was out here to-day.'

'Certainly she's here, sir. Certainly she is.'

'Us came along o' she, on our bicycles,' threw in Lobbie.

'Where is she now, then?' Wolf insisted.

'She went castle-way, I think, Mr. Solent,' said Bob Weevil.

'She said to we,' interjected Lobbie, 'that her reckoned she'd have a quiet stroll-like, long o' they ruings.'

Wolf looked from one to the other. 'So, in plain words, you deserted Miss Malakite?' he said sternly.

'Lob knows what I said when she was gone,' mumbled Mr. Weevil.

'When she were gone,' echoed the boy. 'I should say so!'

'What *did* you say?' asked Wolf.

'He said her walked like a lame hare,' threw in Lobbie.

'I didn't, you little liar! Don't believe him, Mr. Solent! I said she walked lonesome-like with her head hanging down.'

'That weren't *all* you said, Bob Weevil! Don't you remember what you said when us were looking at thik man-monkey? No! 'twere when us seed they girt cannibals all covered with blue stripes. That's when 'twere! Dursn't thee mind how thee said 'twas because Miss Malakite hadn't got no young man that she went loppiting off to they ruings 'stead of buying fairings like the rest of they?'

Wolf suddenly found himself losing his temper. 'I think you both behaved abominably,' he cried, 'leaving a young lady like that to go off by herself! Well, I'm going after her, and I'll tell her what I think of you two when I've found her!'

He strode off in the direction indicated by the boys' words. It was towards the southern extremity of the fair-field that he now made his way, where a dilapidated hedge and a forlorn little lane separated the castle field from the castle ruins. He had not gone far, however, when, glancing at a row of motionless, human backs, transfixed into attitudes of petrified wonder by the gesticulations of a couple of clowns, he became aware that two of those backs were obscurely familiar to him. He approached them sideways, and his first glance at their concentrated profiles revealed the fact that they were Mrs. Torp and old Dimity Stone.

It gave him a queer shock to think that this tatterdemalion shrew in rusty black was actually Gerda's mother. For the least fragment of a second he was aware of a shiver of animal panic, like a man who hears the ice he is crossing bend and groan under him; but he forced himself to walk straight up to them and salute them by name.

'I'm glad to see you, Mrs. Torp,' he said cheerfully. 'How do you do, Dimity? You and I haven't met for several long days.'

'Hark at him, Mrs. Stone,' gasped Gerda's mother. 'Hark at him, how 'ee do coax a body! He do look and speak just as I was telling 'ee, don't 'ee, now? If I hadn't told 'ee, honest to God, how the gentleman spoke, ye'd have never known it, would 'ee, Mrs. Stone?'

The withered face of Mrs. Torp remained turned toward her companion as she uttered this ambiguous welcome. She seemed unable to give Wolf so much as one single glance from her little vixen eyes, over which two artificial pansies, hanging from the battered bonnet on her head, jiggled disconcertingly.

But old Dimity retained Wolf's fingers quite a long while in her bony hand; and with absorbed and searching interest, as if she had been a fortune-teller, she peered into his countenance.

'The gentleman be far from what thee or any others have reckoned,' repeated the crone slowly. 'I've always known you were a deep one, Mr. Solent,' she added.

'I'm glad you think better of me than Mrs. Torp does, Dimity,' threw in Wolf, and he glanced anxiously over their heads toward the boundary of the field, his mind full of the deserted Christie.

'I think of 'ee as one what *speaks* fair enough,' grumbled Gerda's mother, 'but 'tis deeds *I* waits for. As I said to Torp this very mornin' . . . "Thy fair-spoken young gent," I said, "be only another Redfern; and all the country do know how daft *he* were!" Squire Urquhart must have 'em daft! Daft must they be for he, as I said to Torp. And that's because it's only the daft 'uns what'll serve for his cantrips – the girt bog-wuzzel 'ee is!'

Wolf detected a very sagacious expression in old Dimity's eye as she dropped his fingers at this.

'This gent bain't no more a Redfern, Jane Thorp, than a pond-pike be a gudgeon. What I've a-said to 'ee in neighbour-fashion I'd say now to 'ee on Bible-oath.'

There was a dead silence for a moment between the three of them, broken only by the gibberish of the two clowns, which sounded like the chatter of a pair of impudent parakeets amid the slow, rich Dorsetshire speech about them.

Without pausing to think of the effect of his words on Gerda's mother, Wolf could not restrain himself from uttering at this juncture the question which so occupied his mind. 'By the way, Mrs. Torp, have you, by any chance, seen Miss Malakite here this afternoon? I wanted to find her.'

Mrs. Torp nudged her companion with the handle of her umbrella.

'So ye're after her, too, are ye, mister? What do 'ee make o' that, Dimity Stone? Hee! Hee! Hee! The gentleman from London must have a sweetheart for Wednesday and a sweetheart for Thursday. But you have a care, Mr. Solent! Our Gerda bain't one for sharing her fairings; and she'll let 'ee know it! Won't she, Dimity Stone?'

Wolf felt unable to decide whether this outburst, under the pressure of which the thin cheeks of Mrs. Torp tightened over their bones till they were as white as the skin of a toadstool, was just ordinary Blacksod humour or was malignity. He contented himself with taking off his hat, wishing them a pleasant evening, and hurrying away.

As he moved towards the southern boundary of the field he found his mind beset with a burden of tumultuous misgiving. Mrs. Torp's malicious 'Hee! Hee! Hee!' continued to croak like a devil's frog in the pit of his stomach, and he remembered with hardly less discomfort the queer look that the old Dimity had given him. He *must* find Christie! That was the one essential necessity. Every step he took towards that ragged little hedge increased his nervous agitation.

'Why did chance throw them both in my way at this same moment?' he thought, as he walked automatically forward. And then a still more furtive and dangerous whisper entered his mind, *'Why didn't I meet Christie first?'*

The ghastly treachery of this final speculation, coming to him on the very morrow of the 'yellow bracken,' only made him shake his head, as if freeing himself from a thicket of brambles, and stride forward with more reckless resolution than ever.

Long afterwards he could recall every slightest sensation that he had as he crossed that empty portion of the fair-field. One of these sensations was a vivid awareness of the sardonic grimacing of that man in the churchyard. The perversity of his father seemed physically to weigh upon him. He had the feeling that he was himself reproducing some precise piece of paternal misdoing. He felt shamelessly like him! He felt as though his arms were swinging as *his* arms used to ... his legs striding the very stride of *his* legs!

205

He had now left the last tent far behind, and was approaching the low thick-set hedge that separated the castle field from the castle lane.

As he came up to the hedge he nearly stumbled over a half-skinned, half-eaten rabbit, one of whose glazed, wide-open eyes fixed itself upon him from the ground with a protesting appeal.

Mechanically he stooped down, and, lifting the thing up by its ears, placed it among the young dock-leaves and the new shoots of hedge-parsley.

Then he leaned both his arms over the top of the brambles, and, raising himself on tiptoe, peered into the lane beyond.

Ah! He had not then come to no purpose!

A little way down the lane, under a closed and carefully-wired gate leading to the castle ruins, crouched the unmistakable figure of Christie Malakite.

The girl was on her knees, her legs crooked under her, and her hands clasped on her lap. By her side, fallen to the ground, were her hat and some sort of paper parcel. She lifted her head and saw him there; but remained motionless, just staring at him without a sign. Wolf tightened his long overcoat round his knees and forced his way straight through the thick brambles. A couple of minutes later he was kneeling by her side on the grass, hugging her tear-stained face against his ribs and stroking her hair with his hands. 'I've had a hunt for you . . . a hunt for you!' he panted. 'What did you come to this damned place for? Well! I've got you now, anyway. I don't know what I would have done if I hadn't found you. But I've hunted you down . . . like a hare, my dear . . . just like a hare!'

'I'm . . . a . . . little . . . fool!' she gasped faintly. 'I'll be all right in a minute. I ought . . . to have . . . known better than . . . to have come here! The boys were kind . . . but, of course, they wanted . . . to enjoy themselves. I was a burden on them . . . and then I felt . . . I felt I couldn't . . . bear it!'

She pressed her face against his coat, struggling to hold back her tears.

Moving his hands to her shoulders, and bending down, he touched the top of her head with his lips. Her hair, neatly divided by a carefully-brushed parting, was so silky and fine that he felt as if his kiss had penetrated to the very centre of her skull. But she did not draw away from him. She only buried her forehead deeper in the folds of his heavy coat.

There was a tuft of loosely-growing stitchwort in the hedge by the gatepost; and this frail plant, as he surveyed it across her crouching form, mingled with his wild thoughts. Had anything like this ever happened to a man before . . . that on the day after such an ecstasy he should feel as he felt now? 'I must be a monster!' he said to himself. 'Am I going to begin snatching at the soul and body of every girl I meet down here?' With the cluster of stitchwort still illuminating his thought, as a flower-scroll illuminates a monkish script, he now struggled desperately to justify himself.

'This feeling,' he protested, 'is a different thing altogether. It's pity . . . that's what it is! And, of course, Gerda being so beautiful pity doesn't . . .'

Christie lifted up her head now, and sat back, hugging her knees and staring at him. He, too, changed his position, so that his shoulders leant against the lower bars of the gate. 'It's queer how natural it seems to be . . . to be with you like this,' he said slowly.

She gave a little nod. 'I used to tell myself stories . . .' she began, searching his face intently as if what she wanted to say lay hidden in its lines. 'I feel so different now,' she went on, 'that it would be easy to tell you . . .' Once more her voice sank into silence.

'It's better to be alone,' he echoed, 'unless you can think aloud. I've been walking about this fair-field all the afternoon and talking to everyone; but I couldn't think aloud until this moment.'

They were both silent, staring helplessly at each other.

'I wish you were a boy, Christie!' he brought out abruptly.

Something in the peevish gravity of this must have tickled her fancy, for she smiled at him with a free, unrestrained, school-girlish smile.

'I used to wish that myself,' she murmured gently; and then she sighed, her smile fading as quickly as it had come.

He knitted his heavy eyebrows and scowled at her in deep thought.

Two persistent sounds forced their identities into his drugged consciousness. The first was the brazen clamour of the whirligig engines. The second was the whistling of a blackbird. This latter sound had already assumed that peculiar mellowness which meant that the sunrays were falling horizontally upon that spot, and that the long March afternoon was drawing to its close.

It was impossible that this bird's voice could fail to bring to his mind the events of yesterday's twilight and that upturned face at which he had gazed so exultantly in the gathering river-mists. To drown the blackbird's notes, he began hurriedly telling her one thing after another of his afternoon's adventures. When he came to his conversation with Miss Gault, they both instinctively shifted their position, and he found himself helping her to adjust the loosened belt of her old-fashioned cloak with a gesture that was almost paternal.

'One thing I cannot understand,' he said.

'Well?' she murmured.

'I cannot understand how Olwen should feel towards you as they tell me she does.'

The girl's forehead wrinkled itself into a strained, pinched intensity; but all she said was, 'I could never take care of any child as well as Mattie Smith.'

'I don't believe you,' he retorted bluntly.

He avoided her eyes now; and, as he looked away into the great elm tree that grew near the gate, he caught sight of a large nest up there.

'Is that a rook's nest?' he asked, pointing it out to her with upraised arm.

Christie turned and peered upwards.

'A missel thrush's, I think,' she said, after a second's hesitation. 'Rooks' nests are all sticks . . . and they're higher up, too.'

With lifted heads they both stared into the elm tree, and, beyond the tree, into the cold March sky.

'Why not take us as we are,' he said slowly, apparently addressing the missel thrush's nest, 'as two hunted, harassed consciousnesses, meeting by pure chance in endless blue space and finding out that they have the same kind of mind?'

Their heads sank down after this, and Wolf automatically fumbled for his cigarettes and then consciously let them go.

'I've never felt as much at ease with anyone as with you, Christie . . . except, perhaps, my mother. No, not even except her.'

'I think we *are* alike,' she said quietly. And then, with the same schoolgirlish simple amusement that had struck him before, 'We're too alike, I think, to do much harm to anyone!'

Her face grew suddenly grave, and she stretched out her thin arm and touched Wolf lightly on the knee. 'You must be prepared for one thing,' she said. 'You must be prepared to find that I haven't a trace of what people call the "moral sense." '

'I'll risk that danger!' he retorted lightly. 'Besides, if you've got *no* conscience, I'm worse off still. I've got a diseased conscience!'

She didn't even smile at this sally. With a quick wrinkling of her brow, as if under a twinge of physical discomfort, she scrambled to her feet.

'I must get my bicycle,' she said, with a little shiver. 'Father will be waiting for his supper.'

Wolf rose too, and they stood rather awkwardly side by side, while the blackbird flew off with an angry scream.

'Where is your bicycle?' he asked lamely; and as he saw her and felt her, standing there by his side, so pitifully devoid of all physical magnetism, he could not resist a chilly recognition that something of the mysterious appeal that had drawn him to her had slipped away and got lost.

He felt in that second that it had been a piece of pure madness to have wished that all this had happened before yesterday's 'yellow bracken.'

She glanced up at him with a quick, searching look. Then she tightened her cloak resolutely round her. 'It's in the Lovelace stables,' she said. 'I can easily find it. You needn't come.'

'Of course I'll come! I'll go with you and put you on it; and then I'll come back for my mother.'

'It's pity I feel,' he said to himself. 'I've got Gerda for good and all. It's just pity I feel.'

They followed the lane westward, skirting the edge of the fairfield. When they reached the foot of 'The Slopes,' they saw the whole of Ramsgard outspread before them. The sunset mist, rising up from the River Lunt, threw over the little town the sort of glamour that cities wear in old fantastic prints. Vaguely, under the anæsthesia of this diffused glory in the chilly air, he marvelled at the mad chance that had plunged him into these two girls' lives with this disturbing simultaneousness. He began furtively trying to annihilate with his imagination first one life and then the other from his obstinate preoccupation. But the effort proved hopelessly futile! To conceive of the future without Gerda's loveliness was impossible. But equally was it impossible to cover up this strange new feeling. Only 'pity,' . . . but a pity that had a quivering sweetness in it!

'You're all right, now?' he enquired abruptly, as they crossed the railway track.

'Absolutely,' she answered firmly, evidently recognizing that this allusion to her original trouble was a sign of a certain withdrawal in her companion. 'And please, please, believe me when I tell you that I hardly ever . . . no, practically never . . . give way like that.'

'What do you think did it?' he blurted out clumsily. 'Those silly boys deserting you?'

She made no reply at all to this; and he experienced a wave of embarrassment that brought a hot prickling sensation into his cheeks.

'You've been very kind to me,' she said unexpectedly, in a clear emphatic voice. And then she added very slowly, pronouncing the words as if each of them were a heavy bar of silver and she were an exhausted stevedore emptying the hold of a ship, 'Kinder . . . to me . . . than anyone's . . . ever been . . . in the whole of my life.'

These words of hers, healing his momentary discomfort, gave him such happiness, that, as they entered the Lovelace stables, and she moved in front of him across the cobblestones, he furtively rubbed his hands together, just as he would have done if he had been alone.

'What a good thing you came over here this afternoon,' he said, as he wheeled her bicycle out of the yard.

'I don't know about that!' she answered promptly, with a flicker of her peculiar elfish humour; and it turned out to be the tone of these words, beyond all others, that remained with him when she was gone. They had the tone of some sort of half-human personality . . . some changeling out of the purer elements . . . upon whose nature whatever impressions fell would always fall with a certain mitigation, with a certain lenient tenuity, like the fall of water upon water, or of air upon air!

10

CHRISTIE

THE cheap wooden clock on the mantelpiece of his small parlour made itself audible to the ears of Wolf across the little passageway as he stood above his kitchen stove. Eight times the clock struck; and the old vivid consciousness of what time was and was not caught his mind and held it. It was not a consciousness of the passing of time as it affected his own life that arrested him. Of that kind of individual awareness he had scarcely any trace. To himself he always seemed neither young nor old. Indeed, of bodily self-consciousness – that weather eye, kept open to the addition of years and months upon his personal head – he had nothing at all. What he lived in was not any compact, continuous sense of personal identity, but rather *a series of disembodied sensations*, some physical, some mental, in which his identity was absolutely merged and lost. He was vividly aware of these momentary sensations in relation to other feelings of the same kind, some long past and some anticipated in his imagination; but he was accustomed to regard all these not from out of the skin, so to speak, of a living organism, but from a detachment so remote and far away as to seem almost outside both the flowing of time and the compactness of personality.

Eight o'clock in the morning of the first day of June was what that timepiece said to him now; and his mind paused upon the recognition of the vast company of clocks and watches all the world over, ticking, ticking, ticking – sending up, in tiny metallic beats, vibrations of human computation into the depths of unthinkable space.

He pushed open the iron cover of the stove and jabbed with his poker at the fire inside. Then he took up a wooden spoon and stirred the contents of an enamelled pot of porridge that stood there, moving it aside from the heat. A thrill of satisfaction ran through him when he had done this, and he rubbed his hands together and made a 'face,' drawing back his under lip in the manner of a gargoyle, and constricting the muscles of his chin.

In less than half an hour, he thought, he would be enjoying

his breakfast at that kitchen-table with Gerda, lovely and sulky as a young animal after her abrupt awakening.

He ran up the short flight of creaking stairs, carpeted with new linoleum; and with the merest pretence of a tap at the door entered their bedroom. The girl was lying on her back fast asleep, her fair hair spread out, loose and bright in the sunshine, across the indented pillow of her recent bedfellow. Her arms were outstretched above the coverlet, and one of her hands was hanging down over the side of the bed. His entrance did not arouse her, and he stood for a while at her side, meditating on the mysterious simplicity of her especial kind of loveliness.

Then he bent down, kissed her into consciousness, laughed at her scolding, and with one resolute swing of his arms lifted her bodily from the bed, set her on her feet on the floor, and hugged her to his heart, struggling and indignant. The warmth of her body under the childish white nightgown she wore, buttoned close up to her chin, gave him a rough, earthy, animal ecstasy. He had already discovered that it was more delicious to hold her like this, he himself fully awake and dressed, and she as she was, than under any other circumstances. A pleasant element of the unhabitual and the predatory sweetened for him that particular embrace. 'Don't!' she cried, struggling to push him away. 'Don't, Wolf! Let me go, I tell you!' But he went on kissing her and caressing her as if it had been the first time he had ever taken her in his arms.

At last, lifting her clean off her feet, with both arms under her body, he put her back upon the bed and drew the bedclothes over her.

'There!' he cried. 'How does *that* feel?'

But the girl turned round with her face to the wall and refused to speak.

'Eight o'clock, young lady,' he cried brusquely. 'Breakfast will be ready in a quarter of an hour.'

For answer she only pulled the bedclothes more tightly round her neck.

'If you haven't time to wash or do your hair, you must come down as you are. Where's your dressing-gown?' And he looked vaguely round the room. 'Hurry up, now!' he added. 'Remember all that's going to happen to-day.'

There was a movement under the twisted sheet.

'You're a wretch!' she gasped, in a muffled voice.

'Never mind what I am. Keep your scoldings till you get downstairs. I've got an exciting piece of news for you.'

This brought her round with a jerk.

'What are you hiding up in your mind now? Tell me quick! Tell me, Wolf!'

But he only laughed at her, waved his hand and went out.

Running downstairs again, he returned to the kitchen, moved the steaming kettle to the side of the stove, turned the spoon in the oatmeal, and then, crossing the little passage where his own grey overcoat and Gerda's cream-coloured cloak, hanging side by side on their adjoining pegs, regarded him with equivocal intentness, he opened the front door and went out into the road.

In one warm inrushing wave the fragrance of the whole West-country seemed to flow through him as he came forth. Sap-sweet emanations from the leafy recesses of all the Dorset woods on that side of High Stoy seemed to mingle at that moment with the rank, grassy breath of all the meadow-lands of Somerset.

The iron railings in front of that row of meagre, nondescript houses opened upon the airy confluence of two vast provinces of leafiness and sunshine – to the right Melbury Bub, with its orchards and dairies; to the left Glastonbury, with its pastures and fens – while the umbrageous 'auras' of these two regions, blending together in the air above the roofs of Blacksod, merged into yet a third essence, an essence sweeter than either – the very soul of the whole wide land lying between the English Channel and the Bristol Channel.

Number Thirty-seven Preston Lane was the last house in a row of small workmen's cottages at the extreme western limit of the town of Blacksod. What met Wolf's actual eyes as he clicked the little gate in the iron railings and emerged upon the road, was only a small portion of the secret causes of his happiness that June morning. He had long craved to establish himself in just such a nondescript row of unpretentious dwellings on the outskirts of a town. He had always had a feeling that the magic of simple delights came with purer impact upon the mind when unalloyed by the 'artistic' or the 'picturesque.' Large houses and large gardens, pretty houses and pretty gardens, seemed to intrude themselves, with all their responsibilities of possession, between his senses and the free, clear flow of unconfined, unpersonalized beauty. His feeling about the matter had something in common with the instinct that has created the monk's cell – only the cell that Wolf preferred was a lath-and-plaster workman's villa, a place possessed of no single æsthetic quality, except perhaps that of being easily kept very neat and clean.

The fact of living here with Gerda under conditions identical with those of the Blacksod carpenters, bricklayers, and shop-assistants, threw into beautiful relief every incident of his life's routine. Preparing food, preparing fires, the very floor-scrubbing wherein he shared, took on for him, just because of this absence of the deliberately 'artistic,' a rarefied peotical glamour.

He moved out now into the middle of the road and surveyed the landscape. As he did so, two very distinct and contradictory odours assailed his nostrils. There were no houses across the way, nothing but a foul-smelling ditch, the receptacle of sewage from an adjoining pig-yard; and beyond that an enormously high hedge, on the top of which, where no child could reach, grew clumps of honeysuckle and sprays of wild roses. The smell of these flowers contended oddly enough with the smell of pigs' dung; and the two odours, thus subtly mingled, had become for him a constant accompaniment to the thoughts that passed through his mind as he went in and out of his tiny front garden.

The pigsty was on his right as he stood facing the ditch; but on his left there grew in the meadow just beyond the hedge a large ash tree – a tree from among whose grey, upcurving branches a thrush was wont to sing, always increasing the vehemence of its ecstasy till the moment when the road grew quite dark. The bird began singing now, and its thrush-notes made Wolf think of those wild blackbird-notes of Gerda, as they flooded the meadows on the day when she lost her virginity.

Thinking of Gerda as he stared up into the ash tree, he began to meditate on the extraordinary good luck he had had ever since he had come to the West-country. 'I must be born under a lucky star,' he thought; and his mind set itself to review the most recent examples of this good fortune.

He recalled the satisfactory manner in which his iron-willed mother had suddenly receded from all her opposition to his union with Gerda. He recalled the equally satisfactory generosity of Mr. Urquhart, who had come forward with an offer to let her go on living at Lenty Cottage free of rent as long as Wolf himself remained his secretary.

He recalled the extraordinary kindness displayed toward him by Darnley Otter, who had not only lent him the fifty pounds necessary to buy furniture, but had also introduced him to the authorities of the Blacksod Grammar School, where he was now earning a pound a week by giving lessons every morning in English and History.

'Luck! luck! luck!' he said in his heart, rubbing his hands together. Through his thin indoor shoes the magnetism of the earth seemed at that moment pouring into every nerve of his body. Happiness, such as he had rarely experienced, flooded his being; and the fantastic idea came into his head that if he were to die now he would in some subtle way cheat death.

'I must remember this moment,' he said to himself. 'Whatever happens to me henceforth, I must remember this moment, and be grateful to the gods!'

Just as he opened the iron gate and glanced at the two or three newly-budded plants that were coming out in his little patch of garden the owner of the pigsty a ruffianly curmudgeon who earned his living in more than one disreputable way, took it into his head to pour out a great bucket of swill into the pig-trough, an action that caused so ear-piercing a volley of bestial shrieks, that Wolf stopped aghast, his heart almost ceasing to beat, and, turning his head, threw an agitated glance toward that sinister little erection of tarred boardings.

His first idea was that one of the animals was being slaughtered; but the sound of voracious gobbling which now reached his ears reassured him.

'He's only feeding them,' he said to himself, and entered the house. In the kitchen he found Gerda already beginning her bowl of porridge.

'What's the news, Wolf?' she enquired, with the indistinct voice of a greedy child, turning, as she did so, her cream-clogged spoon upside-down in her mouth, so as to lick it clean. 'What's this you were going to tell me?'

'Guess, sweetheart!' he said contentedly, emptying what was left of the cream-jug over his own oatmeal. 'Nothing, in fact, could be better. Urquhart announced last night that he has decided to go slow with our History. You know what a hurry he's been in? But he now says he's decided to make a complete job of it, even if it takes five years to finish.'

The infantile sulkiness in Gerda's face only deepened at his words, and with an impatient gesture she stretched out her arms and tossed back her head. Then she tightened the green ribbon with which she had fastened her locks, and fixed upon him a cloudy, satiric frown. She appeared so enchanting in her crossness that Wolf forgot everything as he watched these movements, and for a moment he just looked at her in silence.

'You don't think much of my news, then?' he said presently.

'But you don't realize how awkward it would have been if this confounded book had come to an end this autumn. Where would we have got another hundred pounds from, eh, sweetheart? Tell me that!'

'A hundred pounds!' the girl muttered sarcastically.

'Yes, a hundred pounds,' he retorted. 'Two-thirds of our income.'

He rose and moved to the stove, to get the kettle to refill their teapot.

'But that's not all; so you needn't look sour. There's something much more amusing than that.' She waited impatiently now, and he went on. 'Urquhart doesn't want me over there this afternoon, and mother's coming to tea.'

The girl's sulkiness changed in a moment to something like pitiful dismay.

'Oh, Wolf!' she exclaimed. 'This is the first time.'

'She's been twice to lunch,' he said.

But Gerda's eyes remained troubled and very wide open, and the corners of her under lip drooped.

'Darnley was here, too – both times!' she gasped. 'We've never had her alone, and I've got no clothes for an afternoon.'

'No clothes?'

'You know what I mean, perfectly well,' she went on peevishly. 'People like your mother don't have the same things on in the morning as they do in the afternoon.'

Wolf watched her with narrowing eyelids. He recalled that first walk with her up the slope of Babylon Hill, and his pursuit of her among the earthworks of Poll's Camp. Why did all girls introduce into life an element of the conventional – into that life of which they themselves were the most mysterious expression? He became suddenly aware of the existence, in the beautiful head opposite him, of a whole region of interests and values that had nothing to do with love-making and nothing to do with romance. Was love itself, then, and all its mysteries, only a kind of magic gate leading into a land full of alien growths and unfamiliar soils?

'Gerda, my sweet Gerda!' he cried reproachfully. 'How absurd! What does it matter? It's only my mother. She must take us as she finds us.'

The girl pouted and smiled scornfully.

'That's all you know!' she retorted. 'Your mother's a woman, isn't she?'

Wolf stared at her. Was there then some queer inner world, parallel to the one that was important to him, wherein women encountered one another, and without whose ritual life was

216

completely unreal to them? 'God!' he thought to himself. 'If this *is* so, the sooner I get the secret of this "other reality," the better for both Gerda and me!'

'Well, I only beg one thing of you, sweetheart,' he went on aloud, 'and that is that you don't try and make those funny scones again that you made for Christie. I'll get some halfpenny buns or tea-cakes at Pimpernel's.'

'Halfpenny buns!' she repeated contemptuously.

He began to raise his voice. 'They're the very nicest things! How silly you are! But I don't care what you get, as long as there's plenty of thin bread-and-butter.'

'I can't cut it! I never could cut it!' she cried helplessly, her enormous grey eyes beginning to fill with tears.

It was then that Wolf began to realize that it was necessary to be as indulgent to the 'realities' of this alien array of feelings as if they had been those of a being of a different planet. He got up from his seat and walked round their square kitchen-table, a table that according to his own caprice had been left bare of any covering. Standing over the girl, he bent her head back with both his hands and kissed her many times.

It seemed to him, as he did this, that he had done this very same thing in another room, and even in another country. He remained motionless behind her for a moment when he had released her, and lifted his head. Where had all this occurred before? A queer feeling came over him as if she and he were acting a part in some fantastic dream-world, and that he had only to make one enormous effort, to find he had destroyed for both of them the whole shadow-scenery of their life.

But Gerda, knowing nothing of what was passing in his mind, turned round in her chair and pushed him away with all the strength of her young arm.

'Don't be so annoying, Wolf!' she cried. 'There! I'm hungry, I tell you. Haven't you got any eggs for us?'

He moved away obediently to the stove, made his arrangements for boiling three eggs – two for himself and one for her – and remained there on guard, his watch in his hand.

The audible ticking of his watch, as he concentrated his mind upon it, answered the louder ticking of the clock in the parlour across the passage. 'Time again!' he sighed. And then he thought, 'But I've got the power to deal with far more serious jolts to my happiness than this finding out that a girl's "reality" is not my "reality"!'

In a minute or two, when he had set a china egg-cup in front of each of them and had placed a brown egg within hers and a white one in his own, and had resumed his seat, he found that his quick adjustment of the wheels and cogs of his mind had proved successful. 'It doesn't matter in the least,' he thought, 'whether we understand each other or not. My existence is necessary to her, just as hers is to me. Neither of us can really spoil anything as long as that's the case.'

Whatever secret ways Gerda had of adjusting the machinery of *her* mind, seemed to have been as successful as his own; for when she had satisfied her hunger and filled her teacup with strong, sweet tea, she lifted her head quite cheerfully.

'I'll go to Pimpernel's myself,' she said. 'I saw something there yesterday that I'm sure your mother would like. And I'll make toast. That'll be just as nice as bread-and-butter.'

Wolf declared himself completely satisfied at this prospect.

'You go up now, sweetheart,' he said, 'and finish dressing, and make the bed. I'll wash up. I'll just have time for that. There, do go quick! I don't want anyone to knock at the door and find you like that. We've got to keep up the prestige of Preston Lane!'

He spoke jestingly, but there was an element of concern at the back of his mind. He had had some uncomfortable moments now and again, when tradesmen's boys had come to the door at an early hour. He hated to think of their *ménage* being a laughing-stock to all the Lob Torps and Bob Weevils of the town.

It was a complete puzzle to him the way in which Gerda made such a fuss about the conventions where his mother was concerned, while to the Bob Weevils of the place she let down every barrier as completely as if she'd drifted into Blacksod from the primeval woods of Arcady.

As he watched her now, rushing upstairs like a young mænad, he remembered how the fancy had come into his mind, that afternoon at Poll's Camp, that the West-Saxon Torp blood in her had been crossed at some very early stage with an altogether different strain.

Hurriedly gathering the dishes together on the edge of the sink, he proceeded to do what would certainly not have passed un-observed by a more practical mistress of the house. He proceeded to hold cups, saucers, plates, bowls, knives, forks, and pots and pans under a tap of perfectly cold water, rubbing them and scraping them with his bare fingers, and then drying them violently – greasy as most of them were – with the kitchen-towel.

218

As he did this, he caught a glimpse out of the window of a stunted little laburnum tree, which grew in their backyard; and he noticed, as he had often noticed before, how one of its boughs was leafless and seemed to be stretching out, in a sorrowful, fumbling sort of way, towards their neighbour's fence, above which grew a sturdy lilac-bush, covered now with glossy heart-shaped leaves.

On this occasion, however, for some unaccountable reason, the sight of this forlorn branch brought vividly to his mind the figure of Christie Malakite, as he had seen her that day, crouched in the castle lane. And with that image there came to him – as if a door had unexpectedly opened in the remotest wall of his mind's fortress – a deep, sickening craving, it was hard to tell for what – a craving that pierced him like the actual thrust of a spear. The bareness and tension of that extended branch had won his sympathy before; but to-day, as he rubbed the porridge-pot furiously with the greasy towel and emptied the hot kettle-water into it, the sight of the thing seemed to disturb the complacency of his whole being.

A minute or two later, when he saw it again from the window of their small privy, which abutted upon the same back-yard, he got a sense of being hemmed in, burdened, besieged, while some vague, indistinct appeal, hard to define, was calling upon him for aid.

He moved out to the foot of the staircase, and, with his hand upon the bannister, stood motionless, lost in strange thoughts. These glimpses of certain fixed objects, seen daily, yet always differently, through bedroom-windows, scullery-windows, privy-windows, had, from his childhood, possessed a curious interest for him. It was as if he got from them a sort of runic handwriting, the 'little language' of Chance itself, commenting upon what was, and is, and is to come. As he stood there, he could hear Gerda moving about upstairs, and he hesitated as to whether to run up and speak to her, or to go out, as he generally did, without further farewell.

He decided finally upon the latter course; something at the bottom of his mind, just then, making anything else seem strained and unnatural. Snatching up his oak stick, therefore, he let himself out of the house with deliberate quietness, and walked with rapid steps down the road.

His way to the Grammar School led him past the confectioner's shop; and at the sight of the name 'Pimpernel' over the door, he decided to run in for a moment and see for himself if the particular tea-cakes that he had in mind were available that day.

Not finding what he wanted, he was on the point of going out again, when he heard a familiar voice proceeding from the interior part of the shop. It was too late to retreat. He was already recognized; and in another second he found himself face to face with Mrs. Torp. Gerda's mother had been engaged in persuading old Ruth Pimpernel to sell her a loaf of yesterday's bread at half-price.

Shaking hands vigorously with this uncongenial apparition, whose shrewish aspect was not modified by the dirty black bonnet she wore balanced on the top of her head, Wolf found himself propitiating the woman to the extreme limit of a somewhat unctuous geniality.

He had often noticed that when his blood had been quickened by rapid walking, he had a tendency to exaggerate his natural *bonhomie* to a degree that was almost fatuous.

'You haven't come to see us for such a long while, Mrs. Torp,' he cried. 'Gerda and I can't get on without seeing something of you. It's too ridiculous' – so he blundered on, in complete disregard of the sly expression in Mrs. Torp's eyes, like the expression of a tethered dog leering at a hutch of tame hares – 'it's too ridiculous to have you in the same place and to see so little of you!'

It was impossible even for the perspicacity of Joan Torp to put down this blustering friendliness to its true account – to the pleasant glow, namely, diffused through Wolf's veins by his rapid walk; and so, with a nearer approach to a benevolent grimace than he had ever seen on her grim features, she assured him with unhesitating emphasis that she would, 'as sure as us be standing here, Mr. Solent,' drop in for tea that very afternoon at Preston Lane.

The appearance of the shop-girl with the stale loaf destined for the monument-maker's table – Mr. Torp abominated stale bread – prevented the woman from detecting the cloud that descended on Wolf's brow on receipt of this prompt acceptance of his hospitality. It was, indeed, only when he was hurrying out of the confectioner's shop that he had the wit to turn round and fling back a suggestion that if Mrs. Torp went over there, now at once, her daughter would be very pleased to see her.

'I'll leave it to Gerda,' he thought to himself. 'She'll manage it somehow.'

His mind, however, remained all that morning, as he sat at his desk in the Grammar School fourth-form room, asking questions about Edward Longshanks, teasingly preoccupied with this encounter.

'She may not go there at all,' he thought. 'It isn't her way to go there in the morning. They're so funny, those two, about their houses. Well, we must chance it and hope for the best!'

And then, as he enlarged to his class upon that formidable black sarcophagus in Westminster Abbey, with its grim inscription, the underflow of his mind kept fretting against all the little incidents that had led to this annoying issue.

'If I hadn't stayed so long at that confounded privy-window, I should have got out of Pimpernel's before she came in. And if I'd stopped to say good-bye to Gerda, she'd have gone before I got there at all. Damn! It's like the rope, the water, the fire, the dog, and the old woman getting home from market.'

When his class was let out and he himself escaped into the street at half-past twelve, it occurred to him that it was curious how faint an impact upon his consciousness this business of teaching history made. He was clever enough to do the whole job with the surface of his mind. 'What the devil do those boys think of me?' he wondered grimly. 'I forget their existence as soon as I'm out of sight of them.'

He met Darnley Otter, at that moment, issuing forth from his Latin lesson with a pile of papers in his hand.

Darnley greeted him with more than his usual cordiality; and as Wolf looked into his friend's strangely-coloured eyes, he felt that peculiar sensation of relief which men are wont to feel when they encounter each other after the confusion of sex-conflicts.

Darnley laid his free hand on his friend's arm, and they moved down the street together; but for a while Wolf heard nothing of what he was saying, so occupied was he with a sudden question, gaping like a crack in a hot stubble-field in the very floor of his mind, that had just then obtruded itself. Was he really 'in love,' in the proper sense of that word, with his sweet bedfellow? 'But very likely I could never be "in love" in *that* sense with anyone,' he said to himself as they walked along.

And then he became aware that Darnley had been speaking to him for some while.

'I don't see why I shouldn't take you,' he was saying now. 'I *would*, like a shot, if she hadn't been so funny the other day when I talked about you. But I expect there's nothing in that! Perhaps you hurt her feelings in some way. She's a queer little oddity. I found that out long ago. One has to be awfully careful.'

These words, and other words before them, now began to penetrate Wolf's consciousness, as they might have done with a person recovering from an anæsthetic.

'Sorry,' he muttered apologetically, standing stock-still on the pavement. 'I wasn't listening.'

Darnley stroked his pointed beard and looked him up and down.

'You're boy-drunk, poor devil,' he murmured sympathetically. 'It does take time to wear off. You're repeating to yourself what you'd like to have retorted to Rintoul Minor when he made you feel a fool. I'm often like that myself.'

'No, I'm not,' protested the other. 'But what *were* you saying?'

'Nothing very startling,' said Darnley quietly, pulling him forward by the arm. 'It's only I thought I'd take you with me to Christie's to lunch. Gerda won't mind, once in a way, will she?'

Wolf drew his heavy eyebrows down so low that his startled gaze gleamed out at his companion like lantern-light from a thatched shed. 'I . . . don't . . . suppose so,' he muttered hesitatingly.

The truth was that Darnley's suggestion had set something vibrating violently deep down within him, like the thuds of a buried drum played by an earth-gnome. So this was what things had been tending to since he had caught sight of that laburnum-branch?

Darnley smiled and shrugged his shoulders.

'Don't say any more,' he cried. 'I see you don't want to come. Well! Off with you, then . . . back to your Saxon beauty. Christie's expecting me, anyway.'

But Wolf held him with an appeal in his eye.

'It's only that Gerda and I have got special things to do to-day,' he said. 'Under ordinary conditions I'd have loved to come.'

Darnley looked at him gravely. 'No bad news, I hope?' he said.

Wolf was silent. All manner of queer fancies passed, like the shadows of rooks over a pond, across the surface of his brain. One thing particularly he found himself dwelling upon. 'Didn't seem friendly to me, eh?' And he recalled the only two occasions on which he had seen Christie alone since his marriage.

On both those occasions she had avoided all allusion to the day of the Horse Show. But she had been self-possessed and natural, had laughed at his jests, had talked freely with him about Mattie, had not even drawn back from a passing reference to Olwen. And though her allusions to Gerda were faint and slight, they were friendly and sympathetic. But Wolf remembered well how he had experienced a profound astonishment at the abysses of pride and reserve into which this frail being had the power of retreating.

'Gerda has been a bit surprised,' he said at last, observing that Darnley was growing impatient to be off, 'that a friend like Christie hasn't been in to see us more often.'

His companion freed his sleeve from the nervous clutch with which Wolf quite unconsciously had seized it.

'That's silly of Gerda,' he said curtly. 'She ought to understand Christie better than that. Christie never goes out to see people. People have to come and see *her*. Look here, Solent' – and as he spoke, a gleam of boyish eagerness came into his face – 'why don't you run back home now, have a bit of lunch, and then both you and Gerda come round to Christie's? I'll tell her you're coming. She'll keep some hot chocolate for you. She makes splendid hot chocolate.'

Wolf hesitated. 'We've got my mother coming to tea.' he said. 'And perhaps someone else too,' he added, thinking of Mrs. Torp.

'That's all right. There'll be plenty of time for that. It's not half-past two, anyway. Do go off now, there's a good chap; and be sure you bring Gerda.'

Wolf remained silent, uncertain, ill at ease, tapping the ground with his stick.

'All right,' he said at last, 'I'll do as you say. We shan't be long over our lunch, that's certain. But make it plain to Christie that we're only coming for a very short time. Tell her we've got to get back to tea. That'll reassure her,' he added sardonically, 'if we get on her nerves.'

'Don't be an ass, Solent,' was his friend's farewell remark as they turned to go their different ways.

It took Wolf as a rule exactly twenty minutes to walk from the Grammar School gate to his own door; but this time he lengthened the way by debouching into Monmouth Street, where there were no shops and scarcely any traffic.

The hot June sun was shining down almost perpendicularly on the warm, uneven cobblestones of this quiet alley, stones that left room for the occasional outcropping of thin moss-soft blades of grass. Wolf walked along slowly, under the high brick wall which enclosed the pleasant garden of a certain Lawyer Gault, a remote relative of Selena's. He came to a spot where the branches of a tall lime tree just inside the lawyer's garden threw a dreamy pattern of motionless shadows upon the stones at his feet. There he stood still, while those dark patterns upon the sunlit ground made that portion of the earth seem porous and insubstantial. And then again that drum-like beating in the depths of his heart brought up the vision of Christie Malakite, huddled and crouched, as he had seen her on the day of the Fair.

Making no attempt this time to restrain his thoughts, he discovered, as he gave himself up to his mental disloyalty, a curious emotional phenomenon. He discovered that the peculiar glamour which had always hovered for him like a diaphanous cloud round the impersonal idea of girlhood, had concentrated itself upon the image of Christie. He plunged into a very strange aspect of his feelings, as he stood on those cobblestones and stared at those dark shadows. The thought of Gerda's warmth gave him a voluptuous thrill, direct, earthy, full of honest and natural desire. But he recognized now that there hovered over the personality of this other girl something more subtle than this – nothing less, in fact, than that evasive aura of mysterious girlishness – the platonic idea, so to speak, of the mystery of all young girls, which was to him the most magical thing in the whole world. What had drawn him from the beginning to Gerda had been her wonderful beauty, and after that her original personality, her childish character. He could see Gerda's face now, at this moment, before him – he could catch the tones of her voice. He could feel how lovely she was, as he held her and caressed her. Christie's face, on the contrary, was all vague in his memory; her voice was vague; the touch of her hand was vague. It was hard to believe that he had ever had his arms about her. And yet it was Christie who had drawn into herself all those floating intimations of the mystery of a girl's soul, gathered here and there, like cowslips in green valleys, which were above everything so precious to him.

The chatter of a couple of starlings that sank to the ground behind the wall, quarrelling and scolding, brought him at last to himself. He pulled down his straw hat over his eyes and moved off homewards.

When he opened the door of Number Thirty-seven, he found Gerda covered from head to foot in a print apron, her head bound up in a green scarf, brushing the floor of their parlour.

'You can't come in now,' she said, 'unless you want to sit in the bedroom. I'll be doing the kitchen presently. It's no good your going in there.'

'Good Lord, child!' he expostulated, coughing and sneezing with exaggerated emphasis, as he propped up his stick in its accustomed corner. 'The place will be covered with dust! Why can't you let things alone? My mother would never have noticed whether the room was brushed or not. It'll take hours for all this to settle!'

She rested on her great broom and surveyed him through her cloud of sun-illumined dust-motes. Under her gaze Wolf felt his actual body stiffen into a pose of clumsy awkwardness. He experienced a sense of humiliating self-consciousness. He felt like a fool, and a treacherous fool. The gaze she fixed upon him was the kind of gaze the Olympian dawn-goddess might have fixed upon her human lover at the moment when he first betrayed the tricky and shifty mortality of his race. He never altogether forgot that experience. It made a hole in his armour which never, to the end of his life, quite closed up. Henceforth, in all his thoughts of himself, he had to allow for a weak and shaky spot in the very groundwork of his character – a weakness that nothing short of the clairvoyance of a woman could ever have laid bare!

'All right,' he murmured stupidly. 'I'll go wherever you want me to go, my dear.' And when he found that she still watched him with a sort of pondering detachment, he made a hopeless effort to read her thoughts.

Her look seemed to express resentment, superiority, irony; and yet there was tenderness in it too, and a sort of pitiful indulgence. It was one of those looks in which everything that is most obscure in the relation between two people rises to the surface and can find no expression in human words. All he knew was that this look of hers let him off and did not let him off; though what she could know of the vague, secret thoughts that had been his that day, he could not conceive!

'I'll go anywhere you like, Gerda,' he repeated lamely; and in order to break this spell, he took up a cloth duster she had laid on the back of a chair, and made a motion to dust the chimney-piece.

She relaxed her reverie at this, and resumed her work without taking further notice of him. This enabled him to turn round again, and, with the duster still in his hand, watch furtively every one of her gestures. The apron she'd twisted so tightly about her body, the bit of green muslin she had tied so quaintly around her head, threw the whiteness of her skin and the softness of her flesh into extraordinary relief. She went on vigorously wielding the broom with her rounded arms, the movements which she made displaying the loveliness of her shoulders and the suppleness of her flanks, till Wolf began to forget everything except the voluptuous fascination of looking at her.

This had not gone on very long before he became aware that she knew perfectly well exactly in what mood he was watching her. Every now and then she would straighten her body to rest her muscles, and then, as she lifted her hands to readjust the green muslin at the back of her head, the contours of her young breasts under the tight-fitting apron assumed the nobility of Pheidian sculpture. Whenever she did this she glanced at him under dreamy, abstracted eyelids, and she seemed to know well that what of all things he wanted most at that moment was just to make rough, reckless, self-obliterating love to her. And she seemed to know, too, that if she let him do that, just then, some indescribable advantage she had won over him would be altogether lost. Across an unfathomable gulf she shot these glances at him, the thick dust-gendered sun-motes flashing and gyrating between them like the spilled golden sands of some great overturned hour-glass.

Under the pressure of his conflicting feelings, Wolf's heart contracted within him; and the pride of his threatened life-illusion gathered about it, like broken bubbles of quicksilver gathering against the sides of a globe of crystal.

At last, throwing down the duster, he sprang towards her, driven by the blind, unconscious cunning of a predatory animal and by sheer, exasperated desire. But the girl slipped away from him, laughing like a hunted oread, and, lifting her great broom between them, escaped round the edge of the parlour table, from which she had removed the cloth. Red in the face now, and breathing hard and fast, he pursued her obstinately; and they both ran, panting and hot, round and round that polished expanse of wood, that mocked him like a shining shield. In her flight she dropped the broom, and he in his clumsy pursuit stumbled and almost fell over it.

Then he gave up; because, in a single flash of the dark-lantern of his self-esteem, he saw this whole incident between them just as Bob Weevil would have seen it, had he been pressing his inquisitive face against their window-pane. But as they stood there, stock-still, panting like two animals and staring at each other across the polished wood, it came into his head that if there had been nothing more subtle than that table between them, this game of theirs would have been full of a rich delight for both of them, Bob Weevil or no Bob Weevil!

Heavily he drew his breath, watching the tiny drops of perspiration on her forehead, and her panting bosom. 'She's a complete stranger to me!' he said to himself, with a puzzled sigh.

'You'll never catch me like that, Wolf,' gasped Gerda, with a melodious chuckle; 'so you'd better give up and admit you're beaten.'

But he thought to himself: 'She thinks she's acting the naughty child. She thinks she's ruffled my dignity. She thinks I'm a pompous ass, who can't play naturally with a girl in that sort of way.' He moved from the table, and, throwing himself into a wicker chair, lit a cigarette. 'But I could, I could,' he thought, '*if only* – oh, damn all this business of loving girls! It's getting out of my control; it's getting too much for me!'

Through their open window came the clear, ringing notes of the thrush in the ash tree, along with that curious scent of honeysuckle mixed with pigs' dung which was their familiar atmosphere. She, too, heard the thrush, and, balancing the broom against a chair, walked to the window and leaned against the side of it, her profile toward him.

'What would I feel,' he said to himself, 'if she started whistling her blackbird-song now?'

But Gerda displayed no desire for whistling. Her face looked pale and a little sad; and leaning there, with her forehead resting upon one of her bare arms as it lay along the woodwork of the window, she seemed to be lost in concentrated thought.

Wolf felt a sudden longing to go across to her and comfort her – comfort her about those errant feelings of his own that it was impossible to believe she had intercepted in their secret passage through his brain! He couldn't, surely, at that moment, announce to her Darnley's plan?

What he actually did was neither to go up to her nor to tell her about the projected visit. He rose to his feet, and said abruptly: 'Well! What about lunch, my dear?'

At this remark she lifted up her head from her arm with a jerk, dropped her hand to her side, and, giving him one quick look of unspeakable reproach, went out without a word into the kitchen.

'Damn!' he thought to himself. 'She can't be a witch! She *can't* have the power to read a person's thoughts! Besides, what *did* I think? Nothing beyond what everyone thinks sometimes; wild, crazy, outrageous nonsense! It must be her mother. Tnat old trot must have come round, after all.'

He resumed his seat in the wicker chair; but he felt too miserable even to light a cigarette.

His obscure distress swathed every one of the thrush's notes with a thick soot-coloured wrapping, so that they flapped at him like so many black flags. On the gusts of hedge scent and ditch scent his discomfort rose and fell, rocking him up and down in swart desolation.

'I wish I'd gone straight up to her at the window just now,' he said to himself. 'I can't bear to have her looking like that. Christ saw a man under a fig tree, or whatever it was; and I suppose a girl can see a man under a lime tree and read his thoughts like a map!'

He threw off his gloom as well as he could, and walked slowly into the kitchen. There he found her absent-mindedly laying the table for a meal of bread and cheese. He mechanically started helping her, getting out the knives and forks from the dresser-drawer and uncorking a bottle of beer.

When the meal was ready she untied her apron, removed the muslin from her head, washed her hands at the sink, and then, instead of taking her place opposite him, stood wavering and helpless in the middle of the room.

'I think I'll go out for a breath of air,' she announced. 'I must have swallowed too much dust. I'm not hungry.'

Wolf had already taken his seat; and, as she spoke, instead of moving away from him, as her remark suggested, she made a queer little helpless movement towards him. This time he *did* know what to do. He jumped up and sprang towards her, and hugged her tightly to his heart, overcoming her weak resistance, pressing her cheek, now quickly wet with tears, against his own. They remained thus for some seconds, with their arms round each other, but without a word, leaving the parlour clock and the incorrigible thrush to deal as they pleased with the passing of time.

At length he withdrew his clasp, and, making her sit down at the table, filled her glass with foaming ale.

The mellowness of the drink, combined with the obvious sincerity of his embrace, seemed to drive away the unhappy mood that obsessed her. She turned to the meal before them and began eating with relish. As they ate they talked quietly of what they would prepare for his mother's tea. Wolf found it wise at present to say nothing of Mrs. Torp.

When they were satisfied, however, and after he had handed her a cigarette – for it always amused him to see the childishly incompetent way Gerda smoked – he plunged boldly into the matter of their visit to the bookseller's shop. With one part of his heart he wished this project at the devil; but he said to himself it would be absurd to disappoint Darnley.

'If you're willing not to wash up and not to dress till we get back, we could easily go for just an hour. We really owe Christie a visit; and Darnley's being there makes an excuse.'

'Why ought we to go to Christie's? She ought to come and see us!'

'Gerda, you know how it is! You know what she's like. Besides, we've only asked her that once, when Bob and Lobbie were here. Let's go now; there's a dear girl! We'll have plenty of time to get cleaned up before tea.'

Gerda seemed to struggle with herself for a moment; and then she yielded with the most charming grace. 'All right,' she said, getting up; 'only we must run in to Pimpernel's on the way.'

Wolf's spirits rose high as they left the house. He chuckled sardonically in his heart at his own elation. 'The truth must be,' he said to himself, 'that I'm simply infatuated with both of them – that I want to snatch at Christie and yet not lose my hold on my sweet Gerda.'

The sight of the shop-girl in Pimpernel's, however, brought down his happiness a great many pegs. He had completely forgotten Mrs. Torp.

But he said nothing till they were well out of the shop, and well on their way down High Street. Then he began: 'Oh, I met your mother this morning, Gerda. We talked a bit, and I can't remember how it came about, but she went off finally with the idea that I'd asked her to tea this afternoon. And I'm afraid I didn't mention to her that my mother's coming; so we'd better be prepared for her turning up.'

The effect of this information was startling. Gerda drew her arm away from him and stopped dead-still where they were, which was in front of a butcher's shop; and they let the afternoon marketers jostle past them unheeded.

'You ... have asked ... mother ... to tea!' she gasped; and he was staggered at the dismay upon her face.

'Well?' he said, pulling her into the butcher's porch to avoid the crowd. 'It won't be so very awful will it? My mother can be adaptable and decent enough at a pinch.'

Gerda looked at him with such flashing eyes that he drew back as if she had hit him.

'Are you mad, Wolf?' she whispered hoarsely. 'I can't understand you to-day! What's the matter with you? You rush off without a word this morning. You come back looking as if you'd met a ghost. You drag me out here to see your friend, who wants

me no more than a cat! And now *this*, on the top of everything!
It's too much! I tell you it's too much! I'm going home.' And
suiting her action to her words, she broke away from him and
began rapidly retracing her steps.

Wolf ran after her and caught her by the arm.

'Gerda! Gerda darling!' he cried, regardless of the people who
were passing them. 'I can't bear this. Let me come back with
you. I don't care a damn about seeing Christie!'

'I won't have you come with me, Wolf. I won't! I won't! Do
you want me to make a scene in the street? Go to Christie's, I tell
you! That's where you belong. I've known you wanted to go
to her ever since she came that day with the boys. Go! Go! Go!
I *won't* have you with me!' And she started off almost at a run, her
face white and her eyes dazed and staring.

Wolf remained motionless and stood watching her while long
minutes passed over his head. It seemed impossible that that
should be his Gerda, going off in a rage! But even as he stood
hesitating, her figure disappeared among the people.

He turned wearily round then and resumed his walk down the
street in absent-minded gloom. He hardly knew what he was doing;
but he had a vague idea of wandering about the streets for a time,
and then returning to Preston Lane. His feet carried him, however,
steadily on till he found himself opposite the bookseller's shop.

'In for a penny, in for a pound,' he said to himself. And then
the thoughts which he believed at that moment were what
dominated his action formed themselves in his brain into some
such words as these: 'I've absolutely no heart for seeing Christie
now, or Darnley either! But I suppose it would be an absurd
piling up of misunderstandings if I disappointed them.'

Grasping the handle of his stick tightly in his hand, and seeing
Gerda's stricken face and wild, tearless stare in the very midst of
the doorway, he entered the shop.

He found the old man amidst a pile of books, murmuring with
bent head over a volume bound in vellum, which he was showing
to a customer, evidently a stranger to the place. Mr. Malakite
did not hear him enter, and Wolf found himself looking with a
queer interest at that bowed back and grizzled head. What did
it feel like, as the days went on, to know that one possessed, only
five miles away, a child like Olwen, the daughter of a daughter?
Did the old man ever see Olwen? Did he know anything of the
child's thoughts? Did he want to know anything? A chance
movement made by the customer brought Wolf now into the

bookseller's vision. A startled look passed for a second over the old man's face, but he betrayed no other sign of embarrassment. 'Good afternoon, Mr. Solent,' he said quietly. 'Have you come to see me or to see Miss Malakite?' And then, without waiting for an answer: 'You'll find her in the room upstairs. Mr. Otter has just gone.'

Wolf passed through the shop, and, hurriedly running up the little staircase, knocked at Christie's door. The effect upon him of this unexpected news of Darnley's departure was something beyond what he could possibly have foreseen. The stricken face of Gerda vanished completely, and Gerda herself became what his mother was, or what Miss Gault was, or what his father's grave was – one of the fixed landmarks in his life's landscape, but no longer the centre of his life. That hidden drum, which was neither exactly in his heart nor exactly in the pit of his stomach, beat so loudly as he waited at Christie's door, that it seemed as if that oblong shape of discoloured wood, the very markings of which were voluble, were ready to open now upon something completely new to his experience. That word of the old man, 'Mr. Otter has gone,' kept repeating itself in his mind as he waited. 'Mr. Otter has gone. Mr. Otter has gone.' The phrase became a floating cloud of tremulous expectation.

When Christie did open the door, and they had taken each other's hand, Wolf felt as if he had been doing nothing all his life but wait for this moment. He had the feeling that the man and girl who now proceeded to utter broken and fragmentary common-places to each other were acting as automatic figures behind whose gestures two long-separated spirits were rushing together.

Several seconds passed before Christie had the power to make a move to find a chair for herself or to give a sign for him to be seated; but when he did sink down at last, still talking of anything that came into his head, a sense of such relief swept into his soul that it was as if some spear-head, that had been in his flesh without his knowing it, for days and weeks, had suddenly been pulled out.

And then, without the least disturbance of the atmosphere of that small room, he suddenly found that those two nodding masks had vanished into thin air, and that there was no barrier of any sort left between the real Wolf and the real Christie. Naturally and easily he found himself taking for granted this strange new discovery of what was between them. He thought within himself: 'She knows everything. I'll leave everything to her.' And he suddenly discovered that he was talking freely and openly about

231

all the people of his life, and about Gerda, too. He discovered that to talk to Christie was like talking to himself or thinking aloud. And he recalled how he had been struck, the very first time they met, by this ease and naturalness with which the lightest thought flowed back and forth between them.

And all the while, even as he was whimsically telling her about the unlucky tea-party arranged for that afternoon, the contour of her half-averted face bending over a piece of needlework she had blindly taken up, and the way her instep looked with the thin leather strap of her shoe across it, gave him a sensation completely different from anything he had ever known before. What he really felt was that this was the first feminine creature with whom he had ever been left alone. In comparison with this diffused and thrilling feeling, permeating everything around them, his amorousness for Gerda seemed like playful lust, directed toward some beautiful statue. The slender little figure before him, with those thin hands and those touchingly thin legs, drew into her personality, at that moment, every secret of girlhood that had ever troubled him. Coming to him like the fragrance of wood-mosses to a city-dweller, the consciousness that this dream-like figure was really alive and tangible seemed to melt his bones within him. Those mystic syllables, 'a girl,' 'a young girl,' had always remained at the back of his mind like a precious well-watered flower-bed, but a bed empty of any living growth. Nothing, he now knew, in his life with Gerda had stirred the earth of that mystic bed. But here, in the centre of that bed, was a living, breathing plant, making everything around it enchanted and transparent by the diffused loveliness of its presence. This passive entity in front of him, with her honey-pale oval face, her long eyelashes, her thin legs, her faintly-outlined childish figure, was the only true, real, actual living girl in all the earth.

The minutes slipped by, and Wolf found himself, to his surprise, even talking to her about Olwen. So far from this extraordinary topic agitating her, she seemed to find a deep relief in speaking of it.

'Were you old enough to realize what was going on between them?' Wolf asked her at last.

Christie nodded her head and smiled a little. 'The odd thing is,' she said gently, 'that there never seemed to me anything strangely unnatural in it. I don't think mother ever was the right person for father. I think from her earliest childhood there was a peculiar link between him and my sister.'

'But it killed your mother, didn't it?' murmured Wolf.

Christie was silent for a moment, a queer, pondering frown on her face.

'I don't think so,' she said in a low voice. 'Everyone said so; but I don't believe it. I think it had begun long before that. It wasn't *she* who did it.'

These last words were hardly audible.

Wolf pressed her.

'Who did it, then?'

Christie looked at him gravely.

'Do you believe in spirits?' she asked.

He laughed a little.

'Oh, no more than in anything else!' he said.

'My mother was Welsh,' she went on. 'She used to tell us the wildest stories about her ancestors. Once she actually told us she was descended from Merlin. Merlin's mother was a nun. Did you know that, Wolf?'

'No wonder you're a bit inhuman,' he said. And then, after a pause: 'Did you and your sister write to each other after they sent her away? Was she unhappy about Olwen?'

Christie's brown eyes became for a minute fixed upon vacancy, as if she were scrutinizing some far-away mental image. When she turned them upon him, however, they had an angry and yet humorous gleam.

'I sent her money to come back,' she said. 'I would have had her here in spite of them. Her last letter – I'll show it to you one day – was full of excitement. If I'd been as old as I am now, they should never have sent her away.'

'Did Selena Gault do it? asked Wolf.

The girl nodded. 'She and Mr. Smith. They had the law on their side.' She paused and drew a long breath. 'Law or no law,' she cried passionately, with flushed cheeks, 'if I'd been older I'd have stopped them! I was too young,' she added.

Wolf got up from his seat and stood regarding her. Every aspect of her figure, every flicker upon her face, gave him the feeling that he was regarding a young aspen tree, porous to wind-blown alternations of light and shadow.

'It's wonderful to be able to talk freely to anyone as I can with you . . . now we're alone.'

'I sent Darnley away,' was all she said.

These words of hers hung suspended in the air between them. They were so sweet to Wolf that he felt unwilling to make the least response. He just allowed them to evaporate, syllable by syllable into the midsummer warmth of that pleasant room. Christie's eyelids drooped over the piece of sewing she held in her hands, and he noticed that she was turning this strip of muslin over and over between her fingers, smoothing it out upon her lap, first one side and then the other. The poignancy of her shyness increased his awareness of the suspense between them; and to loosen the spell he turned his head a little and glanced at the mantelpiece, on which was a china bowl, full of bluebells, late, long-stalked primroses, and pink campions and meadow-orchids. His own mind kept beating itself against the unknown – against that fatal *next moment* which drew to itself the dust-motes of the air, the scent of the wild flowers, the warm wind blowing in through the open window.

'Will she let me make love to her? Will she let me?' was the burden of his thought; and as he stared at that bunch of flowers, especially at one solitary bluebell that hung down over the brim of the white bowl and had gathered a tinge of faint rose-carmine upon its hyacinthine bloom, he felt as though the 'to be or not to be' of that tense moment depended upon chance as inscrutable, as fluct-uating, as the light, falling this way, falling that way – light and shadow wavering together – upon that purple-blue at the bowl's edge.

Never had he been more aware of the miracle of flower-petals, of the absolute wonder of this filmy vegetable fabric, so much older, just as it is so much more lovely, in the history of our planet than the flesh of beasts or the feathers of birds or the scales of fishes!

The girl's words, 'I sent Darnley away,' seemed to melt into that wild-flower bunch she had picked and placed there; and the pallor of the primroses, the perilous, arrowy faintness of their smell, became his desire for her; and the rough earth-mould freedom of the campion-stalks, with their wood-sturdy pinkbuds, became the lucky solitude she had made for him!

'Will she let me make love to her?' The longing to risk the first movement towards his purpose struggled now in his mind with that mysterious restraint, so tenuous and yet so strong, of the girl's obscure embarrassment.

'Did you pick those flowers yesterday?' he broke out suddenly; and he was secretly surprised at the loudness of his own voice.

'The day before,' she murmured; and then, without closing her mouth, which, with the droop of her under lip, took on an almost vacant look, she frowned a little, as she fixed her steady gaze full upon him.

His own eyes plunged once more into the green-shadowed depths of that midsummer nosegay. Its pale primroses seemed to sway in the wind over their crumpled leaves, as they would have done where she had actually picked them among the wood rubble and the fungus growths of their birthplace. The moist bluebell-stalks, so full of liquid greenness beneath their heavy blooms, seemed to carry his mind straight into the hazel-darkened spaces where she had found them. These also belonged to the embarrassment of that figure beside him. These also, with the cool greenery of the sturdy campions, were the very secret of that 'next moment,' which floated now, with the mocking sun-motes, untouched and virginal in the air about them.

Wolf knew well enough the peculiar limitations of his own nature. He knew well enough that any great surge of what is called 'passion' was as impossible to him as was any real remorse about making love. What he felt was an excitement that trembled on the margin – on the fluctuating fine edge – between amorous desire for the slim frame of this mysterious girl and the thrilling attraction of unexplored regions in her soul.

His feeling was like a brimming stream between reedy banks, where a wooden moss-covered dam prevents any spring-flood, but where the water, making its way round the edge of the obstacle, bends the long, submerged grasses before it, as it sweeps forward.

Two images troubled him just a little – Gerda's white, tense face as it had looked when she left him on the street, and, with this, a vague uncomfortable memory of the figure on the Waterloo steps. But, in his intensely heightened consciousness of this 'suspended' moment, he deliberately steered the skiff of his thought away from both those reefs.

Suddenly he found himself risen from his seat and standing against the mantelpiece! He lifted the flowers to his face; and then, putting down the bowl, he inserted his fingers in it, pressing them down between the stalks into the water. He noticed that the water felt warm to his touch, like the water of a sun-warmed pool; and the fantastic idea came into his head that by making this gesture he was in some occult way invading the very soul of the girl who had arranged them there. Christie may or may not have read his thoughts. At any rate, he now became aware that she was standing beside him, and with deft, swift touches was correcting the rough confusion he had made in her nosegay.

'The bluebell-scent is the one that dominates,' he murmured. 'You smell them, and see if I'm not right!'

As she leaned forward, he allowed his hand to slide caressingly down her side, drawing her slender body, with a scarcely-perceptible pressure, against his own.

His heart was beating fast now, and a delicious predatory thrill was shivering through his nerves. Christie made not the least attempt to extricate herself from his caresses. She permitted him to bend her slim body this way and that way in his wanton excitement. But when he kissed her, she bent her neck so far round that it was her cheek and not her lips he kissed; and soon after that she slipped away from him and sank down exhausted in her former seat.

The look she gave him now, as they stared at each other, confused and out of breath, was completely inscrutable to him.

'You're not annoyed with me, Christie?' he panted.

There was a flicker of anger in her eyes at this.

'Of course not,' she answered. 'What do you take me for? I'm not as mean as that. I'm not a puritanical fool.'

'Well, then . . . well, then?' he muttered, approaching her chair and standing over her.

'I'm not one least bit annoyed with you,' she repeated.

The faint flush that had now appeared in her cheeks, and the complicated wistfulness of her expression, disarmed and enchanted him. He stooped down to her and stroked with the tips of his fingers the white blue-veined skin under her lace wristbands; but as he looked at her now, there was a certain virginal detachment about her thin ankles and about those lace-ruffled hands which irritated and provoked him by its inhuman remoteness.

'You puzzle me completely,' he remarked, returning rather awkwardly to his former seat and surveying her with a humorous frown.

She lifted up her head from her work. 'Well? Why not? We haven't known each other very long.'

Her words released his pent-up irritation.

'You make me feel funny, Christie,' he said. 'As if we'd lost each other in a wood.'

She held her head very high at this and her eyes grew defiant.

'I know I'm no good at these things, Wolf. I never have been. Girls are supposed to carry off moments like this. I don't know how they do it. I seem to be completely lacking in that sort of tact.'

His irritation increased as he found it impossible to follow her thought.

'Tact?' he re-echoed sarcastically. 'Good Lord! Tact is the last thing I want from *you.*'

She spoke gravely now, but with evident vexation.

'What's the use of talking like this, Wolf? It's growing only too clear that we don't understand each other.'

His only retort to this was once more to murmur the word 'tact' with a grim iteration.

Her brown eyes looked really angry now.

'Why are men so stupid?' she cried. 'When I said *that*, I meant pretending something that wasn't my real self. It's because I've been absolutely natural with you that you've got angrv with me.'

They were both silent after this, and Wolf stared at the half-open window, through which the summer wind was blowing into the room in little eddying gusts. Christie took up her sewing; and the stir of her thin fingers and the waving of the light curtains were the only movements in that flower-scented air.

By slow degrees, as he surreptitiously watched her, the harmony of his mind began to come back; and with this harmony there came in upon him from all that green West-country landscape stretching away toward the Severn on one side and toward the Channel on the other, a sort of dumb, inarticulate reproach. What were they doing, he and this girl, who were, as he well divined, so exquisitely adapted to understand each other, letting themselves be divided by such straws, such puffballs of difference?

From fading cuckoo-flowers by the banks of the Lunt, from brittle mother-of-pearl shells, wet and glittering on the Weymouth sands, from the orange-speckled bellies of great newts in Lenty Pond, there came to him, between those waving curtains, a speechless protest. Brief was his life ... brief was Christie Malakite's life. ... Times like this at best would be rare. He could see himself returning to his tea-party and letting it all go! He could see Christie pouring out tea for her father and letting it all go! Perhaps – such was his pride and such was hers – this June afternoon, which might have been, but for this trivial discord, as perfect as a green bough, would stand out in his memory peeled and jagged, its sap all running out, its leaves drooping.

'Forgive me, Christie,' he said gravely. 'Please forgive me and don't think any more about it.'

The girl looked up from her work, her hands folded in her lap.

'You don't mean,' she said slowly, 'because of *that?*'

Her nod of the head in the direction of the mantelpiece, where he had first caressed her, made clear to him what her words implied.

He got up from his chair and stood in front of her, looking down at her lifted face.

'No,' he said. 'I didn't mean because of that. I meant because we misunderstood each other; which was all my fault.'

Christie began to smile. 'I'm not prudish or unfeeling in things like that,' she said. 'But I've a queer nature, Wolf. I love the romance of being in love, and I like you, Wolf, better than anyone I've ever met; and I like you to make love to me. It's only . . . it's only that – with the life I've had and the mother I had – I seem to have none of an ordinary girl's feelings in these things.'

Wolf began pacing up and down the room.

'I'm queer myself, Christie,' he said after a pause, stopping once more in front of her. 'So there we are! It appears that we're a fair pair! And if you want to know what I feel at this moment, I'll tell you. I feel deliciously happy. You are a witch, Christie, and I don't wonder your mother maintained she was descended from Merlin. I feel I could tell you every secret thought I have in the world. And so, by God, I will! It's an incredible chance that I should have found you.'

He threw his cigarette into the fire and walked to the window.

'What a view you've got here!' he said. 'That's the corner of Babylon Hill, isn't it?'

The window was already open at the top; but he pulled it down as far as it would go, and leaned out of it, looking across the entanglement of slate roofs to the green incline beyond.

'The wind's north-east, isn't it?' he remarked.

She got up and came over to him and stood beside him, and presently he felt her fingers slip into his own.

'North-north-east,' she said; and these words, when he thought of them afterwards, brought back every flicker of his feelings, as he stood stiffly there clutching her hand.

'Where does that lane go?' he asked. 'Do you see what I mean? That narrow little one below those Scotch firs.'

'Over there?' the girl questioned. 'To the left of Poll's Camp, do you mean?'

'Yes . . . there . . . just there . . . where that clump of bushes is!'

'That's Gwent Lane,' she answered. 'And it leads to a whole maze of lanes further on. I'm fond of going to the Gwent Lanes. You hardly ever meet anyone there. It's as if they had been designed to keep traffic away and strangers away. Sometimes on summer days when father doesn't want me, I take my lunch and a book and stay in the Gwent Lanes all day. I often never meet a soul.'

She was silent for a second or two; and he realized that a crowded mass of personal memories was flowing through her mind.

'Some lovely afternoons I've had,' she went on, 'sitting with my back to a gate and looking at the hedge-parsley. When the corn's yellow and the poppies are out, I always sit inside the field, with my parasol over my book. I can smell the peculiar bitter smell now of the elder leaves behind me.'

She drew her fingers away from him and made of her two hands a support for her chin upon the woodwork of the open window. Wolf thought this chin of hers was the smallest he had ever seen. He, too, remained silent, thinking of similar memories of his own, secret and solitary and personal; and he was astonished to note how natural it seemed to both of them, this deliberate indulgence in egoistic recollections.

'North-north-east, did you say?' His voice sounded irrelevant even to his own ears. In some queer way he felt as if he had been sharing these furtive physical memories with the girl at his side. He even felt as if their having shared them had been a kind of love-making more subtle and delicate than any erotic dalliance.

He felt as if he could share with this elfin creature a thousand feelings that no other person could possibly understand – share with her all those profoundly physical sensations – and yet mystical, too – that made up the real undercurrent of his whole life.

'She would understand my "mythology," ' he said to himself. 'No one but she would; no one!' And then he thought: 'I believe my life is going to open out now, as if I really had some invisible tutelary Power directing me!'

They turned away simultaneously from the window, and once more sat down.

'Do you ever feel,' he said, 'as if one part of your soul belonged to a world altogether different from this world – as if it were completely disillusioned about all the things that people make such a fuss over and yet were involved in something that was very important?'

She looked straight into his face. 'I wouldn't put it like that,' she said. 'But I've always known what it was to accept an enormous emptiness round me, echoing and echoing, and I sitting there in the middle, like a paper doll reflected in hundreds of mirrors.'

Wolf screwed up his eyes and bit his under lip.

'You haven't been as happy in your mind as I've been in *my* mind,' he said with a kind of wistfulness; 'but I often feel as if I were unfairly privileged . . . as if some invisible god were unjustly favouring me . . . quite beyond my deserts.'

'I don't think you're as favoured as you fancy you are,' said Christie, with the ghost of a smile. But Wolf went on:

'Do you know, Chris, I think I'm especially favoured in my scepticism. I'm sceptical about the reality of everything; even about the reality of Nature. Sometimes I think that there are several "Natures" . . . several "Universes," in fact . . . one inside the other . . . like Chinese boxes. . . .'

'I know what you mean,' said the young girl hurriedly; and her eyes, as she looked at him, grew luminous with that indescribable excitement of mental sympathy that can bring tears from something deeper than passion.

Wolf, as he received this intimation, said to himself: 'I can think aloud with her. Perhaps one day I'll tell her about my "mythology"!' And there came over him, like a warm, enveloping undertide in which great crimson seaweeds were swaying, an unutterable sense of happiness. 'Oh, I hope Gerda is all right!' he thought. And then, with a concentrated effort of his will, as if he were addressing a host of servile genii: 'I *command* that Gerda shall be all right!'

It occurred to him at that moment, with a humorous force, that his father wouldn't have been a man to allow such scruples as these to impinge upon his mind at such a juncture.

'Had you any idea,' he said suddenly, 'that Mattie wasn't Albert Smith's child?'

'I soon saw the likeness to you, anyway,' Christie replied evasively, 'the first day father brought you to see me.'

'I like Mattie so much,' he went on; 'but her resemblance to me can't be said to improve her looks. Has anyone ever made love to her, do you think?'

Christie laughed. 'Well, *you* must be nice to her, anyway, Wolf dear, to make up in case they haven't.'

'I should be afraid of Miss Gault's sending her off to Australia!' he said with a chuckle, and then felt curiously relieved to find that the grossness of this rather clumsy jest did not shock his companion. 'Nothing shocks her,' he said to himself; and his mind took a long flight to his years in London, where, except for his mother, there was no one to whom he could have talked as he had done this afternoon.

'Well, I must be off,' he said, rather wearily, when these thoughts had finished their circle and had sunk down in the manner of birds on a bough. 'I've got an uncomfortable home-coming before me, what with one thing and another.'

'Don't make too much of it,' she said, opening the door for him and holding both handles of it with her hands, so as to avoid any definite farewell. 'Gerda will be so thankful to have got through it, that when your two mothers leave she'll be radiant again.'

'I hope she won't be too radiant *before* they leave,' retorted Wolf grimly. 'I don't want many repetitions of this particular tea-party.'

She kept the door open till he was half-way downstairs, and they nodded rather dolorously at each other across the banisters. He heard the door shut as he entered the shop below, and a pang passed through him.

As he walked rapidly home, he found himself engaged in an imaginary dialogue with his father.

The skeleton under those obstinate plantains kept grinning mockingly in reply to every argument. 'Life is short,' said the skeleton, 'and the love of girls is the only escape from its miseries.'

'It's not so short as all that,' retorted the son, 'and in every Paradise there is a snake!'

11

THE TEA-PARTY

He found on his arrival that his mother had already appeared. To his great surprise he discovered her standing by their kitchen-stove, with Gerda's apron over her dress, helping to make the toast. He was still more surprised at the way Gerda received him. She was flushed and happy – laughing and jesting as if they had parted the very best of friends.

'How's Christie?' she asked casually. 'What do you think, Mrs. Solent, of his going off to see Miss Malakite when I've got company? I'm sure that's not what you'd approve of.'

'I don't approve of his saying nothing about that pretty frock you've got on! What do you think of it, Wolf? Do you know, when I got here, she was upstairs, crying her lovely eyes out? And all because she thought she hadn't a proper dress to welcome her grand mother-in-law in! We soon settled *that* little job, didn't we, my dear?' And Wolf beheld, to his amazement, his mother putting one of her strong arms caressingly about Gerda's waist, and Gerda responding to this with a lingering provocative glance, such as he himself was wont to receive when the girl was in her most docile mood.

'I heard her crying up there in her room,' went on the elder woman, 'and I ran straight up, and there she was, pretty as a picture in her white shift, and all the bed covered with frocks! She says she's had this one since she was sixteen; but it suits her perfectly, doesn't it, Wolf?'

Wolf surveyed the girl gravely. She wore a long, straight muslin dress, with short sleeves, creamy-white and covered with pale little roses. Never had she looked so enchanting.

'You're certainly a good lady's-maid, mother,' he said solemnly.

'She's told me you're expecting another mother this afternoon,' continued Mrs. Solent, releasing Gerda and proceeding to arrange the slices of toast upon a plate. 'Now then, where's that loaf? I'll cut the bread-and-butter.'

It became Wolf's destiny to stand for the next quarter of an hour, figuratively speaking, 'upon one leg,' while he watched what seemed to resemble the most piquant of flirtations going on between these two.

The tea-tray was 'laid' at last, in the most approved manner, on that very parlour-table round which he had pursued the girl in such troubled agitation so short a time before; and Mrs. Solent, Gerda's apron removed, showed herself in the most fashionable of all her garden-party gowns. Gerda seemed unable to keep her eyes off her, and kept touching with the tips of her fingers first one elegant frill and then another, hovering about her like a slim white butterfly round a purple orchid.

'There's mother!' she cried at length. 'Fetch the kettle, Wolf!'

The countenance of Mrs. Torp was as a book in which one could 'read strange matters,' as she contemplated the scene before her. Wolf, with the teapot in one hand and the kettle in the other, vociferated a boisterous welcome, drowning the politer words of his mother.

Gerda, having removed Mrs. Torp's tasselled cloak, sat her plumb-down at the table, straightening with a familiarly affectionate jerk the ribboned bonnet which adorned her head.

'Don't 'ee fidget wi' me old hat, Gerdie,' murmured the visitor. ''Tis a very good hat, though maybe 'tain't as aleet as some folks can afford. So thee be Mr. Solent's mummy, be 'ee? Well, and 'a favour'n about the cheeks, 'sknow! A body could reason there was some blood twixt ye; though in these which-way times 'tis hard to speak for sure.'

'Well, we must do our best not to quarrel, Mrs. Torp, as they say all mothers do,' threw out Mrs. Solent briskly, watching with some anxiety the unusual amount of sugar that Gerda was placing at the bottom of all the teacups.

'How much milk, Mrs. Solent?' enquired the girl lightly. 'I don't expect our Blacksod milk is as good as yours at King's Barton.'

This society tone was so obviously put on to impress the young lady's mother, that Mrs. Solent hadn't the heart to explain, till the time for her second cup, that she couldn't bear sugar. She swallowed the sweet mixture in hurried gulps; and Wolf chuckled to see her trying to take away the taste by rapid mouthfuls of bread-and-butter.

'How be thee's schoolmasterin' getting along, Mr. Solent? My old man – that be our Gerdie's dad, ma'am – do always say them Grammar boys be above theyselves, what with one thing and t'other. He cotchit two on 'em, the last buryin' 'ee had, stealing

243

of they bones. Not that they were proper human-like bones . . . if 'ee understand . . . for 'ee do always bury *them* religious-deep. They were hosses' bones, seems so, from what 'ee do calculate. But they were more impident, them Grammar boys, when 'ee were arter they, than if they'd been the bones of King Balaam.'

'What's Lobbie been doing lately, mother?' enquired Gerda, feeling vaguely conscious that the subject of bones, whether human or otherwise, was inappropriate at that moment.

'Lob, do 'ee say? Thee may well ask what Lob be doing, the young pert-mouthed limb! He be bringing his dad's hoar hairs down to Bedlam, and mine wi 'em, *that's* what the owl's pellet be doing!'

Gerda hurriedly enquired in a ringing voice whether Mrs. Solent wanted any cake. 'Pimpernel hadn't any fresh kinds except this. I expect you are so used to London confectionery, Mrs. Solent – '

But the visitor seemed more interested in her fellow parent's conversation than in anything else just then.

'Sons are troublesome beings, Mrs. Torp,' she said, 'but it's nice to have them.'

'What *has* Lobbie been doing?' enquired Wolf, heedless of Gerda's frowns.

'He's been going over with that imp of Satan, Bob Weevil, to Parson Valley's. His dad told 'en he'd lift the skin from's backside if he did it; but he was see'd, only last night, out there again.'

'It sounds very innocent, Mrs. Torp, visiting a clergyman,' remarked the lady.

'Innocent!' cried Gerda's mother indignantly. 'Innocent thee own self, though I do say it! 'Tis pagan deviltries, worse nor Paul on Corinthians. I tell 'ee, they do play blasphemous play-actings out there, same as Lot's wife were salted for.'

'Miracle-plays, is it?' asked Wolf.

'How do I know what they call 'en? 'Tis small matter for the name. Wold Dimity, up to Otters', told I that one girt gummuk of a lad dressed 'isself up as Virgin Mary. If that bain't a blasphemous cantrip, I'd like to know what be!'

'I expect Mrs. Solent knows better than any of us, mother, what's going on out at King's Barton,' put in Gerda diplomatically.

'I did hear something about a miracle-play,' said the visitor lightly; 'but if the subject's a teasing one, for heaven's sake let's drop it! I think it was Mr. Urquhart who mentioned it to me;

and if I remember right he took rather the same view of it as Mrs. Torp.'

'Squire Urquhart ain't got so much standing his own self wi' decent folk for *him* to be top-lofty,' remarked the other. 'They do tell down our way 'twas that man's wicked tempers and sech-like, what drove poor young Redfern into's grave; but maybe, as darter says, you know more'n we, ma'am, about King's Barton ways. I be glad for my part that I lives in a God-fearing daily-bread town like Blacksod.'

'By the way, Wolf,' said Mrs. Solent, speaking in her most high-pitched voice, 'I met your friend Jason the other day in Lenty Lane, and we had quite a walk together. We went as far as the ridge-road to Ramsgard . . . you know? . . . by one of those little field-paths.'

'Mr. Jason, ma'am?' commented Mrs. Torp. '*I* do know he. I'd a-seen he, many a fine evenin', a-traipsin' home from Three Peewits.'

'I hope you enjoyed your walk,' said Gerda, gravely and politely, frowning at her mother.

'How did you and Jason get on?' asked Wolf. 'I somehow can't imagine you two together.'

'Well,' said Mrs. Solent, 'I can't quite tell whether my company pleased him or not. He talked most of the time about my neighbour, Roger Monk. He seems to have got into his head that the poor man spies upon him. I tried at first to disabuse him of that idea; but he got so agitated that I just let him go on. In the end he became quite charming. He recited to me a poem about a woodpecker, which I thought very pretty. He has such a nice voice when he recites, and the evening was so lovely after the rain that I really enjoyed it all very much.'

'No doubt Mr. Otter were sober as a jackdaw when 'a walked with 'ee, ma'am. I'm not saying he isn't a nice-spoken gentleman, for he is. It's not so much the drink they talk of, along of he, down where I do live, it's – '

'Oh, mother, please!' interrupted Gerda. 'Do look, mother, how nicely Mrs. Solent tied my sash!'

The girl got up from her chair and turned herself round. This gesture was evidently adored by Mrs. Solent, for she stretched out her arms and caught her by the waist and pulled her down upon her knee.

'I shall spoil your lovely dress,' Gerda cried nervously.

'You're light as a feather, you sweet thing! You're soft as swan's-down.'

'She weren't that light, ma'am, when she made herself stiff as pikestaff, on the day us bundled she down church-aisle for christening,' said Mrs. Torp. 'But she were light enough, God-sakes, when she did play carry-me-over wi' the lads!'

All this while, Wolf was pondering in his soul how it was that Nature had placed in the minds of all mothers, refined or un-refined, so large a measure of the heart of a procuress.

'And she were light enough – ' Mrs. Torp was beginning again, when Gerda, jumping up in haste, ran round the table and clapped her hand over her mouth.

'Hush, Mummy, I won't have it!' she cried.

At that moment there was a loud knocking at the front door, and Wolf went across the passage and opened it.

Bob Weevil and Lobbie hurried into the room together, their caps in their hands. The young grocer looked a little embarrassed at the scene before him, and made a stiff bow to Mrs. Solent.

'Afternoon, marm,' he muttered.

But Lobbie was quite unperturbed.

'Dad's comed home afore his time,' he cried, 'and 'a be mum-bling about his supper.'

'Shake hands with Mrs. Solent, Lob,' said Gerda severely.

But the boy had turned to his own parent.

'Mr. Valley said I was to ask you proper and right for pro-mission,' he said eagerly, 'promission for – '

'For *what*, ye staring toad?'

'Promission,' the boy went on, 'for thik girt play next Thursday. The day arter to-morrow 'tis; and all the gentry be coming. And I be John the Baptist, what lived upon honey and the honey-comb!'

'Ye'll live upon cabbage and the cabbage-stalk, ye impident sprout! I've a-heered too much of your Mr. Valley and his goings-on.'

'Mother . . . mother!' protested the unabashed Lob. But Mrs. Solent interrupted them.

'Don't you worry, Mrs. Torp. I'm going to that entertainment myself, and I'll see that this young man comes to no harm. I understand just what you feel. These clerical junketings are sometimes incredibly silly. But you can trust me. We'll keep each other in sight, won't we, Lobbie?' And she put her hand on the boy's shoulder.

'Well, of course, if you answer for him, ma'am, I reckon I must be satisfied,' grumbled the monument-maker's wife.

'Oh, I'll look after him. Won't I, Lobbie? And if Mr. Valley keeps us all up till midnight, you shall sleep at Lenty Cottage.'

Lob looked a little nervous at this prospect, but he expressed his thanks politely, and the incident appeared closed.

Meanwhile Wolf overheard the following conversation going on between Mr. Weevil and Gerda.

'Why, if that isn't the very frock you wore, Gerdie, when we went to Weymouth, that grand excursion-day, years ago!'

'Yes, it is, Bob. Fancy your remembering! Mrs. Solent made me put it on.'

'And to think of that! And to think how we climbed down those slippery steps at the ferry, and how frightened you were of the green seaweed getting on you, and how we saw sea-anemones in the pools by Sandsfoot Castle, and you couldn't abide the gun-firing out Portland-way. Think of that, Gerdie, the very same dress!'

'Do you think I'm too old to wear it now, Bob?'

'Ask me another, Gerdie! But it do make anyone feel sort of queer to see you like this. You know? It's all the things it brings up, what a person's clean forgotten.'

'You got no more memory than a pig, Bob Weevil.'

'Depends who and what and when,' was the grocer's retort.

'Well, don't you worry any more about it, Mrs. Torp,' repeated the lady in purple. 'I promise to keep Mr. Valley in order. Or if I can't, I'll get someone who can. Lob shan't make a fool of himself, or disgrace either John the Baptist or you. I quite look forward to it. We'll have a fine bit of sport together, Lobbie, you and I, flirting across the footlights!'

'How did you get over to-day, Mrs. Solent?' enquired Gerda, cutting short Mr. Weevil's memories with a furtive little movement of her hand – a movement that came as rather a surprise to Wolf, as he noted it in passing.

'Oh, Roger Monk drove me,' exclaimed Wolf's mother. 'And that reminds me . . . what's the time, my son? . . . Good Lord! I've kept the man waiting already! I must go at once. I'm to meet him at the Three Peewits.'

'I'll walk down with you, mother,' said Wolf, glad enough to get a chance of escape. 'Good-bye, Mrs. Torp. I know you'll excuse me. Don't hurry off, Bob. Why don't you keep him for supper, Gerda? And Lobbie, too, if Mrs. Torp will let him stay?'

Mother and son walked leisurely down the clattering High Street.

'She's certainly beautiful, your Gerda!' exclaimed the lady, after prolonged silence.

'She is,' admitted Wolf.

'But oh, dear! What an awful woman! Does she worry you much, my dabchick?'

'Worry me, mother? Not one little bit! I very rarely see her, you know.'

There was another long pause between them.

'What's going to happen when the History's done, Wolf?'

'It may never be done, mother! He's got really interested in it at last, thank the Lord!'

'Wolf, dear – '

'Well, mother?'

'I wouldn't let Gerda have a child for quite a long while yet.'

'No, mother.'

'I didn't know that she and this Weevil boy were such old friends.'

Wolf swung his stick. Something about the inflexible determination of his mother's profile, especially of her clear-cut chin, at that moment, roused an obscure feeling of rebellion in him.

'Why the devil not?' he cried. 'Bob's a mere kid. Gerda treats him exactly as she treats her brother.'

His voice had become high-pitched. That curious, furtive little movement of the hand, full of old familiarities, returned to him most teasingly.

'Don't talk too loud,' murmured his mother. 'We're not in Lenty Lane.'

'Why did you say that?' he asked.

'Oh, I don't know,' she said lightly. 'Don't take it too seriously. I only know from old experience that men never can be made to realize how susceptible women are except where they themselves are concerned.'

'Even when they love a person?' he enquired.

'What *is* love?' said Mrs. Solent.

He was silent; and the conversation between them took a less personal tone, till he saw her safely mounted in Mr. Urquhart's dog-cart, beside the tall man-servant.

Instead of going straight home, he walked meditatively and slowly past the Malakite bookshop, and then at a more rapid pace followed the road that led up Babylon Hill. He did not turn till, in the slanting rays of the sinking sun, he reached that corner of the ascent which he had noted from Christie's window.

Could he distinguish her house among the rest? He was not sure. The rays of the great June sun were almost horizontal, as it sank down towards Glastonbury; and it was all he could do, even with his eyes shaded by his hand, to identify the portion of the town where the bookshop was. As to seeing Christie's window, it was impossible.

Annoyed by this refusal of Nature to humour his mood, he advanced obstinately still further up the road, and finally reached the stile into the field-path that led to the turfy ramparts of Poll's Camp.

There he sat down among the tall, uncut grasses of the wayside, and allowed the double stream of memories – those connected with Poll's Camp and those connected with that invisible window below him – to contend for the mastery in his thoughts. The extraordinary thing was that all that poetry of his first encounter with Gerda seemed like something that had happened to some external portion of his nature, whereas this strange new understanding with Christie sank so deep into his being that it invaded regions of which he himself had hardly been aware.

He soon found out, as he sat there, with his back against that stile and the pungent smell of herb-Robert in his nostrils, how far this new feeling had gone.

His life had become so agitated since his arrival at Ramsgard, that now, at this moment, he felt he had more on his mind than he could disentangle. The spirit of the evening fell upon him with a burden that was mysteriously sad – sad with a multitude of gathering omens and indistinct threats. With all the evening noises around him – noises, some of them faint as the sighing of invisible reeds – he became once more conscious that between the iron-ribbed gaiety of his mother and the fixed grin of that paternal skull in the churchyard there was an ambiguous struggle going on, the issues of which remained dubious as life itself.

He found himself crying out to that irresponsible skull under the plantains; but the skull answered him with nothing but cynical mockery. He found himself turning restlessly towards his mother; but he felt that just at the point where he needed her sympathy most the very basic rock of her nature flung him contemptuously back.

On and on he sat, with that sinking sun growing redder and

redder before him, and the evening murmurs gathering in his ears; and as he sat, an immense solitude descended upon him, and he began to realize, as he had never realized before, how profoundly alone upon this planet each individual soul really is.

And with this feeling there came over him a deep, disturbing craving for Christie – a craving so intense that the vision of all the length of all the days of his life without her seemed more than he could bear. 'Only one life,' he thought to himself. 'Only one life, between two eternities of non-existence . . . and I am proposing deliberately to sacrifice in it the one thing that I really want!' He hugged his knees with tightly-clasped fingers, and stared at the red orb before him, sinking now over Christie's very roof.

For the first time in his mortal days this great diurnal spectacle seemed to his mind half-fantastic; as if this were not the real sun, the sun he had known all his life, that was descending; nor the earth he had known all his life that was thus hiding it from his eyes. 'If I do give up Christie for Gerda,' he thought, 'it will simple mean that the one unique experience destined for me out of all others by the eternal gods has been deliberately thrown away.'

He bowed his head over his knees and watched the climbing of a tiny beetle up a bending stalk of grass. 'To the universe,' he thought, 'it matters no more whether I leave Gerda for Christie than whether that beetle reaches the top of that stalk! Gerda? . . . Christie? . . . What are they? Two skeletons covered with flesh; one richly and flexibly covered . . . one sparsely and meagrely covered! Two of them . . . that is all . . . just two of them!' And then, bowing his head still lower, so that the beetle and its grass-stalk almost filled up his whole vision, he began to imagine what it would be like if he *did* make some wild, desperate move. What would happen, for instance, if he were to carry Christie to London and get some job to support them both there, hidden from all the world? Gerda would return to her parents' house. Old Malakite would get on somehow or other. His mother would . . . Well! What would his mother do? She had scarcely anything in the bank. Mr. Urquhart could hardly be expected to support her. No, it was unthinkable, impossible! The existence of his mother, her complete dependence on him, tied his hands fast and tight!

And then, with an overpowering surrender, there came upon him all his old childish clinging to that woman whose heart the licentiousness of his father had been unable to quell. He knew his own nature to be tough enough, but compared with his mother he was like an oak sapling growing in the cleft of a rock. The woman was adamant, where he was merely obstinate. Rock-smooth she was, where he was merely gnarled and knotted and earth-rooted.

'Damn!' he muttered to himself, as he watched the beetle turn back resignedly within an inch of the stalk's point, and begin a patient descent. 'Damn! It's just pure weakness and habit!'

But, oh, dear! How could he desert Gerda . . . how could he do it . . . after three lovely happy months; and without cause or reason save his own fickle madness?

Why had he married her at all? That was the whole blunder! He had married her because he had seduced her. But girls were always being seduced! *That* was no reason. No! He couldn't get out of it. He had married her because he had mistaken a mixture of lust and romance for love; and if he hadn't found Christie, he might, to the end of his days, never have discovered his mistake! Affection would have superseded lust; tenderness would have superseded romance. All would have been well. It was Christie's appearance that had changed everything; and there it was! Christie and he were bound together now, come good, come ill. But as things were, so they must remain! If his soul was Christie's, his life must go on being his mother's and Gerda's. There was no other issue.

Abruptly he lifted up his head. The sun was so low now that he could look straight into its great red circle suspended above the roofs of the town. It resembled, as he looked at it, a vast fiery tunnel, the mouth of some colossal piece of artillery, directed full against him. With screwed-up eyelids he returned the stare of this blood-red cannon-mouth; and as he fronted it, it seemed to him that a dusky figure took shape within it, a figure resembling Jason Otter's abominable idol.

There was something so atrocious in the idea of this dusky demon being there at all – being, so to say, the great orb's final *expression* as it went down – that he leaped to his feet in indignant protest. His movement brought the blood from his head, and the phantasm vanished. Slowly and inevitably, with a visible sliding descent, the red globe sank out of sight; and Wolf picked up his hat and stick. 'It must be long after eight,' he thought. 'I must go home to Gerda.'

12

THE SLOW-WORM OF LENTY

The next two months brought no outward change in the existence of Wolf and the various people of his life; but, when August arrived, all manner of strange developments, long prepared for under the surface, began to manifest themselves.

The trend of these developments began for the first time to grow clear to Wolf himself on the occasion of a small garden-party given by Mrs. Otter in her little front garden. He had exhausted a great deal of energy in an attempt to entangle his mother in a more or less harmonious conversation with Selena Gault; and it was with a queer feeling of triumph that he left these old antagonists drinking tea side by side, in their low chairs, on Mrs. Otter's lawn, to cross the grass so that he might speak to Jason.

He came upon him in the back garden in converse with old Dimity Stone, who fled precipitately into her kitchen at his approach.

Wolf was as careful not to disturb the poet's equilibrium as if he had been a leopard cajoling a nervous eland. He shuffled by his side into a narrow passage between two cucumber-frames, where they both sat down. A solitary wood-pigeon kept repeating its diapason of languid rapture from somewhere high up in the neighbouring trees. In the gravel path, quite close to where they sat, a thrush, unruffled by their presence, cracked a snail upon a broken piece of brick; and as Wolf made one desultory remark after another, to set his companion at ease, he found himself complacently squeezing with the tips of his fingers certain sticky little bubbles of tar that the heat of the afternoon sun drew forth from the warm wooden planks of the frame.

'I composed a poem last night,' said Jason Otter. 'And since you're the only person who takes the least interest in what I do, I'll repeat it to you, if no one comes round the corner.'

'I'd love to hear it,' said Wolf.

'It begins like this.' And in a voice almost as modulated as tne

wood-pigeon's own, the drooping head by Wolf's side swayed
slowly to the rhythm of the following stanza:

> The Slow-worm of Lenty curses God;
> He lifts his head from the heavy sod;
> He lifts his head where the Lenty willow
> Weeps green tears o'er the rain-elf's pillow;
> For the rain-elf's lover is fled and gone,
> And none curseth God but the Slow-worm alone.

'It's about the pond,' said Jason gravely. 'I go there sometimes
in the evening. When it's misty you can easily imagine an elf or
a nymph floating on its surface.'

'Is that all?' enquired Wolf.

'Not quite,' replied the other; 'but you probably won't like the
way it ends. It'll seem funny to you; too remote from your way of
thinking; and it *is* rather funny; but Lenty Pond is a funny place.'

'Do go on,' said Wolf.

And once more in his delicately-modulated voice the poet
began intoning:

> For the newts and the tadpoles at their play
> Laugh at the rain-elf's tear-wet pillow;
> Laugh that her lover had fled away.
> Little care they for elf or willow.
> They flash their tails to a mocking cry –
> 'Slow-worm of Lenty, prophesy!'

'That's not the end, is it?' said Wolf.

The man's head turned slightly towards him; and the one grey
eye which was visible from where Wolf sat passed through some
extraordinary change, as if a glassy film separating the outward
world from an inward abyss of desolation had suddenly melted
away.

'Do you want to hear the end?' said Jason Otter.

Wolf nodded, and the voice went on:

> But never again can God look down
> As He did of old upon country and town!
> In His huge heart, hidden all Space beyond,
> There bides the curse of Lenty Pond;
> The curse of the Slow-worm, by Lenty willow,

Who pitied the elf on her tear-wet pillow,
Her pillow woven of pond-weeds green
Where the willow's twigs made a leafy screen;
And the purple loosestrife and watercress
Whisper above her sorrowfulness.

Once more the voice paused and Wolf listened to those two persistent summer sounds, the tapping of the thrush's beak and the indescribable contentment of the wood-pigeon.

'Is there any more?' he asked. 'I like this style of writing better than what you used to read to me a month ago.'

'A person can't do more than he can,' remarked Jason Otter, while the flickering ghost of a smile came and went at the corners of his mouth. It seemed that even this indication of normal feeling was distasteful to him; for he hurriedly raised his hand in order to conceal it.

This movement of his arm made Wolf aware of the scent of incense.

'The chap's clothes must be saturated with the stuff,' he thought. 'Oh, damn!' he thought again. 'I *must* get that idol away from him.'

'By the way, Otter,' he began, 'while I think of it, don't forget what you promised on the fair-ground!'

Jason turned his head away.

'She'll be out again presently,' he remarked.

Whether this referred to the thrush that had just then flown away, or to Dimity Stone, Wolf could not tell.

'I can give you two pounds of that five pounds straight off,' he said, 'if you'll let me come in with you now and put the thing in my pocket.'

'And the other three?' cried the man, rising to his feet between the cucumber-frames and rubbing the back of his trousers with his hand.

'The other three next week,' said Wolf, thinking to himself, 'I don't care what happens, as long as I dispose of Mukalog.'

'Come on then, quick, before anyone sees!'

They hurried into the house together; and no sooner were they in the poet's room than Wolf boldly snatched at the little demon on the jade pedestal, and shoved it unceremoniously into his side pocket. Jason made a queer, stiff, formal movement of his hand towards this pocket; but when Wolf had thrown his arm roughly off, an expression of something like relief rippled down over his agitated countenance. His lips seemed to be muttering; and Wolf fancied that they were explaining to the object in the stranger's pocket that its devotee had only yielded to sheer force.

Hurriedly Wolf put down two golden sovereigns on the table. He refrained from placing them upon the empty jade pedestal. He placed them side by side, close to an edition of the works of Vaughan the Silurist.

'And now,' he cried, 'let's hear the end of that Slow-worm poem!'

'Not here, not here,' murmured the other, glancing, so Wolf imagined, with lamentable anxiety at the empty pedestal, as if at any moment seven other devils, worse than Mukalog, might take possession of it.

No sooner were they safe back at the cucumber-frame than Wolf resumed his request for the end of the Slow-worm. Leaning back with his hands clasped meekly in front of him, like a child reciting a hymn, the astonishing man obeyed him with docility:

> And the Lenty Slow-worm curses God
> For the sake of the rain-elf's pitifulness.
> He lifts his head from the watercress,
> ·He lifts his head from the quaker-grass,
> From the hoof-marks where the cattle pass,
> He lifts his head from the heavy sod,
> And under the loosestrife he curses God!
> And the newts and the tadpoles who where she lay
> Mocked her from bellies white, orange, and grey,
> Cry now to willow and water and weed,
> 'Lenty Pond had a prophet indeed!'
> For the rain-elf weeps no more to her pillow
> Woven of twigs of the weeping-willow;
> But her lover, come back to the laughing rain-elf,
> Cries, 'The Slow-worm of Lenty is God Himself!'

'Bravo!' cried Wolf. 'Thank the Lord you managed to comfort that poor girl!'

'She wasn't a girl,' said Jason, colouring a little.

'Eh? What's that?' ejaculated the other. 'How could she have a lover then?'

The poet was protected, however, from having to answer this objection by a sudden, happily-timed interruption.

Mr. Urquhart, escorting Selena Gault, came shuffling amiably towards them.

'Our two young friends in the kitchen garden, ha?' was the Squire's greeting. 'I've just been telling Miss Gault, haven't I, lady, how well you and I, Solent, get on together as fellow authors. I never got on so well with our poor dear Redfern, did I, Mr. Otter?'

Wolf was aghast at the complicated significance of the look that his employer fixed upon the agitated Jason.

'Your boots have got something nasty on them,' the poet hurriedly rapped out to Miss Gault; and before the lady could stop him, he was down on his knees on the gravel, wiping one of her shoes with a handful of grass.

'It's only manure,' he said presently, rising with a flushed face.

'Thank you, Mr. Otter, thank you very much,' said Selena Gault. 'I must have trodden on something.'

'I hope you found my mother in her best mood,' said Wolf.

Miss Gault frowned a little and then smiled on him graciously.

'Thank you for helping us to renew our old acquaintance, boy,' she said. 'But it's really Mr. Urquhart who ought to be thanked by everybody for bringing you down to us at all.'

'Thank Redfern, not me,' said the Squire, in his silkiest tone. 'It's quite an art, isn't it, Otter, this business of leaving the world conveniently?'

But Jason was occupied in picking up the bits of empty snail-shell left by the thrush.

'What do they do when there aren't any stones to break 'em on?' commented the Squire as he watched him.

Miss Gault swept them both with her formidable gaze.

'Throw those things away, Mr. Otter, please. When the life's gone that's the end.'

'Not always,' murmured the Squire. 'Not always, ha? What?'

Miss Gault lifted her eyebrows, and her distorted upper lip twitched. 'For the dead, it's the end,' she repeated sternly; 'but it's better to be dead in death than dead in life.'

'I think I'd better go and see if my mother wants me,' murmured Jason uneasily.

'I'll come with you, Otter,' said Mr. Urquhart, making a deprecating little gesture with his hand, as if brushing away Miss Gault's indiscretion.

Then he turned to Wolf. 'Be in good time to-morrow, Solent. I've got a book for you that's more racy than anything we've found yet. Malakite sent it over. The old rogue knows exactly what suits me.'

Wolf felt it hard to believe the word 'Malakite' was something that he had heard many times before quite calmly and casually. It teased his mind now that it should even be uttered by this man, whose pendulous cheek-folds seemed to him, as he looked at them, to resemble the crumpled rattles of a rattlesnake.

Conversing sympathetically with Miss Gault, now, on the harmless topic of Emma and the three cats, he led the lady back into the front garden.

Here he was presently much amused by observing Miss Gault, with the graciousness of a ducal personage, offer to drive Mrs. Solent as far as Lenty Cottage – an offer that was promptly accepted. When both women were gone, and Wolf himself had bidden his hostess good night, he was surprised to hear Jason offering to walk a little way with him towards Blacksod.

Wolf instinctively kept his hand in his side pocket as they walked, with an obstinate determination that nothing should induce him to return Mukalog to his idolater. But the poet's thoughts seemed running in a quite different direction.

'It's very difficult not to curse anyone,' Jason began, hesitating, and reddening a little, 'when a person expects you to do it. But I've got the power of joining in, so as not to annoy, while really I'm thinking just the opposite!'

To himself Wolf explained this ambiguous remark by assuming that Mr. Urquhart had been secretly propitiating 'the drunken individual at Pond Cottage' by disparaging to him his new secretary.

But the poet began again. 'I don't like the way some people egg on that young fool Weevil to boast so grandly of what lecherous things he's done. When people encourage an idiot like that, it's bad for everybody. It puts it into his head to play tricks he'd never dare to think out for himself.'

'Ho! Ho!' thought Wolf. 'What's up now? Now we're beginning to learn something really curious!'

And the poet continued, in an excited voice: 'You married people think you know everything. But no man ever knows what these girls are after; and I doubt if they know it themselves! It's like a gadfly, that first tickles them and then stings them.'

'What's like a gadfly?' enquired Wolf.

'The lust of your excellent young men, such as this worthy Bob Weevil.'

'Ah!' thought Wolf in his heart. 'Now it's coming!'

'I never myself talk of lechery to anyone,' went on the poet;

'but this Squire of yours enjoys his little jest, whether it's with a young man or a boy. I expect he's a bit afraid of you, Solent.'

'I should have supposed,' said Wolf, 'that Mr. Urquhart was too snobbish to treat a Blacksod tradesman like an equal, whatever his age was!'

'There is only one class,' said the poet, with an air of benign authority, 'where these matters are concerned.'

'So you think Mr. Urquhart has been at work encouraging our friend Weevil in some pretty little bit of mischief, eh?' said Wolf.

A look of sheer pain came into Mr. Otter's face. 'What put that into your head?' he cried. 'I've not been talking about anyone *you* know, or anyone *I* know. I've been talking about the general mass of people. A person is allowed to talk about *them*.'

'You're afraid that Roger Monk might be hiding behind that wall?'

The poet turned toward him his sorrowful grey eyes. 'I don't like to be upbraided,' he said gravely.

'I'm not upbraiding you,' protested Wolf. 'Look! There are none but very harmless people in there!'

The wall by which they were now walking was indeed the wall of the churchyard; and the idea of Death, like a flying, sharded beetle, struck them simultaneously in the face.

'I think I'll cancel our bargain, Solent,' said Jason suddenly, 'and give you back that money, and take back my piece of jade!'

It was a transformed countenance that the poet turned now to his companion. Abysmal desolation had descended upon him, and he almost whimpered as he implored Wolf to return his idol.

'It's no use, man. I tell you it's no use. If you went straight down on your knees to me I wouldn't give it up!'

Jason Otter pushed his hat back from his forehead and stood for a moment with his eyes tight shut. Wolf, who had no idea what thoughts were passing through that heavy head, clutched tightly the handle of his stick, thinking within himself: 'He's capable of anything. He's like a drug addict, and I've got his drug in my pocket!'

For a perceptible passage of time, though it may have been no more than a few seconds, they remained thus facing each other, while a group of King's Barton children, running with noisy shouts down the road, stopped and stared at them open-mouthed.

Then Wolf was aware that the man's lips, out of the middle of that eyeless mask of misery, were muttering something – something that sounded like an incantation.

'I'd better sheer off!' he thought; and as he tightened his fingers round the handle of his stick, he overheard one of the children who were looking on say to another in a whisper: 'It be only thik poor Mr. Otter, took wi' one o' they fits, look-see! T'other gent be a-going to hit he, present, 'long-side the ear-hole!'

'Well, good night, Otter!' he called out to him. 'If you don't mind I'll shog on! I've got to walk fast now, or Gerda will be worrying.'

The figure in front of him made a blind step forward like a somnambulist; and in a rapid mental vision as definite as if it were a reality, Wolf saw him fallen prone in the white dust, crying aloud for the return of the image.

'Well, good night!' he repeated brusquely; and turning on his heel, he strode off at a pace which it was not easy to keep from becoming a run.

For some distance he had an uncomfortable sensation in the back of his spine; but nothing happened. With his left hand fiercely clutching the thing in his pocket, and his right hand swinging his stick, he achieved an inglorious but effective retreat.

It was not, however, till he was nearly a mile from King's Barton that he dared to reduce his speed and take his mental bearings. Even then his disturbed fancy mistook the faint thudding of some tethered animal's hooves on the floor of a shed for the patter of Jason's steps in pursuit.

It must have been half-past six before he began to recover himself and to look about him. There was hardly a breath of wind stirring. There had fallen upon that portion of the West Country one of those luminous late-summer evenings, such as must have soothed the nerves of Romans and Cymri, of Saxons and Northmen, after wild pell-mells of advances and retreats, of alarums and excursions, now as completely forgotten as the death-struggles of mediæval hernshaws in the talons of goshawks.

The fields of wheat and barley, pearl-like and opalescent in the swimming haze, sloped upwards to the high treeless ridge along which ran the main road from Ramsgard to Blacksod. On his left, lying dim and misty, yet in some strange way lustrous with an inner light of their own, as if all the earth had become one vast phosphorescent glow-worm, rolled away from beneath that narrow lane the dew-soaked pastures of the Blackmore Vale, rising again in the distance to the uplands of High Stoy.

Wolf was tempted to rest for a while, so as to gather into some kind of focus the confused impressions of that crowded afternoon;

but he found, when he paused for a moment, leaning over a gate, that the dew-wet herbage brought to his mind nothing but one persistent image, an image calm and peaceful enough, but full of a most perilous relaxation of heart and will and spirit – the image, in fact, of a young man lying dead in a bedroom at Pond Cottage, a young man with a shrouded face, and long, thin legs. Who was it who had told him that young Redfern was tall and thin?

He moved on, with a wave of his stick, as if to dispel this phantom; and it was not long before the first houses of Blacksod began to appear, some of them with windows already displaying lamp-light, which mingled queerly enough with the strange luminosity such as still emanated from earth and sky. Wolf noted how different such spots of artificial light appeared, when they thus remained mere specks of yellow colour surrounded by pale grey-ness, from what they would be in a brief while, when they broke up the complete darkness.

And as he began to encounter the evening stir of the town's precincts, and the heavy breath of the Blackmore pastures ceased to drug his senses, he found that what he had gone through that day was now slowly sifting itself out in the various layers of his consciousness. 'Either Urquhart *is* up to something,' he thought, 'or Jason has just invented the whole thing to satisfy his own strange mind! God help us! What a crazy set they all are! I'm thankful I'm out of it down here. Blacksod doesn't lend itself to such whimsies.'

Thus did the outer surface of his mind report on the situation, making use of the artificially-acquired genial optimism of many a forgotten mental *tour de force*.

But another – a deeper – layer in his mind made quite a different report.

'There's something up, over there, that's hostile to me, and to my life. They seem to have nothing else to do, these King's Barton people, but plot with one another against someone. Good Lord! No wonder they finished off Redfern among them all! I can see I'm going to have to defend myself. And easily could I do it, too, if it weren't for mother. Damn! It's mother being up there that's the rub; so dependent on Urquhart. If it weren't for her, I'd laugh at the whole lot of them. I've got my job at the school, thanks to Darnley. What a man Darnley is, compared with these madmen! They've worried *him* a lot, though. Anyone can see that.'

This second layer of his consciousness seemed so crowded with thoughts and surmises that he found himself standing stock-still outside a little greengrocer's shop, the better to get things clear.

A small ornament, perched in the lighted window, among the oranges and lettuces, made him recall the idol in his pocket; and from Mukalog his mind rushed back to Jason.

'I can't understand him,' he said to himself. 'Valley, I know, is a good man. Urquhart is a demon. But Jason baffles me. The Slow-worm of Lenty! That's about what he is. I had a feeling just now, when he stood with his eyes shut and his mouth gibbering, that he belonged to some primeval order of things, existing before good and evil appeared at all. But it's clear that Urquhart's cajoled him somehow. And yet I don't know! I'm tempted to think he'd be a match even for him – very much in the way some cold wet rain from the aboriginal chaos would discomfort the Devil!'

He turned from the shop-window and moved on. Soon he came to where two crossroads branched off from the one he followed, the road to the right leading up Babylon Hill, the road to the left leading to that portion of the town where Christie's house was. Should he turn to the left and return home that way? Or should he go straight on, past his father-in-law's yard?

The hesitation into which he now fell left an empty space in his mind; and at once there rose to fill it, from the invisible depths of his being, quite a new report upon the events of that day. Was there something more than those old sea-beach afternoons, those Lovers' Lane naughtinesses, between Gerda and Bob Weevil? He could not help remembering the exciting photograph of the girl astride of the tombstone which he had seen the two lads enjoying so much, that day he bought the sausages for Roger Monk.

The more rational layers of Wolf's consciousness now began a derisive criticism of this new mood. Had he the instincts of the lord of a seraglio? Did he demand that both Gerda and Christie should be faithful to him . . . while he himself was . . . as he was? No, it was different from that! After his fashion he *was* being faithful to Gerda. It was the nature of this particular case. It was, in fact, Mr. Weevil! To be cuckolded by Bob, the scamp of Blacksod, was not any way a very soothing destiny; but to be cuckolded by Bob as a sort of schoolboy lark, a lark set in motion by the sardonic Mr. Urquhart, was a fantastic outrage.

Still he hesitated at these crossroads, teased beyond his wont by the difficulty of deciding which way to go. He was so pulled at in both directions, that as he wavered he seemed actually to see before him the objects he would meet under either choice, and to feel the sensations he would experience under either.

In the end a motive simpler than love or jealousy decided the point. He took the shorter way, the way by Mr. Torp's yard, because of a secret craving for food in the recesses of his stomach. But though this was his real motive, what he *thought* was his motive was jealousy over Bob Weevil. And the idea of this, that he should have such a feeling at all, in connection with the romance of passing close to Christie's room, at once puzzled and shamed him.

He walked on with rapid strides now; and as he passed the familiar Torp yard, which lay in a hushed and rather ghastly pool of twilight, he thought how little he had foreseen, that March day when he turned into this enclosure, what occurrences would be the result of it! Bound by intimate habit to the one he had married – in love, for good and all, with the one he had *not* married – his situation just then was sufficiently complicated, without all this bewildering turmoil of personalities in King's Barton!

It was with an accumulated measure of sheer animal relief that he found himself entering his own house at last. This was increased by a delicious abandonment to unhindered amorousness when he discovered that Gerda was waiting for him at the kitchen-stove in her nightdress and dressing-gown. The girl had certain very quaint and pretty ways of expressing her desire to be made love to; and she had seldom been more excitable or more whimsically provocative than she was that night.

Though hunger had brought him so quickly home, it was more than an hour after his return that they sat down to their supper; and during the lingered-out and shameless caresses which he enjoyed before he would let her approach the stove, Wolf was compelled to come to the conclusion that erotic delight has in itself the power of becoming a kind of *absolute*. He felt as if it became a sort of ultimate essence into which the merely relative emotions of the two preoccupied ones sank – indeed were so utterly lost that a new identity dominated the field of their united consciousness, the admirable identity of *amorousness in itself*, the actual spiritual form, or 'psychic being,' of the god Eros!

What Wolf found to his no small content was that when this spiritual emanation of sweet delight had vanished away he was entirely free from any feeling of having committed sacrilege against his love for Christie. Whether this would have been the case had Christie been different from what she was, he found it difficult to decide; though in the intervals of pleasant discourse with Gerda, as they sat over their supper, he pondered deeply upon that nice point.

Another side issue that had a curious interest for him was the question whether the accident of his having remembered that wicked tombstone-picture on his way home had had anything to do with the completeness of his pleasure! He had noted before in himself the peculiar rôle played by queer out-of-the-way imaginations in all these things! And finally – but *this* thought did not come to him till their meal was over – he caught himself at least once that night in a grim wondering as to how far the sweet desirability of his companion had been enhanced for him by those sinister rumours of a rival in the field, even though that rival was this water-rat-featured seller of sausages!

Gerda was the first to go to sleep that night as they lay side by side, with the familiar odours of summer grass and pigsty drainage floating in upon them. Wolf had arrived, not without many mental adjustments, during the last two months, at a more or less satisfactory compromise between what he felt for this girl, thus lying with his arm stretched out beneath her, and what he felt for the other one. Christie's inflexible pride, and the faint, hardly-stirred pulse of her subnormal senses, made it much easier for him. An instinctive unwillingness, too, in his own nature, to introduce any strain of harsh idealism, led him to get all the contentment he could out of his life with his lovely bedfellow. As he listened to her evenly-drawn breathing, and felt, through all his nerves, the delicious relaxation of her love-exhausted limbs, he was conscious now more than ever that it was completely un-thinkable that he should be guilty of making her unhappy by any drastic change. In a sense what he had said to Selena Gault was true. He *was* happy. But he knew in his heart perfectly well that he was only happy because the deepest emotion he was capable of was satisfied by his nearness to Christie. Profoundly self-conscious as he was, Wolf was never oblivious of his lack of what people have agreed to call by the name of 'passion.' Luckily enough Christie, too, seemed, as far as he was able to tell, devoid of this exigency; so that by their resemblance in this peculiarity the strange intensity of their love was not disturbed by his easy dalliance with Gerda.

What Wolf at this moment felt, as he listened to the girl's soft breathing and held her in his arms, was a delicious, diffused tenderness – a tenderness which, like the earth itself, with the cool night-airs blowing over it, was touched by rumours and intimations belonging to another region. His sensual nature tranquillized, satisfied, appeased, permitted his spirit to wander off freely towards that other girlish form, more elusive, less tangible hardly realizable to any concrete imagination, which now lay – sleeping or waking, he knew not which – in the room that looked out upon Poll's Camp! There, above the books of that incestuous old man's shop, that other one was lying alone. Was *she* satisfied in this ambiguous love of his? He preferred not to let himself dwell upon that aspect of the matter just then; and holding Gerda fast, and inhaling the mingled night-airs, he let his mind sink into the plenary absolution of a deep, dreamless sleep.

13

HOME FOR BASTARDS

The next day proved to be, as far as the weather was concerned, even more pleasant than its predecessor.

Event followed event in harmonious and easy sequence. Gerda's morning crossness was tempered by an enchanting aftermath of petulant willingness to be caressed. His boys at the Grammar School whom he had laboriously anchored in the reign of the first Tudor were too occupied with thoughts of examinations and the approaching summer holidays to be as troublesome as usual. His afternoon at King's Barton was devoted to a concentrated perusal of the history of the unfortunate Lady Wyke of Abbotsbury; and Mr. Urquhart, crouching at his elbow like a great silky Angora tomcat, was too absorbed in their researches to indulge in more than a very few of his sidelong malignities.

So well pleased with their progress was the Squire, that while he and his secretary drank their tea at the library window he asked Wolf if it would be any help to his mother if Roger Monk were to drive her to Ramsgard and back before dinner.

'Roger declares he wants to go over there,' he said. 'What's he up to I don't know. He never tells me anything. But if your mother or you care for the drive, you can tell him to call for you.'

Wolf knew that Mrs. Solent had in her mind the notion of paying a formal call upon Miss Gault as a sign of their reconciliation, so he hurriedly accepted this offer and went off at once.

'I think I'll go too,' he announced to the big dark-browed servant; 'so, if it won't weigh down your gig, you might put in the back seat for me.'

He found his mother lingering over her tea in the parlour of the trim cottage. He caught a glimpse of her unobserved as he approached the window, and it was rather a shock to him to observe a look in her face which he had never seen before. She was sitting motionless, with her outstretched hands pressed against the edge of the table and her gaze fixed upon emptiness. Her brown eyes, from the angle at which he caught her, had a defeated, weary, helpless expression, and even the contours of her formidable chin were relaxed, crumpled, desolate.

He had a queer feeling of shame for having caught her thus, as though in the indecent exposure of some secret deformity; and he hurriedly and noisily entered the little house.

At his appearance her whole manner changed. She seemed delighted to have the chance of driving to Ramsgard with him, and they chatted gaily till she went upstairs to get ready.

Roger Monk did not keep them waiting; and while he was at the garden gate, holding the horse till the lady came down, Wolf had a word or two with him.

'Mr. Urquhart didn't seem to know what you were up to in Ramsgard,' he remarked, indiscreetly enough, but with no ulterior motive.

'He knew right and fine, Mr. Solent! Don't you make no mistake. There isn't much that goes on up at House – or out of House either, for that matter – that *he* doesn't know!'

'That must be rather uncomfortable sometimes, eh? What?'

This rather ungentlemanly imitation of the Squire's favourite phrase tickled the swarthy giant's fancy, and he smiled broadly. But a minute later his face grew grave and worried.

''Tis a good place with Squire,' he whispered, bending down towards Wolf. 'But I tell 'ee straight, Mr. Solent, sir, if I knew for sure he wouldn't play some dog's trick on me I'd do a bunk to-morrow!'

Wolf stared at him blankly.

'I would,' he repeated. And then, with the scowl of a righteous executioner, 'I'll tap the top of his black head for him one of these days, if God Almighty doesn't do it first!'

In spite of this somewhat ominous beginning, their drive into Ramsgard was a great success. Roger Monk quickly recovered his good humour under Mr. Solent's blandishments; and by the time they reached the school gate they were all three in the best of spirits.

Here they separated, the servant driving Mrs. Solent towards Miss Gault's house, while Wolf turned up the street with the intention of paying a visit to the Smiths.

The door was opened for him by Mattie herself; and the brother and sister embraced affectionately, as soon as they were alone in the cool, dark, musty hall.

'Dad is out,' she whispered, 'and we've only one servant now.'

'One servant?' he echoed, as she led him, with her finger on her lip, into the empty dining-room.

266

'Olwen's upstairs playing,' she said in a low voice.

It was clear to him that she was anxious that the child should not hear his voice; so he shut the door very quietly and they sat down together on two red leather chairs.

'What's the trouble, Mattie dear?' he murmured, holding her hand tightly.

'It's Dad,' she said. 'He's been queer the last few days.'

It was difficult for Wolf to repress a smile; for the idea of Mr. Albert Smith, the great Hatter of Ramsgard School, the sedate Churchwarden of the Abbey, being in any kind of way 'queer' struck him as grotesque.

'What's up with him? Business bad?'

Mattie sighed, and, releasing her hand from his clasp, folded her fingers tightly together.

'It's worse than bad,' she said slowly. 'Do you know, Wolf, I believe Dad's ruined.'

'Good Lord, child!' he cried. 'He can't be! I can't believe it. Mr. Smith? Why's he's been at this job here for as long as I can remember. He must have made a lot! He may have got some mania, my dear, about money. You ought to make him sell out and retire!'

'I tell you, Wolf,' she said emphatically, and with a certain irritation, 'it's true! Can't you believe I know what I'm talking about? He's been investing in some silly way. He's never been as sensible as people think; and now he's hit, knocked over. I believe he's already taken the first step, whatever that is, to being bankrupt.'

'Bankrupt?' repeated Wolf helplessly.

'So that's the state of *our* affairs!' she cried in a lighter tone. 'And now tell me about yourself and your pretty Gerda.'

As she spoke she rose to her feet and flung her hands behind her head, straightening her frame to its full height.

'She's got a fine figure,' thought Wolf. 'What a shame that her nose is so large!'

Mattie's countenance did indeed seem, as he looked at her staring steadily down at him out of her deep-set grey eyes, even less presentable than when he had seen her a few weeks ago.

'She's been having a bad time, poor girl!' he thought. 'How damnable that the gods didn't mould her face just a little more carefully!'

He looked at her as she fixed her eyes on the floor, frowning; and then he glanced away at the mahogany sideboard, where Mr. Smith's heavy pieces of polished silver met his gaze, with the peculiar detached phlegm of old, worn possessions that have seen so many family troubles that they have grown professionally callous, after the manner of undertakers and sextons.

Something about that silver on the sideboard, combined with his sister's news, threw a grey shadow over his own life. His mind sank down into a desolate acceptance of long years of stark endurance, the sort of endurance that wind-blown trees have to acquire when their branches become at last permanently bent, from bowing sideways, away from the north or the east.

'Well, now you know the worst!' his sister murmured at last.

'It might be worse still,' he said lamely.

Her eyes unexpectedly flashed and she gave vent to a queer little laugh.

'I don't care! I don't care! I don't care!' she cried. 'In fact, if it weren't for Olwen, I believe I'd be almost glad!'

Wolf screwed up his eyes and regarded her closely. He suddenly became aware that this daughter of his father had something in her nature that he understood well enough.

'Listen, Mattie,' he said quietly. 'I have an idea that things are going to work out all right – work out better for you, in fact, than they've been doing for a long time.'

She looked straight into his face and smiled, while one of her eyebrows rose humorously and twitched a little.

'You and I are a funny pair, Wolf,' she said. 'I believe we actually *like* to be driven and hunted.'

They exchanged a long, confused look. Then he protruded his under lip, and drew down the corners of his mouth.

'If so, we know where we get it,' he said. And then, in a sudden afterthought: 'Look here, we must slip off one day together and visit his grave. I don't see why Madame Selena should have a monopoly of that spot!'

She made a somewhat brusque and ungracious movement.

'I don't like graves,' she said. 'But come on, Wolf, we mustn't stay down here any more. Let's go up and see Olwen. She'll never forgive me, even now, for keeping you.'

He opened the door for her and they went up softly together. As he followed her form up the dim staircase, the thought came shamelessly into his head that had she been as lovely in face as she was flexible in figure she would have had a sensual attraction for him.

'But I understand her well,' he said to himself. 'And I'll do what I can to make her life happier.'

Mattie paused, when she reached the first landing, till he was at her side. Then she called out: 'Olwen! Olwen! Here's a visitor for you!'

'Olwen! Olwen!' echoed Wolf.

There was a scream and a scramble, and a door was flung wide. The little girl ran out with her hair flying and rushed into her friend's arms.

When at last he disentangled himself from her clinging hands, he held her at a distance from him, pushing her into the stream of light that had come with her through the open door. Holding her in this way he searched her face with a stern scrutiny. 'After all,' he thought, 'she's more nearly related to Christie than I am to Mattie. We might all be in Mr. Urquhart's book!'

But the child pulled him into her room, and, disregarding Mattie completely, began hurriedly displaying before him every one of her treasures.

The summer night was already chilly, and over the half-opened window the muslin curtains swelled and receded, receded and swelled, as if they were sails on an invisible sea. Crouching upon a low straight-backed nursery-chair – the very chair, in fact, upon which her mother had sat to suckle her in her infancy – Mattie sat with her hands clasped round her knees, watching the shadows of their three forms, thrown by the candlelight, waver and hover against the old-fashioned wall-paper.

Wolf began to detach himself, as the three of them sat there, from the pressure of the actual situation, from the awareness even of his own personality. He seemed to slip away, out of his human skin, out of that old Ramsgard house, out of the very confines of life itself. He had the sensation that he was outside life – that he was outside death too; that he was floating in some airy region, where forms and shapes and sounds had been left behind – had changed into *something else*.

Attenuated by the influence of these bodiless fancies, the palpable shapes of Mattie and Olwen seemed to thin themselves out into something more filmy than the stuff of dreams. Mechanically he responded to Olwen's intense preoccupations, mechanically he smiled at his sister across the little girl's flushed face. But he felt that his senses · were no longer available, no longer to be trusted. He had slid away somehow into some level of existence where human vision and human contact meant nothing at all. It was as if these two girls had become as unreal as his own intangible thoughts – those thoughts like tiny twilight insects – which passed without leaving a trace!

'No! Didn't you hear me tell you? That's not Gipsy . . . that's Antoinette!' scolded the little girl, as she snatched a miniature pillow from under one waxen head to insert it violently beneath another.

'Dolls – dolls – dolls!' thought Wolf. 'If we can slip out of reality, why can't they slip into it?' He began automatically swinging both Gipsy and Antoinette from one hand to the other, a proceeding which delighted their little mistress.

'What,' he thought, as he contemplated Mattie's heavy, clouded, patient features, her corrugated brow, her thick nose, 'what am I aiming at, meddling with these people's lives? I do it with the same voracity with which I eat honey or trample over grass. I'm driven to it as if I were an omophagous demon! Is this the sort of thing my father did – that scoundrel with his "happy life"?'

He was interrupted in his thoughts by the sound of a bell downstairs, followed by the opening of a door and by unsteady steps in the hall.

Mattie jumped to her feet and stood listening, intent and anxious. 'I believe that's father!' she cried. 'But why did he ring? He never rings. Excuse me, Wolf, I must run down.'

She opened the door, but remained still listening, as also did Olwen, with wide-open startled eyes, a thin arm thrown round Wolf's neck.

There was a muttering and a shuffling downstairs, followed by the clang of a heavy stick falling on a tiled floor. Then a chair creaked ominously and there was a sort of groan. Then all was silent.

Mattie, with her hand on the door, turned round to them; and in spite of the flickering of the candles he could see that her face had gone white.

'It's father!' she whispered. 'He's ill. I *must* go down.'

Still hesitating, however, and evidently struck by some sort of panic, she continued to waver in the doorway. Wolf remembered afterwards every smallest incident of that occasion. Olwen's little arm had a pulse in it that beat against his cheek like a tiny clock as she held him tighter and tighter. He replaced Gipsy and Antoinette on a chair by his side, half-consciously smoothing down their ruffled dresses. Both doll's eyes, one pair blue and one black, stared up at him. Antoinette's arm stuck out awkwardly, absurdly. He pushed it down by her side with one of his fingers and it creaked as he did so.

'Stay where you are, both of you! I must go!' cried Mattie; and she ran hastily down the stairs.

Then there was a sudden scream that echoed sharply through the whole silent house. 'Wolf! Wolf!' came her voice.

'Stay here, sweetheart!' he cried, freeing himself and rushing to the door. 'Stay where you are!' But the little girl followed him like a shadow and was there by his side when he reached the hall. They had left the door of the dining-room open, and by the light thus flung into the passage he saw Mattie on her knees before one of the hall chairs, on which sprawled the stiff, collapsed form of Mr. Smith. His eyes were open and conscious under his black felt hat, which, tilted sideways, gave him a grotesque, drunken appearance. Mattie was chafing his hands with her own and murmuring wild endearments.

Wolf hurriedly closed the front door, which had been left ajar, and then, with Olwen still clinging to him, proceeded to strike a match, so as to light the hall lamp.

'What are you doing, Wolf? Go away, Olwen. He'll be better in a minute. Father! Darling father, what's the matter? What is it, father? You're safe at home. You're all right now. Father dearest, what is it?' Mattie kept crying out in this way all manner of contradictory commands and appeals, as she went on rubbing Mr. Smith's impassive hands.

Wolf removed the man's hat and hung it carefully on a peg. He remembered afterwards the look of this hat, hanging side by side with his own, calm and a little supercilious, as hats in that position always are.

'Mattie,' he said, 'do you want me to go and find a doctor?'

But at the word 'doctor' the man in the chair found his voice. 'No – no – no! No doctor. I won't have one. I won't! Off! Off! Off!'

'What is it, father dear?' cried Mattie, rising to her feet and pressing her hand against his forehead. 'No, you don't want a doctor. I'm here – your Mattie. You're better now, father, aren't you?'

Mr. Smith stared at her with a heavy confused stare.

'All thieves,' he muttered.

Wolf tried to catch his sister's eye for permission to disobey the sick man, but the girl seemed to have forgotten his existence. It was clear to him that Mr. Smith had had some kind of stroke. His face wore now an unnatural reddish tint, and his head kept drooping sideways, as if the muscles of his neck no longer responded to his will.

Suddenly, he astonished them by calling out, 'Lorna! Lorna!' in a loud voice.

'Oh, he's dying!' sobbed Mattie. 'That's mother he wants. It's your Mattie. It's your dear Mattie,' she repeated, bending over him. But Mr. Smith had begun mumbling now, incoherently, but not inarticulately.

'Home . . . home for bastards. . . . ' Wolf was sure those were the words he used; and he was relieved that Mattie, fallen on her knees again now, was sobbing so violently as to make it unlikely that she could catch what he said.

'Hats . . . hats for bastards. . . . ' Mr. Smith went on. 'No no, Lorna! It was to Longburton he took you. But never mind. . . . Albert Smith, home for bastards. Albert Smith, Ramsgard, Dorset, Draper and Hat-Dealer. To the school, I tell 'ee! No – no – no! She'll never, never, never confess. . . . Longburton barn . . . hay and straw . . . hay and straw in your hair, my dear . . . and long past eleven. . . . What? You pricked your finger? A very pretty hat! Hats for bastards. . . . Home. *My* home. Albert Smith of Ramsgard come home.'

His head had sunk so low now as to be almost resting on Mattie's shoulder, as she sobbed against his knees. Suddenly he lifted it with a spasmodic jerk.

'I'll pay for the child! I've got the money. I'll pay for them all and say nothing. Albert Smith, Draper and Hatter. . . . To the school, I tell 'ee! . . . Pay . . . pay all . . . pay. . . . '

This was really the end now. His body fell forward over the stooping girl, and Wolf was hard put to it to pull her away from between the prone forehead and the stiff, protruding knees. For the moment he feared she would collapse; but he saw the quick protective glance she cast at Olwen, who stood motionless, staring at the dead man like a fairy in a pantomime at the chief clown, and he knew then that she was mistress of herself. She helped him, without shrinking and without any more tears, to carry the body of Mr. Smith up the staircase and into his bedroom. . . .

It was about two hours after this that Wolf entered the room again with Mattie. Here, lying on his own high pillow, the head of the dead man had already assumed an expression of exhausted indifference. Close by his side, on a little table by the bed, as Wolf cast a final glance at him, was a picture of a young woman in the chaste costume of the mid-Victorian epoch. 'Madam Lorna, I suppose,' he thought; and he would have looked more closely at his father's sweetheart, but the presence of Mattie restrained him.

'I'll come over to-morrow evening, my dear,' he said, 'after my work with the Squire. Don't commit yourself to any arrangements or any plans till we've seen how the land lies. You won't, will you, Mattie?' he repeated emphatically. 'I'll be really angry if you make any move that we haven't discussed together.'

They were out on the landing by this time, and the little girl heard them speaking and called out to them from her room.

'Go to sleep, Olwen!' cried Mattie.

'I want him to see Gipsy and Antoinette! I want him to see them!' the child repeated.

'Only for a minute, Wolf, *please!*' whispered his sister. 'She's so terribly excited I shall never get her to sleep.'

They opened the door and went in. There was a tray, with milk and biscuits upon it, on the chest of drawers by Olwen's bed, and near the tray a small night-light burning. By this faint flicker Wolf could see the little girl's dark eyes shining with awestruck intensity, though she was immobile as an image.

'Come nearer! Come quite near! They're as awake as I am.'

He went up to the bed; and there, lying on opposite sides of Olwen's pillow, were the two dolls, with black ribbons twisted tightly round them and their hair brushed smooth and straight.

'They are going to grandfather's funeral to-morrow,' she whispered. 'Don't they look sorry and good?'

A minute or two later he bade his sister farewell at the front door.

'You're sure you don't want me to stay the night with you?' he asked.

Mattie shook her head.

'I shall sleep with Olwen,' she replied quietly. 'We shall be all right.'

'Well, remember you've had no supper. You'll never get through the night if you don't eat something.'

'What about you, Wolf? How stupid I am!'

'Oh, I'll get a drink at the Lovelace on my way,' he said. 'But remember – no plans of any kind till I've seen you again!'

He was indeed only just in time to get into the Lovelace bar before the Abbey clock struck ten. He enquired about the King's Barton coachman and found that Mrs. Solent had left a message at the hotel office earlier in the evening, saying that they could not wait for him, but that they had heard of Mr. Smith's death, and would Mr. Solent come and see her to-morrow.

'I wonder,' he thought, 'how the devil she heard? They must have actually come to the door and been told by the maid about it when we were all upstairs. Well, it'll give her some kind of a shock, I daresay – but not very much!'

He left the Lovelace after drinking a pint of Dorchester ale. The night was cool and fragrant. The sky was covered now by a grey film of feathery clouds, through which neither moon nor stars were visible except as a faintly diffused luminosity, which lifted the weight of darkness from the earth, but turned the world into a place of phantoms and shadows.

Wolf decided to follow the shorter and easier way home. This was the highroad to Blacksod that ran along the top of the ridge dividing Dorset from Somerset; and as he strode between the phantasmal wheatfields of that exposed upland, his thoughts took many a queer turn. So Mattie and Olwen were left penniless! That was evidently going to be the upshot of the hatter's death. And the question was, what was to become of them? If it had not been for the child's insane hostility to Christie, the natural course would have been for Olwen to return to her father's dwelling. The chances were that the local authorities, unless Miss Gault took upon herself to meddle again, would not interfere. Then his mind reverted to his mother.

Would his mother take them in? Roger Monk's house was certainly big enough, and it seemed unlikely that the Squire would object if no one else did. But – good Lord! – he couldn't visualize his mother living with another woman, or indeed putting up with the waywardness and excitability of Olwen. Who would educate her? It was impossible to contemplate Olwen at school!

The problem seemed well-nigh insoluble, as he pondered on it. Then, all in a moment, he thought of Selena Gault. There, no doubt, was the obvious solution! Selena was passionately fond of the little girl, and Selena had a servant. He stared at a fantastic thorn tree, whose largest branch, bare of leaves and apparently quite dead, stretched out a semi-human hand across the tangled foliage of the roadside. As was his wont when confronted by a mental dilemma, he stood stock-still and regarded this silent monitor.

Nature was always prolific of signs and omens to his mind; and it had become a custom with him to keep a region of his intelligence alert and passive for a thousand whispers, hints, obscure intimations that came to him in this way. Why was it that a deep, obstinate resistance somewhere in his consciousness opposed itself to such a solution? He tried to analyse what he felt. Selena was a good woman, a passionately protective woman; but there it was! That interference in the case of the Malakites

274

had lodged a deep distaste in his mind. She might love Olwen; but she probably hated Mattie as much as she did Christie.

Damn! Why had Mr. Smith fooled away his money and shuffled himself off in this awkward manner? 'Home for bastards' – what gross outbursting of the literal truth that was! Well, it was *his* business now to take the hatter's place and find just such a home! That incorrigibly complacent and grinning skull in the cemetery had certainly managed to bequeath burdens to its legitimate offspring which were not easy to fulfil!

Wolf stuck out his under lip at the oracular thorn tree and strode on. What, he asked now, of that grey luminosity above him, and of those diaphanous wraith-like corn-shocks, was why there should be, between his deepest desire and his complicated activity, such an unbridged gulf?

He had only one life. That was a basic and relentless fact. An eternity of 'something or other' lay behind him, and an equally obscure eternity of 'something or other' lay in front of him. Meanwhile, here he was, with only one single, simple, and world-deep craving – the craving to spend his days and his nights with that other mysterious and mortal consciousness, entitled Christie Malakite! And yet, for reasons comparatively superficial, reasons comparatively external to his secret life-current, he was steadily, day by day, month by month, building up barriers between himself and Christie, struggling to build them up, moving men and women like bricks and mortar to build them up!

A villainously evil thought assailed him as he walked along. Were all his better actions only so many Pharisaic sops thrown one by one into the mouth of a Cerberus of selfishness, monstrous and insane? Was his 'mythology' itself only a projection of such selfishness? He carried this sardonic thought like a demon fox pressed against the pit of his stomach, for nearly a mile; and it was just as if the hard, opaque crystal circle of his inmost identity were, under that fox's black saliva, turning into something shapeless and nauseating, something that resembled a mass of floating frog-spawn.

'Come, you demon,' he said to himself at last, 'my soul is going to remain intact, or it's going to dissolve into air!'

He had reached the summit of Babylon Hill now; and precisely where he had first crossed that stile with Gerda, he stood at this moment, rending his nature in a desperate inward struggle.

When, in the middle of the night, lying in his bed by Gerda's side, he recalled this evil experience, he found the explanation of it in a sort of dissolution-hypnosis, or corruption-sympathy, linking him with the actual dead body of Albert Smith!

What he experienced was strange enough. He found himself very soon clutching with his fingers one of the posts of that stile, while with his other hand he dug his stick savagely into the sun-baked earth. And it seemed to him that every revolting or secretive instinct he had ever had took on a material shape and became as an actual portion of his physical body.

He became, in fact, a living human head, emerging from a monstrous agglomeration of all repulsiveness. And this gross mass was not only foul and excremental, it was in some mysterious way *comic*. He, the head of this unspeakable body, was the joke of the abyss, the smug charlatan-prig at which the devils shrieked with laughter.

The queer thing was that his brain moved at this moment with incredible rapidity. His brain debated, for example, as it had never done before, the insoluble problem of free-will, the problem of the very existence of the mystery called 'will.' And then, all in a moment, with a crouching wild-animal movement of his consciousness, he flung a savage defiance to all these doubts. He laid hold of his will as if it had been a lightning-conductor, and, shaking it clear of his body, thrust it forth into space, into a space that was below and yet above, within and yet beyond Poll's Camp and Babylon Hill. And then, in a second, in less than a second, so it seemed, as he recalled it afterwards, there came flowing in upon him, out of those secret depths of which he was always more or less conscious, a greater flood of liberating peace than he had ever known before!

He had the sensation, as he came down the slope, of having left behind, on the top of Babylon Hill, some actual physical body – a body that had been troubling him, like a great repulsive pro-tuberance, both by its appearance and by its weight. He felt lighter, freer, liberated from the malice of matter. Above all he felt once more that his inmost identity was a hard, round, opaque crystal, which had the power of forcing itself through any substance, organic, inorganic, magnetic, or psychic, that might obstruct its way.

There were a few lights twinkling still among the Blacksod roofs. But he had no notion whether Christie's was among them; and at this moment it seemed unimportant. A new fragrance filled the air as he descended; which he defined to himself as the actual smell of Somersetshire, as distinct from the smell of Dorsetshire – the far-off fragrance, in fact, full of the exhalations of brackish mosses, amber-coloured peat-tussocks, and arrow-pointed water-plants, of the salt-marshes of Sedgemoor.

Once in the town, he took without any hesitation – though he did not forget that long vigil of the night in June – the particular way that led past the Torp monument-yard. As he approached Preston Lane through the deserted streets, he found himself thinking shamelessly and contentedly of the pleasure of making love to Gerda before he went to sleep.

His mind after the experience he had gone through, seemed to float lightly and carelessly over every aspect of his existence. The personality of Christie remained the same through everything. It was as if to everything he did, even to making love to Gerda, Christie set her proud and careless seal. This indeed – so he said to himself – was the solution of that dilemma on which he had been impaled. Christie did remain the great aim and purpose of his life; but these innumerable other people were part of the body of that life itself. They were what *he was*, his ways, his habits, his customs, his manias, his impulses, his instincts; and *with all that he was* he had now been drawn to Christie as if by a magnet strong enough to move a great slave galleon of manias and superstitions, *en masse* across the deep!

Airy and light as it now was, his soul seemed to have been liberated in some secret way from all that clogged and burdened it. The slave galleon of his manias rocked and tossed on a smooth tide; but his soul, like a careless albatross, rode on the masthead. There was a strange humming and singing from the galleon itself, as if the immense peace of that summer night had turned it into a trireme of deliverance, carrying liberated pilgrims to the haven where they would be. Something unutterable, some clue, some signal, had touched the dark bulkheads of this night-voyager; so that hereafter all might be different. What was this clue? All he knew about it now was that it meant the *acceptance* of something monstrously comic in his inmost being, something comic and stupid, together with something as grotesquely non-human as the sensations of an ichthyosaurus! But once having accepted all this, everything was magically well. 'Christie! Christie!' he cried in his heart, longing to tell her about it.

He stopped when he was opposite the familiar pigsty, and lifted his head, breathing deeply. At that moment Fate seemed so kind to him that its kindness was almost too great. His love for Christie seemed to touch with a kind of transparency everything that he looked at. Rapidly he crossed the road, entered his house, and ran upstairs.

He found the room dark; but when he had lit a candle he saw that the girl was lying wide awake, her head propped high on the two pillows. He was in such an exalted mood that he was hardly surprised at her first words.

'Oh, Wolf, Wolf,' she said, 'I'm almost sorry you've come so soon. I've been looking through that window for hours and hours. What's happened to me I don't know; but I've not felt like this since that evening when you first loved me in the river fields.'

He stooped and kissed her without attempting an answer; and when he held her presently in his arms and the room was again dark, it was as if they each found an opportunity in their embraces wherein to express an accumulated tide of feelings that spread out wide and far – spread out beyond all that he could feel for her, and beyond – so it seemed to him, as he tasted tears on her cheek – all that she could feel for him.

And now, as their dalliance sank into quiescence, one of Wolf's final thoughts before he slept was of the vast tracts of unknown country that every human consciousness includes in its scope. Here, to the superficial eye, were two skulls, lying side by side; but, in reality, here were two far-extending continents, each with its own sky, its own land and water, its own strange-blowing winds. And it was only because his own soul had been, so to speak, washed clean of its body that day that he was able to feel as he felt at this moment. But – even so – what those thoughts of hers had been, that he had interrupted by his return, he knew no better now than when first he had entered her room and had blown out her candle.

14

CROOKED SMOKE

It was with a fairly untroubled mind that Wolf set off the following afternoon for King's Barton. And it was with a peculiar sense of recovery that he found himself seated side by side with Mr. Urquhart at the littered table in the great library window.

Incredibly fragrant were the garden scents that flowed in upon him, past the Squire's pendulous eye-folds, Napoleonic paunch, and withered pantaloon-legs. The old rogue had discovered a completely new stratum of obscene Dorset legends. He had got on the track now of accounting for certain local cases of misbehaviour, on the grounds of libidinous customs reverting to very remote times. He was, in fact, at this moment gathering all the material he could find about the famous Cerne Giant, whose phallic shamelessness seemed by no means confined to its harmless representation upon a chalk hill.

As he looked down, past Mr. Urquhart's profile, upon the lawn below, and contemplated the rich mingling of asters, lobelias, and salpiglossis in Roger Monk's favourite flower-bed, it seemed to Wolf that certain prematurely fallen leaves, which he caught sight of down there upon the grass, had struck his consciousness long ago with a tremendous significance. Those sultry glowing purples ... those dead leaves ... what *was* that significance? 'This day is going to be a queer day for me,' he thought. For he had become aware that some screen, some casement, at the back of his mind, behind which his most secret impressions lived and moved in their twilight, had swung open a little. . . .

He kept staring down out of that library window past his employer's profile. That purple glow from the flower-bed . . . those dead leaves . . . why was there no dew down there? It was autumn dew he was thinking about that August day . . . silvery mist upon purple flowers. . . . 'The most important things in my life,' he said to himself, 'are what come back to me from forgotten walks, when I've been alone. . . . Dark grass with purplish flowers . . . dead leaves with dew on them. . . . I wonder,' he thought, 'how much room those undertakers left between old Smith's face and his coffin lid?'

And then he thought, 'I wonder if old Smith ever noticed the look of dew upon dead leaves?' and he shifted his position a little, as a cold shiver went through him.

But Mr. Urquhart now broke silence. Some telepathic wave must have passed from his secretary's wandering mind into his own.

'What's this news I hear,' he said, 'about Albert Smith? The old chap's kicked the bucket, eh? Lovelace was over here this morning, and he tells me the fellow died last night and left nothing but debts. A bad lookout for those two girls, what? Lovelace even hints at suicide.'

The Squire paused, and a very curious expression came into his face.

'They talked of suicide when Redfern died,' he went on. 'I'd like to know what *you* think, Solent, about this business of shuffling off without a word to anyone? D'ye think it's easy for 'em? D'ye think they do it with their brains cool and clear? D'ye think they have some pretty awful moments or not, ha? Come, tell me, tell me! I hate not to know these things. Do they go through the devil of a time before they bring themselves to it, eh? Or do they sneak off like constipated beagles, to eat the long ditch-grass and ha' done with it?'

Wolf tried in vain to catch his employer's equivocal eye as he listened to all this. Never in his acquaintance with Mr. Urquhart had he felt so baffled by the drift of the man's mind. Something in himself, rising up from very hidden depths, gave him a hurried danger signal; but what possible danger there could be to him from the man's words he was unable to see.

'Do they mind it or don't they?' repeated the Squire. 'People pity 'em; but what does anyone know? Perhaps the only completely happy moments of a man's life are when he's decided on it. Things must look different then – different and much nicer, eh, Solent? But different anyway; very different. Don't 'ee think so, Solent? Quite different. . . . Little things, I mean. Things like the handles of doors, and bits of soap in soap-dishes, and sponges on washing-stands! Wouldn't you want to squeeze out your sponge, Solent, and pick up the matches off the floor, when you'd decided on it?'

Wolf was spared the necessity of any retort to this by the appearance of Roger Monk. The man came in without knocking and walked straight up to their table.

Wolf peered at him with quizzical screwed-up eyes. He couldn't help recalling that explosion of homicidal hatred which he had listened to outside Lenty Cottage. But the gardener's countenance was impassive now as a human-faced rock.

'Eh? What's that, Monk? Speak up. Mr. Solent will not mind.'

'Weevil and young Torp, sir, round at the back, sir; asking for leave to fish in Lenty Pond, sir.'

Monk uttered the words in a low, discreet, colourless voice.

Mr. Urquhart at once assumed a blustering great man's tone of genial condescension, as if he were addressing himself to the youths in question.

'Sporting young men, ha? Gay young truants, ha? Well, we mustn't be too strict. Do 'em good, I daresay, on a fine afternoon. Probably catch nothing but a perch or two! Certainly, Roger. I've no objection, Roger.'

But the man still remained where he was.

'They *did* say, sir, that you said something the other night to them, sir, about – '

But Mr. Urquhart interrupted him.

'I've no time now. I'm busy with Mr. Solent. Tell 'em to clear off and fish all they like. There's nothing more, Roger, thank you. Tell 'em to fish the pond from end to end, but not to trample down the rushes. Tell 'em to be careful of the rushes, Roger. That's all, Roger.'

His last words were uttered in such a final and dismissing tone, that the man, having given him one quick interrogative look, swung round on his heels and left the room.

The Squire turned to Wolf.

'A little sport for the populace, eh, Solent? Do 'em good, what? Doesn't pay to be too strict these days. Seignorial rights and that sort o' thing grown a bit old-fashioned, ha?'

The conversation lapsed after this, and they returned to their investigations concerning the Cerne Giant.

It was Mr. Urquhart's part to select, from the mass of their material, the particular aspects of Dorset history which lent themselves to their work. It was Wolf's business to purge and winnow and heighten these to the general level of the style which they had adopted.

'Every bibliophile in England'll have this book on his shelves one day, Solent,' remarked the Squire, after about half an hour's work.

Wolf did not reply. For some reason he lacked the faintest flicker of an author's pride in what they were doing.

They worked on for nearly a whole hour after this. Then Mr. Urquhart suddenly uttered these strange words:

'It would be wonderful to see one's sponge and one's hairbrush as they'd look just then.'

Wolf hurriedly gathered his wits together.

'You mean after you'd decided upon it?' he said.

Mr. Urquhart nodded.

'You'd see 'em in a sort of fairy-story light, I fancy,' he went on, 'much as infants see 'em, when they're so damned well pleased with themselves that they chirp like grasshoppers. It would be nice to see things like that, Solent, don't you think so? Stripped clear of the mischief of custom? It ... would ... be ... very ... nice ... to see ... anything ... like that!'

His voice assumed a languid and dreamy tone, full of an infinite weariness.

Wolf found it difficult to make any intelligent comment. His own mind was worrying about many teasing details just then, such as what he was to say to his mother with regard to Mattie and Olwen, and whether he should go to Ramsgard between tea and dinner or wait till later in the evening.

Mr. Urquhart suddenly rose to his feet.

'Let's stroll round to Lenty Pond, Solent, and tell those lads they can bathe if they want to. It's bathing they really like,' he added emphatically, 'much more than fishing. Good for the rabble, too, don't you think so, Solent, to learn to swim?'

Wolf could only patiently acquiesce. He did, however, snatch a brief glance at his watch.

'It's nearly four, sir,' he said. 'You won't mind if I leave you after we've been over there, and run round to my mother's?'

The man waved his hand with a negligent, indifferent gesture. It was a mere nothing, this gesture; but in some queer way it rather chilled Wolf's blood. 'It must have been,' he thought to himself, 'exactly in that way that the high priest waved his hand when he uttered the memorable expression, "What is that to *us?* See *thou* to that!"'

They went out together, and Wolf was almost irritated by the unnecessary speed with which Mr. Urquhart walked.

They did not, for all this hurry, reach Lenty Pond uninterrupted. Just as they were entering the field above the Otters' house, they came unexpectedly upon Jason. The poet had – as far as Wolf could make out – been sitting in the ditch, both for coolness and for seclusion; but he emerged from his retreat in comparative self-possession, and accepted Mr. Urquhart's rather curt invitation to join them with quiet acquiescence.

They all proceeded therefore across the field, Wolf forgetting his personal anxieties in his interest in the way his two companions treated each other.

'Your peaches are very fine this year,' said Jason to the Squire. 'And it was a very good idea of yours to put netting over them. Thieves are afraid of touching netting. It's like the Latin words at the beginning of a psalm. It makes fruit seem more than fruit – something sacred, I mean.'

'You must make my gardener pick you some of the sacred fruit when you next explore my garden,' said Mr. Urquhart.

'You've put your garden-seats in such a very well-chosen place,' went on the poet in an eager, propitiatory manner. 'None of these country fools understand why your garden-seats are between the yew hedges and the privet hedges. They've no more idea of how garden-seats should be arranged – I mean, with regard to shadows – than a Sturminster goose has of the taste of Tangerine oranges.'

'I hope,' said Mr. Urquhart drily, 'that you will not fail to take advantage of *all* the shadows in my garden when you happen to be there.'

Wolf glanced at the Squire's face as he spoke, and was startled by its look of agitated annoyance. But Jason went on rapidly, his cheeks growing more and more flushed and a queer dark glow showing itself in his eyes.

'There are idiots who can't enjoy that shrubbery of yours, Mr. Urquhart, just because the bushes aren't trimmed. Untrimmed shrubberies are by far the best. Children and fairies are safe there. Silly old women can't walk about in them, and God can't get into them.'

'I hope you'll never hurt *yourself*, Otter, when you happen to be walking about in my shrubberies.'

The tone in which his employer uttered these words did not altogether surprise Wolf. In his earlier conclusions about these two men he had taken for granted that Jason was helpless in Mr. Urquhart's hands. He had already begun to waver a little in this view.

They now arrived at the edge of Lenty Pond, and Wolf was amused by the sight of two naked figures, splashing, gesticulating, and clinging to the branches of a submerged willow. It was clear that Mr. Urquhart's 'populace' had not waited for any formal permission to substitute bathing for fishing.

'Hullo, lads! You've done very wisely, I see,' said the lord of the manor, approaching the edge of the water and leaning on his cane.

'Take care of the leeches, you two!' cried Jason with benevolent unction.

If Wolf had been previously struck by the unrestrained manner in which the poet had rallied the great man, he was still more arrested by the change that now came over Mr. Otter's expressive face. It had been stonily self-centred when he came out of the ditch. It had been twitching with mischief as he talked. It now became suddenly suffused with a kind of abandoned sentimentality. Every trace of nervousness passed out of it and every shadow of misery. It seemed to be illuminated by some soft inner light, not a radiant light, but a pallid, phosphorescent nebulosity, such as might have accompanied the religious ecstasy of a worshipper of will-o'-the-wisps.

Lobbie Torp, his thin white figure streaked with green pond-weed, staggered out of the water and sat down by the side of Jason on the bank, beating the flies away from his legs with a muddy willow-branch.

Wolf noticed that the poet's expression assumed a look of almost beatific contentment as he proceeded to enter upon a whispered conversation with the small boy, who himself, as far as Wolf could see, was too occupied in casting awestruck glances at the Squire to give the least attention to what was being said to him.

'It's not too warm, gentlemen,' called out Bob Weevil, with a forced shiver, pulling himself up, rather foolishly and self-consciously, by the tree-trunk in front of him.

'Why don't you take a swim, Weevil?' enquired Mr. Urquhart blandly.

'He dursn't, sir. He's afeared of they girt water-snakes,' cried Lobbie Torp.

Bob Weevil's reply to this taunt was to drop his hold upon the tree, swing himself round, and strike out boldly for the centre of the pond.

'Well done, Weevil! Well done!' cried out the Squire in high delight, watching the flexible muscles and slim back of the swimmer as the muddy ripples eddied round him.

'Float now, Weevil!' he went on. 'Let's see you float!'

The youthful dealer in sausages turned upon his back and beat the surface of the pond with arms and heels, causing a solitary moor-hen, that hitherto had remained in terrified concealment, to rise and flap away through the thick reeds.

284

There passed rapidly through Wolf's mind, while all this went on, a hurried mental estimate of his own feelings. He felt – and he frankly confessed it to himself – in some queer way definitely uncomfortable and embarrassed. The air of excited well-being around him jarred upon his nerves as if there were actually present, hovering with the gnats and midges above that pond, some species of electricity to which he was completely insensitive. He felt awkward, ill at ease, and even something of a fool.

What puzzled him, too, profoundly and annoyingly, was the fact that the psychic 'aura' of the situation seemed entirely natural and harmless. The presence of those two lads seemed to have drawn out of both his equivocal companions every ounce of black bile or complicated evil.

The Squire had the air of an innocent, energetic schoolmaster superintending some species of athletic sports. Jason had the look of an enraptured saint, liberated from earthly persecution and awakening to the pure ecstasies of Paradise.

He himself began vaguely wondering, as Bob Weevil reversed his position and with vigorous strokes approached the willow tree, whether the numerous intimations of peril he had been receiving lately had any reality in them.

He had been, he knew well, taking for granted for many months that between himself and Mr. Urquhart there existed some sort of subterranean struggle that ultimately would articulate itself in some volcanic explosion. But at this moment, half hypnotized by the heavy sunshine, by the disturbed waters of Lenty Pond, by the classic nakedness of the two youths, he found himself beginning to wonder if the whole idea of this psychic struggle were not a fancy of his brain.

The sense that this might be the case had an extremely disconcerting effect upon him, and seemed to menace with doubt and confusion one of the dominant motive powers of his identity.

He knew very well why it had this effect. His whole philosophy had been for years and years a deliberately subjective thing. It was one of the fatalities of his temperament that he completely distrusted what is called 'objective truth.' He had come more and more to regard 'reality' as a mere name given to the most lasting and most vivid among all the various impressions of life which each individual experiences. It might seem an insubstantial view of so solid a thing as what is called 'truth'; but such was the way he felt, and he thought he would never cease to feel like that. At any rate, one of his own most permanent impressions had always been of the nature of an extreme dualism, a dualism descending to the profoundest gulfs of being, a dualism in which every living thing was compelled to take part. The essence of this invisible struggle he was content to leave vague and obscure. He was not rigid in his definitions. But it was profoundly necessary to his life-illusion to feel the impact of this mysterious struggle and to feel that he was taking part in it. What had come over him now as he watched the shining body of Mr. Weevil, surmounted by his impudent water-rat face, as the self-conscious youth once more began his gymnastics with the willow tree, was a sort of moral atrophy. Sitting on the bank, hugging his knees, at a little distance from Jason and Lobbie, he had time to watch the Squire, and he was struck by the purged and almost hieratic look which the man now wore, as he stood leaning upon his cane encouraging the silly manœuvres of the sausage-seller. 'He looks like a mediæval bishop watching a tournament,' Wolf said to himself. And the placid sunburnt sympathy he felt for the man's amiable passivity seemed seeping in upon him like a warm salt tide – a tide that was outside any 'dualism' – a tide that was threatening the banked-up discriminations of his whole life.

Then all in a moment he asked himself a very searching question. 'What would I feel at this moment,' he said to himself, 'if Weevil were a girl and Lobbie a little girl? Should I in that case be quite untroubled by this Giorgione-like *fête champêtre*? No!' – so he answered his own question – 'I should feel just as uncomfortable even then at my complicity. It isn't a question of the sex . . . it's a question of something else . . . it's a question of – ' A noisy splash made by Lob as he darted into the water, and a still louder splash made by Mr. Weevil as he plunged to meet him, interrupted Wolf's train of ideas.

He glanced at his watch. It was a quarter to five. He scrambled to his feet and picked up his stick. 'I must rush off,' he cried. 'You'll excuse me, sir? We'll meet again soon, Otter. Good-bye, Weevil! Good-bye, Lobbie! Don't stay in too long or you'll catch a chill, and I shall get into trouble with the family.'

Mr. Urquhart and Jason seemed as indifferent to his departure as if he had been an inquisitive Guernsey cow who had approached them and then gone off with a flick of her tail. As he walked across the field he had an uneasy sense that he was retreating from some occult arena where he had suffered an irreversible defeat. The stirring of the waters of Lenty was evidently perilous to him!

He found his mother sitting over the tea-table in Roger Monk's
trim house, sewing artificial poppies round her hat.

During their tea together he related all he chose to relate of the
hatter's death. His mother, however, with her accustomed airy
directness, like the swoop of a kestrel, pounced at once on the main
issue.

'That's what I wanted to discuss with you,' she said. 'What's
going to happen to those Smith girls?'

She gave him one of her sharp, quick looks, full of worldly
sagacity, and yet full of a kind of humorous recklessness.

'No one has the least idea,' he responded. 'I wish I could do
something for them. But I don't see how I can.'

His mother looked mischievously and affectionately at him.

Suddenly, coming round the table, she kissed him with a series
of little bird-like pecks. 'There's no one like my Lambkin,' she
said lightly, 'for being too good to live!'

Having thus given him the feeling – how well he knew it! –
that the very deepest stretch of his spirit only appeared as a pretty
little pet-dog trick to her cynical maternal eroticism, she went back
again, round the table, to her seat.

She drank more tea after that and ate more bread-and-butter,
and Wolf received the impression that his obvious concern over
Mattie and Olwen had for some reason given her a deep sense of
satisfaction.

It was certainly a relief to him that this was so; and yet, as he met
her warm, ironical, half-mischievous glance, a glance full of a sort
of gloating tenderness that laughed at both itself and its object, he
felt obscurely uneasy.

'I hope,' he said at last, 'that I shan't inflict my philanthropies
on Gerda. Fortunately she's got a very sweet nature.'

A somewhat grim look passed over Mrs. Solent's face. Her
adamantine chin was pushed forward; and her under lip, like
the under lip of a carnivore, protruded itself in an extremely
formidable manner.

'I don't see your pretty Gerda putting herself out for anybody,'
she said.

Wolf began instantaneously to grow angry – far more angry
than he could himself account for.

'She's as anxious about them as I am,' he retorted hotly.

'She knows you too well, Wolf, to dare to thwart you,' remarked
Mrs. Solent.

'It's her generous nature!' he cried, with a trembling lip. 'It's pure and simple magnanimity, such as not another girl in the world would show!'

His mother's massive face, under her weight of silver hair, darkened to a dull red.

'I'm afraid you spoil us all, Lambkin,' she said with a wicked airy little laugh. 'But your Gerda knows how to play her cards.'

She had never spoken to him in this tone before. The magnetic current of his anger had touched an evil chord in her own nature, and her laugh was sardonic.

'Play her cards!' he cried in high indignation. 'She's utterly incapable of such a thing! I wish you'd learn the same sweet generosity, mother! It's you who "play your cards," as you call it.'

Mrs. Solent rose to her feet, her face pale now and hard-set as flint.

'You'd have done better to have gone back to Blacksod this afternoon, Wolf,' she said, 'if that's how you feel about me!'

'Mother, you are absolutely unfair!' he cried. 'And you've always been unfair about Gerda. You hate her for some unknown absurd reason. Pure snobbishness, most likely! And you'd like to hurt her, to make her suffer, to spoil her life. That's why – oh, I see it now! – you're so glad I'm fussed up about Mattie. You think that will spoil everything for Gerda; and you are glad that it should!'

She came again round the table now, but with a very different purpose from her previous gesture; and yet, as Wolf knew well, it was the same savage eroticism that dominated both these movements.

'I care nothing, not one crow's feather, for your pretty brainless Gerda!' she cried, standing quite close to him, her left hand on the handle of the silver cake basket which formed the centre of the tea-table, and her right hand opening and shutting as if it were galvanized. 'I've been good to her, to please you; and I've been made a fool of for my trouble. Don't you think I don't know how little I count any more in your life, Wolf! Nothing . . . nothing . . . nothing! You just come and see me. You flatter me and cajole me. But you never stay! Do you realize you haven't stayed one night under the same roof with me since you married? Oh, it's all right! I don't complain. I'm growing an old woman; and old women aren't such pleasant companions as brainless little girls! Oh, it's all right! But it's a funny experience, this being shelved and superannuated while your feelings are just as young as anyone's!'

Her voice, as she let herself be overwhelmed by a blind rush of accumulated self-pity, began to break and choke; and then, all in a moment, it rose to a terrible, ringing intensity, like the sound of a great sea-bell in a violent storm. . . .

'It's all right! I can stand it!' she cried. 'I had plenty of practice with your father, and now I'm going to have the same thing with you. . . . Oh, it's a cruel thing to be a woman!'

She pushed back her grey hair from her forehead with one hand, while the other twitched frantically at her waistband. Never had her handsome features looked more noble; never had her whole personality projected such magnificent, such primeval passion.

Wolf, as he watched her, felt weak, despicable, faltering. He felt like a finical attendant watching the splendid fury of some Sophoclean heroine. He became aware that her anger leaped up from some incalculable crevasse in the rock crust of the universe, such as he himself had never approached. The nature of her feeling, its directness, its primordial simplicity, reduced his own emotion to something ridiculous. She towered above him there with that grand convulsed face and those expanded breasts; while her fine hands, clutching at her belt, seemed to display a wild desire to strip herself naked before him, to overwhelm him with the wrath of her naked maternal body, bare to the outrage of his impiety.

In the storm of her abandonment, the light irony that was her personal armour against life seemed to drop from her, piece by glittering piece, and fall tinkling upon the floor. Something impersonal rose up in its place, an image of all the striken maternal nerves that had vibrated and endured through long centuries; so that it became no longer just a struggle between Wolf Solent and Ann Solent – it became a struggle between the body of Maternity itself and the bone of its bone!

She broke now into desperate sobs and flung herself face down upon the sofa. But the demon that tore at her vitals was not yet content. Turning half round towards Wolf, and lifting herself up by her arms, she raised a long, pitiful howl like a trapped leopard in the jungle. 'Women . . . women . . . women!' she cried aloud; and then, to Wolf's consternation, propping herself upon one of her arms, she held out the other with her first finger extended, menacing, prophetic, straight towards him.

'It's he who's doing all this to me! You needn't think that you could do it alone! It's both of you. It's both! But, oh, you great, heavy, stupid, clumsy lumps of selfishness. . . . Something, some day, will make you . . . I don't know what. . . . Something, one day . . . will make you . . . Something will do it . . . one day . . . and I shall be glad. . . . Don't expect anything else. I shall be glad!'

She drew in her arm and buried her face in the sofa, her body heaving with long, dry, husky sobs.

Wolf surveyed her form as she lay there, one strong leg exposed as high as the knee, and one disarranged tress of wavy grey hair hanging across her cheek. And it came over him with a wave of remorseful shame that this formidable being, so grotesquely reduced, was the actual human animal out of whose entrails he had been dragged into light and air.

His remorse, however, was not a pure or simple emotion. It was complicated by a kind of sulky indignation and by a bitter sense of injustice. The physical shamelessness, too, of her abandonment shocked something in him, some vein of fastidious reverence. But his mother's cynicism had always shocked this element in his nature; and what he felt now he had felt a thousand times before – felt in the earliest dawn of consciousness. What he would have liked to do at that moment was just to slip out of the room and out of the house. Her paroxysm roused something in him which, had she known it, she would have recognized as more dangerous than any responsive anger. But this feeling did not destroy his pity; so that, as he now sombrely contemplated those grey hairs, and that exposed knee, he felt a more poignant consciousness of what she was than he had ever felt at the times when he admired her most and loved her most.

He let himself sink down in his chair and covered his mouth with his hand as if to hide a yawn. But he was not yawning. This was an old automatic gesture of his: perhaps originally induced by his consciousness that his mouth was his weakest and most sensitive feature, and the one by which the sufferings of his mind were most quickly betrayed.

Then he suddenly became aware that the sobs had ceased; and a second later he received a most queer impression, the impression, namely, that one warm, glowing, ironical brown eye was fixed upon him and was steadily regarding him – regarding him through the disordered tress of ruffled hair that lay across it.

He drew his hand from his mouth, rose to his feet quickly, and, bending down above his mother, pulled her up from a recumbent into a sitting posture.

'Mother, don't!' he cried. 'You're laughing at me; you're pretending! And I might have done I don't know what, because you scared me so. You've just been teasing your poor son, and frightened him out of his wits; and now you're laughing at me!'

He fell on his knees in front of her and she left her tousled forehead sink down till it rested against his; and there they remained for a while, their two skulls in a happy trance of relaxed contact, full of unspoken reciprocities, like the skulls of two animals out at pasture, or the branches of two trees exhausted by a storm.

Wolf was conscious of abandoning himself to a vast undisturbed peace – a peace without thought, aim, or desire – a peace that flowed over him from the dim reservoirs of prenatal life, lulling him, soothing him, hypnotizing him – obliterating everything from his consciousness except a faint delicious feeling that everything *had* been obliterated.

It was his mother herself who broke the spell. She raised her hands to his head and held it back by his stubbly straw-coloured hair, pressing, as she did so, her own glowing tear-stained cheeks against his chin, and finally kissing him with a hot, intense, tyrannous kiss.

He rose to his feet after that and so did she; and, moved by a simultaneous impulse, they both sat down again at the deserted tea-table, emptied the teapot into their cups, and began spreading for themselves large mouthfuls of bread-and-butter with overflowing spoonfuls of red currant jam.

Wolf felt as if this were in some way a kind of sacramental feast; and he even received a queer sensation, as though their enjoyment in common of the sweet morsels they swallowed so greedily were an obscure reversion to those forgotten diurnal nourishments which he must have shared with her long before his flesh was separated from hers.

Half an hour later he was walking leisurely towards Ramsgard along that now so familiar road. He recalled his first acquaintance with this road, that day he drove over by the side of Darnley Otter; and, as he began to approach the town, he found himself glancing across the fields to his right, toward the lane that led to the cemetery, and then across the fields to the left, toward the broader highway which he had followed on the preceding night, his head full of Mr. Smith's death.

Roads and lanes! Lanes and roads! What a part these tracks for the feet of men and beasts, dusty in summer, muddy in winter, had played in his mental consciousness! The thrill that this idea of roadways gave him was a proof to him that his mind was returning to its independent orbit, after its plunge into that maternal hypnosis. His spirit felt indeed deliciously free just then, and expanded its wings to its heart's content, like a great flapping rook. Every object of the way took on an especial glamour; and never had he enjoyed so deeply one peculiar trick of his mind. This was a certain queer sensuous sympathy he could feel sometimes for completely unknown people's lives, as he passed by their dwellings. He enjoyed it now with especial satisfaction, thinking of the people in each cottage he came to, and gathering their experiences together as one might gather a bunch of ragwort or hemp-agrimony out of the dusty hedges.

Well enough did he know how many of these experiences were bitter and grotesque; but what he enjoyed now, along with all these unknown people, was their moments of simple, sensuous well-being.

Such a moment he himself felt presently, as he leaned over a gate to rest, just before the road he traversed entered the outskirts of Ramsgard. Through the warm, misty evening, full of what seemed to him a veritable diffused essence of gold-dust, there came some quick wandering breaths of cooler air; and these breaths of air, brushing against his face and passing swiftly upon their way, carried a peculiar fragrance with them, a fragrance that made him think of a certain little garden of old-fashioned pinks that he used to pass, on his way to the place where he gave his lectures, down a narrow West London alley. If in Mr. Urquhart's library he had been stirred by Roger Monk's flower-beds, he was more stirred now by this far-off impression. The pinks were meagre enough in themselves. But the thought of them in their sunbaked little garden, so close to the hot pavement, touched some chord of seminal memory that gave him just a transporting thrill.

Where did it come from, this emotion? Was it an inherited feeling, reverting to days when some remote ancestor of his, in cloister or market-place, used to inhale day by day that particular sweetness? Or was it something larger and more general than this? Certainly what he felt just now, as these cool-wafted airs came over the yellow stubble, was not confined to the pinks in that hot little garden behind iron railings. It was much more as if he were enabled to enter, by a lucky psychic sensitiveness, into some continuous stream of human awareness – awareness of a beauty in the world that travelled lightly from place to place, stopping here and stopping there, like a bird of passage, but never valued at its true worth until it had vanished away.

'There *must* be,' he thought, 'some deep race-memory in which these things are stored up, to be drawn upon by those who seek for them through the world – a memory that has the power of obliterating infinite débris, while it retains all these frail essences, these emanations from plants and trees, roadsides and gardens, as if such things actually possessed immortal souls!' He turned from the gate and pursued his road, swinging his stick from side to side like a madman and repeating aloud, as he strode along, the words 'immortal souls.'

Certain human expressions, meaning one thing to the philosopher and quite another thing to the populace, were always fascinating to Wolf. His mind began to dwell now upon the actual syllables of this phrase, 'immortal souls,' until by a familiar transformation those formidable sounds took on a shadowy personality of their own – took on the shape, in fact, of Christie Malakite – and in that shape went wavering away over the fields like a thin spiral cloud! 'These quaint words, used by the men of old time,' he said to himself, 'to describe what we all feel, have more in them than people have any idea of. I must tell Christie that!' And then it occurred to him how impossible it would be to explain to any living intelligence the faltering thoughts that had ended by his invocation of the 'soul' of a tiny London garden and his embodying it in the wraith of the daughter of Mr. Malakite!

It still kept hovering in front of his mind, however – this phrase, 'immortal souls' – even after it had slipped like a boat from its moorings. There seemed a noble and defiant challenge in it to all that petered out, to all that flagged, that wilted, that scattered, that became nothing, in the melancholy drift of the world!

With the cool airs of that summer evening wafted about him, he felt, as he passed now under the vast shadow of the Abbey church, that there were immense resources of renewal, of restoration, spread abroad over the face of the earth, such as had hardly been drawn upon at all by the sons and daughters of men. 'Why is it,' he thought, 'that this particular expression, "immortal souls," should act upon my mind in this way?' And as he moved slowly along now between the sculptured entrance to the school-house and the little low-roofed shop where the straw-hatted boys of the School bought their confectionery, it occurred to him as curiously significant that the syllable 'God,' so talismanic to most people, had never, from his childhood, possessed the faintest magic for him! 'It must be,' he thought, as, passing under a carved archway, he came bolt up on the old monastic conduit, 'that anything suggestive of metaphysical unity is distasteful to me. It must be that my world is essentially a manifold world, and my religion, if I have any, essentially polytheistic! And yet, in matters of good and evil' – and he recalled his sensations at Lenty Pond – 'I'm what they'd call a dualist, I suppose. Ay! It's funny. Directly one comes to putting feelings into words, one is compelled to accept hopeless contradictions in the very depths of one's being!'

He moved right in under the carved roof of the old conduit, between the Late Gothic pillars, and laid his hand on the edge of the water-trough. The traffic of the High Street passed him by, and groups of tall straw-hatted schoolboys brushed past him, cold, remote, haughty, discreet, like young Romans in some Ionian market-place.

A barrel organ was being played where the pavement widened, under the out-jutting gables of a mediæval hostelry; and Wolf couldn't help noticing how the abstracted, impassive expression of the old man who played it contrasted with a couple of ragged little children, glowing cheeked and intent, who danced to its jigging tune.

'Polytheism . . . dualism,' he repeated, trying to retain the philosophical distinctions which he felt crumbling to bits and drifting away. But as he fumbled with his fingers at that conduit-trough and turned automatically a leaden faucet so that water gushed out over his hand, his mind seemed to reject every single one of those traditional human catchwords.

'I just told him it was all bloody rot!' The words fell upon his ears from the lips of a pale-faced quiet lad, who, with an arm round the neck of another, swung past Wolf's retreat; and they served to give his thoughts an edge.

'All bloody rot!' he mumbled, turning off the water and throwing a nervous glance round him, lest his proceedings should have attracted attention. 'But there's more in all this, all the same, than any of these words implies. That's the whole thing. Not less, but more! More; though more of *what*, I don't suppose I shall ever discover! But more of something.'

And as he left the conduit and made his way up the street, he had the feeling that his real self was engaged in an exciting maze of transactions, completely different from those which just now occupied his senses and his will.

He found the Smith *ménage*, when Mattie's little maid, smiling and radiant at the presence of so much drama, admitted him after a long wait upon the doorstep, burdened by the presence of two portly and extremely loquacious undertakers. Contrary to custom, but due to the nature of his illness and the heat of the weather, it had become advisable to place the Hatter of Ramsgard in his elm-wood coffin without further delay.

Mattie had brought Olwen down into the dining-room, so as to remove her from the sound of the hammering; but the child was nervous and preoccupied, and it was with but a languid interest that she busied herself with the black ribbons of Gipsy and Antoinette, laid side by side on the great mahogany table, with the cushions from Mr. Smith's chair under their waxen heads. Even Wolf's arrival did not really distract her; and he would have given much to know what the thoughts actually were that gave to her little oval face that sombre pallor and frowning intensity.

Mattie herself seemed strangely lethargic as she drew up one of the straight-backed leather-covered chairs and sat down by his side; and Wolf found it difficult, as they both stared at the un-sympathetic silver on the sideboard, to broach the subject of her future, with which his mind was so full.

'Knock . . . knock . . . knock,' went the hammer in the room above, accompanied by the low-toned rumble of conversation from the two intruders.

'Death is a queer thing,' thought Wolf, while the weary indifference of Mr. Smith's white face dominated the slow passing of the minutes. 'Would anyone know by that sound,' he thought, 'that those were coffin nails? There'll be another sound when they put him into the hole,' so his mind ran on; 'there'll be that peculiar sound of loose, dry mould flung on the top of a wooden lid. All the world over, those same two sounds. Well, not quite *all* the world over. But how many times had Mr. Smith heard that hammering and that rattle of earth mould? Did he sit in this very place when they were nailing Lorna in? I must break this un-comfortable silence,' he thought. 'There! *That* must have been the last! But what the devil are they doing now? This silence is worse than the hammering. Are they having a drink?'

There was a sharp ring at the door bell; and the three strained faces in that dusky dining-room glanced anxiously at one another, while the patter of the maid's feet on the tiled floor responded to this new sound.

A minute later and they all rose hurriedly while, to their com-plete surprise, Mrs. Otter and Darnley were ushered into the room. The little lady seemed perturbed and embarrassed at the presence of Wolf, but Darnley gave him a quick reassuring nod.

'I heard by chance,' began Mrs. Otter rapidly. 'We were so sorry for you. I wanted to come. My son was very good. He got me a carriage. I hope you don't mind my coming.'

'I am sure it's very nice of you, Mrs. Otter,' murmured Mattie. 'Sit down, won't you? Sit down, please, Mr. Otter. Thank you, Wolf. No, that's been broken for years.' Wolf made a fumbling attempt to replace the piece of carved mahogany that had come off in his hand. This mechanical preoccupation enabled him to notice in silence the manner in which Darnley and Mattie had begun to stare at each other.

'What I had in my mind, in coming to you, my poor child,' he heard Mrs. Otter say, 'was to ask a great and really rather a difficult favour. What I came to say was this . . . oh, I don't know whether I ought to worry you now about it! . . . but my son . . . I mean Jason . . . told me I might do just as I liked. . . . My house is my own, you know!' This last rather unexpected phrase was uttered with such a winning and whimsical smile that Wolf looked hastily at Mattie, very anxious that she should say nothing to hurt this visitor's feelings. He was surprised to observe that Mattie had only in the vaguest manner caught the drift of this speech.

'Yes, Mrs. Otter, you've always been most kind to me,' was all she said in reply.

'My son left everything completely in my hands. Didn't he, Darnley?' Mrs. Otter went on. There was a perplexed frown on her face now; and she made a feeble little movement of one of her hands towards Darnley, as if appealing to him for help.

'Didn't he, Darnley?' she repeated.

But Darnley also seemed to have lost the drift of her remarks.

'You were quite right, mother,' he replied at random. 'You're awfully wise when things are getting serious. . . . She's wonderful in a crisis.' He addressed this last remark to no one in particular, and it did little to help forward the general air of cloudiness into which the conversation had fallen.

'She really is . . . wonderful in a crisis,' he repeated absent-mindedly; and Wolf, as he looked at the lethargic silver on the sideboard, seemed to hear the voice of the cake basket addressing the biscuit bowl. 'She's wonderful in a crisis,' in the tone of an ancient playgoer commenting on an oft-repeated play.

'Mattie doesn't know whatever we shall do.' The words came from Olwen, who now stood close to Wolf's chair; and the words served to bring matters to a head.

'That's just what I'm talking about,' said Mrs. Otter, in such an eager tone that everyone turned towards her with full attention. 'What I came to ask you was this,' she said firmly, addressing herself to Mattie. 'Our Dimity is getting feeble and old, and I'm not as strong as I was. My son – Jason, I mean – is very particular. You know what he is, my dear? What a poet he is. Mr. Solent thinks he's a *great* poet, don't you, Mr. Solent? . . . Well, what I came to say is this. It would be such a pleasure to us all, my dear' – here she laid her grey-gloved hand lightly on Mattie's wrist – 'if you'd come and live with us and help me – you know? – help me with everything. Now don't shake your head like that! I know what you mean. Of course, this little one must come, too, and of course we've got to think of her lessons.' The little lady drew a long breath, but hurried on before Mattie could utter a word. 'It's her lessons I was thinking about. I'm very fond of teaching children, children that I *like*, I mean; and I've got *all* the fairy-stories. I've got the one they wouldn't let me even see the pictures of, when *I* was little.'

Wolf had already screwed his head round so as to snatch a glimpse of Olwen's face, and he was surprised at the grave glow of unrestrained delight that was now slowly beginning to spread over it. But Mattie still shook her head.

'I couldn't,' she murmured in a faint voice. 'Though it's very, very kind of you, Mrs. Otter. But I could never think of such a thing. Olwen and I have been talking about it and we've made up our minds that I must go to work. Olwen says she'll be good when I leave her and not fret or be lonely.'

At this moment there was a sound of heavy footsteps descending the stairs, accompanied by a few muffled remarks of a facetious kind. Mrs. Otter glanced at Wolf, who gave her a slight inclination of the head. She turned to Mattie hurriedly.

'Well, my dear,' she said. 'I don't want to rush you against your will into anything. Though I did set my heart upon it, and I've thought about it from every possible side.'

Mattie's answer to this was to stretch forth her hand and press tightly the gloved fingers of the little old lady. But the look which she gave her showed no sign of yielding. It was very tender; but it was firm and resolute.

There was another pause then among them all; and once more Wolf was aware of a most vivid sense of Mr. Smith's white, set face, exhausted, detached, commenting with a kind of desolating equanimity upon the events that were taking place. Those ponderous silver pieces seemed to Wolf now, as he frowned upon them, to be gathering themselves together in that darkening room, to be shaping themselves with shadowy persistence into funereal ornaments heaped up beside the dead hatter.

One of the windows behind Wolf's head was open, and with the noises of the street there entered and circled round him a deliciously cool air, an air like that which he had been conscious of on his approach to Ramsgard, as he leaned over that gate. Once more the scent of pinks came quivering through his brain and he felt a shameless thrill of pleasure. This time, instead of the wraith of Christie Malakite, it was the body of the hatter that associated itself with that remembered scent – not any repulsive odour of mortality emerging from those nailed-up boards, but rather some spiritual essence from the presence of Death itself. And as he breathed this air, the voices of his companions became a vague humming in his ears, and all manner of queer detached memories floated in upon him. He felt himself to be walking alone along some high white road bordered by waving grasses and patches of yellow rock-rose. There was a town far below him, at the bottom of a green valley – a mass of huddled grey roofs among meadows and streams – round which the twilight was darkening. Along with all this he was conscious of the taste of a perculiar kind of baker's bread, such as used to be sold at a shop in Dorchester, where, as a child, they would take him for tea during summer jaunts from Weymouth. The presence of Death seemed to re-create these things and to touch them with a peculiar intensity.

He was roused from his trance by the clear, shrill voice of Olwen arguing desperately with Mattie.

'I *want* to do what she says! Why *can't* we do what she says? I'll be bad if you don't let us! I won't go to sleep. I'll be far worse than Gipsy or Antoinette. I'll tear my hair out! I'll bite my hand!'

'Hush, Olwen!' he heard Mattie reply. 'Mrs. Otter will be only too pleased I can't accept her offer if you talk like that.'

The little girl gazed at her for a moment with a quaint, solemn scrutiny. Then she laughed, a merry, reassured laugh, and, rushing to where Darnley was sitting, slid coaxingly upon his knee.

'You'll tell her what she must do when everyone's gone,' she murmured softly; and then, with her eyes fixed upon his face, she stroked his beard with her small, nervous hand.

Mrs. Otter and Wolf smiled at each other; and there came into Wolf's mind those scenes in Homer where girlish suppliants, mortal as well as immortal, lay their hands upon the chins of those they are cajoling!

'Would you tear *my* hair out as well as your own,' enquired Darnley, 'if she goes on refusing to let you live with us?' Wolf thought he had never seen Darnley's eyes look so deeply luminous as they did while he uttered those words.

Mattie still shook her head; but although there were tears on her cheek, the whole expression of her face was relaxed and at peace. Indeed, as Wolf kept surreptitiously glancing at her, he got the impression that the girl longed to rush away and burst into a flood of crying, but not into unhappy crying. The kindred blood in his veins made him clairvoyant; and he felt convinced that if the Otters refused to accept her rejection of their scheme, she would eventually be persuaded.

'Well, my dear child,' he heard Mrs. Otter saying, 'you must not answer us in a hurry like this. You see what friends Darnley and your little one have already become; and if only – '

She stopped suddenly; for there came a second ring at the street door, followed by the same impetuous rush of the little maid across the hall. This time Wolf looked with dismay into his sister's face when he heard a well-known voice asking in a loud, firm tone for Miss Smith. They all got up when Miss Gault was shown into the room. Olwen hastily snatched her dolls from the table and carried them off to Mr. Smith's big leather chair by the fireplace; and Mrs. Otter, after a hurried bow to the new visitor, followed the child to that retreat and entered into a whispered conversation with her.

The presence of Wolf did not seem to be any surprise to the formidable lady. She nodded at him familiarly, as she embraced Mattie; but her greeting to Darnley was stiff and formal. Darnley himself seemed quite unperturbed by this coldness. His strangely-coloured blue eyes remained fixed upon Mattie; and he stood with his back propped against a bookcase, toying with his watch-chain.

In the darkening twilight of the room – for no one had thought of asking for a lamp – the man's slim figure, as Wolf glanced sideways at him, had the appearance of some old Van Dyck portrait come to life in a Victorian house. Behind his back the great heavily-bound editions of those *Sundays at Home* and *Leisure Hours*, whose illustrations must have solaced many a long evening in the far-off childhood of Albert Smith, gathered the summer darkness about them with that peculiar mystical solemnity which old books, like old trees and old hedges, display at the coming on of night. And Wolf, as he listened with amusement to the discourse of Selena Gault, became aware that, with one of her chance-flung felicities, Nature was arranging a singularly appropriate stage for what at any rate was an exciting encounter between Darnley Otter and Mattie Smith.

'Darnley *must* have often met Mattie before,' thought Wolf. 'But very likely never in her own house and probably never when they could really take in each other's personality. Besides . . . what do I know about them? All this may have begun years ago . . . before I came upon the scene at all. If so, what secretive demons they both have been!'

He turned once more to his sister. Oh, he couldn't be mistaken! Why, the girl's heavy countenance, even in that gloom, had a look that he could only describe to himself as transfigured. 'There's certainly something up, there,' he thought. 'Well! She'll be a little fool if she doesn't take the old lady's offer. I'd like to know, though, what Jason *did* say when this scheme was suggested!'

And then, seated a little back from Mattie and Miss Gault, and accepting a cigarette from Darnley, who now took a chair by his side, Wolf began to be conscious of the drift of the amazing discourse which the visitor was directing, like a cannonade of lumbering artillery, across the table into the ears of his sister. Selena's attire was in good taste enough – indeed, it was superlatively ladylike; but it was the 'rich, not gaudy' attire of a person quite oblivious of contemporary fashion, and in some queer way it lent itself so well to the quality of that room that it seemed to bring the furniture itself to life in support of everything she said.

The gathering darkness assisted at this strange play. It was as if all the ponderous objects in that room – including the silver, the chairs, the dark green curtains, the grotesque portrait of Mr. Smith's father, the leather backs of the *Sundays at Home* and the *Leisure Hours*, the leather back of a draughtboard, with the words 'History of the World' printed on it, the bronze horses on either side of the mantelpiece, the enormous empty coal-scuttle – combined together to give weight to the opinions of this aggressive woman, whose own childhood, like that of the silent person up-stairs, they had ramparted with their massive solemnities!

And Wolf was astounded at the impertinence of what Miss Gault did say. It was an impertinence covered up with bronze and brocade. But it was an indecent impertinence. It resembled the absurd drapery covering the symbolic figure of Mercy, or Truth, or Righteousness, which dominated the great dining-room clock that stood in the middle of the marble chimneypiece. 'I confess I first thought,' Miss Gault was now saying, 'of having Olwen to live with Emma and me . . . but I couldn't have her teasing the cats . . . or pining for you . . . so this Home is better. I have made a lot of enquiries about this Home. I made them last year, for another purpose; and it's lucky I did, because people don't hear of these things when they really want them. The beautiful thing about it is that they accept mother *and* child . . . and of course Olwen *is* like your child now. Another great advantage about this plan is that Taunton is so near us all . . . only a couple of hours by train.' She made a little nod in Wolf's direction. 'Wolf would be able to run over and see you on Sundays,' she added.

Her voice sank; but the darkened room was full of the echoes of it – the whispering of Mrs. Otter, who was evidently telling Olwen a story, being the only force that resisted it. And the dark green curtains were delighted. 'See you on Sundays . . . see you on Sundays,' they repeated, while the draughtboard 'History of the World' echoed the word 'Sundays,' making it seem like the very voice of that charitable institution which accepted both mother *and* child.

'And the little sum required by the authorities,' Miss Gault continued, 'I shall be delighted to provide. I do, of course, recognize that it was against my advice that you adopted Olwen. But the child's naturally fond of you now; and I think it would be wrong to separate her from you, as would have to be done if you got employment here . . . for the child couldn't be left alone all day . . . and no doubt everything here will be sold. Don't answer me just yet,' the lady went on. 'I want you, Wolf, too, to hear all I've got to say . . . for, of course . . . well! there's no need for me to enter into *that* . . . but what I thought I would ask you now, Mattie dear, is to tell me what particular things in this house you're especially fond of; and then . . . well! I hope I should be able to be present at the auction . . . so that whenever you *do* have a house of your own, they'll be . . . well! they'll be, so to speak, still in the family.' She turned more boldly towards Wolf at this point, as if to ensure his recognition of her old-fashioned tact. But Wolf's impulse at that moment resembled the impulse of King Claudius in the play. He felt a desire to cry out in thundering tones, 'Lights! lights! lights!' So that it was still left to the draughtboard and the bronze clock to appreciate such delicacy and to have the last word.

It was not Wolf, but Darnley, however, who broke the spell

thrown upon them by Miss Gault. He walked rapidly over to his mother, whispered something in her ear, took her hand, and brought her to Mattie's side.

'You'll be a dear girl and do what *we* want you to do?' said the old lady clearly and firmly, taking no notice of Miss Gault.

Wolf thought he caught an appealing glance in his direction, though it was so dark now that his sister's face was a mere blur of whiteness. But he rose hurriedly and came up to where they were all grouped. There was just a half-second's pause, which enabled him to catch an impress of the whole queer scene before he spoke, to catch the bewildered anger on Miss Gault's face, to observe that Olwen had possessed herself of Darnley's hand, to remark how Mrs. Otter was so nervous that the chair upon which she had laid her fingers tapped on the floor; and then he himself spoke out with all the weight he could muster.

'I'm sorry, Miss Gault, and I know Mattie's most grateful for your suggestion; but it had all been settled before you came in. They're going to stay for the present with our good friends here. They're going to do what *I* did when I first came to King's Barton. There'll be time enough later for other arrangements; but for the moment Mattie's going to accept Mrs. Otter's invitation, and Olwen too. As to the furniture here, we needn't decide about *that* in any hurry. It may be that Mattie would be happier to get completely rid of it. I know I should, in her case. But it's sweet of you to suggest buying back some of it. I'm sure Mattie appreciates that very much. But the chief point just now is what she and Olwen are going to do; and that has been quite decided – hasn't it, Mattie? They're going to that hospitable Pond Cottage, where I went for my first night in Dorset!'

Wolf's voice became more and more decisive as he brought his declaration to a close; but with an instinct for preventing any further protests from Mattie, he hurriedly rushed out into the hall and began calling for the little maid.

'Constantia!' he shouted. 'Constantia! Please bring us the lamp!'

What occurred after his departure from that darkened dining-room he never knew. His words seemed to have had the effect of the letting-off of a gun in a soundless wood. For from where he waited at the kitchen-door there came to him an incoherent murmur of many confused voices. When at last he returned with the lamp in his hand and placed it in the centre of the table, Olwen was crying in the leather armchair, where Mattie and Mrs. Otter were bending over her; while Miss Gault, standing erect in the centre of the room, was asking Darnley in a strained, husky voice whether it was true that they had recently discovered in the Abbey-church the actual bones of King Æthelwolf, the brother of Alfred.

'Good-bye, then. Good-bye, all of you! I mustn't be in the way any longer.' With this, Miss Gault bowed to Darnley, nodded in the direction of the weeping child, and walked straight into the hall.

From Wolf she kept her eyes averted as she passed; but the expression of her face shocked him, and he followed her to the street door. As he bent forward to turn the handle before she set her own hand upon it, he caught sight of that deformed lip of hers; and the look of it appalled him. To see such a thing as that was bad enough; but it became worse when the extraordinary visage, that now was face to face with him, contorted itself, there in the doorway before him, into a puckered mask of outrage. He felt a little ashamed of himself for the brutality of his observation at that moment; but he couldn't help noticing that Miss Gault made a much more childish contortion of her face when *she* collapsed than his adamantine mother had done that same afternoon! His mother had 'lifted up her voice,' as the Scripture says, 'and wept'; but Wolf remembered well how, even when she was howling like a lioness with a spear in her side, her fine clear-cut features had retained their dignity. Big tears had fallen, but they had fallen like rain upon a tragic torso. Very different was it with Miss Gault at this moment! Three times she made an attempt to speak to him, and three times her face grew convulsed.

'Wait a minute!' he blurted out at last, and ran back into the dining-room. There he shouted a loud good-bye to them all. 'See you to-morrow, Mattie dear!' he cried. 'I leave you in good hands, Olwen. Good-night, Mrs. Otter!'

'I'll come back and have dinner with you, if I may,' he said, as he caught up Miss Gault on the street pavement. 'Listen! What's that striking now?' He laid his hand on her arm and held her motionless. 'Seven o'clock, eh? Well, you don't dine till eight; so do let's have a bit of a walk before going to your house.'

'Let's go to the grave, boy,' she whispered hoarsely. 'We can talk there. My Emma won't mind, even if we *are* late. But how will you get back to Blacksod?' she added with concern.

'Oh, I'll take the ten o'clock train,' he said. 'That'll mean that I shan't have any more walking and shan't keep Gerda up. It runs still at that time, doesn't it? Or have they changed it?'

But Miss Gault had already given to practical concerns all the energy she could spare just then.

'How lovely this place is at night!' she said, as they passed under the Abbey wall. 'I wonder if Mr. Otter is right and it is really the coffin of King Æthelwolf that they've found.'

They reached the main entrance to the building, and to their surprise they found it open.

'Let's go in for a minute,' said Wolf. His companion assented in silence and they entered together.

'I would have liked to have that child to live with me,' murmured Miss Gault; 'but it would have been cruel to the cats . . . she's grown so rough to them lately . . . and she's not always polite to Emma.'

Wolf made no reply to this remark; and as they moved slowly up the central aisle, which was feebly illuminated from somewhere between the choir-stalls, he allowed his mind to wander away from Miss Gault and her thwarted philanthropies. The few lights that were burning hardly reached – and then only with a dim, diffused lustre, like the interior of a sand-blurred mother-of-pearl shell – the high fan tracery of the roof. Wolf felt strongly upon him once again that feeling of mystic exultation which had been hovering over him all day; and when the presence of the light behind the choir was explained by a sudden burst of organ notes, he felt such a thrill of happiness that it brought with it a reaction of sheer shame.

'Accident!' he muttered to himself. 'Pure accident!' he repeated, as they crossed in front of the altar and made their way to the lady-chapel behind it. And he even felt, as he fumbled about in the dim light, looking for some sign of the Saxon king's coffin, a sense of having feloniously stolen his ecstasy from some treasure-house of the human race! 'Why should I,' he thought, 'be singled out by pure chance for this?' That Waterloo-steps face – no King Æthelwolf for him, no fan tracery, no scent of pinks – Is my gratitude to the gods, then, a base and scurvy feeling?'

Even as this thought crossed his mind he stumbled against some sort of glass framework upon the southern floor of that lady-chapel.

'Here we are, Miss Gault!' he whispered excitedly. 'Only, I suppose we shall get into trouble if that organist hears us. Look here, though, for God's sake! This is the king's coffin!'

He went down on his knees and pulled aside in the dim light a piece of carpet that had been carefully spread over the glass frame. The unwieldy form of his companion was promptly now at his side, kneeling too.

'Dare I strike a match, d'ye think?' he whispered.

'No, no, boy! You mustn't do that. Wolf, you mustn't, you really mustn't!' murmured the daughter of the head master of Ramsgard School.

But he disregarded her protest, and, fumbling in his pocket, produced a match-box and struck a wax vesta.

The little yellow flame illuminated the glass-covered aperture in the floor and threw into such weird relief the lineaments of Miss Gault as almost to divest them of their humanity. Only a dim consciousness of this astounding countenance, so near his own, reached Wolf's mind just then. He was too excited. But afterwards, when he recalled the whole incident, it came back distinctly upon him as one of those glimpses into something abominable, ghastly, in Nature's pranks, such as a person were wise to make note of, with the rest, as he went through the world! Here, in the mere possibility of such a vision – for, to say the truth, Miss Gault's face by that match-flare was rendered nothing less than *bestial* – was an experience to be set against those chance-heard organ notes that had mounted up so triumphantly among the torn battle flags.

Holding the match aloft with his hand, he bent down until his face actually touched the glass. *Nothing.* Certain interesting chromatic effects . . . certain flickers and blotches of colour that was no colour, of sparkles that were opaque, of outlines that were no outlines . . . and then the match burnt his hand and went out. Hurriedly he lit another and held it up, his burnt hand smarting. Down went his face till his hooked nose was pressed against the glass. Sparkles, black, wavering spots, fluctuating blotches of reddish-yellow, little orbs of blackness rimmed with lunar rings; and then again darkness! *Nothing!* Angrily he scrambled to his feet, and with childish petulance thrust his smarting fingers into his mouth.

'The bones are there!' he whispered huskily. 'The bones are there! Æthelwolf himself! But it's no use. We must come again by daylight. It's one of those things that are so damnably annoying. Quick! . . . while the organ's still playing! I know what these people are . . . so touchy about their treasures. Let's get out of here!'

He hurried his companion down the great silent nave and out of the open doorway. He felt much more vexed and perturbed than the occasion warranted. The meaningless sparkles from that tricky coffin lid danced like imps across the back of his eye-sockets.

'I suppose it's too late to go over there now?' he said, turning to her with his hat in one hand and his stick in the other, and a wavering helplessness emanating from his whole figure.

'Not at all, boy – not at all!' pronounced Miss Gault. 'Emma must keep supper waiting for us for once. You'll have time for a bite anyway before you catch that train. Come along! You don't know how fast I can walk.'

Wolf put on his hat and strode by her side in silence. The air began to smell of rain by the time they reached the slaughter-house. There was a figure with a lantern moving about in the yard of the shed; and Miss Gault dragged heavily on his arm as they went past, struggling with the rising wind.

'You'll get no meat with me, boy,' she whispered. 'No meat – no meat. It's the only way to help them. But I'd go and be hanged to help 'em . . . hanged by the neck' – the wind caught her voice and rendered it scarcely audible – 'by the neck, boy!'

Wolf pondered to himself upon the contradictory nature of this woman. She would go to the death to put an end to slaughter-houses; and yet she would pack off Mattie and Olwen to God knows what kind of an institution for paupers!

He felt a secret desire to punish her for this inconsistency, and he suddenly said: 'It's really amazingly good of the Otters to take in our friends. To find such a generous heart in a nervous old lady like that makes you think better of the whole human race!'

A portion of the impulse that led him to this speech as they passed the slaughter-house was doubtless a throb of his own conscience over this matter of eating meat. The sight of that man with a lantern, like some ghoulish wanderer in a place of execution, impressed itself by no means pleasantly on his mind; and it was the electric vibration of this discomfort that gave his voice, as he uttered these words, a certain quivering pitch of unnecessary emphasis.

The malice in his tone communicated itself like a magnetic current to his companion, and she took her hand from his arm.

'The child has wheedled herself round Darnley. That's all it is. The mother is willing enough, because she sees what a good unpaid servant Mattie will make. I won't talk about it any more, and I didn't mean to refer to it; but I think you're simply mad to let her accept such a humiliating position. But there it is! The girl can't have much pride, or nothing you said or they said could have made her accept such charity!'

His remark having brought about this outburst, he was able to exclaim in his heart, 'You rude, ill-bred old woman! You rude, ill-bred old woman!' and, having done this, he felt quite friendly toward her again and quite appeased.

He pretended to be sulking, however, for the whole time they

306

remained in the cemetery; though in reality he was thinking to himself, 'What a spirited thing it was, after all, to stick by my father like that, when he was a complete social outcast!'

They walked home in even deeper silence and at a rapid pace. It was twenty-five minutes to ten when they reached Aldhelm Street, only to find Emma in such an agitated temper that Selena had to go herself into the kitchen and bring out to him in the sitting-room a plate of curried eggs and a decanter of sherry.

He sat on her sofa and swallowed this hot dish with hungry relish, eating it in unceremonious fashion with a spoon, and tossing off so many glasses of wine that Selena glanced at him rather nervously as she herself nibbled a biscuit.

'Emma does cook well!' he said at last, as he rose to go. 'It's all right, Miss Gault, dear. You needn't look so anxious. I've got a head of iron.' And immediately as if to prove he had such a head, he felt it to be incumbent upon him to say something affectionate and tender. 'I believe,' he burst out, 'I must have just the same sort of feeling for you that *he* had!'

These were his parting words; but it was not until he was sitting in a third-class smoking-carriage of the South-Western train that he began to wonder why it was that Miss Gault's face had such a wry smile upon it as he shook hands with her at her door.

He was alone in the carriage, and, windy though it was, he kept the window open and sat facing the engine. The rush of air sobered him, and he observed with interest the scattered lights of King's Barton as the train jolted along its high embankment between that village and the Evershot meadows. He wondered humorously to himself what Jason would say that evening when he learnt of the new invasion of his privacy.

His mood saddened before the train stopped at Blacksod.

'If I knew I were only going to live five more years,' he thought, 'I would give away four of them if I were allowed to spend the other one, day and night, with Christie!' And then, as the cold wind made him shiver a little and turn up his coat collar, 'I wonder,' he thought, 'whether I'm just weak and cowardly in not leaving them all and carrying Christie off to London, let happen what may?'

The train was now following an umbrageous embankment parallel with the River Lunt. The muddy smell of that sluggish water, which the Ramsgard boys irreverently named 'the Bog-stream,' assailed his nostrils, bringing with it a feeling of obscure misery. A chilliness in his bones, a weariness in his brain, gave now to all the events of the day a sombre colour, like the colour of river mud.

As the locomotive slowly lessened its speed, he tried in vain to recall those moments of happiness . . . the vision of the bed of pinks . . . the sweet emanation from the very body of death. But in place of these things all he could think of was obdurate roots in clinging clay, sparkles and blotches that bore no human meaning, hammering of nails into coffins, men with lanterns in slaughter-house yards, and the pallid loins of Bob Weevil streaked with the green slime of Lenty Pond.

15

ROUNDED WITH A SLEEP

Aᴜɢᴜsᴛ was drawing to its end, and, with August, the holidays of the Blacksod Grammar School. The young aristocrats of Ramsgard had several weeks more before *their* new term began, but the humbler pupils whom it was Wolf's destiny to teach were now on the eve of their return to work.

Anxious to make the utmost of these precious mornings of leisure, now so soon to be snatched from him, Wolf had lately got into the habit of persuading Gerda to start out with him, for some sort of rural expedition, directly the breakfast things had been washed up.

They had explored the country in this way in almost every direction; but he found that the easiest thing to do was to have some sort of picnic lunch in the direction of King's Barton, so that when they separated he could reach his afternoon's work at the manor without arriving too tired or too late.

Three days before the Grammar School was to reopen he had cajoled Gerda into accompanying him to Poll's Camp. They had brought their provisions in a basket and had made their meal in unusual contentment under the shelter of a group of small sycamores that grew on the western slope of the camp, overlooking the great Somersetshire plain.

Gerda was now fast asleep. Stretched out upon her back, she lay as motionless as the shadows about her, one arm curved beneath her fair head and the other flung upon a bed of moss. Wolf sat with his arms hugging his knees, and his back against a sycamore trunk.

The weather had been good for the wheat that summer, and not too scorching to the grass; so that what he looked at now, as he let his eyes wander over that great level expanse towards Glastonbury, was a vast chessboard of small green fields, surrounded by pollarded elms of a yet darker colour, and interspersed by squares of yellow stubble.

The earthworks of Poll's Camp were not as deeply dug or as loftily raised as many Roman-British ramparts in that portion of the West Country. They were less of a landmark than Cadbury

Camp, for instance, away to the north-west. They were less imposing than Maiden Castle, away to the south. But such as they were, Wolf knew that the mysterious movements of King Arthur . . . *rex quondam rexque futurus* . . . had more than once crossed and recrossed, in local legend, this promontory of grassy ridges.

The day was warm; but the fact that the sky was covered with a filmy veil of grey clouds gave to the vast plain before him the appearance of a landscape whose dominant characteristic consisted in a patient effacement of all emphatic or outstanding qualities. The green of the meadows was a shy, watery green. The verdure of the elm trees was a sombre, blackish monotony. The yellow of the stubble land was a whitish-yellow, pallid and lustreless.

He glanced at the sleeping figure of his companion, and it seemed to him that the milk-white delicacy of Gerda's face, as she lay there, had never been touched by a more tender bloom than it wore to-day, under this vaporous, windless sky.

Her breathing was so light as to be almost imperceptible, her lips were just parted in a confiding abandonment to a happy sleep; while the rounded whiteness of the bare arm she had flung out upon the moss had that youthful charm of unconscious trust in the kindness of man and nature which, whenever he noted it, always struck him as one of the most touching of a young girl's qualities.

And it was borne in upon him how terrible the responsibility was when a man had once undertaken to 'make,' as the phrase runs, one of these fragile beings 'happy.' It came upon him, as he watched Gerda asleep, that a girl is much more committed to what is called 'happiness' than a man is.

Or is it, he thought, that a man can create happiness by sheer obstinate force out of the machinery of his own mind, while a girl is dependent upon all manner of subtle external forces emanating from nature and returning to nature?

Certainly at this moment Gerda seemed to have most deliciously abandoned herself to the power of the grass, the grey sky, the warm, windless air.

A sad, helpless craving possessed him as he turned from the girl and once more surveyed that undemonstrative, unobtrusive distance. He felt as though he longed to fly across it, in some impossible non-human shape – fly across it, not with any actual living companion, but with some shadowy essence, light as that dandelion-seed, which at this moment he saw rising high above him and floating away westward – with some shadowy essence that at the same time was and was not Christie Malakite – some essence that was what Christie was to her own inmost self, the bodiless, formless identity in that slim frame, that in confronting infinite space could only utter the mysterious words, 'I am I,' and utter nothing else.

If only he could do this now, by some occult manipulation of the laws of nature! Gerda's sleep was deep and sound. To her at this moment Time was nothing. How mad it was that he couldn't plunge with Christie, with the inmost soul of Christie, into some region outside these things, where a moment was like a whole year of mortal life!

The vast expanse he looked at had about it, under this grey sky, something wistful and withdrawn. It resembled those patient, melancholy fields, neither happy nor unhappy, where Dante met the souls of the great intellects in Limbo. With his eyes fixed upon its patient-coloured horizons, it did not seem so crazy a notion that he and Christie might meet and escape, lost, merged, diffused into all this!

And then he turned his gaze upon the beautiful girl lying there outstretched beside him, happy in her timeless dream-world, trusting him, trusting nature, half smiling in her sleep.

Looking at her lying there, he thought what an appalling risk these lovers of 'happiness' take, when they burn their ships and trust their lives to the caprice of men.

As he contemplated the loveliness of her figure, it struck him as infinitely pathetic that even beauty such as hers should be so dependent on the sexual humours of this man or that man for its adequate appreciation.

Beauty like that, he thought, as he looked at her, ought to endow its possessor with superhuman happiness, as in the old legends, when 'the sons of God saw the daughters of men.' There was a cruel irony in the fact that he of all men had been singled out to possess this beauty -- he whose heart of hearts had been given to a different being!

And as he pondered on all this it struck him as strange that such rare loveliness should not protect her, like silver armour, against the shocks and outrages of life. Beauty as unusual as this was a high gift, like a poet's genius, and ought to have the power of protecting a girl's heart from the cruel inconstancies of love.

'I suppose it is true,' he thought, 'that when they have been a man's bedfellow, even for a few months, some peculiar link establishes itself which it is as difficult to break as if one tore a grafted sapling from the branch of a tree. I suppose,' so his thoughts drifted on, 'that my love is really more important, in this blind, primordial way, to Gerda – just because we have now slept together for three months – than it could ever be to Christie, though *she* lives inside my very soul! I suppose it's the old fatality of flesh to flesh, of blind matter, proving itself, after all, the strongest thing on earth.'

And then, before he had the least notion that his thoughts would drift in such a direction, he found himself engaged in a passionate dispute with his father. It was as if the dispute were actually going on down at the bottom of that grave; and though he still found himself calling William Solent 'Old Truepenny,' he felt as if he had become a lean worm down there, in the darkness of that hollow skull, arguing with it, arguing with what remained still conscious and critical, although lost 'in the pit.'

'This world is not made of bread and honey,' cried Wolf, the worm, to the skull of his father, 'nor of the sweet flesh of girls. This world is made of clouds and of the shadows of clouds. It is made of mental landscapes, porous as air, where men and women are as trees walking, and as reeds shaken by the wind.'

But the skull answered him in haste and spoke roughly to him. 'What you have found out to-day, worm of my folly, I had outgrown when I was in the Sixth at Ramsgard and was seduced by Western *minor* in the head master's garden. To turn the world again into mist and vapour is easy and weak. To keep it alive, to keep it real, to hold it at arm's length, is the way of gods and demons.'

And Wolf, hearing this, lifted up his worm's voice within that mocker and cried out upon its lewd clay-cold cunning.

'There is no reality but what the mind fashions out of itself. There is nothing but a mirror opposite a mirror, and a round crystal opposite a round crystal, and a sky in water opposite water in a sky.'

'Ho! Ho! You worm of my folly,' laughed the hollow skull. 'I am alive still, though I am dead; and you are dead, though you're alive. For life is beyond your mirrors and your waters. It's at the bottom of your pond; it's in the body of your sun; it's in the dust of your star spaces; it's in the eyes of weasels and the noses of rats and the pricks of nettles and the tongues of vipers and the spawn of frogs and the slime of snails. Life in *me* still, you worm of my folly, and girls' flesh is sweet for ever and ever; and honey is sticky and tears are salt, and yellow-hammers' eggs have mischievous crooked scrawls!'

Wolf saw himself rising erect upon his tail as he heard these words.

'You lie to yourself, Truepenny! You lie with the old, hot, shuffling, fever-smitten lie. It's the foam bubbles of your life mania that you think so real. They're no more real than the dreams of the plantains that grow over your grave!'

A movement of Gerda, though she still remained asleep, broke up the current of his fancies, and he pulled out his watch.

Damn! It was time for him to start now, if he was to reach Mr. Urquhart's house at the accustomed hour.

'I won't have tea with *him*,' he thought. 'I'll have tea at the Otters'. Then I'll find out if Mattie and Olwen are still all right there.'

He rose to his feet. From the hushed indrawn beauty of the hour he gathered up new strength for the burden of human fate he seemed destined to carry.

Fragment by fragment he collected what was over from their lunch and put it back in Gerda's basket, prodding into the soft earth of a mole-hill, with the end of his stick, the bits of paper in which those things had been tied up.

Then, stretching out his arms and seizing with each hand a branch of a young sycamore, he swung these two pliant limbs backwards and forwards, while his gaze concentrated itself upon the girl at his feet.

But as he did this the transparency ebbed away from the vision of his days, and a fantastic doubt assailed him. Was Gerda's sleep so deep and happy because of some occult affinity between her nerves and this historic hill?

As if to give substance to his fancy, the girl rolled over languidly at that moment and lay prone, burying both her outstretched hands in the soft moss. A deep, shuddering sigh passed through her; and her body visibly quivered under her thin dress.

Was there some strange non-human eroticism, he wondered, in this contact between the heathen soil and that sleeping figure? He smiled to himself and then frowned uneasily. He began to feel obscurely piqued by the girl's remoteness and inaccessibility. He felt as if he were actually looking on at some legendary encounter between the body of Gerda and the crafty superhuman desire of some earth god. He began to feel an insidious jealousy of Poll's Camp, an obstinate hostility to its mossy curves and grassy hollows.

'Very well!' he thought, in his fantastic irritation, as if he actually beheld his companion in the very arms of the hill god. 'If she draws away from me, I can draw away from her!' And his eyes, wandering to the roofs of the town, settled on that quarter where he knew the roof of the bookshop to be. He tightened his hold upon the two saplings; and inhaling deeply that hushed, warm air, he mentally swept off the roof of Christie's house, and lifting the wraith-image of her high into the clouds – he never visualized Christie's actual appearance in any of these cerebral excursions – he whirled her away with him towards that lonely cone-shaped hill, rising out of the plain, that he knew to be Glastonbury.

It was a queer dalliance of the mind that he indulged in just then; for he felt that this airy wraith, that was Christie Malakite, was in some way the child of that mystical plain down there, that 'chessboard of King Arthur'; whereas the girl at his feet was in league with whatever more remote and more heathen powers had dominated this embattled hill. King Arthur's strangely involved personality, with the great Merlin at his side, was associated with both. But Christie's 'Arthur' belonged to Glastonbury; Gerda's to a far earlier time.

Wolf's mind now began analysing in a more rational manner this difference between the hill he stood upon and the landscape stretched out before him. 'It must be,' he thought, 'that this mass of earth is a far older portion of the planet's surface than the plain beneath it. Even if its magnetism is purely chemical and free from anything that reverts to the old religions, it may very well exercise a definite effect upon human nerves! The plain must, within measurable years, have been covered by the sea. Where those elm trees now grow must have been shells and sand and swaying seaweeds and great sea sponges and voyaging shoals of fish. And this recent emerging from the ocean cannot but have given a certain chastened quality, like the quality of old mediæval pictures, to these "chessboard fields." '

He stared, frowning intently, at the curves and hollows of Poll's Camp.

'How many men,' he wondered, 'since the black cormorants and foolish guillemots screamed around these escarpments, have stood still, as I am doing now, and wrestled with the secret of this promontory? Did any of the serfs of Arthur, or of Merlin the magician, lean here upon their spades and let their souls sink down and down, into motions of primal matter older than any gods? Did any of the Roman legionaries, stark and stoical, making of this hill "a sacred place" for some strange new cult of Mithras, forget both Mithras and Apollo under this terrestrial magnetism – this power that already was spreading abroad its influence long before Saturn was born of Uranus?

'Poll's Camp is heathen through and through,' he thought; 'and even if the old gods never existed, there's a power here that in some queer way . . . perhaps just chemically . . . is at once bewildering and hostile to me. But the valley . . . this unobtrusive chastened valley . . . like some immense, sad-coloured flower floating upon hidden water . . . oh, it is the thing I love best of all!'

He released the two pliable sycamore branches and let his hands sink down; while the thick, cool leaves of the young trees, so resilient and sturdy on their smooth, purplish stalks, flapped against his forehead.

'The spirit of this hill escapes me,' he thought. 'I have an inkling that it is even now watching me with definite malignity. But I can't understand the nature of what it threatens. There are powers here . . , powers . . . though, by God! they may be only chemical. But what is chemical? . . .'

He turned his eyes almost petulantly to the south-western limits of the valley, to where Leo's Hill and Nevilton Hill broke the level expanse.

'Those hills are not like this one,' he thought; 'and as for Glastonbury, it's like the pollen-bearing pistil of the whole lotus-vale! But this place . . . on my soul, it has something about it that makes me think of Mr. Urquhart. It's watching me. And I believe at this moment it is making love to Gerda!'

He sighed and picked up his hat and oak stick.

'I must wake Gerda and be off,' he said to himself. 'I shall be late as it is.'

16

A GAME OF BOWLS

Wolf was compelled that particular afternoon to walk a good deal faster than his wont, to reach the manor-house of King's Barton in time for his daily labour. But his work itself was, when he did settle down to it, a great deal pleasanter than usual, owing to the absence of Mr. Urquhart from the scene.

He found it extremely agreeable to sit at leisure in that escutcheoned window, one of whose smaller panes opened to the outside air upon such easy and such smoothly-worked hinges as made it a pleasure to open it or shut it.

The purple asters and blue lobelia borders in the flower-beds below had gathered to themselves a much more autumnal atmosphere than when he last observed them. There were more fallen leaves; and upon them, as well as upon the dark velvety grass, he fancied that he could discern the moisture of last night's dew, giving them that peculiar look for which he had been craving.

The actual work he was engaged on lent itself to the breathless peacefulness of that grey afternoon. He had to take the spiteful commentaries and floating fragments of wicked gossip gathered together by his employer, and translate them into a style that had at least some beauty of its own. This style had been his own contribution to the book; and though it had been evoked under external pressure, and in a sense had been a *tour de force*, it was in its essence the expression of Wolf's own soul – the only purely æsthetic expression that Destiny had ever permitted to his deeper nature.

The further he advanced with his book the more interested he became in this aspect of it. He spent hours revising the earlier chapters, written before this style of his had established itself; and he came to value these elaborated pages as things that were precious in themselves – precious independently of whether or not they were ever printed.

The Cerne Giant was now the subject of his efforts; and his first two renderings seemed to him hopelessly below the level of the rest of his writing.

'She had sat on the knees of the Cerne Giant in her youth, and Sir Walter, robbed of the delectation of prolonged seduction turned, it seems, in infinite weariness, to the more ambiguous tastes that procured him his famous infamy.'

He put his pen through this and wrote in its place:

'Those long, hot summer afternoons spent by her in gathering devil's-bit and hawkweed in perilous proximity to that troubling symbol, had seduced her mind long before Sir Walter seduced her body. It was natural enough, therefore, for this corrupt rogue to come soon to prefer – '

Here he laid down his pen and contemplated once more the Squire's notes, which ran as follows:

'Cerne Giant – real virginity unknown in Dorset – "cold maids" a contradiction – Sir Walter's disgust – His erudition – His platonic tastes – How he was misunderstood by a lewd parson – '

'Good Lord!' said Wolf to himself, 'I must be careful what I'm doing just here. The old demon has changed his tune. This isn't garrulous history. This is special pleading.'

He took up his pen, erased the words 'natural enough, therefore, for this corrupt rogue,' and wrote in their place, 'natural enough, therefore, for this baffled idolater of innocence to become a misogynist and to turn – ' He stopped abruptly, pushed back his manuscript, and stared out of the window. He would have found it hard to explain this pause in his work, but a vague consciousness of the personality of young Redfern took possession of his mind.

'I've never seen a line of that fellow's writing,' he thought. 'I wonder what *he* would have made of this precious Sir Walter?'

The blue lobelias, the blades of dark green grass leaning sideways against the edge of the brown mould, as if some faun's light hoof had trodden them down, came to his consciousness then with such a clear revelation of something in nature purer than anything in man's mind, that he felt a sense of nausea with regard to these lewd preciosities. What was he doing, to be employed at such a job?

If the book were ever published, none of his own stylistic inventions, such as they were, could offset the general drift of it.

And what effect would that drift have? To which side of the gulf between beauty and the opposite of beauty would it draw readers?

Like a drop of ice-cold rain, frozen, accursed, timeless, this abominable doubt fell upon his heart and sank into its depths. The whole subterranean stream of Wolf's life-illusion had been obsessed, as long as he could remember, by the notion of himself as some kind of a protagonist in a cosmic struggle. He hated the traditional terminology for this primordial dualism; and it was out of his hatred of this, and out of his furtive pride, that he always opposed, in his dialogues with himself, his own secret 'mythology' to some equally secret 'evil' in the world around him. But because the pressure of circumstances had made him so dependent on Mr. Urquhart's money, it happened that until this actual moment he had evaded bringing his conscience to bear upon the man's book, though he had brought it to bear freely enough upon the man himself.

But now – cold, frozen, eternal, malignant – this abominable doubt fell upon him like an accursed rain . . . drip-drop, drip-drop, drip-drop . . . each drop sinking out of sight into the dim, unreasoning levels of his being, where it began poisoning the waters.

'How can I struggle with this man when I am exhausting all my ingenuity in trying to make his book an immortal work?' Wolf placed the sheets of his manuscript carefully in order and put a heavy paper-weight on the top of them. Then he set himself to curse the obscurity of his universe as he had never done before.

'Good – evil? Evil – good?' he thought. 'Why should these old dilemmas rise up now and spoil my life, just as it is rounding itself off into a solid integrity?'

He surveyed the great shelves of Mr. Urquhart's library much in the same mood as he had recently surveyed the circumvallation lines of Poll's Camp. 'Come out of your grave, you wretched Redfern!' he cried under his breath. 'And let's hear what *you* made of it! Was it the drip-drop of this infernal indecision that sent you scampering off to Lenty Pond of an autumn evening? Did you feel a knot in *your* head, tightening, tightening, tightening?'

The thought came to him then, 'Suppose I gave up this whole job?' And the image of his mother seeking refuge with Lord Carfax, of Gerda back again in Torp's yard, of himself wandering over the world, far removed from Christie, rose sickening, ghastly, before him.

He lifted the paper-weight from the pile of manuscript. It had its own interest, this paper-weight – a slab of alabaster with a silver eagle upon it. He tilted it up and balanced it sideways, till the eagle looked to him like a fly on a piece of soap.

'Soap?' he thought; and the word put him in mind of what Mr. Urquhart had said about the transfiguration of little things by the decision to commit suicide.

At that moment there was a sharp knock at the door, and Wolf started violently, leaving the paper-weight upside down upon his manuscript.

'Come in!' he cried, in a loud, irritated tone.

The tall figure of Roger Monk entered and walked gravely up to him. It had always been a speculation to Wolf how this great ostler-gardener managed to move so discreetly across these polished floors. The man moved up to him now as if he had been a super-natural messenger walking upon air.

'I came just to tell you, Mr. Solent, sir,' said Roger Monk, 'that there's a bowling-match goin' on at Farmer's Rest. It entered my mind, since Squire's out to Lovelace's to-night, 'twould be a sight you might be sorry to miss, Mr. Solent, sir.'

'Where's Farmer's Rest?' enquired Wolf.

'Why, that's the village pub, sir! Haven't you ever been into it, sir? But I expect it's out of your way. It's out of all decent folk's way, I reckon. 'Tis down Lenty Lane, Pond Lane, and Dead Badger Lane. 'Tis no great way; and I'm thinking of going round there myself. So, if it's no offence, Mr. Solent, sir, I thought as maybe ye'd like to have my company.'

He stopped, and in the manner of the discreet servant of a wilful master, stared impassively at the wall till his gentleman made his decision.

'I'd like to come with you very much, Roger,' Wolf replied. 'But what about tea? I was thinking of dropping in at Pond Cottage.'

'Don't do that, sir. Come, as I'm telling 'ee, to Farmer's Rest, and I'll see to it myself that Miss Bess'll give you as good a cup o' tea and a better, too, than ye'd ever get from that old Dimity's kitchen. Not but what things be much more decent-like down there, since Miss Smith be living with 'em.'

'How does Dimity put up with Miss Smith, Roger?' enquired Wolf slyly.

'Past all expectancy, Mr. Solent,' replied the other. 'But she's a real lady, that young woman, whoever her Dad were.'

'Why wasn't Mr. Smith her father, then?'

Roger Monk winked slyly.

'There *be* as says he weren't, sir. But if you don't mind, Mr. Solent, we'd best be getting along, down-village.'

He moved towards the door as he spoke, and Wolf got up and followed him.

Lenty Lane and Pond Lane were familiar enough, though under that grey windless sky they assumed the kind of expression that Wolf always imagined such places to assume when some disturbing human event was impending; but Dead Badger Lane led him to completely new ground. It was narrower than either of the others and very much overgrown with grass. This grass grew long and rank on both sides of deep cart-tracks, and amid its greenness there were patches of scabious and knapweed.

'Who's playing in this bowling-match?' Wolf asked, wondering vaguely what there was about these patches of country weeds that made him think of a certain dusty road beyond the railway-station at Weymouth. 'Beyond the backwater it was, too,' he said to himself.

'Mr Malakite from Blacksod, sir, be playing against our Mr. Valley. . . . And I be playing myself, sir,' the man added, after a pause, in a deprecatory tone.

Wolf prodded the cart-track with his stick, and, unseen by his companion, pulled down the corners of his mouth and worked the muscles of his under jaw.

'Who are you playing against?' enquired Wolf in a politely negligent tone.

The man gave him a quick glance.

'Hope 'tis no offence to name the party, sir, but I be playing against your Missus's Dad.'

'Against Mr. Torp?' cried Wolf, feeling that the situation in front of him was growing thicker with discomfort every moment.

'None other, sir. The old gentleman be the best hand at bowls, when 'ee be sober, if I may say so, that they have anywhere down these ways. I learned the game myself' – these last words were spoken with extraordinary impressiveness – 'in the Shires.'

Farmer's Rest turned out to be a small, whitewashed, thatched cottage, not very well kept up, and displaying no sign, as far as Wolf could see, of its professional use. The place was open and they stepped inside.

They were confronted by a narrow passageway leading into a garden at the back; and there, framed by an open door, he could see the bowling-green, with groups of grave men moving solemnly across it in their shirt sleeves.

The public bar was on his right, the private parlour on his left; and into this latter room he was ushered by the tall gardener.

'One minute, sir, and I'll fetch Miss Bess. I expect some of the other gentlemen will be glad to have a cup of tea. Her name is Round, sir, if you don't mind. Miss Elizabeth Round.'

Wolf sat down and waited. Sure enough, in about five minutes, a pretty young woman, plump and rosy-cheeked, but in some odd way vacant-looking, brought in a tea-tray and placed it on the table.

Wolf was completely nonplussed by the personality of Miss Round. Superficially she looked clean, fresh, amiable, and a little stupid; but all her movements possessed a queer, automatic quality that made him slightly uncomfortable. He couldn't define it at once; but after watching her carefully for a short space, he came to the conclusion that she was like a pretty doll, or a human mannikin, wound up to perform a given task, but lacking all interior consciousness of what she was doing.

'Mr. Malakite sends his compliments, sir,' she said, 'and he hopes to have the honour of a cup of tea with you in a minute. He's just finishing his game.'

'Don't hurry him. I'll be all right,' murmured Wolf. 'Is your father the landlord here?' This he added rather lamely, as she proceeded with rapid movements of her plump hands to arrange the tea-things on the table.

Miss Bess nodded. 'He's not Dad,' she replied calmly. 'He's uncle. Dad's been gone for years.'

Whether she meant that Mr. Round, for reasons of his own, had bolted, or whether she meant that he was dead, Wolf could not tell. His interest in Miss Bess was faint; in her father, dead or alive, fainter still. His heart was beating at that moment for quite another cause. His glance, fixed upon the door into the passage, kept visualizing the bookseller's grizzled head. His ears strained themselves to catch the sound of the old man's voice.

But for several seconds all he could hear was the knocking of the bowls against one another on the grass outside.

Then he became aware of quite a different sound, a sound that apparently proceeded from above the ceiling of the private parlour. He glanced at Miss Bess, and, to his surprise, she promptly raised a plump finger and pressed it against her lips.

'It's uncle,' she whispered. 'He's heard a strange voice and it's set him off.'

Wolf and Miss Bess both concentrated their attention upon this

321

new sound. It was a thick human voice, repeating over and over again the same two syllables.

'Jesus . . . Jesus . . . Jesus . . . Jesus.'

'Is he ill? Is he suffering? Don't let me keep you if you ought to go up to him.'

Miss Bess removed her fingers from her mouth and smiled a little. 'Oh, it's all right *now*,' she declared calmly. 'It's your voice what started him. He knows every noise for yards and yards round this house. Dogs, cats, pigs, poultry, pigeons, horses, cattle. There isn't a sound he doesn't know. He'll know who's won this match o' bowls afore I tells him a thing.'

The voice above the ceiling continued its refrain.

'Jesus . . . Jesus . . . Jesus . . . Jesus. . . .'

'That's how he goes on – sometimes for hours. But us who knows him takes no stock in *that*. Now, if I'd heard him starting off on God, same as he does sometimes, you'd have seen me running upstairs like greased lightning! It's all as how he gets started. Whichever way he starts he keeps it up till he's tired. Funny, isn't it? But no one knows what human nature can come to, till ye've seen it and heard it.'

'Does he say "God" over and over again in this same way?'

Miss Bess nodded. 'It's *then* I've got to run! It's always the same. I used to let him do it; but one day they found him in a ditch, eating frog-spawn. The ditch were over Lenty-way. I expect you've often seen it. It's where them mare's-tails grows. He had to be pulled out. *That* were one of his "God" days.'

Once more Wolf strained his ears; and, mingled with the clicking of the bowls outside, came that repeated 'Jesus . . . Jesus . . . Jesus . . . Jesus' from above the ceiling.

'He'll go to sleep, present; and by supper time he'll be gay as a lark. It's our Mr. Valley taught him what to do. "When you feel God coming," Mr. Valley said to him, "don't get flustered or anything. Just say 'Jesus' and you'll go to sleep like a newborn babe!"'

'What's the matter with him?' enquired Wolf. The girl fetched a blue tea-cosy from the recesses of a cupboard and pulled it down carefully over the teapot. Then she raised her eyes and looked straight at her guest; and for the flicker of a second her brisk, automatic personality displayed the troubled awareness of a conscious soul.

'Worried,' she said simply. And then, in the old automatic way: 'Excuse me, sir. There's someone in the bar.' And with all the fresh, stupid innocence of her first entrance upon the scene, she hurried across the passage.

Wolf surveyed the admirable preparations for tea that lay spread before him. There were two teacups, two knives, two plates, and two chairs.

'Jesus . . . Jesus . . . Jesus . . . Jesus. . . .'

'What on earth shall I talk about with the old man?' he thought. 'I wish he'd hurry up. This tea will have stood much too long.'

He had not long to wait. There were shuffling steps in the passage, and the bookseller came in. Wolf rose and shook him by the hand.

'Just in time, Mr. Malakite,' he said. 'I was afraid our tea would get too strong.'

The two men sat down opposite each other, and Wolf, removing the blue cosy, filled both their cups and handed the bookseller the bread-and-butter.

'I hope you're ahead in your game,' he said emphatically. 'It must be an absorbing game, bowls. It must be one of the most absorbing of all.'

Mr. Malakite put down his cup and moved a long, slender forefinger round its rim.

'Your father and I had many a game on this green,' he said, without raising his eyes.

And Wolf looked at Mr. Malakite with as many confused feelings as he had ever experienced in the presence of one human head. He thought to himself, 'Was the man ever ashamed of that white beard when he saw himself in the looking-glass, as he went up to wash his hands between dusting his books and sneaking into his girl's room?'

'You and my father, Mr. Malakite,' he said in a low tone, 'must have seen quite a lot of each other in those old days.'

'One more cup, if you please, sir. A lot of each other? Well – no. He was a gentleman, you see; and I've never been anything but a tradesman. But still . . . in a manner of speaking, we *were* friends, I suppose.'

He lifted his eyes now, and Wolf was surprised by the devouring intensity of their gaze. It was a fixed, monomaniacal intensity, and it seemed addressed to no particular object. It was impossible to imagine it softening into tenderness, or abandoned to humour, or melting in grief. It did not seem adapted to looking into human eyes. It seemed directed towards some aspect of universal matter that absorbed and fascinated it. It seemed, so to speak, to *eat the air.* Mr. Malakite himself appeared apprehensive of the effect of his gaze upon his interlocutor; for he lowered his eyelids directly his words were out of his mouth, and once more began following the rim of his teacup with the tip of his finger.

'I know that look,' thought Wolf. 'I've seen it on the streets in London and I've seen it on the esplanade at Weymouth. It's like the passion of a miser. It's horrible, but it's not contemptible.'

'Had you many friends in common?' enquired Wolf; and as he spoke, he leant across the table, and, without waiting this time for any request, filled up the old man's cup to the very brim and placed the milk-jug at his side.

'I can't stand that finger-game of his!' he said to himself. 'He'll have to stop doing that if he's going to drink his tea.'

But not at all! Mr. Malakite bent his furrowed head, but keeping his gaze discreetly lowered, once more commenced circling the vessel's rim with the extreme tip of his long finger.

'Friends in common?' the old man repeated. 'You mean, I suppose, Mr. Solent, to ask whether your father and I had any peculiarities in common? That's a natural question, and if I knew you better I think I could interest you a good deal in answering it. But we don't know each other well enough, sir . . . not nearly well enough. Besides' – and once more Wolf got the benefit of that fixed, monomaniacal gaze – 'I don't approve of exposing a father to his son. It's an impiety, an impiety!'

Wolf finished his tea in silence after this, and handed Mr. Malakite a cigarette. When they were both smoking, and Wolf, at any rate, was enjoying that faint rarefication of human thought, like the distilling of an essence, which tea-drinking can induce, he asked Mr. Malakite with grave directness what was the matter with the landlord of Farmer's Rest.

The bookseller's forehead knit in an unpleasant scowl.

'Been hearing him, I suppose? Nobody bothers about *him*, Mr. Solent. Miss Elizabeth is the boss here, and she don't like people who talk too much about family matters. Why should she? Round's *her* uncle, not yours or mine.'

The brutality of this remark destroyed in a moment all the fragrant clarity of Wolf's after-tea sensations. He received the sort of shock from it that always made him seem to himself a priggish fool, devoid of the degree of humorous toughness which this world requires. At the same time it stirred up all his ill-balanced impulses with regard to persecuted people – impulses that led him to a morbid exaggeration of this particular aspect of life.

He began to indulge in the wildest imaginings about the 'worried' Mr. Round; and he obstinately returned to the subject.

'Has this fellow up there,' he said uneasily, jerking his thumb towards the ceiling, 'lived in King's Barton long?'

But Mr. Malakite rose from his chair.

'Come out and see the game, sir, won't you? There are people everywhere about us whose existence is no affair of ours. To fuss over them like this clergyman here does is only to share their disease.'

'What disease are you talking about, Mr. Malakite?' asked Wolf, as he followed him into the garden.

The sight of the group of men gathered there so disturbed his attention that he could not be quite sure whether he caught correctly the malignant mumbling that issued from his companion's lips. 'The disease of Life!' was what it sounded like.

A little later, as he watched the bookseller calculating with exquisite nicety the 'bias' of his particular bowl, he was conscious of a desire not to encounter again for some while the expression of those deep-sunken eyes.

'What *does* that look of his make me think of?' he wondered, as he nodded to the other players and their absorbed spectators. And it seemed to him that he recalled a sombre lightship that he had seen once in Portland harbour, which every now and then emitted a long, thin stream of ghastly, livid illumination from the midst of waters desolate and disturbed.

There had apparently been time, while Wolf was having his tea, for Roger Monk to defeat Mr. Torp; for that champion, still in his shirt-sleeves, and extremely hot, was arguing in a plaintive voice with Mr. Valley as to what he might have done and didn't do.

Wolf shook hands with Mr. Valley and commiserated his father-in-law on his defeat. 'It's a wonder I didn't lose a lot of money over you,' he said facetiously. 'I backed you to the limit to beat our friend Roger, for the honour of the family; and now you've let us all down, and the West Country too! Mr. Monk, so he tells me, comes from the Shires.'

'Shires be damned, Mr. Solent!' said the monument-maker. 'Tweren't no Shires! 'Twere me wone bloody cussedness. If I'd 'a known then what I do know now, 'twould be he and me' – he nodded in the direction of Mr. Malakite – 'and not he and *him*, for this here final.'

'How is it that *you* got knocked out so soon, Valley?' enquired Wolf.

But the little clergyman made a sign with his hand, and advanced a step or two, intent with all his mind and soul on Roger Monk's massive wrist and the bowl which he was poising.

Wolf had to content himself, therefore, with drawing back his father-in-law to a bench under the hedge, where the game could be watched and Mr. Torp's lamentations listened to in comparative ease and comfort.

'What's wrong with this Mr. Round?' He hadn't intended to say anything like this when he searched about in his mind for a suitable topic; but the words rose to his lips as if from some inquisitive demon pricking up its ears in the pit of his stomach.

'Can't forgive 'isself, I reckon, for they things he said about young Redfern. 'Twere summat o' that, so folks do tell I, what stole the heart out o' that young gentleman and made 'un turn to the wall. Leastways, there were some folks as told 'un 'twere what he did say, down here, at Farmer's Rest bar, that turned that young man's poor heart to stone. 'Twould have jostled me wone innards, I tell 'ee, if any well-thought-of landlord spoke such words of I.'

'What did he say about Redfern?' enquired Wolf, suppressing the absurd image that rose in his mind of a Mr. Torp lacerated by moral disquietude.

His father-in-law, however, at that moment saw fit to display a revived interest in the game of bowls.

'Look-see!' he cried, tapping Wolf on the knee, and leaning forward. 'By jiggers, if that girt flunkey from up at House aren't making Mr. Malakite look like nothing!'

Wolf had indeed for some while been admiring the steady play of the big gardener. The old man opposed to him seemed on the contrary to be growing less and less careful of his aim.

'Something's fretting that wold gent, looks so,' went on Mr. Torp. 'Miss Bess been showing her laces to he, in parlour, like enough! 'Tis a wonderful disposing of Providence, Mr. Solent, when old men can flutter young ladies and make their hands fidget. 'Tis not been allowed to I, such privileges and portions. And yet I be a man, I reckon, what knows the road royal as well as another!'

But Wolf's mind was still hovering about Mr. Round and his remarkable 'worries.'

'What did this man actually say about Redfern?' he repeated.

Mr. Torp turned his head slowly towards him. 'It may be a good world,' he remarked sententiously, and 'and it may be a bad world, but *it's the world;* and us has got to handle 'un with eyes in our heads for landslides. My job mayn't be the job *you'd* choose. It mayn't be the job *I'd* choose, if others offered. But it's my job. And anyone, Mr. Solent, with a job like mine can't afford to stir up trouble among they dead. I were the man who made the headstone for'n. I ask 'ee, should I go spreading trouble about thik quiet lad? They said, when his funeral day came, that he'd got no relation to mourn for'n. Who then, I ask 'ee, Mr. Solent, is to hold their tongue, i' the peace of God, about the poor young man, if it bain't me wone self, who chipped the stone what covers him?'

'Is it true, when his conscience troubles him, that Mr. Round wanders about that field where Lenty Pond is?'

'Never ye mind where 'a wanders, Mr. Solent! Nebuchadnezzar were more than he; for kings be more than publicans; and *he* went on all fours in's day.'

His father-in-law's poetic prevarications had begun to irritate Wolf.

'I wish you'd tell your wife, Mr. Torp,' he burst out, 'not to let Lobbie bathe in that damned pond!'

The monument-maker gave a start and opened his eyes wide. Wolf's intonation evidently surprised him.

He smiled as he answered.

'*She* not let him bathe? She don't let him do nothing – not even breathe, I fancy! 'Twould be somebody very different from our Gerda's Mummy, Mr. Solent, what would make Lob Torp bide at whoam. But what ails 'ee, sir, to speak with such disturbance of a good Darset duck-pond, such as I do mind sliding on, winter come winter, since I were slim as a lath? What's Lenty Pond done to thee, sir? 'Tis no girt place for perch or pike; and to my belief no wild-geese ever settled on it; but 'tis a good pond. 'Tis a pond that would drown the likes of you and me, maybe. But they boys! Why, they'd bathe in Satan's spittle and come out sweet. Lenty Pond's nothing to Lob Torp, sir! You can rest peaceful on that.'

As Wolf listened to all this, with one eye on the final defeat of Mr. Malakite, and the other on the doll-like briskness of Bess Round, who was now bringing out into the garden more chairs and more tables, he began to be aware of a very odd fancy, which he found it impossible to take seriously, and yet impossible to get rid of.

The fancy had to do with Lenty Pond; and the more he thought of it, the more ridiculously it pressed upon him. It was as if every single person in these three Dorset towns were hiding from him something they knew about Lenty Pond, something that was absurdly simple, that fitted together with mathematical precision, but to which he was himself completely blind.

He got up from the bench and went across the grass with the

intention of congratulating Roger Monk on his victory. On his way, however, and before his approach was detected by the gardener, round whose tall figure all the villagers who had been watching the match were now gathered, he caught sight of Miss Bess ushering into the garden the two Otter brothers.

Towards these two men he directed his steps, leaving Mr. Torp to join the loquacious group in the centre of the bowling-green. As he shook hands with the brothers, he detected Mr. Malakite secretively shuffling off by the elbow of Miss Bess, who, with a tray of empty bottles, was returning into the house.

That disconcerting feeling, as though the whole of his life at the present moment were unreal, weighed upon him still. It hung upon him like a wavering dizziness, as full of meaningless blotches and sparkles as the glass coffin lid of King Æthelwolf in the Abbey.

Even as he was describing to the two Otters the portion of the bowling match that he had seen, his eyes remained fixed on a particularly smooth and delicately polished bowl, of a dark chestnut colour, that lay on the grass close to Darnley's feet.

It seemed to him as if he were reading his fate on the polished surface of this object, a fate laborious, complicated, burdened, but at the same time rolled and tossed about at random by many alien hands! Was there *any* portion of his identity, compact, self-contained, weighted with inward intention, like the 'bias' of this bowl?

As he went on talking to the two brothers, he became aware that a small flower-seed had balanced itself, in its aimless flight, on the bowl at Darnley's feet, and he began to feel as if this flower-seed were tickling the skin of his mind, and that he couldn't brush it away. Something was fretting him; something was teasing him. What was it?

Then quite suddenly he knew what it was. It was the memory of old Malakite's obsessed expression – that expression of con-centrated erotic insanity, directed toward universal matter, as he had caught it from under the man's wrinkled forehead across the blue tea-cosy. This, then, was why he was answering Jason's remarks in so perfunctory a manner! Then he gave a quick sigh of irrepressible relief; for he became aware that the doll-like young lady was back again at their side, suggesting that they should all sit down before a rickety garden-table upon which she had placed a fresh tray of mugs.

This they proceeded to do; and while she was supplying them with foaming pints of Dorchester ale, he heard her say to Darnley:

'Mr. Malakite's just traipsed off. He made his little joke, like he always does, the funny old man; but anyone could see he weren't best pleased! 'Tis hard for him, I expect, to be beat like this by a fellow who, as you might say, is a foreigner in these parts. He's been playing on this green, that old gentleman, as long as I can mind anything, and there be few enough who've got the best of him!'

She moved away to persuade the winner of the match and his rustic admirers to gather about another wooden table, leaving the 'gentry' to their own devices.

Then it was that Wolf's mind completely recovered from its sense of unreality and from its hallucinations about Lenty Pond. From where he lay in a creaky straw-plaited chair between Darnley and Jason, he could take in at his leisure the whole characteristic West Country scene. There was a relaxed jocularity about the men's voices, as they rose in that shadowy garden, between the tall privet hedge and the sloping thatched roof, that seemed to contain within it all the rich apple-juices that were ripening in the orchards around them, all the cool sap of the mangelwurzel plants in the neighbouring fields, the good white heart of billions of ears of plump wheatsheaves, awaiting their threshing-day in all the granaries between Parret and Stour!

The sky, as he watched it above that privet hedge, was still of the same filmy greyness as when he had sat, some five or six hours ago, under the sycamore at Poll's Camp; but the gathered volume of masculine personalities, as it surrounded him now – for Miss Bess was the only woman on the scene, and *her* femininity seemed to have no more weight in it than petticoats on a clothes-line – seemed fast building up about him a sort of battlemented watchtower, from the isolation and protection of which his days began to fall into a measured, reasonable order, such as he had not known for many a long week.

That chestnut-coloured polished bowl was still within his vision on the smooth turf; but at this moment, in place of giving him a sense of random helplessness, it gave him a sense of reassured control. In this pleasant retreat, with the fumes of the Dorchester ale mounting into his head, he began to feel his hand firm and unbewildered once more upon his life's rudder.

These worthy men, with their work behind them, seemed to have eluded by some secret pressure of their united force the splash and beat of nature's chaotic waves. They seemed to have dragged their 'hollow ship' out of the tide that summer afternoon – up, up, up some hidden shelving beach, where all agitations were over.

Everything disturbing and confusing sank away out of sight for Wolf just then. Indeed, his whole life gathered itself together with lovely inevitableness, as if it were a well-composed story that he himself, long ago and time out of mind, had actually composed.

And by degrees, while he lazily drank his ale and chatted with Darnley – for Jason had for some unknown reason become suddenly silent – the old fighting-spirit of his inborn life-illusion rose strong and upwelling within him.

And there came to him the vision of one particular rock-pool near Weymouth, to which he had once found his way. He saw the rose-tinged seaweeds sway backwards and forwards . . . he heard the crying of the gulls. . . .

Oh that it were possible to gather together a great handful of such memories and pour them forth out of his cupped hands into the brain above that face on the Waterloo steps! But – but what if there should arrive a day when, by the turning of the terrible engines, he himself should *look like that face*, while some other Wolf, drinking ale on a bowling-green, indulged in benevolent emotions in a creaky wicker chair?

'Are you sure you couldn't come back to dinner with us, Solent?' said Darnley at last, in a pause in the midst of their rambling conversation.

'Impossible!' he said, looking at his watch. 'It's seven o'clock now. As it is, I shall be late for Gerda's supper.'

And then he suddenly remembered that Gerda's last words to him had been: 'Don't hurry back, Wolf, I like waiting for you. I like sitting at the window and doing nothing. That's what I like best of all!'

'Those girls of yours will be very annoyed if you don't come,' said Jason.

'Why, they don't expect me, do they? Your mother doesn't expect me, does she?'

'All women,' said Jason with a chuckle, his spirits reviving when he saw Wolf's discomfort and indecision, 'expect all men!'

'Well, I must come another time,' said Wolf. 'I can't leave Gerda like that without telling her. But I hope "my girls," as you call them, are all right? I hope you don't find Olwen too much of a handful?'

'Darnley is the one to give advice. Do you think he'd better go home, Darnley; or do you think he'd better come to dinner with us?'

'He must suit himself,' said Darnley, smiling. 'I wouldn't care

330

about leaving Gerda alone if I were in his shoes. But then, I've never had a Gerda . . . and am never likely to have!'

Mr. Valley at this point drifted up to their table.

'I've got to be getting back now,' he said. 'Are any of you people coming, or are you going to stay longer?'

The three men all rose. 'We were just talking of getting off,' said Darnley. 'I suppose we all go the same way? At the start, anyhow?'

He beckoned to Bess Round to come to their table, and, drawing a small leather purse out of his pocket, paid for all the drinks they had had except Mr. Valley's. Him Roger Monk had already treated, and treated well.

Wolf went across the grass and said good-bye to Mr. Torp and to Roger Monk, congratulating the latter warmly on his victory.

'I've never known the old man to play so badly,' said Monk, with a deprecatory shrug of his shoulders. 'That cup of tea he had with you in the parlour, sir, must have gone to his head.'

'Give me little darter me love, Mr. Solent,' said the monument-maker. 'And you may kiss she, too, if ye be so minded, from her old Dad. Not that they turns aught but cold maids' cheeks to their Dad's kisses. But that be all the better for thee, sir; and ye are more like to mind me message than if't had been any o' the young gents here assembled.'

Roger Monk's victory at bowls had been celebrated by such copious libations that the gardener had no hesitation now about indulging in a piece of ribaldry from which in more sober mood he would certainly have refrained.

'Young and old is the same to that gender – eh, Mr. Solent, sir? That's what we servants know, maybe, better than you gentlemen. There's not a poor one among that gender, nor a rich one among 'em – eh, Mr. Torp? – that hasn't wished themselves in the bed of somebody that isn't their law-established.'

Wolf went off down Dead Badger Lane side by side with Jason, while Darnley walked in front of them with Mr. Valley.

That remark of Roger Monk teased Wolf's mind. The man had worded it in a coarser, drier, cruder manner than such a thing would have been worded by a man of the West Country. The use of the word 'gender,' for instance. 'That's a touch of Sheffield or Birmingham,' thought Wolf. And perhaps just because of its coarse wording, the thing hit Wolf with a most unpleasant emphasis. What *would* he feel if there were any serious cause for his being jealous? What he did feel at that moment was an actual sense of physical nausea caused by Roger's words. It wasn't only

Gerda. That use of the word 'gender' seemed to have stripped the world of a certain decency that belonged to its inherent skin quite as much as to its external conventions.

He experienced at that moment a wave of positive hatred for Roger Monk. 'He looked as if he might put his hand on my shoulder or even slap me on the back. There's something horrible about a male servant ... especially a big male servant ... when he drops his professional discretion. ... I could find it in me to pity even Mr. Urquhart if this chap *does* ever turn on him!'

His thoughts were jerked back into focus and into the cart-ruts of Dead Badger Lane by a remark from Jason Otter.

'Look at those two, in front there! Your friend Darnley has no more idea of what Valley's after, than that stick of yours has! I suppose *you* think that Darnley's very clever and very gentlemanly. That's what most people think. It's all his politeness. Look at their two heads now, bobbing up and down under their hats! I think cows and sheep are better than human beings. Nicer, I mean. Cleaner, too. Cleaner and nicer. What's wrong with human beings is their minds. Their minds are filthy. The minds of worms are much nicer. Have you ever thought about what really goes on in people's heads? I suppose not. I never thought you really knew very much. You're good at writing histories of a lot of bawdy idiots; and you're good at keeping old Urquhart in a good temper. But I've been thinking about you all this afternoon, Solent, and though you'll probably abuse me for telling you the truth, I think you're a crazy fool.'

By this time it began to dawn upon Wolf that Jason had no more power of drinking Dorchester ale with impunity than had his *bête noire* Roger Monk. He tried to distract the poet's attention from personalities by remarking on the insubstantiality and ghost-liness of the elm trees in the hedges. But Jason refused to show any interest in the beauty of that August night.

'Your friend, Darnley,' he now began again, 'believes in polite-ness. He thinks he can smooth everything down by that. He doesn't know what he's got against him.'

'What has he got against him?' enquired Wolf, wondering at the back of his mind what effect upon this 'politeness' the presence of Mattie in Pond Cottage had been having of late.

The reply of Jason was so violent and so abrupt that it had an uncanny effect upon the placidity of those vaporous elm trees.

'He's got God against him!' cried the poet. 'What he tries to smooth down are the porcupine-quills of God!'

'We'd better walk a little faster,' said Wolf. 'They'll be turning soon, and I've got to go the other way.'

'You're always on the walk, Solent. Walking here, walking there! You'll walk into a pit one day, with that stick of yours.'

But Wolf lifted his voice.

'Darnley!' he shouted. 'Valley! Wait a minute, you two!'

He could see the figures in front of him turn and stand still.

'Your friends over there will say good night to you, Solent. Were you afraid they wouldn't? They'll say good night. All the world over people say good night. They think it does something, I suppose. *I* don't know what it does!'

Wolf could not repress a heavy sigh. For some reason or other, the peculiar nature of this man's pessimism began to affect him as if he had been forced, till his hands were weary, to push away great stalks of deadly nightshade.

Jason caught this sigh upon the air, and it seemed to change his mood.

'I expect, Solent, you poor old devil, that that young lady of yours doesn't cook a good meal for you very often.'

'Oh yes, she does, Otter!' replied Wolf, as jocosely as he could. 'There's hardly a day we don't have meat. But to tell you the truth, I've been thinking of giving up eating that sort of thing ever since Miss Gault talked to me the other night.'

'Do you attend to anything that an ugly old woman like that says to you? She only wants to stir things up, because she's never slept with a man.'

The unkindness of those blunt words roused sheer anger in Wolf.

'Sleeping with people isn't everything in this world, Otter! It isn't even especially wonderful. I should have thought that being a poet you'd know that, and wouldn't go putting such importance on these material accidents!'

His anger, as he recognized clearly enough, was due to the fact that his own erotic feelings were so divided just then. But the tone of his voice was so vibrant with irritation, that its electric current conveyed itself to Jason in a second.

They were now quite close upon the others, however; and there was no time for anything but a swift, bitter, malicious blow, aimed where the opponent was most vulnerable.

'You'll walk into a material accident that'll stir *your* quills, master,' the poet growled, 'though you *do* think yourself a sort of superior being going about among ordinary people. *You'll* walk into the wood where they pick up horns ... clever though you may be!'

333

The altercation subsided as swiftly as it had risen.

'I didn't want to lose sight of you,' said Wolf, 'because our ways divide in a minute. I wish you'd won that match, Valley, instead of Monk. I can't tell why, but there was something about Monk that annoyed me this afternoon. Perhaps servants are always annoying when they're neither one thing nor the other.'

'I hope you didn't bring *me* into your quarrel,' said Jason Otter.

'I'm not as good as any of them,' replied Mr. Valley. 'Even Torp is better than I am. I never allow enough room for the swing of the bias.'

The four men walked on together and soon reached the spot where Dead Badger Lane joined Pond Lane.

'Well, good night,' said Wolf. 'You and I will be seeing each other on Monday, eh, Darnley? Won't you come back to lunch with me then? I'll tell Gerda if you will; and we'll celebrate the beginning of term with some sort of feast.'

'Don't get anything out of the way for me, Wolf,' the other replied. 'You know what I'm like – the most irritating kind of guest. But I'd love to come. It'll make Monday less of a burden to look forward to.' He stopped short and then suddenly added, 'If it wouldn't be a bother to Gerda, I wish you'd really make it a bit of an occasion and ask little Christie? I've had an idea for the last few weeks . . . in fact, since Olwen came to us . . . that she wanted cheering up. But don't say anything if it would be too much for Gerda.'

'But, Darnley . . . you and I know . . . everyone knows . . . that Christie never goes out anywhere.'

'Ask her, my dear man, that's all! I daresay she won't come, but ask her!' He paused for a second. 'Everyone likes to be asked,' he added gravely.

'Hee! Hee! Hee!'

Wolf swung round. It was Jason chuckling like a goblin in the darkness.

But Mr. Valley threw in his word before the electric current of irritation that still connected the two men's minds, had time to explode.

'Let's see,' said Mr. Valley. 'It's Friday to-day, isn't it? Don't forget, all of you, that next Wednesday is our school treat. It begins at two and goes on till seven. The Squire always comes after tea to watch the sports; so I shall expect *you* with him, Solent. But tell Gerda I want her to come too. Lobbie will be there, and our friend Weevil's sure to come.'

334

A muffled chuckle became audible.

'What's the matter with you, Jason?' expostulated Darnley. 'We all enjoy Valley's school treats. Are you going to have the Kingsbury band over here again?' he added, turning to the clergyman. 'What a time we had last year! They wouldn't stop, Solent, until it was pitch dark. When we did get 'em off, they played the Kingsbury jig out there in Lenty Lane, till Roger Monk hit the drummer into the ditch.'

'It was honest of him to do that,' said Jason. 'We all know why these lecherous young men want the Kingsbury jig. It would be a good thing if your friend Solent used his stick for these young dogs, instead of boasting how many miles he can walk.'

'Well, I'm going to walk now, anyway,' broke in Wolf, making a violent effort to keep his temper. 'Good night, Valley! Good night, Darnley! . . .'

He found it impossible to think of anything, either good or bad, except imaginary retorts to Jason, as he made his way eastward through that hushed night. The mere fact that Jason had the power to annoy him so much increased his aggravation; and his inability to lay his finger on the exact nature of this power added the last sharp prod to his irritated spirit.

'I wonder if I *am* the conceited fool he thinks me? Well! I don't care if I am. I have my "mythology," anyway. He's got the terrible instincts of a child in these things,' his thoughts ran on. 'He's so appallingly direct.'

He meditated for about a quarter of an hour upon Jason's personality; while the man's taunt about his fondness for walking and his fondness for his stick took the heart out of every stride he made.

'What really rouses me,' he thought presently, 'is his *desire* to annoy. People can get angry with anyone and say outrageous things. But this is different. He *wants* to make me feel a fool. He *wants* to take the life out of my life.'

Then Wolf set himself to wonder as to why it was that his mysterious psychic struggle with the Squire left him so free from personal hostility; while in the case of Jason he actually felt a longing to be wrestling with him in that very ditch into which he had said it was 'honest' of Monk to hit the Kingsbury drummer!

'It's because he knows by some childish instinct just where my life-illusion is weakest. It's because he sees this weak spot, like a raw scratch in the hide of a bear tied to a pole, and it somehow gets on his nerves, so that he wants to poke at it.'

With this hypothesis in his mind he advanced yet another quarter of a mile between the high hedges, where great bunches of old-man's-beard made large, whitish blurs against the darkness. The trunks of the elms looked now, as he passed them by, as if they were composed of a vaporous stuff that was absolutely liquid. But he hated to see this particular effect, because it made him think of his recent attempts to distract Jason from poking at the spot in his life's conceit where the skin was so tender.

'*That* is what it is,' he thought. 'Jason has deliberately stripped himself of every consolatory self-protective skin. He must see life continually as we others only see it when our life-illusions are broken through. The point is, *is* life what Jason sees, or is it what *we* see?'

Trailing his oak stick now, instead of prodding the ground with it, Wolf lurched forward in that fluid, grey-coloured darkness, as if he'd been some forlorn Homeric ghost whose body had been left unburied.

'It *can't* be as he sees it,' he thought, 'except to him . . . except to him!'

He now stood stock-still, his stick just held, but no more than just held, from falling to the ground.

'I refuse to believe,' he said to himself, 'and I never will believe, until the day Nature kills me, that there's such a thing as "reality," apart from the mind that looks at it! Jason's stripping himself bare is *his* way . . . that's all . . . what he sees when he's like that is no less of an illusion than what I see when I'm plastered with armour. The "thing in itself" is as fluid and malleable as these trees . . . I'm a sharded beetle, and he's one of those naked little green things that live in the centre of cuckoo-spit!'

This comparison cheered Wolf's mind a good deal; and his fingers tightened once more upon the handle of his stick. 'These trees, this old-man's-beard, these dark ditch-plants . . . they all see what they've the nature to see. . . . No living thing has ever seen reality as it is in itself. By God! there's probably nothing to see, when you come to that!'

He heard at that moment a slight, dry rustling in the grass by the side of the road. Inquisitive to know what it was, he went over, and, stooping down, fumbled with his hand among the entangled weeds. A scent of camomile hit his nostrils; but then – with an exclamation of distress – he drew his hand away.

'Damn!' he exclaimed. 'Thorns!' And he thought vaguely, 'How odd that there should be a bramble-bush so low down!'

Once more he heard the rustling; and once more, though with

more caution, he stretched out his hand. This time he knew what it was; and repressing an instinct to hook the hedgehog with the handle of his stick and drag it out into the road, he straightened his own back and walked on.

'Another version of reality!' he said to himself. 'And a bit more armoured even than mine!' And then he remembered what Jason had said with regard to the prickly quills of God. 'I must tell him about this hedgehog,' he thought. 'It's just the sort of thing that'll please him, especially as it's made my finger bleed.'

The notion of communicating this occurrence with self-depreciatory humour to the 'Slow-Worm of Lenty' completed his restoration to good spirits. By the little device of seeing himself in a humorous and yet not in a ridiculous light, he crossed the moat that separated him from his accustomed stronghold, and pulled up the drawbridge after him.

'I'll tell him about the hedgehog on Wednesday,' he thought, 'when I meet him at the school treat.' And thinking of Jason's goblinish laughter when he should be telling him the tale, Wolf entirely forgot the sensations he had recently received from that same sound.

With a mind once more adjusted and fortified to deal with existence, he advanced rapidly towards the outskirts of Blacksod. He knew every mark, every sign of the way, as he came along. In a darkness far deeper than this darkness he would have known them, those grotesque and insignificant little things that arrest a person's attention for so many unknown reasons, as he follows a familiar road.

But all at once Wolf thought vividly, sharply, disturbingly, of Mr. Malakite.

'I hope I'm not going to overtake him!' he said to himself; and then, before this hope was fully registered in his conscious brain, there in the dimness, standing as if she were waiting for him, was Christie herself!

'I knew your step. I knew the tap of your stick,' she said hurriedly. 'I haven't been here very long. Father came back and told me he'd had tea with you and then went off to get supper in the town; for he knew I hadn't anything for him in the house.'

She spoke hurriedly, but quite calmly; and all the while she was speaking she held one of Wolf's hands tightly with one of her own, and kept rubbing his knuckles with her other hand, as if she were rubbing out some stain left by Time itself, some imprint which the days that had passed since they had last seen each other had left there.

'Do you realize,' he said, 'that two seconds before I saw you I thought suddenly of your father? That shows something, doesn't it?'

'I've been thinking of him, and of you, too, Wolf, all the afternoon. When he told me you were watching that game of bowls, I said to myself in a flash, "I'll go out and meet Wolf coming back!" – and you see I did meet you.'

She spoke with a wavering happiness that seemed to be lifting the syllables of her voice up and down on the darkness as the undulations of a full-brimmed tide might lift a drifting boat.

'Let's find a place to sit down for a minute,' said Wolf. 'I can't realize I've got you, when we're just standing up like this.'

He tightened his clasp upon her hand and led her to the hedge. A mass of vague, dark umbrageousness confronted them.

'Stop!' he whispered, 'while I see if there's a ditch.'

He advanced slowly, feeling with his stick among the hemlocks and dock-leaves.

'There's no water, anyway,' he said, stepping down among the obscure rank-scented growths. 'Wait a second,' he cried, 'I believe we can get up over this.'

He felt about with his free hand. He could just detect the faint outlines of the branches of some small tree or shrub. It turned out – well did he know that acrid mind-cleansing pungency in his nostrils! – to be an elder-bush; and he pulled himself up by its brittle stalks till he attained the summit of the hedge.

'Come on! Catch hold!' he cried triumphantly, securing a firm position for himself and stretching out the handle of his stick towards her.

It took her a second or two of struggling amid the mass of weeds, and of fumbling with upraised arm, before she reached the extended support. But when once she felt it between her fingers, she clung tight with both hands, and he soon pulled her up beside him.

They found themselves, by a lucky chance, in a wheatfield that had been cut but not yet carried; and after a step or two across the stubble, they sank down with one consent and with cries of satisfaction against the side of a shock of corn.

The weight of the immense vaporous summer darkness covered them there like a waveless ocean. They floated there upon a cool, yielding darkness that had neither substance nor shape, a darkness full of a faint fragrance that was the sweetness neither of clover nor of poppies nor of corn nor of grass, but was rather the breath of the great terrestrial orb itself, a dark, interior, outflowing sweetness between vast-rocking waves of air, where firmament bent down to firmament, and space rose up to meet space.

He kept fast hold of her hand; and her fingers seemed still cold and stiff and impassive, just as they had done when he first took them in the road. She did not bend her head towards him as they sat side by side, nor did he make the least movement to put his arm around her.

Wolf had sunk a little lower in the corn-shock than she, so that their heads were exactly level; and to any inquisitive owl or night-jar hovering across that stubble-field they must have appeared like two well-constructed scarecrows, good enough to frighten the silly daylight rooks, but quite negligible and harmless to all more sagacious nocturnal eyes.

'When I'm with you like this,' said Wolf, 'I feel as if I'd stripped my mind clean of my spirit; pulled it off as I might pull off my vest when I go to bed! I feel as if I could actually see my mind now, like that terrible flayed skin in the "Last Judgment," lying there on the ground. I can see the rents in it and the stains on it and all the insane zigzag creases!'

'I knew I should meet you to-night,' said Christie, 'just as I really knew, though I wouldn't admit I knew, that you'd come to me that day of the fair. I felt it would be like this the moment my father left the shop. Do you think it's being the daughter of my mother that gives me these feelings, or do you think every girl who's in love has them sometimes?'

The question fell like a ripple of the very sweetness of the night over Wolf's soul, but he went on thinking aloud without replying.

'The odd thing is that when I'm away from you I can hardly call up your face. Mother's face and Gerda's face I know like two books; but it's as if I carried your identity so close to me that I couldn't see a single expression of it.'

'I feel unreal,' said Christie. 'That's how I feel – unreal. I've told myself stories about a lover since I was little. But after Olwen was born – oh, and before that, too – my life was so crushed and inert that I seemed to look at everything from some point outside of myself – as if my mind had been a cold, hard, inert mirror, reflecting what was there, but not feeling anything. But now I've known you it's been all different. My mind has got in touch again. I was a mere husk or shell all those miserable years – without a heart at all. But now the husk has come to life, and my heart with it. But sometimes I think my heart's still partly dead.'

'I'm perfectly satisfied with how your heart is,' Wolf threw in.

'Alive or dead, I've got it now, and I'm never going to let it go. What's so strange is that I don't idealize you one bit; and I don't think you idealize me either. I think it's wonderful how we accept each other just as we are.'

'Whether it's being my mother's daughter or not,' said Christie, 'it's a great comfort to me to have the feelings I have about what you're doing or where you are. . . . I think if anything happened to you I should know.'

'I wonder what it really is in us,' said Wolf, 'that makes us so happy as we are? All other lovers in our position I know very well would be desperate to make love, to live together, to have a child; but here we are, in this field, perfectly content just to be side by side. *You* don't want anything more than this, Christie, do you?'

'I don't know, Wolf, that I'll always feel as I do now. How can I know? But certainly to-night, I don't want anything else.'

She stopped; and then, after a little pause, her voice began again in the darkness.

'But you don't think, Wolf' – her tone had in it now a certain half-humorous dismay – 'that what we feel for each other could ever be called "platonic," do you? I don't know . . . perhaps it's because the word's been so misused . . . but I've always had such an aversion to that idea. The mere possibility of its being applied to the mysterious feeling between us, just because we don't want what people usually do who are in love, reduces everything for me in some way . . . do you know what I mean?'

'Ay, Christie! Christie!' he cried. 'How my father would chuckle if he heard those words of yours! You know how *he* would regard us and the way we behave? As nothing less than stark, staring mad! I'm damned if *I* know what "platonic" does mean . . . but I'm rather inclined . . . to think . . . to think . . . that our way of dealing . . . with things . . . with our feeling for each other . . . is much more mediæval than platonic.'

'Mediæval, Wolf?' protested Christie.

'Don't be cross with me. I know I'm absurd. I suppose I'm more of a slave to philosophical *phrases* than anyone in the whole of England! I love the sound of them. They have something . . . a sort of magic . . . I don't know what . . . that makes life rich and exciting to me.'

'Oh, I know what you mean, Wolf!' cried Christie. 'That's why I've loved reading those books in our shop . . . especially Leibnitz and Hegel. I've never been able to follow their real meaning, I

340

suppose; but all the same it's been a great satisfaction to me to read them.'

'I don't think it's pedantry or priggishness in either of us,' Wolf continued. 'I think we're thrilled by the weight of history that lies behind each one of these phrases. It isn't just the word itself, or just its immediate meaning. It's a long, trailing margin of human sensations, life by life, century by century, that gives us this peculiar thrill. Don't you think so, Christie?'

'What I was going to say,' the girl murmured, 'was that since I've known you I haven't cared so much for these philosophical books.'

'Nonsense!' he muttered. But once more there floated over him an undulating tide of happiness that made the mere tone of her voice seem to him like those fluctuating wine-dark shadows on the deep sea, that suggest the presence of cool-swaying fields of submerged seaweeds lying beneath the water.

'I know they're absurd . . . these phrases . . .' he went on. 'Words like "pluralism" and "dualism" and "monism." But what they make me think of is just a particular class of vague, delicious, physical sensations! And it's the idea of there having been feelings like these, in far-off, long-buried human nerves, that pleases us both so much. It makes life seem so thick and rich and complicated, if you know what I mean?'

They were both silent, and presently she struggled stiffly to her feet.

'And now, Wolf dear,' she said, 'I'm sure it's time we went on! I don't like being the one to say it . . . or being the one to interrupt our thoughts . . . but father will be back, and Gerda will be expecting you.'

He rose to his feet, too, and they stood awkwardly there, side by side in that windless darkness. Wolf had the feeling for one second as if the world had completely passed them by . . . gone on its way and forgotten them . . . so that not a soul knew they existed except themselves. As the shadow of a solitary bird on lonely sands answers the form of the bird's flying, so did he feel at that moment that his spirit answered her spirit.

But the moment passed quickly. A vague, troubling remembrance of that 'yellow bracken' down by the Lunt rose up suddenly without cause. 'Gerda must be thinking of me,' he said to himself. And as this thought came into his head he couldn't resist a savage secret jibing at his own treachery. 'I wonder,' he thought, 'what Jason would say if he knew everything!'

The girl's figure, close to him as it was, seemed like a pillar of mist. 'It's love-making,' he thought, 'just the relief of love-making, that saves a person's touchy mind from these morbid thoughts. But Christie doesn't depend on that any more than I do. What *would* Jason say if he saw us now?' And then there came upon him a curious sense of shame that his mind had the power of wandering so far. 'Is *her* mind wandering too?' he thought. 'What is going on in *her* mind?'

He spoke to her then . . . to that blur that was her face in the darkness.

'As long as we see each other like this, it'll go on being all right, won't it, Christie?'

Her voice replied to his voice with a sound that might have been a whisper out of his own heart or might have been a cry from the other side of the world.

'But it's hard now. It's hard when it ends,' she murmured.

'We might never have met at all,' he said resolutely. 'We've had all we wanted to-night. It's been as if all the noises of the world had blent into one, and then quite died away. Listen, Christie, there's not a stir or movement. It's silence like this that you and I have always wanted . . . all our lives.'

'But it's hard when it ends,' she repeated.

'We mustn't think of that,' he said. 'Our thoughts will always be able to find this silence. We shall always be able to reach each other with our thoughts, wherever we are. Don't you feel like that, Christie?'

'I try to,' she said.

'You *do*. No one else except you could answer a person's thoughts before they've been spoken! You *must* know, Christie, how I go muttering on and on to you in my heart, day and night, telling you every single feeling I have?'

'I tell you things, too, Wolf. I talk to you, too, sometimes . . . but still, but still . . .'

Her voice broke in a light sigh that floated away into the stubble, fainter than the falling of a feather.

'I know,' he repeated obstinately. 'But don't let's be ungrateful to the gods, Christie. Think, how easy for us never to have met at all! Think, how I might have gone on with my life in London, you with your life in Blacksod! But now, it's all different. And there really *is* a sense . . . don't you see, Christie? . . . in which by just knowing each other and being as we are we've got outside Time and outside Space! We've got into a region where all this –'

342

'Stop, Wolf, stop!' the girl cried. 'I can't bear it now. I tell you I can't –'

He moved towards her, seeking to touch her; but she drew away from him.

'Forgive me!' she said, in a low, quiet voice. 'It isn't that I don't understand you. I feel all those things. It's only that . . . at the end . . . when I've got to leave you . . . that all this seems . . . I mean doesn't seem . . .'

The gentleness of her tone softened the reproach if reproach there was; and Wolf was conscious of nothing but an obscure rebellion within him against this mysterious pride in them both which made it so hard for him to risk the relief of the least caress. It was his turn to sigh now – a heavier sigh than hers – and in a second she caught his change of mood.

'I love you so much, Wolf,' she said. 'I wouldn't hurt you for anything. It's what I feel for you that makes it so hard when you've got to go and I've got to go. And I know what you mean . . . I *do* know what you mean . . . about . . . about our thoughts!'

As she spoke she moved towards him a little in the darkness. It was an almost imperceptible movement; but it was enough to send a perilous stab of tenderness through his nerves.

'Christie, oh, Christie . . .' he murmured, involuntarily starting towards her.

But she had already gathered her cloak about her and held it tightly with one hand under her chin.

'It's all right, Wolf! It's all right!' she said quickly, turning as if with a swift impulse for flight towards the hedge.

'It would be mad now, I suppose,' he thought, as he followed her through the entangled branches.

Half an hour later and he was walking with a rapid, pre-occupied step along the lighted pavement of the Blacksod High Street. His head was so full of Christie, as he strode along, that the people he passed were as much phantoms to him as had been the elm trees on the road from King's Barton.

Christie had agreed to come on Monday. That was what he was thinking about now; and it was an imaginary dialogue with Gerda, dealing with this project, that he was now occupied in rehearsing, sentence by sentence, as he hurried along.

'If she refuses, she refuses!' he thought. 'I shan't press her. I'll just have to tell them the thing's off.'

He had just reached the point, close to the market-place, where Preston Lane debouched from the High Street, when he encountered, without any warning of his approach, for the pavement was crowded, the lean Panurge-like figure of Bob Weevil, hurrying along in a new straw hat and new flannel trousers.

'Hullo!' said the young grocer, with a shrinking, startled movement; and then he gave a furtive glance around him, as if to ensure public protection from a possible outburst of physical violence.

'Oh, it's you, is it, Bob?' said Wolf. 'Where are *you* going so fast?'

Mr. Weevil stopped and gazed at him with screwed-up eyelids, as he shook him by the hand.

'Home,' he announced, in a loud, unpleasant voice. 'Home to Dad. "Little Bobbie's Best at Home,"' he went on. 'Where've *you* been? Pursuing the Necessary over at Barton?'

The forced grin that animated the lad's features as he indulged in these pleasantries was so obviously embarrassed and uneasy, that Wolf became instantaneously suspicious. Every word of Jason's innuendos returned to his mind. There also returned to him that still more sinister hint whispered by the poet on the day of the snatching away of Mukalog.

'Where have *you* been?' he asked abruptly.

He did his best to give his voice a casual tone; but the effect of his question upon Mr. Weevil showed that this effort was unsuccessful.

'You're not a detective, are you?' jeered the young man, in a boisterously insolent manner. ' "Little Bobbie's Best at Home," ' he repeated. 'Do you know that song? I'll give you the rest of it some day.'

'Well, good night to you!' rapped out Wolf, brusquely and almost rudely. 'I've had a long day. Good night to you; and don't stay in the water so long the next time you bathe in Lenty Pond!'

He moved off at that, grimly entertained, in spite of his agitation, by the manner in which the young man's eyes and mouth opened at the tone of this remark.

'He's been with Gerda,' he thought, as he hurried on.

17

'THIS IS REALITY'

As soon as he reached Preston Lane, Wolf looked at his watch under the first of the three lamp-posts which were all the illumination that Blacksod had bestowed on that humble district. It was a quarter past nine. He must have been more than an hour in the cornfield; for he had left the bowling-green at seven.

'He's been with Gerda.' This single thought had brought him from the centre of the town to where he now stood, without consciousness of anything in the world except one solitary fish's eye – glazed and staring – that he had caught a glimpse of on a gas-lit counter.

He was too staggered even to experience surprise at his unexpected feelings. No alert, self-watchful demon in him cried out, 'What is this?' or 'What does *this* mean?' He just suffered; and his suffering was such a completely new thing to him that he had no mental apparatus ready with which to deal with it. He was like a man who all his life stalked leopards, suddenly confronted by a charging rhinoceros! All the blood that was in him seemed to have rushed with blind, irrational violence to a portion of his nervous system which he had supposed atrophied and callous. Vividly he recalled Jason's warning to him in the road by the churchyard. 'Those people must have pushed him to this,' he thought. 'Not very nice,' he thought, 'to think of the water-rat boasting up there with them and telling tales about her!'

He stood stock-still beneath the lamp-post. He felt as though a mob of Urquharts and Jasons had burst into the inmost sanctuary of his feelings – of his inarticulate physical feelings – and were jeering at them. He felt as though he had been stripped naked – as though he had become a laughing-stock to the human race. These were just the things – these physical feelings – that in his pride he had hidden from everyone. And now they were held up to derision, and he himself with them! He walked slowly across the road and then stopped and looked about him.

Everything was quiet. Most of the windows of those neat little houses displayed shaded gas-jets between the muslin curtains. From where he stood, the dark outline of the pig-dealer's shed was a small huddled blackness against the tall ash tree further on. Over the top of the shadowy hedge came a faint smell of cattle-trampled grass, a poor antidote to the manure-drain whose stench soon swallowed it up. His own house was still two or three doors off. He could see a thin stream of light emerging from its upper window. Gerda was in her bedroom, then – in her bedroom at a quarter past nine! Had Bob Weevil cajoled her up there, directly they'd finished their supper? 'Where did I once read,' he thought, 'that whatever liberties they allow, they usually fight shy of their man's bed? Good Lord! but what are beds? Beds are nothing. Beds are birth, death, and the morning and evening. But they're nothing when it comes to this! This can take the heart out of any bed.'

He recrossed the road to where the lamp-post was. The particular house just there had no light in the front windows. Instead of this there was a small notice which he could plainly read: 'Furnished Room to Let. Inquire within. Mrs. Herbert.' 'I suppose I've seen Mrs. Herbert,' he thought, 'a hundred times without knowing her. And I shall never know her. I shall die without knowing her.'

He tapped Mrs. Herbert's railings with his stick. 'It's not that I grudge Gerda any pleasure,' he thought. 'It's that I don't like spectators at *my* pleasure. She'll be just the same whatever Bob Weevil did. But he'll always be there . . . hiding behind her thoughts like a rat behind a screen . . . and watching me when I touch her. He'll be in her thoughts when I'm holding her. He'll be always there. I shall be eating with him, sleeping with him. There'll always be a slit in her thoughts through which his eye will be on me.'

He remembered how his mother had once come home in high spirits to their London flat, after a conversation with her cousin, Lord Carfax, and told him how this nobleman had explained to her his philosophy of free love, and how barbarous it was to grow jealous and possessive when you were enamoured. 'Jealous?' he thought. 'Well! He's more sociable than I am, the good Carfax. I like to be alone in my house . . . not to be peeped at by a third person from the back of my girl's head!'

He felt an extreme reluctance to move a step from where he was at the railings of the unknown Mrs. Herbert. 'I've talked a lot about reality,' he said to himself. 'But now I know a little better what *mine* is . . .'

'*This* is reality,' he thought. 'This is the kind of thing that men returning home at a quarter past nine in Colorado, in Singapore, in Moscow, in Cape Town, in New Zealand, see in the darkness! . . . This is reality,' he thought.

He looked down at the tiny gutter at his feet between the asphalted pavement and the road. The lamplight shone upon this gutter, and he observed a torn piece of newspaper lying in it – a headline of the *Western Gazette* – and just tilted against the edge of this headline he saw an empty greenish-coloured tin. He could even read the words upon that torn bit of paper – printed in large, heavy type. 'France distr . . . land.' 'France distrusts England,' he repeated to himself; and then 'Lyle's Golden Syrup.' He could read *that*, without reading it! Much sweetness had he, in his time, watched Gerda imbibing from such a greenish-coloured receptacle!

'Does Mattie make 'em give Olwen *her* "golden syrup" out at Pond Cottage? This is reality,' he thought.

Down under his feet, under this asphalt, under this Somerset clay, down to the centre of the globe, went the mystery of solid matter. Up, up above him, beyond all this thick swine-scented darkness, went space, air, emptiness – the mystery of un-solid matter. 'France distr . . . land' – 'Lyle's Golden Syrup.' Poke them with the end of an oak stick. . . . 'You'll walk into a pit with your precious stick, master!' – was that what Jason had said?

Pluralism, pantheism, monism! . . . Phrases . . . phrases made by men who come home at a quarter past nine. But these sounds too . . . these large, easy, purring sounds . . . part of reality!

Did Bob Weevil pull up her clothes? They like to have 'em unhooked better than that . . . untied . . . slipping down. . . . They never lose that sense . . . They belie 'em when they say they lose that sense. What sense? The beauty of their beauty . . . the sense of being *beautifully* loved . . . 'This is reality,' he thought. 'They belie 'em when they say . . . Up or down, Bob Weevil? That's the question. Up is infinite. Down is infinite. Pantheism, dualism, pluralism! An ounce of civet, good Master Jason!'

He moved on and stood by the little iron gate of his own house. He did not look up, because there suddenly came to him the nervous idea that she was kneeling on the floor in her short 'slip,' peeping out at him; and he didn't feel in a mood to be peeped at!

What he did was to stare at the latch of the gate, wondering if he could lift it without making any sound. She had so often heard that 'click' and come running to welcome him. He felt that to make that particular noise now would be as if he entered her presence with his face blackened all over like a clown. . . .

But now there arose a different question. His mind began tying itself in a knot like a twisting snake. His own voice was in his ears assuring Christie that, all day and all night, he did nothing but

347

live with her in his thoughts, telling her everything! Could he now tell her everything? . . . She who at this very minute was no doubt standing at *her* window? Why couldn't he tell her everything? Why couldn't he tell her that it wasn't that he grudged Gerda pleasure . . . that it was only that he grudged Bob Weevil the *sort* of pleasure he had got from that tombstone picture! Why couldn't he explain all this to Christie; why couldn't he explain to her that it was not the thing itself, but only the way . . . the way in which Bob Weevil did . . . whatever it was he did?

He knew perfectly well that Christie understood his attachment to Gerda. He knew perfectly well that she would understand his resentment at the intrusion of Bob Weevil. What he could never, *never* make her understand would be this cold, sickening nausea he felt toward the simple, actual facts of what must have gone on. How *could* Gerda allow it? How could she?

But perhaps she did struggle a little — if only out of pride — when Bob Weevil began fumbling. But soon there could have been no sound at all except their breathing, except their hard breathing . . . Gerda would suffer, if she knew about Christie, the most secret of feminine sufferings . . . deeper than 'France distr . . . land' . . . But a man coming home at a quarter past nine suffered too, the most secret of male sufferings . . . 'An ounce of civet, good Master Jason!' He bent his head low down over the little iron railings, trying to think — to think and get it all clear.

He leaned against the little gate, while some unperturbed portion of his consciousness set itself to wonder whether it were a marigold or a petunia that emitted a faint, whitish lustre in the darkness. There were plants of both of them there; but he couldn't remember their position — whether the marigolds were there or *there!* Then a thought came into his head that made him straighten his back, click the latch, open it, and walk boldly to the door.

If Gerda and Mr. Weevil were really fond of each other — if the girl had grown weary of him and his heavy lumpish mind — why couldn't they separate . . . he *his* way . . . she *her* way?

To his surprise — in spite of the lighted candle upstairs — Gerda was seated quietly, contentedly, calmly, at a table in their parlour. She was hemming an apron; and before she smilingly rose to greet him, he saw her quickly but carefully fix her needle in her bobbin of white thread. She threw her arms round his neck and kissed him, not passionately, or perfunctorily, but affectionately and gaily.

'I had tea late and waited supper. It's all ready in the kitchen,' she said, releasing him. And then she stretched herself, with both arms outspread; and her careless air of indolent well-being was accentuated by the childish smile that covered a shameless yawn. Wolf returned to the passage to hang up his hat and place his stick in its accustomed corner. He could not help thinking of Jason as he did this.

When he returned she was folding up her sewing and putting it away in a drawer. She looked at him smilingly over her shoulder. 'I've had a visitor for tea, Wolf. Guess who it was.'

'It wouldn't be much of a game for me to guess *that*, Gerda,' he said with all the lightness he could assume. 'Careful! Careful, now!' his fighting spirit whispered to his excited nerves. 'If you make the least false move she'll have you at a disadvantage.'

'Why not?' The girl approached him, as she spoke, giving him a long, scrutinizing glance. 'What's the matter, Wolf? Is anything wrong?' She laid both her hands on his coat, clutching its unbuttoned flaps and tightening them round him with a gesture that was at once imperative and cajoling.

'I met Bob Weevil just now,' he murmured, trying to give the words a natural tone, and smoothing out every sign of treachery from his face.

But with incredible rapidity, even while she was lifting up her chin and opening her lips, the self-protective demon in him cursed him for a blundering fool. 'Why did you blurt *that* out?' said the demon.

'And he told you he'd been here?' Her words were as calm as if she'd said, 'And he told you he'd been playing bowls.' She released her hold upon his coat and with easy naturalness ran out into the passage and thence into the kitchen.

Wolf heard her collecting the supper-things. He heard the sound of running water and the sound of metal against earthenware. He looked round the room. Ah! *there* was something he hadn't noticed before, a draughtboard open, with the black and white disks jumbled in casual confusion over its checkered surface.

So they had been playing draughts!

He walked thoughtfully up to this object and began piling up the round wooden counters, one on the top of another, balancing his shaky tower with his fingers as it began to sway. Then he removed his hand, and his tower fell with a crash and many of the pieces rolled on the floor.

The house was so still that the sudden noise brought Gerda running into the room – to find him standing by the draughts-table.

'What's the matter with you?' she cried peevishly. 'Aren't you going to help me get supper? Aren't you even going to wash your hands?'

'So you and Bob were playing draughts? I never knew you even knew the game, Gerda,' he said.

'Come and wash your hands,' she replied in a calm, scolding tone. 'I've got tomato-soup. It'll be ready in a minute. I'll tell you every bit of the gossip about Bob when we've sat down! Of course I know draughts. Bob taught me years ago, when I was little. To-day I won every single game. I was "huffing" him all the time. But *do* come, Wolf. I'm hungry. Never mind picking up those things!'

He followed her into the kitchen and stood there, awkwardly and sulkily, till the meal was ready.

'I'm going to have beer to-night, Gerda,' he said. 'I don't know if *you* are.'

'I certainly am!' she said in her most cheerful tone, seating herself at the table and breaking a piece of bread with one hand, while she dipped her spoon into the soup with the other.

He went to the cupboard and came back with three bottles.

'Wolf . . . *dear!*' she cried, with her mouth full. 'Who's the third bottle for? Have *you* got somebody coming in?'

'It's for me,' he remarked laconically. 'I'm tired to-night. I've had a long day.'

'But, Wolf – isn't it rather extravagant drinking so much at one meal?'

He didn't reply to this, but busied himself with opening two of the bottles and with filling her glass and his own.

'It's good . . . this soup . . . isn't it, Wolf?' she remarked presently, passing the tip of her pink tongue over one corner of her perfectly curved lip and lifting her spoon once more to her mouth.

He poured half his glassful of beer, froth and all, down his throat without a word! Then he began swallowing the soup in rapid gulps.

'Good soup . . . very *good* soup,' he muttered.

She gave him a quick penetrating look over her own raised glass, just sipped at the white foam, and then replaced the tumbler on the table. The next spoonful she lifted slowly, meditatively, absent-mindedly, a little puckered frown hovering about her forehead.

Wolf set himself obstinately and resolutely to finish the meal. Eating pieces of crumbled bread, hurriedly, intently, as if the process were something important in itself, leading to some desirable consummation, he kept drinking the beer in long draughts. The moment the first bottle was finished he opened the other, and with the same concentrated absorbed determination, disposed of that also.

'Good soup . . . very *good* soup,' he repeated, as if the words were a sop thrown over his shoulder to some insatiable Cerberus of the river of Time.

'I am the weakest, most gullible fool,' he thought, as he watched Gerda spreading a large slice of bread and then very deliberately taking little bites out of it, 'ever born into the world. I oughtn't to be called Wolf Solent at all! I ought to be called Mr. Thin Soup or Mr. Weak Beer.'

'Aren't you going to give me a cigarette?' asked Gerda.

He got up to obey, and it seemed to him as if the physical effort it required to hand her what she demanded and to hold towards her a lighted match, were the heaviest material task he had ever stretched his muscles to perform.

He lighted one for himself, however, and resumed his seat.

In complete silence now, save for the ticking of the clock on the mantelpiece, the greyish-blue spirals of smoke rose from each end of the table and floated hesitatingly, fluctuatingly, towards one another, high up above the two human heads.

'It's the weakness of your nature, Beer-Soup,' he said to himself. 'The weakness and the gullibility.' Then he recalled the sudden bold resolve with which he had clicked the latch of their gate; and he compared that flash of inspiration with his wretched feelings now. Didn't he know himself at all? What he felt now was a complete disintegration of desire and will. He felt as if his consciousness were a tiny fitful flame, no, not a flame even, a scarcely visible vapour, hovering over a chaos of conflicting wishes, purposes, desires, hopes, regrets, that were so disorganized as utterly to cancel one another. They felt remote from him, too, these feelings that ought to have been his – remote and infinitely contemptible! The only desire this weak, floating awareness retained was a desire to escape from them altogether. For, disorganized though they were, a dull nausea, sickening and paralysing, ascended from them, troubling that feeble, free consciousness of his, as a putrefying body might trouble some frail *animula vagula* only half-escaped from it.

He struggled to use his brain, his free brain. 'What *is* the matter with you, you lump of asininity? Speak up, express yourself, Mr. Wolf Beer-Soup!'

Then he suddenly recalled what he had felt as he drank that Dorchester ale in the bowling-green of Farmer's Rest. He had felt completely master of his destiny then. All these disorganized emotions, all these nervous electric currents, were gathered up then and focused. Was he perhaps . . . innately incapable of dealing

351

with women, whether in the way of lust or in the way of tenderness? Was he only *a man* when confronted with men? Thrown with women, did his whole nature turn lumpish, sapless, porous? He began suddenly to have that appalling sensation which had come to him on Babylon Hill, as if his head . . . the thing that said 'I am I' . . . were twisting and turning, like an uprisen hooded serpent . . . above a body of unspeakable decomposition. . . .

Like a drowning man he stretched out his thoughts for help in every direction. To his mother he stretched them out. To his father he stretched them out. Feebly and automatically he carried his thoughts like a basket of dying fish to the threshold of Christie's room. 'Christie! I must tell you . . . I *must*, I *must*, tell you!'

But it seemed to him then as if even Christie's mind were shut to his helplessness. He seemed to hear her cry, 'Stop, Wolf, stop! I can't bear to hear it!'

'This can't go on,' he thought. 'I must end this somehow; or I shall go mad.'

He rose to his feet and began pacing up and down the kitchen.

Gerda watched him in silence for a moment or two; and then, extinguishing the remains of her cigarette against the edge of her empty soup-plate, she said to him, quite naturally and quietly: 'Wolf, darling, just run upstairs, will you, and see if I left my candle burning? I want to wash up before we go to bed.'

He stared at her in bewilderment, blinking his eyes. Then he lifted his hand to his mouth and held it there – held it to hide that trick he had, when he was at the limit of his endurance, of working the muscles of his lower jaw.

Gerda calmly rose from her seat and began gathering together the things on the table. '*Do* run up and put out that candle, Wolf,' she repeated. 'We don't want a fire in our house.'

He obeyed her in silence now, and ascended the creaking steps, dragging his feet. He felt as if some completely different person – some docile, harmless, lumpish idiot – had taken the place of the Wolf he knew.

When he entered the room he found that the candle she had left there was low down in its candlestick, burning and guttering sideways, and dropping grease over the cover of the chest of drawers. He bent down mechanically to blow it out, receiving as he did so the full force of the carbonic-acid gas in his face. With no conscious purpose in his mind, he approached the bed, and, in the darkness, passed his hand hesitatingly over both the pillows, as if feeling for something.

Then he stood straight up against the edge of the bed, his knees touching the sheeted mattress, his arms hanging limp at his sides.

Quite externally and objectively, as if it had been this idiotic other person and not himself at all who formulated the thought, he wondered whether it was *after* she had let Bob Weevil make love to her up here, or *before*, that the game of draughts had been brought out. A hideous commentary upon this problem seemed to arise then from the mass of his own disorganized nerves. 'Why don't you ask Christie what *she* thinks? Christie is a girl. Christie will be able to tell you whether it was before the draughts or after the draughts!'

He left the bed and went to the open window, hearing, as he did so, the sound of Gerda's clattering with the supper-things as she calmly washed up below.

The window was open at the top, so that to get the coolness of the air he was forced to lean his elbows upon the woodwork and rest his chin upon the back of his folded hands.

He remembered to the end of his life what he felt at that moment, while the bone of his lower jaw met the bones of his knuckles pressed so hard against them. He felt absolutely alone – alone in an emptiness that was different from empty space. He did not pity himself. He did not hate himself. He just endured himself and waited – waited till whatever it was that enclosed him made some sign.

By slow degrees it dawned on him that he had been for the last two or three minutes seeing something without being conscious of what he saw. Now it began to grow slowly plain to him, lineament by lineament, feature by feature, what it was he had been seeing in the darkness of that room, in the darkness of this obscure night.

It was the face of the man on the Waterloo steps! And out of his abominable misery Wolf cried a wordless cry to this face; and the nature of this cry was such that it seemed to break – so desperate it was – some psychic tension in his brain. And it seemed to him that what he was appealing to now was something beyond his mother, beyond his father, beyond Christie herself – something that was the upgathered, incarnated *look*, turned toward life's engines, of every sentient thing, since the beginning of time, that those engines had crushed.

The smell of the pigsty across the way must have been the reason why the *look* he appealed to was only partially human. It was an animal look . . . it was a bird look . . . it was the look of the fish's eye that he had seen on a counter as he came along the street that very night; it was the look of a wounded snake's eye that he had had time to mark long ago, out on some country road near London before he ended its suffering.

It was, in fact, the Life-Eye, looking out on what hurts it, that he now knew he had caught glimpses of, all the days of his existence, in a thousand shapes and forms. From air, earth, water had he intercepted the appeal of that little round living hole . . . that hole that went through the wall . . . straight into something else. Into *what* else? No one knew or would ever know. But into something else. It was upon *this* he was crying out now . . . upon that eye . . . upon that little round hole . . . upon that chink, that cranny, that slit, out of which life protested against its infamous enemy!

'Jesus . . . Jesus . . . Jesus . . . Jesus!'

Was that the heart of Wolf Solent howling a wordless howl in a dark bedroom, or was it the voice of Mr. Round of Farmer's Rest seeking escape from his 'worries'?

A sigh of unutterable relief shivered through Wolf's nerves as they relaxed and yielded. He drew back from the window and began with an almost cat-like movement licking his hurt knuckles.

His whole being seemed dissolving into some lovely liquid-floating substance, lighter than human flesh, and he became capable of thinking now with every portion of his identity, easily, freely, spontaneously.

'I've learnt one thing to-night,' he thought, as he crossed the room and felt about in the darkness for the handle of the door. 'I've learnt that one can't always get help by sinking into one's own soul. It's sometimes necessary to escape from oneself altogether.'

He ran down the little staircase with happy agility. He burst into the kitchen, where he found Gerda placidly and abstractedly polishing her knives and forks.

'How long you – ' she began; but the words were stopped upon her mouth by an imprint of impetuous, almost boisterous kisses.

As he held her in his arms, Wolf's thoughts were of the most intense and rapid kind. Why was it that his love for Christie hadn't protected him from all this agitation? Why had he been paralysed by Gerda's calm? How was it that, in the unbelievable relief he experienced now, he really felt as if it didn't *very much* matter what the water-rat had done or hadn't done?

Releasing Gerda now, he seemed to bewilder her a good deal more by his high spirits than he had done by his moroseness.

'Don't let's go to bed *just* yet,' he said. 'Let's go for a tiny stroll down the road.'

'Why, Wolf, how funny you are to-night! A moment ago you were telling me that you were quite exhausted.'

354

She yielded good-humouredly, however, to his caprice, and they went out together into the narrow road.

Wolf had the strangest feeling as he clicked the latch of the gate to let her through. It was as if he were breaking some law of nature – refuting some inflexible scientific category of cause and effect.

He kept his arm tight about her, and led her up the road, in the direction away from the town, till they came to the place where the immense ash tree lifted its branches into the dark air high above their heads.

There was a small gap in the hedge at this point, and Wolf pulled her through it, into the meadow on the other side. 'For the second time to-night!' whispered his demon. But for some reason the mockery glanced off from Wolf's present mood of slippery buoyancy, without causing him the slightest discomfort. 'Very well, then,' he mentally retorted, 'for the second time it *shall* be!'

They found themselves now under the very trunk of the vast tree whose branches they had so often watched from their upper room. One branch bent so low down and stretched out so far that they instinctively put their arms about it and dallied with its cool foliage. Wolf even amused himself by gathering up those great multiform leaf-growths, so different from the foliations of all other trees, and twisting them, without breaking their flexible stalks, about the girl's bare neck.

Gerda remained passive and yielding under this dalliance. It seemed to him that her mind was a little aloof; but he could see, without seeing it, the faint, docile smile, like that of a sweet-natured child drawn into a game it was ready to play without understanding, with which she submitted to his humour.

All at once there came a sudden coolness upon his face and a quick rustling above their heads. The wind was rising. Oh, this was what he had been craving for ever since his return to Preston Lane! It had been – he knew it now – something in the heaviness of this windless air that had caused half his trouble. Had this cool wind been blowing when he crossed the threshold, everything would have been different. It was the wind he wanted, the wind, the wind; to blow away all odious eidolons of Bob Weevil's presence out of his 'sober house'!

He permitted the leafy ash twigs that he had been bending to swing back to their natural position; and snatching at Gerda's arm above the wrist, he drew the girl, like a captive, right up to the trunk of the great overshadowing tree. She remained still passive, gentle, unresisting, by his side, her head drooping a little, her whole being – so it seemed – lost in a calm untroubled quiescence. Holding her thus, but turning away from her, he rubbed the palm of his free hand up and down over the hard slightly-indented surface of the ash trunk, whose bark, thin and tightly fitted, raised no barrier between his human touch and the tree's own firm, hard wood-flesh.

'Human brains! Human knots of confusion!' he thought. 'Why can't we steal the calm vegetable clairvoyance of these great rooted lives?'

'I simply can't understand myself,' he thought. 'Why, after being so happy with Christie, should the idea of Bob Weevil, poor, lecherous little rat, have worried me so? And why didn't I make a scene with Gerda – raise denials, anger, tears, reproaches? Why, instead of that, did I just muddy up my own wits?'

Still retaining his clasp of Gerda's wrist, he leaned forward and pressed his bare forehead against the trunk of the ash tree.

'What's this, Wolf Solent? . . . What's this, you lumpish, mock-platonic, well-cuckolded ass? Ash tree! Ash tree!' Why had he been allowed by the justice of things to deny himself a single embrace with Christie, only to come home at a quarter past nine and find a lit candle in Gerda's bedroom? Platonic cuckold! That was just what he was. . . . Not even platonic . . . for Christie despised that word. . . . Mock-platonic cuckold! Oh, it was all coming back! The knot in his mind was tying itself up again – tight – tight – tight! He continued to lean against the tree in the position of an animal that is butting with its skull against some immovable obstacle.

And then the Waterloo-steps eye, the fish's eye, the snake's eye, the slaughtered pig's eye, the eye of a caged lark he had seen once as a child in St Mary's Street, Weymouth, all seemed to melt strangely together – all seemed to peer out at him from the heart of the tree-trunk against which he was butting with his skull.

And he thought to himself, 'There are ways that I haven't tried at all!' And he thought to himself: 'Endless little things are beautiful and wonderful beyond words. And I can love Christie and forgive her for hating "platonic"; and I can love Gerda and forgive her for letting Bob Weevil pull up her clothes. And if Christie and Gerda knew what *I* know, they'd forgive *me* for loving both of them! Christie would forgive me for not telling her. Gerda would forgive me for not telling her. There are things a person can't tell. But there's a way of floating like a mist out of my pride and conceit. There's a way of accepting myself as Mr. Promise-

356

Breaking-Beer-Soup, and yet not minding it at all . . . just becoming a cloud of mist that enjoys this cool wind . . . a cloud of mist that pities everything and enjoys everything!

He swung away, back from the tree, at this, and let Gerda go. 'You've hurt me, Wolf!' the girl cried peevishly. 'Why did you do that? I haven't done anything to you. I wouldn't have come out with you if I thought you were going to act so funny. Come! Let's go in. What do you think I am, to stand so much silliness? You're drunk – that's what's the matter with you; you're just drunk and acting silly!'

He was so delighted to receive nothing but this very natural piece of scolding, that he only answered by hugging her tightly to his heart. 'Little Gerda! Little Gerda!' he kept repeating. And he thought to himself: 'I've exaggerated the whole thing. She *can't* have let Weevil play with her and be like she is now!'

And then an idea came into his mind.

'Don't be cross, sweetheart,' he said. 'If I *was* drunk, I swear I'm all right now. But listen! Do let me lift you up into this tree, just for a minute! I'd so adore to hear your voice out of the leaves above my head and not see hardly a glimpse of you! *Do* get up into it, Gerda, and let me hear your voice from up there. You needn't climb far. I can't climb trees at all. I get dizzy. Or I'd climb it with you.'

The girl was still apparently enough of a child to be stirred by this unexpected appeal.

'But I'm so heavy, Wolf; and this branch is so high up.'

'Oh, no, it's not – it's not! There – shove yourself up on the palms of your hands. Jump – and lift yourself – you know? Like boys do on walls!'

He bent down and encircled her body with his arms, just above her knees, and lifted her up.

Gerda pressed her hands upon the bough as he had suggested, and after a few struggles was lying prone along it, holding it so closely with her arms and legs that he could hardly distinguish the one living thing from the other.

'Well done, sweetheart!' he cried. 'That's right. Now work your way towards the trunk. Careful now! Straddle your legs – you'll scratch your knees like that – straddle your legs and hold with your hands!'

Again she obeyed him with good-humoured docility. And as he watched her shadowy figure riding the swaying branch, he could not help recalling the wicked tombstone-picture; and the thought – the very last thought he expected to cross his mind that night – flitted into his senses that it would be a desirable moment when he blew out the candle in their room—blew out that candle for the second time!

'That's it, Gerda, that's it! Now get hold of the branch above, and pull yourself on to it!'

He came nearer the tree-trunk and gazed up into the darkness. In a second or two he lost sight of her altogether, for Gerda was an adept at climbing trees. All he could detect was a vague rustling; and even that was very soon swallowed up by the murmur of the whole dark mass of foliage, stirred into movement now by the rising wind.

He waited. He leaned his back against the trunk. He listened to the long-drawn swish — swish — swish of the invisible, rustling leaves.

Then his heart gave a leap within his body and he caught his breath with an indrawn quivering gasp.

A blackbird was whistling above his head! Faint and low at first, each liquid flute-note went sailing away upon the wind as if it had been a separate pearl-clear bubble of some immortal dew. Then, growing louder and clearer, the notes began following rapidly one upon another; but each one of them still remained distinct from the rest — a trembling water-transparent globe of thrilling sound, purged, inviolable — a drop of translunar melody, floating, floating, far above the world, carrying his very soul with it.

Then the notes changed, varied, overlapped, grew charged with some secret intention, some burden of immeasurable happiness, of sadness sweeter than happiness.

Rising still, freer, stronger, fuller, they began to gather to themselves the resonant volume of some incredible challenge, a challenge from the throat of life itself to all that obstructed it. Tossed forth upon the darkness, wild and sweet and free, this whistled bird-song, answering the voice of the rising wind, took to itself something that was at once so jocund and so wistful, that it seemed to him as though all the defiant acceptance of fate that he had ever found in green grass, in cool-rooted plants, in the valiant bodies of beasts and birds and fishes . . . 'mountains and all hills . . . . fruitful trees and all cedars' . . . had been distilled, by some miracle, in this one human mouth.

The whistling sank into silence at the very moment when its power over Wolf's soul was at the flood. But without one single second of delay, when the last note had died, Gerda came scrambling down, laughing, rustling the leaves, and giving vent to petulant little outcries as her clothes impeded her descent. Wolf, when she finally fell, all panting and tremulous with wild gaiety,

358

into his arms, felt that it was difficult to believe that this was the same Gerda whom he had watched, that very noon, asleep on the summit of Poll's Camp.

As they returned hand in hand to their house door, a queer, abashed sense came over him that all the events of this turbulent day had been a sort of feverish delirium. What *was* his mind that it should go through such agitation and remain unaltered – remain the same 'I am I' of Wolf Solent?

But once again his self-knowledge received a shock. For no sooner were they inside their small domicile, no sooner had he glanced at the linoleum on the staircase, the wooden clock in the parlour, the familiar kitchen-table, than all these little objects hit his consciousness with a delicious thrilling sense of happy security, as if he had come back to them from some great voyage over desolate and forlorn seas, as if he had come back to them with his clothes drenched with salt water and his hands wounded by tarred ropes! His mind may have remained unaltered by all this, but it had at any rate been washed very clean!

Upon every tiniest and least-important object he looked, that night, with a purged simplicity, a spontaneous satisfaction. The pine-wood boarding at the edge of the linoleum stair-carpet, the pegs where their coats hung, the handles of the dresser drawers, the rows of balanced plates, the cups suspended from the little hooks, the metal knobs at the end of their bed, Gerda's comb and brush, the candlestick still covered with grease, and two exposed soap-dishes on the washing-stand, one containing a small piece of Pears' soap and one containing a square lump of common yellow soap – all these things thrilled him, fascinated him, threw him into an ecstasy of well-being.

What was it that Mr. Urquhart had said, that day, about these little inanimates? Suicide *he* was talking about. But this was different....

It was a very quiescent Gerda, lethargic and languorous, who lay down by his side that Friday night. It was a very indulgent Christie, grave and tender, who listened now in her room above the shop to his story about ash trees and draughtboards – who listened to every thought he had, as she lay there with closed eyes!

No system at all! Only to dissolve into thin, fluctuating vapour; only to flow like a serpentine mist into the grave of his father, into the mocking heart of his mother, into the ash tree, into the wind, into the sands on Weymouth Beach, into the voice of the landlord of Farmer's Rest. No system at all!

'Jesus . . . Jesus . . . Jesus . . . Jesus. . . .'

359

18

THE SCHOOL TREAT

G<small>ERDA</small> had refused point-blank to invite Darnley and Christie to supper on Monday night, thus bringing to nothing Christie's premonition in the stubble-field. And now it was the middle of the long, sunlit afternoon – relaxed, autumnal, mellow – of Mr. Valley's great gala day.

The *fête* was held in the vicarage glebe, adjoining that portion of the churchyard-wall behind which rose the now four-months-old tombstone of the youthful Mr. Redfern.

The young men and boys of the village, encouraged at their game by Mr. Urquhart and Darnley Otter, were engaged in an interminable cricket match, a match played between those who lived west of the church and those who lived east.

When Wolf first left his employer's library, which he did some half-hour later than the Squire himself, and entered the school-treat field, he felt nervous and irritable. Everyone he knew in the world seemed to be gathered in that enclosure; and, as he stealthily shuffled along the edge of the churchyard, he felt as if he would like to hide himself from them all, down in the silent earth along with young Redfern!

He found himself at a spot where the wall was very low, and, turning his back upon the crowded scene, leaned there for a while unnoticed, gazing at the great perpendicular tower. With the shouts and laughter in his ears, that tower looked incredibly massive and silent. What ebbing and flowing of human lives had it not seen, since unknown hands in the reign of the first Tudor piled it up there, stone upon stone!

Well, at least it was something to face the disquietudes of his own life in the presence of masonry like this, so subdued, so encrusted, rendered so mellow by the passing of the generations! As long as Fate allowed him to eke out his days amid old time-weathered concretions, like this King's Barton tower, he could never touch certain abysses of misery! Here in these West-country places he was at any rate spared the atrocity of feeling the pinch of life's dilemmas against a background of monstrous modern inventions. The long, cold clutch of scientific discovery, laid, like metallic fingers, upon the human pulse, could not despoil the dignity of existence here; though the invasion by such inhuman forces had already begun!

'Long may this tower stand, so that men like me can touch its stones, its buttresses, its lichen, its moss, and escape from the dragon's-tail of the stinging present!'

He was conscious of a stealthy step behind him, and, turning round, he found Jason Otter at his side.

'You are enjoying yourself looking at his grave,' the poet began; 'and I don't blame you. I like looking at the graves of people I've known. But you go further than I could go, Solent. You are the clever one, the wise one, the old cunning one! You can enjoy looking at a grave though you never knew the person who's in it.'

'You can't expect me not to be interested in Redfern, can you?' retorted Wolf, a little crustily.

'Of course not. That's just it. We all feel an interest – a nice, merry interest – in being alive when someone else is dead. He only came down here for money,' he added unexpectedly, 'like you!'

'If I came for it, I assure you I don't get it,' said Wolf.

Jason chuckled a great deal at this remark. Then he grew grave. 'I've got a poem here I'd like to read to you, if it wouldn't spoil your pleasure in looking at this young man's grave. I won't, if it *would*.'

'I've looked all I want to look,' said Wolf; 'so do read me what you've got there. I'm glad of any excuse not to go round the field and hear so much talk.'

'Sit down, then, a minute . . . do you mind?'

The two men sat down at the base of the wall and leaned their backs against it, facing the school-treat meadow. Jason produced from his pocket a small notebook, which he opened very deliberately upon his knee.

'It's about white seaweed,' said Jason Otter.

'I didn't know it was ever white,' said Wolf.

'Everything is white at one time or another,' retorted Jason. '*You'll* be white enough yourself, one fine day!'

'If it only goes white when it's dead,' argued Wolf obstinately, 'I don't think it's much of a subject. I like the idea of seaweed being white in the way chalk is white or daisies are white; but if it just fades and bleaches . . . I don't think much of that.'

'It's no good abusing me before you've heard it,' said Jason; 'but of course we know this business of reading our writings is what your friend Darnley would call impolite.'

'Go on, man, go on!' cried Wolf. 'I'm listening.'

And the poet began to read.

'White Seaweed' . . .

He repeated these words a second time, gathering his energy.

'White seaweed.'

'For God's sake,' cried Wolf, 'get on with it! They'll catch sight of us in a moment and then it'll all be spoilt.'

Jason accepted this impatience with unruffled equanimity, and began in a low voice; but, gathering confidence as he proceeded, he read the poem from beginning to end without a pause:

> White as the foam in the track of a whale
> As he spouts and sports for a thousand miles
> Where the waters slope round the planet's rim,
> Beyond the continents and the isles,
> White as the foam that follows him
> Where there's never a masthead nor a sail.
>
> Drowned and dead from their sunken ships,
> Drift the bodies of boys and girls;
> White are they as they float and drift,
> Their hair like flotsam, their breasts like pearls,
> While the grey tides lift them, or cease to lift,
> And the green tides gurgle between their lips.
>
> Fishes' eyes in the cold grey deep,
> Staring and waiting, waiting and staring,
> Seagulls' beaks on the tops of the wave,
> The same eternal quests are sharing;
> But the dark, wet, purple, slippery grave
> Holds safe those bodies in untouched sleep.
>
> And out of the flesh of those bodies light,
> In their dark, wet, purple, slippery bed,
> A seaweed grows that is soft as silk.
> White as the moon on St. Alban's Head,
> Moss-like, fern-like, white as milk, –
> The fingers of Mary are not more white!

Oh! white as the horn of God's unicorn,
That seaweed lies upon Red-cliff bay,
Lies in the spindrift on Red-cliff sands.
Fling all your wicked thoughts away!
Take off your shoes; anoint your hands!
Than to touch such seaweed with careless scorn
'Twere better never to have been born!

Jason's voice sank; and that peculiar silence ensued which is fuller of electric cross-currents than anything else in the world . . . the silence produced by the falling of the seminal drops of verbal creation . . . upon an alien mind.

'I like it very much,' murmured Wolf at last. And he thought to himself, 'The beggar *has* his own peculiar imagination.'

Then he said aloud: 'It's one of your best poems, Jason. I don't think it's quite up to the "Slow-worm of Lenty," but it does you credit and I congratulate you. What did you exactly mean by that last verse? Did you mean that there are people in the world whose wicked thoughts are aroused by white-seaweed, or did you just mean the ordinary stupidity of human beings?'

'It's not my business to explain what I mean,' said Jason. 'It's my business to write. I can see what you think. You think that I just string words together as they come into my head! It isn't as easy to write a poem as you seem to imagine.'

'Why do you write so often about water and about drowned people?' asked Wolf. 'Your pond-elf in "The Slow-worm" gave me a weird feeling; and this seaweed of yours, growing out of drowned bodies – '

'You needn't go on!' interrupted Jason. 'Of course, I can't expect anyone to like my poetry who lives by copying out the liquorish thoughts of a doting old fool. We all want to be glorified. My poetry is all I've got and I ought never to have read it to you. I ought to have known I'd only get abuse. It's this wanting to be glorified that's the mistake. A person ought to be satisfied if he can get his meals three times a day, without having to dance attendance on some silly old man or some ugly old woman!'

Wolf swept this aside. 'Do you have in your mind any definite people when you make the newts and tadpoles tease the pond-elf, and when you make these fish and gulls want to eat these youthful bodies?'

Jason's face wrinkled with delight at this.

'You're afraid I might bring *you* in!' he chuckled. 'I wouldn't mind not being glorified if I could make your friend Urquhart agitate himself as much as you do over my poems.'

Wolf had no time to reply to this; for, to his considerable surprise, he perceived his mother and Gerda, arm in arm, advancing towards their retreat.

Both he and Jason struggled simultaneously to their feet and moved towards the two women. Mrs. Solent began speaking with her accustomed high-pitched ironical intonation.

'Don't take it off, Mr. Otter,' she said, when the poet raised his hand to his hat. 'I know how you hate the sun; and it *is* hot to-day; though the hotter it is the more I enjoy it, though I think our pretty Gerda here agrees with *you*.'

Jason, who had succeeded with a certain embarrassment in lifting his straw hat a few inches from his head in a stiff, perpendicular direction, pulled it down once more over his forehead with grateful relief.

'What's this?' said Wolf, trying to conceal his discomfort under an airy jauntiness. 'What's this between you two?'

'Your mother and I have had several walks together,' said Jason, 'and she knows my ways.'

'So well as to take a great liberty!' exclaimed the handsome lady, whose brown eyes were shining with radiant exultation. And as she spoke she stepped to Jason's side and poked something, with her light-gloved fingers, into its place under his hat.

While this was proceeding, the expression upon the poet's face made Wolf astonished. It was the queerest mixture of physical repulsion with pleasurable, masochistic submission. He was amazed at his mother's audacity.

'What is it that you wear under your hat, Mr. Otter?' asked Gerda innocently.

The strange man looked at her with a very peculiar expression – an expression that baffled Wolf altogether. Then a most beautiful look came into his grey eyes, a look infinitely wistful and sorrowful, the sort of look that a disguised and persecuted god, lost among some savage race that knew him not nor could have comprehended him if it had known him, might have worn; and he replied gently: 'I feel the sun, young lady. I find cabbage-leaves a great help. But to-day' – and here he smiled a disarming smile – 'to-day it's a rhubarb-leaf.'

Having said this, and with a courtly bend of his body that would have done credit to a royal personage, Jason Otter moved off, making his way, with careful manœuvring to avoid any

364

encounter with the crowd, towards that part of the field where the old men of the village, seated on wooden benches, were partaking of cakes and cider.

'I hope you haven't offended him, mother,' muttered Wolf.

'I don't think so,' cried Gerda. 'What a nice man he is, Wolf! I like him ever so much better than Darnley.'

'That's because Darnley's my best friend,' said Wolf. 'It's a law of nature, sweetheart. Isn't it, mother?'

But Mrs. Solent completely disregarded this little passage between them.

'What Gerda and I came for,' she said, 'was to ask you to show us Mr. Redfern's grave. Gerda's never seen it, though her father made the headstone, and I've never seen it, though I've asked Mr. Urquhart a hundred times to show it to me.'

'It's not hard to find,' said Wolf drily. 'You could have gone any day by yourself.'

'What's the sport in *that*?' laughed the lady, still displaying the same undercurrent of secret excitement. 'The fun of looking at graves is all in the person you look at them *with* . . . isn't it, Gerda? I'm sure *you* must have enjoyed yourself watching all the fuss people make!'

'I can't help my father being a monument-maker,' said Gerda gravely. 'It's a trade, like any other trade.'

'I'm not quarrelling with your father's profession, child,' Mrs. Solent rapped out. 'I'm only saying that there's no sport in looking at graves by oneself; and I *do* want to see this one.'

'There it is, then, mother!' cried Wolf almost peevishly. 'Can't you see? . . . the tall stone one there . . . no! over there . . . nearer the tower,' and he pointed with his stick.

'I want to go up to it,' said Mrs. Solent obstinately, 'and so does Gerda. She told me so just now. We're both sick to death of swinging long-legged girls. I don't want to see any more frills or garters for the rest of my life.'

'Well, come on, then,' said Wolf petulantly. 'You can climb over this, can't you, mother? I suppose Bob Weevil's making himself useful at the swings, eh?'

Whatever demon it was that made him indulge in this jocularity, its result was immediate.

Gerda turned on him fiercely. 'Don't be so vulgar, Wolf. Bob's playing cricket, and so's Lobbie. You ought to know better than to make remarks like that!'

'Don't push me, Wolf.' It was his mother speaking, as she began

scrambling over the low moss-grown wall. 'Give me your hand;
. . . no! give me your hand.'

Soon they were all three standing by Redfern's grave.

'Poor boy!' sighed Mrs. Solent. 'Do you know, Wolf, I heard
Roger Monk talking in a queer way last week. I was asking him
about this boy's death, and he spoke in such a funny tone about it.
He almost implied that it was a case of suicide. Have you heard
anything of that sort?'

'Oh, just rumours, mother,' replied Wolf casually; 'just rumours
and village gossip. I've never heard of an inquest, or anything
like that. I believe he died in his bed.'

'Father talks queer about it too,' said Gerda. 'But do look at
that! Is that a mole or a rabbit?'

'*I* don't know,' said Wolf vaguely. It did not interest him in any
particular way that this newly-grown-over mound should have
been burrowed into or scraped at. After his many years of London
life, the ways of moles, rabbits, dogs, foxes were all equally
arbitrary, equally unpredictable. It was, however, brought home
to him now that there *was* something exceptional in this phenomenon; for Gerda, oblivious of the risk of grass-stains upon her
summer frock, went down hurriedly on her knees and began
fumbling with her bare fingers in the disordered clay, scoop-
ing up little handfuls of dry brown earth with one hand and
filtering them thoughtfully into the hollow palm of the other
hand.

'Are you looking for Mr. Redfern's bones?' enquired Mrs. Solent
in her most airy manner. 'You look like that pretty girl in the
poem, leaning over her Pot of Basil; doesn't she, Wolf?' And
touching the mound with the tip of her green parasol she put her
head a little to one side and began quoting from the poem in
question in a mock-sentimental intonation . . .

> 'And she forgot the stars, the moon, and sun;
> And she forgot the blue above the trees;
> And she forgot the dells where waters run;
> And she forgot the chilly autumn breeze.
> She had no knowledge . . .'

'Don't, mother,' interrupted Wolf crossly. 'Gerda knows what
she's doing.'

The unequalled lines roused their response in him, as independently of the mocking tone in which they were spoken as

366

beautiful limbs under a ridiculous disguise; but this response only annoyed him the more.

'What is it, sweetheart?' he cried. 'Is it a rabbit? I didn't know rabbits ever burrowed in churchyards.'

'It's a mole,' said Mrs. Solent.

It was Wolf's turn to mutter something now ...

'Well said, old mole! canst work i' the earth so fast? A worthy pioneer! Once more remove, good friends.'

'What's that? You know perfectly well it's a mole, Gerda,' said Mrs. Solent. Gerda remained silent. She lifted some of the loose earth to her face and smelt it. Then she leapt to her feet, shook out her skirt, and rubbed the palms of her hands together. 'I give it up,' she said. 'It isn't a rabbit. There's no smell of a fox either. It *may* have been a dog.'

'A mole ... a mole!' repeated the older woman.

'A *mole!*' muttered Gerda, with the profound sarcasm of the country-bred; and Wolf caught a little red flush on her cheeks like a crimson shadow on a mother-of-pearl shell. 'Well! *we* can't do anything, anyway,' she said. 'It's silly to fuss ourselves. Bother! I've got some grit in my shoe!'

'It spoils the look of the grave completely, this great mole-hole,' said Mrs. Solent. Then her face lit up, and she opened her parasol with an eager click. 'This is a bit of sport,' she cried. 'Let's fill the thing up! Never mind about the school treat. Where does Valley keep his spade? We only want a spade and a roll of turf. I saw some loose turf lying about in our garden. Come on, Wolf! Let's go over and get it, and ask Valley where he keeps his shovel.'

Her face was full of animation now, and her eyes shone. Her grey hair and black Gainsborough hat framed the vivid cheeks of youth. The way she tilted her parasol as she spoke had something adventurous, almost hoydenish.

'Come, Wolf, let's get that turf,' said Mrs. Solent. 'We must ask Valley where he keeps his spade.'

As Wolf turned to follow his mother on this impetuous quest, he caught sight of Gerda, struggling with the strap of her shoe, as she propped herself with one hand upon Redfern's headstone. There was such a look of defiant anger on her face that he halted irresolutely.

'Oh, go, if you want to, Wolf!' she cried. 'I'm sure I don't want to keep you. It isn't often, though, that I get a chance of enjoying myself, working like I do in that dark kitchen all the time!'

Mrs. Solent gave her a steady, surprised stare.

'I won't keep him long, if you want him for your game' she said. 'I can fill this hole up by myself, if you just get me the spade and the turf, Wolf.'

The flush in Gerda's cheeks grew deeper. 'I think it's a shame! Why did you bring me here at all, Wolf, if we weren't going to do something nice? I don't want to spend this afternoon doing what I do every day in the week.'

Mrs. Solent gave Wolf a quick, surprised look, full of airy pity – a look that said, 'You poor boy, how awful for you to be at the beck and call of such a child!' But aloud she remarked:

'It's all right, Gerda. We won't spoil your sport. Run along to your friends. I won't keep him long.'

But Gerda's suppressed anger had mounted so high by this time that there could be no such easy *dénouement*.

She held up her rounded chin and tossed back her head. Then, clasping her hands behind her, with her heels close together at the edge of the grave, she regarded Mrs. Solent with flashing eyes.

'Of course Wolf's on your side. Of course he'll love to fool about with your spades and turf, when it's my one real treat of the whole summer! You two are both the same. You only think of yourselves and what *you* want. If it's the silliest thing, like this nonsense about a mole, and every sensible person knows what a mole-hill is, it must come first, before everything, just because you've thought of it! Oh, yes, I saw you smiling at him just now, when my shoe came off. You couldn't have looked much different if my stockings had been full of holes! Everyone can't buy high-class London things; but I tell you our Blacksod shops be as good as they be any day in the week!'

'Well, Wolf,' said Mrs. Solent calmly, holding her parasol at a correct garden-party angle and letting her high spirits drop away, 'the best thing you can do is to take your pretty young wife back to her friends' games.'

'My friends' games!' retorted the indignant girl. 'I'm as old as anyone, considering all I put up with!'

'My dear child,' said the elder lady gently. 'There's really no reason for this excitement. Do try and calm yourself, and let's all go back quietly. I'm sure I'm quite ready to give up my idea if it spoils your pleasure. Don't, for mercy's sake, make such a mountain out of this mole-hill. I only thought of filling up this hole as a bit of sport, and because school treats are so boring.'

Her words were soothing; but there was something in the tilt

of her eyebrows, as she glanced at Wolf, which made him realize
that she was less unruffled than she appeared. He knew of old
that the one thing in the world she hated was any display of temper
or anything resembling a 'scene.' His own mind at this moment
was unable to resist its furtive commentary upon the way Chance
had managed to stage this encounter between the two. He had
noticed these tricks before. It was as if there were some special
æsthetic laws which Chance delighted to obey; and it always gave
him a peculiar satisfaction to contemplate this bizarre rhythm.
At such moments he found himself sacrificing action, emotion,
sympathy, every human attribute, in a sort of ecstatic pondering
over what this artistry of Chance was accomplishing. He felt as
if he were in the presence of the unrolling of a psychic map. The
figures on this map – his mother with her green parasol, Gerda
with her grass-stained dress – were a sort of eddying vortex of
significance upon a stream that was always rippling itself into
mystic diagrams! Chance, in fact, was for ever at work fulfilling
its own secret æsthetic laws; but every now and then, as at this
fatal moment, its creation became especially vivid, and the whole
'psychic map' upon that flowing stream grew violently and intensely agitated. The circle of ripples he was now contemplating
with this inhuman detachment had two circumferences, namely,
the angry consciousness of Gerda and the supercilious consciousness
of his mother; but below them both – down there on the quiet
river-floor – was the discoloured, decomposed, unrecognizable face
of the young Redfern.

'You've never liked my marrying him!' It was Gerda's voice
he heard now, as he awoke from his metaphysical trance to realize
that part of his mother's last remarks had fallen upon nothing but
the surface of his mind.

'I've always been an outsider to both of you,' the angry girl
went on. 'You've always despised me and my family, and done
your best to make him despise us.'

'I have the greatest respect for your family, my good child. No
one who knows your father can possibly help it. Come now!
It really won't do for us to make Wolf embarrassed like this. I've
the utmost respect for your people, Gerda, and I'm sure my son
couldn't have married a lovelier creature than you are, even at
this moment! But do come, now, both of you, and let's get back
to the field. Mr. Urquhart will be quite lost among those boys
without Wolf's help.'

She laid her hand with a soothing gesture upon the girl's wrist;

but the glance she gave Wolf was full of a mocking resignation that threw a screen round them and railed off this ill-advised proletarian. Gerda's behaviour on the other side of this barrier became so irrational that it could only excite well-bred surprise! But the girl tossed her hand away.

'Mr. Urquhart, indeed!' she cried. 'A nice sort you are out here, you King's Barton gentry! Why, I've never cared even to *tell* Wolf all I've heard Dad say about what some folks do in this dirty village.' Her voice grew louder, as her long-suppressed feelings burst forth. Wolf had fancied in his simplicity that his mother's airy propitiations had disarmed the girl; but he underrated both Gerda's perspicacity and her pride.

There was something else on Gerda's mind, too, beyond her personal indignation. What actually, he wondered, *were* these Blacksod gossips saying? He looked at the girl with a kind of paralysed helplessness, and again the thought struck him how neat a stroke of chance it was that Redfern's grave should be the background of her outburst.

'Some of you gentry,' she went on fiercely, 'don't lie abed with decent consciences like my folks! Why, they do say down at Farmer's Rest that landlord Round do keep his bed, and that Squire Urquhart can get no peace by night or by day, because of what do taunt their minds over this poor young man.'

In spite of his discomfort, Wolf couldn't help feeling faintly amused at Gerda's struggle to keep the insidious Dorset dialect out of her speech, a struggle that grew less and less availing as her agitation rose.

'And these be the high-class people that you think so superior to respectable plain folk like my dear Dad!' Her voice had a quiver in it at this point that made Wolf cry out, 'Gerda! Gerda, darling!' But she did not break down. On the contrary, her tone grew stronger and more defiant. 'Like my dear Dad,' she went on, 'who never in his whole life said an evil word to anyone. But you get your spade and your turf and cover up this hole. Maybe you'll catch the fox that made it and be surprised!'

'Come on, come on, Gerda,' said Wolf peevishly, stretching out his hand, in his turn, and trying to seize her fingers. 'We mustn't stay here like this. We shall be attracting attention soon. Come on; let's go back to the field.'

His glance wandered from one to the other of these two figures who held his peace of mind so completely in their power. He could not shake off the profound inertia that had fallen upon him.

'But we *must* go back,' he murmured helplessly. 'Come along, Gerda. Please do stop saying these things.'

His voice sounded in his own ears puerile, feeble, futile. It sounded like the petulance of a child, outraged and astonished by the tenacious obstinacy of grown-up people.

He had noticed on other occasions this peculiar psychic pheno- menon – that when he was with Gerda and his mother together, his personality shrank and dwindled until he felt his actual body grow limp and lumpish. The supercilious calmness of his mother's face under her green parasol, the angry defiance of Gerda's face under her simple school-treat hat, with its pale watchet-blue ribbons, seemed to paralyse him; so that all he could do was to bow before the storm, like a horse with its rump turned to the wind and its forehead turned to the fence! The male animal in him felt quelled and cowed by these two opposed currents of feminine emotion. Both of them seemed to him completely irrational at that moment. His mother's patronizing irony seemed absurd, in conflict with the direct outburst of the other; and Gerda's violence seemed pitifully uncalled-for. If he could have felt any sort of complacent superiority, he could have endured it more easily. But he felt no such superiority! Irrational though they both seemed to him, their personalities had never struck him as more attractive or more mysterious. Their very irrationality seemed drawn from some reservoir of life-energy that was richer, more real, more strange and vibrant than the lumpish bewilderment with which he confronted it.

As he looked from one to the other, and listened, without listening, to the rising torrent of Gerda's wild words, he felt that it was absolutely impossible for him to take whole-heartedly one side or the other. He felt not only inert and helpless; but he felt as if he were himself torn into two halves by their struggle. He felt as if he incarnated at the same time his mother's ironic detach- ment and his girl's passionate grievance. All the long nights he had lain by Gerda's side, all their sweet, secret caresses, clung, like a portion of life itself, to what he felt then for that young, troubled face under the watchet-blue ribbons. But in his mangled bifurcated identity it was impossible to feel hostile to the other figure. Longer nights with him had been hers, and closer caresses! How could he, for all the sweetness of his companion's body, turn away from the flesh that was his own flesh?

Reason? Justice? The forces that victimized and paralysed him now were those that had created the world. Who was he to contend against them?

Gerda came to a pause at last, and without a word to either of them walked off towards the school-treat field.

Then it was that Mrs. Solent turned upon her son with wide-open eyes and gave him a prolonged stare.

'Well!' she exclaimed at last, while her tilted parasol sank down, 'there it is! ... I think,' she resumed, slowly and casually, 'I'll go back to the cottage and do a little gardening before tea. If I mustn't tidy up your graveyard, at least I can tidy up my landlord's garden! Digging in the earth for an hour or two will give me an inspiration perhaps about all our affairs. I'm tired of this treat and I've done my share.'

'All right, mother,' he said, casting a quick glance after Gerda, whose muslin frock and blue hat were now disappearing over the wall; 'I'll take you a little way and then go back.'

They walked round the church and out of the main entrance into the road. When they had passed the gate into the field, and were almost at the point where Pond Lane debouched from the village street, they overtook the furtive figure of Jason Otter, hurrying surreptitiously homewards.

He gave a start of dismay when they came up with him.

'You won't tell Urquhart you saw me,' he said hurriedly. 'The truth is I can't stand it any longer, seeing that great lumbering gardener of his swaggering about at the wicket. No one can get the great fool out. He hits boundaries all the time. They oughtn't to have let him play! He thinks because he won that bowling-match he can do everything. And, of course, with a lot of little boys like that, who consider he's a great batsman – ' A look of dismay covered Jason's face like a frayed shroud as he spoke these words. 'They think he's a kind of county player,' he added gloomily.

'Were you playing yourself?' enquired Mrs. Solent.

'Any one of the Ramsgard second eleven could send his bails flying!' continued Jason. 'Wilson Minor would have got him out for a duck's-egg.'

A faint wrinkling in the lines of the poet's profile indicated that some mental image was exciting his proclivity to roguery.

'I've never heard of Wilson Minor,' murmured Wolf.

Jason cast a sideways glance at him and then looked at Mrs. Solent. He seemed to imply that these intimate affairs of the second eleven of Ramsgard School were, where women were concerned, rather to be concealed than revealed.

'Do you know him?' enquired Wolf boldly, taking the bull by the horns.

There was a moment's hesitation.

'He bowls left-handed,' Jason threw out. 'They twist, too. This stall-fed head-gardener couldn't stand up to them for a moment.'

'Is he a nice boy?' persisted Wolf.

'*I* like him,' said the other nervously. 'I have only seen him three or four times. I took him to tea once at the Lovelace. But that was only because I *wanted tea*; and when I'm alone, that waiter always stares at me so. When I first spoke to him he thought I was a new master.'

'What does he think you are now?' said Wolf.

Jason chuckled. 'An undertaker perhaps; or a private secretary, like you! But he sees I'm honest; and he knows I know a good bowler.' He paused for a second. 'We all like to be praised!' he added grimly.

'Jason,' said Wolf, feeling a sudden qualm about Gerda, 'why don't you take my mother home? She'll give you a splendid cup of tea . . . better than you could make for yourself at Pond Cottage . . . and I know there'll be nobody in your house now. Mother, you'd like that, wouldn't you? I know how well you two always get on.' He felt so impatient to be off, that he cared nothing for the effect of this suggestion upon either the poet or the lady. But Mrs. Solent looked not altogether displeased at this turn of events.

He hurried away now, avoiding any glance at Jason to discover how this prospect appealed to him. He had no difficulty in finding Gerda when he reached the field. She had not yet joined in any game, and it was quite easy to take her aside. She was in a mood of reserved apathy, neither apologetic nor defiant, just remote from the whole stream of events, and a little sad.

'Did you really hear all that about old Urquhart?' he asked her, anxious to distract her mind.

She smiled faintly; and he was so delighted to welcome that sign of a return to her normal self that he gave scant consideration to the substance of her reply.

'Well – not in those very words, Wolf! But Dad do always tell that there was something queer about this young gentleman's end; and if it weren't the Squire, 'twere at least Landlord Round who folks have seen, mooning and mowling round that grave.'

'Come on, Gerda!' – he spoke as energetically and gaily as he could – 'let's hear what you really think! You don't *yourself* think that it wasn't an animal that made that hole, eh?'

'Let's not talk about it any more,' the girl replied. 'I was angry, and you know why; and you know that any girl who wasn't made of rags and straw would have been angry! If I said more than I meant, you must forget it, Wolf, and forgive me.'

Together they advanced now, boldly and unhesitatingly, into the midst of the crowded field. They soon came upon Mattie and Olwen, hand in hand, watching a three-legged race, in which the most buxom and spirited of the maids of King's Barton, tied together in couples, were contending for a bag of sugar-candy.

Olwen greeted Wolf with her usual passionate intensity. 'Mattie won't race,' she cried. 'Do make her do it!'

'But *you* can race if you like,' Mattie retorted. 'That big girl who looks like winning was ready to run with you.' Mattie turned to Gerda, as she said this, with something like an appeal.

'I don't like racing,' she added. 'Besides, I'm not dressed for it, am I? and she glanced down at her new black frock.

'Oh, that's nothing,' mumbled Wolf; and then, observing that Gerda had bent over the child and was diverting her attention, he took his sister's arm and led her aside. 'Everyone I've met to-day seems upset by something or other,' he began, as soon as they were well in the rear of the onlookers at the race. 'I don't know whether it's because I'm nervous myself; but there's a bad wind blowing from some quarter.'

'Do you think there's something the matter with *me*?' she asked. 'You're too sympathetic, Wolf dear. To tell you the truth, I do feel rather grim this afternoon. I *ought* to have let them tie Olwen and me together; but I couldn't bring myself to it. I hadn't the heart for it.'

Wolf glanced back over the heads of the spectators. He could see that Gerda had possessed herself of the child's hand and that they were both watching the proceedings with absorbed attention.

'They're all right,' he whispered. 'Let's go for a bit of a stroll.'

They moved off together towards a vacant portion of the meadow, midway between the cricket match and a noisy group of smaller boys.

'Now, what is it, Mattie?' he said, pressing her unmercifully. 'I've seen you so little lately that I can't follow your moods. But I've never seen such a depressed look. It's far sadder, your face to-day, than when Mr. Smith died. It's a different kind of sadness. It makes me wonder.'

'Dear Wolf! I assure you, you needn't fret about me. I'm all right. You worry too much about people. You can't take *every-*

one's sorrows on yourself. People have to go through things some-times where no one can help them.'

Wolf stood stock-still and laid his hand on her wrist.

'Don't begin those platitudes, Mattie, or you'll make me angry. I don't take anyone's sorrows on myself. But you know . . . I feel as if . . .' He stopped short and stood hesitating, wondering how he would dare to broach the various troubled intimations that had been crossing his mind concerning her and Darnley. They moved on again, and his words still hung uncompleted in the air.

To help him out she tentatively repeated, 'You feel as if?'

'Well . . . don't be angry with me if I'm plunging into something too' – he hesitated for a word – 'too frail to bear the weight of my clumsiness. But I'm not blind. I've seen that you and Darnley have something between you, some subtle understanding. I was glad to see it. You don't know on what a long road it started my fancy! So now, when I see you looking "grim," as you call it, I can't help thinking it must be because of . . . you know? . . . something gone wrong between you.'

Mattie gazed at him dumbfounded.

'But . . . Wolf . . . but . . .' she gasped. She looked so hope-lessly confused and so wretchedly miserable, as she stood there before him, her heavy eyebrows twitching as she frowned and her mouth a little open, that Wolf was afraid he had made some gross blunder that might be terribly hurting to her reserved nature.

'But there's nothing in it at all!' she cried pitifully. 'Darnley and I are just friends. I've always felt he understood me better than anyone I've known. But that's not much, Wolf. You know how many people *I've* known! There's nothing more that's be-tween us, Wolf. What made you think there was?'

'Oh, all right, Mattie,' he muttered, rather sulkily. 'I see you have to keep your affairs to yourself, and I'm not the one to force anything on you.'

He broke off; for he saw her face assume an expression that was completely new to him and to which he had no clue.

Swinging round, and following the direction of her eyes, he saw Darnley and Mrs. Otter coming straight across the grass towards them.

'I came to find Olwen,' the old lady began. 'I'm going home now, and I thought it would leave you freer if I took her with me.'

'I'd much rather come back with you,' said Mattie. 'But I expect I ought not to desert Mr. Valley quite as early as this. What is the time, Darnley?' Darnley looked vaguely round. 'Oh,

375

of course you haven't your watch with you,' the girl went on. 'Have you the time, Wolf?' Wolf looked at his watch, one of the few objects in his possession that was of monetary value. His Weymouth grandmother had given it to him as a child; and there were moments when merely to take it out of his pocket brought him a kind of reassurance, as of things quiet, stable, continuous, in the midst of turmoil.

'It's ten minutes past seven,' he announced; and as they separated he caught a look between Mattie and Darnley that made him wonder if, after all, his instinct had not been on the right track.

'Has the Squire gone home yet? enquired Wolf, as he and Darnley walked slowly towards the cricket-pitch.

'I don't know. I expect so,' the other answered absent-mindedly; and then, as they came nearer: 'No, he's there still.'

When they reached the outskirts of the game they stood for a while in silence, a little behind the player who was fielding at 'point.' Mr. Valley was umpiring on one side and Mr. Urquhart on the other; and it interested Wolf to note that it was his own hand that was instinctively lifted to salute the clergyman, and Darnley's to salute the Squire. One of the batsmen proved to be none other than Bob Weevil; and Wolf was sardonically amused at his own expense when he found that this fact gave him a thrill of unexpected relief. There was little chance, for some while, anyway, for Mr. Weevil and Gerda to pair off, unless the sausage-seller was pre-pared to sacrifice his reputation as a batsman to his amorous propensities; and, as Wolf watched him now, playing with skill and caution, this seemed the very last thing he was prepared for.

'What would you do, Solent,' began Darnley suddenly; and Wolf, glancing quickly at him, observed that his head was turned away and his gaze fixed intently upon the bowler at the further end of the pitch. 'What would you do if you were in love with a girl and had at the same time some peculiarity that made all women repulsive to you?'

Wolf deliberately attuned his voice, as he replied to this, to a flat, dull intonation, as if Darnley had said, 'What would you do if you were bowling at Bob Weevil and he had "got his eye in"?'

'It would entirely depend on who the girl was,' he said, keeping his gaze on the bare arms of the young grocer, as he balanced his bat in the block and bent his slim body forward.

'That's all very well,' rejoined the other, 'but you can't go against nature beyond a certain point.'

376

Wolf raised his voice a little at this, as Bob Weevil, swinging his bat round, slogged the ball vigorously to leg and began to run.

'Nothing is against nature!' he retorted. 'That's the mistake people make; and it causes endless unhappiness.'

Darnley replied in three muttered, disjointed words, stressing each of them with a deliberation that had something ghastly in it. 'Patience . . . pretend . . . perhaps. . . .'

Wolf paused to join in the loud general clapping that indicated that the batsmen had scored six runs. Then he pointed with his stick. 'Come on,' he said, 'there's Miss Gault over there, watching the tug-of-war. Let's go and speak to her. I particularly want to avoid getting caught in a long conversation; but, at the same time, I *must* speak to her. It would be outrageous not to. But if you come with me, Otter, I shall be safe.'

Darnley smiled and took his friend's arm.

It was then, as they moved across the field together, that Wolf discovered that the touch of Darnley's hand on his arm agitated his nerves to a pitch of exasperation. Inexplicable to himself, this mounting anger with the man he loved so well gradually grew so intense that he could hardly endure it. He exerted a superhuman effort to restrain his nervousness; but his friend's very consciousness of his mood was rapidly making it impossible for him to control himself.

The sunshine made Darnley's beard glitter, as if it were composed of shining gold; and this effect, though he noticed it calmly enough with one part of his mind, increased Wolf's irritation. It was all he could do to prevent himself from seizing upon this beard and pulling it viciously. Darnley was now holding Wolf's arm so tightly that he felt a blind impulse of animal resentment rising up within him – an impulse upon which his nervous irritation rocked like a cork upon a wave.

'Avoid! Avoid!' he suddenly flung out; and with the same spasmodic impulse, as he uttered this strange cry, he tore his arm free. 'It's a trick! It's a trick! It's a trick!' He let his voice quiver without restraint, as he hissed out these words, though he knew perfectly well that the ugly contraction of the muscles of his mouth, as much as the word itself, must have been very agitating to his companion. But for this, just then, he cared nothing. If he could have made clear to that anxious face, that now gazed at him so concernedly, what he really felt at that moment, it would have resolved itself into something like this: His mother and Gerda had lost their separate identities. They had become the point of a

377

prodding shaft of yellow light that was at the same time the point of Darnley's trim beard! This shaft was now pushing him towards another misery, which took the form of a taste in his mouth, a taste that he especially loathed, though he could only have defined it, even to himself, as the taste of salad and vinegar! But, whatever it was, *this taste was Miss Gault.* The shaft of yellow light that prodded him on had the power of thinning out and bleaching out his whole world, taking the moist sap quite away from it, leaving it like a piece of blown paper on an asphalt pavement. Between these two things – the blighting light and the corrosive taste – he felt an actual indrawn knot of impotence tying itself together within him, a knot that was composed of threads in his stomach, of threads in the pulses of his wrists, and of threads behind his eye-sockets! Everything in the world that was lovely and precious to him was being licked up by a mustard-coloured tongue, while a taste of constricting, devastating sourness began to parch his mouth.

They were now close behind the back row of spectators. 'She was here just now,' said Darnley. 'She must have gone round to the other side.' Wolf knew perfectly well that his friend referred to Miss Gault, but he only murmured, in a weary, drawling voice, 'Who's that you say's gone over to the other side?'

There was *that* in him that was ashamed of what he was doing ... *that* in him that knew well enough that he was only behaving in this childish way because of his profound reliance upon Darnley's affection and concern; but his nerves were so completely jangled by this time that he was just tinder-wood for any casual spark.

The spark soon came; for, emerging from the crowd, and coming straight to meet them, appeared the familiar figure of Mrs. Torp. Of all people in the world, Mrs. Torp was the very last with whom he felt himself capable of dealing just then. This did not prevent her from approaching them with extended hand, her face rigid and yet festive, bearing an expression like a waxen murderer's in Madame Tussaud's, while from the top of her bonnet a big purple feather nodded with a diabolic gaiety all its own.

If it had not been for this lively and obtrusive feather, Wolf might have retained his self-control; but this, combined with that rigid, festive smile, proved the last straw.

'Mrs. Torp! Mrs. Torp! Mrs. Torp!' he yelled, at the very top of his lungs.

'Stop that, now! Stop that, Wolf!' said Darnley sternly, seizing him by the elbow, just as he had done before.

'Quarrelling, young gents, be 'ee?' said Mrs. Torp; while, in the hurried rush of his shame, Wolf, hardly knowing what he did, shook her vigorously by the hand. 'You be too fine a figure of a man, Mr. Otter, to come to school treat with brawlings and babblings brewed in pub-bar. Mercy! and what a face upon's shoulders have our Mr. Solent got! Don't let my Gerdie see 'ee with thik face. What be come to, young gents, what be come to?'

At this point Mrs. Torp was side-tracked in her volubility by the appearance of her son Lobbie at her side. 'You get back, you limb of Edom, where you belong!' she cried, giving the boy a vigorous push. 'What dost want here, dirty-face; ferreting round like the weasel thee be? Get back where 'ee belong, and don't plague the gentry!'

But Wolf's thundering outcry had made other heads turn about; and soon quite a little group began to gather round them. The voice of Mrs. Torp was naturally penetrating; and the nature of her discourse – intermittently caught by inquisitive ears – did not lessen this effect. Wolf and Darnley soon found themselves, in fact, in the unenviable position of a sort of side-show to the main interest of the tug-of-war. It was clear enough, however, that none of these staring rustics had caught the real significance of Wolf's unpardonable outburst. They must have simply supposed that in some fit of whimsical impatience he had peremptorily summoned his wife's mother to that particular spot.

Such at least was the impression gathered up for future reference by that unclouded portion of Wolf's own mind, which, like a calculating demon perched on the top of his head, calmly contemplated the whole scene. Mrs. Torp herself, as far as he could make out, never deviated one second from her preconceived notion of the incident; which was, to put it bluntly and grossly, that the two young gentlemen had had a drunken quarrel!

It was with a very distinct feeling of relief that Wolf, as he moved forward hurriedly now to meet the approach of no less a personage than Selena Gault, recognized that his father's old friend had no conception of anything unusual in that cry, 'Mrs. Torp! Mrs. Torp!' which, resounding across that small arena, had informed her of his presence there.

'Is poor Mrs. Torp to be dragged into this game, then?' said Selena, as she shook his hand.

Wolf muttered some lame jest about tug-of-wars and lean people, and then found it inevitable that he and Miss Gault should wander off together, leaving Darnley to deal with the Torp family.

His nerves were not yet altogether steady; for he found it necessary to reply in nothing but patient monosyllables to what Miss Gault was saying. By degrees, however, her discourse became so personal that these replies began to gather a dangerous intensity, although they still remained abrupt and brief.

'I'm glad to find you, boy. I've been hoping and hoping I should get a word with you.'

'Dear Miss Gault!'

'You're not angry with me any more for opposing your plan about Mattie and Olwen? I confess it seems to have worked out better than I ever supposed it would.'

'No . . . no.'

'As long as she doesn't meet that terrible old man or that crazy girl – '

'What's that?'

'Oh, I forgot. They tell me you yourself visit those people, Wolf.'

'Who tells you?'

'Of course, you have to go there for books. I understand that. But there are reasons which are hard to explain, boy, why I'd sooner see you enter . . . enter a workhouse . . . than go into that house.'

'Mr. Malakite was my father's friend.'

She raised one of her gloved hands to her mouth at this, as if to restrain the quiverings of her upper lip. 'You don't know what you're saying, Wolf! His friend? That man corrupted his soul; and he did it with his accursed books.'

He was saved from making any answer to this by the sound of a familiar but by no means pleasant voice calling him by name.

'Mr. Solent! Mr. Solent!'

He turned on his heel and beheld Bob Weevil, still in his shirt-sleeves, smiling and perspiring after a violent run.

'What's up, Weevil?' he asked.

The young man bowed respectfully to Miss Gault and gasped for breath.

'Mr. Urquhart sent me to find you, sir,' he panted. 'He says you must umpire now instead of him. He has to go now.'

'Mr. Solent is taking care of *me*, Weevil,' said Miss Gault indignantly. 'What does the man mean by "must" umpire? I don't see where the "must" comes in.'

Wolf looked the excited lad up and down. Miss Gault's words had not abashed him in the least. There was even an air of spiteful arrogance in his manner, an air which seemed to say, 'As the Squire's emissary to his secretary, I am the most important person here.'

'I'm afraid there *is* a "must" in this, Miss Gault,' Wolf said quietly. 'It was agreed between us, before we came on the scene, that I was to umpire when Mr. Urquhart had to leave. It isn't Mr. Weevil's fault that he happens to be the messenger of ill-fortune!'

The lady drew herself up in high dudgeon. 'Well! Run off, both of you, as fast as you can,' she said.

The annoyance of Miss Gault, thus expended upon both men, had the natural effect, as they went off together, of closing up in a measure the rift between them.

They passed the swings on their way, and a common masculine weakness for the sight of ruffled skirts held them for a moment behind a group of hobbledehoys who were enjoying this spectacle.

'They love swinging,' remarked Wolf carelessly, as Weevil and he moved away at last; 'but those boys being there makes it delicious for them.'

Bob Weevil sighed deeply; and this pitiful sigh, rising up from the young man's aggravated senses, went wavering skyward. Past a high trail of flapping rooks, heading for Nevilton, it went; past the flocks of the white clouds. At last, far beyond all human knowledge, it lost itself in the incredible desirableness of lovely blue space, and mingled, for all we know, with the vast non-human sighing of the planet itself, teased by some monstrous cosmogonic lust!

Hearing this sound, Wolf glanced sideways at his young rival, and an unexpected flicker of sympathy for that water-rat profile ran through him.

They crossed the field in silence; and the thought that he was going to meet Mr. Urquhart recalled to Wolf's mind that mysterious aperture in the side of Redfern's grave. Could it be possible that there were in the village people so crazed by remorse for this boy's death that they actually had been making mad attempts to disinter his bones? Such, at any rate, from what Gerda hinted, would not have struck these Dorsetshire gossips as impossible. But impossible, of course, it was! It was one of those morbidly monstrous fancies that, as he knew well from the Squire's own collection of weird documents, did sometimes run the round of these West-country villages, passing from tavern to tavern, and growing more and more sinister as it went. Something in this quarter of the land, as soaked with legends as it was with cider-juice, seemed to lend itself to such tales!

'Well, sir!' he said, as he approached the wickets where Mr. Urquhart stood at attention like a sober sentinel on the ramparts of Elsinore, 'I'm ready to relieve you.'

The cheerful complacence with which his employer accepted his docile obedience caused his nerves to assert themselves again in a surprising manner.

'If you're going to say good night to Valley before you leave, sir,' he said brusquely, 'you might tell him that something or somebody has been stratching a hole in that grave in the church-yard!'

A queer cowardice, or discretion perhaps, prevented him from looking at Mr. Urquhart's face as he tossed out this remark. He followed it up, without a second's pause, by crying out 'Right you are!' to the batsman opposite him, and by moving hurriedly aside into his place, a yard or two from the wicket, so that the new 'over' might commence.

All that he could take in of the effect of his words was the look of his employer's back, as the man moved away, not at all in the direction of the clergyman's black-coated figure, but straight to-wards the little group of spectators who surrounded the seated form of Roger Monk, occupied just then in keeping the score.

Mr. Urquhart's back, as Wolf followed it with his eyes at that moment, seemed to him to resemble the back of Judas Iscariot in that popular picture entitled 'Pieces of Silver,' of which there used to hang a cheaply coloured reprint in his grandmother's house at Weymouth. It did more than stoop with its usual aristo-cratic bend, this back. It sagged, it lurched, it wilted. It drifted towards that bench of heedless spectators as if it had been the hindquarters of the Biblical scapegoat, driven forth into a wilder-ness whose desolation was not material, but psychic. The neat clothes that hung upon it only accentuated the ghastliness of this back's retreat.

It may be believed that Wolf's umpiring was not of the most alert or efficient kind that evening. But it sufficed; it served its purpose. For the game itself was dragging a little tediously now, and most of the lads were weary of it and longing in their hearts for the grand consummation of the eventful day.

This was the hour of the twilight dancing, a celebration that, taking place in a roped-off portion of the meadow furthest re-moved from the churchyard, was the supreme source of responsibility and concern to the authorities – the thrilling climax and crowning episode to the boys and girls of King's Barton!

Long before the cricket-match was over, all the other sports had drawn to a close. Tired groups of children, disputing about their prizes and gorging themselves with butterscotch and barley-sugar torn from sticky paper bags, drifted across the hill towards the gate, followed by voluble mothers with overflowing parcels and sleeping babies clutched tightly in their arms. The older men had found themselves seats here and there, and were smoking their pipes with an air of cautious relaxation, an air that stopped short of the complete abandonment of Farmer's Rest and yet had unstiffened beyond the super-ceremonious atmosphere of the earlier hours of the afternoon.

The youths and the maidens, from all parts of the field, along with a drifting concourse of outsiders attracted by the occasion, gathered now, impatiently and nervously, round the weary cricketers.

The Kingsbury band, duly stimulated by its full quota of traditional refreshment, was now tuning up for the great moment of that gala day. At length, to Wolf's infinite relief, the last bails fell; the captains of the two sides pulled up the wickets; the score was proclaimed in indifferent tones and amid lethargic cheers; and the whole company hurried towards the dancing-plot.

Wolf, as he looked about for Gerda, crossed inadvertently the path of the perturbed Mr. Valley.

'It'll be dark in an hour,' said the anxious Vicar, glancing up at the sky; 'but they will hardly have begun then.'

'There's a nice scent of trodden grass in the air,' remarked Wolf.

'What a time! What a time!' wailed the little priest, disregarding the interruption.

'What's wrong, my dear man?' sighed Wolf indifferently, searching with his eyes the groups who passed by for a glimpse of Gerda's white gown. 'What's troubling you? Dancing's all right. There's no harm in dancing.'

The little priest laid his hand upon the front of Wolf's coat. 'Dancing!' he muttered peevishly. 'Oh, you Londoner! you Londoner! It's not the dancing I'm thinking about. Do you suppose it's only for the dancing that all these men are collecting? I tell you I've never known one single visit of the Kingsbury Band to this place when there hasn't been some girl – and they're always the wrong ones – got into trouble! If I could keep 'em penned up in these ropes, they might dance till dawn!'

383

Wolf made a grimace and moved away. There seemed to him, at that moment, as he thought of Gerda and his mother, such far worse things in the world than the episodes dreaded by Mr. Valley, that he found it impossible to give him the remotest sympathy. Mr. Valley, without knowing it, however, had his full revenge for this callousness in less than a minute from when they parted. For there was Gerda's white gown! And there, side by side with it, were Mr. Bob Weevil's white shirtsleeves! . . . As he walked up to them trying to assume his most invulnerable philosphic calm, Wolf thought to himself, 'I'll let her dance one dance with him and then off we'll go . . . back to Blacksod!'

They did not observe his approach till he was quite close.

'Hullo, Gerda! Hullo, Bob! Look here, you two.' He paused awkwardly, staring at Gerda's sash. 'I don't want,' he went on, 'I don't want – ' He seemed to catch a defiant look on the girl's face. 'I don't want to break this up till you've danced once to-night. So go ahead, for heaven's sake, as soon as they start. . . . Only, listen, Weevil – ' He paused again, and found it necessary to take several long breaths. He had said exactly what he meant to say. He had said it in the tone he meant to adopt. Why, then, were those two staring at him like that, as if he were a ghost? Did his face look funny to them? Was 'the form of his visage changed' upon them? 'I mean,' he went on; but his voice sounded unsure to his own ears now – unsure and queerly mechanical, as if it issued out of a wooden box. 'I mean that you'd better have one good dance, or perhaps two . . . two certainly! Two would be far better than one . . . one dance is nothing. . . . What's one dance? Nothing at all! And then . . . and then . . . what was I going to say? That band's making such a noise! . . . Oh, then we'll walk home, Gerda; and perhaps Bob will come with us. But I expect not, with Mr. Valley so jumpy.'

'What are you talking about, Wolf?' said Gerda abruptly. 'What's the matter with you? Is there anything wrong? I thought we'd agreed that I was to stay for the dancing. You've no objection to my dancing with Bob, have you?'

'I beg your pardon, Mr. Solent,' broke in the voice of the young grocer, 'but what was that you said about Mr. Valley being "jumpy"? I couldn't hear what you said; and I don't see, anyway, what it's got to do with me.'

'Did we decide that I had to wait till midnight for you, Gerda?' said Wolf sternly, disregarding Mr. Weevil.

'Oh, let me be! Let me be, Wolf!' cried the girl angrily. 'I don't know what's come over you to-night . . . you and your mother! I suppose you've been over there again and she's been talking to you again. I don't know what you take me for! I've danced at King's Barton school treat since I was no bigger than Lobbie. I don't know what you've got against it, or against me and Bob. You've been over to Lenty Cottage! That's where you've been; and she's sent you back to punish me for what I said to her. I haven't said I was going to dance with Bob at all. Bob isn't my only friend here. Mother's going to stop to the end. She always does. And I shall go back with her. I don't want either you or Bob, I tell you! You've never treated me like this before and I won't stand it! *You* can walk back with him if you like, Bob. I'll be glad enough to see the last of both of you! I want to enjoy myself to-night ' She moved away as she spoke, and Wolf caught a look of miserable consternation upon the water-rat physiognomy at his side. 'I don't want any men to dance with!' she flung back at them. 'I'll dance with no one but girls. But I *will* enjoy myself in spite of you all! I won't depend on any of you for my pleasure . . . and I'll go home with father and mother!'

She walked off haughtily, her blue-ribboned hat held high, and was speedily lost to sight in the gathering crowd.

Wolf and Mr. Weevil stood staring at each other stonily and awkwardly while the long-awaited music burst triumphantly into the familiar strains of the Kingsbury jig.

After a few seconds, with an abrupt lifting of his hand, Wolf moved away. He pushed through the crowd with the air of a complete stranger who finds his path impeded by some popular transaction that means nothing to him.

On the outskirts of the field he was arrested by the sight of a figure that seemed familiar to him. Yes! It was the automatic young lady from Farmer's Rest. But there was another girl there – a younger girl – and he recognized her too. She was the maid in the white muslin frock whose shameless manner of swinging had arrested Weevil and him an hour ago. This younger girl's head was turned away; but as he approached them, he caught a full glimpse of the automatic young lady's face. She was too absorbed, however, in what she was doing – fastening a safety-pin or something in the other's waistband – to give the least attention to him. But what was this? The look he captured upon her face was a look of unmistakable emotion, rapt, intense emotion, such as a boy would have displayed when he was caressing the object of his desire. Like a flash it came over Wolf, as he wavered there for a second, that he was in the presence of a passionate perversity, kindred to that he had discovered elsewhere in this Dorsetshire village; and he was a little startled to find how the presence of it set his heart beating and his pulses throbbing. Something in him pleaded desperately to be allowed to remain a second longer on this unhallowed ground; but he resisted the temptation, and hurried forward. But what did this mean? How could he explain this in himself? That kindred obliquity, which he had so recently tracked down among the 'higher circles' of King's Barton, had not affected him to anything resembling this degree of vicious sympathy! The vision of those two girls remained like a deadly-sweet drop of delicious fermentation in some vein within him – some vein or nerve that seemed in contact with the very core of his consciousness. Like some virulent berry-juice, insidiously sweet and yet maddeningly bitter, like a drop of that old classic poison distilled from the blood of the enamoured centaur – that look, that gesture of the Farmer's Rest girl teased and troubled him. The averted head of her muslin-frocked companion, the contour of that soft, conscious, youthful profile, stirred his senses even more.

'Damn!' he thought. 'Don't I *yet* know the worst of my vicious, secretive nature?'

He felt startled rather than ashamed by what arose within him; but what *did* trouble him, to a kind of inward fury, as he left those preoccupied girls, was the ricochet of this discovery upon his jealousy over Gerda and Bob! Who was he to indulge in sulky jealous heroics, when he himself was capable of a feeling like this? To be angry with those two, to be bitterly hurt, and yet not to be able to indulge in the undertone of his own grievance without knowing himself to be an unphilosophic fool – *that* was the point of the spiritual wedge that now was driven into his disordered life-illusion!

Was Lord Carfax, that whimsical 'man of the world,' of whom his mother loved to relate the shameless opinions, right after all? Had he always overrated the connection between sex and that mysterious struggle in the abysses, with which his 'mythology' was concerned?

In regard to the perversity of Mr. Urquhart, he had taken for granted that the man's sex-aberration was merely the medium through which unspeakable emanations of evil – beyond sex altogether! – flowed up into the world.

'But what *is* this evil?' he asked himself, now letting his mind

386

hover like a hungry cormorant over the heaving waters of his troubled senses. Vague intimations concerning some sort of *inner malice*, that was beyond all viciousness, rose up within him as his mind's deepest response. Hunting irritably for some gap in the hedge by which to escape, he tried to define this inert malice. Was it an atavistic reversion to the primordial 'matter,' or 'world-stuff' – sluggish, reluctant, opaque – out of which, at the beginning of things, life had had to force its way? Was this, and not his attitude to any youthful Redfern, the real secret of Urquhart's harmfulness?

All the while he struggled with these thoughts, he kept feverishly skirting the hedge, striking it every now and then with his stick. If he could only find a gap by which to escape! This hunt of his for a gap into the next field began to assume almost symbolic proportions. Something within him was tugging at him all the while to make him turn his head and cast another furtive glance at those two girls. Were they still together there, just where he had left them? He began to indulge his imagination, letting it tantalize and provoke him with the tremulous intensity of the feeling that sight might have aroused. He knew he could cool his excitement, blunt it, undermine it, stave it off, by analysing its nature; but the feeling itself was so deadly-sweet to him that it pleaded in 'a still, small voice' for a postponement of this invasion of his reason!

Was it his jealousy over Gerda that had made him so porous to this quivering, breath-taking obsession? Indignantly his soul shook itself to and fro in its endeavour to escape. Like a slippery-scaled fish it shook itself, turning sideways, turning belly-up, as it strove to force its way through the strands of the net that encircled it. Why was it that this glimpse of the amorous feeling of one girl for another girl should send this trembling, dissolving, shuddering provocation through him? Was it that the mere importunity of the feeling, so intense, so sterile, emphasized the mysterious quality of desirableness? Did it imply a diffusion of the magic of beauty through the whole identity of the desired one, such as can rarely take place where great creative Nature, contemptuous towards both lover and beloved, shamelessly occupied with her own enormous purposes, is baiting the trap?

What a queer thing it was that the attraction of this muslin-frocked little hoyden should have been barely emphasized for him by Weevil's desire for her, but increased to a point of shivering, electric sweetness, under the emotion of the 'automatic young lady'! Oh! it had *that* within it that might lead him upon such a quest that nothing else would matter to him any more! He could feel even now, as he went along this stubborn hedge, the sort of scoriac desolation – all delicate intimations become cinders and ashes in the mouth – that would possess him, as this quest grew more and more concentrated! He felt within him the actual *expression* his face would come to wear, as in his maniacal pursuit he went to and fro over the earth, oblivious of all else.

He had just reached this point in his mental struggle, when he suddenly did find a gap in the obstinate hedge. Forcing his way hurriedly through, careless as to how he pricked his face and hands, he descended from the high hedge-bank into a field of mangel-wurzels. Over this field he now strode, while the gathering twilight deepened about him, oblivious of all purpose save to escape – to escape into the peace of his own soul.

The mangelwurzel field behind him at last, he blindly pushed his way through a second hedge, this time caring not even to find a gap. What next awaited him was a succession of stubble-fields, some of which had patches of purple clover growing amid their cornstalks, the dark foliage of which, soaked with heavy dew, quickly penetrated his boots. This physical sensation, the sensation of walking barefoot through an endless dew-drenched twilight, gradually soothed and calmed him.

He went obstinately forward, crossing field after field in the falling darkness, forcing his way recklessly through every sort of rank vegetation, through every sort of arable fallowness. He had left the school-treat field for more than an hour now. He had crossed, almost without consciousness of doing so, the main road between Ramsgard and Blacksod. He had threaded his way through the maze of small, grassy lanes that lay between that highway and the village of Gwent. And now, emerging in the scented autumn night into a rondure of sloping hills, he could see, beyond the scattered lights of Gwent, a vast unbounded region, shadow within shadow, vapour within vapour, a region that he knew to be – though all he could actually see was darkness of a thicker, richer quality than the darkness about him – the umbrageous threshold of Somerset, the first leafy estuary of that ocean of greenness out of which rose, like the phallus of an unknown god, the mystical hill of Glastonbury!

He stretched himself out on the grassy slope of this shadowy amphitheatre and gazed long and long into the vaporous obscurity before him. The quarrel between Gerda and his mother became nothing. Nothing and less than nothing became his jealousy over Weevil . . . his vision of those two girls!

It was as though he had suddenly emerged, by some hidden doorway, into a world entirely composed of vast, cool, silent-growing vegetation, a world where no men, no beasts, no birds, broke the mossy stillness; a world of sap and moisture and drooping ferns; a world of leaves that fell and fell for ever, leaf upon leaf; a world where that which slowly mounted upwards endured eternally the eternal lapse of that which slowly settled downwards; a world that itself was slowly settling down, leaf upon leaf, grass-blade upon grass-blade, towards some cool, wet, dark, unutterable dimension in the secret heart of silence!

Lying upon that rank, drenched grass, he drew a deep sigh of obliterating release. It was not that his troubles were merely assuaged. They were swallowed up. They were lost in the primal dew of the earth's first twilights. They were absorbed in the chemistry, faint, flowing, and dim, of that strange *vegetable flesh* which is so far older than the flesh of man or beast!

He stretched out one of his hands and touched the cool-scaled stalks of a bed of 'mare's tails.' Ah! how his human consciousness sank down *into that* with which all terrestrial consciousness began! . . .

He was a leaf among leaves . . . among large, cool, untroubled leaves. . . . He had fallen back into the womb of his real mother. . . . He was drenched through and through with darkness and with peace.

19

WINE

The three autumn months that followed the school treat became for Wolf, as the days shortened and darkened, like a slowly rising tide that, drawing its mass of waters from distances and gulfs beyond his reach, threatened to leave scant space unsubmerged of the rugged rock front which hitherto he had turned upon the world. Something in the very fall of the leaf, in the slow dissolution of vegetation all about him, made this menace to the integrity of his soul more deadly. He had never realized what the word 'autumn' meant until this Wessex autumn gathered its 'cloudy trophies' about his ways, and stole, with its sweet rank odours, into the very recesses of his being. Each calamitous event that occurred during those deciduous months seemed to be brewed in the oozy vat of vegetation, as if the muddy lanes and the wet hazel-copses – yes! the very earth-mould of Dorset itself – were conspiring with human circumstances.

It was during many a lonely walk among the red-berried hedges and old orchards, where the rotting cider-apples lay wasp-eaten in the tangled swathes of grass, that these events worked their wills upon him. Sunday after Sunday, as September gave place to October and October gave place to November, he would lean upon some lichen-covered gate and struggle to give intelligible form to these 'worries' of his. Threaded in and out of such ponderings were a thousand vivid impressions of those out-of-the-way spots. The peculiar 'personality' of certain century-old orchards, of which the grey twisted trunks and the rain-bent grass seemed only the *outward* aspects, grew upon his mind beyond everything else. How heavily the hart's-tongue ferns drooped earthward under the scooped hollows of the wet clay-banks! How heavily the cold raindrops fell – silence falling upon silence – when the frightened yellow-hammers fled from his approach! He felt at such times as though they must be composed of very *old* rain, those shaken showers; each tremulous globe among them having reflected through many a slow dawn nothing but yellow leaves, through many a long night nothing but faint white stars!

He certainly had anxieties enough this autumn to bring down his happiness to a very muted key. The head and front of these 'whips and scorns of time' had been a complete break with Urquhart. The Squire's obsessions had got upon his nerves to such an extent that he had just recklessly revolted – flung up his work on this detestable history of Dorsetshire scandals – and, cutting his coat to suit his cloth, fallen back upon a rigid monotony and economy between Preston Lane and the School.

The results of this quarrel might have been much more serious than they were, if he had not, by Darnley's diplomatic help, obtained both more work and more income at the Grammar School. But this piece of good luck had been followed by a second calamity; for his mother, in her reckless, irresponsible fashion, had also annoyed Urquhart, and had consequently been compelled to give up Lenty Cottage and join him in Blacksod. Twenty-five pounds, therefore, of his increased salary had to go now to pay for a room she had taken a few doors from them in Preston Lane. Here she lodged in the house of that very Mrs. Herbert whose name was already familiar to him. She had managed to obtain, however, a job for herself in the town, and was highly amused and extremely pleased by her unexpected success in the conduct of it. But this also was attended by an unpleasant consequence, her business being nothing less than the managing of a tea-shop belonging to Mr. Manley of Willum's Mill! Wolf would have been quite resigned to this development, if his mother had not, in her gay, ironic manner, cast a magnetic spell over the bullnecked farmer and entered into some sort of humorous flirtation with him.

As far as those two perturbing figures in the background of their days were concerned – Bob Weevil and Christie – matters relapsed during these long autumn months into a curious state of suspension. He would go to tea with Christie; and once or twice Gerda spoke of a visit from Bob. But as winter set in, and the nights lengthened to the December solstice, it seemed as if the burden of his monotonous work in the classroom, and the rigid economies practised by Gerda in the house, had undermined the spirit of adventure in both their natures.

He was surprised at his own obstinate patience in the tedious routine of teaching history to the Blacksod tradesmen's sons. What supported him were the moments of ecstasy he derived from his long week-end walks. He had the whole of Saturday free, as well as Sunday, and sometimes with Gerda, and sometimes alone, he would follow the wraith-like vapours of autumn as they drifted over the lanes and hills, and give himself up, with a large forgetfulness of everything else, to his sensuous-mystical mythology.

If it had not been for this secret refuge and for the sensations accumulated in these walks, Wolf's first winter in Dorset would have culminated in a miserable inertia, resembling that of the luckless Redfern. For one thing, Gerda seemed completely to have lost her miraculous power of bird-whistling. He caught her making the attempt; but recently, as far as he could tell, she had given the thing up. He suspected, too, that Darnley and Mattie were unhappy; but, ever since that day at the school treat, both those reserved beings had remained completely uncommunicative as to their relations with each other, though on all other topics he found them as affectionate and spontaneous as ever.

There had been little frost and no snow before Christmas. Gloomy, damp days had succeeded one another all through the month; and now, on the last Sunday of the old year, it seemed to Wolf, when he awoke in the darkness, that the air smelt of deep pools of rain. He awoke that morning long before his companion; and once awake he lay thinking intensely and excitedly for several hours. It was of his mother he thought. She had dropped a hint, while he was at Mrs. Herbert's on the previous night, that she would like to start a tea-shop of her own, and that she thought of borrowing the money for this project from her present employer. Wolf was startled at the depth of the hurt to his pride that this information dealt him. In the early hours of that rain-smelling morning he made a drastic resolution. *He would go back to Urquhart!* What did it matter how he outraged his conscience over that accursed book, so long as his mother got this help from *him* rather than from the owner of Willum's Mill? Oh! And what pleasure to be able to hand over a little solid money to Gerda after her long, miserable economies! He knew so well the list of desirable purchases in the girl's mind – from the silver sugar-tongs to a grandfather's clock! It always touched him, the way Gerda put things for the house above things for her own person. Yes! That is what he would do: run round to his mother's after breakfast find out how the land lay with regard to the tea-shop project, and then set off for King's Barton. Urquhart would most certainly be at home on Sunday morning; and he knew exactly how he would deal with the man. He would ask him point-blank for a cheque for two hundred pounds. He would ask for this on the understanding that he should finish the book for him in three months – finish it, in fact, by the anniversary of his first arrival in Dorsetshire!

He was so excited by the idea of this daring move that it was with difficulty he refrained from jumping out of bed; but Gerda being sound asleep, and to wake her a couple of hours before her usual time being likely to make her cross for the whole morning, he restrained his impulse and continued to lie still. . . .

It was early enough, however, when finally he rang the bell of Mrs. Herbert's house; for the landlady, evidently just returning from eight-o'clock Mass, came up to her door at the same moment.

'Good morning, Mrs. Herbert,' he said, as pleasantly as he could. But when the woman had let him in and was proceeding to announce him, a faded picture of 'The Bombardment of Alexandria,' hanging in her hall, brought to his mind all the lodging-houses he had ever entered! It was as if from each of these places some polished banister-knob, some vase of dead bulrushes, some dusty ornamental chair, some vague odour of Indian spice or of dried-up seaweed, added its quota to the accumulated memory.

'Oh, it's you, Wolf!' exclaimed his mother, without rising from her antimacassared chair, where, with a volume of *The Trumpet-Major* open on her tea-tray, she was sipping her tea. 'How grave you look, my son!'

She gave him a glowing smile as he sat down opposite her. But he plunged at once into the dangerous waters.

'Are you really thinking of borrowing money from that brute, mother? You know it's been worrying me a lot.'

She regarded him with eyes that gleamed with mischief.

'Why not?' she said. 'I think the good man has grown quite attached to me. I think he *likes* elderly ladies!'

Wolf was too agitated to keep his seat. He began walking up and down the room. Suddenly he stopped in front of her. 'Are you as happy down here, mother, as you were in London?' he said, looking down on that mocking, invulnerable face.

She settled herself in her chair, stretching out her arms with an almost feline gesture of physical wellbeing.

'I live in hope of greater happiness yet,' she murmured, with a contented yawn. 'Your mother's an unregenerate woman,' she went on, her words rising on the breath of her yawn like fins on a smooth wave. 'She doesn't take life as seriously as her ugly duckling of a son!'

He sighed and sat down again.

'But it's a disgrace I can't support you properly, mother.'

'As well as your wife, Wolf? Sons who have to support wives

393

can't tackle mothers too. You ought to have thought of that six months ago.' The shamelessness of her words was relieved by the ironic glint in her eyes. 'But you must have come to your mother's defence at any rate over that young lady of yours; for, when I met her on the street three weeks ago, she stopped and talked quite pleasantly to me! She told me you were still friends with that bookseller girl; and I told *her* she was far too pretty to be jealous of that melancholy little shadow.'

Wolf frowned, picked up *The Trumpet-Major,* put it down again, and began nervously scratching its cover with his finger-nails. He thought to himself: 'It's absolutely impossible to talk of any woman to another woman without betraying the absent one. They must have blood! Every word you speak is a betrayal. They're not satisfied otherwise.'

To turn the conversation from Gerda he launched out at random. 'I wish Darnley would try and support a wife as well as *his* mother! I hate to see anyone as decent as he is, getting so little pleasure.'

'Mattie, eh? What a boy you are! Legitimate . . . illegitimate . . . you're ready to look after them all! I daresay you're only waiting till my new flame, Mr. Manley, starts me in my own shop, to give my twenty-five pounds to this deserving couple!'

'What's your idea, mother, of how things are at Pond Cottage? I don't believe I've ever asked you that.'

'What do you mean . . . how they are? A good but very plain young woman and a good but very handsome young man . . . isn't that the whole situation? She's in love with him, of course; and he enjoys it. He'd do more than enjoy it if her nose wasn't so awfully like yours!'

'Will they marry in the end, do you suppose?'

'Why not? Didn't we agree he's a *good* man? What's the use of a man being good if he can't make a plain face happy? Besides' – and the brown eyes laughed with the gayest wickedness – 'your sister's got very pretty legs!'

Wolf made a faint grimace and plunged into a different topic. 'Did you really tell Urquhart, mother, that Monk had threatened to kill him?'

Mrs. Solent laughed aloud. 'Don't start me on those two, Wolf, or I'll talk all the morning. Why, they set on me as if they'd been a pair of savage goats that I'd tried to separate. Monk was rude. Mr. Urquhart wasn't rude; but he'll never forgive me.' She laughed again, the gay, mischievous, rippling laughter of a young girl. 'I had the best hit all the same; and I'm glad I did!'

'What did you say, mother?'

'I told him he ought to set a trap for that fox in the churchyard!'

'Why was that a hit, mother?'

'Oh, you know! Anything about Redfern. . . . It bothered him that he couldn't tell what I'd heard or what I hadn't heard. As a matter of fact, Roger Monk told me there wasn't a night he didn't go rambling about. *I* don't think anything of that. I like night-walking myself. But I knew it would be a hit!'

Wolf looked at his mother with frowning brows.

'But, mother, mother; don't you ever take anything seriously?'

'I take my tea-shop seriously,' she said, with a mock-tragic air.

Wolf sighed. 'Sometimes I've fancied, mother, that you'd got some secret philosophy of your own that made you wiser than anyone . . . wise as some great sorceress.'

'Your father thought me a hard, selfish, conventional woman, without an idea in her head. And that's what I probably am at bottom, Wolf!' She paused, and her face grew flinty. 'I can never forgive him for destroying our life. What's the use of that sort of folly? What's the use of tilting against conventions? It's more amusing, it's more interesting, to play with those things. They're as real as anything else.'

'What do you actually want out of life, then, mother?' His tone was naïve and pedantic. And he *felt* naïve and pedantic, as he looked at this woman, the contours of whose countenance were as defiant to ordinary emotions as dark, slippery rocks to the wash of the sea.

She startled him then by suddenly rising to her feet with a movement that seemed to shake off twenty years as if they were nothing. 'I want happiness!' she cried. 'I want a lovely, thrilling, beautiful life. I want adventures, travel, noble society. Oh, I don't want to be shut up all day long in Preston Lane, Blacksod!'

She turned her back upon him and surveyed her own face in the little plush-framed mirror over the mantelpiece.

'Our friend Selena used to tell me I was a woman of the world . . . and I am! I am! What else should anyone be, I should like to know?'

She put her fingers to her cheeks and began tracing their lines as if she were an angry sculptor, feeling for the mistakes of her work.

'I want to drive down the streets of Vienna! I want to float down the canals of Venice! I want to see Paris, Amsterdam, Constantinople!'

Wolf stared at the strong back in its neat tailor-made jacket.

He stared at the loose coils of wavy grey hair; and an odd sensation went through him, as if this extraordinary person were a complete stranger to him. He began to feel that the moment was tense and even dangerous. What a fool he'd been to disturb such ocean-deep waters!

Presently she swung round upon him. 'I suppose you never thought,' she cried in a high-pitched voice, 'that I wanted anything more than to be the mother of a well-meaning ninny!'

'Mother dear . . . my dear mother . . .' he faltered, dominated so completely by the woman's formidable paroxysm as to feel as if she were towering above him in that funny little room, and above the whole of Blacksod.

But she controlled herself now with a suddenness as unexpected as her outburst had been.

'It's all right, Wolf. I only wanted to be petted up a little,' she murmured gently, moving to the table and beginning with agile fingers to pile the breakfast-things on her tray. 'I expect I've worked myself into a fuss by reading Thomas Hardy! One day you shall take me down to Weymouth and we'll walk over to the White Horse and the Trumpet-Major's village. Yes, and we'll go in and see who's living in Penn House now, where your grandmother was. You'd like that, wouldn't you?'

Wolf nodded; but he did not smile. 'If I give her every penny of what I get from Urquhart, will it be enough?' he thought.

'Listen, mother,' he said aloud. 'I'm going to walk over to King's Barton presently to call on the Squire. You'll smile, but I have practically decided to finish that book for him. I can work at it at home with the notes he's made. I could get it done in about three months. It's absurd to be too –' He stopped abruptly, irritated, in spite of his anticipation of that very thing, by the gleam of sardonic mischief upon his mother's face.

'The truth is, mother,' he went on, 'I'd much sooner get this money for you from Urquhart than that you should fall under this brute's thumb!' It was the teasing indulgence in her smile that made him use this crude expression. The sight of the malicious glint still radiating from her eyes drove him to add, 'Will two hundred be enough, mother?'

Her expression became so extremely mock-sentimental at this, that he was completely nonplussed. She even tilted her head a little to one side, just as she had done when she quoted the 'Pot of Basil' by Redfern's grave. Then she laid down her tray and rested one of her hands upon the chimneypiece.

'Perhaps . . . it would . . . be . . . enough,' she said slowly, giving him a long, hard, penetrating look, out of which all sentiment had fled. Then she added, while a dusky red spot appeared in each of her cheeks, 'Don't you see that I've got it in me to make a success of this thing and stand on my own feet?'

She paused and stared into the fire, biting her under lip in concentrated thought, and drawing two of her finger-tips along the edge of the mantelpiece. Then she suddenly burst out:

'Don't you see it's a life of my own I want, now you've deserted me? I've lived in the thought of something exciting that you'd do for both of us, but' – and she made a dramatic gesture with her strong shoulders – 'you won't do anything . . . any more than *he* did.'

'Well, mother,' said Wolf slowly, when her final outburst had spent itself and a tender whimsical smile had settled down upon her face, 'I'm off now, anyway, to see Urquhart. That's *something* to have decided upon, at any rate, isn't it? Oh, I shall get more competent and more scrupulous, if you give me time. Well, I'm off, so good-bye, mother.'

It was at this juncture, after a hurried tap at the door, that Mrs. Herbert appeared upon the scene, to carry off her lodger's tray.

'Can you manage it?' Wolf said politely, balancing a forgotten sugar-bowl among the rest of the things. But his mother came towards him, and, standing with her back to the landlady, made a whimsical grimace. As he bent forward to embrace her, there was a furtive exchange between them of that rapid blood-understanding which human beings share with the animals; but even as she kissed him she whispered in his ear: 'Don't you think any more about the money, Wolf, for I won't have it! And look me up to-morrow, if you have time, either here or at the shop. Good-bye! Don't you bother, Mrs. Herbert! I'll open the door.'

As he made his way through the quiet Sunday morning streets, Wolf found that he had already decided, in the secret places of his mind, to look in at Christie's before he started for King's Barton. This decision quickened his steps, but it did not prevent him from being stared at with the usual rapid curiosity by the few lethargic idlers he encountered.

He tried to analyse, as he went along, the cause that intensified this curiosity, in certain particular eye-encounters, to a malignant hostility. He came to the conclusion that this occurred only when his own mind was especially harassed. It must be, he decided, the same psychic instinct that makes a flock of fowls attack the one that happens to be hurt or sick. Mentally, at such times, he *was* hurt – he was actually bleeding invisible blood – and it might easily be that this wounded 'aura' excited some mysterious irritation in those who caught it.

When he reached the Malakite shop he determined to ring the side door bell; and he entered the little alleyway with this purpose. A certain shrinking from the critical moment that would decide whether Christie were in the house or not led him to gain time by strolling forward into the small garden at the alley's end.

The little enclosure was entirely surrounded by walls; and at that time of year the only greenery visible was a few patches of parsley at the further end. Wolf walked towards those patches, though the soaked earth-mould clung heavily to his boots. Under the wall he did find a couple of dilapidated chrysanthemums, little, drooping, daisy-like blooms, that seemed to have had their very souls washed out of them. Glancing upward above these, he observed a projecting stone in the wall, which was covered by a species of vividly green moss, small and velvety, that seemed enjoying a vernal prime of its own, in the midst of the universal dissolution. In a moment, like a rush of warm summer air, there came sweeping over his mind the memory of certain old pier-posts at Weymouth, covered with small green seaweed . . . and simultaneously with this he heard a sound that made him turn hurriedly towards the house.

It was the opening of the side door. And there was Christie, emerging in her out-of-doors attire!

He called her name loudly before he knew what he was doing, and she turned and looked at him.

With the poignance of that vision of pier-post and green seaweed still in his brain, the sight of her figure there, so quaint and pitiful in her old-fashioned cloak and tightly-pulled-on gloves, stirred in him a sudden sense of something so beautiful in life, that it melted the bones within him. She herself seemed startled and overjoyed at seeing him; and tossing aside her accustomed reserve, she hurried towards him, heedless of the rain-soaked soil under her feet, heedless of any windows that might be overlooking them, her arms impetuously stretched out and her mobile little face working under her tremulous emotion like a ruffled leaf in a gusty wind.

Once in possession of her hand he defiantly retained it; and together they moved close up to the wall at the end of the enclosure where, on their rain-battered stalks, drooped those miserable chrysanthemums.

'I've come to the conclusion, Wolf,' she said, as they stood there side by side, looking down at those forlorn survivals, 'that I must be more frank, as well as more philosophical, about what I feel for you.'

His heart began to beat wildly. The fantastic idea flashed through his mind that she was going to suggest – she herself – that he should come to her one of these nights when the old man was asleep!

'What exactly do you mean, Chris?' he asked, as she dropped his arm and faced him with her steady stare.

'I'm going to keep my feminine nature in control after this,' she said. 'We know what we are to each other . . . and what apparently we have to be . . . so I've decided not to allow any insurrection of my feelings. I've even thought of a *coup d'état* to keep them in their place!'

Quite unconsciously she had lifted her free hand to his coat and was twisting round and round in her gloved fingers one of its buttons.

An electric vibration of understanding quivered between them like a shivering cord stretched between two boats balanced each on its own wave-crest. And then, with incredible swiftness, a deliciously mocking smile came into her face. 'Shall I tell you something, Wolf?' she said. 'I've started writing a story! I began it at one o'clock last night, when I decided to conquer all feminine equivocations. It's about someone quite different from me, but . . . very philosophical. It was the philosophical part I began last night. I wrote page after page . . . quick as that!' And releasing his coat, she made a characteristically girlish gesture with her fingers.

'I believe you could write a wonderful book,' said Wolf earnestly; and then, almost before he was aware of it, as they stood together, the indescribable entrancement of that green seaweed he had visualized a moment ago, and the salty taste of spray, and the touch of sun-warmed sand that had come with it, associated themselves with the delicious peace into which her presence threw him, and he began to abandon himself to the ecstasy of his 'mythology.'

He was stupid enough to dream that he could give himself up unobserved to this egoistic satisfaction. It was therefore with something of a shock that he caught the faint sound of a sigh upon the air.

'I've got to go now,' she said. 'I've got to get something for father's dinner that I forgot yesterday, and there's only one little shop round here that's open on Sunday morning. But don't let me drive you away if you're happy in my garden. Stay as long as you like!'

She was holding out her hand now, and upon her face was a candidly humorous smile. He knew perfectly well that she had discovered, without the passage of a sign between them, that his mind had plunged their paradisic moment into some undersea of its own, where she could not follow. But he saw that she accepted this with complete indulgence; just took it for granted as a masculine peculiarity . . . a different way from hers of being happy!

'When am I to see you again?' he asked. 'Our school-holiday will soon be over . . . and then . . . well, we know how it goes!'

Christie turned her head away from him, and, with puckered forehead and drooping under lip, fell into a fit of deep pondering.

'Now's the time for you to practise your new philosophy, Chris, of being frank with your lover!'

Wolf uttered this lightly, but his heart was beginning to beat again. Something had made him give to her confessed 'decision' a meaning directly the reverse of what her words implied. Wicked, satyrish thoughts flashed through his mind like darting fish through disturbed water. Her frown deepened at his speech and her lip drooped still more. Then, with heightened colour, she turned quickly and faced him.

'Will . . . you . . . be –' she began slowly. 'I mean, will Gerda be –' She hesitated; and then, speaking rapidly, and with wide-open eyes fixed steadily upon his: 'Will you be free to-morrow night, Wolf? Father is going down to Weymouth to-morrow, on some affair of his own, and is going to stay the night there. So, if you like, I could get you supper, and we'd have everything to ourselves.'

It was Wolf's turn now to look away; but he answered her easily and lightly, as if it were quite a small matter. 'Why, Chris, that would be wonderful! I'll snatch at such a chance as that, whatever's in the way. Besides, there's no earthly reason why I shouldn't come to supper to-morrow. So let's consider it settled. No, I mustn't stay longer now; and I mustn't try and help you with your Sunday shopping! I'm off to Barton to see if I can't catch Urquhart at home.' He paused for a second. 'I'm thinking of finishing that book for him, you know . . . after all . . . if he'll pay me in advance.'

Perhaps never in his life had Wolf's mind moved as rapidly as it moved now. His consciousness at this moment became like a wild horse stung by a gadfly or like an ox driven crazy by the eating of some 'insane root.' Those words of hers, 'Father is going to stay the night there,' took to themselves a sweet-shivering identity of their own. But his cheeks were flushed with a queer sense of discord within himself. 'What I feel now,' he thought, 'is not happiness at all. *What is it?*' And then, as the two of them moved away over the wet sods of earth to the alley's entrance:

'That green moss . . . that green seaweed . . . *was* happiness; but this is something else. There is something that will kill my "mythology" if I let it.'

He was taking her hand now to say good-bye. 'What does she care,' he thought, 'about my doing Urquhart's book?' And there came over him, as he looked into her brown eyes, a cold shudder of deadly loneliness. 'She would never understand,' he thought, 'what I am risking by going back to Urquhart.'

'Well, good-bye, Chris, till to-morrow night!' And then, as they released each other's hands, 'You're not to look round now!' he added querulously.

'I've never looked round in my life!' retorted Christie Malakite, as she gave him her parting nod.

It was still about half an hour before church-time when he reached the gate of King's Barton vicarage. And there was T. E. Valley himself, in his ragged brown ulster, scraping with a hoe at one side of the drive!

For a moment Wolf found himself enjoying the lot of this little clergyman. *He* had no worries about girls. *He* had no worries about money. *He* had no mother but the Mother of God.

Wolf advanced slowly up the drive. The click of the hoe on the gravel made so much noise that his approach was unobserved.

Mr. Valley's green-tinted trousers – he thinks nothing of Sunday, thought Wolf – covered such lean flanks, as he stooped, that it was as if the trousers were doing the weeding rather than the man.

'Good morning, Valley! Not started ringing your bell yet, then?'

A twinge of physical discomfort, as he resumed his upright position, crossed the priest's face. He rubbed his spine with the back of his left hand, as he offered his right to his visitor.

'Stiff. I feel rather stiff, Solent. You must excuse my being stiff.'

Wolf sighed wearily. 'I've been envying you, you irresponsible monk.' He turned his head and surveyed the result of Mr. Valley's labour. A small path had been made free of weeds along the edge of the great overgrown drive.

'People won't follow your path, Valley, even if you carry it to the gate. They'll just walk straight up the middle.'

Disregarding this remark, the clergyman screwed up his eyes as if thinking of some important matter. Then he leaned forward and said gravely:

'By the way, Solent, do you know any literary people in London?'

Wolf surveyed him in astonishment.

'Yes, a few,' he said.

A smile like a tiny crack in grey pond-ice crossed Mr. Valley's pallid features.

'Why don't you get them to publish Jason's poems, then? They're good, aren't they? He won't show them to me. You know what he is! He thinks I'd steal the ideas for my sermons. But if your London friends were to see them –'

Wolf felt sheer amazement at the perspicacity of the little man. What a fool he'd been never to have thought of this! Of course, it must be exceedingly difficult to get anything published. Carfax might – he had an interest once in a publishing house. And they *are* –

'I'll talk to Jason about it,' he said gravely. 'Well, I must be off now. I'm going to see Urquhart. By the way, Valley, *I am* going to finish that book of his.'

Mr. Valley's face crumpled into woeful disorder, as if he had received a blow. He turned up his shirtsleeves and resumed his weeding, without a word.

Wolf experienced extreme discomfort.

'You think I'm making a mistake, Valley?' he said.

There was no answer.

'You think the less I see of Urquhart the better, Valley?'

Still there was no answer.

'Don't work at that job too long, Valley, and forget about the service!'

The man gave him an extraordinary sideways glance without lifting his head or ceasing his work. But not a word did he utter.

'Well, good-bye... and I *will* do something about Jason's poems!'

'I wonder if I *am* making the greatest mistake I ever made in my life!' he said to himself, as he emerged into the road. He began to feel almost startled by the blind desire he had to erect this money as an impassable barrier between his mother and Mr. Manley. 'It's only his money. *Of course* it's only his money. She couldn't *like* a brute like that!'

In spite of the lowering clouds hanging like toppling bastions above High Stoy – as if the Cerne Giant himself were heaping up earthworks there – not one single drop fell till Wolf reached the shelter of the manor. He began to feel there was something uncanny about the way the rain threatened to descend and yet did not descend.

'What's the time, Roger?' he asked, nervously, as he followed Monk up the old Jacobean staircase to the familiar library.

'Must be near church-time, I believe, sir; though, I haven't heard the bells yet. Squire'll be main glad to see 'ee, sir,' the man went on, as he opened the library door; 'glad as a hernshaw Squire'll be!'

'He wants to get his book done, Monk, I suppose?'

''Tis all he thinks of, sir. Night and day, 'tis all he thinks of.'

'Why doesn't he advertise for another secretary?'

Roger Monk made a deprecatory grimace and then hurriedly placed his large first finger upon his lips.

'Squire's had enough of secretaries,' he whispered, 'and so, by Grimey, have I!'

His voice resumed its normal tone when they were well inside the room.

'You'll find your old seat just as comfortable as it used to be, sir. Them big logs warms the whole place.'

On the servant's departure Wolf went over at once to the table by the window. How well he recalled the thrill he used to get from the asters and lobelias, down there in that round flower-bed, so dark and bare to-day!

There was a book, lying with others upon the table, that caught his attention at once. He picked it up. The particular pencil-marking in the corner of the fly-leaf indicated to him that it had come into Urquhart's possession through the agency of Mr. Mala-kite. The volume had no connection at all with the rambling chronicles and scandalous county trials out of which Urquhart's History was being framed. It was the kind of book the debased purpose of which is simply and solely to play upon the morbid erotic nerves of unbalanced sensuality. The Malakite shop had, it appeared, inexhaustible resources of this nature, distinct altogether from any merely bawdy local folklore.

He turned over the pages. At once that old wicked shiver, drunken, indescribable, ran through his veins. It was an abomi-nable book! A peculiar tremulousness took possession of the pit of his stomach, and a mist swam before his eyes. The atrocious attraction of a single page that he had encountered drew him towards a region of unspeakable images. Through an iridescent vapour, with the blood rushing to his head, he followed those images. He sank down into the chair, with the book clutched between his trembling fingers. He read voraciously. All those drops of deadly nightshade which, four months ago, had distilled themselves into his nerves as he fled from the school-treat field, began to seethe and ferment again in his secretest veins. Every now and then he was compelled to wipe away the salt sweat that clouded his eyesight. His knees knocked together beneath the table in his absorbed emotion.

It was while he was thus engaged that the library door opened upon him and Mr. Urquhart presented himself in the doorway. The Squire advanced towards him across the polished oak floor, limping and muttering, his cane striking the echoing boards resoundingly at each step.

Wolf rose and met the man with extended hand; but his flushed cheeks, hot forehead, and excited eyes must have betrayed his preoccupation.

'Glancing at our last purchase, eh? What? Can't keep these pretty little books out of you young people's hands! You'll be snatching, by hook or by crook. . . . You'll be snatching, you rogues, eh?' And he dropped Wolf's fingers, only to nudge him familiarly in the ribs.

Mr. Urquhart looked that morning as if something had inordinately refreshed and cheered him. 'Well?' he muttered interrogatively. 'Well?'

Wolf retreated a step or two, and mechanically placed the book he had been reading on the top of another volume, adjusting it evenly and neatly. Then, with his clenched hand resting on the table, and leaning a little forward, 'I've been thinking, sir,' he began gravely, 'a good deal lately about that book of yours; and I've thought I'd like to see you again to find out if we could come . . . if we could come . . .'

'To business, me boy!' threw in the other. 'Quite right. I'm your man. I'm ready to bargain with 'ee.'

Wolf's eyes fixed themselves upon the ebony stick upon which his late employer propped himself. 'As it happens, sir,' he began resolutely, 'my mother is just now in need of a sum of money . . . two hundred pounds in fact . . . to start a new tea-shop in Blacksod. She wants this at once. She's been thinking of borrowing it from . . . from a friend. What I had in my mind, sir, was . . .' He relaxed the tension of his muscles a little at this point, and, in place of leaning heavily on the table, he found himself scratching with his thumbnail a zigzag pattern upon it in the shape of an architectural ornament. 'What I thought was,' he went on, 'that if you could see your way to give me a cheque for this sum . . . now at once . . . I would pledge myself, in any form you suggest, to get the book finished within the next three months . . . by March, in fact, when I first began it. What you'll be doing, Mr. Urquhart, is to pay me in advance for this three months' work on condition that I finish the job in that time . . . but I must be free' – his voice became quite steady now, and he found himself looking at last into the Squire's face – 'I must be free to do this work at home and in my own way, using your notes, of course, as my material. I mean, that with my school-teaching I can't come over here regularly. But if I haven't finished it by the end of March you'll have the right to demand the repayment of this two hundred.'

He paused, a little breathlessly; and, as was his wont in any crisis, he put his hand into his side pocket, produced his cigarettes, and lit one with punctilious deliberation.

'Come over to the fire, Solent.' said Mr. Urquhart. Wolf followed him, as he limped across the room; and they sat down in the two leather chairs against the open hearth, the smouldering logs of which the Squire proceeded to stir up with the end of his stick.

Wolf's heart was now beating fast. 'I shall have the two hundred,' he thought 'I shall have the two hundred!' He became aware that the vision of himself handing over this cheque to his mother was melting now into a vague, delicious sweetness that had nothing to do with either Mrs. Solent or with Mr. Urquhart. It hung quivering – this drop of maddening sweetness – on the edge of those words of Christie's, 'He will stay the night at Weymouth!'

'I'm not a rich man, Solent. You know *that*, I suppose?'

Wolf nodded sympathetically; but he caught no more than the general drift of his companion's words, as the Squire rambled on.

'She's a plucky woman, your mother, and a darned good-looking one still, me boy, if you'll let an old man say so. Shame you had to desert her. But you nympholepts are all crazy. It's beyond me what you can find – But there! It's a matter of taste. But I don't see why you need have bought the filly as well as ridden her. Torp's a reasonable man; though he *is* such a fool. But there! We all have to pay for our little vices. Well! About the two hundred, me boy – I suppose you must have it. Yes, by Jove, Solent, and you *shall* have it! And what's more, we'll drink a glass of my old Malmsey to wash the business down!'

While these words were reaching him across the smoke of the stirred-up logs, Wolf's own consciousness was sounding the depths of an unexpected mental crisis. Intensely did he realize the relief with which he would fling this cheque into his mother's lap. It was against his conscience; but the moment had come when he must sacrifice his conscience! In an irresistible salt tide, over-coming all barriers, the idea of sacrificing his conscience rushed in full force now over the portion of his mind where the words, 'Mr. Malakite at Weymouth,' lay like a drowned sea-reef! And then, as he stared at Mr. Urquhart, it became clear to him in a

405

flash of cruel illumination that these two things – to-day's bargain with the Squire and to-morrow's visit to Christie – would be the end of his peace of mind. To these two things had he been brought at last. This was the issue; this was the climax of the mounting wave of his life in Dorset. He had to outrage now – and it was too late to retreat – the very core of his nature! That hidden struggle between some mysterious Good and some mysterious Evil, into which all his ecstasies had merged, how could it go on after this?

'Do 'ee hear, me boy?' The Squire's voice came clear and straight now into his agitated consciousness. 'Will you do me the favour of ringing the bell? There! Just in front of 'ee!'

Wolf rose and rang the bell, and sank down once more into the depths of the leather chair. As he did so he was aware of a rattling at both the mullioned casements. The wind was rising, then? Let it rise! Let the rain pour down. It would please Mukalog, in his kitchen drawer over there, to hear this sound.

The tall gardener had his black coat on when he entered the room, and his air was the air of a privileged major-domo in a noble house.

'Get my paper and pens, Roger, and my cheque-book, out of my study, please. Oh, and one thing more! Here, you'll want my keys for that' – and he began fumbling in his pockets.

'A bottle of port, sir?' suggested the servant.

'Where the devil *are* my keys?' murmured the Squire petulantly.

'In your dressing-gown, I expect, sir. I'll look for them, sir. Is it the 1880 port that I'm to get?'

'Listen, Monk,' said Mr. Urquhart gravely. 'How many bottles of my father's Malmsey have I got left?'

The man straightened his back with a jerk, and Wolf noticed that his eyebrows went up as if some extravagant and very foolish transaction were in the air.

'Some half a dozen, sir. Them what's in the walnut chest are the last. We locked them up, sir, after Candlemas night, when you and young Mr. Redfern looked at they portfolios of antiquities.'

Mr. Urquhart gave Wolf a rapid but very complicated glance as he answered the man.

'Never mind about the antiquities, Monk. Mr. Solent doesn't care for antiquities. Get a bottle of the Malmsey, and bring my cheque-book.'

Half an hour later, over the same fireplace, Wolf found himself drinking the most nectareous wine he had ever tasted in his life. A cheque for two hundred pounds on Stuckey's Bank lay securely in his waistcoat pocket; and on the silver tray between Mr.

Urquhart and himself, a corner of it beneath the decanter to keep it in its place, was his own acknowledgment of the money and of the obligation which it entailed.

'Fifteen chapters would be a good round number, Mr. Urquhart.'

'Fifteen...thirty...fifty!' cried the other. 'I don't care how many! Order it as you please. My *facts*, my little *facts*, are the main thing – that future generations should have all the biting, pricking, itching, salty little facts about our "wold Dorset" that can be put together!'

'I won't have any of your "facts," sir, that I can't turn into decent English. This book may carry your name, but it will have my soul between its – '

He broke off abruptly. 'What's amusing you, Mr. Urquhart? By God, I *will* hear what's amusing you! Have I said anything ridiculous?'

'Not . . . at . . . all . . . me boy!' gasped the Squire, suppressing his chuckling fit. 'Did you say your "soul" between its pages? "Soul" is good. "Soul" is a good word. So you've got a soul, have you, Menelaus? Or you *had* before it strayed into my book? By Jove, that's a pretty fancy, eh? Like a rose-leaf or a bit of white heather, such as the wenches put in their prayer books!'

Wolf laid his hand on the stem of his wineglass and stared sombrely at the rich purplish umber of its contents. Never had he tasted such wine! He felt irritated with Urquhart for not letting him enjoy it in silence – savour every drop of it – draw it into his heart, his nerves, his spirit. . . .

'Not one fact left out . . . Menelaus . . . that's in the bond, you know!' And Wolf, through that Malmsey-tinctured mist, saw his host tap significantly with his forefinger the sheet of paper that lay under the decanter.

A second gust of rising wind rattled the two window-casements; and this time there came with it the sound of a distant bell ringing.

'It's Tilly-Valley,' said the Squire brusquely. 'Hand me your glass, Solent.'

'Does he have it done when he's saying Mass?' asked Wolf, watching the tilting of the decanter. Then he cried, 'I like to hear it!' with a sudden, fierce emphasis. 'I think I'll open the window.' He rose with meticulous care and moved across the room, lifting his legs with cautious exactitude, as if they were heavy objects totally distinct from his personality.

He pushed open that familiar latched pane of the mullioned window.

'I say, sir!' he cried excitedly. 'It's going to pour with rain.

Ehere's an enormous black cloud out there!'

He strode gravely back to his place by the fire: and the wind followed him, making that paper he had signed rise up like a leaf and tap against the side of the decanter.

'It's going to pour in a minute,' he repeated, emptying his glass.

But he now became aware that his companion's wits had completely succumbed to the influence of the wine. Mr. Urquhart was engaged in a fatuous attempt to measure out the last few drops of the Malmsey equally between their two glasses. 'Empty . . . quite empty . . .' he murmured, with a deep sigh; and then he began muttering something that sounded like 'Who'll toll the bell? "I" said the bull, "because I can pull." '

'I beg your pardon, Mr. Urquhart?'

His recognition that the man had sunk instantaneously through all the intervening stages and was now hopelessly drunk was a sobering shock to his own fuddled mind.

'It's ringing still,' he remarked gravely.

'I'm the only magistrate round here,' cried the Squire. 'What does Torp know of the law?'

Wolf contemplated with some concern the heavy lips in front of him, which were now gibbering incoherently. Valley's Mass-bell had ceased. The wind was rattling all the windows. A wild gust, blowing down the chimney, drove a handful of bitter-tasting wood-ashes against both their faces.

'If I told you three feet was enough, what's that to you? Three feet is deep enough for a boy not twenty-five. They sleep sound then. It's different later. Three feet is a very good depth. Don't throw in any more, I tell you! His skin was always soft. Three feet is more than enough. How do we know they don't feel it falling on 'em? It's clay, mind you. It's thick Dorset clay.'

Wolf drew in his breath with a long-drawn sigh. 'He'll tell me everything soon, if only I can keep my wits clear.'

There was a sharp splash of rain against the open casement, and a violent shaking of the window-catch.

The Squire recommenced his mutterings.

'D'ye think it's an easy thing to walk up and down on the earth with him lying down there? What would it be to stop thinking about it and just do it? . . . Foulness? . . . Abomination? . . . I don't know about that. . . . I . . . don't . . . know. . . .'

His voice died away into complete incoherence. But suddenly it rose once more, shrill and strident. 'It falls off . . . it falls off . . . the sweet flesh!'

Wolf stiffened himself in his chair and leant forward. Big drops of rain were descending the chimney, each one hissing with an angry hiss, as it touched the burning logs.

'The lips . . . the lips . . . where are his lips now?'

The man's voice sank again; but Wolf seemed to catch a low moaning sound coming from him, a strange, sub-human sound, that was ghastly to listen to.

Then there were more articulate words. 'Nothing can make him not to be himself! And if he's himself, and I'm *myself*, 'twould be like my life hugging my life to do it!'

He fell into a silence then; and lifting one of his arms from where it sprawled upon the table, he wiped the saliva from his mouth with the back of his hand.

'I'll find out everything in a moment,' Wolf thought. 'All I've got to do is to keep my brain clear.'

The windows had become so dark with rain that the room was in twilight. The upper portion of his companion's face was almost invisible. Over the lower part of it, however, the smouldering fire threw a wavering illumination. It was this obscuring of the man's eyes in the darkened room that made it a surprise to Wolf when, after a long pause, a voice came from him that was pitched in a completely different key – that was, indeed, crafty and foxy in its sobriety!

'Drunk and chattering, eh, me boy? It's when I think of Torp . . . that's what it is . . . Torp and the mess he made of the grave out there! Couldn't even dig it deep enough. Said he came upon an old coffin or something! Torp and his stupidity always upset me. A stonecutter is what the man is. I was a fool to let him meddle with gravedigging. Torp digging graves is absurd. You can see *that* for yourself, tow-pate, can't you, even though you do go about with Lobbie? What was I saying just now? Oh, I know! That it was all crazy village gossip when they talk of suicide. Don't you listen to 'em, tow-pate! Don't you listen to that ridiculous individual down at Pond Cottage either. He takes drugs, that man. You can smell 'em on his clothes. Suicide? Nonsense. It was pneumonia. If he'd stayed at Lenty, Tilly-Valley would never have got at him. They moved him against my wishes. D'ye hear, Solent? Against my wishes. That Lenty place of mine . . . your mother liked it, didn't she? . . . was just right for that boy. What did they move him for? He wasn't fit to be moved. He might have got well if they'd kept Tilly-Valley away from him and hadn't moved him. That . . . was . . . wrong . . . to move . . . him.'

With these words, Mr. Urquhart's heavy head sank down till his chin rested against his chest. The shock of the jerk to his neck aroused him again, however; and with a crafty, wrinkled leer he glanced at the empty bottle.

'Empty . . . every drop,' he muttered. Then, with his elbow resting on the table, he supported his head with his hand.

'Torp's the fellow who upset me. Why, I can dig a grave better myself! But you must excuse me, Solent. I know you are mixed up with those people. Married the little boy, I mean the little girl, didn't you? Your relative Torp is a prize fool, Solent. Don't defend him! I tell you it's no use. You're . . . a sensible . . . boy . . . Menelaus . . . though you're *not* as good-looking as your father . . . and the best thing you can do is to leave Torp to me. Stonecutter or undertaker, I understand him. I've known individuals of his kind all my life. He's pure Dorset, is the good Torp. Leave him . . . to me . . . leave . . . him . . .'

His arm sank down upon the table and his head sank down upon his arm. A gust of wind from the open window swept across the room and lifted into a spiral dance the scattered wood-ashes that lay on the silver tray. Some of those ashes, as they subsided, fell upon the man's glossy black hair and lay there where they fell; so that Wolf was reminded of the men of old time, who, in their grief, strewed ashes on their heads.

He rose quietly to his feet. 'I'd better hunt for Monk before I go,' he thought, 'and tell him to come up and see him.'

With this in his mind he stole across the polished floor, opened the door with the utmost caution, and let himself out.

The rain had stopped when he emerged into the manor garden; and he decided that the best thing he could do would be to walk off the effects of the Malmsey and remain in the open air until tea-time. Then it would drop in at Pond Cottage, where, no doubt, since it was Sunday, he would find all his friends together.

By the elimination of any lunch he would be all the hungrier to enjoy the homemade bread and flaky Scotch scones and honey in the honeycomb which always made Mrs. Otter's teas such solid and delicious repasts.

Feeling a longing for absolute solitude, he looked about for some unfrequented path. He had not passed, by more than two hundred yards, the well-known house inhabited by Roger Monk, when he came upon a cattle-drove leading due east, which was completely unfamiliar. This he decided to explore; and when it led him into a narrow, grassy lane, heading towards High Stoy, he made up his mind that he would follow this new direction and see what came of it. Every now and then, as he walked, he found himself thrusting his finger and thumb into his waistcoat pocket to make sure the precious slip of paper was still safely there.

He had never been quite in the mood in which he struggled now. The thought of Christie's invitation to him, the tone of her voice as she uttered the words about her father, the expression of her face as she described what she had been writing – all these things fermented in his veins like drops from the sap of a deadly upas tree. To die without ever having slept with Christie . . . No! He *couldn't* submit to such a destiny! His heart beat fast as he gathered up his forces for this challenge to the gods. Between the bare branches of rain-soaked elms and the wet leaves of gleaming holly he strode along now like a centaur maddened by juniper-berries! And yet all the while, below this recklessness, lay a furtive, troubled, ghastly dread. Did not his 'mythology' depend upon his inmost life-illusion – upon his taking the side of Good against Evil in the great occult struggle? And if Urquhart's book and 'Mr. Malakite at Weymouth' killed his mythology, how could he go on living? What feelings does a man have when his inmost integrity is shattered? 'You Dorset!' he murmured aloud, as he trailed his stick through a heap of dead leaves. 'You've not beaten me yet, you Dorset! Ay! I'll be a match for you yet, you dark rain-scented earth!'

But even as he spoke, the thought of holding Christie against his limbs, stripped of her clothes, brought him an intolerable spasm. The words, 'Mr. Malakite at Weymouth,' ceased altogether to be words. They became tiny blue veins just above those slender knees! They became – oh, he couldn't give up such a chance! He couldn't!

He had let Christie become a spirit to him. He himself, with his Pharisaic chatter about 'platonic,' had turned her into a spirit. Men of his type make their girls into anything. He had made her what he wanted her. He had satisfied his sensuality with the other one and gone to Christie for mental sympathy. He hadn't considered *her* side of it at all. But now – to-morrow night – he would be a magician! He would turn this Ariel, this Elemental, into a living girl! His mind reverted to Gerda. 'How pitiful that she should have lost her blackbird-song! That's what I've done to *her*! I've become too solemn. I've wearied her with my pedantic, ponderous thoughts. She's come to feel that I'm "heavy weather," a fellow without humour, without gaiety, a lumbering schoolmaster. That's what it is. She's turned to Weevil, for the simplest of all reasons – for pleasant *camaraderie*!'

Suddenly, with a cynical frankness, he began comparing his feelings for these two girls. 'The truth is,' he said to himself, 'I love them both! I love Gerda because she's so simple, and because I've slept with her all these months; and I love Christie because she's so subtle, and because I've never slept with her!'

He paused by the lane side, and, stepping over some dripping clumps of rank weeds, whose odour seemed like all the vague, anonymous scents that had hit his senses for the last four months, he leaned upon a disused gate and stared northward towards Ramsgard. 'Is that the Abbey?' he thought, as he heard faint chimes upon the heavy air. Hovering about the image of Æthelwolf's coffin, his mind reverted to the idea of Christ.

'How extraordinary it would be,' he said to himself, 'if there really were an incredibly tender and pitiful heart . . . tender to the craziest sentimentalities as well as to the most tragic dilemmas of humanity . . . just outside the circle of time and space!' If there *were* such a heart it would certainly turn all modern scientific theories into something trifling and unimportant. But did he want such a Being to exist? Not to want Him . . . not even to *want* Him . . . would seem an outrageous cruelty to all the Tilly-Valleys in the world. And, besides, such a Being would look after Gerda and after Christie . . . and settle all their dilemmas . . . ultimately . . . 'And yet I don't believe I *do* want Him!' he murmured aloud, as a sprinkling of cold raindrops fell upon his clasped hands from a tree above his head.

As he set himself to answer the question, why it was he didn't 'want Him,' there came into his mind one of Gerda's recent hints, full of her primitive Blacksod mania for gross scandal, implying that the perverse tendencies of Mr. Malakite had not even yet been eradicated by old age.

'If I take her to-morrow night,' he thought, 'there'll exist . . . something . . . in common . . . between the old man and me . . . yes! if it's only a . . . only a . . . Is that the reason why I don't really want "Him" to exist? For fear my feeling for Christie should have to be a thing purer even than "platonic"?'

He stared frowningly at the stubble furrows in front of him. One especial little pool of water caught his attention, between the melancholy stalks, into whose bosom at intervals single drops, from an extended branch above, kept splashing. So this was the inmost law of nature, was it; that if a man had more than one woman in his life he sank of necessity to such base compromises that he *couldn't* want Christ to exist?

Well, he must content himself with thinking of the coffin of King Æthelwolf when he heard the chimes of Ramsgard!

In his defiantly heathen mood he suddenly found himself chuckling, as he stared at those little periodic water-tongues leaping up in that brown puddle; for he recalled the opinion that Bob Weevil had expressed to him recently, that girls' legs were the most beautiful thing in the world. 'Weevil and I are both lucky in one way,' he thought. 'We both have the sort of intense life-illusion that protects human beings from the futility of the commonplace. But, oh God, oh God! I wish I hadn't taken this two hundred pounds, and I wish Mr. Malakite *wasn't* going to Weymouth to-morrow!'

He lifted his eyes from the wet stubble and let them roam at large across the green expanse of the great vale. And there swept over him an immense loathing for the furtive indecencies of human life and beast life upon the earth. 'It would be so much better,' he thought, 'if all men and all beasts were wiped out, and only birds and fishes left! Everything that copulates, everything that carries its young, how good if it vanished in one great catastrophe from the earth, leaving only the feathered and the finned!'

And he tried deliberately, as he moved away from that disused gate and strode further eastward along the lane, to visualize all this patient Sabbath landscape as it would be if it were indeed washed clean of all mammals! He imagined the vast cirque of Poll's Camp, couchant like an heraldic lion, and befouled no more by the rabble of Blacksod. He saw Melbury Bub rising out of the calm rain-drenched fields, free from all the privies and dungheaps and Farmer's Rests and slaughter-sheds that so profaned its leafy purlieus.

The lane rose a little presently, following a slight undulation of the bed of the vale; and when he reached the top of this small eminence, the expanse of country that stretched before him assumed for his imagination that particular look of a land submerged under fathoms of transparent water, which, from his childhood up, had especially thrilled him.

To his left rose the corrugated trunk of an enormous elm tree, about whose roots a thick covering of green moss held the fallen rain like a sponge.

The sight of this moss swept his mind back to Christie's garden and thence to those slippery wharf steps and wave-swept pier-posts that he associated with the first discovery of his mystic ecstasy.

413

So absolutely did he live in symbols of his mental life, that the two things which now threatened this ecstasy – Urquhart's book and a shy, slender Christie, stripped of her clothes – transformed themselves into the wet, uneven bark of this trunk against which he now pressed his hand. 'Two hundred pounds?' he thought. 'What is that to spoil a whole life? A thin, bare figure held tight for a second . . . what is that to change a person's whole idea of himself?'

As he went on pressing his bare palm against the wet corrugations of that inert trunk, it seemed to him imperative to make an attempt then and there to evoke his master-sensation. With a desperate straining of all the energy of his spirit, he struggled to merge his identity in that subaqueous landscape. He had, at that moment, a strange feeling, as if he were seeking to embrace in the very act of love the maternal earth herself! For, as he strained his spirit to the uttermost, the landscape before him ceased to be a mere assemblage of contours and colours. It became one enormous water-plant, of vast, cool, curving, wet-rooted leaves – leaves that unfolded themselves, leaves that finally responded and yielded to the outflung intensity of his magnetic gesture! 'Not dead yet!' he muttered aloud, as, with an exhausted sigh, he turned to retrace his steps. 'Not dead yet!'

In the reaction from this desperate plunge into his mystic vice, Wolf found that he was beginning to feel extremely hungry. 'I don't want to have to wait a minute after I get there,' he thought. 'I can't cope with Jason till I've had my tea. So it's no use walking too fast!'

His mind began fumbling then, puzzled and weary, around that question which always had such a curious interest for him, as to the inner nature of each person's secret life-illusion – that peculiar consciousness people build up as to their dominant 'entelechy' or ultimate life-flowering. Thus it seemed to him now that while his own life-illusion was his 'mythology,' Christie's must be those 'platonic essences' about which she was always pondering, Weevil's the mystic beauty of girls' legs, and Urquhart's the idea of his shameless book. He could not help chuckling a little to himself when his exhausted thoughts, like weary gnats that sink down upon water, began hovering round the question as to what Jason's life-illusion was. 'He has none! He has none!' he cried aloud; and he found himself so excited by this explanation of Jason's peculiarities that, not thinking what he did, he debouched into a field path quite different from the one that had led him into this lane.

After walking nearly a mile, this newly discovered path conducted him, to his considerable surprise, into Lenty Great Field –

into the opposite side of the field to that of Pond Lane. Indeed, so unfamiliar did the field look from this direction, that it was only by the well-known willow trees in the centre that he recognized Lenty Pond at all.

'Why, there *is* Jason!' he said to himself; 'and the girl with him must be Mattie. Damn! How the devil shall I cope with *this* combination?'

Then in a flash he realized that it was only his mental preoccupation with Jason that had given these complete strangers, sitting on the bank of Lenty Pond, *his* shape and Mattie's. Surely this man and this girl were completely unknown to him! But *were* they? The man certainly was. But the girl? Ah, he knew her! She was the 'automatic young lady' of Farmer's Rest! So that wizened old chap in a bowler hat was her uncle . . . the unseen invalid he had heard calling out, 'Jesus . . . Jesus . . . Jesus!'

As soon as he reached the side of the pond that was nearest to him, the two figures, who were seated on the opposite edge, stood up, the girl helping the man to his feet. He could see they were exchanging remarks about him; and knowing the condition of the man, he hesitated and looked away, flicking the dead reed-stalks with the end of his stick.

But as he hesitated there, he gave them a furtive sidelong glance, and he saw they had begun to come slowly along the side of the water, evidently intending to speak to him.

He advanced to meet them, and they met half-way round the circle of the pond.

'How do you do, Mr. Solent,' said the girl quietly. 'This is my uncle, Mr. Solent.' Then she turned and raised her voice, as if speaking to a deaf man. 'This is Mr. Solent, uncle; the gentleman I was telling you about.'

It gave Wolf a queer sensation to see this equivocal 'Miss Bess' again. Was it Gerda who had told him that she was a friend of Bob Weevil's? Little pleasure Mr. Weevil would get out of her, judging by that evening of the school treat!

But as she looked furtively into his eyes now, it was difficult for him to believe that the quiver of chemical attraction which for that single second united their nerves had no normal eroticism in it.

The girl was the first to drop her eyes. 'Uncle here takes all the time I've got, these days,' she murmured; 'uncle and the bar – don't you, you funny old man?'

Mr. Round's countenance flickered all over with little wrinkles of complacent pride.

'She looks arter me as if she were paid to do it,' he remarked in a hollow voice.

'I'm sure she does,' Wolf responded absent-mindedly, his gaze wandering to the surface of Lenty Pond. 'I think you're to be congratulated, Mr. Round, on having so capable a niece,' he added after a pause, with a little more emphasis.

Something about the landlord's disordered physiognomy began to suggest to his mind the head of a decapitated criminal carried on a pole. It was just as he was wondering how he was going to slip away from these two that there came into his head, as if from the lips of a goblin inside him, that queer tag of bawdy gibberish which Manley—or was it Josh Beard? – had chaunted so derisively that night at the Three Peewits. 'Jimmy Redfern ... *he* was there!' mocked this jibing voice.

But the man's face had begun to expand with such maudlin satisfaction that it became absurdly puckered and puffed out, like a toy balloon composed of crocodile skin.

'One who looks after you so well, Mr. Round –' continued Wolf.

At that moment, however, he caught the eye of the automatic young lady fixed upon him so quizzically that he felt the colour mounting to his cheeks.

'Curse the baggage!' he said to himself. 'She's not one to be propitiated.'

'You chose a nice day to bring your uncle out,' he remarked humbly, turning his back upon Lenty Pond.

'She brought me out. That's what she done. And she will take me in, present! We comes out and we goes in; but 'tis they what bides.'

'You're in the right of it *there*, Mr. Round,' said Wolf, meeting the niece's eye as boldly as he could. 'But I don't think it was very wise of her to let you sit down after all this rain.'

'I brought his shawl,' cried the girl, smiling. 'Look, uncle! You've left it over there.'

The innkeeper turned his head. 'Over there,' he repeated; and pulling at his niece's sleeve, he began shuffling back. Wolf accompanied them round Lenty Pond, and Miss Bess picked up the shawl. Bits of rush-seed were adhering to it; and she shook it in the air.

'Good-bye!' Wolf brought out at this point. 'I'm going to call at Pond Cottage before I walk back to Blacksod.'

' 'Tweren't either o' they,' the innkeeper murmured hurriedly, 'what drove him to it.'

Wolf looked questioningly at the girl.

'He's worried,' she said laconically. 'Here, uncle, lean on my arm and we'll soon be home! Have you forgotten what I've got for your tea?'

The puckers and creases came wrinkling back.

'She's got sardines for me tea,' he murmured confidentially.

'Capital!' cried Wolf. 'I hope they'll have sardines at Pond Cottage!'

He was on the point of leaving them, when the innkeeper suddenly stretched out his free arm towards the centre of the water.

'That's where he do bide!' he murmured hoarsely. 'Churchyard can't hold *he!*'

The automatic young lady, to Wolf's consternation, proceeded to shake her relative by both shoulders.

'Stop that, uncle!' she cried angrily. 'Stop that!'

The corners of Mr. Round's mouth fell. 'Don't 'ee take no notice, maidie. I weren't thinking what 'ee do reckon I were.'

He lowered his voice and leaned close to Wolf. 'She were afeard I were thinking of God,' he whispered.

'No I weren't, uncle!' cried Miss Elizabeth. 'So don't tell stories to Mr. Solent.' She looked Wolf straight in the face. 'He's worried,' she repeated.

'I see he is,' Wolf responded feebly. 'Well, I hope you'll enjoy your sardines, Mr. Round.' And he added in a firmer voice, 'Good-bye! Good-bye!' and, lifting his hat, moved away from them.

As he crossed the field he tried to think of each particular spot of ground he had come to be so familiar with in this locality ... Lenty Pond ... Melbury Bub ... Poll's Camp ... the Lunt Meadows....

'These are the reality. These are what will last,' he thought, 'when all those agitated people with their crazy fancies have passed into nothingness!'

At the gate of Pond Cottage garden he glanced at his watch. It was ten minutes past four. 'I should have sworn it was five,' he said to himself. 'Time's like a telescope. It compresses itself or lengthens itself, according to our feelings.'

The mystery of time continued to tease him as he strode up the path. His whole past seemed swallowed up by Mr. Urquhart's two hundred pounds and by 'Mr. Malakite at Weymouth.' 'The misery of these decisions assumes time,' he thought; 'but what if time is itself an illusion?'

After he had rung the bell, he was struck by the curious silence that always falls down on the thresholds of houses, like the feathers of some vast overshadowing bird, when house bells are rung. . . .

But the door was brusquely flung open now; and there were Darnley and Jason!

'You?' cried the younger brother. 'How splendid! Our ladies have gone for a walk; but they'll be back presently. They're sure to be back presently, because it's Dimity's day out. Dimity's gone to tea with Mrs. Martin, up at the House. I've just been making Jason put on a new tie.'

He turned and looked affectionately at his brother, while Wolf hung up his coat and hat.

'There!' Darnley cried. 'You've been fooling with it again. What a demon you are, Jason, after all my trouble!' And lifting his hands to his brother's throat he set himself to rearrange the tie in question, which was of a brilliant vermilion. Wolf was amazed at the amiable gravity with which the poet submitted to this gesture.

'These young wimming,' he mumbled – pronouncing the word more quaintly than Wolf had ever heard Mr. Torp pronounce it – 'like red ties.' And moving to the mirror above the hall table, he proceeded to regard the improved adornment with whimsical complacency.

They had not been seated many minutes beside the drawing-room fire when Wolf took the bull by the horns.

'Look here, Jason,' he began. 'Why don't you let me send a selection of your poems up to London, so that we can see what the critics think of them?'

There was an ominous silence. Darnley's hand went up to his beard; while his eyes fixed themselves frowningly upon the coal-scuttle.

Slowly Jason spoke, putting an abysmal malice into his words. 'You think you're God, don't you?' he remarked; while out of a stony countenance his eyes flashed with nervous fury.

Wolf felt a tremor of anger; but he suppressed it resolutely. 'Those poems of yours ought to be published,' he said.

'For you Londoners to scoff at!' returned the other. 'My poems may not be much,' Jason went on, 'but I don't like their being poked about by you clever dogs, any more than I'd like to have such rogues spit in my porridge.'

'My mother has a cousin,' continued Wolf obstinately, 'who is very good at getting things taken he feels interested in. He happens to be a lord, and had some connection once with a publishing house. I'd send your poems to him first.'

'Will this lord you're boasting about get a share of the money?' asked Jason harshly. 'Why don't you introduce Darnley to him? He might give Darnley a place at that – Institution, where you used to teach Latin!'

'Jason! Jason!' protested the younger brother indignantly.

But the man went on. 'If you're not so much like God as to be angry at everything that isn't praise, I'll give you my advice. My advice is – '

'Shut up, Jason, can't you? interrupted Darnley.

'My advice is that you go back to London. This Dorset climate isn't good for you! Those Londoners would very soon give you plenty of money, when they heard that your mother was cousin to that lord you were telling us about just now.'

'Jason can't forgive you, Solent,' interposed Darnley, 'for having heard his poems at all. Years ago he read some to me, and afterwards stopped speaking to me for three days!'

Instead of being annoyed at this remarkable reminiscence, the Slow-worm of Lenty raised his shoulders and chuckled audibly.

'You schoolmasters!' he cried. 'Your holidays have lasted too long! Teachers of Latin, like you, always get fidgety when you're not with your boys.'

'I don't teach Latin,' murmured Wolf, in a voice almost as silky as the Squire's own. Anger was mounting up within him like a black wave.

'Do you want to know why I advise you to go back to London?' went on Jason, disregarding this protest. 'Not because of Urquhart – though I'm tired of warning you against *him* – but because if you go about with *me* much longer, you'll wake up one fine morning with your merry little ways fallen from you like a snake's skin.'

'What ways?' asked Wolf.

'Oh, do shut up, Jason! Do stop making a bloody ass of yourself!' interjected Darnley.

'Those feelings you have when you stretch out your legs in the morning, and when you walk home to tea, swinging your stick, and when you go up those back stairs of old Malakite's, and when you drink that bottle of gin of yours which I've heard about and forget that it isn't your first night with your young lady, and when you enjoy those books in old Urquhart's library and tell yourself stories about them, and when he brings out his second-best wine and you warm yourself at his fire, and when you look over gates on your walks and think that Nature is something!' He stopped breathlessly, and then added, in the dead silence that followed,

'If you go about with me much longer you'll find yourself falling into *reality*, like ... like an abortion into the Bog-stream!'

'Jason, if you don't shut up,' cried Darnley fiercely, 'I'll go straight off to Preston Lane with Solent and leave you alone!'

'It's all right,' interposed Wolf. 'I don't mind hearing these things. But, if Darnley doesn't object, I'd like to ask you one question, Otter. What is it about me that annoys you so?'

The poet's whole frame seemed to hug itself together, to contract to tighten. Then he said: 'I'm not in the least annoyed by anyone's ways. We're all beetles in the dung of the earth. If you go about with me, Solent, you won't be able to think of yourself like you like to do, or about any of your young ladies either! You'll be glad enough to get three good meals every day and to sleep as long as you can. . . . You'll learn from me more about the value of sleep than about courting young ladies. . . . So my advice is, get back to London, where that lord of yours is, and teach – '

He was interrupted by the opening of the front door and the sound of Olwen's shrill voice rising above those of her companions. As they all hurried out into the hall to greet the newcomers, Wolf thought to himself, 'Now we'll see how three generations of feminine sensibility will take possession of a house!' But things arranged themselves very quietly. Mattie took Olwen upstairs, to tidy her up, while Darnley followed his mother into the kitchen, to help her getting tea. So that soon after their arrival Wolf found himself alone with Jason by the drawing-room fire.

'They'll be a long time,' said the poet, with grave solemnity. 'They always *are* a long time on Sundays.' He then walked gingerly to the door and furtively closed it. Returning to Wolf's side by the hearth, he drew from his pocket a crumpled piece of paper, which he carefully unfolded.

'When you send my poems to London,' he began quietly, while Wolf, watching him with astonishment, possessed himself of a seat from which he could see the window, 'I think it would be a good thing if you didn't leave out the last one I've written. It's called "The Owl and Silence." Do you mind if I read it to you now?'

'I'd like very much to hear it,' Wolf responded humbly; but while the man was thus occupied, he allowed a portion of his consciousness to appropriate to itself a lovely bluish light that, with the falling of that winter twilight, began to fill the uncurtained window.

'Does it mean that the horizon is now clear of clouds?' he thought to himself. And then he thought, 'It seems early for the twilight

to be setting in.' The disarming monotony of Jason's voice blended
with the impalpable colour that filled the window-frame....

When the mossy vistas call to the rain
To ravish their fern-fronds green,
Thro' the dripping hazels they dart again,
These points of damascene!
And each root holds blood in its amber cup,
Holds blood in its emerald bowl,
While the White Owl covers silence up
As death covers up the soul.

The great White Owl, he passes by
Like a ghost among the guests.
The woodmice watch him with frightened eyes;
The birds crouch in their nests;
And Silence asleep on her lichen bed,
Asleep on her fungus sheet,
Feels those feathers sink on her drooping head,
And fall on her tender feet!

They have known each other so long, so long,
That Owl and that Silence deep!
The mosses and ferns to life belong;
But they belong to sleep.
They belong to the land behind all lands
Where the greenest leaves look grey;
Where the tree of the unknown sorrow stands
Weeping its well-a-way!

For the Owl is old and Silence is old,
And that tree is older yet!
Its tears, malignant, drizzling, cold,
Make their love-pillow wet!
New moss, new ferns, the new spring brings;
New primroses in death
Are soothed by new moth-flutterings
Of euthanasian breath;

But the Owl that over Silence sinks,
With strange and drooping feathers,
Eternal rest-without-end drinks,
Absolved from all life's weathers.

Each root holds blood in its amber cup,
Holds blood in its emerald bowl,
But the White Owl covers Silence up
As death covers up the soul.

'Oh, I like that *very* much!' he murmured gently, when the man's voice died away. 'Certainly we will include *that* in what we send to London!' It somehow seemed quite natural to him now, in the fleeting loveliness of this blue light, that Jason should, without retracting his spleen, have accepted his offer. As he watched the man crouching there between himself and that unearthly atmosphere, his sombre figure became for him a monumental symbol charged with feelings beyond expression. At how many hearths, that winter afternoon, were human beings watching this strange blueness, flung against their casements like the dreamy breath of the earth itself, caught ere it dissolved into space! That aerial transparency might easily be something that never again in all the days of his life would appear exactly as it did now! Oh, how he longed to scoop it up in great handfuls and pour it forth over every wounded spirit in the world! How he longed to sprinkle it like holy water over that face upon the Waterloo steps! A strange melting happiness began to thrill through him – and then, suddenly, 'Mr. Malakite at Weymouth.' *No!* He would have supper with Christie; but he would keep his integrity. At eleven o'clock he would go back to Gerda. The idea of this *eleven o'clock* seemed like a penitential offering, heavy to lift, which, by a super-human effort, he would offer up to his Deus Absconditus. But even now, as he heard Olwen's light steps and bursts of laughter in the room above, the thought of the two hundred dragged his resolution down. He *couldn't* give up the relief of flinging this cheque into his mother's lap; and by some intricate psychic law it seemed useless to renounce Christie's bed and yet accept Urquhart's money!

Jason's voice interrupted his meditations. But it was not of poetry he spoke. 'Tell me, Solent,' he said, 'would you prophesy from what you know of me that I would outlive you by ten years?'

'Not ten, Jason!'

'Five, then?'

'No.'

'Four?'

'No.'

'By three years, then?'

422

'Well, perhaps you *may* outlive me by three! But listen, Jason. I wish you'd let me run up for a minute to your room, before they all come in. May I do that?' And he began to move to the door. Jason rose quickly to his feet and followed him. His expression was grave and extremely perturbed.

'I'd go to Darnley's room if I were you,' he said eagerly. 'The basin's much grander there than in mine. But, of course, if you're nervous of doing anything in there . . . and would feel happier in mine . . . but mine wouldn't suit you . . . It's not in your style.'

'I know very well what style it's in,' retorted Wolf, as he opened the door; 'but don't be worried. I'll use Darnley's.'

It was indeed with a curious relief that he found himself in his friend's room. How refreshingly bare it was! The dressing-gown hanging on a nail upon the door, the three pairs of boots placed in a neat row at the bed's head, the grey schoolmaster's suit carefully folded upon a chair – all these objects, combined with the faint sea sand smell that came from the enormous sponge upon the washing-stand, brought to Wolf as he stood among them, washing his hands with Windsor soap, a wholesome and liberating peace.

He, a man, was in a man's fortress, a man's retreat! How cool and quiet did that strip of uncarpeted floor look, with the beautiful blue light lying upon it! How reassuring was the great flat tin bath propped up against the wall!

He couldn't help thinking, as he poured the soapsuds out of the white basin into the white chamber-pot – for evidently Darnley was allowed no slop-pail – how all his agitations had to do with women. 'I'm attracted to them,' he thought, as he instinctively pressed his friend's great sea-smelling sponge against his face, 'but there must be something in my nature that causes them to weary of me . . . that irritates them, that infuriates them . . . unless I behave with diabolical cunning over a long stretch of time . . . and that is difficult . . . that is almost impossible!'

Half an hour later, seated between Olwen and Mrs. Otter, with Darnley and Mattie opposite him, and Jason at the foot of the table, Wolf found that the airy chatter that had been going on, ever since they began their tea, about this and that aspect of the countryside, ended by troubling him with a bitter nostalgia. His brief holiday was already near its close; and how many days and months and years of his life was he destined to spend in that accursed schoolroom! Stirred into magnetic activity by the candlelight and the strong cups of tea, his deepest will set itself to overcome this menace. 'I am god of my own mind,' he said to himself; 'and when I'm not actually teaching history – or "Latin," as Jason would say – I can recreate, out of thin air, the essences of earth, grass, rain, wind, valleys, and hills! I've only to concentrate my mind on the living eidolons *in* my mind; and even if they put me into prison – and Blacksod School *is* a prison – I ought still to be able to cry at the end like my father, "Christ, I've had a happy life!" '

And as he continued to bandy jests with first one and then another, in his heart he thought, 'Lenty Pond, the Gwent Lanes, the Lunt Meadows ... there they remain, all night ... all the long windy nights ... there they remain; and I can see them, touch them, smell them, yes! and become them, whatever burdens Fate puts upon me!'

It was at this point that he found himself arrested by something Mattie had begun to say. She was speaking of some recent argument she had had with Darnley; and as she murmured the words, 'Darnley and I,' Wolf was suddenly struck by the nature of the look she turned upon his friend. It was a glowing, possessive look, full of just that maternal sensuality which he himself hated to receive more than any other look he could think of! But Darnley seemed to derive satisfaction rather than annoyance from this look of hers; for his eyes darkened to a colour like luminous indigo, as he responded to it.

'Ha!' thought Wolf. 'So *that's* how it has worked out! His love for her spirit has been accepted on its own terms; and his inhibition with regard to her body has become a matter of maternal solicitude to her. Ay, what convoluted beings we all are!'

'Go on, my dear,' he said cheerfully. 'Let's have it! Let's hear everything about it.'

Mattie met his eyes with an equivocal response. He knew she was aware of something hostile to her in his mood. There was a flickering half second of actual contention between them as their grey eyes encountered. Then she said, turning to Mrs. Otter: 'It was a long discussion we had ... it would be silly to tell it all. I happened to say something about plants having souls inside them ... no! trees it was ... and Darnley said that the souls of trees and flowers and everything else weren't "inside" at all, but on the surface ... I'm putting it right, aren't I, Darnley?'

'I don't – ' protested the schoolmaster gravely. 'I don't quite know what you mean by "souls"; but if you mean what's most essential to them ... colour ... scent ... expression ... appearance ... yes, it's certainly on the outside!'

'I don't understand, Darnley,' threw in Mrs. Otter, with a face full of nervous concern, 'how you can talk like that! We've been taught . . . haven't we . . . ?' She broke off and looked appealingly at her eldest son. 'What do you think about it, Jason?'

But Olwen, who had been keeping up a surreptitious dialogue with Jason during the whole of tea-time, raised her voice at this.

'*He* knows about it, because he's a tree himself . . . aren't you, Jason? And *I* know about it, because I'm a bird in a tree!'

Jason, who with flushed face had been encouraging her in her mischief – and Wolf fancied that both Mattie and Darnley had been the butts of their roguery – now became gravely sardonic.

'We ought to have Tilly-Valley here,' he said, 'to tell us what he's learnt from the Bishop of Salisbury about the soul!'

'I agree entirely with Darnley!' Wolf burst out with a violence that astonished himself. His annoyance at Mattie's maternal sensuality must have suddenly mingled with a sharp suspicion that Jason and Olwen had been making sport of him too!

'With Darnley?' murmured Mrs. Otter, still anxiously looking at her elder son to see if he had anything further to say.

'Wolf's not a bird *or* a tree, is he, Jason?' whispered Olwen, with teasing eyes.

'It's absurd,' cried Wolf excitedly, while his upper lip began to protrude and tremble so much that an observer might have been reminded of Miss Gault. 'It's absurd to talk of souls being inside things! They're *always* on the outside! They're the glamour of things . . . the magic . . . the bloom . . . the breath. They're the *intention* of things!'

His irritation at this moment was not lessened by a furtive taunt of the demon within himself repeating Mr. Urquhart's biting phrase, 'So you *have* a soul, then, Menelaus?'

'But, Wolf,' protested Mattie, in an obstinate and sulky tone, 'you're contradicting yourself! How can anything be intended and expressed if it isn't there . . . inside . . . already?'

Wolf bit his lip to restrain himself from an outburst of anger.

'It's all so confusing to most of us, Mattie dear,' murmured Mrs. Otter. 'We can only hope and pray that the Judge of all the earth will do right.'

The incongruous piety of this expression seemed to act like the old '*Ite missa est*' to the company about that candlelighted table. As Wolf rose to go, there swept over him a shuddering vision of what such encounters as this might prove to him in the future, when he had lost all his self-respect. As he said good-bye to Mrs.

Otter over the child's head, and felt that hot little forehead pressed against the pit of his stomach, and those long, thin arms clasped passionately round his waist, he realized that to assassinate his self-respect in the manner he intended would be to break the luminous interior lifepool that nourished all his happiness with its fleeting reflections! To feel toward himself in a certain way . . . to recognize himself as a person incapable of doing this or that . . . such apparently was the 'glassy essence' of that ecstasy that was his grand secret.

When at last the garden gate had closed behind him and he had entered the darkness of Pond Lane, he found that in his mental exhaustion all manner of queer little objects, casually noted during his months in Dorset, were floating in upon him. The bell-handle of Mrs. Herbert's door, the white scar on the hand of that old waiter at the Lovelace, the stunted laburnum branch in his back yard—his mind had to make a definite effort to throw off these things.

'I've got a sort of underlife,' he thought, 'full of morbid hieroglyphics. Something must have died down there, and the blowflies are laying their eggs in it.'

Gathering up all the spiritual strength he possessed, he flung his mind outwards, far over those silent reaches of meadow grass and fallow land. He imagined as vividly as he could all that was going on in that darkened margin of Blackmore. He followed the skulking of foxes under the hazels, the stirrings of hedgehogs in their hibernating quiescence, the crouching of birds on leafless boughs, the burrowing of moles under their hillocks, the breathing of cattle in their barns.

He imagined all these things so intensely, one by one, that he began to feel that he shared those nocturnal movements – that he was no stranger among them, but himself a furtive, lonely earth-life among other earth-lives, drawing, as they did, some curative magnetism from the dark greenish-black hide of the great planetary body! And he thought how stoically all these living things – the patient trees most of all – endured those diseased portions of their identities, those morbid under-lives, where the blowflies of dissolution were at work.

'I can do it!' he thought. 'It isn't for ever.' And in his necessity he laid hold of those two dark horns of non-existence, from the cold slippery touch of which all flesh shrinks back – the horn of the ages before he was born, the horn of the ages when he would have ceased to be. 'I can plough on,' he said to himself.

The clock in the mid-Victorian tower of the town hall was just beginning to strike a quarter to seven when Wolf reached the Blacksod High Street. The words of an unknown farm-labourer he had met on the road repeated themselves in his brain as he turned up his collar against a merciless downpour. 'Blowing up for rain, Mister!' and Wolf's mind turned these harmless words into a vast non-human menace, directed against him by some malignancy in the very system of things.

He stopped for a minute at the entrance to Preston Lane, to decide whether to go straight to Mrs. Herbert's and give his mother the cheque, or to let it wait till the following morning.

'If I were a bit more superstitious,' he thought, 'I'd curse Mukalog for this!'

He stood disconsolately watching the splashing of the water-drops in the puddles by the roadside. 'They don't *dance!*' he said to himself. 'Reality's always different from the way people put it.'

With an obscure instinct to postpone giving the cheque to his mother, he stared intently at those splashing drops, to see what they really *did* do under the flickering lamplight!

No, they didn't 'dance.' Each individual drop, as it fell, seemed to draw up the water of that dark puddle in a tiny pyramid; but there were so many of them that it was hard to focus the attention upon any single one of those minute waterspouts. When, however, he lifted his head, the volume of rain driving eastward along pavement and gutter took a continuity of form, like the identity of some desperate living thing bent on pursuit or escape.

Against this cold, blind presence he now resolutely pushed on. 'If there's a light in mother's room,' he said to himself, 'I'll go straight in and give it to her.'

True to the usual caprice of Chance, when it's invoked as an oracle, there *was* a light, and yet there was *not* a light. It was clear to him, as he approached Mrs. Herbert's door, that there was a glow in his mother's room that came from the fire and not from any lamp or candle.

'I'll have done something for *you*, old Truepenny,' he muttered, 'if you care anything what becomes of her!'

He opened the little iron gate and moved stealthily to the door of the house. Before ringing, he peered as closely as he could into the firelit room.

'God!' he gasped, in a spasm of irrational fury, 'if that brute isn't with her now.' There was, indeed, no doubt about it. Mr. Manley was snugly ensconced by Mrs. Solent's fireside, though all Wolf could detect of their two figures was the shoulders of the man, upright in a high-backed chair, and a fragment of his mother's profile as she bent over the fire.

'Oh, the brute! Oh, the brute!' he groaned, as he sneaked back, returning as stealthily as he had come. 'If they'd had the lamp lit –' he added weakly.

He crossed the road; and lurching forward against the torrential rain, he stopped when he reached the pigsty. A fantastic dread lest he should find the same firelit glow in Gerda's parlour – with Bob Weevil installed there, like a maggot in an apple – made him reluctant so much as to glance at his own house. Was Christie, too, sitting by *her* fire, acting the devoted daughter to Mr. Malakite?

Three fires and three women – and Mr. Wolf Solent leaning against the pigsty!

The rain now began to find his skin. A little trickle of ice-cold drops descended between his coat collar and his neck.

As he clung with his hands to the wet railing, he could hear one of the animals rustling in the straw in the interior shed. Was it ill? Was it moving in its sleep? Or was it simply guzzling in there . . . in warm, dry darkness?

He pushed the outer gate open, hardly knowing what he did. So here he was, standing shivering inside that so-often-observed enclosure, from which the familiar stench emerged that had been the accompaniment of all these eventful months!

'Weevil's with her,' he thought. 'I know it as well as if I'd seen his Panurge nose! He's with her. She's going to give him supper . . . or perhaps they're roasting chestnuts! She said once they used to roast chestnuts together.'

He fumbled about with his fingers for the latch of the inner door. How soaked with rain the woodwork was! A second pig began to stir now and emitted a feeble grunt. Then he gave up trying to find the latch; and pressing his two hands against the jambs of the door, he bowed down his head until his forehead rested upon the low wooden lintel. At this moment it was given to him to taste those secret dregs of misery, cold as ice and black as pitch, that lie dormant under the lips of every descendant of Adam.

Here he remained perfectly still, while it seemed to him that the wind was whistling a special little tune, composed for his benefit, through the dripping boards of the pigsty.

'Wishaloog! . . . wishaloog!' whistled the wind. . . . Then all of a sudden he burst out laughing. 'A comic King Lear! That's what I am! There's nothing tragic about this, Wolf, my friend! What you've got to do is to defy omens and fight for your own hand.'

He rose up erect, tightened his fingers round his stick, and straightened his shoulders.

'I've got Urquhart's cheque,' he thought, 'and by this time to-morrow – "Mr. Malakite at Weymouth." ' Once more, while he used these words, what he saw in his mind was the little blue veins under Christie's satiny skin – just above her knees.

It was then – and he had remarked it in himself before – that the constriction of lust endowed his spirit with a recklessness that was alien to his character. 'Wishaloog! Wishaloog!' whistled the wind; but mounting up, out of the chill of the nether pit, something in his nature, some savage stirring of his animal will, mocked back now at this impish derision.

'Whi . . . Hoo! *thee own self!*' he cried aloud, mimicking the tone in which Gerda's father used this West-country retort. Without further delay he left the pigsty, crossed the road, and rushed into his house. . . .

Not a sign of Bob Weevil. But oh, what a relief it was, a relief beyond anything he had expected, when he entered his own kitchen and found Gerda, arrayed in a spotless print apron, laying the supper.

He could see how pleased the girl was at the obvious genuineness of the emotion with which he greeted her. And genuine indeed his feelings were; though not all of them would have caused her equal satisfaction had they been exposed.

He ran upstairs to change his clothes, bringing the drenched ones down with him a minute or two later to dry them by the stove. The warmth of the kitchen, the steam that came from his wet things, the rank earthy smell of boiling turnips, the affectionate scolding of this beautiful young being, betrayed him quickly enough into that peculiar intimacy where the safety of virtue becomes the voluptuousness of content. The beat of the rain on the roof enhanced this security; while everything outside his four walls seemed a sweet shiver of excluded danger.

'I've agreed to finish Urquhart's book,' he said, 'and he's paid me in advance. But the chances are that I'll have to lend this money to mother. Anyhow, I'm not going to think about it to-night. I'll wrap it round Jason's idol for the present . . . then *you* won't want to meddle with it any more than I do!'

Saying this, he opened the dresser drawer with a jerk and thrust Mr. Urquhart's cheque under the stomach of the prostrate god of rain.

Though he did all this with an air of careless decision, it was with several anxious side glances that he scanned Gerda's face as he washed his hands in the little tin basin.

This process of washing his hands before a meal was one that he always prolonged with elaborate punctiliousness; and now, as he played with the iridescent bubbles, and squeezed the yellow soap into a foaming lather, he could not help making a grimace into the little square mirror that Gerda had hung above the sink, as the thought crossed his mind that although he had sold half his soul that morning, and was intending to sell the other half of it to-morrow night, he could still enjoy with childish satisfaction the pleasure of sitting down to supper, in his own kitchen, opposite his own girl!

As far as he could read her thoughts Gerda had decided to remain entirely non-commital over the matter of the two hundred, postponing, he suspected, any struggle about it until she realized more clearly which way the wind was going to blow. She gave him a lively description, as they sat down to their meal, of a visit she had had that morning from her mother and Lobbie. It transpired that Lob was to start his first term at the Grammar School when the holidays ended, and that Mrs. Torp, in complete ignorance of the ways of such places, was assuming that her son-in-law would be her son's constant and indulgent preceptor!

When their supper was finished, Gerda leaned over and reached for an open book that lay on the edge of the dresser. Lighting a cigarette as frowningly and awkwardly as if it had been the first she had ever smoked, she pulled the lamp towards her. 'I've got to an exciting part,' she said. And then, a second later, 'I think *Theodoric the Icelander* is the nicest book I've ever read!'

Her fair head, for she was a little short-sighted, sank down over the open volume; and Wolf, still seated opposite her on his kitchen chair, was left to stare at the polished handles of the drawer that contained both Mukalog and the cheque.

His pleasant relapse into the comfort of virtue ebbed and vanished with the girl's absorption in her story.

To-morrow . . . to-morrow . . . what *would* the upshot be? He sat bolt upright in his chair, holding a matchbox in one hand and an unlit cigarette in the other. It was as if he were secretly praying for some unexpected external event, like a sudden uncharted reef, to break up the dark-swelling wave upon which he was being carried.

Soon he let both matchbox and cigarette slip from his fingers, and, lifting his elbows upon the table, pressed his knuckles against his closed eyeballs. How they throbbed . . . those eyeballs . . . and what surprising shapes and colours those were, that appeared before his inner vision!

With a sort of sullen curiosity he watched those floating geometric shapes – green and purple and yellow and violet. 'Each of these,' he thought, 'might be a world. Perhaps it *is* . . . and from the point of view of the Absolute just as important a world as this of ours!'

And then something completely different from geometric shapes appeared. Well enough he knew what *this* was . . . even before its lineaments had grown distinct. . . . The unhappy one of the Waterloo steps!

'Very well, then,' he muttered under his breath, taking his hands from his face. 'Very well, then, I shall see thee at Philippi!'

And as he folded his hands behind his head, looking across at Gerda and her *Icelander*, he set himself to curse the misery the human mind can go through because of this wretched necessity for action, for decision, for using what is called 'the will.' What did a person feel when the hard little crystal of his inmost life lost its integrity? What did food taste like, what did the warmth of fire mean to such a derelict? A Wolf who had gone back to *that book* . . . a Wolf who had seduced Christie . . . how could such a Wolf ever swing his stick, ever drink up 'the sweet of the morning,' ever feel the wind upon his face, with the old thrill?

Among the fragments of their meal his eye now fell upon a chicken bone upon Gerda's plate, the last surviving relic of their meagre Christmas dinner. It was a 'wishing-bone,' from which Gerda, as they had pulled it between them, had won the right of 'wishing'; and it lay there now, with the library cover of *Theodoric the Icelander* just touching its forked and bare forlornness. But the sight of it sent Wolf's mind upon a long, fantastic quest. He seemed compelled, by some hypnosis proceeding from the wishing-bone, to make a Domesday Survey of all the trivial and repulsive objects he had ever passed by. Wolf and the wishing-bone set out together, in fact, upon a pilgrimage through the limbo of the world's rubbish heaps.

Some of the objects were commonplace enough; others were fantastic. The scavenging obsession of the wishing-bone allowed him to omit nothing that he could rake up out of a thousand obscure half-memories. The thumbnail-parings of a nameless old tramp sitting by a milestone on the Bristol road . . . the amber-coloured drop of rheum in the eye of a one-eyed doorkeeper of a house of ill-fame in Soho . . . the torn-off corner of a butcher's advertisement lying in a gutter outside St. Paul's . . . the left arm of a china doll thrown on an ash-can under the west door of Ely Cathedral . . . the yellow excrement of a dog, shaped like a dolphin adhering to the north wall of the Brighton Aquarium . . . the

431

white spittle of a drunken cabman outside the station at Charing Cross . . . the hair-clippings from an unknown head, wrapped in a French comic paper and dropped in the public urinal at Eastbourne . . . such things, and others like them, all parts and parcels of what humanity *sets itself to forget*, did Wolf and the wishing-bone redeem from the limbo of obliterated memory and gather in a heap on the kitchen table of Number Thirty Seven Preston Lane!

Was it a sign that his 'mythology' was already dying, that his mind became so easily servile to these rakings among the offscourings of the earth?

He struggled to shake off this curious morbidity; and in order to give Gerda a further chance of enjoying *Theodoric* in peace, he rose from the table now, and carrying their plates and dishes to the sink in the corner, he set himself to wash them up with a slow and concentrated nicety. This mechanical task, at which he was inordinately clumsy, acted as an opiate to his mind. He felt, as he proceeded to dry those various objects, as if, with the wet cloth he held, he were obliterating much more than ever the wishing-bone had called up!

Finally, before Gerda and he put out their lamp, he deliberately endeavoured to prolong this pleasant numbness by drinking several stiff glasses of gin. This gin had been their Christmas present from Mr. Torp; and most friendly did Wolf feel to his father-in-law, when under its beneficent influence he slipped into bed beside the already unconscious girl.

'It's the best of all drinks.' he thought. 'By God, I'll be economical with it! It's a good thing Bob Weevil doesn't like it.'

His mind seemed preternaturally clear now, as he lay on his back listening to Gerda's soft breathing, and to the intermittent wind-gusts that kept tossing into that darkened room a brackish odour from the far off Sedgemoor marshes.

'It's the stream of life itself that is important,' he thought, 'not any particular event or emotion! Just to be thrillingly happy over a crowd of little half-remembered, half-forgotten sensations . . . that's the whole thing. And it has got in it something much more than that . . . something more spiritual than anyone knows. It has effects beyond the visible world. It needs an effort of will as great as what saints and artists use! Oh, if only I could find words for this . . . but I never shall, I never shall.'

He stretched himself stiff and tense as he lay there, while like an aerial landscape, luminous and yet minutely distinct, his vision of things gathered, clarified, mounted up, as if out of a transparent sea.

'The stream of life is made of little things,' he said to himself.

432

'To forget the disgusting ones and fill yourself with the lovely ones . . . that's the secret. What a fool I was to try and make my soul into a round, hard crystal! It's a lake . . . *that's* what it is . . . with a stream of shadows drifting over it . . . like so many leaves!'

Instinctively he avoided any definite thought of Urquhart's cheque and of the morrow's supper. But they were both there. They were like a dull throbbing at the back of his closed eyes.

'What people call "futility," ' so his thoughts ran on, 'is just the failure of great emotions. But it's a good thing for them to fail. Let them fail! Only when they fail does the undertide of life itself rise to the surface. Futility is the transparency of the lake . . . what makes the shadows fall and float . . . beautiful . . . like leaves!'

Before he knew that sleep was anywhere near him, he sank, just as he was, like a drifting log in his own leaf-strewn lake, into the region where the living are as the dead. But the suppressed intention at the back of his brain awoke him into full consciousness again, just before dawn.

There was by this time an indescribable chilliness in the room, different from the chilliness of the rain and the wind as they had been when he had gone to sleep. Lying with hunched shoulders and hooked knees close to Gerda's side, his arm flung across the girl's body, he felt through every nerve this new feeling in the air.

His human soul seemed to leave its body and pass out of that small room into the great air-spaces that suspended themselves above the West-country. The interior chilliness of the darkness as the delaying dawn drew him forth, had that within it which corresponded to the spring of the year; only, *this* was the spring of one winter's night! There was a greenish, wet-growing stir in that dawn's approach; and the whole night about him seemed to shudder and contract like the cramped shuddering of an unborn child.

Not a muscle did he move as he lay there, hunched and inert, his stiff fingers folded around Gerda's right breast like the fingers of an infant around the toy with which it has been soothed to sleep. But within his curved skeleton his mind was lucid with the lucidity of something starkly at bay.

'Mr. Malakite at Weymouth' and that piece of paper wrapped about Mukalog had become part of his very brain . . . part of the machinery of his brain . . . but his mind was grappling now with something more than machinery. More? Yes! There was more . . . somewhere . . . more . . . than just this dawn-chilled Space, through which, like a wingless, tailless, beakless bird's head, with oceans for eyes, the earth he lived upon lurched, darted, oscillated, shivered, spun!

433

20

MR. MALAKITE AT WEYMOUTH

Wolf's inmost soul seemed torn up like a piece of turf under a sharp ploughshare, as, driven by a power beyond his resistance, he put one foot in front of the other in his obstinate march to the Malakite house.

As he moved on past the shop-windows oblivious of everything but the drama within him, he tried to anticipate the result of what he was projecting. His 'mythology' had always implied for him some sort of mystic participation in a deep occult struggle going on in the hidden reservoirs of Nature. Stripped of it, there would be nothing left but a stoical endurance – endurance of his own misery and a few attempts to soften the misery of others! He would be left with a soul that had the power of moving his arms and legs, the power of throwing itself into other people's tortured nerves – and that would be all! He would be able to deny himself this and that for the sake of these people, paying back what he owed, sharing the burden of the cruelty of the ultimate Power – but that would be all! The old Wolf, the old, obsessed medium for lovely, magical, invisible influences, would be gone for ever!

And even now, if he could only stiffen his will to leave Christie early that night, he might save what he was losing. Oh, what cruelty the Power behind life possessed, to transfix him upon such a dilemma! Oh, what cruelty it possessed! Well, he would defy it. That was the word. He would defy it. Whether he chose his 'mythology' or whether he chose his satisfaction, this ultimate thing was something so inhuman, that defiance was the only retort! If he chose his 'mythology' it would not be in submission to *this cause of all suffering*. It would be a league with invisible forces that resembled himself – compassionate forces, that were also defying this inhuman thing. Dante had said, *E la sua voluntade è nostra pace.*' He would reverse this saying. The will of the power behind life was clearly that human nerves should be confronted by monstrous, hideous dilemmas. To the end of his days he would protest! He would be the champion of human nerves against this ultimate tormentor. If he kept his self-respect and left Christie in peace, he would use his 'mythology' to defy this power. If he seduced Christie and lost his life-illusion, he would still defy this power. . . .

His mechanical advance had brought him now to the turn into the narrower street. In three minutes he would be in Christie's room! He took off his hat and looked up at the drifting rain clouds. The gusty rain made it impossible for him to keep his eyes open; but with his eyelids tight shut he cursed the power behind life. 'You Mukalog up there!' he muttered. 'You scurvy Mukalog up there!'

It was not ten minutes past nine by the small clock upon Christie's mantelpiece when she and Wolf returned to her sitting-room and closed the door, after washing up the supper-things in the little alcove between that room and the girl's bedroom.

Wolf sank down in the chair by the fire, which faced the window, and leisurely lit a cigarette; while Christie, seated upon a four-legged stool opposite him, a stool embroidered with pale early-Victorian pansies by the hands of her mother, leaned forward towards the bars, and with a thin outstretched bare arm prodded the coals into flame.

This done, she impetuously rose to her feet; and taking a spill from one of the blue vases that stood on each side of the clock, she also lit a cigarette. And then, resettling herself upon the stool, one lean arm encircling her knees and the other holding the cigarette, she turned her head round and surveyed the tumbled litter of books, some open and some shut, that covered the lavender-coloured sofa.

'No; I've tired of *Tristram Shandy*,' she said. 'In fact, I've got at present a reaction against all those old books which are so entirely *men's books* – full of masculine prejudices, masculine vices, masculine complacency! You know, Wolf, I think it's such a pity that the best old books should all be written by men. What I'd like to read would be an Elizabethan Jane Austen, a Jacobean Emily Brontë, an eighteenth-century George Eliot. It's so annoying to me that the best women writers all belong to the time when the custom had stopped of calling a spade a spade.'

There was something so quaint to his mind in Christie's fragile identity being stirred by the urge of drastic realism, that he looked at her in amazement.

'They're not so reticent now, are they?' he said.

But it was difficult for him to give his full attention to this dialogue between them. Another dialogue, far more important, was going on in his own mind. With concentrated interest he had already noticed that she was wearing brown silk stockings under her thin brown skirt. The sight of her bare arms made him shiver at the thought of her slipping off those stockings! It seemed absurd that he dared not even kneel down and unbutton the straps of her little-girl black slippers! The thought, 'She's never had a lover . . . no one has ever undressed her . . . she doesn't know what it is to be idolized from head to foot,' ran like ravishing little drops of quicksilver through his tingling nerves. 'Under that brown dress, under all she's got on, she's as slim and slippery as a bluebell stalk pulled up by the root!'

'I wouldn't call them reticent to-day,' he repeated aloud. But his mind raced back over the whole course of his life in Dorset as he looked at her now . . . so virginal . . . and so free from conscience!

Far more – oh, far more than Gerda, who seemed like a recognized, an *accepted* portion of his destiny – did this evasive little being seem to embody all his hovering, intangible dreams! It was hard to shake off a quivering cloud, beyond the cloud of cigarette smoke, that dimmed his vision, as he looked at her. How he longed to snatch away that brown dress, wintry-withered as it was, that hid her from him!

'Not reticent, perhaps,' she was saying. 'But it's utterly different in these days, Wolf. They don't do it for simple, mischievous pleasure. They do it for principle's sake, for the sake of science, for the sake of a new fashion in art. It's all premeditated and deliberate.'

He began to feel such an overpowering desire to seize upon her now, that the idea of losing his life-illusion seemed like tearing a mask from his face, a mask that hurt his flesh.

'How does your own writing go, Chris?' he asked in a forced, queer voice.

She reached over to the sofa and piled *Tristram Shandy* on the top of *Humphrey Clinker* and the *Anatomy of Melancholy* on the top of *Tristram Shandy*. As she did this she smiled sideways at him, while the smoke from her cigarette rose up as if from a hidden crucible of incense pressed against her knees. He had noticed before, that she never said anything important to him except while making some physical movement to distract attention from her words!

Reaching over still further, in order to balance the *Urn-burial*

436

on the top of the *Anatomy*, 'I've finished,' she murmured, 'my seventh chapter.'

'Is it a real story, then?' he asked, wondering if she would yield to him without a struggle if he took her quickly by the wrists.

Her defensive gesture this time, as she responded to his question, was to flick off a small grey ash upon the cover of *Hydriotaphia*. He had long ago observed with an amused interest what a dislike to the use of ash-trays she had.

'I hope it's real!' she murmured, in her most straw-like voice.

'The best thing would be,' he thought to himself, 'just to take hold of her by her hands and lift her up!' Aloud he said, 'What's its title, if you don't mind my asking that?'

'Guess, Wolf!' she said, without a smile. Indeed, she had never looked graver or more concerned than she looked then. 'I thought of it when I was out marketing in High Street the other day.'

'*The Grey Feather?*' he flung out, as he rose with a bound from his chair and groped on the floor. He had caught sight of the feather lying there at his feet. It must have fluttered out when she moved the book. As he picked it up, his contact with Christie's floor made him think of Gerda's floor . . . which had so different a carpet!

There was a moment, as he replaced the feather, when a feather-weight decided it. What he fancied made him pause was a sudden memory of the confiding repose of Gerda's expression as she bent so closely over *Theodoric the Icelander*; but when he recalled all this later, the conclusion he came to was that the touch of the feather had restrained him!

'*The Grey Feather* . . is your title,' he repeated, while Christie managed with fair success to conceal her face in a dense cloud of smoke.

'No,' she said, 'I've called it *Slate*.'

The astonishment with which he received this piece of news was quite genuine.

'Because of the view from your window?' he enquired.

'No. Because of – '

But the creaking of his wicker chair, as he resumed his seat with a helpless groan, drowned her faint words.

'I didn't hear, Chris,' he said. But he knew by the way she raised her chin that nothing would induce her to repeat what she had just uttered.

'What I'm trying to do, Wolf,' she went on, in a tone that seemed to him to have in it something like a challenge, 'is to express a point of view entirely feminine!'

437

'It will be the view of a feminine Elemental, then,' he said to himself. 'Does she think that she's like the rest of them? God! It'll be the view of a sylph in the Lunt mists, or of Jason's nymph in Lenty Pond!'

'All the clever ones nowadays just copy men,' she remarked, with the same nuance of defiance, holding her chin high and sitting very straight upon her stool. 'And none of the men themselves, or hardly any of them, *enjoy* writing outrageous things. They do it from artistic duty . . . and that's why it's all so different from reality, don't you think so? And so dull, as well as so disgusting! Just imagine what it would be like, Wolf, to have a Jane Austen ready to write of the most scandalous things! She'd write really mischievously, with zest and satisfaction, not like a solemn scientific journal.'

'Well, I'm sure I wish you luck with your *Slate*, Chris! Don't sponge out anything, though, I beg you. I mean, don't tear anything up, however much you revise!'

Even while he was uttering this harmless encouragement, some devilish analytical self-consciousness in him was noting the fact that he didn't like the thought of Christie's appreciation of any sort of Rabelaisianism. 'Christ! What a selfish, lecherous demon I am!' he said to himself. 'I suppose I want her response to *my love-making* to be her one and only awareness of the amorous element in life!'

He became at this moment intensely anxious to clear up certain things in his own mind.

'What feather *is* that, Christie, that you keep in your *Urn-burial?*'

She looked at him very straight now, with the eager, level stare of an interested child.

'A heron's,' she answered. And then, as if for the mere pleasure of repeating the word: 'A heron's, Wolf. I found it just exactly a year ago . . . two months before I first saw you. I was walking by myself in those Lunt meadows that you see from the lower road to King's Barton. You know where I mean? I was walking by myself along the river bank.'

Wolf continued to listen intently to every word, as the girl went on with her story; but even as he listened, his mind was still struggling with the shock of finding himself so shamefully possessive as to dislike the idea of her encountering any sort of amorousness where it was disassociated from himself. 'I really am scandalous,' he thought. 'I'd like her to be virginal in mind, body, soul, spirit, intellect, nerves, humour!'

438

His thoughts, before she had finished her story, had wandered a second time from what she was saying. 'Is this interest of hers in these shameless books inherited from the old man?' he thought. 'Is it a vice in her, like my own?' And his mind recalled the trembling, drunken ecstasy with which he had read that appalling book in the library window.

'And so I picked up the feather out of the mud and brought it home,' she concluded; 'but whether the heron caught another minnow, or whether the hawk frightened it away for the rest of the day, I shall never know.'

'I wish you'd let me see a page . . . just a single page of *Slate*,' he said presently. 'Somehow I cannot imagine the manuscript of a real story of yours. I cannot see you writing it, Chris, nor how you would hold your pen.'

The colour went to Christie's cheeks. 'Oh, Wolf,' she cried, 'don't ever ask me to let you see what I write! I love to tell you about it; but I think I'd die if you ever saw it.'

'Oh, all right . . . all right, sweetheart,' he said soothingly. 'You talk as if I asked to see your shift! By the way, Chris, I suppose you don't realize that I never *have* seen that room in there where you spend your nights?'

Christie smiled with intense amusement at this. She rose lightly, without a trace of embarrassment, took a candle from the mantel-piece, threw her cigarette into the fire, and opened the door into the alcove. A second door on the further side of this recess she opened with the same docile unconcern, standing aside to let him enter, while the flame of her candle flickered in the draught.

Her apparent complete freedom from any self-consciousness as she did all this had a complicated effect upon Wolf's mood. It made it possible for him to sit down upon her bed, and to stare in silence at the darkness between the white curtains of her window. It made it possible for him to ponder as to what her feelings and thoughts were, night by night, left to herself in this oblong little room. It made it possible for him to ask her whether she used the green lamp he saw standing on the chest of drawers on one side of the mirror, or contented herself with a couple of candles which, in old-fashioned Dresden candlesticks, stood on a little table by the bed's head. But it also seemed to make any attempt at love-making curiously difficult!

Christie slid down into a chair between the little table and the window; and as she did so she explained to him that she used the lamp till she was actually in bed, and then lit the candles to read by.

'I've often wondered,' she said to him, 'whether you can see my light as you come home from King's Barton.'

'And I've often wondered,' he answered, 'which of the lights I've seen from the top of Babylon Hill was yours.'

'We neither of us know,' she said sadly.

'Neither of us,' he echoed.

The flame of the candle she had picked up from the parlour mantelpiece was now blowing sideways, and the grease guttering down. 'I'll light the lamp and then you'll see how it looks,' she said eagerly. 'It's not an ordinary green. It's a peculiar kind of green. I wish we did know whether it could be seen from Babylon Hill!'

Wolf turned half round on her bed and let his shoulders rest against the woodwork above the pillow. There he watched her as she stood with her back to him at the chest of drawers, busied with the lamp. As the green light slowly awakened into being, there came over him an overpowering sense of this fleeting moment. Christie's small head, dark and dainty in that emerald-coloured glow, the shadowy nape of her little neck, the dusky fall of her straight sepia-brown dress, hovered before him at the end of that white bed, like things seen in a magic crystal. He dared not breathe lest he should break the spell! It may have been that unusual greenish light, glimpsed across the old-fashioned counterpane stretched before him like an expanse of shining water, or it may have been a hovering emanation from some old forgotten dream, unfolding, like an invisible nocturnal flower, from the girl's pillow. He could not explain it. But whatever it was, the sight of her there, bent down over that lamp's wick, enthralled him with a feeling he had never anticipated, with a sense of the possibilities of *new* feelings beyond anything he had known! When his normal consciousness came back to him, it came back with a heavy sigh; and with it came the thought, like the galloping of a black horse against the horizon, that when this girl was dead and he was dead *that* was the absolute end! Dreams of anything but of such an end were fancies – pitiful human fancies! Moments as perfect as this *required* death as their inevitable counterpoise.

With a furtive movement of his shoulders he suddenly found himself meeting the girl's steady gaze, as her face looked out at him from the little square looking-glass. With her hand still regulating the newly-lit wick of the green lamp, she was staring directly at him out of this looking-glass, staring with a fixed, calm, dreamy stare, like that of one whose mind is full of the end of some exciting book, just laid down.

440

'Take down your hair, Christie,' he said in a low voice, as he met this strange gaze. 'I've never seen you with your hair down.'

She gave him the most whimsical smile at this; but it flickered away as quickly as it came, and a frown appeared between her arched eyebrows.

'I don't mind,' she murmured, with a sigh, 'if you really want me to. But what's the use of it, Wolf? My hair's not pretty. It'll probably spoil your illusion of me.'

But Wolf's heart had begun to beat now with the old unconquerable beating, the beat of the rise and fall of the sea, drawing close to its destined shore. 'Take it down, Christie. I must see you with it down!'

Calmly and quietly, having given the shiny little knob of the lamp its final adjustment, she lifted her thin bare arms to her head and began to take out her hairpins. Her movements as she did this had the obedient docility, humble and submissive, of an Arabian slave.

Wolf's position, as he sat on the edge of the bed, with his back against the woodwork, had grown extremely uncomfortable. Nothing would have induced him to rest his dirty boots upon that glimmering counterpane; but his body was twisted askew in consequence of this self-denial, and the woodwork hurt his head. This physical discomfort had the effect of destroying what remained of that moment of vision, and of once more rousing in his nerves a spasm of the old tyrannous lust.

From that little oval head by the green lamp the waves of dusky hair slipped down now to the girl's slim waist.

'Oh, Chris, it's beautiful! You look perfectly beautiful!' he cried hoarsely, sitting up straight on the edge of the bed and stretching out one of his hands towards her with a fumbling movement. 'Come here, Chris, and let me see you closer!'

Moving calmly, and with perfect self-possession, she came towards him till only a yard of floor divided them. Then she stopped, fixing him with the same dreamy stare as if she had been walking in her sleep.

He got up upon his feet now; and between the light of the candle in the silver candlestick, which she had put down upon the little table at the bed's head, and the light of the green lamp upon the chest of drawers, they stood looking at each other, like two ensorcerized automatons under the power of an invisible magician.

She had pulled the green lamp, after lighting it, to the edge of the chest of drawers, so that its globe was now reflected in the looking-glass, a reflection that seemed to push backwards in some mysterious way everything else reflected there. The whole contents, indeed, of the illuminated mirror seemed to fall into a long, dwindling perspective, like the outlet from a shadowy cave, a tunnel-like outlet, full of mosses and ferns and tree-roots, which were all silhouetted against the round little circle of empty sky at the end.

Contrary to his own will, which would fain have hypnotized her to approach him, he found himself glancing aside from Christie's steady look, very much as a wild animal, hesitating whether to leap or not, might turn aside from the conscious expectancy of its prey.

This avoidance of her eyes gave him a moment's respite, during which his glance plunged into the receding depths of that looking-glass, depths lit up by the lamp as if by the swollen green bud of a luminous water-lily.

Round that green globe little phosphorescent rays flickered and darted. 'If I meet her eyes again,' he thought, 'she will come to me. She will let me undress her.'

A strange fear came upon him; and he felt as if he couldn't take his eyes away from the looking-glass. Those darting radiations became like the transparent moons, surrounded by dim haloes, that move along at the bottom of ponds under the sticky feet of skimming water-flies. In the turmoil of his agitation, with the sense upon him that this was the crisis towards which his life had been moving for weeks and months, that mirror seemed no longer to reflect Christie's bedroom. It seemed to him to be reflecting the mysterious depths of Lenty Pond!

His mind felt as if it were being torn asunder, so terrible was the swaying of his tight-rope of indecision! On the one hand he knew that in a moment he must draw down upon the bed this hushed, submissive figure, standing thus patient and docile before him. On the other hand, a mounting fear – a fear that had unspeakable awe in it, that had a supernatural shudder in it – held him back. Beat by beat of his heart it held him back. It tugged at him like a chain fixed to a post.

'Slip off that sad-looking dress, I beg you, Chris! Let me see you all in white!'

Had he whispered those words aloud? Had he only *thought* them?

The form he loved best of all was here by his side . . . pliant

442

. . . soft . . . submissive. This bed was *her* bed. They two were alone, without the faintest risk of interruption. Long ago had the last train from Weymouth come in!

It was Christie herself who made the next move. Naturally and easily she slid down by his side on the edge of the bed . . . and then . . . what was this? Had those thin bare arms been raised to her shoulders to untie the fastenings of her dress?

But still he was staring, obstinately, almost rudely – staring past her drooping profile into that devilish mirror!

The thought hit him with a kind of mockery how he had played with that lovely Shakespearean phrase about a white peeled willow-wand on his journey down to Dorset. Well, he was in a world of whiteness now. Phantasmal was the glimmer of her white counterpane . . . phantasmal the whiteness of her profile against the silky fall of loosened hair. There were white reflections in that mirror too! It was as if a supernatural musician had suddenly begun playing a 'White Mass'!

'Slip off that sad-looking dress, Chris!' Had he really uttered those words aloud? Or had it been no more than his heart speaking to his heart? Was one of her fragile shoulders free now of that dress . . . and become white, as everything else was white, at that fatal moment?

'You're looking at my mirror, Wolf?' Ah! She was speaking to him at last! But why did not the sound of her voice relax the tension? 'It's old, that looking-glass. It belonged to my mother.'

His eyes seemed to be dimmed now by a film of gauzy mist, which, as it floated before him, made everything vague and fluctuating. And then – without a second's warning – there appeared, at the end of the reflected perspective in that mirror on the chest of drawers, the lamentable countenance of the man on the Waterloo steps!

The pitiful face looked straight into his face, and it was in vain that he struggled to turn away from it.

All the sorrows in the world seemed incarnated in that face, all the oppressions that are done under the sun, all the outrages, all the wrongs! They seemed to cry shame upon him, these things; as if the indecision that tore at his vitals were a portion of whatever it was that caused such suffering. He instinctively lifted his hands to his eyes and pressed his knuckles against his eyeballs. 'Chris!' he cried hoarsely . . . 'Little Chris! my little Chris!' . . . just as if her form were being carried down some receding distance like a lost Eurydice.

443

She moved up closely to his side then, and touched his clenched hands with her own, not trying to pull them away from his eyes, but just laying her own fingers over them. 'What is it, Wolf?' she whispered with vibrating alarm. 'What is it?'

He reeled awkwardly to one side, and, snatching his hands away from her, sank down against her pillow. For a second or two the struggle within him gave him a sensation as if the very core of his consciousness – that 'hard little crystal' within the nucleus of his soul – were breaking into two halves! Then he felt as if his whole being were flowing away in water, whirling away, like a mist of rain, out upon the night, over the roofs, over the darkened hills! There came a moment's sinking into nothingness, into a grey gulf of non-existence; and then it was as if a will within him, that was beyond thought, gathered itself together in that frozen chaos and rose upwards – rose upwards like a shining-scaled fish, electric, vibrant, taut, and leapt into the greenish-coloured vapour that filled the room!

The part of his consciousness that remained still clouded seemed quivering with a vision of the girl with her hands raised to her shoulders in the act of slipping off her dusky dress; but as his full awareness returned to him he saw that she had left his side and was standing by the green lamp, her eyes fixed reproachfully upon him out of the foreground of that mirror of her mother's – of that woman's who believed in spirits – and her fingers occupied in fastening up her hair.

Automatically, and with a hand that shook, like a man's who has seen a ghost, he took out his packet of cigarettes and lit a match.

His cigarette alight, he got up from the bed; and walking with shaky knees across the room – he felt far more dizzy in the head than under the power of Mr. Urquhart's Malmsey! – he offered his packet to her. But Christie, with eyes whose pupils were so large that they completely dominated her face, refused his offer with a wordless shake of her head.

The girl's hands seemed to him to be shaking too, as she thrust in the last hairpins and pressed her two palms against the sides of her small head.

'Come,' she said, 'I'll put out the lamp now, and we'll go back to the sitting-room.'

When they were back by the fire, they both instinctively drew their chairs close up to the bars and held out their arms towards the warmth. Long-drawn shivers kept running through Wolf's body, as if he had been drenched in floods of ice-cold rain; and he felt certain that the slender form by his side was experiencing an identical sensation.

At the moment of seating herself there – it was in a chair this time, and not upon her four-legged stool – she had given Wolf a look that filled him with self-reproach. 'I have hurt her feelings,' he said to himself, 'in the one unpardonable way.'

Listlessly taking up the silver-knobbed poker from the side of the fender, he broke a great smouldering lump of coal into blazing flame.

'Did I,' he said to himself, 'actually beg her to undress, and then, as soon as she began to do it, act like a madman?'

'I can't have done that,' he repeated. 'I can't have done that to my little Chris.'

'The rain seems to have cleared off, doesn't it?'

As he made this remark, he felt as if not he at all, but some sardonic Lord Carfax, were making it, in cold-blooded mockery!

'I hadn't noticed it,' she answered faintly; and then, turning her head towards the window, 'Yes,' she said, 'it seems to have cleared up.'

'I must be,' thought Wolf, 'the most heartless, self-centred brute in Dorsetshire. Mr. Manley must be a considerate man of honour compared with me.'

'The wind's still blowing,' he said aloud. 'Wind without rain,' he said, 'is a different thing altogether from wind *with* rain. Don't you think so, Chris?'

'Very different,' murmured the girl, almost inaudibly.

'If I'd made love to her, in there, on her bed,' he thought, 'would it have meant *everything*? And if it *had* . . . would we have been miserable like this, or happy?' He turned his chair round and reached over to the sofa, picking up the volume of Sir Thomas Browne.

'Let me read to you a little, Chris dear,' he said gently.

'As you like, Wolf,' came the faint response, as she propped her chin on the palms of her two hands and stared into the fire.

He turned the pages of the book, sadly and slowly, carefully moving the grey heron's-feather to the middle of the 'Religio,' where it would not be disturbed.

When he came to one of those majestic, far-echoing passages – passages that had always struck him as superior, after their fashion, to anything else in literature, except certain single lines in Milton – he set himself to intone the familiar cadences in a low, monotonous sing-song.

445

He dared not give more than a furtive glance now and then at the delicate profile beside him; but his impression was – whether a true or a false one he could not be sure – that Christie was not unaffected by those plangent, cosmogonic litanies.

As for himself, as he read on, it seemed to him that the bitterness of their fate did soften a little. These human contrarieties, were they not, after all, so much sandalwood, so much cinnamon, burned in the bonfires of chance, but liberating a sweet, strange smoke, purged of the worst misery of despair? 'But the iniquity of oblivion,' he read, 'blindly scattereth her poppy, and deals with the memory of men without distinction to merit of perpetuity. Who can but pity the founder of the pyramids? Herostratus lives that burnt the temple of Diana, he is almost lost that built it. Time hath spared the epitaph of Adrian's horse, confounded that of himself. In vain we compute our felicities by the advantage of our good names, since bad have equal durations, and Thersites is like to live as long as Agamemnon. Who knows whether the best of men be known, or whether there be not more remarkable persons forgot, then any that stand remembered in the known account of time? . . . The number of the dead long exceedeth all that shall live. The night of time far surpasseth the day, and who knows when was the equinox? . . . In vain do individuals hope for immortality, or any patent from oblivion, in preservations below the moon; men have been deceived even in their flatteries above the sun, and studied conceits to perpetuate their names in heaven. The various cosmography of that part hath already varied the names of contrived constellations; Nimrod is lost in Orion, and Osyris in the Dog-star.'

As he murmured these rhythmical dirges with his lips, and got a kind of comfort from them and a doubtful hope that Christie did too, his own mind – like hers no doubt – went circling the bruised ground of their trouble, of this wretched dilemma of his, like a dragon-fly hovering over a stagnant pool.

'I must have,' he kept thinking, 'the most selfish and heartless soul in Dorsetshire. Mr. Manley of Willum's Mill must be far more aware of other people's feelings than I am! Oh, God, what would Carfax say *now*? He'd say, "So this is your delicacy – this is your precious consideration – to hurt a girl's feelings by your bloody equivocations far worse than by all the ravishings in the world!" ' As little by little the opiate of Sir Thomas's rhythms soothed his remorse, he shook away the thought of Carfax. But Jason's 'Lord in London' had no sooner vanished than his father's

446

skull took up the tale. 'Your metaphysical virtue, my most moral son, has caused more unhappiness this night to this Love of yours than all my sensuality ever caused to any woman! And what's all the fuss about? Nature can right herself. Nature can justify herself. It's these withdrawings and shirkings that do the harm!'

As he went on intoning the sonorous sentences with half his attention, Wolf seemed to see himself, under those imaginary strictures, reduced to the meanness of a cowardly hypocrite. His mother's hard, gallant voice joined in the chorus. 'I have only one word for you, Wolf,' he heard her say, 'and that is contempt!'

But underneath all these fanciful upbraidings, underneath the real comfort of his chanting of *Hydriotaphia*, there steadily went on gathering itself together, in the subsoil of Wolf's being, a certain obstinate recovery of his secret soul.

'It was my snatching at you like that,' he whispered to Christie, in an unspoken dialogue, 'that was the wicked thing! I should have made you far more unhappy if I hadn't seen that face. That face saved us both, and Gerda too!'

What kept hitting him to the heart as he glanced sideways at Christie's profile was its innocence. 'She doesn't look like a grown woman whose deepest self-respect has been outraged,' he said to himself. 'She looks like a proud little girl whose hidden fairy-tale has been violated by some heavy-footed elder.'

Wolf was honest enough with himself, in the midst of all these criss-cross communings, to recognize that there was, somewhere within him, a furtive upwelling of profound gratitude to the gods. His life-illusion *had* been given back to him! He was still the same Wolf Solent who had seen that face on the steps, who had seen that animal feeding in the paddock at Basingstoke, who had heard the milk-cans clattering on the platform at Longborne Port. He would not have to return to Preston Lane, to take up his burden, with his soul a shapeless lump of whale's blubber! He was still himself. He was still the old Wolf, whose philosophy – such as it was – kept its hand on the rudder.

'O Christie, O Christie!' he cried to her in his heart, 'I couldn't have been any good to you, I couldn't have been myself with you any more, if that face in your glass hadn't stopped me! It would have changed everything, Chris! It would have ruined everything.'

The inner voice of self-dialogue died down, as the outer voice of his monotonous intoning sank into silence; and the only sound in the room was the ticking of the clock and the faint, weird whisper of the wind in the chimney.

'Christie,' he said aloud; and so deep had been the silence, and so drowned had they both been in their separate thoughts, that the syllables of her name seemed to fall into an invisible stretch of water.

She lifted her head from her hands and sat up straight, fixing her gaze upon him in the old, steady, unfaltering manner.

'Yes, Wolf?' she murmured.

'I want to tell you something, Christie.'

As he spoke he couldn't help recalling the advice he had so often given to Darnley. He had told Darnley to explain everything to Mattie. Ah, it was easier to tell a person to explain everything than to do it oneself!

'I was reckless just now, Chris. I just snatched at the chance. It seemed so wonderful our being alone. But do you know what stopped me? Don't look like that, my precious! You'll understand when I tell you.'

'What, Wolf?' she whispered.

'The day I left London, from Waterloo Station, I saw a tramp on the steps there.' As he uttered these simple words he experienced a most curious sensation. It was as if he were smashing with his clenched hand one of those glass coverings which on certain express trains preserve from casual contact the electric bell that has the power of stopping the train. 'It was a man,' Wolf went on; 'and the look on his face was terrible in its misery. It must have been a look of that kind on the face of someone – though *his* sufferers were children, weren't they? – that made Ivan Karamazov "return the ticket." But all this time down here – *that* was March the third – ten months of my life, I have remembered that look. It has become to me like a sort of conscience, a sort of test for everything I – ' He stopped abruptly; for a spasm of ice-cold integrity in his mind whispered suddenly, 'Don't be dramatic now;'

'A test for everything you – ' Christie repeated, showing more spirit in her expression than he had seen there since they returned to her sitting-room.

'Well, a test for to-night, anyway!' he added, with the flicker of a smile.

She pondered for a minute with puckered forehead.

'Enough to make me do up my hair again!' she said, while little wrinkles of amusement began to appear at the corners of her eyes.

He longed to ask her whether she had actually heard him beg her to take off her dress. He felt completely confused about that whole scene in her bedroom – confused as to what he had said and what he had only wished to say. Most of all he felt bewildered as to what *her* feelings had been between that green lamp and that glimmering counterpane! Had she really lifted those cold bare arms, that he looked at now, so calmly, to unfasten that old-fashioned gown?

He decided, as he glanced at her shoulders at this moment, that it *would* have been those particular fastenings she would have to unloose to get off the brown dress.

'I wonder whether our time together to-night,' he said bitterly, 'will have helped to make your writing more what you want it to be and less of the sort that "copies men"?'

Christie gave a faint toss of her head and a faint tilt of her arched eyebrows. She got up from her seat and shook out her wide brown skirt with both hands. The combination of these gestures filled Wolf with discomfort; for it was as if he had said to her something so brutal that she had to shake it from her petticoats, like burdock-seed or cuckoo-spit!

'I really was serious, Wolf,' she said gravely, 'when I told you just now that I'd almost sooner be dead than read to you anything I've written. I'm not even sure' – here she moved to the window and laid her hand on the sash of the closed pane – 'that I shan't have to change its title now.'

'I'll forget,' said Wolf grimly. 'It's the one thing I'm good at. I don't know now whether it was *Slate* or *Slates*!'

She turned away and lowered the top sash of the window, letting in a great gust of damp night air.

The flame of the two candles on the chimneypiece blew wildly to the left; and the third one, in the flat silver candlestick, which she had brought back from the bedroom and had put down on her tea-table, began to gutter so extremely that a solid buttress of white grease formed itself against its side. Many loose pieces of paper were swept off their resting-places and were blown across the floor.

'I should think you'd aired your room enough already,' remarked Wolf, pressing his knuckles against the volume of Sir Thomas so that it should not flutter as some of the books were doing.

'It smells of peat-bogs!' cried Christie excitedly, holding her head out of the window.

'It must be a south wind,' he muttered, rising to his feet and moving one of the flickering candles so as to adjust its guttering. 'It must be blowing across from High Stoy; so it can't be peat you smell. I expect it's Lunt mud,' he added morosely.

449

'Whatever it is, it smells delicious to me,' she answered. 'I wish we were both on the top of Melbury Bub!'

'I wish we were both at the bottom of Lenty Pond!' cried Wolf fiercely.

She turned at that, startled by his tone, and closed the window with a jerk.

'What is it, Wolf? Why did you say that? I should think I'm the one to say that, not you! Everything that's happened this evening has been exactly as you wanted it to happen, hasn't it? Why aren't you satisfied, then?'

The indignation in her tone was in a way a relief to him. 'Let's have the worst,' he thought. 'Better in the open, while I'm here, than after I'm gone.'

'Christie,' he began, 'I *have*, I know, thought only of myself . . . and yet I *do* love . . . you know I *do* love you!'

She looked at him scornfully.

'What you always do, Wolf, is to get out of things by accusing yourself . . . but if you really *felt* what other people feel, you would – ' She broke off. 'Oh, I don't know what you'd do! But at least you wouldn't be having it both ways.'

Almost automatically, in spite of his remorse, something seemed to shut up within him like the shutting of a door that closes inwards.

'You're unfair – ' he murmured.

Her eyes flashed. 'Everything that happens,' she cried passionately, 'is only something to be fixed up in your own mind. Once you've got it arranged *there*, the whole thing's settled . . . all is well. What you never seem to realize, for all your talk about "good" and "evil," is that events are something outside any one person's mind. *Nothing's finished* . . . until you take in the feelings of everyone concerned! And what's more, Wolf,' she went on, 'not only do you refuse *really* to understand other people; but I sometimes think there's something in you yourself you're never even aware of, with all your self-accusations. It's this blindness to what you're really doing that *lets you off*, not your gestures, not even your sideway flashes of compassion.'

A certain direct and childish humility in Wolf's nature came to the surface now under this attack.

'I expect all that you say is true, Christie dear, and that you are "letting me off" yourself, in spite of what you say, lightly enough if all were known. I'm a strange one, I suppose, and there it is!' He smiled ruefully. 'But we're a fair pair when it comes to that, aren't we, my dear?' he added. 'And all the same, if I hadn't seen that face – '

All the fire of her indignant arraignment seemed to die out at these words; and as her frail figure sank down on the rose-embroidered sofa, it seemed to be entirely divested of any spirit.

'If that man's face,' she sighed wearily, 'hadn't appeared to you I should have known to-night – '

He moved a step towards her.

'What's that, Christie?'

She leaned forward and her eyes narrowed between her eyelids in an expression he had never seen on her face before. Then she continued, with a peculiar solemnity, almost like a young neophyte repeating a fatal ritual, 'I should have known . . . to-night . . . what . . . now . . . I . . . shall   never . . . know!'

Staring at that little oval face, with that strange expression of finality upon it, he muttered huskily: 'Christie, Christie, I love you. I love you.' His voice had a groaning intensity, like that of a branch creaking in a storm. 'I have been thinking only of myself. But I love you, Christie! I love you more than anyone in the world!'

She looked steadily into his face; and thus they waited, listening as before to the weird wailing sound that the wind was still making in the chimney.

This whistling of the wind brought suddenly to his mind that night at the pigsty when he had gathered together his deepest powers of resistance. He burst out with his favourite quotation from King Lear: 'The goujeres shall devour them, flesh and fell, ere they shall make us weep! We'll see 'em starve first!'

He caught her hands and drew her up to her feet with a flashing look that was almost exultant: 'He that parts us shall bring a brand from heaven and fire us hence like foxes!'

When he released her, a most whimsical and penetrating smile flickered over her face.

'I believe that something has happened to-night, or has not happened, that has taken some great weight off your mind!' she said. 'Is that it? You look relieved and relaxed . . . different altogether from when we had supper.' . . . As she spoke she glanced at the clock, and his own eyes followed. Together they realized that it was a quarter to twelve.

'Oh, what will Gerda do?' he cried. 'Christ! she'll be so vexed!' Blankly and irritably he looked at Christie; and in that expression of confused dismay there was – and he knew well enough there

451

was – a faint tinge of reproach. But the girl was apparently too tired to notice this.

He was unable to catch the faintest irony upon her anxious, sympathetic face, as she let him out by the little side door into the street. It did occur to him, however, as he strode rapidly down the echoing High Street, to wonder a little uneasily what kind of expression her face would wear when, alone in her bedroom, she looked at herself in her mirror. It was not, all the same, till he was opposite Mrs. Herbert's darkened house that the full poignancy of one of her remarks hit him with its barbed arrow-head. 'I wonder if that *will* be her destiny,' he thought.

'She was perfectly right about my selfishness, though. What a brute I am! Oh, my true-love Christie! What I do make you put up with in one way and another!'

He stopped when he reached the pigsty; for there was the light in Gerda's bedroom!

How different this home-coming was from all that he had expected! Well, that was the way things worked out! Instead of either of the great clear horns of Fate's dilemma, a sort of blurred and woolly forehead of the wild goat Chance!

He had managed to keep his life-illusion. His precious 'mythology' could live still. But at what expense?

'If you hadn't seen that face, I should have known to-night what now I shall never know!' O fool . . . fool . . . fool!

He crossed the road with dragging steps and opened the little iron gate as quietly as he could.

'I have thought only of myself,' he muttered, as he shut the gate behind him; 'and yet I love you, Christie. I love you! I love you!'

21

'SLATE'

ALL through January and February, Wolf lived out his life with obstinate, stoical acceptance. He led his pupils at the Grammar School patiently and thoroughly through the reigns of Richard II and Henry IV.

His interviews with Christie had grown gentler and tenderer, though in some ways sadder, since that night of 'Mr. Malakite at Weymouth'; and whatever deception of Gerda they still implied, Gerda herself gave no sign of suspicion with regard to them. His mother's new tea-shop, furnished with money borrowed at reasonable interest from Mr. Manley, had already proved itself a most promising venture; and Mrs. Solent's spirits, as the weeks passed by, were steadily rising. Wolf had worked at top speed during those two months at Mr. Urquhart's book, writing every day between tea and their late supper at the little card table by their parlour fire, while Gerda read a series of romantic tales.

Almost to his own surprise – and certainly to Mr. Urquhart's – the 'History of Dorset' showed signs of drawing to its close. Writing day after day from seven o'clock to ten o'clock, Wolf had come to hit upon a style of chronicling shameful events and disconcerting episodes that cost him less and less effort as the weeks advanced. What really gave him impetus was a trick he discovered of diffusing his own resentment against the Power behind the universe into his commentaries upon these human aberrations unearthed by his employer! The more disgust he felt for his task, the more saturnine his style became and the faster he wrote! Some of his sentences, when he revised them in cold blood, struck him as possessing quite a Swift-like malignity. He astonished himself by certain misanthropic outbursts. His habitual optimism seemed to fall away at such times, and a ferocious contempt for both men and women lay revealed, like a sullen, evil-looking, drained-out pond!

It was a surprise to him to find that this business of writing 'immoral history' lent itself as well as it did to his natural method of expression. Each time he carried his new quota of pages up to King's Barton manor, Mr. Urquhart seemed more delighted than the time before. 'Stick to the facts . . . yellow Menelaus . . . stick to the facts . . . and we'll show 'em for all time . . . eh, me boy? . . . what our "wold Darset" is made of!'

As February drew to an end, it became more and more probable that the anniversary of his reappearance in his native land – the third day of March – would be, as he wished to make it, the date of the book's completion.

As to Mr. Urquhart's cheque for two hundred pounds, it still remained where Wolf had first placed it – under the stomach of Mukalog at the bottom of that unused dresser drawer in Gerda's kitchen.

Several events of importance occurred during those two months of exhausting work. One of these was the acceptance, under Lord Carfax's patronage, of a small volume of Jason's poetry by a well-known publishing house. Not only were these poems accepted, but Jason received – so highly were they praised by the inner circles of London taste – the sum of fifty pounds as an advance royalty, an event which, when it occurred, a few weeks after the book was taken, seemed to impress the author himself a great deal more deeply than the many tactful letters that reached Pond Cottage from 'that lord of yours in London.'

Even more pleasing to Wolf than the success of Mr. Valley's suggestion about Jason's poetry was the upshot of his own advice to Darnley about his relations with Mattie. These two were definitely going to be married on the first Saturday in March, a day that happened to occur just one day after the anniversary of his own appearance on the scene. T. E. Valley had already begun reading their banns in the church; and on the strength of his approaching marriage, Darnley had obtained a small rise of salary at the Blacksod Grammar School.

On Saturday, February the twenty-fifth, Wolf awoke, after writing very late into the night, to a happy consciousness that Mr. Urquhart's finished manuscript lay on the card table in their parlour!

Saturday was a 'whole holiday' for the Blacksod boys, although for Ramsgard it was only a 'half,' so that Wolf had a solid expanse of forty-eight hours before him of delectable idleness before his work began again on Monday. The following Friday, the third of March, was the eventful day when, just a year ago, he had arrived in Dorset; and on the day after that, a week from this morning, Darnley and Mattie were to be married. Wolf surmised that there must have been some eventful conversation wherein Darnley had 'explained everything'; and it was apparently accepted at Pond Cottage that the rise in Darnley's salary – little as it was – would smooth over every new economic strain.

'I shall take the book to Urquhart after breakfast,' were the first words Wolf addressed to Gerda when she opened her eyes.

'And then we can change that cheque!' responded the girl excitedly. 'I've not teased you about it, Wolf; because I know what men are like. But now it's done! Now it'll be just the same as if he gave it to you to-day, won't it? We can change it at Stuckey's this afternoon, if you get back in time. No, I forgot. It's Saturday. Well, we can change it on Monday, anyhow. Oh, Wolf, what a good thing your mother didn't need this money! I'm going to buy a new carpet for the parlour and a set of dinner-plates and a new frying-pan and two pairs of sheets and a set of silver spoons – oh, and something else that I've always wanted, Wolf, and that's a grandfather's clock for the kitchen – same as mother has!'

Wolf's face clouded. 'I'm sorry you brought up that cheque, honey,' he said. 'I've not made up my mind about it. I've got an odd feeling about it. In fact, I have an idea that we'll all be much happier, much more lucky, if I just tear it up and hand back the pieces to him!'

Gerda jerked herself up on her elbow and looked at him with flashing eyes. 'Wolf! How can you think or dream of such nonsense? Of course we must change that cheque! You've worked for it. You've earned it. Do you think I'd have been so good and quiet about it if I'd thought you were going to act like this at the end? I said nothing when you told me it was for your mother. I've got my pride, though you may not think so; and I'd have sooner bitten off my tongue than for her to have said I stopped you from giving her money! But you never *did* give it to her. You just kept it. So I made sure it was only that you didn't want to be paid till you'd finished the job. And now you go and talk like this!'

Wolf's mind was so bewildered and nonplussed by this unexpected outburst, that he just stupidly straightened out the sheet, which had got rolled into a weft under his chin, and slipped slowly out of bed. He certainly *had*, as she said, completely misunderstood her silence about the cheque. Well, here was a new complication. But he must gain time to think. Perhaps, sooner than disappoint her as much as this, he *would* relinquish his idea of 'getting even' with his employer.

After all, he would be glad enough, himself, to have two hundred pounds at his disposal! He had already spent a third of all his and

455

Gerda's savings in the purchase of a cut-glass decanter and a set of wineglasses for Darnley and Mattie. It would be riches to have such a sum as this added to their account in the Post Office! All he knew was that ever since he had wrapped the cheque about the belly of Mukalog he had been profoundly unwilling to touch it. The thing seemed unholy to him . . . unholy. It was a sort of blood-money for the sale of his 'mythology.' He had pilfered back this precious possession . . . desperately, cowardly, meanly done so . . . by his equivocal behaviour to Christie. To fling down the torn bits of the cheque upon Urquhart's table would be an equivalent for many snake-like turns and twists!

But in spite of these thoughts he felt at that moment an uneasy stirring of self-reproach. He had treated Christie abominably that night two months before when Mr. Malakite was absent in Weymouth. Was he going to treat Gerda still worse to-day? 'It's all very well,' he said in his heart, 'to follow these niceties of honour for my own sake. But how arbitrary how monstrous, to snatch this money from Gerda when it means so much to her!'

'There's something in what you say, sweetheart,' he muttered aloud; and he began wrapping himself in his dressing-gown and tightening it round him in the way he liked to do, preparatory to opening the door. 'Don't get the idea I'm going to be silly or obstinate!' he added. 'We'll discuss it all later.'

There seemed to be a cold wind from the east that morning; and Wolf, when he reached the kitchen, was glad enough to find the stove still alight. But just for the sake of getting into the air he unbolted the back door and shuffled in his slippers across the yard. 'I'll fetch two or three pieces of wood,' he thought. The shock of the east wind cutting at his lean frame and whistling past it as if it had been the post of a clothes-line, roused a grim and yet an exuberant feeling in him that sent him back to the kitchen in high spirits.

'Ay!' he thought, 'how it all depends on these little things! What was that that mother told me about Carfax? That he used to "play" with these accidents, like a fisherman with a trout, making 'em serve his sensations!'

Back by the side of the stove he gave himself up to enjoying the flames that came out of that round iron hole. 'Jason was certainly right when he said that to have a roof over you, and a fire to get warm by, and three meals a day, was enough to be grateful for in this world.' And what about the straight, sweet, flexible body of Gerda? Wouldn't he be a fool if he let his craving for Christie kill every element of natural pleasure? And, after all, he *had* Christie. Had her, at any rate, in a sense that was as important to his imagination as Gerda's body was to his senses!

He covered up the iron hole with the bigger of their two kettles. This extra large kettle was a recent present from Gerda's mother; and Wolf suspected, perhaps unfairly, that the gift was an insult to their hand-to-mouth household! He ran upstairs after adjusting this kettle, and with his back to Gerda, who still lay supine, with the blankets tight under her throat, he began his slow process of shaving, while a thin inrush of bitter cold through an inch of open window kept alive the taut stoicism of his mood.

'You needn't think I'll get up while the room's as cold as this,' cried Gerda crossly.

'All right, sweetheart,' he said; 'don't get up. It doesn't matter.' But he thought in his heart: 'Unselfish or selfish, we are all forced to fight for our own hands! If I'm selfish in being happy this morning, if I'm heartless in enjoying this heavenly east wind, I can't help it! If no one were allowed to be thrilled by anything, as long as someone is made wretched by something, the life of the whole planet would perish!'

But his blessedness, whatever its nature was, was brought speedily to an end by Gerda's voice from the bed behind him.

'If you don't change that cheque, Wolf,' came her words, 'I simply won't live with you any more! I'm tired of the life we lead . . . and it seems to me that it gets worse and worse, instead of better!'

At his own image in the glass Wolf made a vicious grimace. But he held his tongue. What a different looking-glass this was from the one inherited from the woman who 'believed in spirits'! . . . But he held his tongue; and by various crafty tricks he turned her thoughts to other channels. It was not till the middle of their breakfast that he deemed it advisable to refer again to the two hundred pounds.

'I'm afraid I must take that cheque back to Urquhart,' he remarked abruptly. 'I have to live with myself, Gerda, as well as with you; and I couldn't endure myself if I thought I'd been paid for a thing like that book.'

She put down her porridge-spoon and stared at him.

'Why did you do it, then, if not for the money . . . working every night and not speaking a word! Do you think *this* is any life for a girl?'

He made a stupendous effort to put a caressing tone into his voice. The justice of her outcry had, however, hit him pretty shrewdly; and feeling ashamed of himself he began to lose his temper.

'It's hard, I know,' he said, 'Gerda honey, to make you understand. I felt on my mettle to get the thing done. And I *wanted* to do it. And in the way I've done it, it isn't such an awful thing.'

'I don't care what it is!' she cried. 'It's not the book I'm thinking about. It's the money. Oh, I do so want to get those plates and that clock! Do be reasonable, Wolf darling!'

She must have made as great an effort as he had done, to take this gentle tone, and he recognized fully the pathetic justice of her appeal; but something obscurely and dangerously obstinate in his nature seemed to rise up against her, something that he could actually feel, like a physical pressure, at the back of his windpipe.

'I won't say I'll tear it up, Gerda, and I won't say I *won't* tear it up. I know you do want those things, and I want you to have them.'

The middle of their breakfast seemed likely to be the end of it too; for both of them, with simultaneous instinctive movements, pushed back their empty porridge-bowls and got up from their chairs, facing each other across the table.

'I *do* want you to have them!' he repeated. 'And you're not playing fair if you think I don't! It . . . it goes much deeper than plates or carpets or clocks!'

His voice had risen now, and to his own surprise he found his lip trembling. What he felt was: 'How *can* she force my hand when she sees it's so serious to me? How *can* she do it when she sees that it's a matter of life and death to me how I act with Urquhart? How can she care so little whether I'm tortured by this cheque or not?' That particular word 'tortured' seemed to form itself into a wicked pellet in his throat, rising up from the nameless pressure at the back of his gullet.

'I never thought,' she cried, 'that you weren't going to be paid! And I sitting so quietly every night and having no life at all!'

Then, as he only fumbled with his unused knife and stared heavily at her, 'It's just what I expected from you 'Wolf,' she went on, a hard, mocking smile coming to her lips. 'I've always known you were the most monstrously selfish man any girl could live with!'

The ugly pellet in his throat became a rough piece of gravel that he *had* to spit out or it would choke him.

'How can you care nothing about my deepest feelings, Gerda?' he cried loudly, while the trembling of his fingers made the knife he held rattle against the porridge-bowl. 'Don't you see it's torture

458

to me ... torture ... torture ... torture ... to change tha cheque?' The nervous emotion he suffered from had grown to something out of all proportion to the occasion.

Frightened by his outburst, but supported still by her burning sense of just indignation, Gerda – still a practical housewife, even at the moment she felt like rushing from the house – went off to the stove to move aside from the fire the saucepan in which their eggs were boiling. Wolf, still shaking from head to foot, strode round the table, and, advancing to the dresser drawer, flung it noisily open. His movement brought Gerda flying to his side. What ensued then was all so violent and instinctive that it hardly seemed to register itself as a real occurrence at all in his agitated brain. . . . Their clock in the parlour had, however, barely ticked two hundred seconds before he found himself standing breathless and shaky on the pavement before Mrs. Herbert's house door, the manuscript of Mr. Urquhart's book clutched tightly in a hand that seemed to be all one single beating wrist-pulse!

'I must see mother,' a voice seemed to cry out from some long-obliterated bruise in the pit of his stomach – some navel-string nerve of prenatal origin. . . . 'I must see mother!'

He went to the door, and Mrs. Herbert promptly answered the ring.

'She's still at breakfast,' whispered the woman confidentially, when she'd closed the door behind him. 'She had a visitor last night,' she added. Wolf hung up his coat and hat on one peg in the little hall, and his stick upon another peg. Each of these pegs looked like the head of Mukalog, as he used them. He received a vague impression that the landlady had jerked an insulting and libidinous thumb towards his mother's room before she went off down the passage!

He knocked, heard his mother's indolent reply, and entered.

She welcomed him radiantly. She was fully dressed and looked surprisingly young.

'Sit down, my dear one,' she said, 'and smoke while I finish my coffee.'

He felt she must have perceived his agitation, but she made no sign of that knowledge; and as they chatted, easily and freely, about her new tea-shop, his heart and his two wrists began to stop their wild dance.

By degrees, under her hypnotic power, he even began to feel that he had made too much of the whole incident. Mentally he qualified and softened both his own anger and Gerda's anger. 'I'll run in and speak to her before I start,' he thought. And then: 'No! I'd better not begin it all over again! But maybe, after all. I *will* come back with the cheque changed!'

His attention gradually became given up, free-mindedly, to his mother's affairs. But he remained touchy and nervous; and when after a time the talk drifted round to Mr. Manley, this touchiness reached a climax.

'I can't make you out, mother,' he said. 'Either that fellow wants to get social prestige by persuading you to marry him, or you are just exploiting him . . . playing on his infatuation and using him. Whichever way it is, I don't like it.'

Instead of replying to him directly, Mrs. Solent glanced at the great manuscript-packet, which he had put down carelessly between her coffee-pot and her loaf of brown bread.

'What's that you've got there, Wolf?' she asked; and though apparently innocent, her question carried for him a mischievous implication.

'His book, mother . . . Urquhart's book. I finished it last night.'

Her eyes glittered like those of a triumphant witch, and her bright cheeks glowed like a couple of russet apples.

'A compromise with Satan, little Wolf! Have you forgotten all you told me when you left him? All that about his book being simply naughty scandal? Will you *never* face the facts of life, my son? Can't you accept once for all that we all *have to be bad* sometimes . . . just as we all *have to be good* sometimes? Where you make your great mistake, Wolf' – here her voice became gentler and her eyes strangely illuminated – 'is in not recognizing the loneliness of everyone. We *have* to do outrageous things sometimes, just because we are lonely! It was in a mood like yours when you came in just now that God created the world. What could have been more outrageous than to set such a thing as *this* in motion? But we're in it now; and we've got to move as it moves.'

She lifted the cold dregs of her coffee-cup to her lips and drained them with a sigh.

'Go on, mother,' he said.

She smiled at him – a swift, mysterious smile, neither bitter nor ironical, but proud and contemptuous, like the dip of a falcon's wing in a farmyard tank.

'Every movement we make must be bad or good,' she said: 'and we've *got* to make movements! We make bad movements anyhow . . . all of us . . . outrageous ones . . . like the creation of the world! Isn't it better, then, to make them with our eyes

460

open . . . to make them honestly, without any fuss . . . than just to be pushed, while we turn our heads round and pretend to be looking the other way? That's what you do, Wolf. *You look the other way!* You do that when your feet take you to the Malakite shop. You're doing that now, when you carry this naughty book back to that old rogue. Why do you always try and make out that your motives are good, Wolf? They're often abominable! Just as mine are. There's only one thing required of us in this world, and that's not to be a burden . . . not to hang round people's necks! My Manley-man, whom you hate so, at any rate stands on his own feet. He gives nothing for nothing. He keeps his thoughts to himself.'

Wolf was listening to his mother at this juncture very much as an unmusical person listens to music, making use of it as a raft whereon his thoughts are free to cross far horizons. It was when he heard her say 'your father' that this voyaging stopped abruptly.

'Your father never once,' she said, striking a match with so sweeping a stroke to light one of her favourite 'Three Castles' cigarettes that he felt as if she'd struck it on that skull itself, 'never once stood on his own feet! He clung to me. He clung to the Monster. He clung to Lorna.'

Wolf might have interrupted this invective, if a portion of his mind had not slipped off again to Gerda's kitchen. What did she mean by what she said at the end?

'He shirked everything,' his mother went on. 'He lapped up the cream of those silly women's love like a leering cat. He laughed at people who did anything in life. He wasn't afraid of being broken, because there wasn't anything in him hard enough to break, He oozed and seeped into women's hearts like bad water into leaky pipes. And he justified himself all the time. He never said, "This is outrageous, but I'm going to do it." He said' – But at this point Wolf began wondering why his mother kept her window shut when the wind was in the east.

'East wind is different from all other winds,' he thought. 'Something to do with the roll of the earth, I suppose.' And he imagined his soul shooting like a projectile out of that closed window – shooting, whizzing, darting against the sharp wind, till it reached the wind's home. And he visualized the wind's home as a promontory like St. Alban's Head. But his mother was still going on abusing his father. 'How she must have loved him,' he thought, 'to hate him like this after twenty-five years!'

'There was no hardness in him, Wolf, no ambition, no pride,

461

no independence! *He* didn't know what it was to feel alone! He sucked up women's life-blood like an incubus; and nothing would make him confess it – nothing would make him say, "Yes . . . it *is* outrageous!" He justified himself all the time.'

Wolf looked away from those fierce brown eyes, out of Mrs. Herbert's front-room window, into the cold iron-coloured sky, a sky swept clean of all softness by the east wind.

'I'm not going to quarrel with you, mother, about him,' he said heavily. 'I suppose I'm more like him than like you. But you're wrong if you don't think I feel alone!'

'My dearest one!' she murmured, with a rich gusto of tenderness in her voice; and stretching out her rounded arm, she stroked the back of one of his hands. As she did this her formidable lineaments assumed the warm, amorous playfulness of a dusky-skinned puma, dallying with its firstborn in a sunlit glade of the jungle!

'How much healthier-minded she is,' he thought, 'than I am! But so was *he*, too, after his fashion. It's the mixture of them in me, I suppose, that creates these miseries of indecision!'

'Well, mother darling,' he said aloud, as he got up from his seat, and, taking her head between his hands, kissed her lightly on the forehead, 'I won't tease you about Willum's Mill, if you won't tease me about the Malakite shop. We'll agree to be indulgent to each other's outrageous behaviour! I'll try and learn your philosophy and accept my badness as part of the game. Good-bye, dear one! I'll come in sometime to-morrow.' And with that he snatched up the manuscript from the table and took himself off.

He looked back at her window, however, when he was in the road – and there her figure was, smiling and kissing her hand to him! 'The truth of it is,' he thought, as he moved away, 'she was intended to be a *grande dame*, with a house and servants and guests, with a *salon*, too, perhaps, where political magnates came that she could chaff and fool and put in their place! It's action she enjoys. I can see it all now like a map! Life's simply tedious to her when she isn't stirring. How I must have disappointed her! How she must have hoped against hope in those London years!'

His mother's personality filled his mind completely, as he passed Pimpernel's and steered his way through the Saturday crowds in High Street. 'Her nature's never had its proper fling,' he thought. 'No wonder she treats people carelessly and ironically. She's like a great lioness whose only food for years has been rats and mice and skimmed milk! The mere brutality of that fellow appeals to her. At least it's something formidable and positive.

462

I wonder' – here he paused on the pavement, just as he debouched into Chequers Street – 'whether she lets the brute kiss her.' As this thought began to transform itself into an impious, unseemly image, he pushed a sprig of greenery of some kind that someone had dropped there, with the end of his stick, along the pavement, till he got it into an empty little space behind some railings, where a patch of grass was growing. 'God!' he said to himself as he recognized this spot; 'this is where I read her letter the day I ate Yorkshire pudding at the Torps', and she first spoke about coming down here! If I hadn't sat by Gerda that day and eaten that Yorkshire pudding and taken her up to Poll's Camp . . . I'd have been free now . . . to . . . to – ' At that point he tossed his thought away from him. 'It's no good,' he said to himself. 'When Chance has once started things, a sort of fate sets in that a person has to accept!' He moved on again down Chequers Street, observing, as he did so, however, that a small single leaf still lay on the pavement. His consciousness of this leaf worried his mind after he had taken only a few steps. He endowed it – thinking to himself, 'I believe it's a myrtle leaf' – with nerves like his own. He thought of it as being separated from its companions and doomed to be trodden underfoot alone. 'Damn my superstition!' he muttered, and forced himself to walk on. But then he thought, 'They'll be treading on it just at the time I'm talking to Urquhart!' This brought him to a stand-still, while indecision took him by the throat. He slipped his fingers into his waistcoat pocket. There was Urquhart's cheque! After that unthinkable scene with Gerda he *had* taken it from under the stomach of Mukalog.

'How can I expect the gods to give me luck,' he said to himself, 'when I leave living things to be trodden underfoot?' He stood quite still now, paralysed by as much hesitation over this leaf as if the leaf had been Gerda herself.

'If I go back and pick up that leaf,' he said to himself, 'I shall be picking up leaves from these Blacksod pavements till next autumn, when there'll be so many that it will be impossible!' He began to suffer serious misery from the struggle in his mind.

'If I force myself to leave it there . . . with the idea that I *ought* to conquer such superstitions . . . won't it really be that I'm getting out of rescuing it from mere laziness and making this "ought" just my excuse to avoid trouble and bother? I'll pick it up now,' he concluded, 'and think out the principles of the affair later on!' Having made this decision, he hurried back, picked up the leaf, and flung it over the railings after its parent twig.

But he had forgotten the east wind. That unsympathetic power caught up the leaf, and, whirling it high over Wolf's head, flung it down upon the rear of a butcher's cart that was dashing by.

'*That* wouldn't have happened,' he thought, 'if I'd left it where it was.'

The sight of the butcher's cart made him think of Miss Gault. 'I wonder what that woman feels,' he said to himself, 'now Mattie is to be married instead of going to a Home in Taunton? Does she realize the amount of old bitterness that underlies her meddling? But she *does* think herself into the nerves of animals in slaughter-houses just as I do into the nerves of leaves on pavements.'

As he moved on he seemed to see the whole universe crowded with quivering sentiences suffering from untimely mishaps, and nothing done to help. 'I don't care if she *is* a bad woman,' he thought. 'I don't care if she is revengeful without knowing it. The more people become *aware* of what goes on, the fewer living things will be tortured. I hope she'll never stop putting her nerves into animals. I love her for it; even if she *does* want Lorna's child to go to a Home in Taunton, instead of being married to Darnley!'

He arrived now at the Torp yard. It seemed hard at that moment to hurry by, as he usually did when he came that way, for fear of a lengthy delay. He glanced across the yard at the covered shed where the work was done. In a second he met the eyes of Mr. Torp, who was resting from his labours with an air of '*Requiescat in pace.*'

His father-in-law beckoned him to come in.

'Well, how be?' was his greeting as they shook hands. ''Tis long since Mr. Solent has stepped into me yard. Though us have seen 'ee, traipsing by, coat-flying as you might say from hell to wold Horny!'

'Rather a sharp wind to-day, don't you think so?' said Wolf genially, stroking with his hand the surface of a large uninscribed tombstone hewn from a block of Ham Hill stone.

'May be. May be. But I be wondrous sheltered in yard from they cruel winds. 'Tis het I do fear more'n cold, mister; though I have heard tell that wind be turble rough on pavement out yonder.'

Mr. Torp smiled complacently and pulled at his pipe. He talked of 'out there' with the superiority of a man who lived, sleek and snug, in the company of artistocratic tombstones. But this slyness and aplomb soon changed, as he led his son-in-law into the interior of his shed; and the two men sat down together on a bench covered with stone dust.

'Say, mister,' John Torp began, ' 'twere only yesterday that I thought deep about 'ee, dang me if I didn't! I were out, passing the sweet of the evening, wi' old man Round, to Farmer's Rest, and who should drop in for a game of draughts or summat but that there Monk from up at Squire's. They be a couple of devil's own, when liquor's aboard, them two; and 'twere good I be the man I be, with a headpiece what no small beer, brewed by the likes o' they, can worrit, if 'ee knows my meaning?'

Wolf nodded sagaciously, resting his manuscript on his knees.

"Twere along o' young Redfern them two sly badgers got to talking, and maybe them forgot I were thee's missus's dad, or maybe they forgot I were there at all, for I sits quiet as stone, 'sknow, when I be out from home. Anyway, they was talking; and what must thik girt bugger from they Shires say but that since you've gone back to Squire, and have took young Redfern's place, that poor lad's sperrit have been quieted down wonderful. He were taunting the life out o' they, seems so, that boy's ghostie! But since you've gone back, mister, like a dog to's vomit, if you'll excuse the word, thik sperrit have let they three parties sleep soft as babes.'

Mr. Torp paused and glanced nervously round him. He then took several long, meditative pulls at his pipe.

"Tweren't pretty,' he said, looking sideways at Wolf with half-closed eyes; "tweren't pretty to hear what they did say about 'ee.'

'What *did* they say, Mr. Torp? Come on! You *must* tell me now!'

The stonecutter looked about for some imaginary spittoon and then spat with extraordinary clumsiness upon the face of the big unlettered headstone in front of him. Wolf watched the white spittle slowly trickling down the yellowish surface, and he thought: 'What things there are in the world that have a definite place in Time and Space! There's Mr. Torp's "gob," as the Ramsgard boys would say . . . and there's that big round tear from Gerda's eyes that I saw this morning on the back of my hand as we quarrelled about the cheque . . . and then there's that leaf on the butcher's cart! Ailinon! Ailinon! What things there are in the world!'

'They said,' the stonecutter proceeded, 'that 'twould be thee wone self what would go next. They said the thing what made thik poor lad's sperrit bide where 'a ought to bide were the comfort of another party going his way. 'Tweren't pretty to hear 'un say that, mister; and 'twere well I *do* sit quiet, in the sweet of me cups, or they never would have spoke such words. But that's what they said; and so now I've told 'ee.'

465

He paused and sighed heavily.

'You've always been what a gentleman *should* be to Gerda's mother and me! But that's what them chaps said.' And Mr. Torp fixed a somewhat gloomy eye upon his own spittle as it descended the uninscribed headstone. 'A scholar like what you be,' resumed the monument-maker, 'won't give no credit to the wambling words of plain men like they. But I bain't no scholar; and they notions taunt me mind. 'Tis all very well for gentlemen to put down their thumbs at Providence. Them whose brains be work-sodden have to guard theyselves from He. If 'twere only plagues and pestilences He showered down, it *might* be all one. 'Tis they lightnings, murders, and sudden deaths what send we to cover . . . same as the poor beasties in field!'

Wolf shifted the manuscript upon his knee into an easier position.

'I confess I *did* notice,' he said gravely, 'about New Year, I think, that when I went back to Mr. Urquhart both Round and Monk picked up their spirits. I had thought Round's wits had gone for good and all. And I had thought Monk was getting much more nervous. But, as I say, I did notice that my going back there seemed to cheer them all up quite astonishingly! So . . . you see, Mr. Torp, I'm not at all ungrateful for your warning.' He got up as he spoke, and thrust his burden under his arm. 'But the point remains,' he concluded, with a hilarity that was a little forced, 'the point remains, what ought I to do to propitiate Providence and escape those terrible occurrences?'

Mr. Torp moved slowly to a mason's shelf at the back of the shed and returned with his chisel. Then, armed with his professional weapon, the good man tapped the great slab of Ham Hill stone.

''Tis no comfort,' he remarked, 'though I be the man I be for cossetting they jealous dead, to think that "in a time and half a time," as Scripture says, I'll be chipping "Rest in the Lord" on me wone son-in-law's moniment. But since us *be* talking snug and quiet, mister, on this sorrowful theme' – Mr. Torp's voice assumed his undertaker's tone, which long usage had rendered totally different from his normal one – ''twould be a mighty help, mister, to I, for a day to come, if ye'd gie us a tip as to what word – out of Book or out of plain speech – ye'd like best for I to put above 'ee ?'

The plump rogue looked up so grave, as he said this, touching the stone with the point of the tool and staring at his interlocutor, that Wolf hadn't the heart to treat it as the man's form of humour.

'I'll leave it entirely to you, Mr. Torp,' he pronounced with equal gravity, as he bade him good-bye. 'I'm surprised Redfern hasn't been content with all you've done for him. I assure you *I* shall be! But we'll hope that empty stone will have to wait a long time yet ... for Gerda's sake! Well, good-bye, Mr. Torp. I won't forget your warning, though. I'll fight shy of "murders and sudden deaths"!'

He walked off along Chequers Street, chuckling rather grimly. Absurd though it all was, he was superstitious enough not to be able to treat that drunken chatter at Farmer's Rest with the contempt it deserved.

He mind began now to revert to that final scene with Gerda. She had actually used physical force against him as he took the cheque from under Mukalog, a thing she had never done before. Her last words, from within the open door, as he went off, had been uttered from a countenance streaming with tears. 'You'll be sorry for this, Wolf! You'll be sorry for this!'

What had she meant by that, he wondered. Bob Weevil again! But he had discounted Bob Weevil altogether. It was just un-satisfied lechery with that boy; and Gerda's own words, referring to her coldness to him, had had the very ring of truth. But one never knew, in these things! Perhaps at this very moment she was writing a letter summoning Weevil to their home.

He had reached the turn to Babylon Hill now, and for a moment he wondered whether he wouldn't take this road and turn off to King's Barton by those larches! But he decided against it and walked on. When he got to the place where the lane leading down to the bookshop was, he found himself stopping again. 'What the devil's the matter with me?' he thought. 'I feel as if a lot of invisible wires were pulling me back to this town! Don't the spirits want me to take Urquhart's manuscript to him? Am I like William of Deloraine, in Scott's poem, with the wizard's volume under my arm?'

He looked at his watch. It was already half-past eleven. It would be after twelve when he got to the manor-house; and the Squire would undoubtedly want to keep him for lunch. 'He'd want to do that all the more if I gave him back his two hundred! He'd be in a royal good temper with me.'

He stood hesitating at this familiar point, where he had so often hesitated before. This, however, was the first time he had done so on *leaving* Blacksod. 'I don't think it would seem absurd to Christie,' he said to himself, 'if I went in for half an hour before going out there? I don't suppose it would make her feel that anything was wrong in Preston Lane?' He put these questions to himself while he stood facing the east wind, turning up his collar with one hand, as he clutched stick and manuscript with the other; and as he did so he thought once more of William of Deloraine burdened with the magician's book.

It always gave Wolf a peculiar thrill thus to tighten his grip upon his stick, thus to wrap himself more closely in his faded overcoat. Objects of this kind played a queer part in his secret life-illusion. His stick was like a plough-handle, a ship's rudder, a gun, a spade, a sword, a spear. His threadbare overcoat was like a mediæval jerkin, like a monk's habit, like a classic toga! It gave him a primeval delight merely to move one foot in front of the other, merely to prod the ground with his stick, merely to feel the flapping of his coat about his knees, when this mood predominated. It always associated itself with his consciousness of the historic continuity – so incredibly charged with marvels of dreamy fancy – of human beings moving to and fro across the earth. It associated itself, too, with his deep, obstinate quarrel with modern inventions, with modern machinery, and his resolve, as far as his own life was concerned, to outwit this modernity – not merely to resist it, but to outwit it – by a cunning as subtle as its own!

Damn these indecisions! This accursed difficulty of deciding, of deciding anything at all, seemed to have grown into an obsession with him. To *have* to decide . . . *that* was the worst misery on earth!

He felt a strong reluctance to see Christie just after he had quarrelled with Gerda. What hit him now most of all was not her streaming face at the end, nor that mysterious threat, which he supposed referred to Weevil, but the single big tear he had glimpsed on the back of his hand when he shut their dresser drawer.

What he fooled himself now into believing to be his motive when he *did* tear himself from that fatal parting of the ways and hurried down towards the shop, was his unwillingness to be landed for lunch with Urquhart. 'I'll catch him about two,' he thought. 'That's the lowest pulse of the day! And I'll get home to tea and make it up with Gerda at the highest pulse of the day!'

An instinctive desire to avoid setting eyes on Mr. Malakite led him to go straight to the side door. What was his surprise when he found that little postern wide open! There was the narrow flight of stairs leading straight up to Christie's room!

This time he did not hesitate. Stick in one hand, manuscript in the other, he ran up those stairs. There was Christie's door, also wide open! He entered and called her name, softly and tenderly. No answer! He passed through the alcove into her

468

bedroom. The cold grey light lay upon her counterpane like the first light of the morning upon a smoothed-out winding-sheet.

As he came out, he caught a glimpse of himself in that Merlinish mirror, and the expression upon his face gave him an unpleasant shock. Returning to her room, he softly closed the door. Then he went to the fire and stood in front of it, warming his hands. There was a tiny bowl of white violets on the mantelpiece, with two primroses among them, one fully out, the other in bud.

He bent forward and smelt this fragile bunch of flowers, and it was as if he had inhaled the very fragrance of its owner's soul. Then, led on rather by a nervous restlessness than by curiosity, he began wandering about the room, turning over books and papers. Suddenly, as he ran the tips of his fingers along the familiar books on her shelves, he came upon a large, thin exercise book wedged in between Spinoza and Hegel. This he pulled out and mechanically opened, his mind still thinking more of Gerda and the two hundred pounds than of what he was doing. But after glancing at a sentence or two in an idle fashion, all at once he began reading furtively and guiltily, standing motionless where he was and turning the pages with the feverish excitement of a sacrilegious thief.

He had not failed to remark the word 'Slate' written in large printed letters on the first page of the exercise-book; but what he was now reading was in the middle of the book, and it was one particular paragraph that caused him to draw in his breath with a faint rasping suction. It read more like notes for a book than anything else; but that might be her style.

'Shame? She felt nothing of the kind! Human tradition meant little to her. Sacred guilt. Forbidden thresholds. Just *custom!* Just old moss-covered milestones of *custom!* But the silence that followed when his footsteps died away? Drops; one, two, three, four . . . *four drops.* Drops of acid on the grooves of a waxed pattern. A girl's excited senses rousing desire in old age. What a curious thing! Filmy butterfly-wings waving and waving; and old cold lust responding. Curious, not terrible. A chemical phenomenon. Interesting in a special way. The opposite of tedious routine! Something startling and primeval. But how curious that a girl's senses, excited from one direction, should wave signals in another! Unconscious. Totally unconscious. Butterfly-wings quivering. Do thoughts come and go in some strange "substance" called mind . . . or are they all

469

there is? Memory. What is memory if there's no "substance"?
... She slid down the old slippery groove into the old deep
hole. Forgetting. A girl dissecting memory and forgetting her
shame! Why shouldn't she forget? He was a very old man. In
a few years, perhaps in less than a year, she would be looking
at his dead face. A few years more and somebody else would
be looking into *her* dead face. "To live so as to regret nothing!"
It must have been a young man who said that. A man, anyway.
Remorse as man's prerogative! Nature. It was in Nature that
girls hid themselves and covered their heads. Nature has no
remorse. Nature has no "substance" behind her thought.
Thoughts without "substance." One ... two ... three ...
Three drops of acid in a grooved, waxed pattern? The girl
smiled into her mother's mirror. Thoughts without "substance."
Butterfly-wings quivering. Unconscious signals. Little fool.
The old man meant nothing at all. It was all your – '

Wolf was interrupted in his reading by the sound of a door
slamming below and by quick steps upon the stairs. He closed the
exercise-book and thrust it back. In his haste, however, he put it a
shelf higher. Not only so, but he left it lying on the top of books
instead of among them. Then he went over to the fireplace. . . .

Christie came rushing in, her arms full of packages, her face
glowing with the self-satisfaction of a girl who has done some
adroit shopping.

'Wolf! ... You frightened me!' She panted a little and laid
down her parcels on the table. Then she snatched off her hat and
dropped it on the top of the books.

'I'm so sorry, my dear!' he said lightly, taking her by the
shoulders and kissing her hot forehead; 'but I found the door open
and came up. You don't mind, Chris, do you?'

He was dismayed to see her eyes turn, like the needle of a com-
pass, straight to the bookcase.

'You've been reading it!' she cried, breaking away from him
and rushing to the shelf. Hurriedly she possessed herself of the
exercise-book. Twisting the thing in her fingers till it became a
veritable trumpet of judgment, she struck the table with the end
of it. 'Wolf!' she cried, 'I'm ashamed of you! I knew I'd left it
out! I always put it away because of father; but I knew I'd left
it out! Directly I saw the door was shut, I thought, "Father's in
there, and I've left it out!" And now it's you who've done it!
Oh, Wolf, how could you, how could you?'

470

Perhaps never in his life – not even when he had to appear before that College Board in London to be reprimanded for his crazy malice-dance – had he felt so humiliated.

'I'm sorry, Christie!' he blurted out. 'It was wrong of me. I did it somehow . . . I don't know! . . . without meaning to.' He made a feeble movement towards her, where she stood by the edge of the table, her chin raised high, her eyes literally flashing, the curved lines of her lips much redder than usual! He had never never seen her look so beautiful. But her anger frightened and paralysed him.

'I only read a word or two, Chris . . . just one sentence . . . that's all.'

She swept the table with her doomsday-trumpet. Backwards and forwards she swung it, as if drawing a furrow in windy sand; and under its stroke the little volume of *Hydriotaphia* went whirling to the floor, where it lay face downwards at Wolf's feet.

Wolf shuffled backwards, expecting at any moment to see his own manuscript follow *Urn-Burial*. The thought of the heron's feather rushed through his mind; but he didn't dare to move lest he should vex her further. Foolishly he clenched and unclenched his fingers and stared at the band round her waist.

'I'd like to go away from you both!' she cried passionately. 'I'd like to go away, far from everyone, where no one could find me!'

'I'm very sorry, Christie,' he repeated helplessly.

'To read it,' she began again, 'when I wasn't there and when you knew what I felt!' Her voice grew husky now and choked in the utterance. Then a shiver went through her and her slight frame stiffened. With a long, scrutinizing look she seemed to stare right through his fumbling, bewildered consciousness.

'I'll go, Christie,' he murmured. 'Don't be too angry. I say I was wrong to do that. I'll go now. I only came in for a minute.'

She dropped the exercise-book upon the table; and pressing both hands upon her face, she drew them apart, against her cheeks and eyebrows, stretching the soft skin tight in a grotesque distortion. When her hands fell, after this, he noticed that the anger had gone out of her. Her expression had become gentle and sad.

'What's that?' she said, in a low voice, pointing to Mr. Urquhart's manuscript. Wolf hurriedly stooped down and picked up *Hydriotaphia*. He caught sight of the feather, lying safe between the leaves, as he put it on the table.

'The "History of Dorset," ' he said eagerly. 'That awful book, you know.'

He tried to speak facetiously.

'I gave the old chap's lechery a twist in my own direction. It's still pretty awful, but it's not just pure bawdiness any more. In fact, I'd like some people I know to read it. It's ferocious. It's like Swift.'

Over Christie's expressive face, its whiteness blotched by faint red marks from the violent usage she had given it, flitted a tender, ironical smile.

'*You're* like Swift, Wolf,' she murmured, 'coming into people's rooms and poking among their things.'

'There, Chris! See what you think of it,' he cried, pushing the great parchment-bound book towards her.

But she only mechanically turned over its pages.

'It's nearly a year since I began it, Chris. It'll be a year ago next Friday, when I arrived . . . going by the *date*, that's to say.'

She bent her head above the white parchment-covered book – it was really a form of ledger-book, that he had bought at the stationer's in High Street, but he preferred it to a pile of loose sheets – and when she lifted her face again, she had an expression exactly like a young archaic priestess.

'Next Saturday, then,' she said, 'isn't only your sister's wedding-day! It's the anniversary of your first coming to this room . . . of our first meeting.'

He made a second rather nervous movement towards her. But she repelled him by taking up the parchment-bound book again.

'I'm glad you went back to this,' she said thoughtfully. 'I always had an instinct that Urquhart would do you some harm if you didn't do what he wanted.'

Wolf laughed a forced laugh. 'You unscrupulous little thing! What if Urquhart *were* the Devil . . . ought I to go back to him just the same?'

Christie shrugged her thin shoulders. 'My mother used to tell me,' she said, 'that all angels could turn into demons, and all demons could turn into angels.'

'Merlin and *his* mother!' he threw out; but his face was as grave as her own. 'Christie!' he cried suddenly, after a pause, 'why couldn't you and I have a day off together, away from here some-where? Couldn't we go down to Weymouth, for instance? Say next Sunday, when the wedding's over? Gerda's mother always likes to have her come round sometime on Sunday; so we shouldn't feel she was – '

He was interrupted by a querulous voice calling Christie's name from the bottom of the stairs.

After what he had read in that exercise-book he had a funny shyness about catching the girl's eye. But she swept this aside with sublime unconsciousness. He couldn't tell whether she even *felt* his embarrassment.

'Good-bye, my dear!' she said with a perfectly candid and affectionate smile. 'Father's getting impatient for his dinner. Poor father! He'll have to wait three-quarters of an hour . . . well, perhaps forty minutes!' Thus speaking, she drew Wolf by the hand to the door. He had already snatched up all his belongings. 'Off with you!' she whispered. 'Quick! Quick! Quick! Father would want you to stay; and I don't like dinners *à trois!*'

He could hear her moving the saucepan over her stove in the alcove, as he ran down the shaky back stairs. His desire to escape from her room without seeing Mr. Malakite was stronger now than it had been to reach her room without seeing him.

Little did he notice of the people or of the things he passed, as he walked away from the bookshop! Once out of Evershot Road, however, his feet dragged slowly. What he had read in 'Slate' – those short, compact sentences – passed through his mind like depraved choirboys in white surplices. 'Have I done what she hinted?' he said to himself. 'Have I troubled her senses by my advances and retreats, until she's lost something that it's essential for a girl to have?'

He groaned aloud as he walked, and trailed his stick along the ground. 'What will the upshot be if that old man *has* begun persecuting her *like that?*'

Bitterly now he reverted to his childish fancy, that his stick was like William of Deloraine's spear. As he shuffled along, he began a deadly interior survey of his mental state. Like a black fly crawling upon walls and ceiling, his consciousness set off to explore its own boundaries. 'I have no certainty,' he thought. 'I don't believe in any reality. I don't believe that this road and sky are real. I don't believe that the invisible worlds behind this road and sky are any more real than they are! Dreams within dreams! Everything *is* as I myself create it. I am the wretched demiurge of the whole spectacle. . . . Alone . . . alone . . . alone! If I create loveliness, there *is* loveliness. If I create monstrosity, there *is* monstrosity! I've got to move this creaking machinery of my mind into the right position; and then all follows. Then I can stop that old man from persecuting Christie. *Then* I can make Gerda happy without the two hundred!'

A bleak, saturnine disgust with the primary conditions of all human life took possession of him. The insane fancy took possession of him that he knew something at this moment of what the guilty lonely Power behind Life knew, as it drove towards its purpose. Was he himself, then, in league with this merciless thing, that from his deepest heart he cursed? Did he know what It felt, confronted by all these shadow worlds, dream within dream, each of them unstable as smoke and reflecting only *thought* . . . nothing but circles of *thought?*

Just as when his 'mythology' was upon him he felt life surging with magical streams of sweet, green sap, so now it seemed as if he could sink through world after world and find them all blighted, all poisoned, all corroded by some perverse defect. The only comfort was that they were all equally phantasmal! Nothing was real except thoughts in conscious minds; and all thoughts were corrupted.

Had Gerda really meant by those final words that she would renew her relation with Bob Weevil? His mind visualized Bob Weevil now with an obsessed intensity. He saw his face, his clothes, his yellow boots. He saw his heavy gold watch-chain. Did the saints teach that one ought to *love*, as well as pity, every living soul? He could pity Bob Weevil. Bob Weevil had not asked to be born any more than he himself had. But to love the Bob Weevils of the world? Well! The great saints could do that. *They* could see the tragic necessity of birth branding the forehead of each child of Adam with a ghastly uniqueness! But it was too much to ask of *him* . . . too much. . . .

It was at this moment in his abstracted progress that Wolf was confronted by nothing less than the entrance to the little driveway – pompously entitled 'private lane' – that led to the villa of Bob Weevil's father.

'It must have been *this*,' he thought to himself, 'that, like a letter at the door, brought the water-rat to my mind!'

Led by a sudden impulse that he made no attempt to explain to himself, he proceeded to walk up this 'private lane.' The east wind moaned forlornly through the laurel bushes on either side of the path. 'He's invaded my privacy often enough,' he thought. 'Why shouldn't I invade his for once?'

'Is Mr. Weevil . . . Mr. *Bob* Weevil . . . at home?' he enquired of the maid who opened the door. She had friendly blue eyes, this maid, but she looked amused and astonished to see him.

'I'll go and see if Mr. Bob has come in,' she said. 'Will you take a chair, sir?'

She went off, and Wolf sat down obediently. The place was certainly the coldest, the most cheerless, the most forbidding entrance hall he had ever waited in. 'I prefer the Mrs. Torp kind of house to this!' he thought, as he fidgeted upon his glacial chair and shifted his shoulders to avoid its pseudo-antique mouldings.

Wearily he fixed a lack-lustre eye upon a heavy marble slab that stood opposite him, supported by carved alabaster columns. 'I suppose,' he thought savagely, as he struggled against a wave of overpowering gloom, 'I suppose Bob Weevil hardly extends his interest in ladies' legs to alabaster sphinxes!'

Not a single object in this entrance hall pleased him. As for the gryphon-clawed feet upon which those alabaster ankles rested, he could feel them raking and combing at his very bowels! He hugged his parchment-book, he clutched his stick; but he no longer felt like William of Deloraine. He felt more like the knight's dwarf, who vanished from sight altogether at last, calling out, 'Lost! lost! lost!'

Nothing mellow or friendly, nothing either rustic or urbane, seemed to have touched, even remotely, the devastating pomposity of this furniture. There was a tiny, shapeless curl of dust at the side of one of those gryphon-claws; and he looked at it with positive relief! There was something reassuring about it! It might have been in a cottage, in a shed, in his own parlour! It was a sign that he had not been transported into a place from which there was no outlet.

But even this bit of dust – *dust* being something that at least had an authentic place in human history! – failed to support him just then in what threatened to become a veritable dissolution of his being! The spiritual 'aura' emanating from the Weevil mansion attacked him like a miasma of desolation, blending itself with Gerda's anger, with what he had read in Christie's exercise-book, and with the thought of having to face Mr. Urquhart. The strength seemed to ebb out of him. Slowly he rose to his feet; and turning his eyes from the marble slab, he stared now at a gilded table, with a fringed mat upon it, supporting a bronze tray containing a solitary black-edged calling-card.

He leaned upon his stick and contemplated that card in an hypnosis of misery. Life seemed entirely composed of weeping faces, old men sneaking up bedroom-stairs, tombstones with spittle trickling down, and black-edged calling-cards. He felt as if the First Cause of the Universe were a small, malignant grub, radiating a deadly blight in withering, centrifugal air-waves!

475

He shifted the weight of the book a little. He shifted the balance of his stick. He felt as if, with stick and book, he were journeying through space; while the malicious grub, out of whose ill-humour time and space were born, aimed a sour-smelling squirt at him.

At this moment Bob Weevil himself came hurrying down the staircase. Wolf moved across the hall to meet him, thinking in his heart, 'The simpleton must have been tricking himself out all this while!' for certainly the suit, the tie, the collar, the socks, the shoes, worn by the 'water-rat' this Saturday afternoon, were at the very top of Blacksod fashion!

The young man hurriedly apologized for keeping his visitor waiting. Mr. Weevil, Senior, it appeared, was already eating his midday meal, but Bob had ordered an extra place to be set, and would Mr. Solent honour them with his company?

The lunch or dinner that followed was something that fixed itself indelibly in Wolf's memory. He decided afterwards that it was only his preceding struggle with the inert malice of the inanimate in that appalling hall that gave him the power to carry the thing through! Carry it through, however, he certainly did, and with an adroitness that amazed himself. For he received a startling shock at the very beginning. The presence of the old dotard at the head of the table, mumbling and spluttering over his food with imbecile gluttony, did not prevent Bob Weevil from laying every one of his 'cards,' if so they could be called, flat down before his successful rival! It appeared that Lobbie Torp had turned up half an hour ago – 'when I was with Christie!' thought the visitor – with a note from Gerda inviting Bob to go for a walk with her that afternoon, 'as Mr. Solent was away and she felt lonely.' Bob Weevil communicated this occurrence shamelessly, as if it were all natural enough. 'I suppose,' thought Wolf, 'it's perfectly natural to him. It's probably not the first time she's sent for him like this!' It also struck him that Bob Weevil was propitiating him by introducing a note of humorous, masculine *camaraderie*, while at the same time he was letting it be clearly seen that he regarded this unexpected event as a personal triumph.

'Can it have been, after all,' Wolf thought, 'just a piece of incredibly subtle cunning, worthy of the father of all water-rats, that chat about the maddeningness of girls' legs? And had Gerda too, after her fashion, fooled him, as men have been fooled since the beginning of the world?'

Following Bob Weevil presently into his own 'den,' Wolf thought he had never seen so many actresses' photographs as he now beheld;

and it gave him a reaction in favour of Mr. Urquhart's vice, as he tried to avoid this concentrated feminine ogling from every wall! . . . However!' He was soon stretching himself out in a low deck chair comfortably enough, while his mind, as he listened to his host's excited volubility, took its soundings of the situation.

Things were always returning upon him, he thought, in great irrevocable curves. A year ago he had found Gerda and Weevil in close association. A year ago he had been introduced by that old man to his daughter; and now, after all the intervening changes and chances, Mr. Malakite was there still, at Christie's side, and Mr. Weevil was here still, tricked out in his best, ready for a walk with Gerda! It gave him a disconcerting feeling, all this, as if he had been wasting his time in a maze, that perpetually led him round and round to the same point!

He wondered that it didn't strike Mr. Weevil as somewhat odd, that Gerda should be talking of 'loneliness' and 'Mr. Solent being away,' when here was Mr. Solent, drifting casually round, up 'private drives,' within half a mile of her! But apparently Mr. Weevil felt that Saturday was a day dedicated to the erratic wanderings of desire-driven humanity! At any rate he took it all for granted, with the easiest facetiousness, when Wolf finally shook hands with him in the 'private road' and made off towards King's Barton.

It was with many queer sensations that he stood at last under that well-known historic porch, waiting for the answer to his ring. A year ago next Friday he had come to this place! How hard it was to think of it all as only a year! It seemed to him as if something in this Dorset air had the power to elongate the very substance of Time.

Roger Monk opened the door to him. Wolf could see at once that something unusual was in the wind. The eye of the man 'from the Shires' was hunted and startled.

'What's wrong, Roger? Has anything happened?' He put all the nonchalance he could muster into this question, but in his heart he felt discomfortable misgivings. Roger Monk carefully and gravely bolted the great door. He had the air of a man who bars out an army of enemies.

'He's up there with him. He's been giving him a bottle of that Malmsey, same as he gave you, sir, but I don't like it when he drinks with any strange party, saving, of course, yourself and his lordship.'

'Who's with him? Who are you talking about?' enquired Wolf.

Mr. Monk bent his head down a little, so as to bring his face nearer to his interlocutor.

'I don't like the way he's talking to Squire,' he whispered. 'I'm glad you've a-come, sir. Maybe you'll be able to do something to stop him.'

'Who *is* he?' asked Wolf again.

'Mr. Otter, sir,' said the servant, straightening his back. 'Not *your* Mr. Otter, if I may say so . . . the other gentleman, sir.'

'Jason, you mean?'

The man nodded.

'He's been using words to Squire such as I never thought to hear spoke to he by a human lip.'

'What's Jason been saying, Monk? I don't see that it's any good my going up there, if they're both drunk? I know how strong that wine is.'

The man's face showed consternation.

'Oh, Mr. Solent, you wouldn't desert us when you've come back to us? . . . come back at the moment we need you as never was! Let me have your coat, sir. I'll take your parcel, sir.' And he laid an almost compulsory hand upon the manuscript book which Wolf was still clutching.

'I've brought this book for Mr. Urquhart,' said Wolf, submitting to have his coat and stick taken away; 'but what's the use, if he's –'

'His book, sir? His book? Is *that* his book?' cried the agitated giant, throwing Wolf's coat down on an oaken chest and approaching him as if he held a precious animal in his arms. 'Ghost of Jesus! What a day is this day! Writ and copied by handiwork! Ghost of Jesus! But I'm glad to see this day!'

His excitement was so great that he ran his fingers along the surface of the great ledger, stroking it as if it had a head and a tail!

'Come along upstairs, Mr. Solent! This is what my master has need of. Come along upstairs, Mr. Solent!'

Wolf followed his enormous figure as he strode up the stately Jacobean ascent, his hand on the carved balustrade. When they were outside the library door, the man paused and whispered in an inaudible voice.

'I beg your pardon?' repeated Wolf; for behind that closed door he began to catch the murmured sound of voices. 'I can't hear what you say, Roger!'

The man raised his voice a little, with a nervous sideways glance at the closed door.

'I took the liberty of asking you, sir, whether you'd step into the kitchen before you leave us. Old Man Round's down there with Miss Elizabeth. They caught some lad or other fishing out o' season in Lenty Pond, and they've come to show Squire a monstrous perch this lad hooked up. I dursn't say nothing, because of *he* in there' – and the man jerked his thumb towards the door – 'but maybe they'd like for you to see the fish. I only mention it, as Miss Martin and our maid be gone to Weymouth for the day . . . so if you'd walk straight in on us, sir, afore you leave, 'twould be a kindness!'

'Certainly I will, Roger. I'll be very glad to . . . as long as I don't have to eat that fish!'

Monk displayed a more earnest gratitude in his gipsy-eyes than the occasion seemed to warrant; and then, opening the door wide with a sudden jerk, he announced in a louder voice than usual, 'Mr. Solent to see you, sir!'

As the door shut behind him Wolf had a momentary feeling that the man was there still, holding fast to the handle, to bar any panic-stricken retreat. But what he saw now swept Monk and his movements completely out of his consciousness.

Hurriedly he moved forward towards the two figures at the fireplace.

They were in the same position as he himself and the Squire had been on that memorable day of the contract; but now, with this finished book under his left arm and the two-months-old cheque in his right pocket, the curve of recurrence leered at him with a sly difference.

Between the two men was the same table, with the same empty decanter upon it; and the logs upon the hearth seemed to glow with the same light. But Jason, instead of being seated, was standing erect, his fingers tapping the table's edge and his eyes burning with a black intensity.

'The Malmsey,' thought Wolf, 'has loosened his tongue. He looks like an avenging demon.'

What gave Wolf an especial shock was the way Mr. Urquhart himself was sitting. He sat, indeed, bolt upright, but he had twisted himself in some odd fashion to the side of his chair, against the arm of which his back was pressed hard. His thin legs were at an acute angle to his Napoleonic paunch, a distortion that endowed both stomach and legs with a disturbing separate identity.

The final token of abnormality in the man's appearance was not connected with his body, however, but with his head; for to Wolf's consternation the glossy black hair upon his scalp had *moved*,

479

moved about an eighth of an inch, pushing the parting over to the wrong place.

Mr. Urquhart's mouth was open; but this was not all, for his thin lips were inward-drawn over the rims of his gums, and there was a staring intensity of outrage in his face, worthy to be compared with that peculiar expression which the sculptor Scopas used to lay upon the hollow eye-sockets of his figures!

Both men were far too engrossed with what was occurring to do more than turn their eyes towards Wolf as he approached. Mr. Urquhart gave a perceptible shrug with his left shoulder. Jason's cheek flushed duskily. But not another sign did either make to greet him.

'You think you are different from other people,' Jason was saying, as Wolf came and stood by Mr. Urquhart's side. 'You think you have deeper feelings, because you own this big house and keep these servants! You think your ideas are wonderful, because you've got a great library. You think you have more respect than other people, because you've got money to buy it. You only asked me here and gave me this wine because those London newspapers praised me. You've always hated me. You've paid your man to spy on me. You're not a bit different from your friend Round. You like good meals. You like watching boys bathe. You like warming your feet by your fire and thinking how great you are because your father left you some foreign wine! You're exactly the same as everyone else, except that you've got an uglier face. You make a mystery of your life, when there's nothing in it to boast about except worrying people with your nasty fancies! You think your life is grand and devilish, when all you are is a silly old man with a boy's death on your conscience. Yes, on your conscience; but no more on *your* conscience than on anyone else's! *He* wasn't upset by you. He hardly gave you a thought. *You* weren't his friend. He used to laugh at you with his real friends! He only thought of you as a silly old man who liked his meals and his glass, just as everyone does. That's all you are. You're no wonderful, mysterious man of evil. You're an ugly-faced pantaloon . . . just greedy and stupid. That's what *he* thought of you, when he gave you any thought at all! Why did you ask me to come here to-day? Only because you heard that Lady Lovelace had been to see me, and that there was an essay about me and my art in the *Illustrated London News!* You think it's grand to have a head-gardener as a servant, so that you can say, "Ring the bell, if you please! Get me a bottle of foreign wine, if you please!" Everyone knows the real reason you pay that man to hang around. Only because you like to feel gentlemanly and refined in comparison with a great bully like that! Here's your new assistant come to ask for his pay, for copying out your liquorish tales! Do you think he takes any interest in you really, or cares a farthing for your writing? Not a jot; not a jot . . . not any more than – '

Wolf interrupted him at this point by flinging down the great white ledger-book on the table. The two glasses tinkled. One of them hit the side of the decanter with a silvery reverberation. Jason turned a stony face towards him. Mr. Urquhart blinked his eyes, moistened his lips with the tip of his tongue, closed his mouth, and shot at him a look like that which an experienced trapper, his right arm in the jaws of an infuriated bear, might cast towards a faithful dog!

'There's your book, sir!' cried Wolf, completely disregarding Jason. 'I finished it last night and brought it straight up to you. It's really something . . . *this* . . . that we've done together! If we can get it printed I believe it'll make an impression . . . even on Otter's attention.'

'Otter's attention' seemed, certainly at that moment, paralysed by the great parchment-covered volume, lying on the Malmsey-stained table.

Very slowly he bent down and opened it at random, letting half the pages lean against the decanter. 'You write like a person who knows Greek,' he said gravely to Wolf. Wolf bowed.

'I know Greek too well,' he replied significantly.

'He means he knows what's made you abuse me like this, eh? what, Solent?' And the Squire jerked himself into a normal position, straightening out his legs under the table and leaning back with a deep sigh of relief.

Wolf felt an absurd, an almost sentimental desire to lay his hand on his employer's head and adjust that unnatural parting. So it was a wig he wore, after all; at least *some* of it was a wig!

Jason bent down still lower over the book, holding the pages back with two of his fingers while his lips mutely repeated the paragraph he had chanced upon.

'I hope you haven't brought *me* into this History of yours,' he remarked, after a pause. 'I don't like to be abused any better than Mr. Urquhart does.' He straightened himself and placed his hands behind his back. 'I expect,' he went on, 'I wouldn't have talked to you like that, Mr. Urquhart, if you hadn't given me your best wine. For your second-best wine I'd probably have flattered you as much as Solent does!'

The Squire disregarded this completely. With a caressing and rapturous hand he began himself turning the pages, running his forefinger along certain sentences, as if he were blind and the letters stood out in relief.

'Are you tired with your walk?' Jason remarked, addressing Wolf, and politely offering him his chair. 'I ought not to have abused anyone like that; especially anyone who has such good wine,' he added, in a low meditative voice.

'You'll see how I've managed, sir, about the way it ends,' said Wolf, still itching to play barber to Mr. Urquhart's disorganized poll. 'It ends with the Puddletown incident; but I've added a sort of conclusion . . . rather a bitter one, I fear, but I thought you wouldn't mind?'

'Wanted the last word, eh, me boy? It ain't the first time you've wanted that! No, no, no, no . . . Gad! *I* have no objection!' As he spoke, the Squire lifted his head and stared haughtily at Jason.

'Otter,' he said. And his tone caused dismay to Wolf; for he thought, 'They'll burst out again in a moment!' 'Otter,' he said, 'I wish you'd do me the favour of opening that window over there.'

To Wolf's surprise Jason made no bones at all about obeying this request. He went off at once with firm, steady steps to one of the great mullioned windows. He went to the nearest one, not the one above Wolf's old place of work, but one much nearer; and when he got to it he turned round, and, with something almost resembling a friendly chuckle, he called out: 'I can't work the machinery of these grand windows of yours! Shall I just unfasten it and let it swing out?'

Mr. Urquhart threw a most whimsical look at Wolf . . . he seemed to have recovered from Jason's tirade very much as a piece of elastic that has been stretched to the breaking point but has been released in time sinks back comfortably to its former state.

'Unfasten it, my good man!' he cried. 'Never mind what happens! Unhook it and let it go!'

Jason shrugged his shoulders, and, seizing the window-catch did exactly as he was bid. The leaded casement swung heavily on its hinges, was caught by the wind, and was blown wide open.

Into the room rushed such a blast of cutting east wind, that Jason came hurrying back to the fire, chuckling, hunching his back, and making a grimace as if pursued by demons. The pages of the open book upon the table fluttered like burdock-leaves in a storm. Wolf closed the volume and placed the empty decanter on top of it.

'Now's the moment,' he thought, 'to give him back the cheque.'

Jason pulled a third chair towards the fire. Mr. Urquhart settled himself deep in his seat, complacent and imperturbable, crossing his legs and swinging one of his slippered feet up and down in a manner that indicated complete self-assurance.

Wolf looked across the table at him. 'Yes, now's the moment to do it,' he repeated to himself. As he made this decision, he thought of Bob Weevil, dressed in his smart suit, sitting with Gerda in their parlour. 'They'll never go for a walk,' he thought, 'in this bitter wind.'

The whole library seemed full just then of a nipping air; and he noticed that both Jason and his host began turning up their coat collars. But the cold was rapidly sobering them. That was one good thing! It *was* certainly the moment to do it now; for the Squire's expression had an ironical aplomb that indicated the return of sobriety, and Jason had poured out apparently all his reservoir of black bile.

But, oh, how hard it was to do it! He thought of Gerda's longing for the pots and pans, the silver spoons, the carpet, the kitchen clock. He thought intensely of his own desire for a dozen bottles of Three Peewits gin. Damn it all! The whole idea of giving it back was fantastic and superstitious. Yes, that's what it was – superstitious. And it was pure selfishness too. Gerda was doing everything for him – what right had he to rob her of their earnings? Those quiet evenings she'd given him for the last two months were what had finished the job.

'They've asked me to send them another volume of my writings,' remarked Jason suddenly. 'What do you two advise me to say I've got to have, before I send it? Darnley thinks a hundred pounds wouldn't be too much.'

'Two hundred,' murmured the Squire, with a sly glance at Wolf.

'Let's have your opinion, Solent,' continued Jason. 'You're one of these cunning dogs who know what's what!'

In a flash Wolf had jumped to his feet.

'Mr. Urquhart,' he cried, pulling the bit of paper from his pocket and spreading it out before the Squire, 'here's that cheque you gave me! I haven't cashed it and I'm not going to cash it. I've done your work for my own pleasure. I don't want a penny for doing it! You see it's the same cheque, don't you? Well . . . here goes!'

As he spoke he crumpled up the precious slip in his fingers; and, just as if he were retreating to make some tremendous leap, he stepped back a pace or two from the table.

The east wind was whirling round and round the room; and

483

both of the men, sitting huddled by the fire, lifted their heads to look at him over their turned-up collars.

But as Wolf jumped back, crumpling the cheque, what *he* looked at was not the face of the Squire, but the face of Jason.

As he lifted his hand, something at the very bottom of his soul fought for release. Jason's face at that moment was a thing he had to challenge, to defy, to surmount. The man's eternal derision of him had suddenly swollen up, towering, toppling, tremendous . . . like an ice wall. It had been gathering weight, this wall, for months and months; and here it was! His impressions moved more rapidly at that moment than light-waves travelling from Betelgeuse or from Algol; and one of these vibrations, flashing through his mind, hinted to him that the menace to his 'mythology' which Dorsetshire had brought, came through Jason and not through Mr. Urquhart. . . .

'Well . . . here goes!' And he flung the crumpled-up bit of paper over the table, between the two men's heads, straight at the blazing logs!

His action would have fulfilled his intention to a nicety, if he had not neglected, for the second time that day, to take into account the power of that east wind.

The little ball of paper was caught midway, whirled in an ellipse, and neatly and accurately – with what might have seemed demoniac intent – deposited in the centre of the Squire's stomach! Mr. Urquhart secured this unintended missile as it rolled down between his legs, and laid it with a careless gesture upon the table in front of him.

Wolf made a dash forward, but stopped abruptly; and very deliberately the Squire unfolded the cheque and smoothed it out before him.

'That's just silly, me boy,' he remarked calmly. 'No need to insult a person, when you've picked him out of the ditch! That's just rude and uncivil. That's unkind. There you are!' And with a gesture as grandiose and princely as if he were returning a rapier to a disarmed antagonist, he raised his arm and stretched out the thing for Wolf to take back.

Without a word Wolf submitted – received the slip of paper from that outstretched hand and replaced it in the identical pocket where it had lain since morning.

As he did so, he was conscious of two dominant feelings, a sensation of sickening shame, as if he had been caught stealing a piece of silver from the communion-plate, and a puerile thrill of

484

delight to think of Gerda's pleasure over the carpet, the clock, and the new spoons!

As this event occurred, the countenance of Jason Otter relaxed into a thousand wrinkles. Up went his hand to his mouth, to hide a chuckle worthy of Mukalog himself. But the only comment he uttered was a murmured 'Boss-eye!' . . . a preparatory-school expression that had not entered Wolf's ears since his childhood in Ramsgard.

'May I ask you to close that window again, Otter?' said Mr. Urquhart in his silkiest tone, removing, as he did so, with the tip of his finger, a drop of wine that had trickled down from the outside of the decanter upon the cover of the manuscript.

While Jason was fumbling with the window, Wolf had begun a series of preoccupied pacings, up and down, across and back, over the expanse of the room.

When the window was closed he stopped and spoke.

'Monk tells me that Mr. Round is in the kitchen and has brought a fish to show you – a large perch – caught out of season. Do you mind if I run in and see it before I go? I'm afraid I must be off now. I'm glad you're pleased with the look of our book, sir! And I thank you for this money. It was ridiculous of me to – ' He broke off. 'I shall change it at Stuckey's on Monday. It'll keep the pot boiling splendidly, sir.' . . .

The time that passed between his utterance of that final word 'splendidly' and the entrance of all three of them into Mr. Urquhart's kitchen did not present itself to him in the form of the passing of so many minutes. It presented itself as one shattering question, addressed by Wolf Solent *to* Wolf Solent, as to whether this crowning defeat over the cheque had really done at last the thing he dreaded! Would he find, when he took up his life again, that his 'mythology' was stone dead . . . dead as Jimmy Redfern?

Beautiful in their blue-black intensity, the great dark stripes over the metallic scales of the perch – caught out of season – brought back to Wolf's mind a certain inland pool, near Weymouth backwater, where he had once hooked a small specimen of this particular fish, which his father had made him throw back again. As it had swum away through the aqueous dimness, between two great branching pickerel-weed stalks, he had had an ecstasy in thinking of that lovely, translucent underworld, completely different from his, in which, however, the pale-blooded inhabitants knew every hill and hollow, just as intimately – nor with such very different associations either – as he knew his own world.

Spacious and noble was the kitchen at Barton Manor; but somehow, as Wolf took that fish into his hands and entered into the overpowering emanation of its dead identity – its pale blood drops, its sticky iridescent scales, its mud-pungent smell – he was seized with a sudden shock of intense craving for that barren, brackish country around Weymouth where his 'mythology' had first been revealed to him. 'Which of us five men,' he thought, 'is most like a fish? It's the best symbol of the Unutterable that there is!'

Laying the fish down, while Mr. Round explained to the Squire and Jason how his niece had caught the poacher – and it turned out, as the innkeeper went on, that this poacher was none other than Lobbie Torp, who had been over there soon after dawn – Wolf stood aside, conversing with Miss Elizabeth.

'I congratulate you on your uncle's recovery,' he said. 'I often felt so sorry for you after that day we met at the pond.'

The 'automatic young lady' wetted her lips with the tip of a little snake-like tongue and whispered something almost inaudible. Wolf drew back further with her till they were out of hearing of the rest.

'I don't know why I should tell you this, Mr. Solent,' she said, with an air of sentimental hestitation.

'I'm afraid I didn't hear,' he replied rather coldly.

'I don't often tell strangers anything,' she went on. 'But seeing your lady's brother, at *that* time in the morning, and finding him with this fish and everything, put it in my head to tell you . . . and then I heard you were here.'

'I am sure I'm much obliged to you, Miss Round,' he said, with a lack of curiosity that verged on impoliteness. 'It's . . . very kind of you . . . to . . . remember me.'

But as he lifted his fingers to brush away a fly from his face, Miss Round, Mr. Urquhart, Jason, Monk – all receded and faded before him, till they became small, insignificant, wavering shadows! The smell of the dead fish, as he caught it from his raised hand, touched that spacious kitchen and turned it into thin air. In its place there appeared the hot, powdery sands by the King's statue at Weymouth, the tethered donkeys, the goat-carriages, the peaked bathing-machines. In its place appeared the grass-green seaweed clinging to the black posts of half-obliterated breakwaters. In its place appeared the bow window of the draw-ing-room in Brunswick Terrace, where, in those early mornings, as he watched his grandmother's maid shake the duster over the sill, there always hung a peculiar odour of sun-dried woodwork, mingled with the salt of the open sea!

'Your wife's father was there, sir,' was what he heard now, with at least a quarter of his mind. 'But he had been drinking and was all so mazed-like that he couldn't hear what uncle and Monk were saying. But *I* heard them, though they didn't know I heard them. And oh, Mr. Solent, they're all after you; they're all watching you like dogs at a rabbit-hole! They're just pushing you on to it . . . and that's God's truth!'

She had been whispering all this with flushed cheeks and an intense gaze fixed upon him.

Wolf's attention began to return.

'Pushing me on to what?' he replied, in equally low tones.

'I were born in Barton,' the girl whispered. 'I know every stick and stone of the place; but I didn't know 'twere as bad as I learned it that day.'

'What do you mean?' he murmured.

'They said,' she continued rapidly, 'that every Urquhart what's lived at House since Noll Cromwell's reign has drove some young man into Lenty Pond! They said 'twere only the Reverend Valley's league with Jesus what made young Redfern die in's bed, 'stead of drowning hisself! They said for certain *sure* you'd be the one to go next. All the aged folk in village do be watching for it, they said – them as is wise in what was and must be! They said 'twere a good day for King's Barton when you came here, foreign as you be! Uncle said there were Scripture for it. He first knew there were Scripture for it, he said, when Mr. Valley drove his voices away from his poor ears and he stopped worrying. "Some *must* go that way," he said, "while pond be pond. And if it ain't I, 'twill be he," he said. I knew who 'twere they were talking of by their fleering nods.'

The girl paused. Wolf noticed that her eyes had grown liquid and soft. A feeling of undeniable discomfort rose up within him. 'What a superstitious idiot I am!' he thought. 'The automatic young lady has taken a fancy to me, that's all it is! This is her way of starting an intimacy. Well, Miss Round,' he said gravely, 'I think it's very nice of you to be so concerned about me. But you can set your mind at rest. All villages have these legends. Besides . . . who knows? . . . I may be such a crafty scapegoat that I'll bear the burden without turning a hair!'

She opened her mouth; she opened her blue eyes wide; she distended her little round nostrils.

487

'Go back where you came from, Mr. Solent dear!' she whispered. 'Go back to London afore anyone can push you to it! I shivered in my breasts, for fear for 'ee, when I saw how bitter cold that pond were in the horns of dawn! 'Tweren't only the sight of Lobbie Torp fishing against the law what made me shake. I've thought of you and dreamed of you, Mr. Solent, yes I have; and I'm not ashamed of it, ever since I first set eyes on you!'

Wolf glanced nervously across the kitchen; but what he heard and saw reassured him. His singular interview with Miss Bess seemed totally disregarded by the others. Jason was evidently propitiating Roger Monk with the most fawning civility; while the Squire and the innkeeper were occupied in weighing the perch.

Wolf was impressed more than he could have foreseen by the girl's manner; nor had he missed that poetical expression of hers – 'the horns of dawn.' He began a humble and equivocal answer to her startling outburst, trying to explain to her the subtle manner in which these wild rumours, drawing their sap from the human passion for the supernatural, gathered weight in the countryside. He was a little dismayed, however, by the reckless response in his own fingers, which seemed to be reciprocating the ardent pressure of hers, as he bade her good-bye! Had he lost *all* integrity of emotion, he asked himself, as he went across to take leave of the others? Had his retention of that cheque undermined the whole dignity and self-control of his nature? Or was it that what he had accidentally discovered as to the Lesbianism of this strange girl appealed to something perverse in his imagination?

Once out of the house, however – once clear of the bare raked-over flower-beds, beds whose patches of yellow crocuses and jonquil buds seemed shrinking back into the earth under that biting wind – he threw those feelings from him and took the shortest way to the Blacksod road! This led him past the church-yard and the vicarage gate; and he scarcely knew whether his jarred nerves sympathized more vibrantly with the frostbitten population under the grass or with the obsessed little priest drinking his brandy amid all the trash in that desolate study!

When he got clear of the village he struck westward across the fields, so as to hit the upper road; and it was not till he reached Babylon Hill that he paused to take breath. There he decided to skirt the edge of Poll's Camp and avoid the more familiar descent into the town.

'You two down there,' the demon within him began muttering, as his glance swept over Blacksod, from Preston Lane to the Malakite shop, 'you two down there . . . when are you going to stop rending me and tearing my vitals?' This was not the first time lately that he caught himself coupling Gerda and Christie together. 'These Bess Rounds,' he thought, 'are a lot easier to manage than *my two!*' Repeating the syllables 'my two' with all the more bitter relish because of his realization of their outrageousness, Wolf began descending the westerly slope of Poll's Camp, with the intention of discovering some unorthodox way of striking Preston Lane without having to walk the whole length of the High Street.

When he reached level ground he found he had to cross several enclosed orchards, which he did by scrambling through three successive hedges. Pricked by thorns, stung by nettles, his hands smelling of the bitter sap of elder twigs, he made his way through those ancient enclosures, noting how their lichen-covered branches reproduced almost exactly the colour of the grey sky. In spite of the bitter wind, he stopped in the middle of one of those orchards to crouch down over a patch of shining celandines. The valiant lustre of those starry petals in the dark green grass gave him a confused hope. No scent had they in themselves; but as he pressed his forehead into the cold roots of the grass around them, the smell of the earth, sucked up through mouth and nostrils, entered into the very nerves of his soul with a long, shivering, restorative poignance.

'Is it dead?' he said to himself. 'Well, even if it *is*, I've still got *some* sensations left!' When he thought in this way about his 'mythology,' it was queer how he always endowed it with a visible shape. He thought of it as 'it,' and this 'it' was always compelled to take the shape of large, succulent leaves, the leaves of a waterplant whose roots were hidden beneath fathoms of greenish-coloured water.

'*Some* sensations left, even if it *is* dead!' And he rose heavily to his feet and moved on.

He emerged into a narrow, unused cart-track between overgrown, neglected hedges. As he made his way down this path, treading on young nettles and upon old burdocks, he couldn't help thinking how charged with a secret life of its own, different from all other places, a deserted lane like this was. 'What a world it is in itself,' he muttered, 'any little overgrown path!'

The curious satisfaction which this secluded cart-track gave him caused him to stand still in the middle of the path. The hedges sheltered him from the wind. The spirit of the earth called out to him from the green shoots beneath his feet. Faint bird-notes kept sounding from unseen places. The cold sky prevented them from completing their songs; but the stoicism of life in those feathered hearts refused to be silenced.

His consciousness, as he stood there, seemed to stretch out to all the reborn life in the whole countryside. 'Good *is* stronger than Evil,' he thought, 'if you take it on its simplest terms and set yourself to forget the horror! It's mad to refuse to be happy because there's a poison in the world that bites into every nerve. After all, it's short enough! I know very well that Chance could set me screaming like a wounded baboon – every jot of philosophy gone! Well, until that happens, I must endure what I have to endure.'

His mind returned again to the scene about him. 'What a world it is, a little overgrown path, especially in the spring, when it isn't choked up!' He tried to imagine what such a place must be to the rabbits, fieldmice, hedgehogs, slow-worms, who doubtless inhabited it. 'Very much what Lenty Pond is to its frogs and minnows!' he thought. And then his mind, from visualizing those remote backwater worlds, turned once more to Redfern.

'I'm Redfern Number Two,' he thought. 'There's no getting over *that*.'

The path he followed soon emerged into the back premises of a small dairy-barton; and these in their turn opened out into one of the outlying streets of the town.

'Redfern must have been an idiot,' he thought, as he made his way towards Preston Lane, 'to contemplate drowning himself over Urquhart's manias. King's Barton isn't everything. King's Barton isn't a shut-off world, like that deserted path!'

He looked at his watch as he approached the door of his house. Just five o'clock! 'Will she have got rid of him? Will she be away and the place empty? She knew I was coming back to tea. It will be the first time she's ever done it, if she *is* away.'

As he fumbled with the latch of the gate, he found that once more he was associating Gerda and Christie together.

There were four purple crocuses and two yellow ones in the flower-bed on his left; and, on his right, three impoverished hyacinth-buds, of a pinkish colour; and they all seemed to be doing their best to sink back into the earth out of a world that contained, among its possibilities, such a thing as this wind!

'Is Bob Weevil in there with her?' he thought, staring at the crocuses till they ceased to be crocuses. 'He may not be ... but one thing is absolutely certain, and that is that Christie and the old man are having tea together! If not now, they will be, soon. What more natural? "The dear father would with his daughter speak." '

He did his best to peer into the parlour window, but the afternoon was so dark that all he could make out was a faint glow from the firelight.

He looked at the closed door and made a step towards it; but a leaden weight seemed to oppress the muscles of his arm. He glanced down now at those wretched hyacinth-buds. How miserable they looked! The strange thing was that he had the feeling now that to open *this* door would be opening the *other* door too!

He stood hesitating, listening to the wind whistling along the rain-gutter upon the roof above him. At last, with a violent effort of his will, he lurched forward, opened the door with a jerk, and walked into the house.

The kitchen door was open, and from the middle of the hallway he could see the kettle steaming upon the stove. The parlour door, however, was shut. He hung up his coat and hat, and with a beating heart he opened the parlour door. There, by a low red fire, with the tea-tray between them on the little card table, sat Gerda and Bob Weevil, drinking their tea.

He was conscious, as he entered, of an atmospheric density in the room – a density that seemed both material and psychic.

'The place smells of Bob Weevil's new clothes,' he thought, moving forward towards them.

The young tradesman rose to greet him, but Gerda retained her seat.

'You were so late that I thought I wouldn't keep Bob waiting for his tea,' she said; 'but I've got your cup here, and it's only just made.'

'Bob was good enough to give me lunch,' he remarked; 'so you are right to treat him nicely. Sit down, Bob,' And pulling a third chair towards the table for himself, he held out his cup for Gerda to fill.

'Well,' he said, after he had tasted his tea, 'I found Urquhart at home, and I met Jason there too . . . oh, and a friend of yours, too, Bob! Guess who that was!'

As he spoke, he tried to catch Gerda's eye, but she successfully evaded the attempt.

'I don't mix with any such swells,' remarked Weevil, with a facetious grimace. 'I'll try another piece of that cake, Mrs. Solent, if you don't mind.'

The emphasis he laid on the words 'Mrs. Solent' was jeering and impudent.

'It was Bess Round,' Wolf brought out grimly; 'and the joke

of it is she'd come with a great perch that she'd found our Lobbie catching out of season.'

Gerda flashed a glance at him that even in that dim light was like the blade of a knife.

'Bess is no friend of mine,' said Weevil. 'She caught that fish herself, I've no doubt, and palmed it off on Lob. Lob don't need to go as far as Barton for his fish ... season or no season ... does he, Gerdie?'

'*I* don't know, and none of us here know either,' the girl rapped out. 'Lob does what he likes these days when he's out of school. He's got to fish early, if he's to fish at all.'

What came suddenly into Wolf's head at that moment was an excited wondering why it was that a fish once had been a symbol for Christ. This thought, however, vanished as quickly as it arrived; and he soon found himself trying in vain to exchange an intimate look with Gerda. More and more strongly, as he sat there sipping his one bitter cup of tea — he had no spirit to ask for a second, no spirit to ask for more hot water – was the conviction growing upon him that something really serious had happened. Gerda had a look on her face utterly different from any he had ever seen there. It was a hard, reckless, unhappy look, resolute, reserved, indrawn. She looked five years older than when he had seen her asleep in her bed that morning.

He furtively felt in his pocket, to make sure that the cheque was there still. He had an uneasy feeling, after all those agitating occurrences, that he might have lost it. He longed for the moment of Weevil's departure, that he might throw it into her lap!

'What did you think of my poor old dad, Mr. Solent?' enquired the visitor, munching his cake with relish. Wolf was conscious of a ridiculous insistent wonder as to when it was that Gerda had run over to Pimpernel's for this luxury. 'He's not much to look at when he's at meals, or to hear from either,' went on this pious offspring; 'but he takes notice after supper. Last night, for instance, if you'll excuse my mentioning it, he began jawing away like a dissenting minister about my having no purpose in life. What's *your* purpose in life, Gerdie?'

'Don't talk nonsense, Bob,' replied the girl.

'What's *yours*, Mr. Solent?' pursued the incorrigible young man, while Gerda was bending over the lamp.

Wolf had by this time become so certain that something fatal *had* happened, that in his nervousness it was very hard to restrain himself from a violent outburst.

'Purpose?' he repeated; and the word sounded pure nonsense.

'She must have given herself to him,' he thought, 'out of blind anger, just to spite me! If it isn't that, what is it? Something's happened. She's either given herself to him or promised to!'

'Purpose?' he repeated aloud, turning the word over in his mind as if it were a stone or a shell. 'I suppose to get at reality through experience? . . . No! How shall I put it? . . . To enjoy reality through sensation? I expect that's it. Through certain kinds of sensation.'

The illuminated lamp threw its light upon Gerda's face as she resumed her seat.

'What would you describe as your purpose, Bob?' he went on, thinking to himself: 'She's gone through something that's startled and shocked her . . . or she's made up her mind to go through it. She's not the same Gerda that I left this morning with her face drenched with crying.'

Bob Weevil rose to his feet. 'My purpose is to get home to supper,' he said. 'I told Dad last night that it was to serve my God, and he told me not to be so cheeky . . . so you see he's not such a fool after all, the funny old chap!'

Gerda displayed no emotion of any kind on Weevil's departure. As soon as the door was shut upon him, Wolf produced Mr. Urquhart's cheque and pressed it into her fingers. 'You shall have your clock and your carpet and your spoons; and everything else, honey,' he whispered, clutching her by the wrist.

They were back in the parlour now, and she smoothed out the crumpled piece of paper upon the tea-tray. Then she folded it up, as mechanically as if it had been a napkin, and handed it back to him, looking at his fingers, but not at his face.

'Do you want to wash up these things for me, Wolf?' she remarked coldly to him over her shoulder, as she took up the tray and carried it into the kitchen.

As she passed him again in a couple of seconds, moving with a candle in her hand, he made a tentative caressing gesture. 'Don't Wolf!' she murmured, pushing his hand away. 'I'm tired. I'm going to bed.'

He followed her to the foot of the staircase and looked up at her as she walked upstairs. 'You'll be able to get all those things now, Gerda!' he cried.

Her face, as she held the candle level with her breast and turned to look at him, was white and set. For the first time that evening she stared into his eyes.

'It's too late now,' she said quietly, and passed on into their bedroom.

493

22

THE QUICK OR THE DEAD?

GERDA was asleep, or pretending to be asleep, when Wolf got into bed beside her that night on February the twenty-fifth. He was physically so exhausted with walking, and so drowned by exposure to the wind, that he soon sank into oblivion himself; and all night the two lay side by side, their heads, their hips, their knees frequently touching, but their souls restlessly wandering far apart.

The first feeling he had when he awoke was a faint impression of moss and earth mould. Then he realized that the sky between the curtains was of a deep blue. He had opened the window wide before getting into bed; and the room was full of a delicious relaxed air that must have blown over leagues of Somersetshire pastures.

'It's impossible,' he thought, 'that I shouldn't be able to deal with everything, when Nature can produce mornings like this!' He propped himself up on his arm and gazed down upon the figure by his side, struck once again, as he always was, by the freshness of her beauty. She stirred in her sleep and turned her head.

'Her profile is flawless,' he thought. 'How do these classic faces come to exist in these parts at all?'

He bent down over the sleeping girl as tenderly as he might have done over the first cuckoo-flower of the season. 'It's happened at last,' he said to himself. 'She's let him have her . . . just to revenge herself about the cheque and about everything else she endures in her life with me! I'm a cuckold at last. I've always wondered what it would feel like; and now I know. I don't feel anything! I'm just a mirror for *her* feelings. It's been so bad for her that it's of *her* I think . . . entirely . . . absolutely!'

The girl stirred again, more uneasily than before. There came a frown between her eyebrows, and her nostrils quivered. She turned her head from side to side, like a person in a fever or a person whose limbs and arms are paralysed. Deep in Wolf's heart, as he stared at her, there gathered a fundamental decision. Formless at first, it rolled together in the recesses of his nature like a rack of clouds on a misty horizon. Then suddenly it tossed forth a coherent resolution. 'I won't let the water-rat keep her. Cuckold or no cuckold, I love her. She's been miserable about it. I won't give her up!'

At that moment, disturbed by the magnetism of his look, Gerda opened her eyes. He bent and kissed her; and as he lifted his head again, he saw a lovely smile flicker across her face. 'She'd forgotten the whole thing!' he thought, as he watched this smile vanish away and the same rigid, unhappy look come back. She made a movement to extricate her arm from the bedclothes, but the look upon her face was sufficient. He scrambled to his knees and slipped out of bed.

The day being Sunday, there was no need for them to have their breakfast as early as this; but the bright sunshine and the warm, spring-scented air made the hour seem later than it really was.

All that morning they were both like persons on the deck of a becalmed ship, who move restlessly, hurriedly, through familiar tasks, in preparation for some drastic event. Over and over again Wolf was on the point of launching forth into a passionate declaration that what had occurred made no difference . . . that he loved her just the same . . . that he blamed himself over the matter of the cheque. But every time he formulated such words and was on the verge of expressing them, that look of hers froze them in the utterance. She held him helpless and mute by that look. It was like a ceremonial death-cloth wrapped round a living head.

When the housework was quite done – and he noticed that she did it much more conscientously than usual, as though making excuses to prolong it – she announced her intention of going over to Chequers Street. 'If Lobbie hasn't gone out yet,' she said, 'and I'm pretty sure he won't have, I'll get him to go down by the river with me.'

'You'll be back for lunch, won't you, honey?' He threw into these words all the supplication he could.

'No, Wolf, I don't think so,' she replied slowly. 'I think I'll get mother to make up some sandwiches, like she used to in the old days, when Lob and I went down to the Lunt. I'll be back for tea, though. You can put on the kettle at five, if I've not come then. I won't be much later than that.'

Wolf's memory rushed away to that March evening by the banks of the river . . . to the shed in the middle of the wet grass . . . to the yellow bracken. It struck his mind as ominous, if not tragic, that at this juncture she should instinctively revert to Lobbie and the Lunt. But he made no attempt to dissuade her. 'She thinks it's

495

pride in me that I don't,' he said to himself. 'It isn't that! It's respect for her. It's respect for her life. It's respect for her identity.'

'Where will you get *your* dinner?' she said at last, standing between the crocuses and the pink hyacinths, while Wolf still held their front door open. His heart leaped up at this word. Was it an overture, a motion towards him?

'Oh, I expect I'll find enough in the cupboard, sweetheart,' he said lightly; but into these words also he threw a caressing supplication. 'If not, I'll see if my mother's in . . . or Christie,' he added.

At the sound of Christie's name she did fumble for a second with her gloved fingers upon the top of the iron gate, while her head sank down in intense thought.

'Wait a minute, Gerda!' he cried, noting this hesitation. He ran back into the hall and returned with his hat and stick. 'I'll come with you as far as their house.'

She made no objection to this; and as he shut the gate behind them, the particular feel of the ironwork and the noise of the latch brought back to his mind some occasion in the past when they had embraced each other, just there, in a rush of happy reconciliation. He glanced at the pigsty across the road. There wasn't a hint upon the air to-day of anything but the spring.

'Gerda,' he said, when they were well past the street corner, a vantage-ground that served the idlers of their quarter in lieu of a tavern bar, 'I don't want you to think I'm a bit jealous of poor old Bob. It's only fair you should have a friend you're fond of, in the sort of way I'm fond of Christie.'

She was silent for a couple of seconds; and his words seemed to make the lines between the paving-stones, as he stared at the ground, turn into the rungs of a ladder upon which it was necessary to place his feet very carefully, because the space between gaped and yawned.

Then she said slowly: 'There . . . would . . . have . . . been . . . a time . . . for telling me . . . that, Wolf. Better say no more about it to-day.'

He held his peace after that, and they reached the monument-maker's house, just as the 'five-minutes' bell of the parish church began to ring, indicating that it was service-time.

The warmth of the day was phenomenal. A light, vaporous mist, balmy and fragrant, as though millions of primrose-buds had opened beneath it and millions of jonquils had poured their sweetness into it, hung over the lintels of the houses and floated in and out of the doorways. Filmy white clouds, so feathery that they faded into the air at their outer edges, swept northwards over the roofs of the town; while the liquid blue of the sky, visible in fluctuating pools and estuaries between those fleecy vapours, seemed to obliterate everything that was hard and opaque from the whole terrestrial globe. So flowing and so diffused was the heaven above, that it seemed to spill and brim over, making the pavements underfoot appear like clouds too, and the patches of grass in that or this little garden like interstices of another, a second sky, whose receding depths were green instead of blue!

Groups of churchgoers were moving languidly past the gate of the Torp yard under the urge of their various pious purposes; and in his growing distress at the set, indrawn look on his girl's face, Wolf felt mocked and taunted by the somnolent leisureliness of those people's voices and by the fresh neatness of their clothes.

Not another interchange of real feeling could he obtain with her until they knocked at her father's door; and it was a sharp stab to him to think that this was actually the first time since their marriage that they had presented themselves together at this threshold.

Lobbie himself opened the door to them, and they found the whole family collected in the front room. Mrs. Torp, having obviously finished making the beds and tidying up the kitchen, for she wore a dirty apron over her Sunday dress, had recently dropped into a chair opposite her husband, from which island of peace she had clearly been flinging abroad volleys of belligerent eloquence; for the plump shirtsleeved monument-maker had a fixed expression upon his face, at once crushed and protesting – an expression that remained visible even after the stir of their arrival.

'I've only come in for a moment,' said Wolf, taking Mrs. Torp's vacated chair, as the lady led her daughter away to pour her troubles into a feminine ear; 'but I think Gerda intends to stay. Well, Lobbie, you certainly caught a big fish yesterday! I must congratulate you. Season or no season, it's the biggest perch I've ever seen!'

'My old woman have been skinnin' the poor lad like a fish 'isself, just as you were coming in,' said Mr. Torp. 'She says I encourage he in they scallywag larks. I don't encourage yer, do I, Lob Torp?'

The boy glanced uneasily at the kitchen door, from behind which his mother's voice was still audible.

'She were out for mischief, mister,' he whispered solemnly, 'else she would never have meddled wi' I! What did she reckon she wanted, walking in they wet fields afore 'twas light? And she spoke to I twice afore I hooked thik girt fish. Be I'd been little, like I were wunst, she'd have made I run home quaking and shaking! Do 'ee know what she said to I, mister? Her came 'long o' thik hedgeside path what leads from Farmer's Rest to Pond Lane. I saw she coming and I wished myself anywhere; for I reckoned the wold chap had gone and hid 'isself; and her were after he; both on 'em nigh crazy, as you might say! Her came walking straight to where I were, stepping silent, like any wold cow, and when she'd looked at that cold water awhile her kind o' shook. "Have 'ee seen it?" she said. "Seen what, Miss Bess?" I said. "The face under the water," said she, "what they all talk of up at Rest." "I bain't looking for no faces," said I. "I be fishing for perch." "'Twill be seen," she said, "'twill be seen, till one that be living now be where *it* be ... then 'twill fade out." It were when she were saying "fade out," just like that, that I saw me float bob down. You can believe, mister, that a fellow had no time then for a woman's foolishness! But 'twere nought to she what my float were doing. "'Twas thik face in this here water," said she, "what worried uncle. Thik face will be seen by all and sundry," said she, "till the time come when –" '

Lobbie's discourse was interrupted by a sudden movement by his father. Mr. Torp got up from his chair. 'You stop that now!' he roared. 'You stop that or I'll call your mother to 'ee! Sunday be Sunday, I say, and Mr. Solent be our visitor. If Providence have on's mind to afflict such a gentleman, 'tis his wone concern! This house be my house, Lob Torp; and this morning be Sunday morning. So shut thy mouth about faces in ponds!'

So loud was the voice of Mr. Torp, that no sooner had he resumed his seat than his wife and Gerda burst in.

'What's this about Sunday, John?' said the lady sharply. 'Can't you leave that boy in peace for a moment when my back's turned? If it *be* Sunday, what of it? Here's our Gerdie asking for nice meat-sandwiches for to take the lad picnicking. Mr. Solent says he can't stay, so me and you can do what I was telling 'ee just now ... go quiet and natural to Nevilton meeting. What do 'ee think I went to the trouble of putting my best dress on for? To hot up yesterday's Yorkshire pudding? If some can eat cold meat, *others* can eat cold meat. There'll never be, all spring I tell 'ee, such a day for me and you to cover them quiet miles.'

Mr. Torp permitted himself a swift, humorous leer at his preoccupied son-in-law.

'What *is* Nevilton meeting, Mrs. Torp?' enquired Wolf, with forced vivacity.

''Tis mother's favourite preacher,' interposed Lobbie. 'Old Farmer Beard, Mr. Manley's friend, fetches he in dog-cart, from Ilchester. 'A be a Baptist, mister, the kind that washes grown folk all over like babies. Mother goes to hear he, because 'a says all drinking-men, like our Dad, will be burnt cruel, come Judgment. Mother likes for Dad to hear they things; but Dad be a churchman, same as I be, what don't hold with such conclusions. Dad and me be High-Church. Mother be Evangelic.'

Mrs. Torp untied her apron and began folding it up. It was clear from her expression that wrath at her offspring's impudence was qualified by pride in his capacity for fine theological distinctions. She began a rambling eulogy upon the preacher from Ilchester, punctuated by irritable exclamations, as she hunted in vain about the room for some tract or hymnbook connected with this celebrity.

But Wolf had no attention just then for anybody but Gerda, whose abstracted look of settled misery, as she sat upright upon a straight-backed chair against the wall, pierced him to the heart.

'She's given herself to that little ass,' he thought, 'out of pure spite; and it's broken up all her self-respect.'

Mrs. Torp's project of making Mr. Torp walk five miles that afternoon to hear himself damned became a desolate background now – like that marble table in the Weevil villa – to this wretched crisis in his life. The idea of some stuffy little room in Nevilton – a village he particularly admired – resounding to the voice of this protégé of Mr. Beard, on a day like this, seemed to paint the whole Dorset landscape with a mud-coloured pigment. A bitter, masculine anger stirred within him at the destructive emotionalism of these women, unable, as they always were, to 'leave well alone.'

And it did not lessen his agitation to think of Gerda's blind, desperate instinct to take refuge with Lobbie, her old childish companion, down there in those Lunt meadows! Just exactly a year ago since the three of them had come home through the spring twilight . . . and now she was to carry her sandwiches to the very spot, eat them with Lob on the trunk of that very tree, set eyes, perhaps, on that very shed, and nothing to persuade her to let him join them.

A pitiful craving came upon him to take her in his arms and purge her bedevilled memory of every trace of that lecherous water-rat. And Christie too – why must Christie, in some crazy psychic mood, go and stir up the villainous fires of that old man's smouldering lust? The words that he had read in that fatal exercise-book wrote themselves on the Torp wall as he stared at it. If he hadn't made love to her and then drawn back in the way he did, she'd be still just as she used to be, immune as the flowers on her mantelpiece to that old satyr's approaches.

Gerda's abstraction had by this time become so extreme, her face so sad, that he couldn't bear it any longer. He walked across to her; and in a low, emphatic voice, under cover of Mrs. Torp's voluble hunt for her lost pamphlet, he begged for leave to accompany them in their excursion.

'It's too late, Wolf!' she repeated, looking at him with eyes that seemed five years older than they'd been yesterday. 'Haven't I told you it is? Why do you keep teasing me so?'

He bent down above her now and lowered his voice to a whisper.

'It *isn't* too late, Gerda. You're taking everything much too hard! I love you far too much for anything to be too late!'

But the tenderness in his voice only seemed to irritate her. She flashed a look at him of aversion, of contempt. 'You are a fool, Wolf,' she whispered. 'I never supposed you were quite such a fool!'

Then she jumped to her feet. 'Come on, mother! Never mind those Nevilton hymns. Lobbie and I want to start in a minute. Come, both of you, and let's make the sandwiches!'

Her mother and brother followed her into the kitchen, and Wolf was left alone with Mr. Torp.

'Cold meat for me dinner, and hot damnation for me pudding, seems so!' remarked that good man. 'Well, if I've got to walk to Nevilton this afternoon, I shall traipsy round to ostler Jim's this morning. He'll be finished cleaning up in Peewits back yard by now; and him and me can sit snug for a while . . . "doors all locked and maids all mum," as the saying is.'

Even while he was still speaking, Mr. Torp was shuffling into his Sunday coat and straightening his Sunday tie. Wolf picked up his hat and stick.

'Well, I'll be moving on too, I think.' He spoke louder than was necessary, in order to let Gerda know he was going. But there was no voice or sign from the kitchen.

'Good-bye, Mr. Torp,' he said, shaking his father-in-law's hand warmly. 'Be careful of that ostler's back room, or your preacher will catch you on the hop.'

'Don't 'ee worry, Mr. Solent,' returned the other; 'and do 'ee bear in mind thee own self what I told 'ee yesterday. Not a man of us, these shifty times, nor a gentleman neither, can see what bides for'n. 'Tisn't as 'twere when I were young. Life be a wink of the eyelid, these times; and only them as jumps the ditches goes dry to bed!'

Once back again in the sun-warmed quietness of Chequers Street, Wolf, after walking a step or two, paused to take counsel with himself.

'She'll be back for tea,' he thought, 'and then I'll talk to her. I'll make her take this affair lightly. But no more of Weevil. She must be quit of Weevil. Cuckold I am. Wittold I refuse to be!'

He drew pensive patterns on the sunlit pavement with the end of his stick. All manner of contradictory projects floated through his brain as to how to spend the long, tantalizing hours between this and five o'clock. Of these notions, one lodged itself finally in his mind as the very thing indicated by the occasion. He would consult the most cynical of all his oracles! How many months was it since he had last been over there . . . since he had gazed straight down through the clay to where the skull grinned back at him? Too long . . . too long! Yes, that is what he would do. He would visit 'old Truepenny.' Nothing would make the hours pass quicker than that!

He looked at his watch. It was a quarter to twelve; and he knew there was a Sunday train to Ramsgard at twelve-fifteen.

'I'll have hours for walking back . . . hours and hours,' he said to himself. 'I'll come by the highroad. I'd like to find a way through the Gwent Lanes, if there be time.'

Then suddenly an idea came into his head that brought a rush of blood and a faint, pricking sensation to the flesh that covered his cheek-bones. Why not run in to Christie's for a second, and see if she'd go with him? Damn! – but there might be somebody he knew on the platform or in the train. They'd probably – just because it was such a heavenly day – find Miss Gault at the cemetery!

No, it was too risky. 'But I'll run in a second, anyway,' he thought, 'and see what she says.'

A few minutes later he found himself ringing the bell at the Malakite side door.

All was silent in the little alley. He could see some brilliant patches of green, swimming in pools of sunlight, in the small garden. Then a faint shuffling of feet came along the pavement, outside in the road. That shuffling and the beating of his heart were the only sounds. All Blacksod lay immersed in a golden mist of quiet. He rang the bell again. 'In a minute,' he thought, 'I shall hear her coming down! The old man may sleep late o' Sundays; but she'll be up.'

The shuffling steps in the road came to a pause.

'Mister!'

He turned towards the voice. It was a little, old-fashioned maid carrying a prayer book.

'If it's the Malakites you want, mister, I saw them pass my house, down-street, an hour agone. They were dressed for travel; so it did look to me! I reckon they were minded to catch the eleven-three to Weymouth.'

Wolf left the door and advanced to meet the speaker. He knew her now as one of the shop-girls in Pimpernel's. He had often bought cakes of her for Gerda. She was reputed to be a Roman Catholic.

'Dressed for an excursion, eh, miss?' he said lightly. 'That eleven-three goes straight through to Weymouth, doesn't it? Well, they certainly have a lovely day!'

The little Catholic walked hurriedly on. 'She'll miss her great miracle if she's not quick,' he thought. 'Don't they say the words exactly at noon?'

All the way to the station he tried to concentrate his mind on the mystery of the Mass. 'The Christ of these priests,' he thought, 'is a totally different god from the Jesus of Mr. Beard's preacher. Which of 'em would help me most at this juncture, ha? Which of them?'

It was only when he was sitting alone in a third-class smoking-carriage, staring out of the window at Melbury Bub, that the full bitterness of this last piece of news grew ripe for tasting.

'She ought to have known I'd look in to-day,' he thought. 'She ought to have known it.' And then he thought: 'Natural enough to go to Weymouth on a sunshiny March day! Mr. Malakite . . . and his daughter . . . at Weymouth. I expect they'll lie down on those dry sands where the donkeys are. They'll probably have lunch at the "Dorothy" and then go for a row, or cross over the ferry to the Nothe and walk to Sandsfoot Castle. Perhaps they'll go past Brunswick Terrace and walk across Lodmore.'

Oh, it was all natural enough! If only he hadn't come across that exercise-book. But an imaginative girl like Christie might exaggerate a thousand little nothings. Besides, 'Slate' was a story.

It wasn't a diary. It revealed nothing . . . nothing at all . . . except her thoughts!

Gerda too. . . . He hadn't seen anything. He hadn't caught them at anything . . . except sitting in the dark. What if *that* also were a fancy of his own? He leaned forward and clasped his hands over his knees. Oh, this was the worst state of all! Not to be quite sure. The train was passing close to King's Barton now. There was the great perpendicular tower ... there was the church-yard! He unclasped his hands and sat sideways against the window, trying to make out Redfern's headstone; but the train moved too fast. He thought he caught a glimpse of it, but he wasn't sure. He wasn't sure of anything!

Hardly anyone else got out when he reached Ramsgard. 'If I meet Miss Gault,' he thought, 'I shall be rude to her.'

He skirted the Public Gardens and hurried past the Lovelace. 'Is that old waiter there still?' he wondered. At the sight of the workhouse, the personality of his father seemed to beckon him, to welcome him; but it was still only as a skull. The skull knew he was coming, though; and it was glad! The skull of 'old Truepenny' was the only brain in the world whose thoughts he *could* read! Eyeless sockets deceived no one.

He was passing the slaughter-house now. 'I've only touched meat once,' he thought, 'since she talked to me that day. But if I see her at his grave I shall sheer off and not go near it!'

When he came to the hole in the fence that led to that portion of the cemetery where the paupers were buried, he recalled how startled he'd been when he saw Miss Gault go down on her hands and knees to get through this aperture. So well did he remember that incident as he himself now went down on his hands and knees, that while a clump of dock-weeds struck cold against his face, he became suddenly certain that Miss Gault was there now.

Yes! If she wasn't there, her spirit was most certainly there. He scrambled to his feet, feeling sure that he would see her; and there she was! She was seated upon a grave over against William Solent's. On her lap was a paper of sandwiches, in her hands a book. She was munching and reading at the same time, her hat on the grave by her side, her large black boots emerging from beneath a voluminous skirt, whose stiff folds suggested the *Melancholia* of Albert Dürer.

He had vowed he would bolt if he saw her that day, but instead of that he pulled off his cloth cap with effusive humility and stepped over the intervening mounds.

'Miss Gault!'

She must have marked him down while he was under the fence, and been merely gathering her wits; for all she did now was to raise her eyes and blink at him.

'So you've come at last, boy!'

He moved up to her, laid his hand upon one of hers, as it still clutched the paper of sandwiches, and sat down.

'Every one seems eating sandwiches to-day,' he threw out.

'Best thing to do, boy,' she replied; 'best thing to do! They're lettuce.'

'What a day it is, isn't it, Miss Gault?' he murmured vaguely, glancing at the words 'William Solent,' upon which the sun was pouring its friendliest benediction.

She peered obliquely into his face. 'What's the matter with you, boy?' she said earnestly; and then, with a nervous apology in her tone, 'It's Emma's day out; so I thought I might as well have a picnic.'

'Oh, I'm all right, Miss Gault! Tired of school, perhaps. But we've all got to feel the pinch somewhere.'

'Take off your cap, Wolf, and let me look at you.'

He threw his cap down on the grass and accepted a sandwich which she held out to him.

'Why, you've got grey hairs!' she cried. 'You hadn't. one when you came to me a year ago.'

'Dorset air,' he remarked grimly.

'And you've got lines there; and your mouth is different; and you're a lot thinner!'

'Hard work!' he threw out. 'I've done Urquhart's book for him though ... and I've been paid for it.'

She turned round fully towards him now and laid both book and sandwiches on the ground. He noted that the volume was Palgrave's *Golden Treasury*. He also noted an empty medicine-bottle beside her, blurred with the whiteness of milk, upon whose orifice three black flies had settled.

'You're thoroughly unhappy, my dear,' said Miss Gault. 'I can see it in everything about you. What is it, Wolf? It's ridiculous not to confide in an ugly old woman like me! What is it, Wolf?'

A sound of bells came to them at that moment, carried on a gust of soft air that was like dark, sweet rain-water.

'The Abbey,' murmured Miss Gault. 'They're out of church; but they always go on ringing those bells.'

'I like to hear them,' he responded; and then, with a sigh: 'I suppose it's the same with every one. Life doesn't get easier.'

A kind of disintegrating softness had fallen upon him. The vaporous sunshine, the dreamy light-blowing air, the imponderable fragrance, seemed to combine to melt some basic resistance in his bones. He felt as if there were arising from that place of mortality a sweet, faint, relaxing breath, full of the deliciousness of luxurious dissolution.

The distant bells suggested the greenish fluidity, flowing and fluctuating, of the fan tracery under the Abbey roof. They suggested the centuries of calm, irresponsible repose that weighed on that royal coffin under the Abbey floor! What did it matter that a girl called Gerda had abandoned her body to a youth called Weevil? What did it matter that a lecherous old bookseller was giving his daughter a day on Weymouth beach?

So indifferent to all human fates did he feel just then, that, after swallowing the last morsel of his sandwich and wiping his fingers on the grass, he stretched out his feet in front of him, brushed the flies away from the empty bottle, and gave himself up to a physical sensation of being an integral portion of this wide, somnolent landscape!

'I am Poll's Camp,' he would have said, if the sensation had articulated itself. 'I am Lovelace Park. I am the Gwent Lanes. I am Nevilton Hill. I am Melbury Bub. I am Blackmore Vale and High Stoy. It is over me that Gerda and Lob are now walking, down there by the Lunt.'

'Why don't you tell me what's the matter, boy?' repeated Miss Gault. 'Don't you care anything about me? Is my friendship of no value to you at all?'

Her words seemed as much a part of the balmy light-fluttering air above him as his own body was a part of the earth mould below him.

Feebly, with less energy than he had used to brush away the flies from the bottle, he analysed his inertia. 'I have killed my life-illusion,' he thought. 'I am as dead as William Solent. I've got no pride, no will, no identity left.' He fixed his eyes on his father's headstone, across which there kept fluttering the shadow of an unbudded branch from a little tree near the fence. He tried to visualize the skull under that mound. It was still of the skull, rather than of coffin or skeleton, that he thought! But this also seemed to have lost its identity. No cynical grin came back towards him from down there. No sardonic commentary upon his predicament rose to mock him or to reassure him.

Suddenly he was aware that Miss Gault was speaking rapidly, excitedly.

'But you needn't tell me, boy. I keep my eyes and my ears about me. I know where you're always going! It's those Malakites have got hold of you. It's that Malakite girl that's the trouble. You're being unfaithful to that wife of yours. I knew it would end like this. I knew it was all a woeful mistake. These marriages out of one's class never do succeed and never will. The truth is, boy, that you don't know yourself, or what you really need, any more than that stick of yours does! You're making yourself ill with remorse, when neither of those little Blacksod hussies cares a fig about your feelings ... or about your faithfulness either. Why, they've been brought up to be as indiscriminate as flies! You don't know our Dorsetshire lower classes, boy. They haven't the same feelings, they're not human in the same way as we are. And what's more, Wolf, let me tell you this' – her voice deepened to a discordant harshness, and she seized the *Golden Treasury* and beat it against the ground – 'you're not really in love with either of them! If you were, you'd choose between them. You're one of those men like Jason Otter, like Mr. Urquhart, who in their hearts hate women. It was sheer madness your ever picking up this Torp girl. If Ann hadn't been such a feather-headed fool she'd have stopped you! Ann is so full of her own pranks, that you're just a pet to her, a great baby pet! If Ann had been a different sort of person, you'd never have got mixed up with these Malakites. I told her myself what would come of it! I told her in my own drawing-room while Emma was spoiling the tea-cakes, that day she called on me. I said to her, "If you can't keep your boy from that bookshop he'll go the way his father went!" That's what I said to her. I remember it, because I was unkind to Emma afterwards about the tea-cakes! But Ann only laughed. That mother of yours doesn't any more know the difference between good and evil than between – ' The excited woman broke off in a half-humorous chuckle.

But before this diatribe had finished, Wolf had pulled in his legs and straightened his back. Something deeper in him than the grin of that skull down there, deeper than the drowsy deliciousness of the day, twitched, contracted, tightened. The ancient, unconscious tug of the navel-string, or what bound his flesh to the flesh that had conceived it, roused him from his torpor.

He saw that hard, ruddy, ironic face. He saw that gallant chin. He heard those light, reckless, defiant tones.

'I'm with you, mother!' he thought, while his lip trembled. 'I'm with you, whatever any of them say! Good or evil, I'm with you!'

506

Miss Gault paid no attention to this stiffening of the figure at her side. Her thoughts too, it seemed, had wandered to the roots of the past.

'William! William!' she groaned aloud. 'I'd have held you. I'd have peaked and pined to hold you. I'd have slaved for you, watched for you, wasted for you, and always forgiven you!'

Completely unaware of the effect of her words upon her companion, she turned her great wild-horse eyes, the whites of which showed desperate in the sunshine, from Wolf to the grave, and back again from the grave to Wolf.

'I only pray, boy,' she went on, 'that you'll never meet a woman who'll love you as I loved him down there. If you do, you'll kill her with the Ann Haggard in your brain. We're all of us flinty enough, boy base and flinty; but I've never met a person who gloried in it as your mother does! Oh, love him, boy! Love him, love him, as I've loved him for twenty-five years!'

Wolf lurched to his feet and stood erect. The struggle that had been going on so long within him between his father and his mother had reached a crisis. He had come here to range himself with that skull, to cry to it for a sign in his trouble; but this woman's desperation had wrought a change in him. His mother's words of yesterday rose up in his mind. His father must have lodged himself like an undying snake in Miss Gault's bosom! Would it be with his mother or with his father that he would range himself now, were this accusing creature with the pendulous lip and the vast black lap the very Judgment of God? With which of them? With which of them?

With his mother! Out of that hard, ironic flesh he had been torn. Good or bad, he was on her side. Good or bad, he would be judged with her!

'I've listened long enough,' he said sternly. 'I came to him alone. I came for my own reasons. I didn't come to side with you against her.'

Miss Gault jumped up so impetuously that one of her feet tripped upon the empty bottle. Her intention was apparently to rush over the grave; but this misadventure sent her stumbling towards it, her great body bent forward and her arms outspread, till she fell on her knees against it. Crouched and hunched there like an immense black dog, she emitted a pitiful, hardly human groan. Then she twisted her head round so that one of her troubled eyes was just able to meet Wolf's indignant stare.

From the depths of this eye – as from a waterhole in the crust of nature – a look shot at him that he never forgot. But he moved forward until he faced her; and she sank then into an easier position, yet still remained upon her knees.

'He had you always in his mind,' she gasped. 'You've never thought about *that*, have you? He was too proud to say a word. Oh, he had a soul worth a dozen Anns!'

The challenge of Miss Gault's spirit, flung at him through that wild-horse look, was a challenge from his mother's enemy.

It was then that anger overcame pity in Wolf's heart. 'Do you understand,' he burst out, 'I happen to care a good deal for my mother? We've lived together more closely than anyone knows. Do you understand? More closely than anyone knows.'

The crouching woman jerked out two long, dark-sleeved arms.

'Go back to her, then!' she screamed, waving her hands as if she were driving off a jackal from a dead body. 'Take her back to London! Don't let us see either of your faces again!'

Without a word or a gesture in response to this, Wolf wearily picked up his stick from the grass and strode over the graves to the gap in the fence.

'Back to London?' he muttered, as he went down on all fours and butted his way through the opening. 'That's what Jason said. They'll get it lodged in my brain before they've done! But I *won't* go. "There's a special providence in the fall of a sparrow. If it be now, 'tis not to come; if it be not now, yet it will come; the readiness is all." '

Once outside in the road, there came to him a troublesome stab of remorse. He had always been so indulgent to what Miss Gault had to say about his mother. Why should he have turned on her like that just then?

He was half tempted to drop down on his knees again and crawl back. He stood still, listening attentively; but there was not the faintest sound from in there. The living woman was as quiet as the dead man. Ay! the god of human sorrow is a man; but Love crucifies women.

Grasping his stick below the handle, he hardened his heart and hurried off towards Ramsgard. When he reached the workhouse, he looked at his watch. It was only half-past two. He had two hours and a half before tea-time.

On the side of the road opposite the workhouse was a low stone wall. The garden of some tradesman's house was separated from the pavement by this wall, on the top of which grew thick, green moss. The Ramsgard people being all at their noon meal, he had the pavement to himself; and he stopped and stared at this coping of moss. Hooking his stick on his elbow, he laid both hands upon the top of this wall; and the life of the moss seemed to pass into his nerves. It was at this moment that he heard a boy's shrill scream from an unseen playground behind the house which appertained to this garden. The sound was not repeated; but Wolf clenched his teeth. 'It's one of the Houses of the School. It's a bully,' he thought. And then he found himself muttering a deadly curse. 'You brute! you brute! – Never, till you die, shall you dare to do that again.'

Then it suddenly occurred to him that he had his back to the workhouse.

'I wonder if my father could see this wall from the room where he died? I expect he could.' He walked on into the outskirts of the town. The lane which he followed emerged into a narrow road, where the chilly, newly budded hedges alternated with small stone houses, standing back from the thoroughfare and approached by little stone paths. He caught sight of an old man, sitting on a trim bench in one of those little gardens, with a look of the most supreme contentment on his face as he smoked his pipe and watched the passers-by. There was a white cat at his feet and a clump of daffodils in the flower-bed beside him; and bathed as he was in the mellow afternoon light, his leathery, secretive, roguish countenance – he might have been the owner of some little shop or a retired gardener – seemed to gather to itself the whole long history of Ramsgard and its famous School, from the time when King Æthelwolf was buried in the Abbey to the time Miss Gault's father became head master!

This sly, sagacious, whimsical old man had nothing of the taciturnity of a remote village about him; still less had he the urbanity of a large town. He was as much a product of certain peculiar local traditions – in this case urbane gentility mingling with urbane obsequiousness – as if he had been a rare beetle in the hazel-copses of High Stoy, or a specimen of the 'Lulworth Skipper' butterfly on the Dorsetshire coast!

Wolf couldn't resist a spasm of envy as he paused for a second to peer up at this old rascal, sucking his pipe, cogitating upon his savings in Stuckey's Bank, leering at the lads and lasses who passed his gate. . . . Free from all remorse, all misgiving, how greatly did that old villain enjoy life! Ay, he was as selfish as his cat – as those yellow daffodils in that flower-bed! Before he left him Wolf had a queer hallucination. He saw this perfectly well-behaved old man in the shape of a plump, blunt-nosed maggot, peering out from a snug little crack in the woodwork of a blistering cross, on which hung, all in her long black skirt, the form of Selena Gault!

Wolf walked on, but he couldn't help pondering on the kind of self-centredness that had enabled this old demon to last so long. What would *he* have made of it if, on some business trip to London, he had encountered that Waterloo-steps face? Just thought: 'That fellow ought to be in the workhouse. They oughtn't to allow such people here.' Or he would have simply regarded him as part of the station, no more than a door, a post, an iron orna- mentation, an advertisement board!

Very likely this old man was the head master's gardener, and had worked in his day for Miss Gault's father. Well, which had got the most out of life – Miss Gault, hunched up over there in the paupers' plot, or this merry old man with his white cat?

Miss Gault loved cats too. Some who loved cats had to eat their sandwiches upon graves. This citizen of Ramsgard had a different destiny. . . .

Wolf moved on up the road, passing an increasing number of lively Sunday-afternoon strollers. What, he wondered, were Gerda and Lobbie doing at that moment? Where were Christie and the old man? He came to a halt just then. Should he, after all, go to Ramsgard station and take the train, instead of walking? No sooner had this idea entered his head than he decided to follow it. He would have plenty of time to change his mind again if there were no train.

'I'll go into the Abbey for a minute,' he thought. He turned northward and entered the town by way of a field path past the massive wall of the Preparatory School. When he got close to the Abbey, he encountered several groups of straw-hatted boys, and the sight of them put him in mind of Mr. Smith. What would *he* have felt about the marriage of Lorna's daughter? From the straw hats his mind slid to Mattie, like a loaded trunk down a ship's gangway. Would she make Darnley happy? Would she be happy herself?

He caught sight of a pair of immaculately handsome lads, arm in arm, each radiating delight in the touch of his companion. He saw them reject with mechanical indifference the appeal of a dilapidated tramp who had evidently singled them out from the rest, hoping that the happiness which surrounded them like an aura would redound to his advantage.

It was at this moment that he heard himself called by name.

'Wolf! It *is* you! I saw you first!'

He swung round, and there were Mattie and Olwen.

As he responded to the little girl's excited embrace, which was so emphatic that it attracted a glance of haughty disapproval from one of the straw-hatted pair, he had time to note that this was the second time to-day that a person's presence had communicated itself to him before it appeared in the flesh.

He made no bones about kissing his half-sister very tenderly across Olwen's woollen cap; and the two straw-hatted ones drew away, evidently feeling that the emotions of the populace were a discordant note in that privileged place.

'We walked over, Wolf,' the girl said. 'That'll do, Olwen! Darnley wanted to have a walk with his mother. Jason's writing poetry in the back garden. So I said I'd show her the King's tomb. She's been learning about King Æthelwolf – haven't you, Olwen?'

But Olwen displayed scant interest in royal dust. 'I want to sit outside with Wolf,' she remarked, clutching his fingers with an impatient hand. 'I want to talk to Wolf while you go back to church.' Mattie took not the least notice of this remark, and they all three moved slowly round the corner of the Abbey towards its front entrance. The bride's eyes were brilliantly animated. And Wolf felt as if a warm globe of magnetic power were shooting out rays of exaltation from her strong, virginal body. There was that in her excitement that at once irritated Wolf and touched him to the heart.

'I was going to write to you, my dear,' she said eagerly, 'in case I shouldn't see you before Saturday. We're going to Weymouth, Wolf!'

He looked at her closely. The heavy, sulky face was gleaming. He commented, with shame in his secret heart, upon his lack of spontaneous sympathy. What did it mean, this cold, tightening sensation within him? Was it that the figure of Darnley, urbane, melancholy, unattached, had become a sanctuary of refuge for him? He found himself responding to the clutch of Olwen's feverish fingers with a significant and treacherous pressure.

'I'm glad you're going to Weymouth. What a splendid idea!' he replied, as enthusiastically as he could. 'Weymouth has always been –'

At that moment they reached the wide-open door of the church.

'You go in first, my dear,' he said, in a tone of command. 'I'll just smoke a cigarette, on that seat, with Olwen, and then we'll come. Don't sit too far in. But we'll find you. It won't be crowded. Oh, we'll easily find you! But Olwen and I have a very important secret we want to talk about.'

He gave her a reassuring little push, half playful, half paternal, and watched her figure vanish in the cool dimness of the nave.

Olwen positively danced with glee as they moved across to a vacant seat under a yew tree, not far from the grotesque little statue of the poet-courtier.

'She thought we were going to talk about her *presents*, didn't she?' said the little girl, as they sat down and he lit a cigarette. 'But we're not, are we, Wolf?'

'Perhaps *I* am,' he replied with a smile. 'But how do you like all this marrying, Olwen?'

The child's eyes were fixed upon the hazy outline of 'The Slopes,' just visible in that shimmery air beyond the Public Gardens and the railway. 'Oh, don't talk about it, Wolf! Jason and I never talk about it. Jason says the only nice part of it will be the wine. They're going to have Sauterne.'

Wolf began to realize that Mattie's nature was not one that a love-affair expands and widens. It dawned upon him that this little Malakite waif was being thrown more and more upon the indulgence of Jason.

The child's mood this afternoon was evidently wistful. She seemed to take Wolf's sympathy for granted; and now, with her hand in his, after uttering the word 'Sauterne,' she relapsed into silence.

He too was silent, repeating to himself an imaginary dialogue with Gerda, over their tea in the kitchen. The disagreeable thought came into his head, 'Shall I feel any difference when I lie by her side to-night?'

'Wolf!' The little girl's voice had a solemn intensity, and she stared at him with grave eyes.

'Say on, Princess Olwen.'

'Do you think people are always treated as they treat *other* people?'

The child's question, directed against the very heart of the universe, disturbed Wolf profoundly. It was the sort of remark that indicates something materially wrong in the person who utters it.

'I can't say I do, Olwen. Life is far more unjust than ever King Æthelwolf was.'

'You like Miss Malakite very much, don't you, Wolf?'

He gave a palpable start and flung away his cigarette. What *was* coming now? This warm spring air seemed to be bringing all human troubles to the surface as the hot day brings forth the adders!

'Very much indeed, Olwen. Christie is very nice indeed. She's rather – she's rather like you.'

'I want to see her, Wolf. I want to tell her that I'm *sorry* I wouldn't ever speak to her when I was a little girl.'

'What made you so unkind, Olwen?'

'Shall I tell you, Wolf? You won't tell anyone, will you, if I tell you?'

He shook his head with all the solemnity he could muster.

'Don't look at me while I tell you!'

'All right. I'm not looking.

'Grand-dad Smith told me when I was very little' – the voice in which the child said this was low and restrained, and her words came slowly – 'that . . . Miss Malakite . . . was . . . a . . . leper.' Having overcome the difficulty of her confession, her expression became entirely different. She seemed as relieved to have brought this thing into the light as if she'd pulled a thorn from her hand.

'But, Olwen darling' – Wolf spoke with as much intensity as if he were addressing an intelligence equal to his own – 'your grandfather didn't mean a *real* leper! He meant that people shunned Christie because of her father . . . because of her father's bad character.'

The child's eyes opened wide. 'Then Miss Malakite is not a leper at all? Not all white and horrid under her clothes?'

'Of course not! She's sweet and lovely under her clothes . . . just as you are!'

The child looked away again towards 'The Slopes,' her forehead puckered in concentrated thought. Then she turned to him with flushed cheeks. 'Oh, Wolf, I want to see her! I want to see her soon . . . to-day . . . to-morrow! I want to tell her how glad I am she isn't a leper!'

It was Wolf's turn now to look at 'The Slopes' with a pondering frown.

Suppose he *did* take Olwen to see Christie? What harm could come of that? He rose from the bench. 'Come on, sweetheart,' he cried, 'Mattie will wonder where we are!'

They met Mattie coming out of the church; and at that same moment the tramp he had observed talking to the two boys drew near. Where had he seen this fellow before? The tramp approached them, and began begging. Good Lord! It was that old, courteous waiter at the Lovelace! Mattie was now pulling Olwen away. 'No, no!' she murmured in reply to the man's supplication. But Wolf fumbled in his pocket. He could tell by the feel of the coins that he had half a crown and a few halfpence there. That was all he had. At that moment the great clock in the tower above their heads began striking. It must be four o'clock! He must hurry to the station. Like a flash he thought, 'If I give him the half-crown I shan't be able to buy a ticket!' and he put the few halfpence into the man's hand. As he did so he noticed that very scar which had struck his attention a year ago. The ex-waiter's eyes met his own, but without recognition. 'It must be drink,' Wolf said to himself, as he hurried away after the two girls.

Half an hour later and he was safely ensconced in a crowded carriage, from the windows of which he could see only the blue sky.

'*I might* have given him that half-crown,' he thought. 'I could have done it.'

The incident taunted and teased his mind so unmercifully that it was not till he had left the train and was nearly at his own door that he could harden his heart against it.

'It's just pure chance that I'm not in the same boat as that waiter,' he thought. 'He's got a look . . . it's a different expression, but he's got a look of that Waterloo-steps man!'

He rushed into the house, calling Gerda's name in a low, eager voice. There was no answer. He went into the parlour, the kitchen, the back yard. He ran upstairs and looked into the bedroom. No one! The familiar furniture wore that peculiar air of desolation that of all things he especially disliked. The beauty of the day seemed to have completely passed it by. It looked cold and unhappy. It looked like a child that has been left indoors when all the world has been out at a festival.

And yet he had to admit there was something dignified, even *spiritual*, about those quaint, cheap objects, waiting there for their absent mistress. 'They are the extreme opposite,' he thought, 'of that self-satisfied old rascal with the white cat.'

He busied himself with careful preparations for tea, and grew peevishly puzzled at the unexpected difficulties he encountered. 'Girls do things so mechanically,' he said to himself, as for the tenth time he walked round their kitchen table, altering this and that. When all was ready he opened the dresser drawer, took the cheque from beneath Mukalog, and placed it under Gerda's plate.

Then he sat down on a hard, high chair and waited, listening to the clock in the parlour. He felt too excited even to smoke a cigarette.

'What *is* it that worries me?' he thought. 'Not fear lest she has some crazy love for the fellow. I know very well she hasn't. Damn! I suppose Carfax wouldn't believe it if I said I was thinking simply and solely about *her* feelings. But there it is! You can't sleep with a girl for twelve months and not feel what she feels! I don't believe his having gone to the limit will change her at all for me. I don't want to set eyes on the chap again . . . but that's another thing. How sleek he looked in that new brown suit! I suppose he hung that brown coat over the bottom of our bed. That's not a very nice thought!'

Suddenly the idea came to him that perhaps she would never come back – that he would have to eat this meal alone, and all other meals! He hurriedly looked round for something belonging to her wherewith to reassure himself. He saw no sign anywhere of a small work-basket that she was in the habit of using for her occasional young-girl struggles with needle and thread.

Restlessly he got up and began looking about for this. The little work-box became the most important of all objects in the world at that moment. If it were here, why, she would soon be safely home again! Where the devil was it? He went into the parlour. He even went upstairs. Not a sign! 'But I've seen the thing . . . I know I've seen it . . . since I came in!'

With a sudden inspiration he opened the dresser drawer. There it was . . . and protruding from its edge a ragged glove! He left the drawer open, went to the front door, and looked out. The light was waning. At the first approach of twilight that lovely day began yielding itself to its death with a precipitate eagerness!

He stood in the doorway listening. Ah, *there* was the sound of her footsteps coming along the pavement! No. It was the slouching form of their neighbour, the owner of the pigsty. Silence again! Then again footsteps! No. This time it was a pair of lovers, returning from their Sunday stroll, the boy's arm round the girl's waist.

He felt unwilling to close the door, and he went back to the kitchen, leaving it wide open.

She was with Lobbie anyway. Surely she would never do anything wild or rash with Lobbie at her side!

Such light wind as there had been during the afternoon had dropped completely now. How still everything was! He and the furniture sat waiting, while this perfect day sank willingly into oblivion.

'Gerda, my precious! Gerda, my darling!' He kept forming words of this kind in his mind, as he fidgeted on his hard chair, facing the hallway. 'It was all my fault, Gerda, that you gave yourself to your water-rat!'

He began to long for her coming, as he had never before longed for any human step. He seemed to realize the helpless pathos of her beauty, as he had never realized it before. He saw her bending naked over the stove, as he had seen her once, when, for wantonness, he had undressed her downstairs. He saw the calves of her legs, the curves of her thighs. He saw the peculiar loveliness of the back of her neck and the way her eyelid drooped upon her cheek, giving her profile such evasive innocence.

'You *must* come, Gerda! I don't care for anything, except for you to come! If you come in now . . . safe and sound . . . you can sulk and scold and cry as much as you like!'

How late it was getting. The clock would be striking six soon! She had never been as late as this before. Something *must* have happened! He got up from his chair and looked round the kitchen. Mukalog lay on his back in the open drawer; and suddenly the sight of the idol's fleering face transported him with fury. The 'god of rain' seemed the epitome of everything that was making him suffer. Jason's contempt, Gerda's absence – they were both gloated over in that little monster's abysmal leer!

Recklessly he sized the idol, as he might have seized a dead rat, rushed with it out of the kitchen, out of the house, across the road, and flung it with all the force of his arm high over the pigsty into the darkening field beyond.

The pigs, aroused by his approach, set up a hideous hullabaloo; and the foul smell of their enclosure followed the indrawn panting of his breath. He paused for a minute, with his hands on the fence of the shed, uttering a foolish malediction upon the screeching snouts raised towards him. Then he turned with a groan and shuffled back across the road.

Standing disconsolately by the table, he mechanically lifted up Gerda's plate and surveyed the cheque beneath it. He recalled how she had folded it up with cold, indifferent fingers. He pressed it with his clenched knuckles and re-covered it. Could he do nothing to make her come now, this very moment? 'My "mythology"!' he thought. Up went his hands to his eyes; and pressing his eyeballs tightly, so as to blot out everything, he concentrated his whole nature in one terrific effort to summon up that formidable magnetic mystery.

His will, strained to its uttermost, gave him a sensation as if an obstinate, taut rope were tugging at a water-logged bucket. Not a stir, not a vibration, in those dark interior gulfs!

Removing his hands from his face, he swayed a little against the table, dizzy with his mental struggle. It was no use. His 'mythology' would never help him again. That ecstasy, that escape from reality, was gone. Dorsetshire had done for it!

He subsided into the same chair and waited, his hands outspread, palms down, upon his knees, his heels together, his head bowed.

A kind of waking trance took possession of him, in which he had the illusion that the smell of the pigsty and Gerda's absence were the same thing. 'I shall have to go to the Torps' and ask about her,' he said to himself; but the words only tapped against one another in his brain like dry peas in a sieve.

Then he heard the gate click.

He rushed to the door, out of the house, and, heedless of everything but overwhelming relief, hugged her to his heart.

Her mouth was cold. Her cheek was cold. He pulled her into the hall and slammed the door with a jerk of his shoulder; but not for a second did he let go his tight hold of her. His relief was so great that, as he pressed her against him, he gave vent to several long-drawn breaths that had in them the catch of sobs.

He had felt from the very first touch that she would not resist him, that the barrier between them was broken. When at last he got her into the kitchen, and she had taken off her things, he was hit to the heart by the haggardness of her face. Till now she herself had been tearless. Emotions must have done their worst with her all that day, and she had nothing left. But the sight of the carefully-laid tea-table stirred up too many old associations. She stood staring at him, her hands hanging down limply by her sides, her great eyes fixed upon him. Then, without the least contortion of her face, a torrent of tears descended. . . .

It was after eight o'clock when they got up from their tea-table. Neither of them had said a word about Bob; but Wolf felt convinced that the girl, without using one single articulate syllable about the matter, indicated that henceforth she would close her door to Mr. Weevil.

It was with a strange sensation that he found his thoughts reverting to Christie and her trip to Weymouth – a strange and peculiar sensation. He felt as if Christie had grown thin and frail as a ghost

– remote and far off, too – like that day when he saw her crouched in the Castle lane! She seemed to have become once more what she was in the beginning of their friendship . . . a disembodied entity dwelling in his consciousness like a spirit in a cloud, immaterial, unreal . . . near to him as his own thought, and yet far removed in body.

One by one, holding a blue-bordered napkin in his hands, he dried each cup, each saucer, each plate, each knife, each spoon, as Gerda handed them to him out of the wash-pan in the sink. Sometimes in light, sometimes in shadow, as his own figure came between her and the two candles on the table, her face still showed fluctuating signs of uneasiness. But these signs grew fewer and fewer as he told her about Miss Gault and her sandwiches, about the waiter at the Lovelace having become a beggar, about the extreme emptiness of the outgoing train, and its crowded state returning, about the crafty old man with a white cat – he suppressed all mention of Mattie and Olwen – until at last an expression came into her face that he knew well, an expression of sleepy, infantile amusement.

He paused in his narration directly he caught sight of that look, and hung up the blue-bordered drying-cloth in its place, and proceeded to wash his own hands at the tap.

He got into bed that night some while before she did; and he lay quietly watching her, while she brushed her hair at their chest of drawers between the two half-open windows. This little wooden-framed looking-glass, on this clumsy pinewood object, had been Gerda's only toilet table from the start. 'She shall have more of these things,' he thought, 'when we've cashed that cheque!'

As he watched her candle-flame bend towards her in the faint airs that came wandering out of the night into the room – as he watched the careful gesture with which she pushed back the candlestick as she stood there in her long-sleeved nightgown – he pondered upon the death of his 'mythology.'

'Perhaps it was an escape from reality,' he thought, 'that I was *bound* to lose, if reality got hold of me! Dorsetshire, at any rate, seems to have got hold of me. No, no, I am *not* going back to London; and I am *not* going to drown myself in Lenty Pond!'

When Gerda had finished brushing her hair and had tied it with a thin blue ribbon – he had long since remarked that this was one of the few personal peculiarities she never deviated from – she seemed inclined to loiter awhile before coming to bed. She closed the window at the top, opened it at the bottom, and, drawing a chair close to the sill, sat down there, leaning one of her arms on the woodwork.

It was odd how one single gross image annoyed his mind to the exclusion of all others. This was the image of Weevil in his brown suit, with most of the buttons tightly buttoned, making love to her in that white, high-throated nightgown! Of course, it couldn't have been in the nightgown . . . but still he must have . . . and his brown suit had so many hard, impudent, shiny, cock-crowing buttons!

'Don't catch cold, sweetheart!' he cried suddenly, while a very disconcerting doubt shot through him. Was it revolting to her feminine life-illusion to slip into his arms, easily, naturally, after the shock of what she had undergone? Did *she* feel Bob Weevil's brown suit, his impudent buttons, too nearly, too closely, to bear the thought of any love-making that night? He longed to call out to her bluntly and directly, 'Come on, you sweet little fool, I won't touch you!' . . . or better still perhaps, 'Come on, you beautiful distracted creature, I'll soon make you forget your water-rat!' Instead of uttering a sound, however, what he really did was to jump out of bed, snatch his own warm dressing-gown from the door, and wrap it about her shoulders.

He was very anxious not to bother her with either his sensuality or his sentimentality. His feeling for her at that moment was objective, almost impersonal. He returned to bed, lit a cigarette, propped himself up upon both pillows, and smoked meditatively.

'Christie must be safe back now,' he thought; and there moved slowly across his innermost consciousness the evil suggestion that it was because of what he had read in that exercise-book that the girl's thin frame seemed to him so unearthly to-night, her shadowy personality so remote. 'She's lodged in my mind, though, come what may,' he said to himself. 'I *will* take Olwen to see her,' he thought. 'She *shall* find out she's not a leper!'

From Christie his mind rushed away to that little house in Saint Aldhelm's Street. 'I suppose Emma's come home by now, and Miss Gault's in bed! I wish I'd gone back and kissed her, huddled up like that on his grave – kissed her right on her de-formed lip!'

The night air was stirring again now, and the flame of the candle upon the chest of drawers flickered up and down, throwing queer shadows about the room. The air was sweet with vague earth-odours – not the least tincture of the pigsty perceptible – and as it blew in upon him, past the motionless figure by the window, it seemed like a host of air-spirits journeying on some errand that had no connection with human affairs.

Suddenly he drew in his breath with a startled, hissing sound, and sat bolt upright, staring at Gerda in rapt attention.

The girl had fallen upon her knees at the window, and was making little, tentative, whistling sounds. She was trying to catch the notes of her blackbird-song! First one note she would try, and then another; and each one, as she tried it, broke off in mid-air, ineffectual and futile. . . . Her fingers were clutching the window-sill now, and her head was tossed back. The gown he had thrown over her had fallen away. Her shoulders looked cold and pitiful. Her body trembled and swayed. Her back being turned to him, he could not see that desperately pursed-up whistling mouth; but most vividly he imagined it, and imagined too the piteous contortion of that face against the warm, green-growing darkness outside.

'Gerda . . . my darling!' This was what he wanted to cry out; but he did not dare to utter a whisper. The room had become enchanted. It was a dedicated place – set apart . . . and there was he, foolishly propped up on their two pillows, mute, helpless, like a witness at the birth of a stillborn child!

Again and again did the girl make desperate, discordant, whistling sounds; but it was all to no purpose!

'Don't mind, my darling!' murmured Wolf, when, in a troubled pause after these attempts, he noticed her back shaken by weeping. 'Come on to bed, honey – to bed, to bed! You're lucky not to have started a hoot-owl answering you. I fancied I heard one of those demons, when I woke up in the middle of the night last night. Come on, Gerda; there's a good girl!'

He had never heard a human sigh so deeply drawn as the one he heard now from that open window. But she got up slowly upon her feet and blew out the candle.

He threw back the bedclothes and smoothed out the pillow for her head. Tightly he held her when she stretched herself out by his side.

'Well, there it is!' he thought. 'Life has scotched her just as it has me. Urquhart's cheque has brought me down. Weevil's brown suit has done the same for her. Well, we must get on somehow. Shall I say good night to her before I let myself go to sleep? No; better not! Better just hold tight to her . . . and drift on in our barge – down, down the stream . . . drift on in our barge!'

23

LENTY POND

'Don't you ever say "It's too late" again, missy!' were his parting words, as he kissed Gerda, a few days later, across their iron gate.

It was Thursday now, only two days before the King's Barton wedding, and events had moved rapidly since that agitating Sunday. He had cajoled his Pond Cottage friends into allowing Olwen to pay a surreptitious visit to what after all was her paternal home; and the child had fallen in love with Christie to such an extent that the visit had been repeated within forty-eight hours. And this very day Darnley was driving her in, as he came to School with the idea that she should stay a couple of days under the Malakite roof.

'No one will interfere; it's all blown over,' Wolf had said. 'It would have to be some enemy if any fuss were made. But there won't be any fuss. A little gossip, when Christie goes out with her in the street . . . nothing more . . . and perhaps not even that!'

The only opposition to these proceedings came from Jason, who, though he would not confess himself jealous of this new passion in the child, brought forward the darkest suggestions as to the dangerousness of Blacksod as a place for little girls. 'These large towns,' he had said to them all, speaking as if Blacksod were a second Birmingham, 'these large towns are full of disgusting goings-on. These tradesmen think of nothing but their merry little ways. And, of course, if you want Olwen to have her meals with Mr. Malakite – ' But to Wolf's delighted surprise he had received emphatic support in this enterprise from Mrs. Otter. He had, indeed, been quite as astonished at the insight displayed by that timid lady as by her defiance of the protests of her eldest son. 'Olwen will only do them good, Jason,' she had said. 'There's a special providence over a child like that. She'll turn that sad little Christie into a different girl.'

It was just after eight o'clock when Wolf swung round to wave a final farewell to Gerda. He had begged her to let him have a very early breakfast that morning; for Mrs. Solent wanted him to see her tea-shop with what she called 'clear decks.' Everything had always been in confusion near closing time, when he came in at the end of the day; but this morning, full of pride that her son should see her shop before her waitresses appeared, Mrs. Solent had unlocked and cleaned up the place herself at an incredibly early hour, and was waiting for him there now.

The new tea-shop was not far from the Grammar School, but it was in a side street that branched off towards the meadows where the Lunt encircled the town. The town, in fact, melted into the country here even more quickly than it did on the Babylon Hill side or in the direction of Preston Lane. It was a more umbrageous country, at any rate, into which that little side street led.

Into this quarter of Blacksod, cutting its way through heavy clay hills, diving between tall ferny banks covered with beeches and Scotch firs, following swifter streams than the Lunt, ran the great Exeter highroad; and it was the tourists from that direction that were now to be waylaid and entertained.

This process had apparently already begun; for when Wolf approached the neat little square building, lying back from the road, with a garden in front of it yellow with daffodils, his feeling was unmistakable that prosperity was in the air. The wind was keen and invigorating this morning, the sky clear; and as he strode up the path between the swaying daffodils, he had a sharp, prophetic sense of his mother's future. He saw this little shop moved to one of the main streets of the town. He saw still more of the savings of that enamoured farmer swept into the business! He saw his mother's grasp upon life growing more drastic, more daring, more debonair. He saw her power over material things increasing, her strange pride and exultant loneliness keeping pace with her power. 'She'll leave me far behind,' he thought. And there swept over him a wave of bitter shame at his own incompetence.

'She'll be doling out bonuses to Gerda and me,' he thought. 'We shall be hanging on to her skirts! We shall be a dead weight upon her.'

Vividly he recalled the discussion that had taken place in the last few days between himself and Gerda on the subject of how to spend Mr. Urquhart's two hundred pounds. How childish Gerda was, and how reckless he was! The whole thing was ridiculous . . . with their tiny income to think of spending all this on just smartening up their house!

He knocked lightly now at the tea-shop door and entered with-

522

out waiting for a response. He was amazed at the neatness and elegance of what he saw.

His mother greeted him in the highest feather. Laughing and jesting, she showed him the kitchen, the scullery, the sanitary arrangements, the furniture. 'The rooms are empty upstairs,' she said; 'but do you know what I'm going to do? I'm going to leave Herbert-land, with its dust and its smells, and move over here! I'm going to use one of my waitresses – I've got two, you know – as a maid. She and I will both sleep up there. There are three rooms. And I'll have a regular drawing-room. I'll have the kind of drawing-room I've always wanted – different altogether from that old place in town.'

Mother and son were now seated on two immaculate wicker chairs. Wolf had not yet dared to light a cigarette; but Mrs. Solent, with a quick, radiant gesture, offered him one of her own.

'You won't get enough exercise, mother, if you live where you work; and your precious drawing-room will always be full of the smell of cooking.'

'Oh, we won't think of that!' she cried, making a stroke in the air with her cigarette as if condemning to annihilation every trick of hostile chance; and as he watched her, he realized for the first time what a power she had of forcing external events into line with her wishes. Never had he seen her so full of zest for labour and trouble and tension as she was that morning. Wolf himself felt sick with dismay when he thought of this place filled with tourists from Exeter, and the rooms upstairs reeking of culinary odours!

'What are you making that face about?' his mother asked.

'Am I making a face? I was wondering how much spirit you'll have left for those evening walks you're so fond of.'

Mrs. Solent laughed gaily. 'I had one, last night,' she said, 'towards Pendomer. There are lovely fields over there' – she nodded her head towards the west – 'and delicious woods. I couldn't want anything nicer. I went out there last night . . . up the hill and over the hill . . . I half thought of waylaying you at the Grammar School and taking you with me. But you know what I am! I love my Wolf.' Here she extinguished her cigarette and rose from her seat. 'But I *have* to be alone for these walks. I tell myself stories; I let myself be as romantic and excited as I can. That time of twilight stirs me up . . . like a nightjar, I suppose . . . and I have lovely sensations!'

She moved past him; and as she passed she bent down, took his head between her two hands, and kissed it. Then she went to the door, and, flinging it wide open, inhaled the cool, strong north-east wind. As she stood thus, with her straight, sturdy back turned to him, he seemed to get a supernatural glimpse of the whole power of her personality. This tea-shop and that hill 'towards Pendomer' were only little, material symbols of a Napoleonic campaign that she was working out . . . not necessarily in *this* world at all, but in *some* world, some level of psychic conflict, parallel with his 'mythology.'

'Well, I've got to be off, mother!' he cried. And as he extinguished his cigarette by the edge of hers, in one of her new ash-trays, he instinctively squeezed it into an identical perpendicular position. Then jumping up from the creaking wicker chair, 'I'm late as it is,' he murmured. 'I suppose Mr. "Willum's Mill" comes here for his tea every day?' He strode to the door and stood there by her side. Mrs. Solent laughed, with the rich, careless, high-pitched laugh of a Ninon or a Thais.

'Only on market-days, my son. But I'm going to tea with *him* next Sunday.'

Wolf disregarded this confession altogether. 'I say, mother! You're coming to the wedding on Saturday, aren't you? The day after to-morrow. You haven't forgotten that?'

She turned towards him her radiant cheeks and glowing eyes, 'Will the monster be there, to see Lorna's child married to your respectable friend? If she's there, I *must* come. What sport it'll be! The monster and I in the same pew, and your sister landing her patient fish!'

Across Wolf's mind flitted the image of that unwieldy figure stumbling over the milk-bottle at the grave.

'I haven't the least idea whether Miss Gault means to come,' he said. 'But *you* must come, mother! You must leave your work to your two girls. I'll call for you at Mrs. Herbert's . . . about half-past nine . . . and we'll walk over. Well, I must run. Good-bye, mother.'

She met his embrace with a swift, almost greedy kiss, but immediately afterwards whispered with airy mockery: 'Mattie Smith must be very grateful to you for giving her her darling! That pointed beard would never have been caught if my Wolf hadn't played matchmaker.'

'What the devil are you talking about, mother? They knew each other years before *we* came down here.'

There shone in her brown eyes such a well-spring of satirical mischief, he found it hard to tear himself away. A spasm of vicious sympathy with this dark-spurting jet of malice produced the sensation within him of a nervous twinge that was half a tickling delight to him and half an adder's bite.

His mind reverted in a lightning-flash to his father's skull. Oh, how gentle, oh, how kindly that grin of death seemed, compared with this inhuman glee in the presence of perverse fate! A malign voluptuousness rose up within him, like an intoxicating bubble out of the very abyss, spilling black bile through veins. Ferociously he offered up that poor skull to this radiant sorceress. 'You look just as you did, mother, when you teased Mr. Smith so much, that Horse Fair day. I hope *his* ghost won't be there on Saturday !' His words were innocent enough; but he knew too well what passed, under their cover, between himself and this woman. For good and evil he had made his choice between the living and the dead.

'I *could* not feel like this,' he thought, 'if I were the Wolf Solent I used to be. Good-bye!' he repeated. 'I must run.' . . .

All that morning, as he faced the Grammar School boys, his mind squeezed out the essence of this scene with his mother. He had gone over to her altogether! He had deserted the 'fellow i' the cellarage.' He had betrayed his 'old Truepenny.' All that long morning, while those boys' faces scattered themselves into his mind like grey ashes into a pail, he struggled to make clear what had happened to him.

He had no longer any definite personality, no longer any banked-up integral self. Submission to Urquhart had killed more than self-respect. He could never have gone over to his mother like this if his 'mythology' had survived. He could feel now that greedy kiss of hers upon his lips! He had come to Dorset . . . he knew it well enough now . . . to escape from her, to mix with the spirit of his father in his own land. But Fate was hunting him 'back to London,' and he began to have an inkling as to what the alternative to London was. The alternative to London was the bottom of Lenty Pond!

Wilder and wilder grew his thoughts as he rounded off the destiny of the House of Stuart to those furtive listeners. Rows upon rows of dwarf-men . . . that is how he saw them now, these boys of his . . . embryo-men, with a kind of distorted, atrophied intelligence, full of a jeering, idiotic cunning! Oh, how he hated them and the task of teaching them!

Suddenly in the very middle of his lesson he felt his voice changing and becoming strangely vibrant. Good God! What things were on the tip of his tongue to say to them! Was he going to 'dance his malice-dance' before them, as he had danced it before that London audience? Life upon this earth began to show itself to him in a most evil light.

This killing of his 'mythology,' how, could he survive it? His 'mythology' had been his escape from life, his escape into a world where machinery could not reach him, his escape into a deep, green, lovely world where thoughts unfolded themselves like large, beautiful leaves growing out of fathoms of blue-green water!

What were his sensations to him now? What was the air of a morning like this, without those mysterious emanations from the glimmering depths?

He had comforted Gerda; and the way she was happy now in her childish delight over that two hundred ought to have given a fresh glow to his days. But it didn't. That startling alliance between Christie and Olwen, which he had plotted in the face of so many difficulties, and which was apparently absorbing both of them in its excitement, ought to have satisfied him. But it only made his thoughts gloomier. The last time he had seen Christie, her mind was so full of Olwen and Olwen's future, that she scarcely listened to what he was telling her!

Through the dizzy foreground of these boys' heads, white collars, sharp elbows, and scratching pens, through the patient 'notes' he himself was dictating to them, floated in long procession all the people of his life.

Urquhart was sending his book in instalments to Bristol to be printed. He appeared to be thinking of nothing else. Jason was revising another volume of poetry, which promised to raise him into the innermost circle of modern literature. Darnley, Mattie, Mrs. Otter – they were all happy just then. He found himself sheering off any thought of Miss Gault. But apart from Miss Gault, all his friends were in calm waters. Even T. E. Valley, so Darnley had informed him, was in a state of comparative peace of mind.

He found himself and Miss Gault to be the only unhappy ones. Yes, and they were the only consciousnesses in the whole circle who gave a thought to that cemetery! When he and Miss Gault were dead, not a living soul would remember William Solent, Why, Mattie, the man's own daughter – not even once had Wolf been able to persuade her to visit that grave!

Oh, how he hated his work in that classroom! He did not only know in pitiless detail every map upon the wall . . . and feel toward it as something removed from every tincture of happiness . . . he also knew every ink-stain and fly-stain upon the wall. Those dirty marks were of equal importance with the maps. Both the marks and the maps represented a world that was totally bleak . . . a world of doleful invention, of disconsolate fancy . . . and yet a world in which he had to spend by far the larger part of his life.

He had just managed to cope with this desolate world by giving himself up to his secret vice the very second he left the school gate. But those ecstatic sensations were now gone for ever! He might tear his nerves to pieces with his effort to get those feelings back. They would never come back! They were lost. How did human beings go on living, when their life-illusion was destroyed? What did they tinker up and patch up inside of them to rub along with, to shuffle through life with, when they lacked that one grand resource? . . .

He hurried back to Preston Lane for lunch, and was more than successful in hoodwinking Gerda as to his secret desolation. The girl chatted all the time about the spending of the two hundred! So far she had bought nothing but one small pair of silver sugar-tongs. The cheque had been deposited in Gerda's name, and the girl was touchingly proud of possessing her first 'fortune,' as she kept calling it. She apparently intended spending every penny in the next few weeks! At least that was the implication of her excited chatter; and Wolf was quite prepared to submit.

He derived a sardonic amusement from noting the fact that this 'spiritual blood-money,' which had cost him his secretest happiness was apparently smoothing away altogether the moral bruise left by the Weevil incident. That 'brown coat' might return to *his* mind now and then. Hers it seemingly troubled no more. As for the luckless water-rat, he did not show his face again. Wolf's private inkling was that he had been indignantly dismissed, once for all, in some brief scene to which the girl never alluded. But it may easily have been that the lad himself was frightened by the length to which he had gone. Wolf certainly found, in his own weary introspection into the feelings of a cuckold, that he had a tendency to avoid that part of the town where the sausage-shop was! . . .

His lunch over, Wolf strode back more dispirited than ever to the scene of his pillory.

He had come to loathe every aspect of that chair and desk which made up his spiritual scaffold. There he talked and fidgeted while those rows of cropped heads and protruding ears nodded and swayed like shocks of ruffled wheat under the conscientious, pitiless repetition of a recurrent winnowing. And this was destined to be his life indefinitely, *sans* the remotest chance of a change for the better, unless his mother, as a successful business-woman, gave him a pension!

What a mess he had made of his life! As he surveyed those spots and blurs and marks on these odious walls, he began to recognize the fact that until the last two or three days he had never faced reality at all. His heavenly vice, hugged to himself like a fairy bride, had protected him from reality. Here he was, thirty-six years old, and as far as *real reality* was concerned – the reality his mother lived in, the reality Darnley lived in – he was as innocent and preoccupied as a hermit who reads nothing but his breviary.

He had lost his breviary now, his Mass-book, his Mass! He had lost his whole inner world; and the outer world – what was it but rows of puzzled, protruding ears, into which, for an eternity, he had to pump tedious, questionable information?

When he left the classroom that evening, he waited for Darnley outside the building.

'I must see Christie first!' he kept repeating, as he watched the boys file out.

'Will you do something for me, old friend?' he said, as soon as his colleague appeared. Darnley fixed his mackerel-coloured eyes upon him in patient surprise.

'Even into the third part of my kingdom, Solent!'

'Well, keep Mattie waiting for once, and go to tea with Gerda. Will you do that? Tell her I've got one of my walking-fits upon me and *have* to have some air. Tell her not to be worried, even if I'm late for supper. Of course, I don't mean you to stay all that time. But just tell her I shall be late; and she's not to worry.'

'But what on earth's up, Wolf? Where, if a person may ask, are you going to run off to?'

'Oh it's all right,' Wolf said quietly. 'I'm not sure yet where I *shall* go. Possibly I'll pay a visit to Mattie and tell her to expect *you*! Don't bother me with any details, my dear! Only, if you love me, go over to Preston Lane and make yourself amusing to Gerda and enjoy her tea. And make her understand that it's all right. That's the great thing . . . that it's all right!'

Wolf fancied there was a dim expression of disquietude in his friend's face as he nodded to him and hurried off; but he felt as if he would have run a worse risk just then than to disquiet Darnley.

Hurriedly he made his way to the Malakite shop. 'She's got Olwen in there now,' he said to himself. 'She won't want to see me.'

But while he still kept repeating the words, 'She won't want to see me,' he rang the bell in the little side alley.

To his surprise the door was opened immediately, and Christie herself, in cloak and hat, stood before him. 'You!' the girl cried. 'Well, you'd better come with me! Olwen has begun murmuring something about cake; and I've got none in the house. I've left her with father, over their tea. They're both slow eaters; so we needn't rush *too* madly. Let's go this way!'

She led up the quiet incline leading to the King's Barton road. He could guess now which was the actual confectioner's to which she was hurrying him . . . a little shop he had often passed on his way in and out of the town.

The horizontal sun was shooting its rays through great dark banks of western clouds as they approached this shop; and from its windows the fiery reflections fell upon the road like the reflections of barge-lanterns into an estuary.

'Wolf! I never knew how exciting she was, how intelligent she was! Oh, Wolf, it's wonderful! We suit each other down to the ground.'

He snatched at her hand and pressed it hard. Never in all his relations with her had he caught such a tone in her voice.

When they turned into the Barton road, there was wafted into their faces one of those wandering winds that seem to carry a burden of earth-mysteries from one unknown spot to another.

'What an evening it is!' she cried. 'I smelt primroses then!'

'It's moss, I expect, and dead leaves,' he said, 'from the woods over there.'

They soon reached the little shop; and he entered it with her, and helped her to choose the cake.

'Where are you going, Wolf? Over to Barton? Over to Pond Cottage?'

He held open the door for her in silence. There was a bell fixed upon the top of this door, which rang noisily as he closed it behind them. His nerves were so strained that this harsh jangle above their heads seemed ominous to him – seemed to have a sound of warning, like a reef-bell at sea.

'Yes,' he said dreamily. 'Over to Barton . . . over to Lenty Pond.'

The girl missed this slip of the tongue.

'Is your sister happy, Wolf?' she asked. And then, without waiting for an answer: 'Do you know what Olwen said just now? She said she'd like to live with me when Mattie was married!'

Wolf prodded the ground with his stick. 'Did she really? What a wise little girl! And what did you answer? I don't see why you shouldn't have her! I'm sure it would be all right now.'

Christie sighed deeply, a long breath.

'*Would* they agree to it? Do you think they'd agree to it?'

'I don't see why not,' he repeated in a low voice.

'If you see Mattie to-night, Wolf, I wish you'd sound her about it . . . and Mrs. Otter . . . just to see how they'd take it.'

He made no reply to this; but drawing under his arm her free hand, and straightening his shoulders, he gazed up the road.

'Do you remember our night in the cornfield, Chris? After that game of bowls?'

She lifted her head and looked sharply at him, and he received the impression that he had struck an unseasonable note.

'I'm not one for forgetting, Wolf. You ought to know *that* by this time.'

'Urquhart gave me two hundred pounds for finishing his book, Chris. I've never told you that, have I?'

But she had turned her face away now and was evidently thinking about Olwen, and getting anxious to return.

'Oh, I'm so glad, my dear!' Her voice was sympathetic, but it was the calm sympathy of a friend, not the vibrant sympathy of a lover.

'What a detached little thing she is,' he thought; and the memory came over him, with a rush of wild self-pity, of all they had whispered together in that cornfield. 'I've never told her about my "mythology" . . . but she ought to know, she ought to know what that two hundred means!'

'Well, I must run back. Olwen will have finished her tea.' And she tightened her hold upon the cake and made a little movement to draw her arm away. But Wolf burst out then with a final impulse of desperation:

'It was a vile job. It's a vile production to be paid all that for! He's printing it in Bristol *now*. It'll just suit your father's clients! How do you think I'll appear to myself after this, Christie?'

The girl tossed her head proudly. 'Oh, the clients!' she cried. 'You're extremely moral to-night, Wolf! I daresay you thought *my* book would please the clients!'

'I read just a page,' he said. But he released her arm now and only held her there by the grimness of his mood. 'To sell my soul to Urquhart! . . . to do what young Redfern *wouldn't* do!'

She did look up at him now with a flash of penetration.

'But, Wolf – any deviltry he threatened you with, was to *make* you do it, wasn't it? Well! You've done it. You've submitted. He can't hurt you now, can he?'

'But the book – the book, Chris!'

The girl gave a faint little laugh . . . the laugh of an air-sprite for whom these human scruples were growing intolerably tedious. . . . 'Well, there are plenty of things Gerda will be glad enough to buy with this money. You're different from what I thought you were, Wolf, if you let an absurd fancy, like this prey on your mind!' She paused a moment and then said gravely, 'But mother would have understood what troubles you.'

She seized the sleeve of his coat with her fingers, and then stood silent, looking fixedly at him. Then she sighed very heavily, and, lifting up his arm to her face, pressed her lips to his wrist. After that she stared at him once more, in intense contemplative scrutiny.

He looked away, across her shoulder, over the scattered Blacksod roofs, over the Lunt meadows. Her sudden gesture of affection and something in the white immobility of her face made him think of the warning he had received in Urquhart's kitchen from that Farmer's Rest girl.

'I'll take a look at that pond to-night,' he thought grimly. 'If that's to be the upshot, I'd better see how it looks of a fine March evening!' . . .

'Well, give Olwen a kiss for me, Chris; and if I find Mattie at home I'll certainly try her out about that. I believe myself that she'll agree to it. She's so self-absorbed just now that I think she'll be glad to be left free. Well . . . God bless you, Chris! Don't drop the cake. Good-bye . . . good-bye!'

He did not look back after they separated, but the sound of her light running footsteps made his heart feel desolately empty.

His last hope of recovering his old self seemed to sink down like a child's sagging balloon, pricked by a bodkin.

'She doesn't know. She's full of Olwen; and she doesn't know,' he said to himself. But could he have *made* her know, even if he'd gone back with her? She didn't ask him to go back. Why should she? *But could* he have made her know, even if she had? He had never told a living soul about his 'mythology.'

He grasped his stick by the middle now; and in place of William of Deloraine, there came into his head the Homeric description of Hector of Troy, when, with his great spear held in just that way, he imposed a truce upon the combatants!

531

As he caught himslf with this thought in his mind he smiled at his own grandiose self-consciousness. Stoicism! That's what a man needed, made as he was made! Stoical endurance of whatever fate the gods rained down upon his head! No Trojan, no Roman, would blink and whimper at the thought of Lenty Pond.

It was not long before he reached the very spot where on the night of the bowling-match he had climbed over the hedge with Christie, into the cornfield. . . .

Moved to what he did by an obscure sense that this might be 'the last time,' he hurriedly scrambled through the thickset hedge. The field was evidently destined to lie fallow that season. He found a rusty barrow, with its wooden shafts protruding into the air like the horns of a buried monster, and upon this he sat down. The sun had disappeared now, and he felt disposed to let the twilight fall about him in that place of memory.

Slowly, as he waited, did the earth swing into greyness, into dusk, into darkness. Cramped and chilly, he felt as if it needed more energy than he possessed to clamber down again into the road! A sort of waking trance fell upon him as he crouched there, growing more and more cold and numb; and it was almost quite dark when he resumed his walk.

'I am like a ghost that's been damned,' he thought, as he moved on. And indeed it was just as such a ghost would have felt that he had the sense of being cut off from all the magnetic reservoirs of the planet! He experienced a physical sensation of lightness, of hollowness, as he walked – as if he had been a husk, blown by the faintest of all winds!

When he reached the path that crossed the fields to the main highway, 'I suppose,' he thought, 'the whole business has been inevitable since the beginning; the sort of thing that *had* to happen, if a nature like mine lost its pride?'

As he began to approach King's Barton he noticed that the night was going to be one of those clear, vapourless nights, when the sky is velvety dark and the stars exceptionally large and bright. He was walking with his head turned towards a specially luminous constellation, just above the arable uplands, a little to his left. Suddenly he became conscious, as an absolute certainty, that just above the horizon *behind* him, somewhere between Melbury Bub and Blacksod, there was a crescent moon. He swung round on his heel. Yes! There it was . . . the thinnest, most disembodied new moon that he had ever seen!

He surveyed that fragile-floating illuminated curve, comparable to nothing above or beneath the earth, and there came over him an inexplicable desire to do reverence to this immortal visitant. How had he known with such certainty that there *was* a new moon behind him? He was not yet enough of a countryman to keep any account of these things. Well! whatever perch were left in Lenty Pond would know about this new moon!

When he reached the wall of the churchyard, he noticed that there was a light in one of the lower windows of that great Perpendicular Tower. He paused and contemplated this light. In that vapourless darkness its effect in the middle of a great mass of masonry was singular and arresting. While he leaned upon the low, crumbling wall and surveyed this light, he became aware of the sound of men's voices – voices whispering . . . whispering furtively and suspiciously. Suddenly, by means of a light much less clear than the light in the window . . . 'It's a lantern!' he thought . . . he detected the forms of three men, one of them much taller than the others, grouped around the boy's grave. He had no sooner caught sight of this group of noctambulists than the light in the tower went out.

Never had he felt less inquisitive, less concerned. He was tempted to walk forward and let the whole thing go. However, where all motives were equally futile, let a straw turn the scale! He climbed stealthily over the wall and advanced to the church door.

The door was wide open, and he entered the central aisle, moving as cautiously as he could. Past the christening-font he moved; past the back of the rear pews. All was pitch dark, and the peculiar smell of the church, suggestive of mildew and worm-eaten woodwork, was like a second darkness within the darkness. He was arrested in his advance by the sudden appearance of a flickering light, which proceeded from the space under the tower where were the stone steps that led up to the belfry.

'Tilly-Valley!' he muttered to himself, as once more – as had been happening to him so often these last few days – he knew without question who this light-bearer was.

Yes! He was right! Descending the belfry steps, with a flickering candle in his hand, came the figure of the little priest, his thin legs first, then his cassocked body, then his agitated white face, then his bare black scalp!

The expression of the man's face, when he caught sight of Wolf, was an epitome of consternation and relief, the latter emotion rapidly overspreading the former, like a kindly shadow crossing a distorted gargoyle.

533

'What's up, Valley?' whispered Wolf, taking the vicar's cold, limp fingers in his own. 'What are they doing out there? Is it Urquhart? There were three of them. They had a lantern. God, man! You're trembling like a leaf!'

'I was in my garden . . . I saw them come in . . . over the hedge. . . . For a long time I watched them. I ought to have gone down to them . . . I know I ought . . . I've betrayed the Sacrament by not going down to them. . . .'

'It's all right,' whispered Wolf soothingly. 'You couldn't have done anything. They've probably been drinking. Monk's with him out there. I saw him . . . the great devil! The other one's that fellow Round, no doubt.'

The priest broke away from him and began hurrying up the aisle towards the altar, Wolf following at his heels.

'There would have been a time,' he said to himself, 'when . . . when . . .'

Wolf thought the clergyman was going to kneel down or even prostrate himself; but instead of this he placed the candle carefully upon the top of the altar, made a hurried genuflection, and then ran round like a panic-stricken thief to a small window in the side transept which overlooked the invaded spot.

Here Wolf followed him and peered out too, leaning over his shoulder.

There were only two men to be seen now . . . and they were both busy filling up the open grave. The lantern was on the ground, and by its light they were seen working hard, stamping down the loose soil with the utmost concentration and scraping away all the tell-tale rubble from the surface of the grass. Not a word did the men speak to one another; but it was easy enough to recognize Monk. The other was undoubtedly the landlord of 'Farmer's Rest.' Mr. Urquhart had disappeared.

They worked at their job so rapidly that it was not long before the carefully folded rolls of turf-grass were being pressed down upon that oblong heap, concealing the raw clay. Wolf fancied he could even detect a patch of daisies upon this replaced turf. There was a patch of something, at any rate, that showed whitish, as the lantern-rays fell upon it.

Mr. Valley's cassock, as Wolf bent over the little priest, smelt unpleasantly of gin. The wall against which he himself was pressing the palm of his hand, as he leant forward, felt damp and chilly under the touch, like the flesh of a corpse.

'They can't see our light, can they?' groaned the vicar, half

534

turning his head. 'I'll blow it out!' whispered Wolf in reply; and leaving the man's side, he walked over to the altar-steps, extinguished the flame, and came back with the candlestick swinging from one of his fingers, and a fume of carbonic-acid gas floating round his head.

Shifting his stick to the hand from which the smoking candle was swinging, Wolf peered again through the narrow window. He could feel the body of Mr. Valley shivering; and to give the man some reassurance in the darkness he placed his free hand upon his shoulder. Then, bending down, he laid both the candle and his oak stick softly on the flagstones.

The two men at the grave seemed resolved to complete their job with the utmost scrupulosity. 'I can't believe they *are* drunk,' he thought. 'He must have appealed to their superstition. He must have scared them into it.'

What the man has said over the Malmsey returned to his mind. 'He must have forced the coffin open!' he thought. And then, as he stared above Mr. Valley's head at those two figures beating the turf down, he was surprised to find himself completely indifferent and impassive. Whether Mr. Urquhart had been content to press his perturbed face against the cold featurelessness of Redfern's mortality, or whether, like Isabella in 'The Pot of Basil,' he had carried 'so dear a head' back to his secret chamber, seemed at that moment a question that left him utterly incurious!

'There *would* have been a time for such a word,' he said to himself; 'but *now* all is equal!' He saw Roger Monk straddle over the grave with his long legs, move the lantern, and whisper something to Mr. Round. From the road outside there came the sound of children laughing and chattering. 'I wonder Urquhart didn't wait till midnight. Anyone might have drifted in here; but I suppose they'd just take 'em for grave diggers . . . or be too scared to go near 'em!'

'Thud! Thud! Thud!' went the spades of the two men against the sides of the grave. Valley's shiverings had stopped now. Wolf heard the little man's lips moving in the darkness. He was muttering a Latin psalm. Wolf now began to feel like a mute sentinel – a sentinel at the grave of everything that had ever enjoyed the sweet sun! Vast tracks of Dorset earth seemed spread out before him. He could hear a low wind in the sycamores of Poll's Camp. He could hear the wide expanses of Blackmore Vale sighing in their sleep. He recalled what he had felt at his first encounter with Urquhart . . . that vague awareness of something new and strange to him in the secret of evil. He seemed totally indifferent to all that now! Good? Evil? It all seemed to belong to something unimportant, irrelevant, remote. What did it matter? This grave those two were stamping down so smoothly ... it was only one of thousands under that crescent moon! With the heart of life killed, what did it matter what happened to anyone?

The two men were exchanging whispers now. They were gazing with satisfaction at their work. Wolf recognized that his bare hand, whose outspread fingers were pressed against the cold stone, had grown numb as he leant hard upon it, bending forward over Valley's shoulder. Ay, but what an unpleasant odour ... like dissolution itself ... emanated from the cold sweat of the little priest! But the man's shivering had subsided. That was a good sign. No doubt the departing of Mr. Urquhart had relieved the situation for him. As for himself, he felt an obscure regret at the Squire's withdrawal. So deadly callous had his emotions grown, he experienced at that moment nothing but a weary curiosity. Yes, it would have been interesting to see that convulsed white face bending down over the form in the coffin! The old villain must have crouched on the grass, when they got the lid off, undeterred by the smell! Had Valley seen what happened from up there in the belfry? Probably he *had*; and the shock of it had brought him scrambling down, torn between the outrage of the sacrilege and his fear of the Squire.

The two men were standing erect now and staring straight towards him. Of course, they couldn't see anything, now that the church was dark. They must be *feeling* the vibration of his and Valley's intense scrutiny.

How long had his hand been lodged on Valley's shoulder, and why was he gripping the man so hard?

He raised his arm, so that both his palms were pressing now against the coping of that narrow slit in the wall. One of them was numb, but the other was hot and pulsing feverishly. Ah, the foul fiend Flibbertigibbet! But a time will come when there'll be no more lanterns!

'Damn that beggar Monk! He's not satisfied yet. There goes his spade again. Yes, take the lantern away, landlord Round! Yes, nudge the great brute and call him off. Yes, there *are* steps in the road. You'd better clear off, both of you! God! I believe they're going to quarrel! But it's all nothing to me now. What is a quarrel over a boy's grave when the "hard little crystal" of a person's inmost self has dissolved.

'It'll be a quaint moment, though, when that great beggar gets back to the house and has to answer his master's bell! Will he say, "Yes, sir . . . no, sir," in his usual tone? He talked to me once of killing the man. Why does *that* come into my head at this moment? But no! He'll never do that. He'll carry up the hot drink and turn down the bedclothes just as usual; and Urquhart'll say, "The moon has gone down, eh? what?" just in his ordinary tone! They *have* done now . . . at last. . . . Oh, that's right! Don't forget the crowbar, Mr. Round! A crowbar? So they did intend to open the coffin!'

Wolf watched the two men make their way, slowly and carefully between the graves, towards the wall that divided the churchyard from the meadow where the school treat had been held. Once over this wall, only an occasional flicker of the lantern revealed their path; and soon even that vanished.

He turned from the window, pulling his companion after him. It was like touching something that had no feeling with something else that had no feeling, to tug at Valley's arm with his benumbed fingers.

After three of four futile efforts, he managed, however, to strike a match; and by the aid of this match, moving across to the altar-steps, with his fingers guarding the flame, he relit the priest's candle. With a cold, weary impassiveness . . . allowing this impulse to reach Lenty Pond, which was indeed the only definite impulse he retained just then, its fullest sway . . . he suggested to the silent figure at his side that they might walk over together to Pond Cottage. 'It'll cheer the little beggar up,' he thought, 'to have a chat with the bride and bridegroom; and I can drop him at their gate.'

T. E. Valley seemed glad enough to postpone his return to the desolation of his littered study. 'But I mustn't stay long!' he murmured.

During the first part of their walk together some common instinct prevented them from referring to the scene they had just witnessed; but at last, when they had reached Pond Lane, Valley burst out:

'I hope you're right . . . from a secular point of view . . . about my not interfering just now, Solent. From my own point of view I shall find it . . . hard . . . yes, very hard . . . no, I don't mean that . . . did I say hard? I meant that I shall find it . . . very . . . you know, Solent? . . . very shameful . . . to . . . to . . . forgive myself!'

They were walking now where the hedges were very high and

thick. Wolf began to experience a confused exhaustion, that seemed to weigh upon his head as well as upon his arms and legs. It was as though a knot had been tied in the recesses of his being, which interfered with the flow of his blood. A heavy, inert apathy settled down upon him, which he vaguely associated with these high hedges. 'It would have been ridiculous to meddle,' he said. 'You'd have done no good. Do you know, Valley, I think I'd like to rest for a minute!'

'To rest? Certainly . . . of course. You mean it would be nice if we sat down? But it's very dark, isn't it? There's usually water in both these ditches; and they are very deep. Hadn't we better wait till we get to the Otters'?'

'Better wait,' repeated Wolf wearily, feeling as if it would be a heavenly thing to slip gently down now into Lenty Pond and have done with it all; 'better wait till we get to the Otters'.'

'You're not feeling shaky, are you, Solent? I'm rather shaky myself. Take my arm. The air will be better soon. It's these hedges. I never come here alone, because of these hedges – and – well! you know? because of that pond over there. Don't mind them, Solent. They're only high hedges and deep ditches.'

Wolf stopped motionless in the middle of the road. 'I really would like to sit down,' he said. 'I mean, to lie down! I think I must be, as you say, shaky. I expect it's from standing so long at that window. Would you mind if I tried, with my stick, to feel if there *is* water in the ditch?'

'If you feel dizzy, Solent, why don't you lie down where we are – in the road? I've often done that myself. Here; lean on me! I'll help you. That's right. It's quite dry, isn't it? Here; I've got a handkerchief in my pocket, a big red one . . . it's as big as a scarf. Here; I'll put it under your head . . . so . . . so . . . so. Do you feel all right now, Solent? You *will* soon, anyway. Do you know. I've had some of the happiest moments of my life lying down in the road? The road to Blacksod is very good for lying down on, because there's grass at the side of it and very few carts go that way. How do you feel now, Solent?'

A relaxation of every muscle and fibre in Wolf's body seemed to have taken place. He gazed up at the obscure form of the priest and at the shivering stars in the blue-black sky.

'It's–just–what–I–wanted,' he murmured, with a luxurious sigh.

Mr. Valley was delighted. He hovered over him as if he had ensconced him in his own bed. 'I thought you'd like it, Solent,' he murmured. 'Sometimes when I've been like this on the Blacksod road I've felt as if, with the round earth beneath me carrying me between the constellations . . . and the Blessed Sacrament waiting my return . . . I've felt as if – What's the matter, Solent? Is the road too hard?'

But Wolf had only been fumbling with his hand to make sure he hadn't lost his stick. He felt extremely unwilling to move or to speak. But he was conscious of a stronger wave of affection for Valley than he had ever known before.

'Does your forehead feel feverish?' his companion enquired now, touching Wolf's head in the darkness with the tips of his fingers. 'Don't think I'm inquisitive, Solent; but I'm a priest of God, and I . . . I notice people that are . . . people that are . . . disturbed.'

'You're very nice to me, Valley. Please don't kneel in the road! I'll get up in a minute. It does me good lying here.'

'Don't think I'm inquisitive, Solent; and don't answer if you don't want to. But am I right in thinking that you've got something on your mind . . . something that troubles you till you feel dizzy, like you did just now?'

'I'll get up in a moment, Valley. I'm only lying like this now because it's such a nice sensation! Why do you think it's so dark, when the stars look so large?'

'It's these hedges, Solent. They keep the light out.'

'The moon's gone down. Do you mean the light from Pond Cottage?'

'Solent! You won't mind if I say something?'

'No. I'm listening. Please get up. I don't like your kneeling.'

'Shall I tell you what's troubling you, what's made you so dizzy, Solent? It's because Darnley is going to be married. I know exactly what you feel. I know well what you and Darnley are to each other. Do you know what I think, Solent? I think it's a shame you two didn't have the happiness of living together before you both married. It's *that* that's troubling you; aren't I right? It's thinking that your friend's lost to you?'

'Nonsense, my good man!' cried Wolf, scrambling hastily to his feet. 'What has been weighing on my mind has nothing to do with this wedding. Come! Let's be getting on! I left Darnley at tea with my wife; I mean I sent him off there.'

His words were casual and careless; but Valley's suggestion hit him hard. It was the same hint that Miss Gault had made last Sunday. Was it possible that the accursed mood he'd fallen into . . . this mood of miserable apathy . . . had as much to do with the wedding as with the loss of his great secret?

His companion had difficulty now in keeping up with him, so fast did he walk. Presently he said: 'Tell me this, Valley, if you don't mind . . . did you *see* what Urquhart was doing just now?'

They were close to the Otters' house when he spoke. He could distinguish the light from the drawing-room shining between the branches of the poplars. Valley laid his hand on his arm and clutched it tightly, compelling him to stop. The man's face was a patch of wavering greyness against the blanket of the dark, but he could detect its extreme distress.

'I can't – Solent – you know what I mean? – I can't tell you anything. It's all misery. Yes, I saw him. It was a long way from the tower. The belfry's high up. I think he loved him. *That's* what I *have* to think; but I can only bear it, Solent, by . . . by a little trick of mine.' He paused; and then, to his companion's consternation, he uttered a ghastly little laugh.

'What trick, Valley, are you talking about?' Wolf instinctively swung his arm free, for the priest's finger-nails were hurting his flesh. 'What trick do you mean?'

His tone was irritable, for he was pondering in his mind how to get rid of the man and slip off. 'I *must* set eyes on that pond before I see Mattie,' he said to himself.

Valley's reply seemed to come from the darkness that surrounded them, rather than from any localized spot. 'If . . . you . . . must . . . know . . . I have . . . to pretend . . . that I *was* Urquhart . . . myself!'

Wolf made no comment upon this. He looked up at the poplars in that well-known garden. They were illuminated on one side by a faint glimmer coming from his old window, the window of the room where he spent his first night in Dorset.

'What a man-lover you are, Valley! *My* trick is to escape from humanity altogether.'

To his dismay the priest's reply to this was a repetition of the same cackling laugh.

'Yes; to escape from it altogether!' Wolf went on. 'I don't know why that should amuse you, Valley.' As he spoke he became aware of something burning at the back of the house. 'Dimity must be burning refuse . . . some sort of greenery,' he thought. 'It's like the smell of dead flowers. It's like a bonfire of dead crocuses!'

This aromatic smoke, poignant and penetrating, floating on the air, gave him a very queer twinge. His nerves reached out invisible tendrils to respond to it; but under the disturbed contact between his sensations and his *enjoyment of his sensations*, this motion of response only caused him tantalizing discomfort. It caused him, indeed, a discomfort of so peculiar a kind, that he prolonged his silence almost rudely, while he gave way to it. It was a sharp, thin, long-drawn-out sensation, like some erotic agitation that is motiveless, meaningless, irritating.

What he felt made it more imperative than ever that he should get rid of his companion and hurry across that field! He turned round, tightened his hold on his stick, and spoke with a tone of quiet authority. 'Valley,' he said, 'I can't go in at this moment. I've got to think a bit . . . out here . . . by myself. You go in and tell them so, will you? I'll follow you in, in a second or so, when I've thought something out . . . in my mind. Mattie will understand. She knows my ways. Apologize to Mrs. Otter. No! Why should you do that? Just tell them that Darnley's with Gerda in town and that I'll be in in a minute. That's all that's necessary.'

But the priest's fingers only tightened upon his arm.

'In town? With your wife? Darnley?'

'Having tea with her, my good man! Those body-snatchers have upset you completely. There! Go in and tell them!' And with a quick movement of his wrist he released himself from Valley's clutch and rushed off.

He found it an incredible relief to scramble over the familiar gap in that high hedge and run with long, swift strides across the field. It was as if all the rumours in the village about that pond had gathered to themselves invisible arms and were pushing him towards it. What he felt in his own consciousness was not a simple nor was it a very complicated feeling. It was exactly as if the loss of his spiritual vice had left him inordinately thirsty and he had an inkling that just to stare at the waters of Lenty Pond would give him some inexplicable satisfaction.

He blundered over the dark expanse of that great field as if Jason's water-nymph herself had been calling to him. Blindly, recklessly, he ran across it, stumbling over the mole-hills, not once glancing up at the starry sky, his stick clutched in his right hand as if it had really been the spear of William of Deloraine, and his panting breath coming in deep gasps. As he ran he did notice one thing, and that was the shadowy leap of a startled hare. The creature rose and dashed away from under his very feet; but instead of disappearing into the darkness, he could see, as he ran, where it had risen erect, a short distance off, and was watching him, motionless and with a frozen intentness.

Ah! There it was – Lenty Pond in the cold starlight!

He moved close up to the edge of the water. He stood with both hands pressed hard upon the handle of his stick. He flung his consciousness, as if it were a heavy stone that all day long he had been carrying in his pocket, down into those silent depths. And then his body – not his mind, but his body – became acquainted with shivering dread. Was his mind going to issue the final mandate now, at this very moment? What was his body doing that it revolted like this? What was his body doing that its foot-soles clung to the mud as if they had been rooted there? It was not only his flesh that now turned sick with fear. The very bones within him began screaming – a low, thin, wire-drawn scream – before what his mind was contemplating. It was not that life – merely to be alive – had suddenly become so precious. It was not fear of Nothingness that made his body quake. *It was Lenty Pond itself!* Yes, what his flesh and his bones shrank from was not eternity. It was immersion in that localized, particular, cubic expanse of starlit oxygen-hydrogen!

He visualized Mr. Urquhart and Jason surveying his dead face. Would someone . . . the 'automatic young lady,' perhaps . . . have closed his staring eyes before those two looked at him? A fish hooked out of season! 'He ought to have taken my advice,' Jason would say, 'and gone back to that lord in London!'

A phosphorescent Redfern began to manifest itself now in that unruffled water . . . a Redfern with no features left!

'This may be,' he thought, 'the exact spot where he stood.'

A spasm of shame oppressed him, that he should be so preoccupied with himself that the weight of all that boy's sufferings meant so little to him. Well, clean out of it now was Jimmy Redfern! But that did not erase the invisible pattern of misery traced upon the air at this spot.

'I'll ask Jason how he knew that the boy used to come here. I'll ask him as soon as I get back.'

Get back? *Get back where?* So he wasn't going to utter that mandate to his panic-stricken body. . . .

How queer that he had nothing now left to decide! His future was already there, mapped out before him. It was only a matter of following the track. Yes! The track was already there . . . leading back again! All he had to do was to accept it and follow it from moment to moment, like a moving hand that threw a shadow over an unfolded map!

But where did that map, that track, that diagram come from,

across which, like a sneaking shadow, he saw himself returning to Pond Cottage?

His consciousness, hauled up, as if by a string, from the bottom of the pond, began beating now against the dark wall that separated him from the portion of his being which was unrolling that map! Without his life-illusion he was at that moment completely devoid of pride. Afraid to jump in? Afraid of that cold water down there? It was nothing to him if he *were* afraid! There was no 'I am I' to worry about; no Wolf Solent, with a mystical philosophy, to look like a cowardly fool! But whose hand was it that was unrolling the map? His own hand? Was he, then, a furtive, secretive, desperate life-lover? Or was it the hand of Chance? But how could Chance unroll a map?

What was left of consciousness within him flapped like a tired bird against the whole dark rondure of the material universe. If only he could find a crack, a cranny in that thick rotundity. But the thickness was his very self! He was no longer Wolf Solent. He was just earth, water, and little, glittering specks of fire!

For the tenth part of a second there seemed to be a faint cracking in this huge material envelope. But no! All was sealed up. The monstrous cube of black immensity remained intact . . . darkness upon darkness. Drawing a heavy breath, he jerked himself upright. He had been leaning forward eagerly, preposterously, over the handle of his stick. But now, with a peevish effort, he tugged the thing out of the mud into which he had been pressing it. His mind had suddenly grown cloudy, lumpish, cloddish. He sighed deeply and let his stick swing loosely in his limp fingers. Then bending down with slack knees over Lenty Pond, he set himself to splash the water, foolishly, aimlessly, with his stick's end. This way and that he splashed it, in the immense stillness, under the flicker of those countless stars. And as he splashed it he began wondering to himself in a heavy loggerheaded way why it was that when all was pitch dark except for those pin-pricks in the firmament, he could distinguish so clearly between the liquid darkness of the water and the solid darkness of the surrounding earth.

He swung round at last, like a man who turns away from the extinguished footlights of an empty theatre, and began retracing his steps across the field. His dominant sensation, as he performed this retreat, was a singular one. He felt as if his consciousness were already ensconced, like Banquo's ghost, at the Otters' table, while some quite alien force was dragging across the field a numb, inert, apethetic human body, that raised one leaden foot after the other.

There was such a hubbub of voices issuing from the drawing-room of Pond Cottage, that with a sulky motion of the muscles of his chin, repeated several times as he stumbled over the flower-beds, he went round the house to the back door. There, at his petulant tap, Dimity Stone let him in. 'Mis-ter So-lent!' the old crone exclaimed, in her most quavering voice. 'And where, for Lawky's sake, be Master Darnley? Sit 'ee down, Mister Solent, while I gets me breath. These goings-on do daunt a body terrible. 'Tis first one thing, 'sknow; and then be another! First there be talk of a cold bite o' summat to save I trouble. Then what do Master Jason do but come wambling in about hotting up they wedding-pasties what I've hid all day from they since a week a-gone, 'cept what Miss Olwen coaxed out of I.'

The old woman kept shuffling her utensils about, as she spoke, from one orifice to another of her vast kitchen-stove. A most fragrant steam emerged from more than one lid; and Wolf, as he sat on a hard chair, with one limp hand dangling his stick and the other dangling his hat, was aware of a pang of extreme hunger.

'And then,' she went on, 'must Parson come whiffling in, white as a lassie's petsycut, and Mistress must uncork a sip o' Scotch for he; and Miss Mattie, all of a tremble with her bride's-night depending', must start crying about Master Darnley, where 'a be and what's keeping o' he.'

'I told Mr. Valley to tell them,' threw in Wolf, in a low voice. 'I told him to tell them.' The heat of the kitchen, after the chill night air, and the stress of his recent experiences, were beginning to make him feel dizzy again. 'I told him to tell them,' he repeated, trying to concentrate his wits upon the confused voices from the drawing-room.

Dimity looked shrewdly at him. 'Why, ye be dodderin' yourself, Mister Solent! Here' – and she hurried to a cupboard and poured something into a glass – 'here . . . drink this. 'Tis me wone cordial.' And she watched him intently, with a hand on his shoulder, as he drained it off. 'That's better, eh? Why, you be near as white as thik parson! 'Tis beyond I, what be coming to this house, these turnover days.'

'What is it?' he murmured, spluttering and gasping while the blood surged back to his head; 'what is it, Dimity?'

'Nought but a drop o' elder-wine,' she said, soothingly, patting him on the head.

The hubbub of voices from the drawing-room of Pond Cottage began to grow more relevant and natural. A moment ago they had sounded in his ears as if he had been a spirit – a spirit whose body was left far behind, under the water with Jason's nymph.

'I told Mr. Valley to tell them,' he repeated firmly.

'Missus said thik parson brought such a word,' muttered the old woman, returning to her steaming saucepans. At that moment there reached them both the sound of an opening door and a man's steps in the front hall. 'He've a-come! Master Darnley be come!' cried Dimity, hurrying out of the kitchen.

Wolf rose from his chair, hat in one hand, stick in the other, and followed her out.

The sight of his friend's yellow beard against the lamp on the hall table completed his restoration to normal intelligence.

'Oh, *there* you are!' cried the bridegroom cheerfully. 'I told Gerda I knew you'd be here all right. She was a bit nervous about you.' He paused to hang up his coat. The sound of their voices brought the drawing-room door open with a fling; and Mattie rushed out, flushed and excited. Even at the moment this occurred, however, Darnley had time to turn a quick sideways glance towards Wolf across the uplifted overcoat. 'She's a darling, your wife!' he whispered emphatically.

Mattie's arms were round Darnley's neck before his hands were free. Wolf had never seen the two of them embrace; and when he awoke that night by Gerda's side, before a window pallid with dawn, he recalled the expression of his friend's mackerel-coloured eyes. They were like those of a man who pulls himself together, naked, tense, exultant, on the brink of a rapid torrent.

It was Mrs. Otter herself who took Wolf's hat and stick away from him now; and as he shook hands with the little lady, he was driven by an unexpected impulse to bend down and give her a hurried kiss.

'It seems the fashion,' he muttered awkwardly, as he turned to greet Jason and T. E. Valley.

'I mustn't stay for more than this,' he found himself saying presently, as he emptied his soup-plate and lifted his wineglass to his lips. 'Darnley says Gerda won't touch her supper till I get home.'

'You don't know, of course, how our little girl is behaving?' said Mrs. Otter. 'Miss Malakite isn't spoiling her too much, I hope?'

Wolf felt very grateful for all the easy implications of this little speech.

'Yes, I do, indeed,' he said, rising to his feet. 'I met Christie as I passed the shop . . . when was it? . . . oh, about half-past five, I think! . . . and she said Olwen was perfect.'

He felt himself blushing as he caught Jason's sardonic eye. Why had he said 'perfect'? But Mrs. Otter continued quite naturally:

'It's rather a test for the little thing. But Miss Malakite, I know, will make it easy for her.' She paused and sighed rather sadly. 'It's strange not to have her here,' she added. 'I feel as if she'd been here all her life.'

'Your friend Miss Gault,' said Jason, 'would like to send the police after her.'

His words produced an uncomfortable silence. Darnley rose to his feet and began sprinkling salt with his finger and thumb upon a wine-stain he had made on the tablecloth.

'If they want to keep her,' said Jason, 'are you going to let them, mother?'

'It's for Mattie to decide that,' murmured Mrs. Otter.

'Your friend Miss Gault would soon decide it,' repeated Jason. 'She's like to send her, and Miss Malakite too, to the Ramsgard Workhouse!'

'Things will work themselves out as God sees best, Jason,' remarked Mrs. Otter reproachfully. Wolf noticed that as the lady spoke she surreptitiously laid one of her hands on Mattie's knee.

It was at this point that Mattie herself turned to Dimity. 'You're tired,' she said. 'Do sit down now. And listen! I don't want you to do anything more to-night in my room.' Wolf had always regarded it as a touching peculiarity of Pond Cottage that the aged servant entered freely into every conversation, as she moved about behind the chairs; but to-night he had a premonition, before the old woman opened her lips to reply, that she would say something unlucky.

'You can't see no corner of Miss Olwen's bed, Miss Mattie,' was what she now brought out. 'They things what I've been ironing be all spread out over'n.'

Her words produced a silence even more disconcerting than Jason's reference to the police.

'You needn't . . . tell me . . . *that* . . . Dimity!' cried Mattie, in a strange, high-pitched tone; and then, snatching her hand away from Mrs. Otter, she suddenly burst out: 'You can cover up her bed with all my new things – you can all of you do it . . . yes, you can all of you do it!'

546

The girl thrust the back of her hand into her mouth, biting the skin. Her heavy face was distorted, her bosom was heaving. 'Oh, I want my mother, I want my mother!' she wailed, clapping both hands over her face and swaying to and fro in her seat.

This unexpected reference to a woman dead so many years – he had no notion even as to where Lorna Smith was buried – gave Wolf a queer shock. Mrs. Otter rose hurriedly and threw her arms round Mattie's swaying head, pressing it to her breast. 'My child! My child!' she kept repeating, while Wolf prayed desperately that the girl wouldn't thrust her away.

'I'm all right . . . I'm sorry, Darnley!' came her muffled voice at last.

Mrs. Otter let her go and slid back into her seat.

'I'll help you with the plates, Dimity,' Mattie murmured, rising and straightening her shoulders. Darnley held the door open for her to pass out. She had snatched up Wolf's soup-plate and Jason's, which were the only empty ones.

'I'll say good night, then,' cried Wolf, looking at Mrs. Otter, 'and I won't be late at the church!'

He gathered together his belongings in the hall, while Darnley, with his arm held tight round Mattie's shoulder, fixed his eyes gravely on every movement he made.

When Wolf had got his coat on, his friend left Mattie standing there frowningly, with the plates still in her hand, and opened the hall door.

'Good night, Wolf,' he said quietly. 'She'll be all right now. Give my love to Gerda. By the way' – and he lowered his voice so that Mattie shouldn't hear him – 'Gerda says your mother wants to come; and for that reason she'd rather come independently of you, with her father. I told her it should be exactly as she wished.'

Wolf at that moment found it difficult to concentrate his mind upon this nice point.

'We'll all be with you anyway, Darnley. As long as we're all there, it doesn't matter *how* we turn up, does it? Well, good luck to you!' But he had no sooner got his friend's fingers in his own than he impulsively dropped them. Catching the man's head between his hands, he kissed him rapidly several times on the forehead. 'Good luck to you!' he repeated, as he strode off down the garden. 'I kissed the mother; why not the son?' he thought, as he reached the gate; but something produced a constriction in his throat that was akin to a sob. 'Down, wantons . . . down!' he murmured audibly, as he fumbled for the latch of the gate.

547

He had scarcely found it, however, when the house door behind him opened and a hurly-burly of voices reached him.

'But you've not even finished your soup!' ... 'You've only had one glass!' ... 'You might wait till Dimity has brought – '

His first idea was that these cries were intended for himself; but as he wavered there, in puzzled indecision, there came hurrying down the path, like a stray dog bolting for home, the agitated figure of T. E. Valley. The little priest was struggling into his overcoat as he ran, and repeating, 'I've had all I want! I've had all I want!'

'Good night, Wolf! Take care of him, for heaven's sake!' rang out Darnley's voice from the door, as the two men emerged into Pond Lane. They saw the light vanish away. They heard the door close. They were once more alone together.

'Well,' said Wolf, 'I suppose we go *this* way, eh?' and he made a motion to turn to the right.

'Would ... you ... mind ... Solent,' pleaded the man piteously, 'if we went the *other* way? I *could* go alone ... but ... you know? ... I'm feeling a little upset to-night ...'

'Right you are, my friend!' said Wolf, with a sigh. 'I daresay Gerda will forgive me. But I'm already a bit late; so let's walk briskly! Why' – he was already moving in the required direction, with the man's arm in his own – 'do you want to go so far round?'

But Valley's mind had reverted again to the scene at the grave. 'The belfry-window was a long way off. I was fretting so much, too, thinking I ought to go down and stop it. Perhaps it *was* natural. ... I should feel like that myself if it weren't for the Sacrament ... I mean if ... you know? ...'

The priest's mutterings rose and fell like a cloud of weakly-humming gnats, over a twilit towpath. Wolf continued to feel as if he were a wooden puppet galvanized into meaningless activity by a complicated system of wires. 'If only they'd let me lie down,' he thought, 'just lie down for a hundred years, I'd deal with them all!'

Once more alone and striding homewards, he teased his memory about the name of an especially luminous constellation that hung in the west directly over Blacksod. 'The most contemptible people are allowed to enjoy the stars,' he said to himself; and then he thought: 'A lump of cowardice without past or future! But this lump has two legs to carry it, and a stick to prod the ground with. Ailinon! Ailinon! But I'll make Gerda laugh when I tell her about Tilly-Valley.'

It gave him one of the first pleasant feelings he had had that evening, to think of making Gerda laugh. 'I won't tell her till we're in bed,' he thought. And then he thought: 'I wonder if Olwen and Christie will sleep together to-night?'

As he moved between the well-known hedges of that road, along which just a year ago he had been driven by Darnley, he experienced a singular sensation. He felt as though he were beginning a *posthumous* life – a life that his own cowardice had snatched from the end intended.

It was as if such an end *had* actually been reached upon some psychic plane; so that now he but 'usurped his life.' Never would he know what actually happened at that King's Barton grave, any more than he would know what Miss Gault did after he left her in Ramsgard Cemetery. But such things could not altogether pass. Must there not be some imprint of them left upon space itself? If so, such air-pictures might easily remain intact, even after the planet itself was uninhabited and frozen.

In his agitation he began fumbling at the handle of his stick, and he noted how the deep indents cut by Lob Torp on that night of the 'Yellow Bracken' had grown smooth and slippery with handling.

'What I really am is dead,' he kept saying to himself. 'That's what I am . . . *dead*.' But out of his balanced indifference, like a man astride of a floating log, who by a miracle has escaped a whirlpool, he began to feel conscious of a faint satisfaction in the mere fact of having experienced that rush of the cold air about his ears and that splash of froth upon his cheek.

What he had to do now was to gather his forces together for a daily and nightly dialogue with the Cause of all Life and of all Death! As he came along into the outlying district of Blacksod, he visualized this Cause as an enormous shell-fish placidly breathing in and breathing out on the floor of a sea-like infinity.

He was staring at its fixed idiotic eyes, and at its long, motionless antennæ, when he passed the turn to the Malakite shop. Then something in him, beyond all reasoning, loosened, stirred, leapt up . . . 'Oh Christie! Oh, my little Christie!'

24

'FORGET'

In the middle of that night Wolf was aroused to consciousness by the voice of Gerda anxiously soothing him; and even in his confusion he was aware at that moment of something exceptionally tender in her tone, something protective, something different altogether from a young creature's spontaneous alarm at being disturbed in its sleep! It was as if all the agitations of that last fortnight had unfolded some psychic bud or frond within her being, changing her from a capricious child into a full-grown sweet-natured woman.

'What did I say?' he asked, as his head fell back upon the pillow.

' "I shall break between you," you cried. "I shall break between you!" And then, when I said, *Between who, Wolf?*" you said "Between *them!* Can't you see? Between those two men!" '

'Men, Gerda? Did I say *men*?' And then suddenly, like a retreating image in a deep mirror, he remembered what his dream had been. He was himself a brittle stick, a piece of dead brushwood. At one end of him was the Waterloo tramp. At the other end of him was that complacent old man with the white cat. He had awakened in terror because he felt himself beginning to crack, as those two antagonists tugged.

After caressing Gerda with an emotional relaxation, such as the self-pitying weakness of a fever might have left, he settled himself again to sleep. His final thoughts were concerned with the meaning of his dream; but beyond a fumbling association of the Waterloo waif with the loss of his 'mythology,' and the sleek cat-man with an acceptance of life on its lowest terms, the riddle remained unsolved.

He awakened next morning to a vivid awareness that this Friday was the eve of Darnley's wedding. He recalled his first encounter with his friend in that tea-room of the Lovelace Hotel; and his mind reverted to the waiter who was now a beggar. 'Stalbridge,' he thought. 'A good man. I wish I'd given him that half-crown.'

As he shaved himself at the familiar looking-glass, he entered upon a cheerful discussion with Gerda as to what they had better decide to do on the following day. Gerda displayed no hostility to Mrs. Solent's company, but indicated that it would please Mr. Torp if she went with him rather than with them; and as for their return to Blacksod after the wedding-feast, *that* could be left to chance!

'There'll be lots of carriages coming and going,' she said, 'and it'll be fun to see what happens! I shan't mind,' she went on, 'if we all walk home in a crowd. But I *would* enjoy going with father. It'll be like the old days, when I used to go to funerals with him. He likes to go to places with me when I'm all dressed up.'

'I suppose Darnley will be at school to-day just as usual,' said Wolf; 'but they've given him a week off. They're going to Weymouth. Did I tell you that?'

'To lodgings?' enquired Gerda. 'We all took lodgings once, Wolf; one Whitsun . . . in Adelaide Crescent.'

'No; it was an hotel, I think,' said Wolf.

'The Burden?' she cried excitedly. 'Oh, how I'd love to stay at the Burden! I've never stayed in an hotel in my life. I've never been *into* an hotel except the Three Peewits.'

Wolf was silent for a second. Then he said slowly, contemplating his half-shaven face in the mirror with as much detachment as if it had been a cat's saucer of milk, 'Well, we might go in to see them next Saturday. They wouldn't be leaving till the afternoon, I suppose. We could all have lunch at the Burden.'

'Wolf,' she cried, sitting up straight in bed – a movement that brought her head into the square of his mirror – 'Wolf! why can't we spend of our money in a week-end at the Burden? Not this week, of course; but next week, just as they're coming back! Oh, I would love that so much!'

A wave of sadness swept over him. It was on the tip of his tongue to reply to her in her own words of last Sunday – 'It's too late, my dear, it's too late!' For that beach in front of Brunswick Terrace came back to him, with the cries of the fish-sellers, with the dazzling sun-path on the breaking sea, with the wet planks and the painted boats. Ay, how he would love to see it all again – but who was he to see it? Hollow! Hollow! A drifting husk, empty of purpose and hope!

'I don't see why we shouldn't do just as you say, sweetheart. But let's get through to-morrow first, before we decide. But I don't see why we shouldn't stay one night, at any rate, at the Burden.'

551

He caught her eyes in the glass, and they were radiant. She was actually clapping her hands, as she heard him; and the cry of delight she gave seemed to him to have the sound of whistling in it!

Yes, even if he were doomed to drift now like a purposeless automaton, it was something to be able to cause such childish exultation.

Gerda wanted to be free that day from the trouble of preparing a midday meal, so it was arranged that he should get a bread-and-cheese lunch at the Three Peewits. Perhaps Darnley would be ready to share it with him! At any rate, Gerda should be left to her own devices until tea-time.

All that morning, as he supervised his boys' lesson, his mind ran upon what she had said about Weymouth. How strange that he had himself proposed to Christie that *they* should go down there this very Sunday ... quite independently of the Burden Hotel! Everything in his life seemed gravitating just then towards Weymouth – towards that birthplace of his murdered 'mythology' – but too heartless was he now to care a straw!

'I won't spoil Gerda's happiness by breathing a word about *this* Sunday,' he said to himself; 'and very likely, anyway, Christie will have forgotten. Olwen has cut me out. That's the long and the short of it. Olwen has cut me out!'

As he stared at the ink-stains on the wall, he found himself selecting one particular stain to serve as a raft in the Dead Sea drift of his trouble. This stain was an elongated one; and before he knew what he was doing, he had turned it into a road – a road like that road in the Gainsborough picture.

As one boy after another came up to his desk with some sort of written answer to the tedious historic question he had propounded to them, his mind began to envisage, with a rapid bird's-eye glance, all the years of his life, and the dominant part that had been played in them by this *ideal road*. He seemed to be able, as he stared at that elongated ink-stain, to recall fragments of old memories such as he had not thought of even once during the last twelve months! The longer he stared at that mark upon the wall the more rapidly those memories crowded in upon him. A village green where a hollow tree had its roots in a duck-pond ... two high banks covered with patches of purple clover and yellow rock-rose, where the dusty highway under his feet led to the top of a hill, from which he knew, by a sure instinct, the sea was visible ... a deserted garden at the crossing of one thoroughfare with another, outside some cathedral town, where nettles mingled with currant-bushes and where an old woman was shouting to an old man across a brook full of watercress ... images of this kind, like mystical vignettes in the margin of an occult biography, kept passing and repassing along the road of his life – that is to say, along that elongated ink-stain.

So fast did such memories crowd in upon him that he grew consciously surprised at their presence, as a drowning man might be surprised at the concentration of a whole life's experience into a second of time!

He even remembered one particular occasion, in the outskirts of London, when he had made up his mind that those glimpses of things seen under a certain light were the sole purpose of his existence! He recalled the exact spot where he reached that conclusion. It was upon a bench, somewhere beyond Richmond, under some enormous lime trees. He remembered how he had decided then that these particular episodes, snatched out of the flowing stream of visual impression, were more charged with the furtive secret of life than any contact with men and women. He remembered how he had pulled up a cool dark green tuft of grass by the root, so excited had that conclusion made him; and how afterwards he had busied himself for some while in a conscientious attempt to replant it, using his stick as a trowel, greatly to the amusement of a flirtatious pair of shop-girls, who regarded him from a recumbent position under one of those trees.

It was ironical that at this very moment, when the power of his enjoyment of it had been killed, he seemed able to articulate his philosophy of the *ideal road* more definitely than he had ever done before. What it really had meant, this philosophy, was a power of seeing things *arranged under a certain light* ... a light charged with memories of the past ... a light capable of linking his days in flowing continuity! Well, it was all lost now ... lost because it implied a certain kind of Wolf who was enjoying it; and *that* kind of Wolf was stone dead.

'Harrison *minor*, what are you thinking of? You've cribbed this straight from Martin *major* !' ...

His voice must have assumed something of the harsh bitterness of his mood; for a lot of heads were raised from the desks, and there was a hurried whispering in Harrison *minor's* corner.

'Reality has beaten me,' he said to himself. 'What I feel now must be exactly what religious people feel when they believe themselves to be damned! They can talk of other matters; they can respond when you approach; but while they are chatting with you of this and that, there is always *perdition* lying at the bottom of their thoughts!'

'Every boy whose paper has been marked must go on quietly, please, with the Restoration!'

'Olwen has cut me out. That's the long and short of it. It was all in vain, that day in the cornfield! "Mind touching mind, without need of words," did we say? But she'll be happy with Olwen. Mattie will *have* to let her have Olwen. . . .'

When he met Darnley, after that heavy morning was over at last, he learnt that Jason too would be at the Three Peewits. Darnley was silent and preoccupied as they walked through the streets; and Wolf set himself to accept the fact that they were destined to go on drudging at this School, side by side, *sans* intermission, to the end of their days! Precisely as they walked through these streets to-day, between School and Tavern, so would they be found walking twenty, thirty years hence, each meditating his own secret cares!

Chance had ordered it that not Jason only was awaiting them in the Three Peewits dining-room. There, in the best window-seat, with a bottle of Burgundy in front of him, sat Mr. Urquhart himself! Jason was drinking beer from a two-handled pewter flagon and helping himself with relish from a large rook-pie, covered with a crust of flaky pastry, that stood before him.

Both he and Urquhart had an air of having been established in their places for many hours. They were, however, as far removed from each other as two guests in the same dining-room could possibly be! Wolf and Darnley went across to the Squire and shook hands with him; and then, sitting down at Jason's table, they both ordered the same brand of Dorchester ale, but in lesser proportion.

'There's enough for you two,' said Jason, referring to the pie before him. 'You're allowed second helpings here. I've had mine.'

'How did those rogues make 'ee come in to town to-day, Otter?' remarked Mr. Urquhart, pulling his chair round, but keeping his elbow on his table and his fingers on the stem of his wine-glass.

'They've given me all next week off,' replied Darnley.

'I've been saying that *I* ought to have a holiday too, just in his honour,' threw in Wolf, feeling as if there were a pail of ashes in his belly that nothing he drank could so much as moisten.

This intercourse between the two ends of the room seemed to

displease Jason. His face assumed its most stony expression, and he bent low over his plate.

'They've good custards here,' he remarked, after a pause. 'Custard's much better than those puddings that your friend Mrs. Stone makes.'

'Don't call her Mrs. Stone, Jason,' murmured Darnley, with a peevishness unusual to him in addressing his brother. 'Wolf's as much a friend of Dimity as any of us.'

For half a second Jason's brows contracted ominously; and then his whole countenance relaxed into a thousand humorous wrinkles.

'He'll be a better friend to her still, when he's tasted those wedding-pasties of yours, Darnley!' he said, holding up his tankard, and making a sly motion with one eyelid and one shoulder in the direction of Mr. Urquhart, to whom his back remained turned.

There was a moment's interruption at this point, while the waiter was laying in front of the newcomers the beer and cheese they had ordered.

'You needn't look like that at my pie,' said Jason. 'Everyone isn't going to be married to-morrow!'

'Hurry up with your new poems,' retorted Darnley, 'and then you'll be able to treat us all to these luxuries.'

But Jason had turned his sardonic eye upon Wolf.

'Solent can tell you what marriage is. He can tell you! You needn't think a person doesn't know what *you've* got in your head as you see me enjoying myself.'

'What have I got in my head, Jason?' asked Wolf. His tone was meek enough; but the black bile of reciprocal malice was seething in the veins of his throat.

'Abuse of me, because of these rooks,' chuckled the other. 'You're longing to spoil my pleasure by telling every one about their cawings and their proud nests. But *you'd* like a taste as well as anyone . . . if there were no one here to see you!'

These words of Jason's, and the look that accompanied them, caused Wolf a discomfort that resembled the squeezing of a person's tongue against a hidden gum-boil. It was impossible for him to help endowing with glossy, outspread wings the unctuous morsel into which the poet just then dug his fork! He felt the blood pricking him under his cheek-bones. He thought of Miss Gault. He began to suffer from that old, miserable sensation that his body was a lump of contemptible putrescence, on the top of which his consciousness floated. This was the sort of occasion when in former days he used to summon up his 'mythology.' Well, that was all over now. He felt as disintegrated as the remnants on the poet's plate. He *was* those remnants. Dorsetshire had eaten him up!

The voice of Mr. Urquhart became audible to him. The Squire was explaining in a querulous voice that the man Monk had been so truculent that morning that he had set the whole household by the ears. 'Mrs. Martin came to me like a virago and threatened to give notice,' he said. 'I thought it best to beat a retreat. Always beat a retreat when servants mutiny, eh? What?'

As Wolf blinked at him across the foam of his beer mug, he began to feel as if that vigil of his at the church window had been a pure hallucination. 'Redfern's grave will look the same as it always has,' he thought, 'when I next see it.'

'Did you enjoy your walk this morning, Jason?' enquired Darnley, pulling at his beard. His brother regarded him with a long, sad, intent look.

'The clouds were like gentle spirits,' he repeated slowly. 'They were coming from eternity and could not stay. The fields were wet with dew for them. But they could not stay. The hazel-bushes were sobbing with sap for them. But they could not stay. The daisies were white with love for them. But they could not stay.'

As the man spoke, he placed his knife and fork carefully side by side, drank what was left of his great tankard, and replaced it on the table as scrupulously and softly as if it had been a living thing.

'They were going *to* eternity,' he added in a low voice. And then, while his melancholy grey eyes assumed a look of such abysmal sorrow that Wolf wondered to behold it, 'God comes and God goes,' he said, 'but no one feels Him except moles and worms. And they are blind and can't see. They are dumb and can't speak. I thought this morning, Darnley, that my poetry is no better than the tunnels of moles and worms.'

'What's that your brother's saying, Otter,' came the voice of Mr. Urquhart across the room. 'Is he making rhymes about the waiter? Do'ee tell him to be careful! Lovelace says a man was kicked out of his club in town for doing less than that; and besides ... in this room, you know ... though we've got –'

He was interrupted by the clatter of a hc se's hooves outside the windows, and Wolf could just see, out tl re, the corner of a nursery-gardener's cart crowded with blue hyacinths.

As Wolf stared at those flowers, he caught Urquhart's eye.

'It's nothing to you, Solent, I suppose,' he remarked, 'but the proofs of my book came from Bristol this morning!'

Wolf murmured his congratulations; but into his mouth rose the sensation of the colour brown.

'He has got his wish over Redfern,' he thought, 'and now he's got his book too.'

Mr. Urquhart was addressing the young waiter.

'Didn't know I was an author, Johnnie, did you? Mr. Solent there and I have just brought out the very book for a sly rogue like you! I'll send 'ee a copy, me boy! Don't forget, now! Ask me for it, if you don't get it soon!'

What Wolf felt, as he listened to this, was that all the mysterious evil that he had associated with this man was in reality nothing more than senile perversity. Jason was right. But if Jason was right with regard to Urquhart, wasn't he likely to be right with regard to Wolf Solent? To Jason's mind . . . to Jason's peculiar satisfaction . . . evil was no more than a thin-drifting, poisonous rain, that seeped through into everything. Nothing was free from it, except perhaps the passionate heart of Olwen! But it was just a slimy rain. It had no spiritual depths. Mr. Urquhart and himself had been playing together a pleasant theatrical drama . . . all gesture, all illusion! Upon Jason's plate of well-cleaned rook bones lay the fragments of their high Satanic play!

Mr. Urquhart had called the young waiter to his side now. Darnley and Jason were talking in low voices about the arrangements for to-morrow. . . .

It was then that an incredibly sweet fragrance came in through the open window! It may have been only the hyacinths; but, as Wolf breathed it in, it seemed to him much more than that. It seemed to come from masses of bluebells under undisturbed green hazels!

This happy sensation, however, was not permitted to him for long. In a second there followed a vibrant, penetrating drumming . . . an aeroplane! . . . with the beat of a demon's sharded wings this sound drew nearer . . . steadily nearer and nearer. . . .

Mr. Urquhart turned his head.

'Those young airmen are fine lads,' he remarked. 'I'd let any one of those chaps carry me to Tibet or Cambodia if he'd give me the chance.'

Wolf noticed a strange light of excitement come into Darnley's blue eyes; and it was Darnley who spoke now.

'Yes . . . to fly!' he cried. 'To clear your soul of all the earth-horrors! To wash your mind clean, in a blue bath of air! Think of it! To fly over land and sea till you realize the *roundness* of the earth! To feel your mind changing . . . becoming a purer instrument . . . as you leave this cluttered world!'

The drumming of the aeroplane was now accompanied by the harsh snorting and snarling of a large motor-car.

'Whether it's by air or by road,' observed Jason, in the tone of a very old hermit, 'these young men come down upon us; and it's best to win favour of the Lords of Science.' He glanced sideways at the waiter. 'They come by sea too, sometimes,' he added, hunching his shoulders in mock alarm. 'This young man looks like a chief engineer on a liner,' he went on, lowering his voice to a whisper, and glancing at his brother.

Wolf began to feel as if he were stranded alone on a high, exposed platform, hooted and shrieked at by thousands of motors and aeroplanes. . . .

Beads of sweat stood out on his forehead. It was as if he searched in vain for any escape into the silences of the earth. No escape was possible any more! He was combed out, raked over, drained of all sap! His destiny henceforth must be to groan and creak in the wind of others' speed. . . .

'It's a miracle,' repeated Darnley, 'to be able to transform the whole bias of the mind by turning away from land and water and making the air our element!'

The man's singular-looking eyes were literally translucent with excitement.

'I'm afraid it's not of Mattie he's thinking,' said Wolf to himself.

But Mr. Urquhart had just made some remark to his ex-secretary that Wolf had been too absorbed in his thoughts to hear. 'I beg your pardon, sir!' he murmured.

'That's the value of a book like ours, eh, me boy?' cried the Squire. 'It'll be kept on newspaper-stands on the top of great iron landing-stages for people to pick up as they start for Australia or Siberia! It'll tickle their fancy, eh? What? By Jove it will . . . to learn what lecherous snakes their ancestors were.'

'I didn't tell you, did I, Solent,' said Darnley innocently, 'that when I called at the Malakites' to let Olwen know I'd take her home this evening, the little minx refused to budge? She swears she won't leave Christie for a single night! There'd have been tears if I'd insisted. Well! It'll be . . . perhaps . . . easier' – he spoke pensively and slowly now – 'if she does remain . . . where she is.'

'Girls are all the same,' remarked Jason. 'They all like sugar and spice. Old Malakite probably buys more tasty sweets for her in this town than she gets with us.' There was something about

558

this speech that was more than Wolf could bear. He rose abruptly to his feet.

'Sorry, Darnley,' he said. 'I forgot something I have to do before afternoon school! It won't be more than that, will it . . . what I've had?' and he laid down a shilling and three pennies upon the table. A grotesque consciousness of the way his quivering upper lip projected and the way his hands shook, filled his brain as he spoke; but he bowed to Mr. Urquhart as he went out, and nodded civilly at Jason. 'We'll meet later,' he said, giving Darnley one rapid reproachful look as he left the room.

Once in the street, he paused, hesitating. He felt as if he were as much exposed to the gaze of the crowds as if he had been one of the featherless birds of Jason's pie!

Instinctively he began to make his way through the crowd towards the Malakite shop. Recognizing the import of this movement, he mentally confronted the only alternative to it . . . that of hanging about for half an hour in his deserted classroom. No! *That* would be misery too great! But when he reached the shop and had rung the bell in the side alley, he felt tempted to bolt. The presence of Olwen seemed to change the whole situation. It was as if the little girl were clinging to both Christie's hands, held behind her back; so that she lacked the *power* . . . whatever her *will* may have been . . . to help him at this crisis!

He could not recall ever having waited so long at that door as he waited now. What a lovely day it was! But that balmy spring air . . . and he could see several clumps of pale jonquils in the little back yard . . . floated over him as if he had been a dead man, as if he had really been drowned last night in Lenty Pond.

Here she was, running rapidly down the narrow staircase. . . .

'Oh, I'm so glad to see you, Wolf! I'm in such trouble! I've been thinking and thinking what to do. . . . I prayed that *anybody* might come . . . and now it's you! Oh, I'm so glad!'

He followed her into the house and she shut the door; and they stood close together in the little dark entrance. Unaware of any conscious impulse, he hugged her tightly to his heart and held her there . . . his brain a complete blank to everything except the sense of holding her.

But this relief from reality was not destined to be permitted to him for long. The girl plucked at his wrists, turned her head away from him, struggled to release herself.

'Don't, Wolf! Not now, Wolf! I want your help . . . don't you understand? I don't want *that* now.'

559

He sighed heavily, but let her go, and stood by her side, clutching the banisters.

'What's the matter, Chris?' he murmured humbly.

'Olwen wants to stay with me . . . to *live* with me . . . you knew that, didn't you? But this morning she's been fretting about Mattie. Ever since she woke up she's been fretting. And now she says she'll be quite happy with me again if only she can go to the wedding and see them married! She wants to go *to-night*, Wolf. That's what she wants . . . to have a last night with Mattie . . . and come back here when they leave for Weymouth; but, you see, I had no way of reaching Darnley. Is Darnley at school to-day, Wolf? I don't know what I should have done if you hadn't – '

She was interrupted by a sound in the bookshop; and Wolf saw her stiffen and lay her finger on her lip, and turn a tense, concentrated, narrow-lidded stare at the door leading into the shop.

Wolf did not like the manner of this intense listening. He had liked still less the tone in which she had welcomed his appearance, not for his own sake, but as a means of reaching Darnley! The truth began to deepen upon him that between Olwen and the old man Christie's world had never been more occupied, had never promised less free space for him and for his affairs.

The sounds within the shop, whatever their nature, ceased now, and she turned, smiling. She laid two small finger-tips, light as that feather in her *Urn-Burial*, upon his coat sleeve.

'I won't ask you to come up now, Wolf. You always excite her so, and I've just got her quiet.' She paused and hesitated; and in the faint light of that little passage he could see she was anxious as to just how he would react under her appeal. 'Will you see Darnley?' she murmured. He moved back a step and nodded gravely.

'Well, listen, Wolf dear!' she went on. 'Bring him to tea here, will you? And ask him to hire a trap at the hotel, so he can take her out there to-night. You'll be able to bring her back to-morrow, won't you, Wolf . . . when the wedding's over?'

He promised submissively to do exactly what she wanted; and opening the door to let him out, she closed it quietly behind them both and stood by his side in the narrow alley.

Once more Wolf was aware of the humming of an aeroplane above the roofs of Blacksod! Those aeroplanes were becoming a kind of devilish chorus to his comic tragedy!

The girl lifted her head, trying to get a glimpse of it, while he himself stared obstinately at the narrow velvet band that encircled her waist. 'Damn these machines!' he muttered bitterly. 'It'll never be the same world again!'

She lowered her chin and looked into his face. The sound of the aeroplane had actually brought – or so he thought to himself in his stubborn resentment – the same gleam into her eyes as into those of Darnley. All were against him now ... all, all, all! These demons were ensorcerizing every soul he knew. The Powers of the Air! No, he would *never* yield to them! While a single grass-blade grew out of the deep earth, he would never yield to them!

'Oh, Wolf, you are wrong, my dear!' she cried fervently. 'It *is* a new world! It is! It is! But it's a beautiful world. It means a new *kind* of beauty: glittering steel, gleaming wings, free spaces –' She stopped suddenly. He thought afterwards she must have seen something in his expression that troubled and puzzled her.

'I must go to Olwen,' she murmured; and then, just as she had done before, she snatched at his hand and raised it to her lips. 'Don't mind about the machines, Wolf, dear. Bring Darnley to tea, won't you? And tell him to order a trap. She *could* walk, I know. But I don't want her to get to Mattie all tired out. *Au revoir*, my dear!' And she slipped away into the house, giving him, as she went, one of those especial smiles of hers that were always so baffling.

Back at his desk again, Wolf was compelled to bestow so much attention upon his boys that it was only once in all the afternoon that he fixed his eyes upon the mark on the wall, and gave himself up to his sullen meditations.

'This is the kind of thing,' he thought, 'that I've got to endure for the rest of my days, unless mother, with her tea-shop money, pensions me off! I could bear it! I know well enough I could bear it, if only – It's nice making Gerda laugh. It's nice doing what Christie tells me. But it'll be hard to go on in this room for thirty years.'

He had occasion to denounce a couple of boys, ere the lesson was over, for a flagrant case of cribbing; and the way in which the elder of these boys – a great, hulking lubber-head called Gaffer Barge – took all the blame upon himself, struck his imagination far more than he permitted that poor, sweet-natured lout to discover! When the clock finally struck the hour, and he found himself free, he stopped Gaffer Barge as the lad was slouching off.

'Barge,' he said, 'I wonder if you would be so awfully good as to do a little errand for me on your way home?'

There came into the boy's face, on hearing these words, a smile of such sheer, innate sweetness and goodness, that Wolf was staggered. He had been, if anything, rather abrupt and distant with the fellow in their daily relations, and the pleasure with which the boy responded to this unexpected request struck him in his present mood as no less than astonishing. It was as if in this desert of grim reality upon which he had been dropped from the back of his divine steed, he had heard the most heavy-humped camel utter melodious words.

'How good of you, Gaffer!' he cried eagerly, using the lad's nickname to indicate his appreciation of this response. 'One minute, then; and I'll write a note.'

He incontinently scribbled a line to Gerda, telling her not to expect him home till after tea. This missive he folded up and directed to 'Mrs. Wolf Solent, 37 Preston Lane.'

'Here you are, Barge,' he said, handing it to him. 'It's not much out of your way. But I'm really most extremely grateful to you.' Whereat the lad slipped off, as shyly exultant as if he had made a hundred runs in a cricket match.

There arose no obstacle, in the sequence of events that now occurred, to upset Christie's prearranged plan. With the fly from the Three Peewits safely ordered for seven o'clock, Darnley and Wolf took their places at the Malakite tea-table; and a situation that certainly possessed elements of awkwardness flowed forward as smoothly and easily as if the girl had possessed a social genius worthy of the subtlest adepts of high society.

Mr. Malakite was himself unusually voluble during the earlier part of the meal, and Wolf's attention was thoroughly arrested by the drift of the old man's loquacity.

'And so Urquhart wrote to him,' the old bookseller was saying, 'and I got his reply yesterday . . . by the second post. Olwen met the postman and brought it to me in the shop. You weren't afraid of your old grand-dad, were you, my chick?' He looked round the table, as he said this, with an expression of crafty triumph.

'We musn't bore Darnley with our business affairs, father,' interrupted Christie, 'on the very eve of his wedding-day.'

But Darnley, too, had caught the unusual quiver of excitement in the old man's voice, and had fixed his blue eyes intently upon him.

'No, no,' he said. 'Please go on, sir; please go on.'

'It's a relative of yours, Mr. Solent, as well as of the Squire's, so he tells me,' continued the bookseller. 'He knew I wanted to sell out, and he sent this gentleman my catalogue, and now I've got his reply . . . by the afternoon post. Olwen gave it to me while I was on the ladder, didn't you, my pet? You didn't know your grand-dad could climb a ladder, did you, my pretty?'

Wolf experienced an intense distaste for the tone the old man adopted in thus addressing his daughter's child. He couldn't resist a furtive glance at Christie. But the girl was staring with one of her fixed, inscrutable looks at Darnley; and all he could interpret of her feelings depended upon a certain disturbing droop of her under lip. Like a flash there shot through his mind a startled doubt at the wisdom of the human race in allowing family life to be so unapproachable, so fortified, so secretive. In spite of what he had often said to Gerda, it came over him now that there *was* something rather ghastly in letting this girl and this child be shut up with this senile nympholept.

'From London, by the afternoon post,' insisted Mr. Malakite. And Wolf, nervously receptive of every psychic current just then, felt more uneasy still at this imbecile repetition of so unimportant a detail.

'Is it Lord Carfax you are talking about?' he hazarded – thinking to himself, 'How oddly that fellow keeps up his rôle in my life!'

But the bookseller nodded eagerly. 'Did *you* write to him too about my stuff?'

Christie turned her head sharply at this. 'I've never told Wolf anything at all about your catalogue, father,' she cried. 'He doesn't approve of our selling' – she hesitated a moment, and then smiled her most mischievous smile – 'the sort of books we *do* sell!'

This identification of herself with the worst aspect of her parent's business was a new shock to Wolf. He looked at her reproachfully; thinking of the nature of that book from Paris compared with which the lewdest court trials in Dorset history were a mere pinch of honest dirt; but the girl's head was held high, and her eyes were flashing ominously.

'His lordship says he'll take the whole lot!' concluded her father trimphantly. 'So *that* means, my pretty ones, that your silly old man has done the best stroke of business of his whole life!' He turned his eye defiantly upon Wolf as he spoke, as if challenging the whole world to interfere with him. 'I shall be able to retire from work after this,' he added, with an unpleasant complacency, 'and we'll go and live at Weymouth, won't we, my treasures? The silly old man will sit on the esplanade all the morning, and play bowls all the afternoon!'

Christie got up at this point and moved round to the little girl's elbow. While she was spreading a slice of bread for her, Wolf muttered something about goat-carriages. The child was all attention at once.

'Did Cinderella's coach have goats to pull it? she asked. 'Do goats go faster than donkeys?'

'I'll just run down and see if I can see anything of your fly,' said Christie suddenly. And she slipped from the room with a movement as swift, and almost as imperceptible, as a breath of that day's soft wind.

The old man took advantage of her absence to begin retailing to Darnley the names, editions, and prices of some of his most curious and expensive volumes. Olwen, at this, left her bread and jam, slipped out of her chair, and, coming round to Wolf's side, scrambled up upon his knees and demanded a story.

Wolf felt sure that, in spite of her ranging herself so definitely on her father's side, Christie was embarrassed by the old man's excitement; and he had an inkling that she would remain down there in the doorway, looking for the carriage, until it actually drew up.

'Well, sweetheart,' he whispered, 'I'm not very good at stories; but I'll try.' He clasped the child closely to him and shut his eyes so as to collect his thoughts.

'At the very moment,' he began, 'when we were all waiting for the cab to come, you and I saw an enormous swallow . . . the ancestor of all swallows . . . big as a golden eagle, hovering close to the window.' Olwen twisted round her head at this, in order to see the window.

'Without a moment's hesitation,' he went on, 'we opened the window together and got on the bird's back.'

'Leaving everyone, Wolf?'

'Certainly. Leaving everyone! This great swallow carried us then over Poll's Camp and over the Gwent Lanes toward Cadbury Camp. It let us get down off its back at Cadbury Camp . . . which really is Camelot . . . and you and I drank at Arthur's Well there; and the effect of drinking that water was to turn us both into swallows, or into some strange birds like swallows. We sat, all three, in a row, on a sycamore branch above the valley; and we wondered and wondered where we'd fly to. And a lovely wind, blowing over the dark rain that is held in the hollows of old trees, ruffled our feathers; and we knew, being birds, the language of the wind; and it said to us: "The cuckoo flowers have come out down by the Lunt!" And it said to us: "If you stop chattering, you silly birds, and listen, you will hear the earth murmuring to itself as it sweeps forward through space." '

'What did I say to it then, Wolf?' whispered the little girl, glancing axiously at the door.

But he continued to hug her closely to him; and with his eyes still tightly shut, he went on in the same low tone: 'You said to it, "Blow us all towards Weymouth, wind, and be quick about it. I want to dig in the sand!" ' . . .

'Wolf!' It was Darnley who was addressing him across the table.

He opened his eyes; as he did so he became aware that his friend was looking at him with that same appealing glance that had arrested his attention when they first met at the Lovelace Hotel.

'Yes, Darnley?'

'Mr. Malakite was alluding to your father just now; and it just occurred to me that I've never told you what *my* father used to say when I had to go back to school. He used to say to me: "Man can bear anything, if it only lasts a second!" '

Something behind his friend's mackerel-coloured eyes seemed at that moment of time to be reaching out to his inmost soul and crying to it for some answering signal. The fact that Mattie only yesterday had called upon her mother, so long dead, and that Darnley was now reverting to a father he had never even mentioned before, struck Wolf's mind as an ominous glimpse into the central nerve of life upon earth. He felt at that moment an out-rushing wave of intense affection for Darnley. But what could he do? Olwen refused to let him so much as even smile at the yellow beard across the table. She turned his head towards her with one of her sticky little hands.

'What did the wind say then?' she cried. 'What did it say to me when I told it to blow me to Weymouth?'

'It said: "You want too much!" ' he went on. 'It said: "I'm afraid you're not a real bird at all! If you were a real bird you wouldn't care what you did or where you went, as long as you were flying. You'd hover over Dorset, looking at everything – looking at every cuckoo flower in the Lunt fields, and every nest in the Gwent Lanes. You'd hover –" '

'Where is Christie?' came the voice of Mr. Malakite from across the table.

Wolf had to reopen his closed eyes at this. 'Downstairs, I suppose,' he responded brusquely. And then, catching hold of the child's hot hand as it clutched at his chin, 'The wind,' he went on, 'lifted all three birds from off the branch and carried them north-east, where not one of them wanted to go! Over hill and dale it carried them, towards Stonehenge. And when it had let them sink down upon the highest stone of Stonehenge, it said to them – '

He was interrupted by Christie's reappearance.

'The fly's here, Darnley!' she cried. 'Come, Olwen; let me put on your things.'

'It said to them,' Wolf concluded, ' "I can only take one of you to the house of my father. You must decide among yourselves which it is to be!" '

There was a general hush in the room as these words fell.

'Don't let it be me!' whispered Olwen hurriedly, clapping her hand over his mouth.

But Wolf's half-muffled voice must have been audible to them all.

' "Let the one who can best bear to be alone be the one to go," cried the swallow. And as he spoke, he snatched up the trembling Olwen-bird with his beak and claws, and spread his great, pointed wings for flight. Over Wilton he flew, over Semley over Gillingham, over Templecombe, over Ramsgard, over King's Barton! And as he flew, the Olwen-bird's feathers were so ruffled by the speed, that she turned into a little girl again; and when he set her down at last on the window-sill, and she clambered back into the room, and called down the stairs to Christie and Darnley, it seemed as if she had never been out of the house at all.'

Wolf was almost embarrassed by the grave hush that followed his conclusion.

'Heavens! I didn't know you were such a story-teller,' murmured Darnley, as he picked up his overcoat.

'Did the wind take you to its house?' panted Olwen, flushed and fidgeting now, as Christie buttoned round her a grey-blue jacket with a rabbit-fur collar and proceeded to smooth down her hair under a small, stiff Russian cap; 'and did you *like* being taken away from everybody, Wolf?'

He made no answer to the child's question. A deadly sadness had suddenly descended upon him; and through this sadness, as if through a screen of Mukalog's most disastrous rain, he fancied he caught an odiously possessive look shot forth upon Christie's bending figure out of the old man's narrowed eyelids. . . .

A few minutes later, as the faded vehicle drove off, with Olwen's thin little arm protruded from its side, like a white stalk out of a black bag, and he turned to Christie in the doorway to bid her good night, he found an expression upon her face that sent a queer shiver through his nerves.

'I must go, Wolf, dear,' she whispered. 'Don't forget all about me in the excitement of to-morrow.'

They remained silent for a second, side by side, as if the physical chemistry of their two frames had its own occult understanding, beyond anything that could be said or done by either. Then she hurriedly touched his hand, turned from him, and entered the house without another sign.

For some mysterious physical reason, the familiar sour smell of the pigsty, when he finally reached Preston Lane, brought to his mind that incredibly beautiful look, of sheer, native goodness, on the face of Gaffer Barge.

That look had surged up from the depths to greet him when he was in his worst danger of being swamped by 'reality.' Gaffer Barge was certainly too unimaginative to blow any ideal bubble! Not even that old rascal with the white cat was more embedded in actuality.than was this generous lout.

Wolf paused for a moment and ran the end of his stick along the railing of the pigsty, as an unmusical man might draw his thumb across the strings of a violin.

He crossed the road and opened the gate into his puny garden. To his surprise, as he moved up to the door, he saw that their front room was brilliantly illuminated. Hurriedly he let himself in; and he was no sooner in the hall than he was aware of youthful laughter proceeding from the parlour.

He burst in upon them, his hat and stick still in his hand. But it was only Lobbie Torp and Gerda, engaged in a vociferous game of cards!

Gerda's cheeks were burning and her eyes were brilliant.

'Lobbie's brought us a real pack, Wolf!' she cried excitedly. 'They've got pictures on 'em, same as they have at Farmer's Rest!' shouted Lobbie in an ecstacy, pushing a card into Wolf's hand.

'Why haven't we ever thought of buying such nice ones, Wolf?' echoed Gerda.

'A pretty sort of game for a schoolboy to bring into my sober house,' began Wolf, smiling; 'but you two are certainly enjoying yourselves.'

'Well, we must stop now,' said Gerda, in her most grave house-keeping tone. 'I've got to get supper. He can stay to supper, can't he, Wolf? she added, throwing into her voice a cajoling little-girl inflexion.

'Oh, don't let's stop, Gerdie! Don't let's stop!' cried Lob Torp. 'Why can't we take sides again, with him joining in?'

But Wolf's presence had already produced a certain restraint and Gerda did not find it difficult to slip away into the kitchen.

Wolf took off his coat, and, throwing it upon a chair, flung his hat and stick on top of it. He noted in his mind that this was the first time he had ever dispensed with his habitual hanging-up of these objects upon the pegs outside.

He lifted the table out of the way, and the two of them sat down by the fire. A couple of cards on the floor made Wolf recall, as he stooped to pick them up, that game of draughts he had intruded upon between Gerda and Bob Weevil.

'How's your friend Weevil?' he asked Lobbie at random.

'Pining for Gerdie,' was the boy's startling answer. 'I went long o' he to Willum's Mill last Tuesday night when Mr. Manley were out courtin'; but he were too lonesome to put a worm on a hook! He said Gerdie never liked they wriggling worms and he weren't never going to disturb they again. He said he reckoned them had *their* feelings, same as other folk. I told 'e 'twere all a girl's foolishness, and that we were men; but he said he had sworn a girt oath to do everythink what our Gerdie wanted, though he reckoned he'd never set eyes on she again.' Lobbie paused, and, feeling about in his pocket, produced a packet of peppermints, one of which he put in his mouth and another he handed to Wolf, who accepted it gravely.

'He made a vow,' the boy repeated, staring solemnly into the fire, as if completely weighed down by the strange aberrations of human passion; 'a vow like what King Harold did make, on they unknown bones.'

'Have you seen him since, Lobbie?' enquired Wolf.

The boy hesitated and glanced rather uneasily at his host.

''Tisn't that I haven't seen him,' he murmured obscurely. 'If you *must* know,' he burst out, ''twas when I asked he to come to Grassy Mound, out Henchford way, where the girls do enjoy theyselves rolling down thik bank. And do 'ee know what he said to I?' Lobbie fixed a portentously dramatic look upon his hearer, the undissolved peppermint in his cheek increasing rather than diminishing its impressiveness. 'He said there weren't no pleasure in 'em! 'Twas upsetting to a person to hear him; but that's what he said ... "no pleasure in 'em" ... meaning, *you know what!*'

'Your friend is in love with our Gerda, I'm afraid,' said Wolf coldly.

"Tisn't adultery, be it,' enquired Lobbie, 'for he to carry on so about another man's wife?'

In place of answering this question, Wolf escorted his brother-in-law into the kitchen. There the boy's youthful spirits, as he helped his sister dish up the supper, left Wolf time to slip out into the yard and possess his 'soul,' such as it was, in five minutes' solitude.

Actuated by one of those capricious motions which he habitually obeyed, he moved over to the stunted laburnum bush by the wall. On one branch only were there any buds; whereas their neighbour's lilac, growing in the pig-man's back yard, was covered with embryo leaves. He laid his hand on the trunk of this abject tree and looked up at the great velvet-black concavity above him, sprinkled with its minute points of light.

It was then that he distinctly heard, just as if the trunk of that little tree were a telegraphic receiver, 'Wolf! Wolf! Wolf!' uttered in Christie's voice, but with an intonation twisted out of her normal accent by some desperate necessity.

As he heard these words he seemed to see her face, exactly as he had seen it at that open doorway a couple of hours ago, only with a look upon it that forced him to make an immediate drastic decision.

He went back into the kitchen.

'Come on, Wolf!' cried Gerda, 'we are ready to begin.'

Not for one single second did he doubt the truth of what he had heard under that tree. 'I must get away without upsetting them,' he thought. 'I must get away without their guessing that anything's wrong!' He nodded his head with a forced grimace.

'Sit down and start, my dear! I've got to run out for a minute to get something.' By the light of the parlour fire he pulled on his overcoat. His fingers shook so much, as he tightened the collar round his neck that it was not easy to button it. Then he went into the kitchen again. The brother and sister were seated at the table now, laughing and jesting with absorbed hilarity. 'There's something important I *have* to get, Gerda! Keep my plate hot for me, will you? And enjoy yourselves till I come back. Don't wait dessert for me! But I'll come back all right . . . before long.' Throwing these words among them in a voice full of exaggerated cheerfulness, he snatched at his stick and was out of the house before they had time to realize what he was doing.

Like a stage group in a charade, just glimpsed by some hurried messenger through an open doorway, as he rushes on his way, those two laughing faces at the table lined themselves against his agitation. He even retained enough detachment, as he strode along, to note how easily these children of Dorset made a natural circle for their festivity, from which he was inevitably excluded. Still there arose no flicker of doubt in his mind as to the truth of the summons he had received. It tugged at him so hard that before he reached the bookshop he was actually running. . . .

God! There was a man talking to Christie at her door.

He approached them breathless, his heart beating violently. He felt the complete confusion which a person feels when he sees some utterly alien object in possession of a familiar spot!

The stranger was talking in authoritative tones to Christie, who herself stood exactly as he had seen her last.

'I'll be back in a couple of hours,' the man was saying. 'But if he *should* regain consciousness before that, you must let me know. You've got someone to send, haven't you?' He remained for a moment hesitating, his bowler hat in one hand and his black bag in the other. His countenance was illuminated by a faint flicker from behind the form of the girl. She must have laid down her candle upon a step of the staircase.

The first impression Wolf received was of an old photograph-album in his grandfather's drawing-room in Brunswick Terrace; the second, one of a certain hospital entrance in a street in London. It was later that these impressions explained themselves. The man had the drooping moustache and unintelligent wooden forehead of an old-fashioned army officer. About his person hung a smell of laudanum or chloroform.

'What is it?' cried Wolf as he approached. 'Can I help? Can I do anything?'

Dark as it was, Wolf was conscious that the fellow gave him a look of frigid suspicion as he bowed himself off. 'You can send for me if anything – otherwise in a couple of hours,' were his final words as he moved away. . . .

Christie led him then up the well-known staircase. 'He is dying,' she said, as they entered the bedroom of Mr. Malakite, a room whose existence was barely known to him. Then there commenced a strange vigil beside the unconscious form of that old man.

Christie herself sat on a chair on the left of her father's bed; he, on a similar one on the right. In broken whispers the girl told him how her father had fallen backwards, down that narrow staircase, soon after he and she had been left alone.

'I think I lost my head, Wolf. I think I ran crying into the street. Anyway, people came round . . . a lot of people . . . and they fetched Doctor Percy. Father's been like this ever since. Doctor Percy examined him. It's some internal injury, he thinks. He says he thinks his spine is hurt in some way; but the worst injury is internal. He thinks' – here the girl spoke in a voice that startled Wolf a good deal more than the meaning of her words – 'that he's bleeding to death inside.'

Each five minutes that passed in this singular interlude seemed as long as twenty minutes of any ordinary time-flow. Christie was completely different from her ordinary self. She avoided Wolf's eyes. She repelled his touch. She seemed reluctant to resume anything approaching their old intimacy.

He longed to ask her whether she had actually called out his name aloud, or whether that psychic summoning had conveyed its message independently of either of their two conscious minds. But he was too troubled by this unusual look upon her face, and this unnatural reserve, to ask any questions. He longed to enquire how the old man had come to have such an accident at all; but he dared not refer to it. There emanated from the girl an ice-cold barrier of inflexible pride, setting him at such a distance that no real exchange of feelings was possible.

Every now and then she would get up and move the bedclothes under the old man's chin, as if fearful lest he should be suffocated. But the particular way she did this struck Wolf as having something unnatural in it, for she did exactly as if the old man were already dead. She touched him differently from the way she would have done it had he merely been unconscious. Her attitude seemed to display the shrinking abhorrence that living people experience at contact with inanimate flesh.

To Wolf, who was both ignorant and very unobservant in matters of this sort, it did begin to present itself at last, as he watched the old man's face, that he really *was* dead . . . had died, in fact, while Christie and he had been watching over him! Incontinently he muttered something to Christie, and, bending over the bed, inserted his hand beneath the clothes and felt for the old man's heart. What he actually said to Christie was, 'I'll find his heart, shall I?' But in all the agitation of that moment he was still shockingly aware of the girl's avoidance of his eye.

'I can't feel it. I don't believe he's breathing!' he blurted out. 'Look at his lips!'

The girl did not answer him. She bent low down over her father's face; so low that a loose tress of her hair fell against the old man's closed eyes.

Then she straightened herself up with a jerk, and Wolf pulled his hand from under the bedclothes. He felt inert, utterly unable to deal with this crisis. Stupidly he watched her across the old man's stiff figure. He had been by degrees noting the aspects of this room which was so completely strange to him. *Mr. Malakite's bedroom!* He had even permitted himself to wonder what kind of spiritual eidola ... the creation of the thoughts of this singular old man ... lived and moved, like invisible homunculi, in this bare room! For the room was absolutely bare. With the exception of a small framed picture, in staring colours, of Raphael's *Transfiguration*, propped up upon the mantelpiece, there was nothing upon the walls. The only thing to be seen in the room now was death – death upon the bed, and the daughter of death standing at the window!

Mr. Malakite's bedroom lamp was of a very different appearance from that old green one in Christie's room. It was a small ship's-lantern; and her father was wont to read deep into the night, so Christie had once told him, with this lantern balanced upon his knees as he lay in bed.

The ship's-lantern did not throw a very strong light; and Wolf, as he laid his fingers on the old man's forehead, with a vague notion of establishing the fact of life's extinction, was aware of Christie's figure at the window as a taut bowstring of quivering feeling.

'He does not breathe. It must be the end, Chris,' he murmured gently.

The girl turned abruptly and came back. Twice, as she crossed that little space between the window and the bed, he saw her straighten herself up, hold back her head, and shut her eyes, clenching her fingers tightly as she did so, and making an odd little indrawn gasp, as if she were swallowing the very dregs of all human bitterness.

'Shall I go and fetch Doctor Percy?' he asked, moving round the foot of the bed.

He caught her eye for a moment then, and it was like the eye of a wild bird imprisoned in a boy's hand. She huddled herself against the wall at the bed's head, her head bowed upon her folded arms, her body as rigid as the form on the bed.

Something about the nape of her small neck, as she hung there, with drooping head and tense, taut limbs, hit Wolf through the heart.

'Don't you mind, O my dear true-love! Don't you mind!' he whispered desperately, clasping and unclasping his fingers, but not daring to approach her. His consciousness of her mood was so intense that when he thought of trying to take her in his arms he saw her wild, white face and flashing eyes turned upon him – turned against him with terrible words!

'Do you want me to go for that doctor, Chris?' he repeated, in a dull, flat, wooden voice.

A long shiver passed through her body, and she turned round, her arms hanging limp by her sides.

'I'd. . . rather go . . . myself,' she said in a low, heavy tone. 'Go . . . myself,' she repeated.

With stiff, leaden movements, after that, she went into her own room and came back in her loose winter coat and woollen cap.

'O Chris!' he cried, as he saw her there, hovering in the doorway; 'O little Chris!'

But she made a movement with her hands, as he approached her, that was almost peevish – the sort of movement with which a little girl beats down the jumping and barking of an excited dog.

'I'll be back in about twenty minutes, Wolf,' she said calmly. But he noticed that not one glance did she cast at the form on the bed, not one glance at him. The words she uttered, natural and commonplace as they were, were addressed to that gaudy rendering of the *Transfiguration* on the mantelpiece.

And then she was gone . . . melting away, so it seemed to him, as if she had actually been a spirit. The sound of the opening and closing of the street door affected him like an everlasting farewell. He recognized in that second that something had happened in his own heart that was like a wall falling outwards . . . outwards . . . into an unknown dimension.

In addition to the bookseller's ship's-lantern, which stood on a small table, there were two candles on the bare chest of drawers, one on each side of a faded leather case, containing two hairbrushes. Wolf sat down again and watched his own shadow sway, with the flicker of those two candle-flames, across the countenance upon the bed.

Very faintly, from the parlour on the other side of the landing – for the door was still wide open – came the ticking of Christie's clock.

His consciousness, like the man at watch on a ship that has been submerged in some terrific wave and rises to the surface cloudy with salt foam, turned instinctively to his lost 'mythology,' turned

573

to it as to something lying dead on the floor of his soul. And it came over him, by slow degrees like a cold glimmer of morning upon a tossing sea, that the abiding continuity of his days lay, after all, in his body, in his skull, in his spine, in his legs, in his clutching anthropoid-ape arms! Yes! that was all he had left . . . his vegetable-animal identity, isolated, solitary . . . hovered over by the margins of strange thoughts!

The intense reality of Mr. Malakite's figure beneath those bedclothes, of his beard above them, of his nostrils, his old-man's eyelids, his ugly beast-ears, narrowed the reality of his own life, with its gathered memories, into something as concrete, tangible, compact as the bony knuckles of his own gaunt hands now resting upon his protruding knees! Thought? It was 'thought,' of course! But not thought in the abstract. It was the thought of a tree, of a snake, of an ox, of a man, a man begotten, a man conceived, a man like enough to die to-morrow! With what within him had he felt that shrewd thrust just now about his true-love Chris? Not with any 'glassy essence.' Simply with his vegetable-animal integrity, *with his life*, as a tree would feel the loss of its companion . . . as a beast the loss of its mate!

His thoughts focused themselves mechanically upon the white lips of the man on the bed and upon his wrinkled eyelids, but they were no longer occupied with these things. His mind reviewed the loss of his life-illusion. How many chances and casualties, how many little criss-cross patterns, puffs of aimless air, wandering shadows, unpredictable wind-ripples, had combined to disintegrate and destroy it!

'I must not let slip what I found out just now,' he thought. And then, as a triangle of tiny wrinkles upon one of Mr. Malakite's closed eyes wove itself into his mental process, 'Whatever,' he said to himself, 'Christie may feel, I know that she, and no other, is my real true-love! Yes, by God! And I know that my "I am I" is no "hard, small crystal" inside me, but a cloud, a vapour, a mist, a smoke, hovering round my skull, hovering round my spine, my arms, my legs! *That's what I am* – a "vegetable-animal" wrapped in a mental cloud, and with the will-power to project this cloud into the consciousness of others!'

As he articulated this thought he gave himself up to a vivid awareness of his body, *particularly of his hands and knees*, and, with this, to a vivid awareness of his mind as a cloudy projection, unimpeded by material obstacles, driven forth in pursuit of Christie.

574

'I command that she shall be all right!' he muttered audibly, addressing this word to the universe in general.

All these thoughts raced through his head, while, for no earthly reason, he transferred his gaze to the bookseller's eyelashes.

'But if I send my mind after her, where is the will that sends it? In my hands and my knees?'

But with the help of Mr. Malakite's eyelashes, which were of yellowish white, he decided to suppress all those logical ambiguities. 'The great thing is to have a *feeling* of my identity that I can strengthen, whatever happens! Perhaps my will *is* in my knees and my hands. It doesn't matter *where* it is, as long as it can drive forth my mind to look after Christie!'

At that point he was aware of a cold, sickening doubt with regard to Christie. Strange that he should only discover what love for her meant at the moment when that closing door rang in his ears!

What a childish optimist he was! Were gorillas like that? *Their* identity, anyhow, was in their hands and knees!

A middle-aged gorilla, watching the dead face of an old gorilla – such was his present situation. . . .

Suddenly the left eye of Mr. Malakite – the one upon which Wolf's gaze had so mechanically been fixed – opened perceptibly and looked at him.

'She'll be back soon, Solent,' said Mr. Malakite.

'Do you want anything? Can I do anything for you. Are you suffering, sir?' Wolf found himself on his knees at the side of this awakened eye. The lid kept flickering up and down, raising itself with difficulty and then closing again; but the amount of conscious intelligence revealed by that life-cranny, when Wolf was able to peer into it, was terrifying.

'She pushed me down,' said Mr. Malakite.

A preposterous nursery-rhyme about an old man 'who wouldn't say his prayers' came into Wolf's head. But he murmured gravely, 'Can I get you a drink of water or anything?'

'Your father.' These two words came very faintly. The flickering eyelid sank down and stirred no more. . . . 'I think I see your father.' This time the voice was almost inaudible. But the next word was clearer. 'Good,' said Mr. Malakite.

Wolf had risen from his knees now and was hanging over the dying man, his face a few inches from his face, his hands, palms down, pressed into his pillow. . . .

'And great.' These last two syllables seemed uttered rather by

575

the old man's spirit than by his lips; for the latter were closed as tightly as his eyes.

'He . . . will . . . for –' The sound of this ghastly susurration seemed to come from under the bedclothes, from under the bed, from under the floor, from under the bookshop beneath the floor, from under the clay-bottom of Blacksod . . . .

'For –' The repetition of the syllable seemed like the echo of an echo; but Wolf became aware of a shocking twitching in the muscles of the old man's face.

'For –' . . .

A wave of atavistic sentiment rose up in Wolf's throat from countless centuries of Christian unction. He found the word 'forgive' quivering on the tip of his tongue, and recklessly he let it descend, like a drop of consecrated oil, on the man's dying. His idea was that Mr. Malakite was confusing the one person he had ever respected with some obscure First Cause. Then he found himself staggering back.

With a convulsion of his whole frame, the bookseller jerked himself to a sitting posture. Spasmodically drawing in his legs, like a frog swimming on its back, he kicked off every shred of clothing. . . .

'Forget!' he shrieked; and his voice resembled the tearing of a strip of calico. He was dead when he sank back; and from one of the corners of his mouth a stream of saliva, tinged with a red stain, trickled upon the pillow.

Hurriedly Wolf pressed down those elevated knees and pulled the bedclothes up to the man's chin. Then, taking out his handkerchief, he wiped the mouth with it, screwed it into a tight ball, and wedged it between the blankets and the jaw of the dead. That done, he drew a long breath and stared at Mr. Malakite. But where *was* Mr. Malakite? The face above the stained handkerchief seemed a *new phenomenon* in the world – something that had no connection with the old man he had heard crying the word 'forget' just now. It was as if the thing he had known in his experience as Mr. Malakite had completely vanished; and *from somewhere else* had arisen this frozen simulacrum.

'Forget,' he murmured to himself; and then he felt a longing to convey at once to Miss Gault the news that a man upon his death-bed had confused William Solent with God!

But at the image of Miss Gault, tumbling over her milk-bottle upon his father's grave, a sudden moisture seemed to flow into the cavities behind his eyeballs.

'It's not for you,' he said grimly to the figure on the bed, as he recognized this tendency to tears. 'It's for Miss Gault.' And actuated by a queer desire *to prove to the corpse* that it was not 'for him,' he laid the tips of his fingers on the bookseller's forehead.

'How soon do they get cold?' he said to himself. . . .

At this point he heard the door opening down below, and the sound of voices and footsteps. He hurried out of the room and met Christie on the stairs.

'He's dead, Chris,' he said. 'I couldn't do anything.' This addition to his news sounded singularly foolish as soon as it was uttered. Even at that inadvertent moment, on the eighth step of those back stairs, he blushed to have spoken such a banality.

'It's too late, doctor,' said she, turning her head towards the man behind her.

'I feared so,' said Doctor Percy.

'Poor old gentleman!' repeated Doctor Percy. 'He is spared a great deal.' The tone in which this amiable epitaph echoed through that house and penetrated into the shop, with its shelves of perverse erudition, had an irritating effect upon Wolf's nerves.

He felt a malicious desire, as he moved aside to let Christie pass, to catch the man by the sleeve of his neat coat and whisper in his ear something monstrous. 'She had to throw him downstairs, you idiot; she had to throw him downstairs!'

Mr. Malakite's daughter was standing by his bed's head when the two men entered the room. Her arms, with the fingers clasped desperately inside the palms, hung down by her sides like torn tree-limbs in a deadly wind. Her head drooped upon her chest. He fancied for a moment that her profile was contorted with crying; but when she raised her head, her brown eyes were dull, abstracted, and completely tearless.

After bustling about the body for a minute or two, as if professional nicety required more evidence of death than nature in decency could afford, Doctor Percy bowed himself off.

'Come into the other room, Chris! No! . . . Come along! You *must*, my darling.' Holding her by one of her clenched hands . . . and she obeyed him like a somnambulist . . . he led her into her parlour, where he made her sit down on a chair, over the glowing heap of cinders.

He sat down close to her side; and without looking at her, but still holding tightly that small clenched hand, he began speaking rapidly, emphatically, monotonously.

'Chris, there's nothing about all this that I don't know *as well*

577

as you do ... nothing, my darling! It's as if some crust were shattered for a moment and we looked through ... into those horrors that are always there! It's the same with us all, Chris! It's the same with the whole world. There's only one thing for us to do if we're to endure life at all, Chris; and ... and your father said the word himself before he died. Are you listening, Chris? He became conscious for a minute; and he said it to me like a message for you. ... O Chris, little Chris, it was a message to both of us!'

She did not lift her head; but he knew, from the quiver in the fingers he held, that her attention was arrested.

'He said "forget," Chris ... just that one word. O my love, my only love! From now on that is the word for us. We know wha we know. We bear it together. Listen, little Chris! You've got to go on living, for Olwen's sake. I've got to go on living for Gerda's sake. When you went away just now, I knew, in one great flash, what you and I are to each other. We shall be *that*, my dear, dear love, till we both are dead! Nothing can change it any more. Nothing can come between us any more. As to everything else ... are you listening, little Chris? ... we've both got to "forget" – just as he said. It's the only way, my precious. When that crust breaks, as it did just now, it's madness to dwell upon it. It's the unbearable. No one can bear it and go on living. And you've *got* to live, Chris, for Olwen's sake, just as I've got –'

He was interrupted in the middle of his speech. The daughter of Mr. Malakite sprang erect upon her feet and uttered a piercing scream. Then she beat the air with her clenched hands.

'Damn you!' she cried. 'Damn you! You talking fool! You great, stupid, talking fool! What do *you* know of me or my father? What do *you* know of my real life?'

Wolf drew away from her, his body bent forwards, his hands pressed against the pit of his stomach, his eyes blinking.

For a second he saw himself and his useless words exactly as she described them. He saw all his explanations as if they had been one prolonged windy bellow, covering the impervious grazing of a complacent ox!

But grim terror swallowed up this spasm of personal humiliation. What if this tragedy were to unsettle Christie's wits?

He used his will now as if it had been a master mariner giving rapid, desperate orders in a deafening storm! He deliberately smoothed out of his face every shade of feeling except a thundering anger.

'Stop that!' he cried, as if he had been speaking to Olwen. 'Stop that, Christie!' And he made a step towards her. She had never seen him in such a mood, never heard such a tone from him. His nervous concern gave vibrancy to his pretended anger. Her contorted features relaxed, her clenched hands dropped down; she stood there before him like a solitary pier-post – desolate but unbroken – about whose endurance the last waves of the storm subsided in foamy rings.

Then, to his infinite relief, she burst into a flood of tears. He never afterwards forgot the extremity of those tears. Her face seemed literally to dissolve; it seemed to melt, as if the very stuff of it were changing from moulded flesh into streaming water!

She flung herself down on the sofa and buried her head in its faded embroidered roses. Approaching the back of the sofa, and leaning against it, he watched her huddled form lying on its bed of relief, very much as a master showman might watch the performance of a darling puppet, over whose form and gesture he had worked in secret, by the light of an attic candle, for many a long, starved month!

The lamp Christie always kept on the sewing-table in her parlour must have been burning steadily ever since they had had tea. The chimney was black now with soot; and Wolf moved across and turned the wick down a little. As he performed this small action, he received, to his astonishment, an inrush of furtive, stealthy satisfaction.

This was the first of such feelings that he had enjoyed for many a long day. '*Mr. Malakite is dead.*' Was it *that* particular collocation of words, as his mind visualized them, that gave him this physical thrill of relief? Or was it just the change of the girl's mood?

He could see, even by that diminished lamplight, when he returned to the sofa, that her streaming tears had made a dark, wet stain upon that pink embroidery. Oh, she would be all right now! Whatever had passed between her and the old man – whatever plague-spot of unspeakable remorse had appeared upon some sensitive fibre in her consciousness – these tears would wash out everything!

How could there be so much salt water in one tiny skull?

The tears of women! How from the beginning of time they had washed away every kind of evil thing, every kind of deviltry! Down the centuries had flowed those tears, clearing our race's conscience from poisons, washing clean the mind of man from the torture of rational logic, washing it clean from the torture of memory, recreating it, fresh, careless, free, like a child new-sprung from the womb! But how could such a wide, dark, wet stain upon those pink roses have come from so small a skull!

He didn't dare to speak to her as he pressed his hands upon the back of that familiar sofa and stared across her form, curved there like a dusky tree-rod, into the dying fire.

As had happened once or twice before to him in his life, he fell at this crisis into a kind of waking trance. That flood of tears became a river, swifter, deeper than the Lunt, and on its breast he was carried, so it seemed to him, into an imaginary landscape, far enough away from the corpse of Mr. Malakite and his ambiguous books! It was that same landscape which the Gainsborough picture had conjured up. But instead of a road there was this river; and the river carried him beyond the terraces and the gardens into less human scenery. There, between high, dark, slippery precipices was he carried by the water of Christie's weeping; and there he encountered in strange correspondency those same towering basaltic cliffs past which he had drifted in a similar hallucination nearly a year ago, as he waited for his mother's train on the 'Slopes' of Ramsgard!

He was brought back from this drugged condition by the sound of the street-door bell; but it was not at once that he realized that he was the one who had to answer this summons! Staring at the curve of Christie's wet eyelashes on her drowned cheek, as that dark stain on the pink roses grew wider, he was startled by the idea that this particular grouping of material substances might be no more than reflections in a mirror. There, below this girl's figure, below these darkened roses, was there not hidden some deep, spiritual transaction? The feeling passed away quickly enough; but as it passed, it left behind it a stabbing, quivering *suspicion*, a suspicion as to the solid reality of what his senses were thus representing, compared with something else, something of far greater moment, both for himself and for her!

All this while the street-door bell continued to ring; and it was ringing now with violent, spasmodic jerks.

He straightened his back, and, moving away from the sofa, stood motionless in the middle of the room, listening.

'I must go down,' he thought. 'It's most likely that doctor come back, to make sure once more that the old man's dead!'

Again the bell rang, this time with a long, continuous, jerking pull. . . .

Wolf glanced at the back of the sofa. There was no movement

there, not any sign. He went out on the landing and waited for a moment at the door of the dead man's room, which they had left wide open. How different was the immobility of that form from the motionlessness of the one he had just left!

He listened to the silence, waiting for the bell to ring again. 'Why is it,' he thought, 'that I find it so hard to go down?' He moved to the head of the stairs. 'Why do sounds like this,' he thought, 'hit corpses in the face and outrage them like an indecency? Does death draw up to the surface some new kind of silence, to disturb which is a monstrous abuse?'

Brought back to reality by the cessation of the ringing, and a little fearful as to what the doctor might do if thwarted in his professional zeal, Wolf ran down the stairs and flung open the street door.

There, in his Sunday clothes, and with an expression of extravagant decorum upon his whimsical visage, was Mr. John Torp!

'Doctor told I, master –' he began.

'Come in, Mr. Torp,' said Wolf helplessly, wondering vaguely what new process of pious science that stark figure upstairs was to expect. 'Come in and sit down, will you, while I tell Miss Malakite you're here?' He let his father-in-law into the house and closed the door. It was easier to tell Mr. Torp to sit down than to give him anything to sit upon. 'I don't know,' he began awkwardly. But Mr. Torp caught him by the sleeve with one of his plump hands.

'It came over I,' he whispered, 'that Miss Malakite wouldn't be wanting one of they arrogant death-women with her dad. And as I were an undertaker meself afore I took to me stone-job, I thought I'd run round and help she out.'

'I'm sure it's most kind of you, Mr. Torp,' murmured Wolf, noticing now for the first time that his father-in-law was carrying a heavy carpet-bag. 'I'll go up and tell Miss Malakite you're here. I expect she'll be very grateful for your help.'

'Don't 'ee say more than just that one word, mister,' replied the other, in a tone of such unctuous slyness that Wolf made a grimace in the darkness. 'Some relatives do like to use a common sheet. But I do say 'tis the corpse's feelings what us have to reason with. These here shrouds' – and he tapped Wolf's knee with the carpet-bag – 'be calculated to lie as soft and light on they, as lamb's-wool on babes. 'Twas one of these here shrouds that thik bull-frog Manley cheated his wone mother of, by his dunghill ways; and her a woman too what always had a finicky skin. But don't 'ee say more than just that one word, mister. Missy up there, 'tis only likely enough, will give no more attention to these here shrouds than if she were tucking her dad in's bed. But "Leave it to Torp" is what thik corpse would say, were speech allowed 'un. They be wonderful touchy, they corpses be, if all were told; and it be worse when folk's tongues run sharp upon 'un, as we know they do on he above-stairs. 'Twere me thoughts of *that*, mister, that made I reckon Miss Malakite would be glad to see I, sooner than they death-nurses, who be all such tittle-tattlers.'

It had by this time begun to dawn upon Wolf that his eccentric father-in-law had been genuinely actuated by a philanthropic impulse in making his appearance at this juncture. With this in mind he caught the man's hand and shook it warmly. 'I'm sure we're much obliged to you, Mr. Torp,' he said.

'And don't 'ee worry about your Gerdie,' concluded the worthy man. 'Missus went round to she when I comed away. Our Lob runned in, 'sknow, with a tale of your leaving your vittles and the Lord knows what! So when doctor told I you was here, I let *she* go to Gerdie and came round here me wone self. Ye knew, I reckon, that there were trouble in this house? Well . . . no matter for that! Every man to his wone concerns, be *my* motto.'

The rough tact of this little outburst of indulgent interpretation was the final touch in the winning of Wolf's gratitude.

'I'll go up and see Miss Malakite,' he said. 'You wait here, Mr. Torp. I'm sorry there are only the stairs to sit on.'

He found Christie putting coal on the grate in the parlour. She had closed the door of her father's room. She turned to him a face flushed by her struggle with the fire, but bearing the impress of her desperate crying in some fashion he could not just then define. At any rate she appeared in full control of herself; and he felt intuitively that as far as remorse went, her reason was clear and unpoisoned.

He shut the parlour door and hurriedly explained Mr. Torp's mission.

'He knew I was with you. Doctor Percy must have told him. He knew you'd want some undertaker's woman to do what's necessary . . . to "lay him out," as they call it. He knew what gossips these demons are. So he just came himself. It was nice of the old chap, wasn't it?'

The psychic tension between them, as he hurriedly communicated all this, was so great that he found they were both on the verge of a childish giggling-fit. Wolf took advantage of this mood to tell her about the contents of the carpet-bag. 'Oh, Chris,' he found himself saying, with a queer chuckle in his voice, 'when the old man used that particular word, I had such a weird sensation! I thought of the shroud in which Samuel appeared to Saul. I thought of the shroud in which Lazarus came out of his grave. I thought of the shroud that Flora MacIvor made for Fergus before he was executed. And then to see that carpet-bag! It might have been a monstrous thing, eh Chris? Nobody but this old fellow could have carried it off. Gad! but what a word it is! A *shroud!* Doesn't it make you want to be drowned in water, Chrissie, or burnt into cinders?' He paused for a minute, struggling to keep back from her one of those forbidden thoughts to which he was so hopelessly subject. But their mood was too close. They were like a couple of excited starlings perched on a gallows that sways in the wind. . . . The love that was between them gave a mad gusto to that incongruous moment, with Mr. Torp waiting below-stairs to wash an incestuous old man with soap and water, and Christie's parlour door shut for ever to Mr. Malakite!

'Isn't it awful, Chris,' he whispered, 'to think of what Redfern's shroud must have looked like when they – ' He suddenly remembered that he had never told the girl a word about what he and Valley had seen; and he stopped abruptly.

'When they?' she echoed faintly.

'I'll tell you another time, Chris,' he flung out; and he seized her fragile figure in the most self-effacing embrace he had ever bestowed on anyone since he was born.

25

RIPENESS IS ALL

'You'll be sure to be back for tea!'

These words were uttered by Gerda as she stood in their doorway, with Lobbie Torp at her side.

'Make it fairly late, then,' said Wolf. 'I don't want to cut short our walk.'

'The best part of our walk will be looking forward to our return,' remarked Wolf's companion, with a smile that Wolf saw reflected, as if it were a bunch of honeysuckle, in Gerda's delighted face.

'Well, I'll have tea ready for *you*, whether Wolf's home or not!' cried the excited girl.

'And I'll get back from *my* walk as soon as you do,' threw in Lobbie Torp. 'I'm going down by the Lunt to cut a new walking-stick. . . . Bob's going with me. He likes the *other* kind . . . proper shop sticks . . . but he's coming all the same. Shall I cut you a stick too, Lord Carfax?'

The visitor turned to the boy with the gravest attention.

'An ash stick, Lobbie? Could you grub up an ash *root?* No! I suppose it wants a spade for that! But an ash stick, with its own root for handle, is just what I *am* on the look-out for.' He turned round to Gerda with sly, screwed-up eyelids. 'You're sure you won't change your mind, Mrs. Solent, and come with us? . . . and Lobbie too?' he added, with an afterthought that brought wrinkles of roguery into his face.

Wolf had already caught the amorous glances with which their visitor had enwrapped Gerda. It was just as if some drooping 'Gloire de Dijon' rose in a deserted garden were enwrapped by a rich slant of August sunshine, full of the heavy poppy-scents of all the yellow cornfields it has crossed, negligent, careless, and yet massively intent! 'Why *don't* you and Lobbie come with us?' Wolf feebly muttered; but as he spoke, there surged up within him a flood of black bile. Oh, how he hated just then, as he stood with his fingers on the iron rail of his gate, every one of the people of his life, except Christie! The maliciousness he felt at that moment amounted to a deadly distaste. He hated his mother, he hated

Gerda, he hated Carfax, he hated Urquhart, Miss Gault, Jason! He hated them all, except Christie . . . and, perhaps, old Darnley with his yellow beard.

'We'd help you get tea, Gerda?' he murmured obstinately. 'Or we could get it in Ramsgard!'

How queer this malice within him was! It made his pulse literally thud with its crazy violence. It gave him a savage, animal-like desire to dig his chin, in a tumbling, tossing wrestle of hate, into the flesh of Lord Carfax.

'Do come, Gerda!' he repeated, in a stubborn refrain. The girl shook her head; but the radiant expression she had been wearing in the last two hours did not pass from her face. It was evident to Wolf that Lord Carfax had completely won her heart during the short time he had spent under her roof.

'Do you really want to see where he's buried?' he asked, as he conducted his visitor through that grassy lane he had recently discovered, which made it possible to reach Poll's Camp without passing through the town.

'I like all graveyards,' replied Lord Carfax, 'and I've always been interested in your father.'

'It's a cemetery,' remarked Wolf sulkily. 'He's been there a long time,' he added.

The weather-beaten countenance of 'the lord from London' wrinkled itself into many genial wrinkles as it glanced indulgently at Wolf's surly profile.

'I was a good deal more interested in him than *she* thought quite decent,' he went on. 'I used always to tell him I'd visit his grave when he was dead. It was assumed between us, you know, that he *would* die. He always talked of being dead. It seemed to please him in some way. It certainly never gave *me* any great pleasure, that particular thought!' As his visitor said this he fixed upon Wolf a look of such humorous whimsicality that it was almost impossible to see it and remain morose and truculent. It was a look of penetrating sweetness, and yet it was shamelessly cynical. Wolf found himself softening; but this in itself was a thing that increased his secret irritation!

'I'd like to show you his grave,' he said bluntly, feeling as if he would be glad to strike that kindly visage, and then to kiss it and ask its pardon for the blow!

He tried to transfer his attention, as they left the lane and entered the first of the orchards, to the beauty of that particular afternoon, the last Saturday in May. It was warm and windless; but a screen of thin, opaque clouds obscured the sunlight, filtering the hot rays, as in some old picture, into a mellow spaciousness of watery gold. In fact, the atmosphere resembled nothing so much, to Wolf's mind, as the look of a great glass jug of cowslip wine, which about a month ago his mother, in her drastic, picturesque manner – quite shameless about the number of flowers she sacrificed for such a thing – had held up to his lips.

He had plenty of time, as they drifted through the long grass of those three hedged-in orchards that led to the foot of the hill, to note every feature of his visitor's appearance. Lord Carfax was to all intents and purposes an old man; but he held himself so erect, and he walked with so resolute a step that Wolf would have taken him for a man of fifty. He was in reality rather short – not much taller than Lobbie; but the massiveness of his great square head, combined with the solid sturdiness of his frame, produced the constant illusion that he was of normal height.

He was certainly eccentric in his clothes. His attire on this occasion gave Wolf the impression of a seafaring man. He might have been the elderly skipper of an old-fashioned packet-boat, bound from Weymouth for the Channel Islands! Wolf had been fascinated by many things in him from the very start. Partly owing to his mother's sardonic predilection, but much more owing to the man's own unique personality, he felt completely at ease with him. The fact that it was due to this man's initial intervention – as a relative of both Mr. Urquhart and Mrs. Solent – that he had come to Dorset at all, combined with the part the fellow's shameless opinions had played in his own secret thoughts, gave to this rugged and leathery countenance, now that he saw it at close quarters, an almost legendary glamour.

A flicker of snobbishness entered into his feelings too. But he salved his conscience over this by assuring himself that he would have been in any case attracted to a person of this original character. He smiled grimly to himself, however, as he assisted 'Cousin Carfax' in pushing his way through the hedge-gaps, to discover that he was already hoping that Jason would never learn of this prolonged visit! Carfax, he knew, was generally supposed to have left for London on the previous day. His remaining at the Three Peewits last night was a sudden caprice, of which even Mrs. Solent was unaware. Wolf suspected that Gerda's beauty had more to do with it than anything else!

They had hardly got through the last hedge, and were just about to ascend the southern slope of Poll's Camp, when they came upon a shabby-looking man – something between a tramp and a poor workman – who was resting himself on a turf-covered mole-hill.

To Wolf's surprise this man turned out to be none other than Mr. Stalbridge, the ex-waiter of the Lovelace Hotel!

The man rose at their approach; and Wolf, ashamed of his behaviour at their last encounter, greeted him with exaggerated deference, shaking hands with him and introducing him to his companion. The ex-waiter professed a vivid memory of their meeting in the Lovelace Hotel more than a year ago, and explained that he had got a temporary job in Blacksod and was now returning to spend the Sunday in Ramsgard.

Mr. Stalbridge's ceremonious manner offered such a contrast to his shabby attire, that Lord Carfax, who seemed to collect human curiosities as boys collect butterflies, entered into a lively conversation with him, and finally appeared prepared to receive him into their company as a fellow-traveller. Wolf felt a little piqued by this; for though he had allowed for Gerda's attractiveness as an element in their visitor's interest, he had assumed that this excursion to the father's grave implied a certain desire on his guest's part to exchange ideas with the son! Apparently he was mistaken; Carfax's attention promised to be totally absorbed by Mr. Stalbridge, whose humorous anecdotes about the Lovelace family and other local magnates continued with small abatement until they reached the summit of Poll's Camp.

Wolf's original sensation of pique at this encounter had increased to a pitch that needed the control of some quite serious effort of mind, when they stood at length on the top of the grassy eminence.

Gerda's radiance under Carfax's admiration returned to him now as an integral portion of the slight he was enduring. 'If she sees much more of these sophisticated people,' he thought, 'she will lose all the simplicity of her nature!'

He flung his gaze round the immense expanse revealed to them, while Lord Carfax drew heavy breaths, leaning on his stick; and Mr. Stalbridge continued the sly process of his courtly seduction. Without being obtrusive in any particular detail, the lavish waves of the season's fertility, feathery grasses, green wheat, new budding honeysuckle, buttercups in their prime, red and white hawthorn, seemed to flow over every field and every hedgerow, between where he stood now on Poll's Camp and the mount of Glastonbury.

He felt at this moment as though humiliation were dripping into his heart, drop by drop, like carefully poured medicine into a tumbler of water. So this 'lord from London' took really not the slightest interest in him! Anxious to help his mother, to help Jason, to help Mr. Stalbridge, the great man had evidently found Wolf himself tedious and uninspiring!

'Damn the fellow! What do I care what he thinks of me?' he said to himself; but as Mr. Stalbridge became more and more voluble, and the leathery creases of my lord's hewn and quarried physiognomy wrinkled themselves in increasing appreciation, he found that his humiliation grew unbearable. That luminous look upon Gerda's face! Why, he had not been able to summon up that look for the last six months! She had become a grown-up woman with him these latter days, tender and considerate; but this man's admiration transformed her back again into an irresponsible little girl!

As soon as the visitor had got his breath, they all moved on, following the outer circle of the camp and heading for Babylon Hill.

Wolf was the last to climb across the stile into the highroad. How rich with the season's overbrimming vegetation that hedgeside was! What intoxicating earth-smells hung about that wellknown stile! Trailing dog-roses that carried frail green buds, whose sweetness resembled the fragrance of apples and sunburnt hay, mingled there, as he climbed that stile, with the white blossoms of tangled umbelliferous growths, their stalks full of warm, moist sap.

He glanced at the two men's faces, as they stood, quite oblivious of him, conversing there in the road. Yes! There was a scooped-out misery in the ex-waiter's eyes that reminded him of the man of the Waterloo steps! He was evidently making some personal appeal to Carfax now. Perhaps he hoped to get employment from him. Perhaps he *would* get employment from him! What a thing it was to be possessed of the power that Carfax had! Carfax was now succouring the Waterloo-steps man!

He remained for a minute balanced on the top of the stile, hugging his knees. He would give this poor devil every second he could snatch for him of this lucky chance! Slowly he turned his head and looked down upon the roofs of the town. 'Christie! Christie!' And there flowed over him the memory of the day, just three weeks ago, when he had gone down to Weymouth. There he had seen her – seen her with Olwen in their new home by the backwater. Till the last minute of his departure, he and she had sat together on the dry sand under the Jubilee Clock, while Olwen paddled among the other children in a sea that danced and glittered in the jocund sunshine. He could smell the sharp sea-smells now. He could taste the salt. He could feel the living slipperiness of a broad brown ribbon of seaweed that Olwen had picked up, and that both he and Christie had pressed against their mouths. He could see the name 'Katie' painted in green on a boat stern, and the far-away look of the sailor who leaned against it, thinking God knows what!

It was owing to Carfax – owing to his unstinted purchase of all those ambiguous books – that these two had enough to live on. He remembered the night when Christie had yielded to the little girl's mania for the seaside. 'It's our fate, Wolf, dear,' she had said, as he touched her cold cheek. He remembered those last minutes under the sea-wall; how they had sat so stiff and straight, letting the loose grains of sand run through their fingers, staring into each other's eyes!

There was no bookshop any longer under that roof down there! Someone else, some overworked greengrocer's woman, was at this moment washing her dishes in Christie's little alcove, between that parlour and that bedroom. . . .

'Are you ready, Solent? I promised your wife to keep you alive-o!'

Carfax's voice was friendly. 'I'm a fool to feel so touchy,' he thought, as he jumped down into the road and joined them.

'He's won his fling,' he thought, glancing sideways at the ex-waiter's face, as they moved on together. It was queer to see that film of unspeakable relief forming itself, like 'cat-ice' over a pool, above those sockets of despair. Ailinon! but the chap *was* like that Waterloo-steps man. He was at least that man's representative! He had denied him half a crown that day outside the Abbey; and now Carfax had stepped in. Everything he would like to have done Carfax had done. And now he was dragging along at Carfax's heels to visit 'old Truepenny!' What a humorous fiasco his whole life down here in Dorset had been! He had been defeated by Urquhart . . . paid off, fixed up, bribed, squared! He had betrayed that skull in the cemetery. He had let his true-love slip through his hands. His 'lord in London' had recognized Jason's genius, discovered Gerda's beauty, poured oil and wine into the wounds of Mr. Stalbridge, added a new glory to the tea-shop. Why the devil should he find anything worth bothering about in Mr. Wolf Solent, teacher of history in the Blacksod Grammar School?

As the three men approached a certain group of larches where Wolf had once wondered what it would be like to live with Darnley, it became clear to him that Mr. Stalbridge *was* to leave his present miserable job. Apparently he was to be transformed into some part of leisurely factotum, or assistant major-domo, in

my lord's London house. What incredible luck for the ex-waiter!
Wolf at this point did feel a certain glow of admiration for this
rugged collector of human butterflies. 'How the devil does he
keep that seafaring air,' he thought, 'among his servants in
London? Anyway, the hiring of Mr. Stalbridge is just the kind
of thing I'd like to do myself.'

The ex-waiter's affair being settled, Wolf began to assume a
more prominent place in the attention of the great man.

'How's my crazy cousin Urquhart?' he enquired. 'I gave his
house a wide berth this time! He's become "heavy weather"
these days, with his fixed ideas. Don't you feel the same?'

'What ideas do you mean?' murmured Wolf.

His companion gave him a slow, quizzical smile. 'That book
of *yours*, for one thing! And his absurd idea that he killed that
boy Redfern. I met Doctor Percy at your mother's last night,
and he told me the boy had died of double pneumonia. Percy
attended him . . . saw him die, in fact . . . had to turn out that
precious vicar of theirs, who was howling like a poisoned jackal.
Urquhart himself's going to die, Solent. By Jove! I felt death in
his hand a year ago. I like the fellow; but when he idealizes his
confounded peculiarities to quite such a tune you get dead sick
of him! I'm all in favour of honest bawdry myself; but why sing
such a song about it? Natural or unnatural, it's nature. It's
mortal man's one great solace before he's annihilated! But all
this bladder-headed fuss about it – about such a simple thing –
one way or the other – I don't like it. It's not in my style.' Wolf
was astonished at the massive foursquare tone in which the man
uttered these last words . . . as if he'd been a great admiral-of-the-
fleet criticizing some popinjay captain for a frivolous manœuvre.

'What do *you* think?' he enquired of the ex-waiter. 'Do *you*
agree with Lord Carfax that annihilation is not to be gainsaid?'

The old man appeared to hesitate for a moment. Then he bent
his head and took off his hat. 'I believe in the Resurrection of the
body; and the Life everlasting,' he said gravely, 'if it's no offence
to his lordship.'

'Put on your hat, Stalbridge; put on your hat.' said the other.
'What do *you* think, Solent? You don't seem to enjoy expressing
your views. You're like Ann. She covers everything with such
malicious sarcasm that she makes everything equally unimportant.
Do *you* believe in a future life, Solent?'

They were now passing one of the numerous cattle-droves that
led into that maze of grassy paths, bordered by high hedges,

which Wolf had come to know as the Gwent Lanes. Wolf himself was walking on the right of Lord Carfax, the ex-waiter on the left; so that as he turned to answer this historic question, he caught the profiles of both these old men silhouetted against the rich vegetation of this avenue of grass and greenery.

'Sometimes I agree with Mr. Stalbridge,' he said, 'and sometimes with you. At this moment I think I agree with you; but that is probably due to the fact that I've been rather hard worked at the school lately.'

Carfax made no comment upon this; and presently Wolf heard him begin to give a humorous account to the new servant of what he described as his 'open house.'

That glimpse of the Gwent lane behind those two faces had brought to Wolf a sickening sense of what he had lost in the disappearance of his 'mythology.' A year ago, how little would it have mattered that he should have replied so lamely to the great question Carfax had put to him! He would have let it go. He would have fallen back on that sense of huge invisible cosmic transactions, in the midst of which he played his part, a part totally unaffected by any casual mental lapse.

As they walked on, and he listened with a negligent ear to the discourse between this master and this servant, he recognized that the corpse of his life-illusion had received two fresh spadefuls of earth.

The resemblance, faint though it was, of Stalbridge to the Waterloo waif, considered in the light of that unbestowed half-crown, gave to this generous caprice of Carfax the quality of something that stepped in 'between the election and his hopes.'

But worse than this were my lord's words about Urquhart. Ailinon! Ailinon! Was all the agitation, all the turmoil, all his consciousness of a supernatural struggle with some abysmal form of evil, reduced now to the paltry level of a feeble old bachelors fantastic self-deception?

If his imagination had been so moonstruck as to make so much of a pure phantasy, was it any wonder that this sagacious man-of-the-world turned away from him with indifference – turned to his wife's beauty, turned to the ex-waiter's idiosyncrasy, found in him nothing more than a pedantic usher in a provincial school? He had been living in a vain dream all these years of his life, living in it ever since he sat in the sunshine in his grandmother's bow window, watching those painted boats rock and toss on the glittering Weymouth waves.

'Christie! Christie! O my lost darling, O my true-love!'

They had now arrived at the point where it was necessary to

follow a field path across the pastures in order to reach the cemetery. Mr. Stalbridge proceeded with elaborate ceremony to bid them both farewell, touching his uncovered forehead to his new master and extending his hand to Wolf.

'The seven-o'clock train, at Ramsgard, then,' were Carfax's last words to him; 'and don't bother about a ticket. Look out for me in a third-class smoking-carriage!'

As they crossed the fields towards the cemetery, Wolf visualized the journey of those two old men that night. In some queer way he felt as if Carfax were a competent actor, naturally assuming the precise rôle in which he himself had failed! Carfax would hear that imbecile youth cry out 'Longborne Port!' and rattle the milk-cans on that little, deserted platform! Carfax would see the tower of Basingstoke Church. Carfax would see that placid-grazing cow. Carfax would observe, crossing the same coloured picture of Weymouth Bay, the same bluebottle fly . . . or his exact representative . . . in the whirligig of chance!

His companion's feet seemed to drag a little now, as they made their way between a flowering hawthorn hedge and a field of green barley.

'I expect we'd better take a carriage back,' Wolf remarked.

'It's not my boots,' growled Carfax. 'I always have them made at the same place. It's my socks. A person knits them for me who was my nurse in former days. She's getting old, and her stitches gather into knots that seem dedicated to gall my kibe.'

'I wonder if we shall find Miss Gault at the grave,' Wolf said, as he lifted up a barbed-wire rail with the handle of his stick for Lord Carfax to crawl under. 'I hope we shall. The last time I saw her was when she tripped over a milk-bottle and I got angry with her attitude to my mother.'

The deep-set eyes of his companion had a whimsical gleam in them as he struggled to his feet.

'It was your father's affair with Miss Gault,' he gasped, 'that gave me my chance with Ann. God! how Urquhart used to gird at me for my mania for that sweet creature! I suppose you have no more idea than a leopard's cub, Solent, how enchanting she was in those days!'

Wolf stopped short as they picked their way between the graves. 'What was it you said made you want to see where he's buried?' he enquired in a high-pitched voice.

The ancient mariner's visage before him contracted itself into what almost amounted to a gamin's grimace.

'I detect,' he said, 'a tone in your voice, Solent, and a quiver in your lips, that suggest I'm on dangerous ground. But the truth is I swore to him once that if he caved in before me I'd come and make a signal to his old cadaver. That's twenty-five years ago, Wolf Solent; and I've never done it till this moment.'

'One minute!' interrupted Wolf, as the visitor made a motion to advance. His voice certainly had a vibration in it that was a surprise to himself. It was apparently no surprise to Lord Carfax; but the man gave him a quick, penetrating, suspicious glance. Wolf flung a hurried look sideways. It was impossible to see William Solent's headstone from where they stood. No stranger could possibly find the spot unless led to it by an habitué of that place.

'Did you have an exciting love-affair with my mother?'

The remark sounded quite as childish, quite as insolent, to his own ears, as doubtless it did to those of his interlocutor. But he followed it up with a further challenge.

'My mother treated my father abominably!'

His lip *was* trembling now. Violent pulses throbbed in both his wrists, like Lilliputian engines. He knitted his eyebrows and glared at the rugged folds of tanned skin that surrounded this man's eyes, giving them the guarded alertness of a kindly, but very wary, deer-stalker.

Carfax squared his shoulders; and then, without removing his gaze from Wolf's face, he proceeded to button his overcoat tightly about his neck. The next thing he did was to fold both his hands – one of them holding his ash stick – massively behind his back. The measured gravity of this gesture, as Wolf recalled it afterwards, resembled that of some seventeenth-century cavalier accosted by a highwayman!

His compact, sturdy figure, his formidable, level stare, presented themselves to Wolf like the embodiment of every banked-up and buttressed tradition in English social life.

'You were very young at that time, Solent,' he remarked in a guarded tone.

'You must have got enormous satisfaction,' Wolf went on, 'in punishing my father for his rascality. You and my mother must have felt like avenging angels!'

The weather-beaten creases about the man's eyes thickened so shrewdly that no more than two gleaming little slits of menacing roguery confronted Wolf's vibrant nerves.

'I don't think we felt exactly angelic,' chuckled Lord Carfax.

The curious thing about what happened then was the ferocious lucidity with which Wolf ransacked his own emotional state.

He recognized that one part of his nature was stirred in an

593

affectionate response toward the rugged face before him. What he felt was that the skull under that mound in the paupers' plot *must* be championed at this crisis, or it would be betrayed beyond recovery.

'You think all scruples are uncivilized bigotry where sex is concerned; isn't that it?'

Carfax merely bowed.

Wolf knew perfectly well that what he was yielding to now was an insane desire to make this man responsible – as if he had been fate itself – for all the convoluted bitterness of his dilemma between Gerda and Christie! Those imaginary dialogues with the fellow, over the kitchen stove, seethed in his mind like steam under a lid. He knew, too, that he was revenging himself now for Carfax's attraction towards Gerda, for his indifference to himself.

'Come!' he cried in a trembling voice, 'come! There isn't time to hunt about here for the place they used to bury workhouse inmates in twenty-five years ago!'

Carfax took off his hat and rubbed his corrugated forehead with the palm of one of his hands. When he removed his fingers, Wolf caught a glimpse of a pair of agitated eyes roving in troubled scrutiny over the headstones to his left. The man's eyes had indeed become so much like those of a nervous hunter, that his whole face assumed a disarming and boyish anxiety, as if he were watching for the head of an otter or the fin of a pike in a disturbed stream!

'Come!' repeated Wolf. 'I'll put you on the road to the Lovelace, and you can get a carriage or something to take you back to Blacksod. I'm going to walk back; but Gerda won't forgive me if you're late, and if you get a cab you'll be with her long before I am! I'm sure she's buying cakes for you at Pimpernel's this very moment!'

Before he had reached the word 'Pimpernel' in this speech, at which point the lips of Lord Carfax broke into a smile of roguish gusto, he was aware of a very stern, straight look from the man's grey eyes.

'I've annoyed you for ever now, I suppose,' Wolf murmured in a low voice. Lord Carfax surveyed him sternly.

'I don't like it when people's nerves get out of control,' he said. 'My instinct is to beat them down, as a menace to civilized behaviour! But after all, Solent, here I am, at your father's request! If you'd rather not show me his grave' – it was at this point that Wolf caught that disarming glint again, like the baffled innocence of a fisherman, emanating from beneath the old man's eyelids – 'I don't want to annoy you. But don't be too leisurely over your stroll back, my lad. If you are, there won't be many of those Pimpernel cakes left!'

'This is your nearest way out,' said Wolf laconically. Stepping carefully, in advance, between the rows of green mounds, upon many of which grew little patches of yellow buttercups and white clover, he guided his mother's and his wife's admirer to the main cemetery entrance. He managed to cast a quick glance in the direction of the grave. No! Miss Gault was not there.

Once in the road, he began giving his companion careful directions how to reach the Lovelace.

As he repeated those directions, he was aware of the man's attentive countenance, bent a little sideways towards him, wearing something of the expression with which an experienced ostler would attend to the inarticulate language of an erratic horse!

The effort of formulating those practical instructions in that silent spot, while the invisible magnetism of so much death nourished vegetation permeated his senses, threw Wolf's brain into a confused stupor. He found, while he was slowly explaining to Carfax how to take the short cut under the Preparatory School wall, past the head master's garden and the entrance to the Abbey, that he was *surprised* at having seen nothing of Miss Gault. He kept glancing at the deserted roadway before them, so warm, so opalescent, in the diffused light. He had an obstinate feeling that Miss Gault *must* be upon that road, either coming or going – a feeling that resembled some kind of chemical clairvoyance in the very marrow of his bones.

His mind, preoccupied with Miss Gault, became now most vividly conscious of the slaughter-house. The slaughter-house looked especially harmless at that moment; but he regarded it with sick aversion.

'These deeds must not be thought after these ways; so, it will make us mad.'

Of course, even while he saw her standing there, he knew he was imagining it, and that she had no palpable reality. This phenomenon, this visualizing of a bodily image that was *known* by his reason to be unreal, was one that he had suffered from before.

'You'll find her,' he was speaking of the sedate lady in the hotel-office, 'very stiff but very polite.' But while he was uttering these words, he saw Miss Gault's figure quite palpably before him. He saw her bony shoulders turned to him, black in the roadway. And there was her arm, with clenched hand, lifted up in prophetic malediction!

'They're killing something in there,' he thought. And then, for the infinitesimal part of a second, there arose within him an awareness of blinding pain, followed by thick darkness smeared with out-rushing blood. As this sank away, there ensued a murky dizziness in his brain, accompanied by a shocking sense that both his father's skull and this woman's arm were appealing to him to do something that he lacked the courage to do. His legs had turned into immovable lead, as happens in nightmares.

'Very stiff . . . very polite,' he repeated mechanically, perfectly conscious that he was smiling into the man's face with a forced repulsive smile.

But Carfax had suddenly become an alert, compact man of action. His expression was more mariner-like than ever. Wolf's eccentric maliciousness might have been a troublesome wave risen from an unexpected reef. Carfax looked curiously at him, his heavy eyelids screwed up, his mouth a little open, his chin set square in his muffler.

'Off with you, lad!' he said in a pleasant voice. 'It'll do you good to have that walk back alone! Off with you; and look alive-o now! . . . if you're going to get home before I finish up those cakes!'

Not Mr. Stalbridge himself could have obeyed his new master more submissively than Wolf obeyed this command. He was well inside the cemetery before Carfax had gone half a dozen steps. From behind the hedge he followed his measured and resolute advance up the road, up the warm clover-scented road, past the slaughter-house.

It was through the tangled greenery of a clustered tuft of budding honeysuckle that he watched Lord Carfax. The faint sweetness of that leafiness remained with him, like a covering of ointment round the bloody stump of an amputated limb, when finally he left his vantage-ground and strode over to the paupers' plot.

The first thing he noticed was a pair of white butterflies flying awkwardly together, linked in an ecstasy of love. They seemed to float upon the warm clover-scented air as if their four wings belonged to one single life . . . an insect-angel of an Apocalypse of the Minute!

'I should not have had the courage to interfere,' he thought, even if an animal *was* being killed. But Miss Gault would. She'd have rushed straight to the place!'

He dug the end of his stick into the turf by the side of the mound and leaned on the handle, frowning down upon what he visioned six feet below.

'O Christie! O my true-love!'

Stubbornly he set himself to analyse how it was that with the loss of his life-illusion he could yet feel as he did about Christie!

There hung about the idea of her still . . . yes! still, still, still! . . . and it was *this* that he must explain to that skull down there

. . . a sweetness as exciting as the wildest fancies of his youth, as those dark, secret fancies where the syllables 'a girl' carried with them so yielding an essence that breasts and hips and thighs lost themselves in an unutterable mystery!

'Do you hear me, old Truepenny?' and it seemed to him, as he stared at the grass, that his soul became a sharp-snouted mole, refusing to cease from its burrowing till it had crouched down close beside those empty eyeholes, and had fumbled and ferreted at that impious, unconquerable grin!

His father *must* hear him! Surely, between those bones that had set themselves against his mother's bones, so that he might be born, and his present living body, there must be something . . . some sort of link!

That was what he wanted, some ear into which he could pour the whole weight of his seething distress. Where else could he go?

Back once more across the grave floated those interlaced, fluttering wings. The contrast between the clover-scents that his nostrils inhaled and the desperation of his mood seemed to him like a well-aimed shaft of derision.

'If there *is* some monstrous consciousness behind all life,' he thought angrily, 'it's responsible for *all* the horrors! Come on, old Truepenny; let father and son celebrate this meeting with a private little curse at God. Let the worm in your mouth be the tongue shot out at Him! Let the look in the eyes of that Waterloo-steps man be His eternal peace!'

No sooner had Wolf articulated this catapult of malice against the unknown First Cause, than, without any apparent reason, he suddenly bethought himself of the boy Barge.

'Barge would never curse God,' he thought. 'Under the worst extremity of suffering he never would! Barge would forgive God instinctively, without an effort.' Barge did, no doubt, forgive Him every day! If Barge had the power of causing God to be tortured for all the torture God had caused, Barge would refrain, *as naturally as the wind blows*. Barge would let the great evil Spirit completely off!

As he meditated upon this forgiveness of God by Barge, Wolf found himself pulling his stick out of the earth and wiping the end of it, even as a duellist might wipe a sword, with his bare hand.

'But to forgive *for oneself* is one thing,' he thought. 'To forgive for others . . . for innocents . . . for animals . . . is another thing! Barge *is* an innocent; so it may be permitted to *him* to forgive. I am not an innocent. I know more than Barge. I know too much.'

He remained in deep, fixed, wordless thought, after that, for several minutes. Then he opened and shut the fingers of his left hand with a convulsive movement. Had his father's skull been able to cast a conscious eye upon him, through the intervening mould, it would have supposed he was freeing his fingers from the clay which, a moment ago, he had wiped from the stick; but what he really was doing was getting rid of the contamination not of clay, but of thought.

He had told himself a story in that brief while! He had imagined himself meeting Jesus Christ in the shape of the man of the Waterloo steps. He had imagined the man stopping him – it was by the stile on Babylon Hill – and asking him what he was doing. His answer had been given with a wild, crazy laugh. 'Can't you see I'm living my secret life?' he had said.

'What secret life?' the man had asked.

'Running away from the horrors!' he had cried, in a great screaming voice, that had rung over the roofs of Blacksod. But immediately afterwards he had imagined himself as becoming very calm and very sly. 'It's all right. It's absolutely all right,' he had whispered furtively in the man's ears. 'You needn't suffer. I let you off. *You are allowed to forget.* It doesn't matter what your secret life is. I've told you what mine is; and I now tell you that it can be borne. So you can stop looking like that! Any secret life can be borne when once you've been told that you have the right to forget. And that's what I've told *you* now.'

It was when he was imagining the man's answer that he had been compelled to practise his own doctrine with violent rapidity; and the next thing he did was to stoop down and dig his fingers into the roots of the grass, where he supposed his father's head would be. 'Good-bye, father!' he muttered; and straightening his back, with a sigh he turned sharp round, and without further parley moved from the spot.

He began by directing his steps towards the main highroad by which they had come; but he hadn't gone far when he suddenly swung about and made for the King's Barton lane.

'I don't want him to pick me up,' he thought. 'They're sure to take him that way.' As he followed the familiar road to King's Barton, he recalled his first drive along it, by Darnley's side, fourteen months ago.

How he had stared into the future then . . . that future which was now the past! How he had hugged his 'mythology' to his soul, during that drive, feeling so confident that nothing in that fertile land could arise to destroy it!

As he went along now, trailing his stick behind him, he became aware that with the approach of the end of the pearl-soft afternoon the voices of countless hidden blackbirds were mounting up, rich and sweet, from the green depths of the hedges.

'She's lost the power to whistle,' he said to himself, 'just as I've lost my "mythology!"' And the identity of Gerda, her excitement about their new silver, their new curtains, their new clock, her radiance in being attractive to Lord Carfax, melted into the sad-gay music poured forth from those invisible yellow beaks, until he felt as if he were walking along a road that passed through her heart, a road the very atmosphere of which was the breath of her young soul!

Those blackbird-notes in the hedges seemed to allay the tension of his nerves as if they had been the touch of the girl's flesh. His outraged mind, with its grievance against the First Cause, seemed actually to float away from his body as it moved quietly along. Between his body, thus freed from his tormented spirit, and the increasing loveliness of that perfect day, there began to establish itself a strange chemical fusion.

He came upon a certain gate now where he had once wondered what it would be like to live with Darnley. Once more he rested there, leaning his arms on its grey top bar and staring over the expanse of greenness separating him from Melbury Bub.

Yes, without any conscious motion of his will something was softening within him towards the long future stretch of the days of his life!

He began to grow conscious of how separate his assuaged senses were from that tormented spirit of his that had just cursed God. What was it that had worked this change in him? Those blackbird-notes? Was it merely that his body, hearing those sounds, plunged into the sweetness of Gerda's body? But now, from the thought of Gerda his mind reverted to Christie. After all, it was the same First Cause which tortured him that had made it possible that such a being as Christie should exist. God must be something that all conscious lives are doomed to curse and to bless in eternal alternation!

After all, Christie *did* belong to him, as she had never belonged, and never *would* belong, to anyone else. So easily might he never have met her – never met the one person he could love with all the worst and all the best in his contradictory nature! Many would be the Saturdays, many the Sundays, he would walk with her now, along the backwater, along that familiar esplanade! In an up-welling of sad, sweet tenderness, he saw himself as an old grey-headed schoolmaster . . . still at his job in that ink-stained room

599

. . . walking with Christie on one arm and Olwen, grown tall and disdainful, on the other, past the bow windows of Brunswick Terrace!

Certain little physical tricks Christie had, separating her from everyone else, came back to him now. The way she would turn her face sideways to speak to him when she was poking the fire, the way she swayed her wrists as if over an old-fashioned harpsichord, when she was arranging her teacups, the way she would hitch up her skirt when it hung too loose over her straight hips, the way she would stretch her head out of the window, drinking up the air with a kind of thirsty fury after struggling to express some subtle metaphysical idea that had baffled her power of words – all these things hit him now with no empty finality of loss, but with a sort of mystic consummation. It was as if, utterly beyond his effort – as it was beyond his merit – Chance itself had caused the earth to whisper some clue word into the ears of his flesh, a word that his *body* understood, though his mind was too humiliated to focus itself upon it.

Pondering upon what was happening to him, he turned from that gate and continued his way; but his stick was held firmly by the handle now, and his feet were no longer dragging as they moved.

He began obscurely to feel that he might get *some* happiness out of his life after all . . . even if he had to work at that school till he died . . . even if he never were allowed so much as to kiss Christie again!

He became more and more aware that it was just the simple chemistry of his body that, under the beauty of this hour, was coming to its own conclusions! It was as if his flesh were drinking in and soaking up this beauty, while his soul, cut into pieces by his recent humiliation like a worm by a bird's beak, wriggled and squirmed somewhere above his head!

His outward skin luxuriated in all this loveliness. It drenched itself in the pearl-soft air, like a naked swimmer in a glimmering sea. But his mind was still malcontent. It kept wincing under its own recent twinges. But it was divided from him in some way, so that it was no longer able to turn a torturous screw in his living brain! It was just as if some heavenly music were pouring into an entranced ear, while the brain behind the ear was beating about in chaotic misery.

Chaotic indeed! The core of his mind felt as though it were a multiple thing and lacked a centre. It felt as though its disintegrated consciousness resembled that of an amœba, of a zoophyte. It felt envious of the human happiness that had begun to penetrate its attendant body. Wolf knew that the man holding that oak stick was himself; he knew it was Wolf Solent, on his way home to eat Pimpernel's cakes and to watch his wife flirt with Lord Carfax. But he felt that the identity of his soul and his body was broken. His soul had received such crushing disgraces that like a thousand globules of quicksilver it no longer dwelt where normal souls *ought* to dwell!

It was out of all this chaos within him that he now set himself, as he strode along, to concentrate his will upon Christie and upon her life by that Weymouth backwater. 'Oh, may she be happy!' he cried bluntly to the grass and the trees. And then a queer psychic inkling came upon him, an inkling that it would be possible for him, now that he no longer had anything left but certain bodily sensations, now that he had become a depersonalized inhuman force, without hope or aim, to exercise a genuine power, an almost supernatural power, over the future of the entity he loved. The more he pondered on this, the more possible did the thing appear to him! As he surveyed the blossoms of a great lilac-bush in the first King's Barton garden he reached, he seemed to visualize the demiurge of the universe as so much diffused sub-conscious magnetism submissive to nothing but commands . . . commands rather than prayers!

The luminous enchantment which this perfect afternoon threw upon those blossoms caused him to stop dead-still in front of them.

'I *command*,' he uttered in a grave, loud tone, 'I *command* that she shall be happy!' And then, with a grotesque solemnity, as if for a second of time he had been given the power to destroy all ordinary sense of proportion, he repeated, as though addressing a slow-witted interlocutor, 'It's Christie Malakite I mean, who lives by the backwater at Weymouth.'

He concluded this fantastic ceremony by an audible chuckle; but his steps, as he strode through the village of King's Barton at a swinging pace, were freer and stronger than they had been for a very long time.

Still, however, he could not shake off the feeling that his soul had become a drifting multiplicity without any nucleus. There had occurred an actual 'resurrection' of his body, which was now giving to his behaviour the aspect, the motions, the gestures of exultant wellbeing, while his inner nature remained a blur of disgusting confusion.

'Walking is my cure,' he thought, 'As long as I can walk I can get my soul into shape! It must have been an instinct of self-preservation that has always driven me to walk!'

601

He had reached the churchyard-wall now; and he couldn't resist the temptation of stopping for a minute to visit Redfern's grave. As he was scrambling over the low rampart of crumbling yellowish stone, he heard the droning of an aeroplane somewhere above his head.

'Mine enemy hath found me out,' he said to himself. 'I suppose walking up and down upon the earth will cease altogether soon. Well, I'm going to walk till I die!' And to avoid giving his airy antagonist even the honour of one inquisitive glance, he proceeded to keep his eyes in religious malice rigorously fixed upon the grass beneath his feet.

His method of advance was more conducive to cerebral revenge than to alert vision; and when he did reach his destination he found a wheelbarrow full of grass by the side of the grave, and beyond the wheelbarrow, bending low and armed with a pair of gleaming shears, the figure of Roger Monk.

The peculiarly subtle smell of the green grass in the wheelbarrow gave him a thrill of such strange contentment that his greeting of his old acquaintance was cordial in the extreme.

'How's the Squire?' he enquired after a minute or two's discussion of the weather. Roger Monk chuckled grimly.

'There was a time, sir,' he replied – and Wolf noticed that the gardener's accent still wavered between the intonation of the Shires and the intonation of Dorset, 'when, as you know, sir, I could have given that man his queetus. But he's not what he was, Mr. Solent, and that's the long and short of it.'

The word 'queetus,' in place of 'quietus,' so tickled Wolf's fancy that he could only make an amiable grimace in response, a grimace that implied that the world had long been aware that Mr. Monk's bark was worse than his bite.

'How does he sleep these days?' he enquired.

'Much better, sir, thank 'ee. In fact, he's slept wonderful sound ever since Master Round and me dug this 'ere grave as 'twere right it should be dug. Old Jack Torp, if I may say so, made a poor job of this burying! Squire was worriting himself over it fearsome. That beer-barrel of a Torp, if you'll excuse such speaking, Mr. Solent, of a party a gentleman like yourself be allied to, ain't no more a sexton than he be an undertaker! Them stonecutters should leave the spade alone. They should leave burying alone, and stick to their own job.'

This plausible and innocent explanation of what he and Valley had witnessed did not by any means convince Wolf. But neither did it lessen his humiliation. He began to feel as if the perversity

of Mr. Urquhart, the incest of Mr. Malakite, the lechery of Bob
Weevil, the morbidity of Jason, were all of such slight importance,
compared with the difference between being alive and being dead,
that he had made a fool of himself in making so much of them.
Such, at any rate, seemed to be the opinion of his body; and it
was his body now that had taken the rudder in its hand! His body?
No! It was more than his body! Behind the pulse-beat of his body
stirred the unutterable . . . stirred something that was connected
with the strange blueness he had seen long ago over the Lunt
meadows and more recently at the window of Pond Cottage . . .
something, too, that was connected with that heathen goodness
that came so naturally to Gaffer Barge.

'How is Mr. Valley, Roger?' he asked. 'I haven't seen him since
before the Otter wedding.'

Monk lowered his voice and jerked his thumb in the direction
of the vicarage. 'Squire's gone to drink tea with him this very
afternoon,' he whispered. 'Squire don't know that I know it.
Nor do he know that Mrs. Martin and our maid knows it. He's
a proud old gent, is Squire; and he's cursed the Reverend so bitter
that 'twould be awkward if all were known.'

'Are they friends again, then?' asked Wolf.

Mr. Monk gave a furtive glance at the church and another at
Redfern's grave. He seemed to suspect invisible eavesdroppers
from both those directions.

'Squire ain't, and never has been, what you might call religious,'
he said, 'but he's got fixed in his mind, since his sleep returned to
him, that our parson have worked a miracle. 'Twould be all my
place is worth if he knew I know what he's up to.' Here the man
came extremely close to Wolf and almost touched his face as he
whispered in his ear, 'He've a-been over there three times this
week already!'

Wolf drew away as discreetly as he could. Mr. Monk's breath
smelt so strongly of gin that he wondered if the servant hadn't
been drinking with the clergyman in the kitchen prior to the
master's refreshment in the study!

A queer notion seized upon him now, as he looked this man up
and down – a fantastic and even obscene notion. He mentally
stripped the tall rascal of every rag of clothing! He visualized his
heavy chest, his huge knees . . . he saw them unwashed and dirty.
. . . But suddenly, in the twinkling of an eye, he knew for a certainty, beyond all logic, that this astronomical universe, of which
the monstrous frame of Mr. Monk occupied the foreground, was

merely a filmy, phantasmal screen, separating him from an indrawn reality into which at any moment he might wake – wake despoiled and released. It was the feet of Mr. Monk, or rather the dirty nails of his huge toes, observed with this grotesque maliciousness, that seemed the seal of certainty upon this mystical knowledge!

'Well, I must be emptying this barrow and getting home,' said the innocent Roger.

'Good luck to you!' replied Wolf in a loud, hollow tone, as he recovered from his trance.

When the man had gone off and he was left to himself, he had time to note that not a sign was left now of the grave's recent disturbance. Redfern's mound, neatly sheared by the gardener's shears, looked just the same as all the other graves in the vicinity.

Wolf sighed wearily. That last piece of information about Mr. Urquhart seemed to have landed him on the deepest bed-rock of his self-contempt. What? Had he seen himself all this while as a great spiritual antagonist to the Squire, only to find at the last that the man was paying surreptitious visits to T. E. Valley?

'Probably,' he thought, 'he's begging Tilly-Valley to let him take the Sacrament!'

He stared at the mound in front of him, wondering, with cynical indifference, whether the body of the boy had been exposed or not. But now, at any rate, he was 'free among the dead.'

'Christie! Christie!' He tried to visualize that fragile figure at this very moment coming back to tea from a stroll along the backwater, where she had gone with Olwen to see the Abbotsbury swans!

Death and Love! In those two alone lay the ultimate dignity of life. Those were the sacraments, those were the assuagements. Death was the great altar where the candles were never extinguished for such as loathed the commonplace.

And it was just this that these accursed inventions were seeking to destroy! They would dissect love, till it became 'an itch of the blood and a permission of the will'; they would kill all calm, all peace, all solitude; they would profane the majesty of death till they vulgarized the very background of existence; they would flout the souls of the lonely upon the earth, until there was not one spot left by land or by water where a human being could escape from the brutality of mechanism, from the hard glitter of steel, from the gaudy insolence of electricity!

' "Jimmy Redfern – *he* was there!" ' he hummed savagely as he moved off; and then, as he scrambled back into the road, he

604

wondered to himself what new mood it was that he had detected in Roger Monk. The man seemed to speak of Mr. Urquhart with a completely different intonation. Wolf's morbid imagination began at once picturing a new Mr. Urquhart, a Mr. Urquhart in an old age of dotage, fallen entirely into the hands of Mr. Monk and of that precious crony of his that he called 'Master Round!'

'I'll call at the Manor House next Saturday,' he thought, 'and find out what Tilly-Valley has done to him.'

He glanced at his watch. Oh, he would be hopelessly late for tea! Well, Gerda wouldn't mind; and Lord Carfax would be thoroughly delighted!

He soon found that the faster he walked through that unequalled atmosphere, the stronger and calmer grew his mind.

The muscles of his body, his skin, his senses, his nerves, his breath, seemed to be gathering up from the soil a new power, a new endurance. The final stamping-down of the earth upon his old life-illusion was the vision, though it may well have been imaginary, of Mr. Urquhart pleading for the Sacrament with Tilly-Valley. He recognized now that his secret motive of all these months . . . yes, he had felt it by the banks of the Lunt, the day of the 'yellow bracken' . . . had been his faith in some vast earth-born power within him that was stronger than the Christian miracle! Had Tilly-Valley won, then? Had he beaten them all? Had the absurd little fool mesmerized the soul of the great John Urquhart, even as he had mesmerized the soul of Mr. Round?

'Jesus . . . Jesus . . . Jesus . . . Jesus. . . .'

No! He would *not* yield! The inborn goodness of Barge . . . a thing natural and inevitable as the rising of the sap in the tree . . . was stronger than all the 'white-magic' in the world.

Oh, Christie! Oh, Christie! Would Gerda mind if he went down to Weymouth to-morrow week? He felt a longing to ask Christie what *she* thought about the difference between the 'goodness' of Barge and the 'faith' of Tilly-Valley. Perhaps, now it was dead, he would tell her about his 'mythology.'

Quicker and quicker circulated the blood through his veins as he entered Blacksod and reached the familiar parting of the ways. There was no hesitation there now. He had never once gone past the bookshop since she had left it!

He found himself dallying with many happier thoughts as he hurried by the Torp yard. Surely he had fallen as low as he could fall! The loveliness of this day . . . a gift thrown out to him by Chance, the greatest of all the gods . . . seemed to have touched his body with a kind of blind new birth. He began to feel conscious again, as he had done over the corpse of old Malakite, of himself as a moving animal, full of a vivid, tingling life that extended into the very fingers with which he clasped his stick. And not only as an animal! The immense vegetable efflorescence by which he had been surrounded seemed to have drawn his nerves back and down, soothing them, healing them, calming them, in a flowing reciprocity with that life that was far older than animal life.

Ah! His body and his soul were coming together again now! Emanating from his lean, striding form, from his spine, from his legs, from his finger-tips, his spirit extended outwards, dominating this forked 'animal-vegetable' which was himself. And with this new awareness as his background, he set himself to face in stoical resolution all the years of his life, as he saw them before him, dusty milestones along a dusty highway!

He said grimly to himself, 'No gestures now!' And it was *not* a gesture that he made at this moment, as he gathered himself together to be an usher in Blacksod Grammar School for the remainder of his life! He kept his spirits down on purpose, visualizing the innumerable moments of discomfort, of nervous misery, that lay before him. He stretched out his hand to pluck at those wretched future moments, so that he might appropriate them now and grapple with them now. . . .

'But it isn't all there is!' he said to himself as he approached Preston Lane. 'The whole astronomical world is only a phantasm, compared with the circles within circles, the dreams within dreams of the unknown reality!'

He passed Mrs. Herbert's house and came to the pigsty. Ailinon! The memories! Peering furtively up the street to his own threshold . . . yes, he could see that the parlour windows were both open. He came to a pause now, hot and breathless from his rapid walking, and leant upon the pigsty railing. That smell of pigs' urine, mingled, just as it was a year ago, with the smell of the flowering hedge, gave him a thrill of delicious sadness, and all Dorset seemed gathered up into it! Little wayside cottages, fallen trees, stubble-fields, well-heads, duck-ponds, herds of cattle visioned through the frames of shed doors – all these things flooded his mind now with a strange sense of occult possession. They were only casual groupings of chance-offered objects; but as they poured pell-mell into his memory, across the reek and the jostling of those uplifted snouts, he felt that something permanent and abiding out of such accidents would give him strength to face the ink-stained classroom – to face the days and days and days – without his 'myth-ology' and without Christie!

He must have been at the cellar-floor of misery when he licked with his mental tongue the filthy toenails of Mr. Monk.

And yet it was from that very beastliness that he discovered the fact that beyond all refutation an actual portion of his mind was *outside the whole astronomical spectacle!*

More heavily than ever now did he lean on that railing, while the pigs, to whom all human heads were the same, grunted and squealed for their bucket.

Then he straightened his back, waved his hand to the dis-appointed pigs, and moved on.

He had hardly taken a step when he suddenly thought of Poll's Camp. What was it? An entrancing bird's note made him stop again and glance up the road to where the great ash tree extended its cool, glaucous green branches against the pearl-soft sky.

Another yellow-beak! It had been a thrush last year. Were Gerda and Lord Carfax listening to this liquid music as they ate their Pimpernel cakes?

Fool! Fool! Fool! It was not in the tree at all. Oh, he had known it all the while! In the deepest pit of his stomach he had known. It was the girl herself. The blackbird's notes were issuing from that open window. It was Gerda's whistling. That strange power had been given back to her at last!

For a second he just abandoned himself to the beauty of the sound. It was this pearl-soft day itself, consummated, incarnated, in flowing drops of immortal ichor!

Then a queer transformation automatically took place in him. His ripened 'soul,' that magnetic cloud about him, drew close to his body like a garment of flexible steel. His muscles contracted, like those of a feline animal stalking its prey. His whole personality became a tense, bent bow of cold, vibrant jealousy, the string pressed taut, the arrow quivering.

Hunching his shoulders, his stick held by the middle – but he had no thought of either Hector of Troy or William of Deloraine! – he ran across the road and advanced stealthily and rapidly along the pavement. His gaze was fixed on the dark aperture of the window through which the whistling came. He intended to *see*, at least one good second, before he *was seen*! . . .

Yes. He had known it. He had known it far down in his con-sciousness all that long day! His glance, when he reached the window, was swift, decisive, devastating. It lasted less than a third of a second; and then he drew back and shuffled out of sight against their neighbour's railings.

The teacups had been used, the cakes eaten. And there, seated in the low chair by the side of the littered tray, was Lord Carfax, with a look of the most sun-warmed aplomb that he had ever seen on a human countenance; and there, seated on his knee, with her lips pursed-up and the expression of a radiant infant upon her face, was Gerda . . . whistling . . . whistling . . . whistling! . . .

'Ripeness is all.' The words seemed to come into his mind from nowhere . . . to come into his mind from that region, whatever it was, that was *not* the universe!

They certainly had not their ordinary meaning for him, as he recoiled from what he had seen. They meant that the lords of life had now filled his cup – filled it up to the brim. Little had he known how much this girl's devotion to him had come to mean. Christie was his horizon; but this girl was the solid ground beneath him. And now the ground had moved!

Like a man who sees his foothold cracking between his feet, and, instead of hurrying forward, looks down, in curious interest, one foot on each side of the crevasse, at a disturbed beetle scrambling up one of the edges of the chasm, Wolf stood on the pavement outside the pig-dealer's house and stared at the shed across the way.

If only she hadn't let him take her on his knee! How *interested* all the people of his life would be that she had let him take her upon his knee! He felt as if Carfax had come into his life for this sole purpose alone – to take Gerda upon his knee! How he could see the nodding heads of all the people of his life, as they glanced at one another *displaying their interest* in what had happened!

Carfax had saved the man on the Waterloo steps. At least he had saved Stalbridge! Carfax had paid Christie five times their value for the books in the shop. Carfax had condemned Urquhart to a harmless dotage. And now, with the crumbs of Pimpernel's cakes strewing the tea-table, Carfax had restored to Gerda her unique gift.

Bob Weevil had had to be cajoled into that bedroom before he grew daring. 'Lords in London' had none of these Blacksod scruples. To Carfax it was nothing . . . a trifle, a bagatelle . . . and yet it was pleasant . . . to feel the warmth of a girl's body pressed against him, while by his glowing sympathy he gave her back her youth, gave her back the life that she had lost in her twelve months with a priggish schoolmaster!

Wolf found it necessary at that moment to act in an almost

jaunty manner. He balanced his stick under his arm – a thing he had never done before; and he thrust his hands into his trouser-pockets – a gesture that was completely unnatural to him. He began moving along the pavement towards the town; but when he found himself opposite Mrs. Herbert's door, he remembered . . . he must have been instinctively turning to her, like an out-raged cub to its dam . . . that his mother lived now above her grand new shop!

It was at this point that he realized that he must find some immediate purpose . . . something that it was *imperative* for him to do. As his eyes fixed themselves upon the green hedge opposite him, he became aware, through a small children-made gap, of the amazing gold of the meadow beyond. Why, the field was full to the very brim of golden buttercups! It was literally a floating sea of liquid, shining gold!

He felt drawn towards the meadow by a bodily necessity, as if he had been a sick dog seeking certain particular grass-blades by the side of the road! Nothing at that moment short of physical force could have prevented him from climbing through that gap and entering that field. In the stunned condition of his emotions, his actions were obedient to the crude craving of that bodily necessity. The automatic movements of his muscles necessary to reach those yellow flowers followed one another with the inevitableness of water seeking water.

Once in the field, it was just as if he were wading through golden waves. And then he suddenly remembered that it was into this very field that he had flung Mukalog. What a shining mausoleum for that little demon!

He couldn't resist the distraction of fumbling about at random with his stick among the buttercup-stalks. What if he *should* by some crazy chance, just at this juncture, stumble upon the obscene idol? How would those long weeks of exposure to the weather have affected it?

While all these notions were pursuing one another over the surface of his mind, like criss-cross ripples over a wharf-brimming tide, something else within him was thinking: 'In a few minutes I shall be entering that parlour and shaking hands with Carfax. In a few more minutes Carfax will have gone off to his train, and Gerda and I will have been left alone.' He suddenly ceased fumbling in that golden sea with the end of his stick. There was nothing else for it but to take up, like a camel with the last straw laid upon his hump, the swaying burden of his life! 'Carfax will probably stay over Sunday. He'll be infatuated. Her whistling will hold him like sorcery. But on Monday he'll take his train . . . and I shall go back to the School; and everything will be as it was before.' But then he remembered the visitor's arrangement with Stalbridge – how the ex-waiter was to meet the seven-o'clock train at Ramsgard.

'No! By God, I believe he'll clear off as he said! He's not a fellow to play fast and loose with a hired servant.'

He began walking to and fro now, with a firmer step, across that field. Back and forth he walked, while the sun, fallen almost horizontal, made what he walked upon seem unearthly. Buttercup-petals clung to his legs, clung to the sides of his stick; buttercup-dust covered his boots. The plenitude of gold that surrounded him began to invade his mind with strange, far-drawn associations. The golden ornaments, tissue upon tissue, leaf upon leaf, covering the dead in the tomb of Agamemnon, the golden pilasters of the halls of Alcinoüs, the golden shower that ravished Danaë, the golden fleece that ruined Jason, the cloud of gold in which the doomed Titan embraced Hera, the flame of gold in which Zeus embraced Semele, the golden fruit of the Hesperides, the golden sands of the Islands of the Blest – all these things, not in their concrete appearances, but in their platonic essences, made his mind reel. The thing became a symbol, a mystery, an initiation. It was like that figure of the Absolute seen in the Apocalypse. It became a *super-substance*, sunlight precipitated and petrified, the magnetic heart of the world rendered visible!

Up and down he went, pacing that field. He felt as if he were an appointed emissary, guarding some fragment of Saturn's age flung into the midst of Blacksod!

'Enjoying the sweet light of the sun . . . deprived of the sweet light of the sun,' these phrases from Homer rang in his ears and seemed to express the only thing that was important. Carfax taking Gerda upon his knee, Urquhart begging Tilly-Valley for the Sacrament, his mother borrowing from Mr. Manley, Roger Monk trimming Redfern's grave – all these human gestures presented themselves to him now through a golden mist, a mist that made them at once harmless and negligible, compared with the difference between being alive and being dead!

With his face turned westward, as he stared in his march at the great orb of the horizontal sun, which by reason of the thin screen of clouds that covered it was no more dazzling to his eyes than the periphery of a full moon, he realized that long ago, at Weymouth, he had had an extraordinary ecstasy from the sight of the dancing ripples of the wide bay turned into liquid gold by the straight sun-path.

'Was it sunrise or sunset?' he wondered; but he could not remember anything beyond that dance of gold and the rapture it caused him.

The deeper the enchantment of the moment sank into his being, the clearer became his conclusion with regard to the whole matter.

In the recesses of his consciousness he was aware that a change had taken place within him, a rearrangement, a readjustment of his ultimate vision, from which he could never again altogether recede.

That sense of a supernatural struggle going on in the abysses, with the Good and the Evil so sharply opposed, had vanished from his mind. To the very core of life, things were more involved, more complicated than that! The supernatural itself had vanished from his mind. His 'mythology,' whatever it had been, *was dead*. What was left to him now was his body. Like the body of a tree or a fish or an animal it was; and his hands and his knees were like branches or paws or fins! And floating around his body, was his *thought*, the 'I am I' against the world. This 'I am I' included his new purpose and included his will toward his new purpose. 'There is no limit to the power of my will,' he thought, 'as long as I use it for two uses only . . . to forget and to enjoy! Ha, old Truepenny, am I with you at last? Air and earth mould, clouds and a patch of grass, darkness and the breaking of light . . . Ay, it is enough! And with this as my background, why can't I be as heavenly "good" as Gaffer Barge? My will can do *anything*, when I limit it to "forget . . . enjoy." '

And there suddenly came upon him, as he thought of these things, the memory of another blundering mystic, another solitary walker over hill and dale, who in his time, too, discovered that certain 'Intimations of Immortality' had to take a narrower, a simpler form, as the years advanced!

> 'But there's a tree, of many one,
> A single field which I have looked upon,
> Both of them spoke of something that is gone.'

Increasingly as he stood there, quite motionless now, did the golden sea around him clarify his thoughts. 'I must have the courage of my cowardice, he thought. 'I can never be brave like you, old Truepenny; but I can plough on and I can forget.' He dug the end of his stick resolutely into the roots of the grass, into the grave of Mukalog; and there slid into his mind an incident from a visit he had paid long ago to Weymouth . . . *before Christie had ever gone there*. . . .

He was drinking tea alone, drinking it from a particular china 'set' belonging to his grandmother, a 'set' called Limoges. Beside him was a book with a little heap of entangled bits of seaweed lying upon it, which he was separating and sorting. There came a moment when he suddenly realized that the book, beside which was his teacup and upon which was the seaweed, was *The Poems of Wordsworth*. A thrilling ecstasy shot through him then. In a flash he associated the heightening of life that came from his tea-drinking both with the magic of the floating rock-pools where he had found the seaweed and with the magic of Wordsworth's fluctuating inspiration; and there came upon him a sense of such incredible loveliness, 'interfused' through existence, that he jumped up from his chair and began rapidly pacing the floor, hunching his shoulders and rubbing his hands together. . . .

That experience came back to his mind now. 'If I can't enjoy life,' he thought, 'with absolute childish absorption in its simplest elements, I might as well never have been born!'

And then there came over him a feeling that he could never have expressed in definite words. It was as if an intangible residuum of all the emanations from all the places in town and country through which he had passed, hovered about him now, like the sea-smell of those seaweeds about that book!

From this feeling his mind reverted easily enough to the thought of death. 'Death, the sweet sleep; death, the heavenly end,' he repeated. And as though the words had been the burden of an old sentimental song, he felt something within him respond to them with a melting nostalgia. . . .

Then, as he turned eastward, and the yellowness of the buttercups changed from Byzantine gold to Cimmerian gold, he visualized the whole earthly solidity of this fragment of the West Country, this segment of astronomical clay, stretching from Glastonbury to Melbury Bub and from Ramsgard to Blacksod, as if it were itself one of the living personalities of his life. 'It is a god!' he cried in his heart; and he felt as if titanic hands, from the horizon of this 'field of Saturn,' were being lifted up to salute the mystery of life and the mystery of death!

What he longed to do was to plunge his own hands into this Saturnian gold, and to pour it out, over Mr. Urquhart, over Mattie, over Miss Gault, over Jason, over all the nameless little desolations –broken twigs, tortured branches, wounded reptiles, injured birds, slaughtered beasts – over a lonely stone on which no moss grew, n the heart of Lovelace Park, over a drowned worm, white and flaccid, dropped from the hook of Lobbie Torp into some Lunt pool, over the death-pillow of old Mr. Weevil, deprived now of his last conscious gluttony, over the lechery of the 'water-rat' himself, so pitiful in its tantalized frustration! All . . . all . . . all would reveal some unspeakable beauty, if only this Saturnian gold were sprinkled upon them!

Reversing the position of his stick in his fingers as if he scrupled to touch this golden sea with anything but its handle, he did his best to turn this new clairvoyance upon the knot of his own identity. Hardly knowing what he was doing, he moved up close to the back of the pigsty; and as he swung his stick by the wrong end, its handle brushed the tall weeds that grew against the shed.

'It's my body that has saved me,' he thought; and as if to assure these patient senses that his spirit was grateful, he abstractedly pinched his thigh above the knee with his left hand.

Behind the pigsty! It seemed to him odd that he had lived here a whole year and had never seen this familiar shed from the back. It was queer how he always shirked reality, and then suddenly plunged – plunged into its inmost retreat! Behind the pigsty! It was only when he got desperate that he plunged into the nature of human beings – that he got behind *them*!

Ay! How coldly, how maliciously, he *could* dive into the people he knew and see their inmost souls . . . from behind, from behind! Poison and sting . . . the furtive coil and the sex-clutch; yes, a spasmodically jerking, quivering ego-nerve, pursuing its own end – that was what was behind everyone!

Behind the pigsty! How often had he visualized every single person of his life, in some treachery of meanness! How often had he caught them in some incredible posture of grotesque indecency! Oh, it was his own mind that was diseased . . . not Nature. Well, diseased or not, it was all he had! Henceforth he was going to take as the talisman of his days the phrase *endure or escape*. Where had he picked up that phrase? Behind a workhouse? Behind a madhouse?

Between himself and what was 'behind' the Universe there should be now a new covenant! The Cause up there could certainly at any minute make him howl like a mad dog. It could make him dance and skip and eat dung. Well, until it *did* that, he was going to endure . . . follow his 'road,' through the ink-stains, and endure!

His eye happened to catch sight of a large grey snail with its horns extended, ascending the tarred boards of the shed. It had just left a pallid dock-leaf that spread itself out against the boarding, and to which its slime still adhered. His mind rushed off to thousands and thousands of quiet spots, behind outhouses, behind stick-houses, behind old haystacks, behind old barns and sheds, where such grey snails lived and died in peace, covering docks, nettles, and silver-weed with their patent slime! How often had he hurried past such places with hardly a glance! And yet their combined memory reconciled him more to life than all Roger Monk's flower-beds.

By God! He must be crafty in dealing with these modern inventions! He must slide under them, over them, round them, like air, like vapour, like water. *Endure or escape!* A good word, wherever it was he had picked it up.

Well, never mind the motors and the aeroplanes! King Æthelwolf was at rest, staring up at that fan tracery. It only needed an adjustment . . . and he could be as much at peace in life as that king was in death!

Was Carfax making love to Gerda now, all soft and yielding and relaxed, after her whistling?

Everyone had to *feel* according to the fatality of his nature; but who was he to make pompous moral scenes?

Alone! That was what he had learnt from the hard woman who had given him birth. That every soul was alone. Alone with that secret bestower of torture and pleasure, the horned snail behind the pigsty!

Endure or escape. He must spread the wisdom of that word over all the miserable moments that were to come.

Oh, Christie! Oh, Christie!

Well, he must go in and face those two now.

He took up his stick firmly and securely by its proper end, and for a few paces moved forward blinking, straight into the circle of the sun, as it aimed itself at him over the rim of the world. Then he swung round, scrambled through the gap, and hurried across the road.

'I wonder if he *is* still here?' he thought as he laid his hand on the latch of the gate. And then he thought. 'Well, I shall have a cup of tea.'

THE END